She was Isabel Valderocas, a vibrant Spanish beauty
blessed by the privileges of one of the finest,
most loyal Christian families in all Spain. Until she
learns that she is a Jew—a Marrano—
fated to die at the stake if her heritage is revealed.

And yet she carries her secret bravely, spying
in her daily sojourns to the court of Philip IV, working
always for the freedom of her secret people—
the hidden Jews like herself.

But Isabel keeps yet another secret; the man she
loves—even as she loves her persecuted
people—is the ruthless, ambitious Rafael Cortés,
determined to become the Grand Inquisitor
of all Spain, sworn enemy of...

# THE MARRANOS

D0720339

# "Don Rafael, What Do You Want from Me?"

He took her face in his hands.

"I want you to trust me," he said. "I want you to trust me implicitly, no matter what I do, no matter who I become, no matter what my title in the Church, no matter what you hear said about me, I want you to trust me. You must never doubt me or fear me. If you give me your full trust, if you will never question anything I do, if you will never again ask me to quit the order to marry you, if you will never try to interfere with my work, then we might be able to go on seeing each other from time to time. You say you will try never to lie to me. I do not want to lie to you either, but you may have questions which I must not answer, so I prefer you do not ask them."

As she looked into his eyes and listened to him, she longed to kiss him and swear eternal trust and loyalty, but how could she give him that precious gift, when she had already bestowed it upon another?

# THE MARRANOS

## Liliane Webb

PUBLISHED BY POCKET BOOKS NEW YORK

Distributed in Canada by PaperJacks Ltd., a Licensee
of the trademarks of Simon & Schuster, a division of
Gulf+Western Corporation.

**POCKET BOOKS**, a Simon & Schuster division of
**GULF & WESTERN CORPORATION**
1230 Avenue of the Americas, New York, N.Y. 10020
In Canada distributed by PaperJacks Ltd.,
330 Steelcase Road, Markham, Ontario.

Published by arrangement with Andrews and McMeel, Inc.
Library of Congress Catalog Card Number: 80-10635

ISBN: 0-671-42388-6

First Pocket Books printing January, 1982

10 9 8 7 6 5 4 3 2 1

POCKET and colophon are trademarks of Simon & Schuster.

Printed in Canada

*for Monique and Benjamin*
*and with loving thoughts to David*

# Prologue

*Extract from the expulsion order signed on the 31st of March 1492 at the Palace of the Alhambra at Granada by the Catholic Kings of Spain: Ferdinand of Aragon and Isabel of Castile.*

"When we were informed that because of their numerous relations with Jews, certain bad Christians of our Kingdoms persisted in Judaizing and in Apostatizing our Holy Catholic Faith, We decreed, at the Cortes assembled at Toledo in 1480, that the Jews should have a residence apart in all towns, cities and villages of our States. Thus we confined them to *Juderias* in the hope that this separation would put an end to our troubles. In addition, We ordered the establishment of tribunals of Inquisition in our Kingdoms and Counties. These tribunals have functioned for twelve years now, and have already led to the condemnation of many persons found guilty. Nevertheless, the great prejudice caused to Christians has continued to exist as a result of their participation in many practices of the Jews who have shown by all means that they pursue a project of subversion, meaning to turn away the faithful from our Holy Faith, remove them from it, attract them, convert them, and pervert them to detestable beliefs, by instructing them in the ceremonies and observances of

their laws, causing them to circumcise themselves and their
sons, offering them bread without leavening and meat from
animals slaughtered according to their rites, and persuading
them to observe the Law of Moses as the only true one. All
this appears clearly from many avowals and declarations
made not only by the Jews themselves, but by those who have
been perverted by them and dragged into evil, causing our
Holy Catholic Faith great wrong, disgrace and detriment. . . .

"For these reasons, and with the consent and upon the
advice of many prelates, nobles and knights of our Kingdoms,
and of other knowledgeable and conscientious persons, and
after due consideration of the subject, We have decided to
order all said Jews, men and women, to leave our Kingdoms
and to never come back. With the exception of those who will
accept baptism, all must leave our territories on the first day
of July, fourteen-hundred ninety-two, and never return,
under penalty of death and of confiscation of all their
belongings. . . ."

# 1.

Valderocas was a name any strangers coming to Seville would doubtless hear soon after their arrival, since much of the wealth of Europe's most fascinating harbor city passed through the hands of the haughty and shrewd Old Christian merchant Don Fernando Valderocas Dominguez. The landing of a Valderocas galleon drew to the wharf of the Torre de Oro as big a crowd as the coming of the royal silver fleet, because the Valderocas cargo was not transferred to the King's treasury, but on the contrary spread out for all to admire. All of Seville could purchase the cargo in the streets around the Cathedral, where daily auctions offered Moorish slaves and East Indian jewelry, ivory artwork from Goa and Chinese enamelled vases, colorful Persian rugs and ebony cabinets with inlaid mosaics of rosewood, exotic fabrics and rare spices, and—more important than all these—sugar from the New World.

Fernando Valderocas was an Old Christian—a man with impeccable family credentials. But what made him unique was his success as a master trader at a time when all other Old Christian Spaniards insisted that work was beneath the dignity of a people whose ancestors had reconquered Andalusia from the Infidel.

The natives' distaste for labor had attracted thousands of adventurers to Seville. When more than half of the Spanish population were strangers, the bulk of private trade fell into the hands of Genoese, Germans, Frenchmen, Italians, and Portuguese. Although the Portuguese were not actually foreigners, since their country had become an integral part of Spain, they were even more disliked than the foreigners. Portuguese blood was tainted, because they could not rid themselves of the terrible blemish of being New Christians.

Not all the newcomers to the city sought to make their fortune by honest work. Many were idlers and ne'er-do-wells, pickpockets, cardsharps, hustlers, and whores, lured from other parts of the country by the reputation of Seville as a world marketplace unsurpassed in magnificence. Lumped together under the name of *pícaros,* they loitered in the streets on the lookout for easy victims.

Doña Isabel Valderocas Sanchez understood with perfect clarity the reasons behind her father's strict order that she should never venture into the streets unchaperoned. Having inherited Fernando's stubborn disposition, however, she did not bow to his wishes. On the contrary, she tried to escape her parents' house as often as she could, though always dressed like a servant girl and never without hiding all of her hair and part of her face under a black scarf. She was almost twenty, a spinster by the standards of her country, but because of her wealth and her astounding beauty, she was still the most sought after woman in Seville. Neither too tall, nor too small, she had finely chiseled features and fair skin. Her thick, wavy, and dark blond hair was overcast by a reddish golden shimmer. Her exceptionally large and clear gray eyes reflected hues of blue or green depending upon the light and the color of her garments.

Spanish girls of good families grew up in ignorance and virtual seclusion until they married or joined a convent. Such would have been Isabel's fate, had she not early in life rebelled against this passive role. Through tears and pleading, she won her father's permission to share her older brother Pedro's private lessons. By the age of twenty, she had finally become that suspect creature, a learned female.

Many times Pedro had left for long trips on one or the other of the Valderocas galleons to acquire the practical knowledge of navigation and the overseas business. In between voyages, he also took special lessons at Seville's maritime university, where Isabel also yearned to study, if only the idea of a young woman studying nautical science had not been as absurd as her becoming a Barbary pirate or a mercenary in Spínola's army. Since she did not share her cousin Pepita's passion for embroidery, she found little to do except study and devour her father's library. Over the years, her parents had offered her all the eligible bachelors of Andalusia, including a few noblemen. But Isabel refused to marry, even a younger member of the Guzmáns, the noble family of the Royal Favorite, Count-Duke of Olivares, and of the important Duke of Medina Sidonia. She gave no explanation for her unwillingness, except that she did not feel any affection for these men, and that was not considered an acceptable reason. She was told that it was not possible to fall in love with a man before marriage, since unmarried ladies of good Spanish families were not allowed to remain alone with any man, even for a few minutes. Isabel, however, was not willing to accept a marriage of convenience.

A slight rain was falling as Isabel picked her way home from the wharf where she had watched the arrival of Pedro's ship. Hiding herself in the crowd, she had seen Pedro, looking older with the beard he had grown, and she had seen her father greeting his son warmly. She had also seen the stranger from Madrid, Don Rafael Cortes, shaking Pedro's hand and slapping him on the shoulder. She had wished to be able to run forward and throw herself in Pedro's arms, but she had not dared to show herself. She was expected to wait demurely at home, reading, or perhaps playing the guitar. Even more than to welcome her brother, she wished to meet her father's guest, a former Sevillean who had arrived from Madrid with an invitation for Fernando Valderocas from the Count-Duke of Olivares. According to Olivares's letter, His Majesty, King Philip IV of Spain, was taking a great interest in the rising fortunes of the Valderocas family and had asked Don Fernando to appear for an audience. Isabel had wheedled the information out of her mother; her father never told her anything.

Valderocas House was a two-story building surrounding a square central court or patio. In order to reach her room, Isabel had to walk from the iron grille entrance gate through a wide hallway, past the doorman's open window, and into the patio, where a curved marble stairway led to the upper floor gallery. The doors of all bedrooms opened onto the gallery which ran around all four sides of the house. It was impossible to enter the building unnoticed and, although the doorman had never betrayed her, her heart beat faster each time she came home from one of her secret excursions. Usually, there were dozens of servants swarming about the patio, but today, because of the rain, it was empty, and Isabel ran upstairs, lifting her skirts to take two steps at a time. She sighed with relief when she reached her room.

In spite of its high ceiling and carved oak door, Isabel's room was an austere chamber. Most bedrooms and drawing rooms contained an *estrado,* an elevated platform covered with thick carpets and floor cushions. Ladies did not use chairs but sat fashionably cross-legged on a pillow, to eat, to chat, to do needlework, or simply to rest. Isabel, however, had had the *estrado* removed and had replaced it with a desk and a chair. The walls were covered with maps she had copied herself, and her bed, chest, and wardrobe were simple pieces of furniture without carvings or other baroque adornments.

Isabel had barely slipped out of her soaked woolen dress and into a dark blue velvet gown, when the doorknocker was tapped gently three times. She swirled around to open the door.

"Pepita! Come in."

Her cousin came inside and closed the door.

"Isabel, where have you been? Mother was looking for you. You should tell me what to say when you leave."

"What did you tell her?"

"That you went to buy a gift for Pedro."

"Alone?"

"No, with two of my friends and their mothers."

"And why didn't you come?"

"Because I had to finish the shirt I am embroidering for Pedro."

"You are so good to protect me!"

Their eyes met, and they smiled in complicity.

"Now please tell me the truth. Where have you been?"

"I went to the wharf."

"Oh, Isabel! Did you see Pedro? Did he see you? What does he look like?"

"He has grown a beard. I could not let anyone see me. While I was there, Father and Don Rafael Cortes were talking to Pedro."

"Don Rafael Cortes? Is that the man from Court?"

"Yes."

"Have you met him?"

Isabel shook her head. "I hope we will meet him this evening. Perhaps we can persuade Mother to allow us to eat with the men."

"There will not be any supper tonight."

"Why not?"

"Have you forgotten? Tomorrow is our spring reception, and Mother says one should fast on the night before a feast."

"I wonder where those rules come from," Isabel said with a scowl. "I think she makes them up herself to make life more complex. Oh, if only I were not a woman!"

"Isabel, why?"

"Because then I could travel like Pedro, and carry on Father's business, and go to Court. I could participate in the long discussions Pedro and Father have at night. Do you never wonder what they talk about when they stay for hours in the library? Or on the nights when visitors come? Do not tell me you have never noticed."

"I have noticed. But our place is not with the menfolk. Mother does not join them either."

Isabel threw her cousin an exasperated glance. Pepita was the perfect embodiment of Spanish female charm. She had olive skin and ebony hair, with dark expressive eyes and a playful disposition. She liked to sing and dance as well as embroider, or sew, or cook. She could be serious—but never for long—and she would one day make a wonderful wife for Isabel's brother Pedro. She was patient and loving, and now she tried to soothe Isabel's rancor.

"Oh Isabel, why are you never happy? You could have gone to live at Court, if you had married one of the noblemen who asked for your hand. Mother thinks you want to join a convent. Is that true?"

"Most certainly not. I will never take the veil. Can you picture me in a nunnery?"

"Why not? Most convents have libraries I have been told, and you love to read. Father said all great families give at least one son or daughter to a religious order, and that since he is not a nobleman, you should consider it an honor to live among the daughters of Grandees."

"An honor I can well do without."

"Well, what do you want to do?"

"I want more freedom to move about and to help with Father's affairs. If a woman could once rule Spain and another England, I don't understand why I cannot at least rule a merchant's empire. Pedro does not like to be a trader—he told me so himself. He only likes the seafaring part. I want to help Father with everything he does. I have learned almost as much as Pedro, and I am certain I could oversee the accounts and correspondence. I despise being shut in."

The door had opened during her last words, and Isabel's mother walked in, looking as always impeccably clean, smelling of orange blossoms, and smiling at her daughter's outburst.

"*Mi reina,* you have not been too much shut in today, have you?"

Isabel looked at her mother, and as their eyes met, she grew red to the roots of her hair. She realized for the first time that her mother knew where she had been, had perhaps known all the time, and yet she did not intend to punish Isabel. To her mother she was always *mi reina,* "my queen," the daughter who ruled her heart.

Catalina Sanchez de Valderocas was a round and motherly woman. Her chief virtue lay in her compassion, and she had chosen as her goal in life the welfare of her family. She presided over Valderocas House by following an unspoken set of guidelines which Isabel had never quite understood. In Catalina's world there was order. Certain things were done a certain way, and certain objects were used on certain days. Catalina's sense of cleanliness, physical as well as moral, approached the unquestionable firmness of dogma. She enjoyed preparing delicacies for her husband, she embroidered white silk shirts for her son, and she designed fancy gowns for her daughter and her niece. She dressed simply herself. Only twice a year, when Fernando and she gave a reception for all their friends and acquaintances, would Catalina wear jewels befitting a queen, and her dress would be the most elegant in Seville.

Isabel had not answered her mother, but Catalina looked at her questioningly and seemed to expect an explanation.

As she had done before, Pepita tried to come to Isabel's rescue. "Mother, I would like your advice about that embroidery of mine. . . ." But Catalina lifted her right hand in a gesture she used when she wanted to silence her children or her servants.

"Pepita, I think you had better leave Isabel and me alone for a few moments."

Pepita curtsied and left the room.

Isabel watched her mother with apprehension.

"What is it, Mother?"

"*Mi reina,* your father and I are worried about you. Until now I have always taken your side, thinking that you were happy with your books, your maps, and your studies, but now I have learned from your own lips that you feel shut in, and it may well be that you are unhappy. It is time for you to make up your mind. You know we want to see you well married. It so happens that there is another candidate for your hand."

"There is?" Somehow Isabel felt sure that her mother must be referring to the man who had come from Madrid, and without knowing why, she sounded hopeful.

"Well, should you finally become a woman?" her mother said with a surprised smile. "Yes, there is. And a promising one at that. He is Carlos de Queras, and he will one day be Grandee of Spain. His father, Count de Queras from Granada, is tremendously wealthy. They own almost as much land as the Duke of Medina Sidonia, and they belong to a very old and noble family."

"Oh, Mother," Isabel's heart sank. "Not him. Not that unsightly old man."

"That is no way to talk about a future Grandee. Why, he can hardly be over forty, and you are almost twenty. There is that much difference between your father and me, and we have always been very happy."

"Yes, but Father is a handsome man. Carlos is as ugly as a reptile."

Catalina sighed. "You have only seen him once, and you were younger then. You have never talked to him, nor really met him. He is very intelligent, they say. He is coming to the reception tomorrow, and I expect you to be kind and polite to him."

"Well, I have heard that he does not have a *maravedí* to his name; that is why he wishes to marry an heiress. It is common knowledge that his father is the biggest miser in Spain."

"For a young lady who is not allowed outside her parents' home, you are remarkably well informed." Catalina could not help chiding her daughter, but she did it with a friendly lilt in her voice.

"Oh Mother, I promise I will not go out anymore. I will act properly, just like Pepita, but please, please do not make me marry Carlos."

"You know that we have never forced you to do anything against your will. But I promised your father I would talk to you about it."

"Yes, Mother, I will think it over." She could see on her mother's face that her answer was kinder than Catalina had expected. "May I ask you a favor, Mother?"

"What is it?"

"May we have a family supper tonight? In Pedro's honor?"

Catalina lifted her eyebrows.

"Have we ever had supper on the eve of our spring reception?" she inquired calmly.

"No, but this is an exception. You know it is. Pedro is back, and Don Rafael is here, and . . ."

"Oh, so that is the reason. What about Don Rafael? Do you really think Father would let us have a family supper when he has company from Court? Why, it would be highly improper."

"I watched Don Rafael last night when he arrived. I was up on the gallery behind the maids, so he did not see me, but then I saw him again. . . ." She stopped short before telling her mother that she had been to the wharf, "Well . . . I do wish to meet him."

Catalina smiled. "He will be staying at our house for several weeks, I think. He is a former friend of Pedro's. So you will meet him eventually. But I am afraid there will be no dinner tonight. It is not good to eat on the night before a feast."

Her mother's strange rules always annoyed Isabel. "Is that what you are going to tell Don Rafael and Pedro?"

"Daughter, I am sure Pedro has not forgotten how we live at home, and Don Rafael will be served, of course. Now, I wish you would get Don Rafael out of your head and instead concentrate upon the prospect of becoming Countess de Queras. It is the best offer you have ever had, and I wish you would not throw it away lightly."

Catalina left. Her footsteps were swallowed by the mats and carpets that covered every inch of the gallery floor.

For a while, Isabel walked aimlessly around her room. She did not even have to consider the possibility of marrying Carlos. She already knew that she would never accept him. The question was rather which convent she should choose if her father insisted that she enter a religious order. It might not be so terrible to join a nunnery, provided she could join an important one. She had heard that the most influential political circles met in the drawing rooms of the Carmelites, since many of those ladies had taken the veil and vows not out of love for Christ, but because it was an enjoyable way to spend one's life if one had not found a husband. Ex-mistresses of King Philip IV usually joined a religious order, too, after they had fallen from royal favor, and there were many of them, since the King had an understanding and forgiving wife and an insatiable appetite for lovely maidens. But the Carmelite convents were at Madrid, and how would she ever reach Madrid, when her native Seville was graced with dozens and dozens of convents?

Pasquito's voice outside her door startled her out of her musings.

"Doña Isabel, would you be so kind as to open the door?"

She let him in. Pasquito was a small plump Moor, a slave, the son of the cook, and his duty was to see that there was enough oil in the lamps and to bring light from the kitchen fireplace to wherever it was needed in the house. He also ran errands and watered the many plants distributed around the patio and along the street balconies. He had brought a fresh supply of candles, and with a long taper, he lighted all twelve wicks in the black wrought-iron candelabra next to Isabel's writing desk.

"Doña Isabel, will you tell me another story about the time of the great Caliph?" His round eyes shone like black cherries. He was about eleven years old, and Isabel loved him like a younger brother. She had taught Pasquito to read and write, and she took pleasure in telling him of the former greatness of his people. She did not want him to feel ashamed that his ancestors had not been Christians.

Although she had realized long ago that her own knowledge was of no practical use to her in a world where women were held to be inferior beings, her mind was overflowing with boundless curiosity, and she could not understand why the other younger women she knew did not feel the same way. She had tried to pass on her own learning to Pepita, but her cousin shrugged and laughed and returned to her embroidery.

Pasquito, however, had been a diligent pupil. And he seemed to share Isabel's fascination with history.

"Doña Isabel?"

"No, Pasquito, not today. Another time."

He nodded gravely and left, the lighted taper in his hand.

Taking one candle out of the holder, Isabel walked to one of the maps on the wall. She had expertly copied it from the globe her father had bought for the library. The most recent discoveries were charted, and the map showed the world as it now was. It showed four continents, not two. And Spain was in the center of the world. But the actual center, she knew, was Madrid. From Madrid the Spanish Court sent its gover-

nors to Lombardy, Sicily, Flanders, and America and its
explorers all over the face of the earth. Yes, Spain was the
center, and it was good to be a Spaniard and a Valderocas.

Why should Isabel Valderocas marry a nobleman? Her
father could buy a title of nobility for himself, if he so desired,
since the name Valderocas carried with it a certificate of
*limpieza de sangre,* of purity of blood. The certificate had
been drawn up for Isabel's grandfather during the reign of the
great Emperor Charles V in whose realms the sun did not set
and who was also King Charles I of Spain.

Yes, it was good to be a Valderocas, except . . . except that
there was something about her family that Isabel did not
know. Some well-hidden secret intrigued her. Pedro knew,
she was certain, even though he had called her Isabel la Loca
when she had tried to wheedle the secret out of him. Her
mother knew, and it might even be the reason for her
seemingly far-fetched rules. But her father, Fernando, was
the principal preserver of what Isabel had come to think of as
the mystery. Pepita knew nothing, probably did not even
suspect that anything was . . . well, not wrong but . . . but
not quite right either.

Sometimes Isabel had thought that perhaps her father had
not come by his wealth in an honest way, that perhaps he ran
pirate ships or stole from the royal silver mines. But she had
finally concluded that this was not possible, because Fernando
was too honest and too well-known a man to engage in
fantastic exploits. A shrewd businessman yes, a crook no!
Yet, he did spend hours with Pedro talking about things she
was obviously not allowed to hear, and sometimes, late in the
night, several men came to the house to meet with her father
and brother in the dark library where book-lined walls
muffled every sound.

And now there was the visitor from Madrid, summoning
her father to Court. She wondered whether the nighttime
visitors would also come to meet the stranger and if so, why?
It might mean that her father was involved in some political
intrigue. But why could they not trust her? She knew more
about history and politics than most men, and she knew the
history of the house of Valderocas six generations back
directly to Manuel Valderocas who had lived around 1400.
And the Valderocas ancestry could be traced still farther into
the past. Even if they were not noble, her family was as good
as any in Spain. Why then could she not be trusted with

whatever secret was being kept hidden from the rest of the world?

Isabel had never spoken these thoughts to anyone except to Pedro, because she believed she was the only one to harbor such suspicions. Pepita was happy to be some far-removed cousin on Catalina's side who had been adopted by Fernando and now bore the famous name Valderocas. And the dozens of servants living in the house, as well as the scores who came in to serve during the day, had never indicated that anything might be amiss.

There was a shout outside in the patio. A deep voice called her name.

"Isabel! Where are you?"

At long last! Pedro was home. Quickly placing the candle back in its holder, she rushed out onto the gallery. Down in the patio Pedro stood with one arm around his mother, and with his other arm, he waved up to Isabel. At the same time, he turned to another person and with a quick movement of his head indicated: Look there is my sister!

"Pedro!"

Isabel hurried along the gallery and swept down the broad carpeted stairway straight into Pedro's arms. He kissed her on both cheeks, tickling her with his short round beard, held her at arms' length, and exclaimed how she became more beautiful during each of his journeys. Then he turned to the man at his side.

"I suppose you have met my sister?"

Before the stranger could answer, father Fernando intervened: "No, Pedro, I am afraid that I have taken all of Don Rafael's time since his arrival. Don Rafael Cortes, may I have the honor of presenting my daughter Isabel."

Isabel sank into a deep curtsy, while Don Rafael bowed. Then both looked at one another, and Isabel knew why she had rejected every other suitor until now and why she would continue to do so if she could not have this man.

He was tall and lean with curly black hair. His narrow, closely clipped beard framed his face. An equally closely clipped moustache circled his mouth and joined his beard, leaving his lips and chin fully visible. His nose was long and remarkably straight, but his most striking feature was his eyes: as black as his hair and beard, deep-set, and burning under thick black brows. Altogether, he had about him a look of pride and fierce determination—the look of a warrior or a fanatic—but there was the barest hint of a smile at the corners of his lips.

He murmured a few words to Isabel, and she smiled and gave the proper reply, but she did so without realizing what she was saying. She felt as if she were under a spell. His eyes seemed to search into the very essence of her being. The pulse of excitement she experienced was a feeling she had encountered several times in dreams, but never in reality. She half-expected him to carry her off with him at that very moment, and she hoped his searching look would discover her knowledge that they were destined for each other.

"Well, then, let us go to the library," Fernando proposed, and Isabel was grateful to her father for letting her remain with them. Catalina clapped her hands twice, and Pasquito appeared. He was sent to fetch Pepita.

In the library hundreds of precious manuscripts and printed volumes filled rows and rows of oak shelves. The floor was covered with colorful rugs woven by Morisco artisans in the old *mudéjar* style, developed by their ancestors during the glorious days of the great Caliphate of Córdoba. The latest acquisition to the library was a huge globe from which Isabel had copied the maps for her room. The Spanish territories of the Americas were shown on it in great detail, and Fernando had marked the location of his silver mines by chips of silver and the trade routes by threads of gold.

Don Rafael touched such a golden thread, and Isabel watched his slender fingers slide caressingly over the face of the ocean. Pedro stood next to him and put a hand on his shoulder.

"Don't you wish you had stayed with me at the Casa, instead of seeking your fortune at Madrid?" he asked.

Isabel was surprised. Pedro's question implied that Rafael had studied with him at the Casa de Contratación, the official clearing house for all trade with the Americas, where young men could learn cartography, navigation, and the use of nautical instruments. Yet, to her knowledge, he had never brought Don Rafael to the house.

Rafael sighed. "It was difficult at first, but now I have made all necessary contacts, and the Count-Duke has been a gracious master. If everything goes well, I can expect to obtain my goal this spring, and then I will quickly advance."

At this moment, Pepita rushed in. She wore a pink silk dress spread over an enormous farthingale, her black ringlets were held back by a velvet band into which she had slipped a flower, her cheeks glowed, her long dark lashes fluttered, her love for Pedro danced in the dimples of her flushed cheeks.

Pedro greeted his cousin in much the same way he had greeted his sister, admiring her beauty and kissing her on both cheeks. Don Rafael smiled openly as he bowed to her, and all his seriousness vanished. Isabel, who had not stopped watching him, felt an instant stab of jealousy. Just like everyone else, Rafael was drawn to Pepita. It was obvious. No one, not even Catalina, was ever cross with Pepita, not even when Pepita pretended to be a gypsy who could tell fortunes and danced wild suggestive gypsy dances, nor when she clowned in the patio with Pasquito and the other servants' children. Pepita had a special way with children; she made them laugh with the sheer ecstasy of being alive, and she had a way with old people, too. Sometimes, when Fernando was worried about a ship being late, she would dance around him and smile candidly and flutter her eyelashes until he chased her away, laughingly, of course. And now she was casting her innocent net of charm about Rafael, the only man Isabel had ever found attractive.

Isabel became angry. Something had to be done. She took a step forward and although her heart beat so loudly she feared the others would notice it, she interrupted the concert of smiles.

"Don Rafael, forgive me for being curious, but I do wish you would tell me something of your life at Madrid. I have never been farther than Córdoba. What is Madrid like? Is it very different from Seville?" She held out her hand to him, inviting him to lead her to a group of chairs near the fireplace. She knew that she was being bold beyond etiquette, but she was determined to attract his attention, even if she would have to resort to fluttering her eyelashes like Pepita.

He took her hand and bowed to her father. "With your permission, Don Fernando." Then he nodded briefly to Pedro and Pepita and led her to the armchairs. Her hand rested lightly on his, but when he gave it a sudden squeeze, Isabel felt a delicious shiver traveling through her body. She glanced at him, and his eyes were again looking straight into hers, but this time he was smiling at her, a different smile from the one he had given Pepita. As she sat down, she saw Fernando coming to join them, but Catalina held him back by tucking at his sleeve and whispering something, whereupon he turned around, and they joined Pedro and Pepita at the other end of the room.

"Your cousin is charming," Rafael began, still looking into Isabel's eyes. "She reminds me of a young actress at Madrid, a favorite of the King. But why are you jealous of her?"

Isabel blushed and was angry at herself for having been so obvious about her feelings.

"Is this the kind of small talk you learn at Court?" she asked, trying to hide her confusion.

"I never engage in small talk," Don Rafael continued softly, "but since I have abandoned science and navigation in the quest for a certain power, life at Madrid, in the midst of political intrigues and Court gossip, has made me a student of human behavior. You thought I liked your cousin more than I liked you, but you should not . . . no, let me finish." He held up his right hand, fingers spread wide, to stop her from interrupting him, and Isabel resigned herself to hearing a lecture he should not dare deliver. "You must not be jealous of her, because she is a happy, uncomplicated girl in love with your brother, who does not seem sure whether he wants to return her love."

In spite of her embarrassment, Isabel nodded, amazed that he should have been able to observe so much in so short a span of time.

"Now then, you are a young woman who is not only very beautiful, but also very intelligent. You have studied more subjects than many learned men. You were able to do your brother's lessons for him. . . ."

"Pedro must have told you that," she interrupted. "You could not have guessed that."

He laughed soundlessly at her scowl and his teeth flashed. "Yes, he did. Pedro used to tell me that he taught you most of the things we learned at the Casa."

"Why did you never visit us when you lived at Seville?"

"Oh, I did, but somehow you and I never met. I think you were courted by sons of noblemen. I could not have competed with them, and your parents very wisely kept you away from unpromising orphans. I had the impression that Pedro himself did not want me to meet you."

"But now you say you will reach your goal very soon," Isabel said with a hopeful glance at him. "I suppose that means you will be ennobled and obtain power at Court?"

He shook his head. "No, it means I will become a Dominican friar and be ordained as a priest, and, who knows, perhaps rise to become a Prince of the Church."

"No!" It was more a soft shout than a word, and Isabel

covered her mouth with her hand, wishing she could take it back.

If he was surprised by her reaction, he did not show it. On the contrary, he continued to speak in his slightly husky voice with the slurred Andalusian accent, telling her of life at Madrid, as if to indicate that his personal life was not to be under discussion.

"Madrid," he said, "is a city unlike any other in Spain. Madrid has no walls. It is a city spreading in all directions, a city where streets are paved. You see, it was built after the wars of reconquest were over. Actually, it is being built right now. They put up entire blocks so quickly, we always joke that we cannot recognize our street at night after leaving it in the morning. Nothing ever seems permanent in Madrid. There are palaces under construction and buildings several stories high with apartments that are rented as fast as they are finished. We have beautiful new theaters, inns, restaurants, and shops. There are new shops all over the city. Did you know that Madrid is the world's biggest marketplace for rare perfumes and spices, for silks and jewelry, for artwork and strange objects from Asia and the New World?"

"No, I did not. I thought Seville's market was unsurpassed. Who buys all these things? And who moves into all those new buildings? Spaniards from the countryside cannot have that much money, and I do not think I heard of many people leaving Seville or Córdoba for Madrid. The only person I ever knew who left for Madrid to make a fortune is Don Diego, the painter."

"You mean Velázquez? Did you know him?"

"Yes, when I was a child, he used to come here and draw sketches of some of our servants. And we knew his wife. She is the daughter of Pacheco, the artist who does all the altar paintings. How do they like Madrid?"

Isabel, too, had adopted a casual tone of voice. She was still upset by Rafael's intention to become a monk, but since there was nothing she could do about it, at least not right away, it seemed best to try to encourage him to talk to her as long as possible. She wanted him to have time to study her oval face, her fine complexion, her gently curved lips, her clear eyes framed by thick golden lashes, her beautiful hair which Pedro had once called as soft and lustrous as fresh orange blossom honey. When she was a child, Isabel had sometimes cried because she wanted to have black hair like everyone else, or at least definitely green eyes, instead of vaguely blue ones, since green eyes were thought to be most beautiful, whereas blue eyes notoriously brought bad luck. She did not want to be different, but as she grew older, she had come to realize that far from being a freak of nature, she was a rare beauty. And now, for the first time, she wanted to please a man, to fill his mind with enticing pictures of herself, so he would be unable to think of anyone else, and she was thankful for every outstanding feature she could display.

"I think, Velázquez should like Madrid very much," Rafael said, after looking at her for a long time. "He is extremely busy, everyone wants to be painted by His Majesty's favorite artist. The King has given him the title of Gentleman Usher and put him in charge of the lighting and rooming arrangements at the palace. Velázquez is also helping the Count-Duke to prepare all special festivities, and he makes himself generally indispensable at a Court which prides itself on being a Court of muses. I doubt whether Doña Juana Pacheco de Velázquez likes Madrid. I think she hardly sees her husband, considering all the work he must do. But to return to your question about who moves into all the new houses, I think we must have more foreigners in Madrid than natives. They rent the apartments, they and the younger sons of the noblemen. You see, life is so much more attractive in the capital than in the old family castles. On the Calle Mayor, at the hour of the *paseo*, you can see many a fashionable lady courted by young *hidalgos,* and on the promenade of the Prado, the coaches of the elegant world are surrounded by cavaliers who ride highly trained horses to show off their equestrian tricks. In the evening, there are concerts in the parks, and everyone strolls up and down among the fountains and the flowers, and people chat and start amorous adventures."

"Don Rafael, how very charmingly you speak. You hardly sound like a man ready to take the vows."

He grinned. "I see that you are not happy with my choice of profession. But I can hardly aspire to a real place at Court. I am not a nobleman, and I am not rich. I am not an artist either, nor a general, nor a writer, nor a philosopher, nor a scientist. That leaves only one career, does it not?"

Isabel wished she could mention that this career required complete abstention from love affairs. Then it occurred to her that this concept might be a childish one, in view of the many bastards priests and even bishops were rumored to have. Why, even the Popes were not above suspicion, and the many scandals said to happen in convents seemed to bear out that chastity was not one of the chief virtues of men and women entering religious orders. There was one thing they could not do, however; they could not marry. But she could hardly say to Don Rafael: I object to your plans because I want to marry you. I have enough money for both of us. You do not need to become a Dominican friar. You need only to fall in love with me. As she thought all these things, she wished he would read her mind now, as he had done before.

He did not. He continued his tale of life in the capital. "A favorite pastime of Madrileños are soirées, given by Grandees or courtesans. There you can meet writers and painters, intellectuals and actors, ambassadors and bankers, explorers and poets. Very often people bring art objects to these meetings, and they swap and buy and sell paintings and sculptures. Collecting art has become a great fashion among wealthy people. The King himself often sends representatives to these gatherings to buy artwork for him. Young as he is, the King has a great appreciation for art, which is good for the artists, but often bad for him."

Rafael looked up and Isabel, turning around, saw that her parents, as well as Pedro and Pepita, had joined them to listen to Don Rafael's story.

Now they all sat down in a half-circle around the fireplace and Fernando asked, "Why is it bad for him?"

"Because the Court is one large pool of intrigue for favor and position. The Court positions assigned by the King are the goal of much zeal and effort, especially among the younger sons of noble families. So they try to bribe His Majesty with the best artwork they can afford in order to attain a Court position. Life is becoming terribly expensive. Since we have encouraged learning and the building of schools everywhere, people do not want to cultivate the soil. Everyone wants to become an employee of sorts, and the country is barely able to feed its inhabitants."

"What does that have to do with Court positions?" Pedro inquired.

"Well, a Court position entails room and board at the royal palace or in one of the apartments near the Alcázar. Can you imagine that about a thousand persons receive daily rations of meat, fowl, venison, fish, chocolate, fruit, oil, candles, coal, everything . . . all free from the Court? In addition, none of these people are required to pay taxes. It is an easy life."

"And so some people use the King's love for art to influence him and to obtain such easy positions," Isabel said pensively.

Rafael nodded. "And others want different favors. Even the Grandees, who already own most of Spain's soil, want still more power. And foreign emissaries try to convince the King to put the interests of the Austrian Habsburgs above the interests of Spain, while native politicians intrigue against the Count-Duke of Olivares. No means are too evil, no plans too foolhardy, and no artwork too expensive, if only the desired favor can be obtained."

"How did you get involved in all of this?" Pedro asked. "I cannot imagine that you would offer anyone priceless gifts."

"No, I had the good fortune of being able to save someone's life, and that someone, whom I do not want to mention by name, had the grace to find a place for me in the office of the Count-Duke himself."

"What is Olivares like?" Catalina asked, and Isabel was astonished to detect eagerness in her mother's voice. Catalina hardly ever spoke in front of company, since she considered it bad upbringing for a woman to speak to her husband's guests, unless spoken to. Pedro and Pepita also looked at her in surprise.

Rafael answered immediately and with much fervor. "The Count-Duke is a most formidable man. I consider him the most intelligent ruler Spain has ever had."

"Really?" said Pedro. "Is he still that firmly in possession of power?"

"Yes, fortunately he is. Not without bribing His Majesty, of course. As you know, Olivares was one of the King's tutors, and he has learned how to keep Philip happy. I say Olivares is the greatest ruler, because his ideas are brilliant. He thinks that Spain's weakness lies in her subdivision into separate provinces. He wants to unify Spain, to reform the appalling abuse of her working population, to encourage more Spaniards to become merchants and traders. I am convinced that he also wishes to end this ridiculous war draining our wealth."

"How is that?" Fernando asked. "I thought he was the one who renewed the war with the Netherlands after the end of the twelve-year truce. We have been fighting again for eleven years now, and we do not seem to be able to win. Why did he have to start again?"

"He could not do otherwise. He could not reverse the

inane policies of the Duke of Lerma, his predecessor at the
Court of Philip III. Actually, our whole foreign policy has
been handed down to us since Philip II. It is an absurdity. But
Olivares's hands are tied by too many intrigues, and his worst
enemy is the Queen, who, of course, secretly sides with our
adversaries, the French, since she is of French royal blood."

"So he is also concerned with the scarcity of Spanish
merchants, eh? I hope he does not intend to take all the
Valderocas wealth to finance his plans of reform," Fernando
said with a twinkle in his eye. "Right now there is hardly a
Spanish merchant left in the country."

"That is precisely what the Count-Duke worries about.
Almost all the commercial wealth has passed into the hands
of the Genoese. Something must be done to reverse this state
of affairs."

"That," said Fernando, "is because Spaniards are either
peasants or *hidalgos*. None of them knows how to do
business. There was a time when we had burghers, but the
burghers are gone, and no Court intrigues can bring them
back."

"That is where you come in," Rafael said. Both Pepita and
Isabel leaned forward to exclaim, "How is that?"

Rafael smiled, "That is a state secret."

Catalina rose. "It is getting late, you must be tired, Don
Rafael. You will find a tray with refreshments in your room."
So there was no dinner, after all. The men bowed, the ladies
curtsied, all wished each other a good night, and they retired
to their rooms.

## 2.

It was well past ten o'clock the next morning when they met
for breakfast around the heavy oak table in the room
adjoining the kitchen. Pedro clamored for fresh milk and for
his favorite kind of fried cakes made from bread batter
dropped into boiling olive oil. The girls and Catalina sipped
steaming chocolate, a tremendously popular beverage since
the time the first *conquistadores* had brought it back from
Mexico. Afterwards Fernando proposed to let them all taste
something new and very special. It was an infusion of a dark

brown powder obtained by crushing dried beans from a plant grown in Turkey. Fernando had bought it from a trader who had gotten it in Constantinople. It had a strange bitter flavor unlike any other beverage. In the Moslem world, everyone drank it, Fernando told them. Some people even mixed it with milk or sugar. But in Spain, as in the rest of Europe, the powder was still unknown, except to a few master traders who planned to import it on a large scale.

Fernando himself prepared the brew by boiling a few spoonfuls in a measure of water. Its strange perfume soon filled kitchen and breakfast room. It had to be poured through a special filter into the cups, and when Fernando finally declared, after taking a sip, that indeed it was ready for consumption, everyone wanted to taste it.

Doñas Catalina, Isabel, and Pepita wrinkled their noses and said they did not think much of it. Pedro tried the experiment of mixing it with milk and sugar and said thus prepared, it was much better than chocolate. Fernando liked it hot, black, and sweet, and Don Rafael, after trying all three versions, thought the pure bitter taste was strange but superb.

"What is it called?" he wanted to know.

"The Turks call it *qahveh,* the Arabs *qahwa,* the trader who sold it to me said the Italian merchants call it *caffé.*"

"Caffé, then," Rafael said. "I wonder how long it will take before we can buy it at the Madrid marketplace."

"Another year or two," Fernando said. "In the meantime, if you like it, we can take a small supply with us to Madrid. If we can get the royal household to use it, we stand to make a fortune."

After breakfast, Fernando called for his coach and four. He had to return to the wharf. The young people begged to be allowed to accompany him and then continue on a ride through town. Fernando hesitated, then gave in. Pedro could be trusted to guard his sister's honor. Isabel was ecstatically happy. She had never seen her parents in such a permissive mood.

Seville had hardly changed at all during his absence, Rafael remarked. Church and 'Change were still close neighbors, with merchants assembling on the open space in front of the Cathedral to carry on their bargaining, and there were as many people fingering rosaries as picking other people's pockets. Isabel half-expected him to suggest that they all go in and hear mass when they were driving by the Cathedral, but he said nothing, and she was relieved. Still, the fact that he

intended to give his whole life to the service of the Church
caused her mind to turn to thoughts of religion. Her father
was no eager churchgoer. Fernando judged it was enough to
go once a week to Sunday morning mass, driving up to the
Cathedral in great pomp, and making sure that everyone saw
him. What more could be required of a busy man from
impeccably Old Christian stock? After all, he was not the
King of Spain who had to attend mass and see his confessor
every day.

Fernando had imparted his own liberal views to his wife
and children, and although both Pedro and Isabel had been
made familiar with the scientific and artistic achievements of
their time, they had never been indoctrinated in the exact
beliefs of their faith.

When the Valderocases went to confession, an act required
of every person at least during Holy Week and whenever
some fanatical preacher caused an outbreak of religious
fervor, they always confessed to the same old priest who had
known them for years and was a close personal friend of
Fernando.

Could it be for this lack of deep commitment that Isabel
hesitated to take the veil? God the Father, God the Son, God
the Holy Ghost, Mary Mother of God, Saints and Salvation—
to her it was all words, words, words. Nothing of it touched
her as much as the sudden understanding of a mathematical
formula, or the knowledge that the earth was a sphere that
could and would be explored in all directions, the first tips of
green sprouting from the damp ground of the wheat fields,
the song of the cicadas in the olive groves, the bright eyes of
Pasquito when she told him of the Great Caliphs, the perfect
beauty of the Giralda, no less impressive for having been a
Moorish construction before becoming a Christian cathedral
tower.

However little importance Isabel attached to outer forms
of religion, if anyone had asked her to define what she
believed, she would have answered, after some reflection,
that she thought there must be a creator, but that she doubted
He took as much interest in people as they thought He did.
She never considered that such an answer would send her
without delay into the deathly embrace of the Inquisition.

Overnight the weather had changed; the sky was a soft
silken blue, and the air smelled of spring and wet earth. Pedro
asked the driver to take them to the entrance of the public
garden in back of the old Moorish palace and to wait for them

while they went for a walk among the palm trees, the budding oleander and hibiscus, and the fountains and statues. On a weekday morning, except for a few gardeners, no one came to the park. Pepita, picking up her skirts, danced around the remaining mud puddles and soon disappeared behind a hedge, all the while teasing Pedro into following her.

Rafael and Isabel walked slowly and seriously, as befitted a future Dominican friar and the daughter of a good Spanish family, but when suddenly they found themselves alone, they stopped and looked at each other. His eyes again seemed to look into her very soul, and again she felt her legs growing weak and her desire for him breaking the chains of convention and upbringing. On the rare occasions when she had accompanied her mother to the harbor to say good-bye to Fernando and Pedro, she had seen girls cling to men of the crew, and she had considered it a vulgar spectacle, thinking she would never be able to offer herself like that to any man.

Don Rafael Cortes was an orphan without family, without money, without title. He had been deliberately excluded from meeting her when he still lived at Seville, but he was the man she wanted. She felt an urge to throw herself into his arms and to allow passion to take its course.

"Doña Isabel," he said with the soft Andalusian veil in his voice, "Doña Isabel, you are a very desirable woman. You must stop tempting me like this."

"Don Rafael," she answered, "you are a very desirable man."

"There are other desirable men, Doña Isabel, men with fortunes and titles. I am sure you will find one who is worthy of you."

Isabel realized that this might be her only opportunity to have a few moments alone with Don Rafael, and she was determined not to waste them. If he refused her, she might be so ashamed that she would never wish to see him again, but she had to take that risk. There was no other way, and she knew she had only a short time before they would rejoin Pepita and Pedro.

"Do not join the Dominicans," she said quickly. "If you do not want to remain in the Count-Duke's service, you could work for my father. He often said we should have a branch office in Madrid. Please, I beg you, do not enter an order."

Again her outbreak did not shock him. "I know you are an exceptional young woman," he said calmly, "I have no doubt

that you will succeed in whatever you do, but I cannot marry
an heiress and live on her family's money. That is impossible."

Isabel was stubborn. If he found her alluring, he should be
delighted to know that she desired him. He must not try to
find obstacles where there were none. When she looked into
his eyes, she felt ashamed of her outburst. Yet, he had said he
could not marry an heiress. The word *marriage* had entered
his mind. If she could make him fall in love . . .

"If you married me, we would not need Valderocas
money," she said softly. "We could live frugally."

He shook his head but smiled gently, as he would at a hurt
child.

"Upon returning to Madrid, I shall enter the Dominican
order. I must."

"But why must you?"

"That I cannot tell you."

Never even considering for a moment that he might have a
vow to fulfill or obligations to keep, that he had had a life
before meeting her, she only thought of her own deep
disappointment. If she could not have him, she wanted no
one. She might as well become a nun herself.

Tears welled up in her eyes, tears of wounded pride, as well
as tears of confusion. She turned away her face and walked on
quickly. He kept up with her in silence. Searching for Pedro
and Pepita, they followed a path leading to a circular clearing
surrounded by tall hedges. In its center a goldfish pond caught
and reflected the sunlight. Here they stayed for a while,
watching the fish dart about in the gold-green water. They did
not speak. Isabel could think of nothing more to say without
betraying her hurt and disappointment. Involuntarily, she
gave a sigh.

"Is this what you want?" he asked her then and slowly drew
her into his arms.

He kissed her gently at first, and when she offered no
resistance but seemed to let herself melt into him, his mouth
and tongue grew hard and hungry. She had never been kissed
before; there was a strange foreign sweetness in her mouth
which sent darts of pleasure all over her body. Yes this was
what she wanted, and she would give up everything she had in
order to attain it and keep it. When her own tongue began to
respond to his, he let her go abruptly, gripping her shoulders,
and pushing her away. For a second, he stared at her, then

with a moan he pulled her back in his arms. There was desperation in his voice, "Why did I finally have to meet you?"

This confused her even more, and she freed herself from his embrace and left the enchanted circle around the goldfish pond. He came to her side, and they walked along quietly.

Presently, they heard Pepita's laughter. "Pedro, our serious couple is finally catching up with us." Pepita bowed to them in mock reverence, "My Lady, My Lord, have you solved the problems besetting Spain?"

Rafael joined in her laughter. "Not quite," he said, "give us more time."

What an actor he is, Isabel thought, he should become an actor, not a monk. A monk, there it was again, that painful word. She must not think about it. She must think instead of a way to capture him.

After lunch everyone retired to take a nap. Throughout the realms of the Spanish Crown, the afternoon siesta was an unshakable tradition, observed by high and low alike.

Isabel went to her room but did not even try to lie down. When she felt sure that the others must be sleeping, she took clean clothes and stole downstairs to the women's bathroom. It was empty and cold. There was water in the jars, but that, too, was cold. There was no wood in the fireplace, and it was impossible to start a fire and heat the water without waking up someone and attracting attention to herself. The house was still, the tables for the party had been set, the food stood prepared in the pantry, either finished or ready to be cooked, even the servants were sleeping. Carefully, she poured some water into a flat basin, undressed, and proceeded to sponge herself quickly, rubbing her skin until it was warm and red.

People said it was sinful to uncover yourself; you should wash only one part of your body at a time, covering it immediately when it was dry—a very complicated procedure that kept most people from washing at all. But that did not matter. Too frequent washings were considered a heretical custom. It had never made sense to Isabel. She loved to take baths, and she found her flawless skin with its short golden hair delightful to look at.

Back in her room, she rubbed fragrant oil over her skin and brushed her hair. Then she finally put on a nightgown and sat on her bed.

When she heard three knocks at the door, she went to slip back the bolt and let her cousin come in.

"Were you sleeping?" Pepita asked.

Isabel shook her head.

"I cannot sleep either," Pepita said.

"Why not? Is anything wrong?"

"Oh, Isabel, I am so excited because Pedro is home. You know, I love him so much I am crazy. I think I will go out of my mind like that young queen you told me about. By the way, I like his beard, don't you?"

Isabel had to admit that Pedro looked older and wiser and somehow more adventurous with his well-kept chestnut brown beard. As for Pepita's going mad like Juana la Loca, there was no chance of it. She was much too gay by temperament.

"What is the future priest like?" Pepita wanted to know. "He looks terribly somber to me, even when he plays at being a King's nobleman."

"What do you mean?"

"Well, he pays us compliments, but he is not sincere. He does it without putting his heart into it, just like something he learned at Court but does not care for."

Isabel was torn between her desire to talk about Rafael and her fear that the family would find out how much and how deeply he had affected her. To distract her cousin, she proposed that Pepita help her get dressed, and she would then do the same for her. To dress for a formal occasion took a long time. First, she had to get laced into a tight-fitting bodice that lifted her breasts. Attached to the bodice were several petticoats into the top one of which were sewn elliptical hoops to give the skirt its tentlike appearance. The gown itself was made from thirty yards of shimmering emerald satin trimmed with gold. In the satin's reflection, Isabel's eyes looked almost green.

Pepita's skillful fingers fashioned Isabel's hair into a resplendent golden crown held in place with pearl-studded hairpins. Finally a ruff, consisting of layer over layer of starched lace, was placed around the neck to form a frame for Isabel's face. If they had lived at Court, both young women would have painted their faces. They owned the necessary cosmetics, but they knew Fernando would never permit it.

Pepita's room was located a few yards from Isabel's on the same side of the gallery. It had equally high ceilings and large dimensions, yet it presented a completely different picture from Isabel's quarters. An abundance of gaily colored wall hangings woven by Pepita herself, hand-embroidered curtains, a spinning wheel, and a weaving loom, an *estrado* covered with velvet floor cushions, a low chest holding bits and scraps of material, needles, and pins, and rolls of thread—and not a book or a map in sight. It was exactly the kind of room one would expect of a well-brought up Spanish young lady.

Pepita had to go through the same succession of lacing and petticoats and what seemed to be hundreds of tiny hooks and buttons. When all was done, she emerged as a pure Andalusian beauty, her ivory satin dress trimmed with silver and pink coral. She, too, wore a ruff, but her black hair was strong and wild and most difficult to tame into any hairdo. The best Isabel could do was to braid it on top of her head, and then to wind a string of pearls through the braid.

"Ayayayay!" Pepita intoned the proud call of a gypsy dancer and assumed her pose: head thrust back, nostrils haughtily inflated, one hand on her hip, the other behind her back.

When the girls came downstairs, Fernando, Pedro, and Rafael sat in the drawing room playing cards. Isabel's heart jumped when she saw them. Playing cards, indeed, the future monk! Another good omen. She already knew that he did not intend to join the order out of any religious sentiment. It was a career like any other. She must show him that there were certain pleasures he would have to forego if he became a friar.

Catalina was still busy surveying the kitchen and dining room. Isabel offered to help her.

"I can take care of everything, Mother."

Catalina gave a little chuckle. It was the first time Isabel had expressed any interest in the duties of a housewife.

"No, dear, you might stain your dress. Leave everything to me. I am almost finished. Why don't you play a few songs instead?"

So Isabel went to fetch her guitar from the music room and sat on the upholstered bench running along one wall of the drawing room. Playing the instrument proved a bit difficult in her starched finery. She struck the first chord hesitatingly, but then her fingers found their way into the lamenting melody of Andalusian folk music, and with every vibration of the guitar, her heart cried out to Rafael. Soon the men laid down their cards and listened to her haunting rhythms. When she played the prelude to an old Córdobese *caña*, Pedro came over to sing it for them, his deep voice translating its tragic anguish into a long string of *ayes:* "Ay, ayayayay . . ."

Pepita bent over to whisper into Isabel's ear, "How sad can you be? That is enough of *cante grande*." Then Isabel played what her cousin wanted to hear, the seductive challenge of a love song.

Both Pepita and Pedro knew well how to interpret the impetuous courtship of a Spaniard and his chosen lady. He stamped his feet impatiently, he implored and beguiled, she turned her head and would not be conquered. When he pretended to give up, she teased him with husky exclamations. He had to do better than that. In the meantime, Fernando and Rafael, as well as a number of footmen and servant girls, had formed a half-circle around the guitarist and the dancing couple. They all clapped their hands rhythmically, but none of them smiled. Spanish folk music was always a serious affair, with more tragic events than comic ones, and even courtship and love were gravely portrayed and often ended unhappily.

While she played, Isabel looked steadily at Rafael. She was a good musician, and her fingers found their way to the right strings without effort; she could afford to call out to him with her changing eyes, to try to draw him into the magic field she was creating for him. He too stared at her, his hands stopped clapping. Was he ready to give in?

Whatever happens, thought Isabel, whatever happens to me hereafter, I shall always remember this moment. If he goes back to Madrid and I never see him again, I shall remember this day as one of happiness. In her heart she did not believe that he would actually leave her; it seemed impossible. And besides, she still had two weeks—enough time to make her head spin with plans.

She struck a few rapid, violently happy chords and stopped. Everyone applauded and laughed and shouted *olé*. Then the servants hurried back to the kitchen and patio. The first guests would arrive shortly.

Later, Isabel stood with her parents and Pedro next to the well in the patio, greeting guests she had not seen since their last reception in the fall. She smiled forgivingly when her mother's old lady-friends chided her for not being married yet, she curtsied to the old Alcalde who was her father's best friend, she inquired of her own former girl friends how their children came along.

The patio was enclosed on all four sides by arches and columns which were overgrown with rambling shrubs. From the upper floor balustrade fell green cascades of asparagus plants. Up to shoulder height the walls of the house itself were covered with a mosaic of blue, white, black, and orange tiles. Fernando Valderocas's home was one of the few in Spain that could compete with the splendor of a nobleman's palace.

The last people to arrive were a group of musicians hired by Fernando to entertain his guests. Since the night air was mild, the musicians stayed in the patio—a colorful spectacle in the shine of torchlights.

Inside the dining room, guests were crowding around Catalina's buffet, tasting salmon, praising swordfish, savoring game birds, exclaiming over a whole roasted lamb. There was wine, too, but Spaniards drank little if any alcohol; they preferred snow-cooled almond water. Isabel had expected Don Rafael to be the center of attraction, yet no one took notice of him, and her father did not once mention that he had been convoked by the chief minister. She went from room to room, exchanging small talk and pleasantries, all the while searching for Rafael. At last she found him in the patio, leaning against a pillar, listening to the guitars and tambourines.

"Why do you stay out here alone?"

"Oh, I do not like to chat unless I care for the audience. Besides, I love guitar music."

"Do you really?"

"You play very well. When I am back at Madrid, I shall remember today, and I shall think of you, and I shall hear your songs in my mind."

"I will play more for you, tomorrow, if you like. Do they have guitar music at Court?"

"No they usually have stage plays that are getting more and more elaborate every year. Since the King called Cosme Loti to Madrid, we have had the most fantastic shows one can imagine. I do not know whether you have heard of the Italian Loti; he is an architect, engineer, and theatrical director, all at once. A wizard at combining the ingenuity of Italian engineering with the artistry of Spanish playwrights. He has given us Court spectacles of unequalled realism. We have seen fire-spitting volcanos, flying dragons, and wriggling sea-monsters. Absolutely nothing is left to the imagination."

"You do not sound enthusiastic about it," Isabel said.

"I am not. I think the Court is wasting money, while the country sinks into poverty."

"Last night you said the Count-Duke was Spain's best ruler. Why does he not stop the extravagance?"

"The Count-Duke has made many enemies through his reforms. If he wants to see any of his ambitious plans for Spain succeed, he must first assure his own position. This he can do only by pleasing the King. Philip is a man of good intentions but he has a weak sense of responsibility. He is a great wit, a good horseman, an excellent marksman, and a passable actor. But that is all. No, not quite. He is also a man of great amorous passion."

"I do not suppose he needs the Count-Duke in that field," Isabel remarked.

"There are rumors Olivares has helped the King seduce more than one beautiful maiden, some of them nuns, but I suppose it is just a rumor."

"An interesting one, though. Could you fall in love with a pretty nun?"

"I am too much in love with you to even consider the possibility of falling in love with someone else," Rafael said caressingly.

"And if I took the veil?" Isabel asked, excitement vibrating through her voice.

Immediately, he became serious. "You must not," he said sternly. "You must absolutely not enter a nunnery. You are not suited to that kind of life. Promise me you will never enter a convent."

"Then promise me that you will never enter a monastery," she retorted.

"That I cannot do. I told you I must join the Dominicans. Perhaps one day you will understand why."

"No, I will never understand why," Isabel replied in a vehement whisper. "I do not understand you at all. Here you stand telling me you are in love with me, and you even presume the right to tell me what I should or should not do, but you insist on getting a tonsure. It makes no sense to me."

He took her hand, turned it around and placed a kiss on the inside of her wrist.

"You do not have to understand me, and you know it," he said. "If you were an ordinary woman, I would not have dared speak to you of love, because an ordinary woman would expect me to marry her if I said I loved her. And the rules of honor would require that I marry her. But you are different. You live in a world of your own, a world of thoughts. . . . Let me be one of your thoughts, that is all I ask."

"Then why should I not take the veil?"

"Because then your thoughts would have to include a lot of saints. And I do not care for the company of saints."

He was the most self-centered man she had ever met, Isabel reflected. He seriously wanted her to spend her life thinking about him. What impudence!

He leaned back against the pillar, and she studied his profile, calm and proud against the flickering shine of the torchlights. She was not sure anymore that her inspiration would work. She had planned to charm him into making love to her, and her intuition still told her that she would achieve that much. The question was, could he then be pressed into marrying her? This morning her mind had answered YES, tonight she sensed it was NO. He turned his face to look at her. His penetrating glance made her shiver; did he implore or did he command? She turned around, picked up her skirts, and slowly walked away to join the party inside.

She saw Pedro watching her as she came into the library. Presently, he left the group of men gathered around the globe and walked over to her.

"Isabel, I must talk to you."

"Yes, what is it?" ·

He led her away from the others to a quiet corner.

"I have been watching you and Rafael. I do not know whether he told you that he will join the Dominicans. . . ."

"He seems to talk of nothing else," she interrupted him.

"That is all right. I was afraid he might forget it. When I knew him before he went to Madrid, he was . . . well, let us say acquainted with a great many young women."

"Oh? Is that why you never introduced him to me?"

"Possibly."

"Why does he want to become a friar?"

"The Dominicans are the most powerful order in Spain. A Dominican priest may rise to become confessor to the King or to the Queen or to the Royal Favorite. Rafael is an ambitious man. He will do anything to achieve his objective. He will be ruthless if he has to; a broken heart will not bother his conscience the least. I want to warn you about him. Do not trust him. He may say sweet things to you, but he will never marry you."

Her pride was stung. "Who says I want to marry him?"

"Your eyes do when you look at him."

She hated herself for having shown her feelings. Yet, the more Pedro warned her, the more she yearned for Rafael.

"Thank you for your advice," she said. "I will remember what you have said."

Pedro shrugged and turned back to the circle of men. He had done his duty. Contrary to tradition and code of honor, he had always treated his sister like a good friend. Studying the same subjects had brought them very close, but tonight he was worried about her.

So, Rafael was what common people called a wencher, Isabel thought. According to Pedro, she was just another girl to him. That meant she must make him jealous. She must make him want her more than he had ever wanted a woman. Her glance fell upon a group of young men who were obviously courting her dimpling cousin. Pepita was the most desirable woman in Seville, next to Isabel herself. But Isabel had been written off as unattainable by the dapper young swains. She was much too bookish. Now she decided she would show them what she could do.

At parties and gatherings, it was customary for hosts and guests to entertain each other with songs, dances, or sketches. At Valderocas House, it was usually Pepita who gave these little presentations. Now Isabel joined the musicians in the patio and briefly conferred with them.

After a soft prelude, her voice rang out, pure and clear, as she sang the lamentation of a beautiful Moorish Queen who saw her lover beheaded by her jealous husband. Slowly, one after another, the guests drifted into the patio to listen to her ballads of the loves and sorrows of past generations. If the King could play in his own theatrical productions, the daughter of a merchant could sing in her own concert. When applause rose, she smiled and curtsied to them, but not once did she look in the direction where she knew a solitary figure was leaning against a pillar. She only hoped he saw the adoring glances of all the men present. She only hoped he understood that tonight she could take any heart and trample on it, if she so pleased. Spite him and his Dominican order!

Pedro and Pepita stared at her and then at each other in disbelief. Whatever had possessed Isabel? She was not usually interested in entertaining the guests. Then, suddenly, Pepita understood. Isabel was doing this for one reason only.

"Go up to her and dance the ballad of the Alhambra," she suggested to Pedro. "Isabel has seen us so often, she will know the steps."

"Why?" Pedro whispered. "She does well enough for herself."

"Do it, please, you will see why," Pepita said and gave him an encouraging nod.

Pedro joined his sister. After talking to the guitarist, he became the supplicant admirer of the haughty Moorish princess who would not have him. Isabel had started to perspire under her heavy dress, and she was glad now that Pedro had to do most of the dancing, pirouetting around her and stamping his feet. Almost everyone knew the old folk dance; in the end the princess would relent. But now the spectators were in for a dramatic surprise. Pepita whispered to the young men who had followed her outside, and they, one by one, joined in the dance, presenting their charms to the arrogant lady, each one of them hoping against hope to win the prize.

The people of Seville had heard that the daughter of Don Fernando Valderocas could rival in haughtiness the Moorish princess she portrayed. The dance became reality. Whom would she choose? Pepita had hoped Don Rafael might enter the ranks of the dancers, that was what Isabel would want, but he never moved from his pillar.

Isabel herself knew that choose she must, the dance demanded that the princess make up her mind. She looked over all her suitors and found them wanting. She considered briefly the possibility of walking off alone, but that would defeat her purpose. She wanted to impress Rafael. Unfortunately, there was no man good enough to impress him with. Or was there?

Out of the crowd came a frail-looking, elegantly dressed individual who had spent most of the evening at her father's side. But smart or handsome he did not have to be, for he was Carlos de Queras, scion of one of Andalusia's noblest families. A future Grandee of Spain! Despite what she had said to her mother, there was nothing particularly ugly about him. Only his manner was cold and forbearing, and his eyes had a nasty glimmer in them when he walked up to Isabel, smiled condescendingly at the dancers and, after bowing low and sweeping off his plumed hat, offered her his arm. She hated him for being the one she must choose, but it was obvious to her, as to everyone present, that she could not refuse him.

Betraying no hesitation, she curtsied to him, took his arm, and walked with him over to her parents.

"I heard that your daughter is learned," Don Carlos said to her father. "I did not know she was also very beautiful and talented. My compliments."

"She surprised all of us tonight," Fernando answered. "Could it be that your presence inspired her?"

Isabel listened to them with broken spirits. She wished now she had never tried to draw attention to herself. Even though Carlos would one day be called cousin to His Majesty, he filled her with so much repulsion that she could hardly bear a polite conversation with him, much less consider becoming his wife. Luckily, there was no chance for any more talk. The first guests came to take leave, and Catalina and Fernando had to rise and bid their company good-bye. Don Carlos de Queras bowed to Isabel again, and she dropped him a deep curtsy; then he was gone.

When all had left, Isabel said to her mother that she had a headache and wanted to go to sleep right away. Fernando heard her. He stood in front of his globe.

"Isabel, come here."

"Yes, Father?"

He looked at her and suddenly Isabel saw that he was old and tired. His carefully barbered gray beard hid the lower part of his face, but there were pouches under his eyes, deep lines on his forehead, and his eyes had a weary expression. Little sweat pearls stood on his temples, and his skin had a greenish tinge to it, something Isabel had never noticed before.

"Father, you look ill. Are you feeling all right?"

"I am a little tired, that is all. That was quite a spectacle you gave tonight. I am afraid you furnished the town with enough gossip for a year. But all is well that ends well. Do you want to marry him?"

"Who?"

"De Queras. He seemed absolutely smitten with you."

"With my dowry, you mean."

"Well, yes, that enters into consideration. But I also think he fell in love with you. I saw him fight with himself. It cost him some effort to walk out there to get you."

"Oh, how I wished he had spared that effort."

"Then I take it you do not like him?"

"Oh Father, I loathe him."

"He will become a Grandee, you know."

"I know."

He gave her a feeble smile and pinched her cheek.

"Don't worry, daughter, I don't like him either. I rather did like young Guzmán. I wish you had taken him."

"Why do you always have to try to find a husband for me? You never ask Pedro to get married."

"That is not the same. It is a father's duty to find a husband for his daughter. Well, good night, dear. I will have to think of a good excuse to refuse his offer."

"Good night, Father, thank you." She bent over her father's hand to kiss it, and he laid his left hand on her head as if to bless her.

As she crossed the patio on her way to the staircase, she noticed that her headache was gone. Queras was no more than a harmless nuisance. For once, her father had understood her aversion to a pretender, and he had even shared it. She knew that his word was good. She need not worry about Don Carlos anymore.

The torchlights had been extinguished, and the curving stairway was dark. She was up on the landing, when a dark figure detached itself from the wall.

"Thank you for the concert," said a husky Andalusian voice, and again her heart stood still, then pounded wildly.

"Rafael," she whispered.

He pulled her in his arms and she bent her head back to receive his kiss. But when her arms went around him, he freed himself quickly. She knew they were courting danger. Still, he walked with her to the door of her room. There he bowed formally and kissed her hand.

"Good night, Doña Isabel."

She wished she were able to invite him in. That was impossible, however, because the chambermaid was waiting to help her out of her clothes. She thought briefly of inviting him to visit her later, but she was afraid he might not come, and then she would wait and fret. Also, there was the danger of her mother or Pepita coming in. No, it would be far better if she went to his room. But did she dare to defy a convention and bring dishonor to her family? Was she not risking death both for herself and Rafael?

"I have something to tell you," she whispered. "I will come to you later in your room." Isabel trembled when she realized what she had done, but she slipped into the chamber before he had time to answer and before she had time to change her mind.

After Teresa had helped her get ready for bed and had left, Isabel put on a simple gown without stays, hooks, or petticoats. Her decision had been made, and she would not waver any longer.

The guest rooms were on the opposite side of the gallery. When she stepped out of her room, everything was quiet. Barefoot, she ran to the other side. Her heart was beating in her throat. She had never been more frightened. If her father caught her, the code of honor gave him the right to kill her immediately and demanded that he kill Rafael. Otherwise, the name Valderocas would be dishonored forever. A blemish on the family honor could only be washed with the blood of the offender. It was a sacred rule.

He had left the door open.

When she entered, he sat at the desk, writing. The goose quill made a scratching sound on the paper. She thought he would jump up and take her into his arms, but he continued to write. She closed the door softly and slipped the bolt into place. Finally, he rose, and his eyes questioned her. He seemed more annoyed than happy to see her.

"You wanted to tell me something? Let me guess. You are going to marry Don Carlos de Queras."

"Most certainly not," she muttered.

"You still want to enter a convent?"

She shook her head.

"My curiosity is aroused. What is it?"

She held out her hands to him, palms up, in an age-old gesture of pleading.

"Rafael."

He stopped teasing her then and pulled her close, and his mouth came down hard on her parted lips.

Her eyes closed, and she leaned against him, dizzy with desire, hardly noticing how he undressed her between caresses and led her to the bed. An intoxicating fragrance emanated from his skin and invaded her senses; she opened her thighs willingly. There was no pain at all. She felt like the overtight string of a guitar, vibrating at the finest touch, and then suddenly bursting from too much pressure. *Ay, ayayayay.* He moved deep within her, increasing her desire, until she spilled herself around him in recurring waves of exquisite pleasure. Then he pulled away unexpectedly and slumped down on her, moaning, "I love you, I love you, I love you. . . ." Afterwards, she felt happy and drowsy, but not too drowsy to wonder what he thought of her now.

She did not have to wonder very long. Presently, he rolled over on one side and, leaning on his elbow, looked at her pensively.

"You should have married a long time ago. Few girls can feel so much the first time they make love. My dearest, you are a fountain of paradise."

"Well, I am glad I am not married," she said, thinking she could never have given herself to another man.

"Have you never fallen in love with anyone? You proved tonight that you have swarms of admirers."

"No, I have not. I have never even kissed anyone. Nothing like this has ever happened to me."

"Well, I am sure you will marry soon, and then it will happen quite often."

"I only want to marry you." There it was. She had said it and could not take it back.

"I know, my darling, but that is not possible. I have work to do. Important work, and in order to do it, I must become a Dominican friar."

She remembered Pedro's words and wondered whether he had lain with country wenches on his way down from Madrid. At any rate, he had seduced the daughter of his host. Do not trust him, Pedro had warned. But, of course, it was too late now. She had trusted him, and, oddly enough, she could not stop herself from trusting him. Then she recalled her plans to capture him. She had thought he would change his mind and marry her if she proved to be with child. Now, all of a sudden, she feared he might tell her to go and marry Carlos de Queras, so his bastard could one day be Grandee of Spain.

She lay quietly, thinking. One half of her knew that she had fallen desperately, irrevocably in love; the other half was confused about the consequences.

He was watching her intensely.

"Are you worried?"

She looked at him, not sure what he meant.

"I was careful, nothing will happen."

"Oh," was all she could say. She did not know a man could be careful. The King himself had bastards all over Madrid.

"I love you, Isabel. You are beautiful, intelligent, strong, and entirely unlike any woman I have ever known."

"How many times have you fallen in love?"

"Never like this."

"Then . . . ."

"Shshsh!" He softly placed two fingers over her mouth, and a wave of happiness surged through her body. Suddenly, nothing seemed impossible.

It was getting cold in the room. They lay close to each other under the blankets, his slender fingers were softly exploring her body, and soon she was aroused and ready to spend herself anew. He took her again, more forcefully than the first time, and she was more certain than before that she would never belong to anyone else. If she could never see him again, she might yet enter a convent. Still, there were two weeks left before Rafael and Fernando would set out for Madrid. Perhaps, she would find a way to make him love her as much as she wanted him to. There must be a way.

In the early morning hours, she left him and went back to her own room. She would probably not be able to sleep she told him, she was too excited. He had laughed his soundless laughter and suggested that on the contrary she would fall asleep right away and dream of him. He would do the same, and they would meet in their dreams.

# 3.

"Isabel, hurry, wake up."

Still drugged with sleep she went to open the door. Pepita came in. "Have you been sleeping through all this commotion?" she asked. "Get dressed, quickly. Father is sick."

"My Lord, what is the matter? What is it?"

"We do not know yet. He has a terrible fever. Mother is afraid it might be the pox. Dr. Rojas is with him now. Please hurry and come."

Not the pox, Isabel thought, now wide awake. It cannot be.

"Why?" she asked Pepita, while slipping into a simple woolen dress. "Why would it be the pox?"

"Because some workers at the shipyard recently died of black pox, and Father has been in contact with them and their families."

"Does Don Rafael know?"

"They are saddling his horse; he is leaving for Madrid."

"Leaving, now?" Isabel felt the blood drain from her face.

She held herself at the bedpost, thinking she would faint. "Is he afraid he will catch it?" she asked weakly.

"No, I doubt he would be afraid of that. A special courier arrived this morning. He has to return to Madrid immediately."

"Why did you not wake me up earlier," Isabel asked with a scowl. "You know I would want to be up."

"Mother said to let you sleep. There was nothing you could do to help."

The sun was shining into the patio when Isabel stepped out of her room. Down by the well Pedro and Rafael were conferring rapidly in low voices. On the gallery, in front of her parents' bedroom, Dr. Rojas talked to Catalina. Isabel rushed to join them.

"Mother, I am sorry I did not wake up earlier. Dr. Rojas," she curtsied to him.

Dr. Rojas was a small rotund man with a white beard and a receding hairline. He had been the Valderocas family physician for many years. He had helped bring Pedro and Isabel into the world and had cured their various childhood diseases. Now he looked at Isabel with sad eyes.

"Your father is very ill."

"He has had a bad ague before and you cured him."

"This is not an ague, there is more to it. We will know for sure by tomorrow night. In the meantime, do not go near him. I will see if I can find a nurse."

Catalina shook her head. She would not let anyone come near her husband, she said, no one except Dr. Rojas and herself. She would take the best care of him; she would stay with him day and night. Dr. Rojas must not send anybody to help her.

"I will help you, Mother," Isabel said, but both her mother and the doctor protested. She was not to enter her father's room under any circumstances. She bowed her head. Then with a heavy heart she went down into the courtyard to bid Rafael good-bye.

Pepita had joined the two men and now, when she saw Isabel coming, she pulled Pedro away and whispered to him, whereupon both went into the kitchen.

Rafael was dressed in simple riding breeches and a short coat. He was riding back to Madrid with the courier who had come to call him back. The man was holding the horses and waiting in the street. Isabel stared at Don Rafael with tears in her eyes. She could hardly believe that only a few hours ago she had lain in his arms. With difficulty she kept her voice steady.

"Will I see you again?"

"I do not know."

She felt like a wounded animal and swallowed hard to repress the hurt and anger welling up within her. She must be strong. She must be stronger than any woman he had ever known. She must never let fate reduce her to a whining, hysterical creature. She must be able to find a solution to her own problems. If she could not do that, she was not worthy of him.

She saw her mother and Dr. Rojas look down from the gallery. She extended her hand to Don Rafael Cortes. As he took it and bent over it, she said quickly:

"When my father is well, I will accompany him to Madrid. Look out for me in the park of the Prado, or on the Calle Mayor. I will be one of your fashionable young ladies, courted by *hidalgos*, giving no one her favor, but waiting for the one she loves." She dropped her voice to a whisper. "Watch out, Don Rafael, for I am not done with you."

He had kissed her hand lightly and now his somber deep-set eyes burned again into her, as if he wanted to etch her features into his memory. She could not hold back her tears any longer. She swirled around brusquely, picked up her skirts, and ran upstairs to her room, where she threw herself on the bed and broke into uncontrollable sobs.

# 4.

Day and night Catalina remained at her husband's bedside, fighting his mounting fever with compresses and herb teas, watching with terror the first lentil-shaped red spots appear on his lips and chin, seeing them spread to the rest of his body and grow and grow until his face was a swollen mass of yellowish white skin ready to erupt at the merest touch. By then he was completely covered with pustules that slowly took the shape of little volcanos. If the pustules could break and suppurate before Fernando's strength was exhausted, he had a chance to live, Dr. Rojas told them. The entire household prayed for him, and Pepita spent the whole day lighting candles in front of every altar in Seville.

But Fernando could not escape the clutches of the terrible fever, and he died shortly after the first pustules broke.

Neither Pedro nor Isabel was allowed to enter his room nor even look at their dead father through the door. Father Tomas, the old priest who had been Fernando's confessor, arrived too late to do more than console the widow. In his last will and testament, Fernando asked to be buried in a wooden coffin in the oldest part of the graveyard and to have as simple a funeral as possible.

His wishes were respected. Nevertheless, on the day of the funeral, half the inhabitants of Seville came to pay their respects to the grieving family. Among the mourners was Carlos de Queras, but neither Isabel nor Pedro gave him any special attention.

# 5.

The Valderocas reception had been held shortly before the beginning of Lent, the forty days of fasting and penitence preceding Holy Week. Fernando had died after the first Sunday of Lent. The following Saturday, Seville began its yearly pageant of awe and secret terror.

The Alcalde, the town crier, and the Secretary of the inquisitorial tribunal of Seville, as well as all unpaid collaborators and informers bearing the title of "Familiars of the Holy Office," assembled on horseback at the Castle of Triana and formed a procession which wound through the city behind a corps of drummers and trumpeteers. It stopped at eight principal places to read the proclamation requiring all persons over the age of twelve to assemble on the following day either at the Cathedral or at the Church of San Salvador to hear the Edict of Faith, under pain of excommunication and of fifty ducats.

The Edict of Faith was a formal declaration designed to make every man and woman aware that their lightest word or act might subject them to prosecution by that Holy Court whose very name inspired dread. The whole population was called upon, once a year, to remember their religious duty to spy upon their neighbors and friends, even upon the members of their own families, and to report within six days any word or act sounding heretical or suspect, erroneous, rash, scandalous, or blasphemous.

Since mourning was no excuse for absence from the soul-lifting experience and privilege of hearing the Edict of Faith, Catalina, Pedro, Isabel, and Pepita, followed by all their servants, freemen and slaves, filed into their pew at the Cathedral.

Every year on this occasion, Isabel had sat at her father's side, confident that none of the terrible things threatened from the pulpit would ever apply or happen to her. She had felt safe and secure in the knowledge that Fernando Valderocas Dominquez and all his family were Old Christians and that they could never be accused by anyone of the crimes enumerated. The thunderous voice of the Secretary of the Holy Office had rolled over her in waves without making a deep impression. Now, in her heartbreak, for the first time, she really listened. A Dominican friar was reading the Edict—one day Rafael might be standing there in his place. She listened to the long list enumerating all Jewish rites and customs, all Moslem rites and customs, all Protestant rites and customs, and the particular heresies of a sect called Illuminists. Next in line were sorcery and witchcraft. She had never realized there were so many ways of calling demons and keeping them by special pacts locked into mirrors or rings, so many ways of consorting with the devil and of practicing devination. It was also a crime to say that fornication was not a sin. Would she be sent to prison if someone denounced her for having given herself to Rafael? Had a servant noticed? Would she be sentenced to wear the sanbenito, the dreadful garment of shame?

She listened with mounting horror, when she learned that she was a culprit on many accounts: She continually disbelieved or doubted articles of faith; she had read books condemned by the Index; she also knew that in her father's library there was a Bible in the vernacular; she believed fornication to be no sin; she was in love with a man who wanted to enter the orders; and she was determined to become his mistress in order to distract him from his holy career; she had told her little slave Pasquito that his Moslem ancestors were heroes to be proud of—oh, there was no end to her sins. If anyone found out, Pepita or Pedro, or a maid, anyone at all, she would be lost. They would have to denounce her, or they would all be thrown into the deepest dungeons of the secret prisons. They would be tortured for names of accomplices, and they would be condemned to eternal shame, unless she denounced herself during the period of grace, during the six days following this Sunday, in which case she might hope to be forgiven by the church. At least she gathered that much from the menacing formulas pouring forth from the black friar standing in the pulpit. She considered briefly confessing herself to the old family priest, truly confessing instead of inventing a few harmless lies as she had done in the past, but then she heard at the end of the reading of the Edict that confessors were ordered, under the same penalties, to withhold absolution from penitents who had not denounced all offenses to the Inquisition. She knew that she would drag her whole family into shame and destitution if she so much as breathed a word about her true feelings.

She was frightened. She stole a couple of sideward glances at the other worshippers, and she thought she sensed fear all around her except in Pedro's face, where she saw strength and a mouth which had become a stubborn thin line. But there was horror in Pepita's wide open eyes, there was fear stamped on the features of every man, woman, and child in the crowd. Six days were left to confess and denounce and repent. Then, on the following Sunday, there would be a second Edict and a sprinkling of holy water to drive out the demons who kept the contumacious sinners from confessing and denouncing. They would be publicly excommunicated, which meant that although no one knew who was a sinner, all the sinners would know in their own hearts that they were condemned to eternal hellfire. There would be a last urgent call for people to come to the inquisitorial tribunal and denounce even the slightest suspect; there was no danger in this for the informants, since no prisoner of the Inquisition was ever told who denounced him nor what the charges were. And then finally, after this last period of grace, there would come the dreaded Sunday of the Anathema.

Isabel left the great Cathedral in a daze. Usually, she enjoyed the end of mass. She liked to come out into the sunshine, to be free of the oppressive odor of incense, to look back with a smile to the graceful lines of La Giralda, but not today. Today she walked heavily, eyes cast down, soul in turmoil. She dared not talk to Pepita or to Pedro, lest they guess her fear and conclude that fear could only be caused by guilt. Never before had her mind been so paralyzed. She could not even think clearly, nor decide what was right and what was wrong. She only knew dully that something was wrong, something was all wrong, but was it her attitude? Was it the fact that for the first time she had consciously listened to all the threats and terrors of the Edict, had grasped the murderous efficiency of the Inquisition, its ever-present power, its calculated method of creating suspicion not only among strangers but among families, its oppression of free thought, its despicable excuse of wanting to purify the faith? Or, was it actually that she had fallen from grace, that she had sinned, that the Church was right, and that she was a heretic deserving to be punished?

For the first time in Isabel's life, she trusted no one. She wanted to see no one, talk to no one. She wondered briefly whether she would feel the same if her father had not died, but she thought that she would not have trusted him either, not anymore, not after she had met Rafael.

Rafael, oh Rafael! Knowing she should feel that he had led her into sin, her guilt redoubled when she realized she believed her salvation lay with him.

The entire Valderocas household was mourning the death of its master, and therefore no one noticed that Isabel was unusually silent. She took her meals without looking up, hardly eating anything, and after a few attempts, Pepita gave up talking to her.

The Sunday of the second Edict came and went, leaving Isabel numb in the knowledge that in the eyes of the Church, she was now excommunicated even if no one else knew it. The more she meditated, the more sins she discovered—her whole system of thought was faulty. She was unquestionably guilty enough to be burned at the stake. She slept little these nights, turning and tossing, and her short snatches of slumber were filled with nightmares of horrible contorted faces of sinners and penitents, wearing sanbenitos painted with devils and flames, indicating that they were to be burned alive. Finally, one night she dreamed of Rafael in the black cloak and hood of the Dominican friar. A rosary was hanging from his hip, and the rosary grew bigger and bigger with each pearl representing one of Isabel's sins, until they crowded around her, engulfing her, suffocating her. Rafael's face, too, grew bigger and bigger, and there was lightning coming from his eyes, condemning her to eternal hellfire, because she was unfit for the company of saints. She awoke trembling, covered with sweat and wishing she knew how to pray, how to invoke the help of a saint. But what saint would listen to her after her mind had denied the very existence of saints? As she lay, shaking with fear, there was a voice speaking to her, a soft Andalusian voice, saying, "I do not care for the company of saints."

She sat up in surprise.

Rafael was a heretic! No matter what anyone else might think of him, Rafael was a sinner. He obviously believed that fornication was no sin, he spoke derogatively of saints, he had tried to dissuade her from entering a nunnery, and he planned to become a monk for personal profit.

All this made him a sinner. But human beings were expected to be sinners, that was the whole idea of religion, that one's soul had to be saved. So being a sinner was not bad in itself, as long as one confessed and repented, but being proud of one's sins was what made one a heretic.

And she had never met a prouder man than Rafael. Pride! Pride was what they had in common, Rafael and she, pride in being what they were: people who thought for themselves, people who knew they had a mind of their own, who were capable of judging, capable of ruling. Rafael, too, knew that he was capable of ruling, and this was why he had chosen the only career where the ruling class was open to a commoner. The Dominican friars ruled the Inquisition, and the Inquisition ruled Spain. They ruled Spain by instilling terror in the people, by reducing the population to blind obedience.

A strange calm started to replace her fear, and with amazement, Isabel felt her powers of reasoning return to her. Why, fear was an emotion for illiterates, for ignorant souls who believed every nonsense they heard. Rafael was fearless, just as her father had been fearless—and she, too, would be fearless from now on.

With relief sweeping through her body, she realized that she had simply lost her head during the reading of the Edict, due to her father's death, no doubt, and Rafael's sudden departure. There was nothing to fear. She was Isabel Valderocas, daughter of an ancient Old Christian family, capable of marrying into the ranks of the Grandees of Spain, heiress to a shipping empire. No one would ever reduce her to a victim of superstitions. Not the King, not the Pope, and not the Inquisitor General of Spain. "And may it spite the Holy Ghost!" she said aloud to her own great satisfaction, for it was one of the curses enumerated by the Secretary of the Inquisition as being particularly blasphemous.

She continued to fortify her mind against the fear pervading all of Spain at the approach of the dreaded Sunday of the Anathema, telling herself over and over again that all others were wrong, that she alone was right, repeating with all her might that there was no devil, no hellfire, no purgatory, no demons, no witches, no sorcery, and, in all probability, no Holy Ghost either. About God's existence or nonexistence she felt not so confident. Atheism was not unknown. On the contrary, it was one of the crimes punishable by death at the stake, but Isabel felt it was just as unreasonable to deny the existence of an ever present force regulating the universe, as it was to attribute human qualities to that force or being.

Then she thought for a long time about the Inquisition, the institution she had always accepted as necessary—like schools or hospitals—and now she asked herself whether it was not more evil than the evils it sought to combat. She could not agree that burning heretics was an act pleasing to God, nor that it was a vindication of God's honor, although she knew this to be the official doctrine of the Holy Office.

She wondered whether there were other people in Spain who thought as she did. It seemed impossible that everyone in this world believed in a God whose honor demanded the odor of burning flesh. If only they could all speak freely, if only people could say what they really believed. Then the world would be a paradise.

But there was no chance of her ever meeting anyone in Spain who dared to protest openly. Not in Spain! Her heart gave a leap. Spain was not the only country in the world!

Yet, leaving Spain was impossible. What excuse would she find for wanting to leave her country? What could she do somewhere else? Where would she go?

There were the Protestant Netherlands, where the Inquisition could not reach, but what would she do there? Besides, she did not want to leave Spain. She wanted to stay with her family, especially now after her father's death, when she knew she could urge Pedro to let her help him direct his business. No, she would always stay in Spain. It would be enough to remind herself every night before going to sleep that no curse pronounced by her fellow Spaniards could do her harm, as long as it was clear to her that God took no orders from any man, that all the curses, all the anathemas were only words, words, words.

Alas, her resolve did not last very long. The middle of the night was not an easy time to be brave. Doubts lurked in the shadows and fear could never be banished entirely. On the day of the great Anathema, she trembled as much as everyone else.

# 6.

There was an oppressive silence in the great Cathedral of Seville as the clergy marched in procession behind a huge cross shrouded in black and flanked by two flaming torches.

Again the words rolled like thunder and filled the high gothic vastnesses with the menace of death and destruction and eternal suffering as the followers of gentle Jesus spoke in his name:

"We excommunicate and anathemize, in the name of the Father and of the Son and of the Holy Ghost, in form of law, all apostate heretics from our holy Catholic faith, their faultors and concealers who do not reveal them, and we curse them that they may be accursed as members of the devil and separated from the bosom and unity of the Holy Mother Church. And we order all the faithful to hold them as such and to curse them so that they may fall into the wrath and indignation of Almighty God. May all the curses and plagues of Egypt which befell King Pharaoh come upon them because they disobey the commandments of God! May they be accursed wherever they be, in the city or in the country, in eating and in drinking, in waking and in sleeping, in living and in dying! May the fruits of their lands be accursed and the cattle thereof! May God send them hunger and pestilence to consume them! May they be a scorn to their enemies and abhorred of all men! May the devil be at their right hind! When they come to judgment may they be condemned! May they be driven from their homes, may their enemies take their possessions and prevail against them! May their wives and children rise against them and be orphans and beggars with none to assist them in their need! May their wickedness ever be remembered in the presence of God! May they be accursed with all the curses of the Old Covenant and of the New! May the curse of Sodom and Gomorrha overtake them and its fire burn them! May the earth swallow them alive, like Dathan and Abiram for the sin of disobedience! May they be accursed as Lucifer with all the devils of hell, where they may remain with Judas and the damned forever, if they do not acknowledge their sin, beg mercy, and amend their lives!"

The terrorized crowd responded, "Amen."

The priests, who had stood in silence during the pronouncement of the Anathema, now took up their procession again and sang the Miserere. Then, as the great bells tolled as for death, the bearers of the torches extinguished them in the font of holy water, saying: "As these torches die in the water, so will the souls of sinners in hell!"

# 7.

On the day following the Anathema, Catalina fell ill. Again Isabel was the first one to notice the greenish tinge of her skin, the dampness of her forehead, and the sweat pearls on her temples.

Since her husband's death, Catalina had hardly eaten anything. Her figure had lost its plumpness, and her grief had turned her slightly silver-streaked hair into a dullish gray. She offered no resistance when Isabel put her to bed and sent Pasquito to fetch Dr. Rojas.

The physician disagreed with Isabel's wish to take care of her mother's nursing needs.

"I cannot let you do that, child. Your mother fell ill because she did not follow my advice. She tired herself out, watching day and night over your father. You may take care of her part of the time, but you must also get lots of sleep, good food, and fresh air. If not, you too will catch the disease. I will send you a nurse."

Pedro had been shaken by his father's death more than Isabel. Now in charge of the business, the more he delved into his father's affairs, the more he became convinced that he was not cut out to be a master trader and banker. Happy though he had been sailing the seas, contacting his father's customers and suppliers and overseers, carrying out his father's decisions, he could not see himself in the role of decision maker. He could not be the head of a vast mercantile empire. Hardly aware of what was going on around him, he was startled to come upon Dr. Rojas and Isabel. He heard only the doctor's last words.

"There will be no nurse," Pedro said abruptly. "I myself will take care of my mother."

"Pedro, that is a woman's work," Isabel objected. "And I think a nurse would be helpful. She could tell us what to do, and we could take turns."

"There will be no nurse," Pedro said stubbornly and glared at Dr. Rojas. "No stranger will come near my mother, do you hear me?"

"As you wish," Dr. Rojas said, taken aback by Pedro's vehemence. "Then you better listen to my instructions. You must make cold compresses for her legs and feet to pull the fever down. You must keep her out of drafts, keep her windows closed, see that she drinks plenty of the herb infusion. . . ."

"What herb infusion?" Isabel asked.

"I will give you the recipe. It has to be made fresh twice a day. Now the most important precaution for you is not to touch your mother's skin, nor anything she is in contact with."

"That is impossible," Isabel objected. "We will have to change her linen, keep her clean, wash her. . . ."

"Absolutely not. If she has the strength to pull through the initial period of fever, nausea, and headaches, she will reach a stage when the pustules forming on her skin will be so big that they break. You must not clean off the pus, it must remain to form a crust. When the crusts begin to darken and dry out, she will be through the worst. When they turn black and fall off, she will live. And let me warn you, there is nothing at all to protect yourself, except to stay away from her as much as you can. Against pox as against plague, there are no secret formulas, no charms, no special incantations. Here"—he bent over his bag and took out a sheet of paper—"here are my instructions. I will be back tomorrow." He bowed and left.

Pedro took the sheet from Isabel's hand. "I will see that this is properly prepared. And you heard the doctor. Everyone will stay away from her. I will take care of her myself."

"And I will," said Isabel. "She is my mother, too, you know."

He gave her a sharp glance, but she held his eyes and did not relent.

They went up to the bedroom. Catalina was asleep. She breathed regularly and looked peaceful.

"Perhaps we are mistaken," Isabel whispered. "Perhaps it is just fatigue."

Pedro nodded. "Let us hope so. Call me if anything is wrong."

Isabel sat down on a floor cushion on the *estrado* and from there she watched her mother.

She reflected that she knew very little about her, having never tried to enter into any serious discussion with her, having taken for granted that Catalina was the shadow of Fernando. Father's opinions were what counted; Mother was merely the preserver of family peace and well-being. Now she wished she had asked more questions of her mother and tried to please her by being more interested in feminine pursuits.

"Pedro, are you here?" Catalina asked feebly, keeping her eyes closed.

"It is I, Mother. Isabel."

"Isabel, I am going to die."

"Mother! Do not say such a thing. Dr. Rojas says you do not have pox. It is just an ague. You will be all right."

"Dr. Rojas lied to you. Isabel, the basin, quick."

Catalina sat up and held one hand in front of her mouth. Isabel got the small water basin and held it for her. She threw up and fell back. "I am burning, Isabel, I am burning."

The cool wet compresses gave her some relief, and she fell asleep again. Isabel sat and watched her. She was not afraid of catching the disease. She had always been healthy and strong, despite her delicate exterior, and since her night with Rafael and her defiance of the Anathema, a wild, angry recklessness had overcome her. If she could stand the curses of the Church and if she could stand being separated from Rafael, she would not be felled by such a common disease as smallpox.

For the remainder of the day, Catalina lay softly moaning in her bed. She did not throw up again, but she refused to drink the herb tea. At night Pedro came in and insisted that Isabel go to sleep.

"Be sure to eat the dinner Pepita prepared for you," he said, "and take a hot bath. The maids have been heating the water for you. Wash off the sickness."

"I will go if you promise to call me if she is worse."

"I promise. Go now."

In the early morning hours, Pedro called to Isabel's room

to wake her up. "She keeps asking for you," he said. "I do not know whether she is fully conscious, but she insists she wants you."

Isabel threw a cape over her nightgown and followed him. When they entered the bedroom, Catalina was sitting up. Her eyes were brilliant with fever, no red spots had yet appeared on her face, but it had started to swell, smoothing her wrinkles and making her look younger and more like a stranger.

"I am here, Mother," Isabel said.

"I must talk to you," Catalina said.

"Not now," Pedro said, "not now, Mother. You must rest. Isabel can stay with you, but you must rest."

"Pedro, get out!" Catalina ordered. "I want to talk to Isabel, I told you."

Bewildered, Isabel glanced from one to the other. It sounded as if they had quarreled about this before he had come to fetch her. Catalina obviously wanted to be alone with her daughter, and Pedro had tried to stop her. Resolutely, Isabel pushed Pedro toward the door.

"Go, Pedro, I can stay with her."

"She is having fantasies," Pedro whispered. "She thinks she is someone else. It is the fever."

"Yes, yes, leave us alone." He left, and Isabel pulled a chair near her mother's bed. She echoed Pedro's words, "You must rest, Mother, please. You must rest."

"I have not much time left," Catalina began, "and there is so much to say, Isabel. Listen carefully. You know about the Moriscos, don't you?"

"Of course, Mother." It was a strange question. Everyone knew that in Spain there were still some descendants of the Spanish Moslems who had become Christians.

Catalina nodded and continued, "It has been twenty years now that the Moriscos were expelled from Spain, like the Jews before them. There were many of them living in Seville and many of them used to work for us." She breathed with difficulty and started to speak in a staccato whisper, "When they were driven away . . . a few families . . . were allowed to stay. They were indispensable, you see. They had to stay for a few more years to teach their skills to the Old Christians. Then they, too, were chased from the country. But there remained a few exceptions. There was that family of tilemakers . . . they made tiles for mosaics like the ones around the house . . . and they managed to stay. . . ."

"Rest for a while, Mother," Isabel pleaded. "You can tell me tomorrow about the Moriscos."

"There will not be a tomorrow for me," Catalina said softly. "I must tell you now." But instead of saying what she wanted her daughter to know, Catalina closed her eyes and sank into the past. . . .

# 8.

It was an early summer day, quite hot already, and Catalina was walking down the narrow dusty lanes of the old Moorish quarter to Yussef's house. Yussef was called José by his Old Christian neighbors, but Catalina had known him all her life and continued to call him Yussef. His parents had worked for her parents, and now, in turn, he was working for Catalina and her husband Fernando. She had asked him to draft a design for a dining room mosaic and in her mind she was redecorating her home. She walked quickly, looking forward to spending a pleasant hour in Yussef's atelier, inspecting the designs he would submit, sipping hot mint water, and tasting the sweet almond cakes Yussef's young wife Aicha knew how to bake, better than anyone. The narrow unpaved street was full of noise and commotion. Half-naked children chased one another, chickens cackled, pigs grunted and dug their noses in the garbage, women squatted in doorways, the waterseller rang his bell and pointed to his goatskins filled with precious drinking water, peddlers sold everything from used clothes to fresh sardines, the vegetable man pushed his wheelbarrow—it was an ordinary sort of day. Then, all of a sudden, a continuously swelling wave of screams rose in the air, women grabbed their babies and toddlers, the older children fell over each other trying to get into the houses, everyone found some open door, and in a few moments the street was cleared of every human being. An old woman dragged Catalina into her patio, hissing, "Quick, my lady, they are coming."

As the lane lay still, except for the eternally cackling chickens and the grunting pigs, they could hear the drunken voices of an unruly mob coming nearer and nearer, menacing death to heretics, shouting obscenities, and causing bloodcurdling shrieks along their path.

The old woman had locked the gate to her small patio. Now she made a sign with her hands begging Catalina to follow her into the front room and there, joining others behind the wooden shutters, Catalina could get a glimpse of the most frightening scene she had ever witnessed. A throng of perhaps two dozen men was pushing through the narrow street, carrying axes, spears, knives, and crudely made crosses. A few brandished human heads impaled on pikes. One of them pulled the corpse of a little girl by its long black hair. Catalina stood petrified with horror. The old woman was crossing herself, no one dared move or speak; the children around them seeing their parents mute with fear, remained paralyzed themselves. When the terrifying gang had passed without so much as looking at the house where she had found refuge, Catalina breathed deeply.

"Who are they?" she whispered. "What are they doing?"

"They are good Christians, and they are going to rid us once and for all of the Moorish devils still living among us," a loud-voiced woman said. "They sweep away the scum who still insult our good Lord Jesus. And who are you to ask?" She took two steps to stare at Catalina's white face. "What are you doing here, hiding in my house?"

"Leave her alone, you," the old woman muttered. "This is my son's house, not yours. Can't you see she is a lady? Mind your manners."

A new wave of piercing screams sent everyone back to the window, but the mob was far down the street.

"That must be at José's," another woman said.

"Yes," said the one who had claimed to be the owner of the house. "That will take care of that Moorish pig trying to pass for a good Old Christian. We ought to take a look at his cellar, probably hoarded the gold he's been getting for his stinking tiles."

"Please," Catalina said to the old woman, "I must go home. Thank you for your hospitality." She took a handful of coins from her purse and handed them to the old woman.

"No," said the old one, "you are a guest in my house."

"My ass," said the younger one and grabbed the coins. "It is my house and she pays."

They opened the gate for her, and Catalina was glad to escape the suspicious eyes of the younger woman. She had planned to run straight home, but when she saw that the mob had left the street, she felt strongly drawn toward Yussef's house. When she reached it, a few neighbors had already started to come out into the street. They all had the same goal and pushed behind her. During the short time the mob had spent there, Yussef's house had been sacked. Doors and windows were broken, furniture smashed, plants and curtains torn, sharp pieces of tile littered the street and courtyard. The crowd forming behind Catalina pushed more rudely, because she did not enter the workshop fast enough. But when they were inside, a gasp went up. In a pool of blood, there lay Yussef and his gentle wife, hacked to death. . . .

# 9.

With a scream Catalina sat up in her bed.

"What is it, Mother? I am here, don't worry. I will take care of you," Isabel spoke soothingly, and she renewed the cool compress on her mother's forehead.

"Yussef, Aicha . . ." Catalina moaned.

She had a nightmare, Isabel thought; she was in another world. Pedro was right.

"It is I, Isabel," she reminded her mother.

"Isabel? No! Sara, Sarita . . ."

"Mother, it is I, Isabel. Your daughter. You have had a bad dream. Mother, wake up. You wanted to tell me something. It is I, Isabel."

Catalina found her way back from the past.

"Oh, yes, Isabel," she said slowly. "There were those Moriscos, you see. And their little girl, who was only two, she had been playing at a neighbor's, you understand? And then she stood there, in the middle of the street, clutching a doll and looking at me. Just looking at me . . ."

"I understand, Mother," Isabel said, although it did not make any sense to her.

"I took her with me," Catalina said. "She was so little, so precious, with big black eyes, and I thought she could play with you and grow up to be happy, never to be hacked to death."

"Yes, of course, Mother," Isabel said softly. "You must forget your dream. It was just a nightmare. No one was killed. It is your fever."

"No! No! You don't understand! They did kill Yussef and

Aicha. But I got their baby. I saved their child. As Pablo had done, don't you understand? God asked me to do it. I did not know her name. It was an Arabic name. She had never been baptized. They wanted to leave for North Africa, to live among their own people, as Moslems. I liked Yussef, he was a good man."

Then Isabel understood.. Her mother had once saved a Morisco baby. Isabel knew that many similar cases had occurred at the time of the expulsion of the Moriscos. Many times, children had been torn from their mothers' arms and taken to Christian homes.

"What happened then?" she asked while she changed the compress on Catalina's legs.

"Pepita," Catalina said.

"You want me to call Pepita?"

"No, no. She is Pepita. The little girl. We called her Pepita."

Isabel was stunned. Pepita a Morisco. Not a distant cousin as she had been told, but a complete alien, of a race and creed not to be tolerated in Spain.

"You baptized her?" she asked.

"No!" Catalina answered with more vigor than she had ever shown when she was well. "No! No one noticed that I took her, and at home we said that she had come from Toledo. That she was a niece of mine."

"Does Pedro know this?" Isabel asked with apprehension, thinking that she would never be the one to tell him.

"Pedro knows."

"Oh." Perhaps he had wanted to prevent Catalina from telling her this, Isabel thought.

"And Pepita?"

"Pepita does not remember anything of her childhood before she came to live with us. We have brought her up as our own. You will soon know why, if I have the time left to tell you."

"If you could sleep a while, you would feel better."

"Pepita does not know," Catalina continued, disregarding Isabel's admonitions, "but your father told Pedro and I think that you, too, should know. I don't want you to tell Pepita. I want you to promise me that you will always look after Pepita, that you will never quarrel with her, and that you will try your best to make her happy. Most of all, let her be happy always, for I saw what was done to her parents, and I cried."

Catalina stared at her daughter with feverish eyes, then she started to talk in a tongue Isabel could not understand. She seemed to recite poems or plaintive songs. Then she interrupted herself and mumbled, "Sarita, Sarita."

"I am here, Mother," Isabel said again, knowing her mother must be speaking to persons she had known in the past, a most bewildering terrifying past, if one could believe her outbursts.

Isabel would have liked to call Pedro to whom Fernando had told so much, but remembering her mother's wish to remain alone with her, she refrained from leaving her bedside.

Catalina was again rallying her strength. Recognizing her daughter, she smiled weakly.

"About the nunnery," she said. "It was your father's idea. It is a good thing for families like ours to have a son or daughter join a religious order. But it never seemed honest to me."

Isabel nodded blindly with tears in her eyes. Her mother was dying and she had hardly known her. She had lived at her side for years and years, never once suspecting that a strong individual lived inside the formal outer shell of Catalina Sanchez de Valderocas. Yes, her mother had been a strong person, and now when Isabel was yearning to confide in her, she was dying.

"There is so much more to know," Catalina mumbled. "Ask Pedro. . . ." Isabel forgot the doctor's warnings. She sat down on the side of the bed, took her mother's burning hands in her own, and slowly blew her own healthy cool breath like a breeze over Catalina's agonized face. As she did this her mother seemed to sense relief. Her features relaxed, and she said something in the strange tongue Isabel could not understand. Then she pulled her hands away, turned halfway toward the wall, and gave a last almost inaudible moan.

At first Isabel thought that she had fallen asleep, but when after some time Catalina did not move, she bent over her and she noticed a strange stillness in her face. Alarmed, she touched Catalina's cheeks, picked up her lifeless hands. Where fever had raged a few moments ago, there was now the chill of death.

Isabel sank down on her knees and sobbed, burying her face in the bed linen.

# 10.

After Catalina's funeral, Valderocas House fell again into mournful silence. No visitors came to the home twice marked by death. The servants would have liked to escape from the danger of contagion, but they could not find another employer and therefore stayed, with fear in their eyes. Pepita cried a lot and went to mass every day, but her friends and neighbors avoided her. Everyone from Valderocas House was now a possible carrier of the terrible black pox.

Pedro refused to talk to Pepita or Isabel. He took his meals alone and spent day and night in the library and in Fernando's office, writing long letters to business correspondents, sorting papers, and making plans for leaving part of the work in the hands of Uncle Jaime of Toledo. When Isabel approached him a week after Catalina's death to ask what his plans were for her and Pepita, he snapped at her to go look for a place in a convent.

"For Pepita too?" she asked.

"Never mind Pepita. Take care of yourself!"

Pedro looked tired and haggard and for a moment Isabel suspected that he, too, had been gripped by the illness. But when another week elapsed without any of them falling sick, she took courage and made up her mind to show Pedro that she was someone to be reckoned with. She expected that a storm would break loose if she told him of her intention to take over the business as an equal partner with him, but she was determined not to let him bully her. On Sunday morning she asked all the servants to accompany Pepita to mass in order to say special prayers for her, because, she said, she was not feeling too well. As soon as they had left, she went to the library for her confrontation with Pedro.

He was pale, and his downward slanted eyes had dark rings under them. His beard had grown shaggy, his shoulders sagged forward, and he seemed to be a man in need of help.

Instinctively, she stretched out her hands to him.

"Pedro, let me help you. Please. You must trust me. I am a

Valderocas, just like you. I can do more than you think. If only you would confide in me."

"What are you talking about?" he said gruffly. "There is nothing to confide." He turned away from her, avoiding her eyes, and she knew she must shake him with a strong jolt.

"I think you are scared of something," she said. "Is it because we have given shelter to a Morisco? Or rather to an Arab girl who was never even baptized?"

He was next to her in one jump and clapped his hand over her mouth.

"What are you saying? You must be crazy!"

She shook him off. "No one can hear me," she said hoarsely. "I sent everyone to mass with Pepita. All the servants have gone with her."

"Never mind the servants. The air itself has ears. You must never say such things. Who told you that nonsense?"

"You know it is true," Isabel said. "Mother told me, before she . . . before she turned to the wall . . . and . . ." Isabel fought the lump in her throat. She managed to swallow and continued in a more steady voice. "Mother also said to ask you. She said there was so much more to know. She said, 'Ask Pedro.' Well, I am asking you now. And I warn you, Pedro Valderocas Sanchez, I am going to stay here until I find out the truth about our family, whatever it is. Mother told me that Pepita does not know and should never find out. Well, to me, she is like a sister, and I will always love her and protect her. I thought you would marry her one day, but now I suspect you are ashamed of her. I cannot say that I approve of your attitude. You should love human beings for their own goodness. Pepita is kind and affectionate. She adores you and would make you a good wife. And I do not think it matters the least whether she was baptized or not, and may it spite the Holy Ghost!"

Overcome by grief and anger, she had to swallow again before she could go on. "I will never betray Pepita as long as I live. And something else. I do not intend to enter a convent, not now, nor next month, nor ever. Mother did not approve of it either. I want to go on living with Pepita. I also want to help you carry on the Valderocas business. You know very well that I learned and studied as much as you did. But even if you do not want me, if you persist in shutting me out of your work as Father and you have done before, I will not be pushed into a nunnery. No matter what you tell me. . . ."

"Isabel, Isabel, calm yourself. Here," he offered her one of the handkerchiefs Pepita had embroidered for him. Isabel took it and touched her cheek. She was surprised to find that tears were rolling down, after she had thought she had cried all she could possibly cry.

He walked up and down for a while, and Isabel composed herself.

"I have known about Pepita for many years," he said, "and I love her as much as you do, probably more. The reason why I cannot marry her has nothing to do with her ancestry. It is that I cannot marry at all."

"Not you!" Isabel said quickly. "Not you, too! You won't join an order!"

"Heavens, no!" A brief smile lit up his face and died out as fast as it had come. "No, Isabel, I will surely never become a monk. But there is a different reason why I must remain single. I have a task to fulfill. And that is also the reason why I intend to give most of the business to Uncle Jaime. The task I speak of requires all my time."

"Can I help you with it?"

He turned away from her to think. Finally, he seemed to make up his mind. "Yes, I think you might be able to help me. But first I must tell you what you have wanted to know for so long. I often begged Father to tell you. He always said the time would come. And now the time has come. If Mother told you about Pepita, she must have wanted you to know the rest. Tell me—" He stopped for a moment, and Isabel realized that the next words would be hard for him. "When she turned to the wall, did she say anything?"

Isabel nodded. "Yes, she mumbled something I could not understand."

Pedro covered his eyes with his hand. "Shema," he said, "she said the Shema."

Without knowing what she was doing, Isabel sat down in a chair and stared at her brother. Her mouth was slightly open, but she did not utter a sound. The word "shema" meant nothing to her, yet she dimly felt that it was the key to the mystery. She waited.

The next thing she knew, Pedro was kneeling in front of her, taking both her hands in his. She looked down into his sad, slanted eyes, and she saw agony. He was not scared of storms at sea, of pirates, of sickness, of death, but he was afraid of whatever he was about to reveal to her, of what it would do to her. She pressed his hands as if to reassure him.

"Tell me, Pedro, I beg of you, tell me. I want to be with you, whatever happens. I am a Valderocas. I wish I were a man and could be your brother. Please let me help you in whatever it is you have to do. Please Pedro, let me stay with you."

He got up. "You are not a Valderocas," he said softly, and yet it sounded brutal.

No! Not that! She wanted to scream, louder than when she had found out that she could not marry Rafael. It could not be true! She could not be a foundling like Pepita! She was a Valderocas. Fernando and Catalina were her true parents! She knew it; she felt it in her blood!

But she stifled the angry scream in her throat. She forced herself to remain quiet, although it took all her energy to keep from falling apart.

Pedro watched her silently and for a time neither of them moved. Finally, she gained control over her emotions and over her voice.

"Who am I then?" she asked quietly, and at her words a look of admiration crept over Pedro's face, as if he had given her a difficult test, and she had passed it.

"You are my sister, of course," he said. "You are the daughter of Fernando and Catalina."

She knitted her brows. "Pedro! Stop this! If I am not adopted like Pepita, then why do you say that I am not a Valderocas?"

"Because none of us are."

"Pedro! Have you lost your senses? We know our ancestors. Who are these people, if not Valderocases?" She jumped up from her chair and pulled him over to the wall, where among maps and sketches of ship models, an elaborate chart showed the ancestry of the house of Valderocas.

On the bottom line were their own names: Pedro, born 1609 and Isabel, born 1612. Like all Spaniards, they had a paternal and a maternal surname. Valderocas, from their father, and Sanchez, from their mother. Pedro Valderocas Sanchez and Isabel Valderocas Sanchez. In the line above were their parents, Fernando Valderocas Dominguez, born 1567, married to Catalina Sanchez Raíz. On the same line as Fernando, there was Jaime, born 1569, who lived at Toledo. On the next line above were Isabel's paternal grandparents, Enrique Valderocas, born 1528 and his wife Isabel Dominguez. Above them was her great-grandfather Manuel, born 1498, and above him her great-great-grandfather Juan, born

1452. Juan's father, Rodrigo, was born in 1420, and then, at the very top, there was another Manuel, born in 1377. But this was just the male Valderocas line. There were also the names of the wives and their ancestry. All together the families shown on the chart represented the six generations of pure Old Christian bloodlines required by the *limpieza de sangre* laws. And there was more. The first Manuel Valderocas on the chart came from Segovia where his father Pablo, whose birth date was not known, had lived, as had apparently all the Valderocases before him.

"Well?" Isabel said, "Who are these people?"

"It is a very long story and a very complicated one. I do not know whether I can tell you everything at once. I am not even sure whether I remember everything. Father told it all to me during the nights when we sat alone here in the library. I will try to start, as he did, by asking you how much you know about yourself."

"Nothing. I know nothing."

"Yes, you do. You know how much importance we Spaniards attach to our purity of blood. You know that it is considered a tragedy to have a heretic in the family, or worse to be descended from a Jew or a Moslem. You know that we distinguish between Old Christians and New Christians and that New Christians are much discriminated against, especially if they are well off, and that they live under constant fear of the Inquisition."

"Everyone does," Isabel exclaimed bitterly.

"Yes, but New Christians more than others."

"I thought that is because they are not sincere in their faith," Isabel echoed common knowledge.

"How could they be sincere, if no one took the pains to instruct them properly?" Pedro countered.

"Well, I do not know. I thought all Jews were converted generations ago, after the great massacres of 1391 and again after their expulsion in 1492. That was a long time ago." She wanted to add that surely by now they should have become true believers, but then she remembered her own doubts and disbeliefs.

"Yes," Pedro said. "Have you never wondered why father made us memorize those dates? The days of the mass conversions, when hundreds of thousands could choose between death or baptism. A free choice it was called, and would you have chosen death?"

There was pent-up bitterness in Pedro's voice, and suddenly the truth flashed through Isabel like a stroke of lightning in whose aftermath she wondered how she could have missed it for so long. It was so obvious, so incredibly obvious, and so deathly dangerous. Now she was the one to fear listening ears.

"Pedro," she whispered, "are we New Christians?"

"More than that, Isabel," he said slowly, weighing each word as he spoke it. "We are Jews."

Abruptly she sat down. "Jews," she said. "Mother, Father, you . . . Does Pepita know?"

"No, of course not. She knows nothing. She must never, never know. She is an Arab girl, as mother told you, but she must not know that either. Nor must anyone else ever know. No one, except you and I. You must never, never trust anyone. You know what happened to La Susana."

"No. Who is she?"

"It is a true story. Father told me so often, I think he must have evoked it whenever he felt the desire to take you into his confidence. It happened here in Seville, almost a hundred and fifty years ago. There was a man called Diego de Susán, a rich and powerful leader of the city, officially a Christian, but, in reality, a rabbi to all the other forced converts who kept alive in their hearts the religion of our forefathers. At that time, the Inquisition was called into existence by the Catholic kings, and thousands of families took flight. Diego de Susán and other important *conversos* of Seville thought they could oppose the coming of the Inquisition to Seville by means of a general uprising, and they raised the necessary arms, men, and money to stage it. You see, this was still in the early stages of the Inquisition, and an armed revolt might have succeeded. The men were betrayed by Don Diego's daughter, the beautiful Susana, who confided the plans unwittingly to her Old Christian lover. So all the men were arrested and six of them, including Susana's father, were burned at the stake. And from that time on, for generation after generation, the New Christians have suffered persecution and torture and horrible death."

Isabel stared at her brother and said nothing. The chart of the Valderocas ancestry had been started by Isabel's great-grandfather Manuel during the early reign of Philip II, probably with the intent to prove the purity of blood of the Valderocases. Such an undertaking was a complicated matter, involving checking entries in old church and municipal registers, sworn statements by witnesses, and verification of old documents. Isabel did not see how the Valderocases could have dissimulated the facts of their conversion, if, indeed, they had once been Jews.

"What about our *limpieza* certificates?" she asked. "Do they not prove that the Valderocases are an Old Christian family?"

"They do. But as I told you, you are not a Valderocas, nor am I, nor was Father, nor were all those people of the genealogical chart."

"I do not understand."

"Our real name is Benahavel. We are lucky that we know as much about our past as we do. You must understand that all the things which I am going to tell you have been told to me by our father, who learned them from his father, and that all I know has thus been passed down from father to son, since Manuel Valderocas, the first on the chart, revealed the truth to his son Rodrigo.

"Manuel Valderocas was born in Seville in 1377. His father was a merchant named Isaac Benahavel. And Manuel's real name was Joseph. Joseph Benahavel. There were other children in the family, and they all lived in a small street of the old Jewish quarter, presumably a relatively happy quiet life. Now and then there must have been outbreaks of violence against Jews, but Seville had a prosperous Jewish community which continued to flourish when the city passed from Moslem into Christian hands. In the year 1391, however, the constant hate preachings of a handful of fanatics set off an orgy of massacres throughout the Iberian peninsula. It started right here at Seville, where four thousand men, women, and children were slain in one day, and the Jewish quarter was sacked.

"Joseph Benahavel was fourteen then, a man according to Mosaic law, but in reality a frightened child who escaped the carnage, because an Old Christian friend of his father's from Segovia happened to be visiting Seville at that time and had invited Joseph to accompany him to Cádiz which was the next stop on his trip. When they heard what was happening all over the country, the friend, whose name was Pablo Valderocas, found a hiding place for Joseph. Then he alone rode back to Seville to discover that all of Joseph's family had perished in the mass murder. The Jews who had neither escaped nor been slain were forcibly baptized. This man, Pablo Valderocas, was a good and true friend. He explained to Joseph that Joseph could either remain at Seville and accept baptism or come with Pablo to Segovia in Old Castile, where Pablo himself would spread the news that Joseph was the son of a sister of his who had died and that he would bring up Joseph, now to be called Manuel Valderocas, as his own son. Joseph chose to go with him.

"Pablo was a wealthy man, much respected in his community, and he had no trouble adopting Joseph as his legal son and heir. Since Pablo had no children of his own, Manuel eventually inherited the Valderocas wealth. It is possible that he married a woman of Jewish descent and because of his standing was able to conceal her background, as Pablo had done for him, or perhaps she accepted his true faith when she married him. Whatever the case, we know that he taught Hebrew to his son Rodrigo and brought him up, secretly, of course, according to Mosaic law. Later on, the family moved back to Seville, but all these years, down the line to our own father, the secret of our true name, as well as the most important aspects of our faith, were passed from father to son. We do not consider ourselves New Christians; we consider ourselves Jews."

Isabel had listened with growing amazement but also with growing relief. In a land ruled by religion, where faith was a matter of life or death, Pedro's revelations were startling but at the same time utterly acceptable.

To be a crypto-Jew in a Christian world bent on burning you alive—that was the ultimate challenge. A challenge Isabel would never be able to refuse. Up until now, she had been merely a frustrated young woman, prospective material for a nunnery. Now, she was a Jewess with a definite mission to fulfill and with so much to learn.

"And Mother?" she asked. "Mother knew everything, didn't she?"

"Yes, Mother herself came from a family of *conversos*, and all the other Valderocas women were secret Jewesses or at least accepted crypto-Judaism as righteous proselytes when they married a Valderocas, or rather a Benahavel."

At his words, a cascade of insights hit Isabel like a spring shower. She could not catch them fast enough. "The reception," she said, "twice a year, on special dates . . ."

"Yes, she tried to have her spring reception on the day called Purim, and she had to find out every year when that day would fall on the Christian calendar. Sometimes we had to have it earlier though, because it could not be held during Lent. That would have been too suspicious."

"And why could we not eat the night before?"

"Because we all try to keep the fast of Esther. Queen Esther is very important to us, because she saved our ancestors from oppression."

"And the fall reception?"

"It was always given a day after Rosh Hashana, our own New Year's Day."

"Why a day after?"

"Again, not to arouse suspicion."

"And Pablo, she mentioned Pablo to me. He had saved our forefather, and so Mother felt compelled to save Pepita. Oh, Pedro! Everything makes sense. And what do you think Mother said when she, when she . . ."

"I think she said one of the few Hebrew prayers I myself know: 'Shema Yisrael, Adonai Elohaynu, Adonai Echod.'"

"What does that mean?"

"Hear, Oh Israel, the Lord our God, the Lord is One."

"The Lord is One? Is that what we believe?"

"That is what I believe and always have and always will. I believe that there is one God who created us and that He is who He is. That He has no mother and no son. That He needs no saints, no pomp, and no Inquisition. That He requires nothing from us but our good will and love. This is what I believe, but I would never force anyone to believe as I do. I do not mind if people prefer to make themselves a more human God, one who has a mother. I do not object either to those who call Mohammed the greatest prophet. There was a time when three religions could live peacefully side by side in Spain, and it was a time of great prosperity, because it was a time of mutual understanding and cooperation.

"Now everything has gone from bad to worse. Since we have expelled the Moriscos, it has become impossible to get anyone to do a decent day's work. We have no shoemakers, no cabinet builders, no seamstresses, no potters, no spinners, no weavers, no silversmiths. In short, we have no skilled workers at all. With the expulsion of the Moriscos, we have divested ourselves of all the craftsmen we had. The same thing occurred when our Spanish merchants were destroyed with the expulsion and destruction of our Jewry. The Inquisition, by its steady persecution of New Christians, be they of Jewish or Moorish ancestry, has driven all of the trade into the hands of foreigners. By confiscating the property of New Christians who are imprisoned and convicted on false or trumped-up charges, the Spanish Church seems more interested in sending ducats into her treasury than souls to heaven. For, you see, the confiscated wealth does not go to the King; it goes to make the so-called Princes of the Church more powerful."

Princes of the Church. The expression conjured in her mind a picture of grave men in splendid robes, carrying bejeweled crosses and blessing the kneeling multitudes. Rafael wanted to take his place in the ranks of those men.

The thought of Rafael immediately tore at her heart and took precedence over everything else. She must know what part, if any, he played in her changing world.

"Don Rafael Cortes wants to become a Prince of the Church," she said. "Does that make him . . . our . . . enemy?"

Pedro looked at her long and hard, and again there was anguish in his eyes.

"You know that the Dominican friars are the most ardent supporters of the Inquisition. They furnish most inquisitors; they see to it that the people continue to spy upon every person who behaves the slightest bit differently from the majority; they encourage denunciation of people who commit no worse crime than washing their hands more than twice a day or changing their linen on Friday. You heard the Edict. Of all the religious orders, the Dominicans are the worst enemies of the New Christians."

"Then I hope that Rafael knows nothing about our being Marranos," Isabel said, purposely using the derogatory name crypto-Jews were given by Old Christians throughout the Spanish realms.

"Isabel," Pedro said, gripping both her hands tightly, "do you realize that I have put my life in your hands? That if you talk to anyone, Rafael, Pepita, Pasquito, anyone at all, about my being what they call a Marrano, a filthy execrable swine, I will be taken to prison, put through the whole gamut of tortures, and finally burned alive?"

"And if you confessed and repented?" she asked, and the grip on her hands tightened so much that she feared her bones would be crushed any moment.

"If I confessed, they would still burn me and take our property, and they would torture all of you, and even if they let you free, which they never do with suspected Judaizers, you would remain under close surveillance for the rest of your lives. Then, the slightest error, such as omitting to cross yourself when others did, or taking one bath too many, or refusing a dish that might not agree with you, or swearing when someone provoked you . . . any of these minor events would make you a relapsed heretic who must be eradicated from the face of the earth." He released her hands and turned away from her to walk aimlessly up and down.

Isabel knew that he had spoken the truth. The yearly Edict of Faith told everyone by what trivial actions a Jew could be recognized, such as avoiding certain foods, putting on clean clothes on Friday night, washing hands frequently, fasting on certain days, asking pardon of one another, blessing their children in a certain way without making the sign of the cross over them. Searching her memory, Isabel now discovered that her parents had done all of these things, especially the frequent washing of body and hands. There were two bathrooms in the basement of their house with colorful tiles in *mudéjar* patterns, and Catalina had encouraged her family and her servants to use the bathtubs often. The servants, being mostly descendants of Moors, needed no encouragement. Arabs loved bathing even more than Jews did. Isabel herself loved to soak in hot soapy water—as far as she knew, it was the only way to keep free of lice. But apparently not all Spaniards shared her love for cleanliness. And in the eyes of the Holy Office, frequent bathing was an incriminating sign of heresy.

She considered the matter a little longer. There might be one solution to all their problems.

"Why do we not go abroad?" she proposed. "It should be easy enough for us. With all the connections we have all over the world, we could load our galleons with everything we possess, pretend to sail to the New World, and go instead to Amsterdam, or to another place where Jews can live in peace. We do not have to stay here."

Pedro stopped and turned to her, resting his hand lightly on the globe. "There are some people who do just that. They leave Spain in order to be able to revert openly to the faith of our fathers. But could you do that? Are you a Jewess? Are you Sarita Benahavel? Or are you Isabel Valderocas, the heiress with the *limpieza* documents?"

"Sarita? Is that my real name? Sarita Benahavel?"

He nodded. "Sara or Sarita, that is what Father told me. Perhaps I should not have burdened you with all this." He sighed. "Perhaps I should have insisted that you join a convent, but I, I just could not bring myself to do it. I need your help; I want to be able to trust you. Father taught me never to rely on anyone, never to trust anyone, never to confide in anyone. This was possible for me while he was alive, but I cannot continue like that now."

"He himself relied on Mother, did he not?" Isabel asked harshly, as she realized that no one but Fernando himself had objected to her being told the truth.

"Yes, he did. I think Mother was his spiritual backbone. She wanted to tell you all of this a long time ago, but you were always so aloof, so different from her, so involved in your studies, and you never asked her anything. . . ." His voice trailed off.

"Oh, but I wanted to know desperately. I was so full of doubt, always. You know I talked to you about it. And now I am sure Mother was about to reveal it to me. She called me Sarita several times that night. I thought she meant someone else."

They both remained silent. Isabel shivered. Pedro added some wood to the fireplace, and new flames began to leap up. Isabel stared into the flames.

"There are many more things you will have to tell me," she said at last. "I must learn to be a Jewess. There is no other choice for me now. I was born into a family who never ceased to worship the God of their fathers—the God of our fathers—even after they had been offered a new name and a chance to erase their past. I cannot but be one of you. How could I ever live with myself if I betrayed my people?"

"You speak like a true Spaniard. We may be Jews, Isabel, but we are Spaniards, too. Never forget that we were Spaniards before the first Christians set foot in this land. Some of us were living in this land, which the Bible calls Sepharad, long before Christ was born, long before the Visigoths came and accepted Christianity as a state religion. Why should we be the ones to leave? Spain is our country. We must help Spain to overcome her errors. This is why we must stay here."

"How can we help Spain, when no one else can? What can we do?"

"We must bring religious liberty back to our country. I realize this is an unheard of idea under the Inquisition, but religious liberty breeds tolerance, and tolerance breeds cooperation, and cooperation breeds prosperity. We must make this clear to our monarch."

"But Pedro, how?"

"I will tell you all about it. Listen, Isabel . . . oh, Isabel!"

He interrupted himself and suddenly drew her up in his arms, "You will help me? You will be on my side? You will be one of us . . . Marranos?" He spat the word with all the contempt he had for it. Swine they were called, swine after the filthy animals from which his people had always shrunk in disgust.

She hugged him and laid her head against his chest. "Yes, Pedro, if God lets me live, if I do not die of pox, I swear to you that I will be with you forever and ever. I want you to trust me, for I will never reveal who we are."

He sighed deeply, and the look of pain vanished again from his face to make room for one of joyful determination.

"Listen," he said again, "this is what Father and I have done. We have smuggled people out of Spain. People who want to leave but cannot do so officially, because New Christians are not permitted to leave the country. We have been taking them secretly as cargo on our galleons, and then instead of sailing directly to the New World, we did exactly what you suggested; we took them to Amsterdam or to Hamburg. For in the Americas, the Inquisition is as bad as it is over here. Once under suspicion, no man can escape its clutches as long as he stays on Spanish soil."

"And the crews? Do they not know?"

"The crews ask nothing as long as they are treated as well as I treat them. Our crews are the best in the world, which is why we have never fallen prey to pirates. In all their lives no one has ever treated them as well as I do. I never use galley slaves or convicts. Every man is fed and paid well. And they get time off—with pay—between trips. No shipowner in the world would consider doing as much. So my crews are loyal and would die for us. But all this is not enough. I want to do more. I want to travel all over Europe and to North Africa and Turkey to set up a network of friends. It is easy enough for me to get refugees out of Spain; the trouble begins at that point. We are not wanted in England or France. Italy's Inquisition is getting tougher, too. In North Africa we are theoretically welcome by the Moslem rulers, but the local population often massacres groups of strangers whether they be Jews or Moslems. They even slaughtered hundreds of Moriscos who tried to find refuge there. Turkey is still one of the best places to go, but is far and difficult to reach. So is the Holy Land, where some of us have been settling with the help of Marrano money."

"Under what pretext can you travel like that? You need to

have an official reason to even leave the country, unless you want to go to Spanish lands overseas."

"I intend to find an official reason. More than that, I intend to offer my services to the Count-Duke of Olivares. With all our wealth and the gloriously unsullied name of Valderocas, I should be able to buy a position as ambassador in charge of international trade or something of that sort. We know that the Count-Duke is extremely concerned about the commercial decline of our country. After all, he was inviting Father to consult with him about the situation."

"Yes, why Father?"

"Well, first of all because the Valderocases are one of the last Spanish banking families, and second, and more important, because the Valderocases are considered to be impeccably Old Christian: That makes us exceptional. Not that religion matters to Olivares personally. I understand he is extremely liberal, but it does matter to the King, since he is the preserver and guardian of the Faith and, as such, must give preference to Old Christians."

"But Pedro, if you are that deeply involved with saving *conversos,* you may get caught any day."

"That is a risk I have to take. I could not live abroad and read the lists of *autos de fé* and discover that friends whom I could have saved are being burned alive, *relaxed in person,* as the official term goes. I have to help as long as I can."

"But you seem to be doing the opposite of what is needed," Isabel said, with a deep frown of concentration. "You are smuggling refugees out of Spain, when you say you want to bring religious liberty back into Spain."

"Please wait," Pedro said. "You do not know the rest. There is an important group forming at Madrid, a group composed of powerful *conversos* and enlightened Old Christians who are determined to save Spain from ruining herself. This group tries with all the means at its disposal to influence the Count-Duke and King Philip himself against the Inquisition. This is extremely secret, you understand. I myself do not know all the men involved, but I know that their ultimate goal is to abolish the Spanish Inquisition and to insure that Spain becomes once again a country where all people can live free of fear. We must join this group, because we are in the unique position of being known as Old Christian, yet we have close ties with the Marrano community because of the help we have given to refugees. We must move to Madrid and once there, we will see how we can be most useful. The Inquisition has been strong for over five generations, but it must come to an end eventually. With Olivares in power, I think that we have a chance."

"Tell me, those men who sometimes came late at night, are they members of that group?"

"Yes, you will get to know some of them. But you must learn never to conjecture about anyone being a secret Jew or a secret this or a secret that. To me, being a Marrano is a state of mind more than anything else. It is the refusal of the individual to be swallowed up by the masses; it is the victory of enlightenment over superstition. Our faith is very simple. We believe that God created us, watches us, and judges us, but not that He died for us to redeem our sins. If we commit a sin, it is up to us to atone for it. After living for generations without prayer books or any other written instructions, our knowledge of Jewish practices has become scant. There are hundreds of thousands of New Christians in our country, but I do not know how many still consider themselves Jews."

"But I want to learn more," Isabel said.

"Ask Uncle Jaime, when we get to Toledo. But always remember that being a Marrano is a terrible secret. It weighs upon you. You must never let it slip from your lips. You must lock it securely into your heart."

There were voices in the patio. Pepita and the servants were returning from the Cathedral. Pedro put a finger to his mouth, and Isabel nodded. Neither one would mention their secret anymore. They were united by a bond of loyalty stronger than any other in Spain. No matter what happened, as long as they both lived, they would find strength in each other.

"When shall we leave for Madrid?" Isabel asked.

"Let us wait another few weeks. Then, if none of us fall sick, we will go."

"Who will you leave in charge here? Alfonso?"

"No. I could not get along without him. And I suppose you and Pepita will want to take Teresa with you. Actually, we should take with us most of the servants we trust. What do you think of leaving Pasquito's parents in charge?"

"But they are slaves," Isabel reminded him.

"I told them they were free to do what they wanted when Father died. I even offered to buy them a house so that they could live by themselves and work as cooks for hire. But they

want to remain our slaves. It is safer for them, since they are
descendants of Moors."

"I would like to take Pasquito to Madrid with us," Isabel
said. "He is a bright boy."

Pepita burst into the library.

"Here you are! How are you feeling, Isabel?"

Isabel smiled. "A lot better."

"That's wonderful," she turned to Pedro, "But look at you,
much too thin. You are driving yourself too much. Let Isabel
help you. She could run the business as well as you can."

For the first time since Fernando's death, Pedro actually
laughed.

"Why Isabel, listen to our cousin. I did not know she was
your ally. I capitulate." He pointed to the desk stacked with
parchment rolls. "From now on, you have the honor of
sharing all my troubles."

# 11.

They set out for Toledo early in May. Two coaches each
drawn by six mules held all their baskets and trunks. Isabel
and Pepita traveled in the first coach, Pasquito and the
chambermaid Teresa in the second. Pedro, Alfonso, and ten
other servants rode along on mules.

The trip would be slow, because the roads between Andalusia and Madrid were little more than tracks, and the passes
through the Sierra Morena narrow, winding, and rocky. Since
the Spanish countryside was notoriously infested with high-
way robbers, Pedro would have preferred to have everyone
ride on horseback, the women wearing men's clothes. But the
idea proved infeasible when they showed him the number of
garments and objects a lady could not do without.

At the beginning of the journey, everything was exciting:
the vast green hills of the Guadalquivir valley, the air smelling
of rich fertile soil and of the sweet scent of myriads of wild
spring flowers, even the dirty villages where country folk
stared at them as if they were a royal cortege.

They stopped over at Córdoba and walked through small
narrow lanes of whitewashed houses, because Isabel insisted

that she wanted to show Pasquito the Mesquita, the great cathedral which had once been the most magnificent of all mosques.

North of Córdoba traveling became difficult. Spring rains had turned the tracks into rivers of mud, and it took a day to advance but a few miles. Now and then, they met groups of vagrants, peasants who had left their lands to roam the countryside like gypsy gangs. But Pedro and his men displayed their rifles, and none of the gangs were strong enough to molest them.

"Who are these people?" Pepita asked Pedro at their next stop.

"Country folk who cannot make a living anymore. They are being taxed so heavily, they prefer to abandon their land rather than be thrown into prison for not paying their property taxes."

"But then who is going to produce food?"

"Most of the land belongs to the nobles and to the Church. The nobles employ farmworkers and thus produce part of what is needed. The Church lands are being wasted as sheep pastures."

"Why do those big landowners not pay taxes?" Isabel asked. "The Church is rich enough."

"Ah, but the nobles and the Church are exempt from taxation. Only the common folk have to pay. That is why the only common folk left are beggars."

"We are not noblemen," Pepita said, "and we are not beggars."

"That is why we are going to Madrid. To show His Majesty that there is still another possibility for raising money."

"How?"

"By encouraging industry and commerce," Isabel said.

"By encouraging freedom," Pedro muttered.

At the end of a week, they reached Toledo, the fairest city of Spain, the ancient capital protected on three sides by the Tajo river, and accessible only from the south over a 1600-year-old Roman bridge. Formalities at the city gate were brief. In Toledo, as in Seville, Valderocas was a welcome name.

Although smaller in proportion to theirs, Uncle Jaime's fourteenth-century house was not much different from the Valderocas home in Seville. There was the same kind of inner court, overgrown with climbing roses, and the same four wings with rooms for guests, servants, living quarters, and the master's office. There were no balcony galleries here, just upper-floor windows and, on the ground floor, doors opening onto the patio.

Uncle Jaime lived alone, except for a few servants. He had lost his wife and his three children to various infectious diseases. At first, after each death, he had wept and cursed, but with the passing of years, he had grown philosophical. When one day, as if by miracle, he had come into the possession of old Hebrew texts, he had turned into a scholar and become the most learned man among the Marranos of Toledo. He was their rabbi now, performing secret Jewish marriages after the official Catholic rites were over, wiping the remainder of holy water from little babies' foreheads to erase the sign of baptism, dispensing advice to those who came to seek it, and saying the old biblical blessing over his frightened brethren: *May the Lord Bless You and Keep You. May the Lord make His Countenance Shine upon You and be Gracious unto You. May the Lord Lift His Countenance upon You and Grant You Peace.*

He was too old to travel, being of fragile health himself, and he had not been able to come to the funerals at Seville. But he was overjoyed to receive Pedro, Isabel, and Pepita in his house. It would be their home for as long as they chose, and even if they decided to settle at Madrid, they would always be welcome at Toledo. He kissed and embraced all three of them and assured them over and over again that he would be their father from now on.

The long trip had exhausted both young women, and shortly after dinner, they went to their room and to bed. After sleeping for the past three nights in the coach, because they could not find an inn, they could hardly wait to slip between the clean white linen sheets. Even Pepita was too tired to talk, and both fell asleep at once.

Isabel awoke in the middle of night. She did not recall immediately where she was, but she was certain she had heard Pedro's voice. A ray of moonlight came in through the slits in the wooden shutters. After orienting herself for a few seconds, she tiptoed to the window and opened the shutter a little. It creaked, and she was afraid Pepita would awaken, but a glance backwards assured her that her cousin was in deep slumber. Gazing down into the patio, she saw two figures, walking on soft soles toward the gate leading to the basement. When she finally realized that they were Uncle Jaime and Pedro, she called out to them softly.

"Wait for me."

She did not know what time it was, nor how long she had slept, but suddenly she was wide awake and determined to find out what was happening. Snatching her hooded cape and a pair of Moroccan leather slippers, she hurried downstairs into the patio.

The men looked at her in surprise. Jaime carried an oil lamp.

"Is anything wrong?" Pedro inquired.

"No," she said. "You woke me up."

"I am sorry, child, you might get a chill coming out of bed like this. I suggest you go back to your room. Pedro and I were talking business," Uncle Jaime said gently.

"Yes, that is what I thought," Isabel said, "and if it is Valderocas business, I beg of you to let me participate in your discussions." Then her voice became almost inaudible. "If it is Benahayel business, I *must* be included. Whatever you would have shared with Catalina Sanchez, you must share with Sarita Benahavel."

Uncle Jaime gasped. "You did not tell me. . . ."

"You did not give me the opportunity to. . . ." Pedro apologized.

"She is one of us?"

"I am," Isabel said and Pedro nodded.

"Come along then."

Jaime was leading the way, holding an oil lamp in front of them. They went through a heavy oak door, down a flight of steps, and into the wine cellar. They walked along racks filled with skins and vats until they came to a tremendous vat leaning against the wall. To their astonishment, the front of the vat was a door leading to another staircase. They were going down again, and Jaime explained that they had reached the network of subterranean passageways that joined all the houses of the old Jewish quarter of Toledo.

"These underground galleries reach seven levels deep into the ground," Uncle Jaime explained. "They were built several centuries ago and lead down to the river. In times gone by, our people have used them to flee whenever a persecution was threatening their lives. Now most houses have closed their entrances to the cellars with brick walls. But a few of us still use the passageways to meet underground. When I bought my house, the entrance had been blocked, but I removed the bricks and added the vat in front of the entrance." He led them deeper and deeper into the ground, along damp, musty-smelling corridors, until Isabel was sure she would never find her way back. Finally, they reached a dead end. Uncle Jaime lifted the lamp, and in its dim light, Isabel saw a brick wall.

"There is one loose brick in here," Jaime said. "You find it."

Both Pedro and Isabel strained their eyes and touched the stones. Every one seemed firmly set in mortar. But Jaime bent down and removed one of them easily. He reached into the hole and pulled a bolt. Thereupon the whole wall swung back: the brick had merely been a veneer on a thick wooden door. They now entered a small chamber, about five feet wide by twelve feet long. Jaime lifted his lamp to let them look around.

"The treasure chamber of the Benahavels!" Pedro exclaimed in a low voice. "Father told me about this, but I did not really believe it."

Isabel stood and gaped. There were chests filled with old gold coins and precious jewels. There were stacks of pure golden plates and jugs; there were silver swords and daggers inlaid with precious jewels. There were also ceremonial objects and two Torah scrolls, which Uncle Jaime and Pedro kissed reverently by touching them with a corner of their cloak and then bringing the spot that had touched the scrolls to their lips.

"You two are the last of the Benahavels," Jaime whispered. "Our family has spent much time and effort amassing these treasures over many generations. When I moved to Toledo, your father and I decided that this would be the best place to keep them. They must not be removed from here until our people are free again. When the day of freedom comes, when the cursed expulsion order of Queen Isabel will be revoked, then we can use this gold to build new houses of God and to help our poor brethren abroad come back to Spain and live honorably once more. Until that day, the treasures must remain here. No one must know about them. But once in a generation the secret must be passed on, lest it be forgotten by the time the glorious day of liberty comes."

He closed the door, replaced the brick, and again they followed him through endless dark corridors, descending flights, climbing others, until they came to another oak door. Jaime knocked five or six times in a special rhythm, and the door opened.

A tall old man welcomed them. He led them upstairs where

they met a plump woman of fifty who drew Isabel in her arms and kissed her on both cheeks when she learned that this was Catalina Sanchez's daughter.

"Your mother and I are first cousins," she said. "I am Juana Sanchez de Raíz, and this is my husband Pablo."

The old man shook hands with them, and his hand was firm and strong. Isabel liked both of them immediately, although she did feel somewhat ill at ease when she noticed that spider webs and mud had collected on her cloak. But when other guests arrived via the same underground passageways, she saw that they were not dressed fashionably either, and her uneasiness vanished.

The Raíz house had only a small covered entrance hall, no open patio, and they were led directly into the sitting room. Including Señora Raíz and Isabel, there were half a dozen women and nine men.

The men filed into the adjoining dining room.

"It is time we started," Jaime muttered. "Why are they not here yet?"

There was another knock at the door, and the host quickly went to open it and let in a young couple. The man was carrying a sleeping baby in his arms.

While the young mother stayed with the women in the sitting room, the father was taking his son to the men, and presently Isabel heard her uncle lead the others in the Hebrew chanting of a psalm. She did not understand a word and would have loved to ask her hostess what the ceremony meant, but she kept silent, for fear of appearing ignorant of her faith.

Juana Sanchez de Raíz seemed to read the uncertainty on Isabel's face, and she bent over and whispered into Isabel's ear, "It is the eighth day. He should be circumcised today, but, of course, that is impossible, so all we do is say the prayers and benedictions."

Isabel nodded and marveled at the exquisite strangeness of the situation. Here she was engaged in an act of such blatant heresy that it would earn her a flaming death, should they be discovered or betrayed, and yet their meeting could not be more innocent: it was a baby naming. Afterwards their hosts offered wine and sweet almond cakes, and then everyone departed as they had come, through the subterranean corridors. Thus, to the outside world, no one at all had come to the Raíz house on that particular night in May of 1632.

When Isabel finally rejoined Pepita in the bedroom, her

cousin—for Isabel would never consider Pepita anything less than her true cousin—hardly stirred in her sleep.

The following Sunday all of them went to mass at one of the most beautiful churches the girls had ever seen. Although its interior pillars and graceful arches were of pure Moorish style, Santa Maria la Blanca had the form of a Christian basilica, an interesting fact for those who knew that the building had originally been erected as a synagogue. It was the perfect monument to the once possible harmony of three great religions living side by side under the enlightened government of King Alfonso the Wise. Uncle Jaime said he did not usually go to mass at Santa Maria la Blanca, but he wanted them to see it first, because it was the oldest synagogue building in Toledo. He usually went to the Tránsito, a logical choice, since it was adjacent to his home.

In the afternoon, Pedro, Isabel, Pepita, Pasquito, and Uncle Jaime, followed by their footmen and servant girls, went to Vespers at the Tránsito. Here they met most of the friends Isabel had seen three nights before at the Raíz house.

The structure and arrangement of the Tránsito was typical of old Spanish synagogues. When the Jews had been expelled from Spain, they had taken with them the architectural plans of this simple yet richly adorned building, and wherever they went, they tried to build their new house of prayer in the same style. It was basically a rectangular hall, with a now unused woman's gallery far up on one side.

After the members of the Valderocas household had dutifully crossed themselves, bent their knees to the main altar, and filed into one of the back pews, Isabel let her eyes wander over the plaster decorations of the walls. Red, green, and golden pineapples, flowers, grape and oak leaves formed a tight geometrical lacework, interrupted here and there by the coats of arms of Castile and Leone and by that of Samuel Ha-Levi, treasurer of King Pedro the Just. Samuel Ha-Levi had built the synagogue and developed most of the subterranean passageways. The windows were covered with lattices to filter the light in intricate designs, and all around the upper part of the four walls Hebraic inscriptions still reminded every worshipper that this had not always been a church. Bending her head back, Isabel stared at the ceiling, a masterpiece of *mudéjar* carpentry, as beautiful as a prayer turned into cedar wood.

Isabel sighed and was nudged in the side by Pepita. She had not realized that everyone was already kneeling, and she quickly slid forward to join the others in a mumbled Hail Mary.

A few days later, Pedro left for Madrid. He was anxious to obtain an audience with the Count-Duke of Olivares, the Royal Favorite—that was one of his titles—and de facto ruler of Spain.

Pedro explained to Uncle Jaime that there was really no need for Pedro to sail to the Americas as regularly as he had done. The overseers of the Valderocas silver mines were trustworthy; all Valderocas affairs had run smoothly for generations; and none of their ships had ever fallen prey to English or French privateers.

Isabel had offered to take over a great part of the correspondence and bookkeeping, because no strangers had ever been hired to supervise the financial operations of the family.

Pepita busied herself immediately, adding the needed female touch to Uncle Jaime's womanless household. She sang and laughed and seemed entirely happy with the world around her, so much that Isabel envied her. Isabel would have liked to be able to talk to Pepita about what weighed upon her heart, about the inner confusion and turmoil that threatened to engulf her, but not knowing the truth, Pepita would not understand, and the truth was too dangerous. Thus, Pedro's absence proved more painful to Isabel, who needed him as a lifeline to her Benahavel identity, than to Pepita, who simply loved him as a young woman loved a young man she hoped to marry.

Pepita was anxious to see Madrid, though, and to meet the elegant Court society, and she kept teasing Isabel about finding a precious Grandee to marry.

"You know my low opinion of Grandees," Isabel said with a shudder, thinking in particular of Carlos de Queras, the last noble candidate for her hand.

"Are you still thinking of that monk?" Pepita asked candidly.

"Who is that?" Isabel retorted, but Pepita's innocent question had landed like a dart into her heart.

Yes, she was still thinking of Rafael Cortes. Not a day went by without his memory being revived in her mind and body. She longed to see his face again, to feel his touch, and the crushing weight of his body on hers. She could not forget him, and whatever she did, secretly in the most inner part of her being, she did to impress him. There might never be a real opportunity to impress him, except possibly an occasion to beat him in the deathly game she was about to start, where he would be the enemy, particularly if he had indeed joined the Dominicans.

The days without Pedro went by slowly. Finally, he returned to fetch them to Madrid. He had not been able to see Olivares; both the King and his Favorite were in Catalonia arguing with the obstinate Catalan Cortes, the parliament of Barcelona. But Pedro had made friends at Madrid. He had found an old palace for sale in the Calle Santiago, near the Alcázar, and he had bought it, because it was located in the most desirable neighborhood of Madrid. He was anxious for Isabel to join him.

But when he started talking to her, Isabel was shocked.

"It would help if you could marry into the right circle," he told her. "You would be invaluable. Or perhaps you could get the King interested in you, for you are certainly beautiful enough."

"Pedro! What are you saying? What outlandish spirit has gotten into you?"

"I am just waking up, Isabel. My God, Seville is behind times. You should see life at Madrid. It is unbelievable. Just wait until you see with your own eyes what is going on. The night life! The theaters! Duels being fought to the death! Intrigues! And love affairs wherever you look. You know I swear I saw a couple make love in a church pew?"

"Pedro!"

"Well, it is true. I also heard a scandal about a confessor raping all his juvenile penitents." He grabbed her by the shoulders and stared into her eyes. "Isabel, with your beauty and intelligence, with our name, and our wealth, with my connections . . . We are the ideal combination. We are going to beat them. We are going to win."

"Beat who?"

He bent to whisper in her ear, "The bigots, the parasites, the murderers, the greedy minds behind the Inquisition."

"And why should it help if the King took an interest in me?"

"Because we must work at the highest level. We must be everywhere. Someone must work on Olivares, and someone else on the King. Now Olivares is a woman-hater, while the King has nothing in mind but his . . . er . . . physical passion."

Isabel was not slow in adjusting to Pedro's new style of talking.

"Well, forget about me as royal mistress," she said. "I heard they end up in convents."

Pedro laughed out loud.

"What is wrong now?"

"You should be indignant! I am supposed to defend your honor to the death, and here I stand giving you a lesson in loose morals. Yet, I cannot help thinking of you as a brother and friend."

"And that is what I want you to do. Do not worry. I will know how to manage myself at Madrid. But what about Pepita? Where does she fit in?"

"Pepita, yes, Pepita," he was subdued. "Where is she now?"

"Probably visiting one of the many friends she has already made. Pedro, are you going to marry her?"

Pedro shrugged helplessly. "Do you not think that she has toyed with that idea for so long that she has talked herself into being in love with me? I do not want to marry just now."

"Pedro, she adores you; she worships the air you breathe."

He glanced around and bent toward Isabel to whisper, "Isabel, I am going to marry a Jewess."

"Who?" It came out as fast as a pistol shot.

"Oh, I did not mean it that way. I am not engaged. I only meant that I must marry one of us, or one who honestly converts herself to our faith. This is a problem you do not have. You are a Jewess, if you want to be, and your children will be Jews if you want them to be." He had continued to whisper this explanation, although no one else was with them in the upstairs study where their conversation took place.

Isabel frowned in dismay.

"I am sure Pepita would do anything you required of her. It would break her heart to know why you reject her. You must tell her."

"Are you out of your mind? She always goes to Church. I am convinced she thinks of herself as the perfect Catholic."

"But she is a Moor, is she not?" Isabel whispered. "She was never even baptized. So why can't you marry her?"

"Because that makes her a Moslem, doesn't it?"

"Pedro, couldn't we just pretend we all are . . . well . . . simple human beings? Are you not the one who wants to fight for religious liberty?"

Pedro stared at her, and a mask fell over his face. "You do not understand," he said. "Forget it. It may only be a cowardly excuse. I don't know whether I love her enough or not. I don't want to marry her yet. She is free to marry someone else, or to join a convent, or to stay with us as a member of the family that she is and has always been."

"Oh Pedro, it is hard on her."

"I know. Isabel, listen. We must not think of our personal lives. We are working for Spain, for a rebirth of the ancient, glorious, and humane Spain our ancestors helped to build. We want a country where Christians, Jews, and Moors can live again in harmony and peace, which does not mean they have to intermarry. Just live side by side. It is not a dream, because it was possible in former times. We must make personal sacrifices, if they are required of us. The brainless masses always do as they are told. When government policy orders them to get along with their neighbors, they do. When they are told to persecute others, they do that, too. We must try to influence those who govern Spain. We cannot sit still and let the country become a hell on earth. You still want to help me don't you?"

"I will always help you, Pedro," she reassured him. "And I will do whatever you ask of me—short of accepting undesirable assignations," she added with a grin.

# 12.

Don Gaspar de Guzmán y Pimentel, Rivera y Velasco y de Tovar, Count of Olivares and Duke of Sanlúcar, Royal Favorite, Grandee of Spain, Great Chancellor of the Indies, Lord Chamberlain and Lord Grand Master of the Horse of His Majesty, and holder of numerous other titles and positions, in short, the ruler of Spain, known to one and all simply as the Count-Duke, sat at his desk, pushed aside the mountains of documents and petitions, bent forward to cradle his massive head in his folded arms, and let himself sink deeper and deeper into his terrible private hell.

His heart and mind were flooded with tears he could not hold back, as once again he was overcome by the insurmountable obstacles in the path of his plans to bring Spain back to her former glory. He knew his country was taking a course of national disaster; he knew that any day could bring the debacle of what was still the world's greatest power; he knew it was impossible to raise more money from a starved population; he knew the various provinces should unite in order to remain great; and he also knew that his monarch was too volatile and too debauched to truly understand the desperation of the situation. He knew and generally he carried this burden with equanimity, but sometimes, especially when he was alone, he would break down under the sudden realization that even if he worked himself to death, he was only one honest idealist in a society of slovenly, lazy, and corrupt noblemen.

Apart from these occasional bouts of depression, the Count-Duke did not know fatigue. Every day he rose at five o'clock in a country where all others started the day at eleven. He saw a hundred petitioners in one morning. He only interrupted his work once a day for a quick midday meal. He then continued at his desk until late at night. He read reports; he composed instructions to the commanders of the armies; he studied the feasibility of special projects such as the canalization of rivers; he proposed the introduction of new industries; and he encouraged the scientists who hoped to extract pure silver from cheaper compounds.

He labored tirelessly for the good of crown and country, since in the depths of his inherited pride and love of Castile, Olivares had discovered the source of a superhuman energy which he spent wildly and without fear of ever exhausting it.

He could go on for months without recreation, almost without sleep, working his secretaries to death or nervous breakdown, getting fresh air only when he had to accompany the King to some state function or official entertainment. Even then, if he did not have to sit in the royal coach, he would continue to do his paper work. There was a special desk installed in his carriage, and he often used that office-on-wheels to receive foreign ambassadors or other persons to whom he wanted to speak without fear of spying ears.

He also had an enormous capacity of concentration. He could recall any problem, any situation, any face, immediately and completely, so that he was able to decide on the spot what to do for a petitioner or emissary. He never wasted a minute of his time. He did not care for titles and honors—although his grateful sovereign flooded him with them—he wanted nothing but power. Not power for power's sake, but power to improve the lot of Spain, power to strengthen the throne of the Habsburg weakling who was his monarch, power to lift Spain out of her threatening decadence into a strong, healthy, and rich future.

When he had started his mission, in the spring of 1621, he had thought it would surely not take him more than ten years to do away with the consequences of the rule of his predecessor, the inefficient and corrupt Duke of Lerma, to bring back justice and prosperity, to renew Spanish claims as the foremost world power, to recapture the fading shine of past accomplishments. Instead, one misfortune had piled upon another. There was the war with the Netherlands for which the people held him responsible, although he could have done little to avoid it, short of completely reversing previous foreign policies that were closely tied to the political interests of the Habsburg dynasty—something he dared not do to a Habsburg king. The war was devouring money and men and pushing Spain to the brink of bankruptcy, but Olivares's warnings, as well as his pleas for help from the other provinces, fell on deaf ears. The Cortes of Aragon and Catalonia stubbornly refused to grant the badly needed subsidies and insisted on all their old regional privileges instead of uniting with Castile, Andalusia, and Portugal to form the strong Spanish superpower Olivares envisioned. No one understood his plans; no one sided with him. The Grandees hated him with the special hatred of equals who feel themselves physically, mentally, and morally inferior to a hard-working, dedicated upstart. The King persisted in his pleasure-seeking attitude, only too thankful to leave serious affairs in the hands of his Favorite and adding on to that business by requesting that the Count-Duke himself organize extravagant festivities costing almost as much as the unfortunate campaigns. The people, the starved masses, the nation of paupers and bandits, the people blamed Olivares for every misery, every defeat, every pestilence, every personal misfortune, and every sorcery, theft, or murder.

After eleven years of these and other false accusations, was it surprising that the Count-Duke encountered moments of such dark despair that he earnestly wished to die?

Especially in the early summer of 1632, after traveling with Philip to Aragon and Catalonia on a trip that cost more money and stirred up more trouble than it was worth, he tormented himself with the thought that in order to punish him for his insufficiencies and mistakes, God Almighty let the whole nation suffer. The suffering of the nation, that was what hurt him most, that and his own impotence to alleviate that suffering. It nearly drove him to madness.

More than once he begged the King to relieve him of his duties, more than once he complained bitterly to his wife and his friends that he was surrounded by empty heads, that he could not be everywhere at once, that he had no helpers.

But the slightest encouragement would pull him out of his self-pity. He would find his strength, his readiness for action, his radiant vitality, his conviction that he alone was destined to lead Spain back to greatness, that in a few more years the other Grandees and with them the nation would recognize his uncontestable genius and would exclaim their gratitude to the savior of Spain.

If only he could find more funds. He was already using his considerable personal wealth. If only he could find more soldiers; if only one of his many brilliant projects would succeed quickly; if only he could convince the pig-headed Catalans that they owed Spain the same fealty as the Castilians; if only he could give the country what it so desperately needed: a few hundred well-to-do merchants from the burgher class.

This last thought pulled him back to sanity. He sat up straight, feeling a warm stream of hope surge through his heavy thickset body. He grabbed the silver bell on his desk and rang it forcefully.

Immediately, one of his secretaries appeared.

"Why hasn't Valderocas come to see me yet?"

"Your Excellency, I am sorry. I am not sure I know the case."

"Must I think of everything myself? Fernando Valderocas the banker from Seville! Oh, damn your dim-witted brain. Get me Simón Rodríguez."

Simón Rodríguez came and supplied the answers to Olivares's questions.

"Don Rafael Cortes was working on that," he said, "just before he joined the Dominican order. But in the meantime, old Valderocas has died. I believe his son has tried to see Your Excellency."

"Thank you, Simón. Get him for me, will you?"

Rodríguez bowed. He would send a runner to the old Santana town palace recently bought by a newcomer to Madrid and renamed Valderocas House.

# 13.

When Pedro had arrived at Madrid, both the King and the Count-Duke had been absent. Since the latter's return, Pedro had tried almost every day to present himself to the chief minister, always with the same negative results.

Today finally was his day. He came not as a petitioner, but as an invited and awaited personage. Doors opened as he walked through the crowded antechambers, and when he crossed the last threshold, he was thoroughly surprised by the smiling informality of the tyrant who made a nation tremble. In accordance with etiquette, Pedro swept off his plumed hat and went into a deep respectful bow. To his astonishment the Count-Duke rose, walked around his desk, and greeted him with cordially outstretched hands.

"My dear Don Pedro, with sorrow have I learned of the passing of your father. Don Fernando Valderocas Dominguez was a man to whom Spain owes admiration."

"My most sincere thanks, Your Excellency."

"I hear that you have taken up residence in the capital. What brings you to Madrid?"

"I have come because I would like to serve Your Excellency," Pedro answered without hesitation. He had prepared a small speech fairly bristling with laurels for Olivares, but something in the Count-Duke's face made him drop his flatteries. He could see that Olivares was startled by his answer, and he decided to wait.

Olivares was smaller in height than Pedro, hardly taller than five and a half feet, but he was extremely broad-shouldered and heavy without being fat. His face was square-jawed with a sunken mouth, a black chin beard, and a strangely brushed-up moustache. His nose was long and fleshy with unexpected curves and bumps, but his dark eyes under wide and unruly black brows were friendly and kind, betraying intelligence as well as sadness. His forehead was high and remarkably smooth for so tireless a worker. He wore a handsomely styled black wig. At forty-five years of age, Olivares was one of the most powerful statesmen of Europe, and this was what made him a giant in everyone's imagination. Stories were told of his indescribable rages, obscene insults heaped on adversaries, his boundless conceit, his overbearing attitude toward the other Grandees, his almost magical power over the King—stories invented afresh every day by his numerous enemies.

Now he turned away from Pedro, returned to his desk, signed a few papers, powdered sand over the wet ink, and rang his silver bell.

Again the secretary appeared, and Olivares gave orders to clear the antechambers. He would not receive any more petitioners for the day. He then asked Pedro to follow him through a back door.

"And now, Don Pedro, let us go for a ride."

Three coaches were waiting in readiness at all times. The first one was Olivares's office-on-wheels; the two others usually carried his secretaries whom he called into the first one whenever he was ready for dictation.

This time he chose one of the plain coaches where he and Pedro sat across from each other. A petitioner who had obviously waited for just such an opportunity approached them and humbly asked to be heard. The man was simply dressed. Olivares stepped out of the coach, listened to his request, thought for a moment, then gave his advice. The man seemed content and left. Olivares climbed back into the coach, the groom closed the door, and as they started to move, Olivares pulled the curtains for privacy.

Pedro had observed all this, and although he had not been able to hear what the request was, the courteous attention of the prime minister impressed him more than any of the foul rumors running through the drawing rooms of Madrid.

"Now, in what way do you think you could serve me?" the Count-Duke asked, coming back to the answer Pedro had given him previously.

"In whatever task Your Excellency sees fit to entrust to me. I have many business connections abroad. I will have to continue to travel for the Valderocas interests, but I would also like to do something for Spain. I presume Your Excellency knows best in what capacity a mercantile and financial expert would do the most good for the country."

Olivares watched him pensively.

"Would you offer the Valderocas wealth to the Crown, if it were needed?"

Pedro was prepared for that question. It was the crucial

point. If the Count-Duke was as brilliant and perceptive as Rafael Cortes had described him, Pedro's scheme would succeed. If, on the contrary, he was as greedy and incompetent as the people rumored, Pedro and with him the Valderocas wealth might be lost. He would have preferred not to have to answer that question so soon, but it was a point in Olivares's favor that he had asked it right away.

"If Your Excellency will kindly permit me to be frank, I would like to give an honest answer."

By a movement of his expressive hands that accompanied all his speeches with convincing gestures, the Count-Duke indicated that Pedro was welcome to speak as he pleased.

"If it would actually help the Crown to save and secure the economic future of Spain, I would not hesitate, nor would any member of my family, to put all our holdings at the disposition of His Majesty. This being understood, I would like to venture the opinion that such an act would be nothing but a drop of water on arid ground. The money would be spent in a day, and nothing could be gained for the future. This has been proved in the past by the confiscation of the wealth of Spanish bankers, with the sorry result that all Spanish money now goes to foreign usurers. Foreigners cannot be expected to feel any loyalty to Spain. Spain's money, and especially the treasures from the Americas, should be kept in Spain. For this we need more native bankers, we need experts. International finance is a complicated affair. It cannot be learned in a matter of months or even in a few years. The Valderocases have been bankers for generations, so have the prominent Italians. I am thinking of the Paravicinos, the Guistinianis, the Piquenottis, and before them the Grimaldis, the Calvis, the Centurionis. They have practically taken over Spanish finance. For a while, it was the German Fuggers. Now there are the Genoese, who have maintained a stronghold at Seville for generations. They dominate our trade with the Americas, our lifeline. Ever since Her Most Catholic Majesty, Queen Isabel, started to rely on the Genoese, Spanish finance has slipped into foreign hands. It is my humble opinion that this trend must not only be stopped but reversed."

What Pedro said was part of a carefully prepared speech. He had not said anything heretical. He had not mentioned the Inquisition or the lack of religious liberty. He had simply talked of high finance—a most suitable subject for an Old Christian banker and presumably the only one that could interest Olivares. Yet the Count-Duke's next remark showed that he understood their talk revolved around more than simply Spanish wealth.

"You speak of the confiscation of the property of Spanish bankers," he said. "Do you realize that the Crown does not confiscate anyone's wealth without a good reason?"

"I realize that," Pedro said, and both of them knew they were starting to tread on dangerous ground. It was Queen Isabel who had expelled the Jews from her realms after her victory over the last Moorish kingdom of Granada in the same month and year that she had sent a certain Christoph Colón—Genoese by birth but Spaniard by conviction—on his fateful journey. It was also Queen Isabel who had called the Inquisition to Spain, the only institution greedy enough to confiscate anyone's wealth, and the main culprit in the disappearance of the Spanish banking families. Even for generations after the expulsion, *converso* families had continued to flourish and to provide Spain with the keys to her wealth. But little by little, the Inquisition had been successful in eradicating a group of people who were distinguished both in lineage and in cultural and economic achievements and who since ancient times had been one of the main pillars of Spanish grandeur.

Pedro Valderocas, as a simple citizen of Spain, could go no further without compromising himself. So much as suggesting that Spain needed Jews was a heresy entailing the gravest consequences. He stared into Olivares's eyes and waited.

The Count-Duke, too, stared into Pedro's eyes, and thus with interlocked glances each searched in the other for assurance of trustworthiness.

"Not all Spanish banking families have perished," Olivares said finally. "For several decades now, Portugal has been an integral part of Spain, and there are Portuguese bankers in Castile, as you must surely know. But, unfortunately, the most important Portuguese have moved to the Low Countries where they contribute to the increasing wealth of Amsterdam."

Pedro understood that even a prime minister had to be careful. The Catholic Church had not hesitated to imprison one of her own greatest archbishops, Cardinal Carranza, when he was suspected of heresy. Olivares knew that the Valderocases were of Old Christian stock, but the elementary law in Christian Spain was to trust no one. It was up to Pedro to establish how his anguish about Spain's economy took precedence over his impeccable Old Christian feelings. As Pedro had explained to Isabel, if they wanted to attack the Inquisition, it had to be done in a round-about way. Officially, neither Jews nor Moslems existed in Spain. In order to insure their religious liberty—and eventually the liberty of all Spaniards—such persons must officially be called into the country. This could only be done by proving that they were indispensable to Spain's welfare.

"There is a definite need for us to instruct more Spaniards in the art of international trade and finance," Pedro said to Olivares. "The problem is simple. We need teachers. We had the same kind of difficulty on another level when the Moriscos were expelled from the country. At that time, the father of our present monarch in his great wisdom ordered that a small percentage of Moriscos should stay to teach their trades to Old Christians." King Philip III had been extremely stupid to order the expulsion in the first place, as both Pedro and Olivares knew, but the monarchy itself was a sacrosanct subject. The kings of Spain, past, present, and future, were to be praised forever.

Olivares leaned forward. His voice dropped to a shade above a whisper, and a mad spark lit up in his dark eyes. "Don Pedro, do you mean to suggest that Jews are the only ones able to instruct good Christians in the art of finance?"

Pedro gathered all his courage. "Precisely, Your Excellency, precisely."

Olivares leaned back with a satisfied smile. One of the many reproaches made openly by the other Grandees was his preference for the company and advice of commoners. Yet, he had often found that commoners possessed better sense and often a better grasp of reality than the lazy nobility.

"You mentioned that you might have to travel abroad," he now said to Pedro. "Are you actually in contact with Jews in other countries?"

"Yes, Your Excellency."

"The Valderocases are not *conversos*, are they?"

"No, Your Excellency."

"Why then are you interested in Jews?"

"I am interested in Spain. We need a revival of industry and commerce. For that we need money."

"And money knows no religion," Olivares added.

The Count-Duke was known to be a deeply religious man, in the sense that he saw his confessor every day, that he went to mass regularly, that he built convents, that he believed in supernatural phenomena and feared the practices of black magic. Yet, he never went so far as to let his religious feelings interfere with the practicalities necessary to further his ambitions. His foremost ambition was to be the savior of Spain. That dream required money, and if money could only be obtained through the presence of Jews in Spain, then there would be Jews in Spain. It might take years to work out the details. No Jew could reasonably be expected to come back to a country where secret believers in his faith were burned at the stake. But come back they must. And if there were a man in Spain who could accomplish their return and oppose the frightening bureaucracy called the Inquisition, that man was Gaspar de Guzmán, Count of Olivares, Duke of Sanlúcar.

"Tell me, where are you staying at Madrid?"

"We bought a house in the Calle de Santiago."

"Oh, so you bought the old palace of the Santanas. But who is 'we'?"

"I have a younger sister and a cousin. Since my parents are dead, I am responsible for both young women. They are living with me."

"Do they plan to enter a convent? Or will you have to arrange suitable marriages for them?" Olivares's questions implied that he intended to use Pedro's services, and Pedro relaxed enough to confide his personal plans.

"Your Excellency, I myself will marry my cousin one day. As for my sister, she is an extraordinary young woman, and I shall let her make up her own mind."

Olivares smiled, but Pedro could not tell why. Then the Count-Duke rapped the coach window with the handle of his walking stick, and they stopped. A groom opened the door.

"Back to the Alcazar," Olivares ordered. He pulled back the curtains and they saw that the streets had started to fill with chatting promenading people. It was the hour of the *paseo*, the most joyful time of day for Madrileños, especially in the summer, when after the heat of day, a cool breeze came down from the Sierra de Guadarrama.

"Tomorrow night the Countess and I are giving a small reception. Don Francisco de Rioja will read us some of his poetry, and we will have a pleasant exchange of ideas. I would be delighted if you, your sister, and your cousin would join us."

The invitation exceeded Pedro's wildest hopes. It meant

that he had found favor in Olivares's eyes. It also meant that the Count-Duke intended to watch him closely for a certain period of time before trusting him with any special mission.

Olivares could not know that Pedro had already made contact with the group of men eager to obtain privileges for the *conversos* still living in Spain and who were planning to invite Jewish families who had fled to North Africa, Turkey, and to the Netherlands to come back to settle at Madrid. Pedro had heard that Olivares listened to the main spokesman of that group with more than a mild interest, that he had already promised to encourage commercial undertakings by New Christians, and that he intended personally to protect all Jews who ventured into the country. That was the reason which had prompted him to be candid during his audience. But Pedro himself did not know who that Marrano spokesman was. No one seemed to know his identity. From rumors alone, Pedro judged that he must be a man with high connections. Recently, he had apparently been able to obtain the release of a Judaizer already in the hands of the Inquisition. It had been leaked down to the other members of the group that this unique feat had been accomplished with the help of Olivares.

Thus, Pedro decided he knew more about Olivares than the Count-Duke knew about him—a definite advantage.

As far as the organization of the secret group concerned him, Pedro was not curious to know all its members. Too much knowledge had proven fatal for many a man in the Spain of the Inquisition. The less one knew, the less one could betray under torture. Ideally, each conspirator should have only two contacts: the man who worked for him, and the man for whom he worked. In Pedro's case, the only person who could be said to work for him was his sister Isabel. The person for whom he worked directly, in the sense that he would pass hints and bits of information on to him, was a man whose name he would never reveal to anyone, not even to Isabel. He did not know how well he would stand up under torture, if it had to come to that, but he hoped that he would be able to live up to the precepts of his faith: to die rather than to betray a fellow human being.

Besides his one certain contact, Pedro had met several Old and New Christians with ideas liberal enough to make them possible members of the conspiracy against the Holy Office. They were a philosopher, a playwright, a university professor, several artists, and some *converso* merchants. All of them had access to Olivares; any of them could be the chief spokesman. There were even a few bishops, a Benedictine and a Geronimite whom Pedro suspected of philojudaism. But as he had told Isabel, it was far safer never to speculate, and between them, they never discussed any names.

# 14.

"It is an incredible honor that he invited not only me, but both of you as well," Pedro said to the young women when he returned from his interview with Spain's master. "I can scarcely believe it."

"Why is it so extraordinary?" Pepita asked. "I remember well how Don Rafael told us all about those charming Madrid soirées. I kept wondering whether it was true. Perchance we shall find out." She stood in front of an oval gilded mirror in the drawing room, a small jar in her left hand, and applied rouge to her cheeks.

"What the devil are you doing?" Pedro asked, taking the jar from her hand. "You look like a painted doll. Go wash your face."

"Do not scold her, Pedro," Isabel pleaded. "It is the fashion, you know. You would not want us to look like peasants from the Sierra. Here, let me tell you," she enumerated on her fingers. "No more ruffs but soft lace collars, hair falling in waves to shoulder length or hidden under a wide puffed-up wig, cheeks highly rouged, eyebrows well plucked and arched, lips moist and pouting, waists thin and long, skirts terribly bulky, that is what a proper Madrileña should look like, and do not tell me you had not noticed."

He shrugged and grinned. "Do as you like, but please cause no gossip. The Countess Olivares sets a high standard of morals, and if you do not please the Queen, we are also in trouble."

"You mean we will meet the Queen?" Pepita asked, her voice trembling with awe.

"What about the Count-Duke?" Isabel asked at the same moment. "Is he not the one we should try to please?"

"The Count-Duke thinks women are good for two things:

praying and bearing children," Pedro said. "I have been told he mostly despises female company."

"Poor Countess," Isabel remarked.

"Not so. She is chief Lady-in-Waiting to the Queen, and she also supervises the education of the little crown prince Balthasar Carlos. Between the two of them, the Olivares couple have the royal pair well under control."

"Then he thinks more of his wife than of women in general?" Isabel asked.

"His wife is probably the only person he trusts."

"How do you know all this?" Pepita asked suspiciously.

"Oh, gossip, just gossip."

"Yes," Isabel said. "Where do you get your gossip? Here Pepita and I have been at Madrid for a week now, and we have not met a soul yet, except for a bookseller and a dressmaker."

"Well, tonight should make up for that." He grabbed Pepita's arm, "Now go and wash off that paint, and I will forgive you for your haircut."

"Oh, you noticed?"

"Haven't I! One more thing. Do not smile too much at the King. I hear he goes for raven-haired beauties like you."

Pepita giggled and danced out of the room.

As soon as she was gone, Pedro turned to Isabel. "You must make a favorable impression on the Countess," he urged. "She is the most important woman at Court. And keep out of the way of the King."

"That is contrary to your previous instructions. Do you really think he will be there?"

"I don't know." He whispered, "Olivares is our man. Of course, he does not know our true goal. He thinks we are only interested in Jewish bankers. But that is enough for now. At any rate, I am convinced that he is a brilliant and perceptive man. Rafael was right about him."

Her knees shook at the mention of Rafael's name.

"Have you seen Don Rafael lately?" she asked, glancing into the mirror and trying to make her voice sound unconcerned.

"Isabel, turn and look at me! Are you still in love with him?"

"In love? Where did you get that idea? You and Pepita are the ones who keep talking about him."

"Isabel, Isabel. I told you to get that man out of your mind. No, I have not seen him since he left Seville. I was only reminded of our conversation, since Pepita brought it up. I do not know where he is. Rotting in some monastery, I suppose. I really don't care."

"He used to be your friend."

"That was when he was normal. To actually join the black friars a man must be either a lunatic or a fanatic. Not someone I would value as a friend."

She forced a smile on her lips, determined to become a better actress for future occasions.

# 15.

Their names were announced by the usher, and they walked slowly into the richly decorated drawing room of the Count-Duke's apartments. Pedro wore a splendid coat of black velvet with the new neckwear fashion launched by King Philip and Olivares: the high cardboard collar called *golilla* which was gracefully curved and covered on the inside with light gray silk. The replacement of the ruff by lace collars or by *golillas* had been one of the Count-Duke's money-saving ideas and one which had almost torn Court society apart.

As they walked at his side, both Pepita and Isabel could feel the curious glances and delighted smiles of the guests grouped about the room. They were a handsome addition to any social gathering. The name Valderocas meant money, Spanish money, Old Christian money, and of the two young women accompanying the owner of all that wealth, each represented a type of beauty celebrated by Spanish poets since ancient times: one the golden-haired lady with carnation cheeks and emerald eyes, the fair damsel of knight-errantry, the other the dark-haired seductress with full red lips and flashing eyes, the proud *morena* of Andalusia.

When they approached their hosts, the hum of chatter around them stopped. Everyone watched to see how well these newcomers would be received, because their importance stood in direct relation to the welcome extended to them by the Royal Favorite and his wife.

Doña Inés de Zúñiga y Velasco was officially supposed to stand as high in the favor of Queen Isabelle de Bourbon as her husband stood in the favor of King Philip IV. She was a plain woman with severe features etched in thick layers of powder and rouge. She wore a formal wig and a black silk gown. Only her eyes looked alive, keen and capable of acute judgment. She sat at the far end of the room on a chair with a high carved back, in a straight regal position, quite as if she were the Queen and not the Lady-in-Waiting.

Isabel's heart pounded so much she was afraid it could be seen under her pale green silk bodice, but she kept her eyes straight ahead, not looking at the Countess but at Olivares himself.

He stood next to his wife, an imposing figure of a man, every bit as powerful as Pedro had described him. When he heard their names, he looked up, and for a moment Isabel thought a smile spread over his face, but then he bent down to talk to his wife.

Finally, they arrived within six feet of the proudest, most talked about couple of Spain, and Pedro went into a deep bow, while Pepita and Isabel sank into curtsies formal enough for royalty.

The Countess's eyes, seen from nearby, were shrewd and calculating, as if to ask whether these people were worth the trouble of a smile. Then her glance softened, and warmth came into it as she stretched out her hand so that Pedro could bend over it and bring it to within an inch of his lips. At the same time, Olivares stepped forward and took Isabel's hand to draw her up from her curtsy.

"What charming company you bring us, Don Pedro," the Countess said in a clear voice for all to hear. "We are delighted that you have moved to Madrid." She smiled at Pepita and asked, "Is this young lady your sister or your fiancée?"

"My cousin," Pedro answered with his most boyish smile.

"Well, cousins are known to make good wives, are they not?" the Countess said, and her husband winked and said they did. Everyone knew that Olivares and Inés de Zúñiga were first cousins, and Pepita blushed becomingly.

Suddenly, Isabel realized that Olivares was still holding her hand, and she looked at him in surprise. He was hardly taller than she, but she did not think she had ever seen anyone more masculine than he. She liked him. In fact, she liked him very much. It was not the spontaneous attraction she had felt toward Don Rafael, whom she had desperately loved from the first moment she had seen him, but, nevertheless, it was a stronger feeling than she had experienced with any other man. A warm current seemed to run from his hand to hers, and she could not believe that he was really a woman-hater. She withdrew her hand softly, and when he looked into her eyes, she responded with a smile, a searching smile, telling him that she found him attractive, not because he was the Favorite, not because she wanted to flatter him, but simply because at this very instant she liked him, his massive thickset body, his beautiful forehead, his square jaw, his brilliant eyes, his thick black eyebrows, and his well-shaped beard.

She did not know that Olivares was in one of his buoyant moods when nothing was impossible for him, when he was riding the top crest of success. She did not know that he could be mean and ugly, insulting and overbearing, a man as much despised as feared by the Grandees of Spain.

Tonight he was in good form, such good form that Hopton, the English Ambassador, would hurry home to compose a long diplomatic note warning Windebank, King Charles's secretary of foreign affairs, that something new must be afoot in Spain, for rarely had he seen the Count-Duke so full of sparkle.

"Doña Isabel, I believe?" Olivares said, and through his deep resonant voice, there ran a faint echo of its original Andalusian accent, although he spoke the purest form of Castilian Spanish. "You look as fresh and charming as the first spring flowers of Seville. If I had not left poetry to my dear friend Don Francisco de Rioja, I would surely be tempted to pour my admiration for you into verse form."

"You are too kind, Your Excellency."

"One cannot be too kind to a beautiful young lady. Come, let me introduce you to a man who should be flattered to paint your portrait. I am sure a more perfect model he will never find."

And so Isabel met Diego Rodriguez de Silva y Velázquez, King Philip's personal painter. Velázquez had been discovered and brought to Madrid by Olivares and had now won the friendship of the young monarch. He was thirty-three, just six years older than the King, a handsome man, but of quiet, serious exterior. His manner was straightforward; he looked into others and with a few strokes of his brush was able to convey the inner life of his subject. He and his family had apartments in the palace, very near the King's own rooms, so that Philip could stroll over easily and often to watch his friend at work, something he liked to do at least once a day.

Isabel reminded the master that she had watched him as a

child sketch several of her parents' servants, and he remembered Fernando Valderocas and invited her to come visit his wife Juana Pacheco. Juana stayed in their apartments to care for their children, he said, because she disliked the social whirl of the Court in which he had to participate as Chief Gentleman Usher.

Velázquez, in turn, introduced her to Pedro Calderon de la Barca, an upcoming young playwright whose religious allegorical plays had drawn the approval of the more conservative elements of the Spanish Court. Calderon's future success seemed assured by the interest of Philip, for here was an opportunity for the young King to prove that he was capable of appreciating serious plays as well as the light banter of Lope de Vega's comedies. His Majesty liked to call himself a passionate patron of artists, and he was fond of taking part in private theatricals for which he even had written a few plays. Calderon told Isabel that His Majesty was hard at work translating stage plays from the Italian, and that if he were not a King, he might make a good poet.

More and more guests arrived, few of them Grandees or outstanding nobles, most of them artists, writers, and scientists. Each time the usher announced a new name, the conversation stopped while everyone turned to welcome the new arrivals. The most striking guest, Isabel thought, was Francisco de Quevedo, a man she had wanted to meet for a long time, since she counted herself among the admirers of his mordant satires. She had always pictured him as a highly polished man. Instead, he turned out to look unkempt. His hair was growing wildly against fashion, an unbecoming black pince-nez framed his wide-set shrewd eyes; his moustache and narrow chin beard drew attention to his sarcastically downturned lips; and he eloquently conveyed the idea that it was condescending of him to appear at the Count-Duke's reception—which in a way was true, for he praised or blamed Olivares to his convenience. Lately, he had blamed him more often than praised him, mostly for the extravagance of his spending.

Of the noblemen, the most important one, according to Isabel's guess, was the Count of Monterrey, brother-in-law of Olivares and owner of a vast town palace and extensive garden where elaborate festivities took place in honor of Their Majesties.

Another celebrity, Francisco de Rioja, Olivares's truest friend and confidant, was not only a poet but also the

Count-Duke's most reliable worker and helpmate. He composed many state documents, and it was rumored that the Count-Duke's reports to his monarch were often successful only because of the masterly persuasive prose of Rioja. From canon of Seville to member of the Supreme Council of the Holy Office of the Inquisition, Suprema for short, Rioja had advanced in life at a steady pace with Olivares, the friend of his youth. In addition to becoming a member of the Suprema, he had also acquired the title of official historian of the Kingdom of Castile, but he still found time to turn out fine lyrical poems, as Olivares had indicated to Isabel.

These famous names she had heard before and therefore remembered, but Isabel also found herself introduced to dozens of courtiers and courtesans, and soon her head spun with a colorful assortment of long complicated family names. As soon as it became known that she had just arrived at Madrid, dozens of ladies were eager to inform her of the latest Court gossip. In a time when news was released only sporadically in published bulletins called *relaciones,* every real or alleged happening was widely circulated by means of gossip and became more embellished or more hideous each time it was told.

To the courtesans, Isabel was a heaven-sent opportunity to rehash old scandals, such as the number of the King's illegitimate children; his current affair with the singer of a theatrical company; his past passionate affair with La Calderona, an actress by whom he had a son he was said to prefer to the royal heir, the crown prince Balthasar Carlos; his nocturnal excursions incognito into the streets of Madrid where he was whispered to pick up any wench he fancied; the Queen's hatred of Olivares, whom she suspected of fostering the King's licentiousness; the yearly special hunting parties where ladies were invited despite the Queen's and the Countess Olivares's disapproval; the secret orgies supposedly taking place during those week-long hunts; and the various ruses by which pretty girls could manage to stay away from their lecherous monarch.

". . . and then she locked herself in her room, and when he knocked at the door, she screamed—loud enough for all to hear—'Go away. Leave me alone. I do not want to end up in a nunnery'. . . ."

"No, did she really?"

"I swear on my eyesight. I would have done the same. Who wants to wither away in a convent?"

"Unless it is San Plácido. . . ."

Isabel listened, confused, and not knowing what to believe. Surrounding her were giggling female members of the minor nobility, bored wives of young Court fops, or mistresses of elderly courtiers whose main occupation consisted of flattering the Royal Favorite.

"Why San Plácido?" she asked and was submerged in a wave of laughter.

"Don't you know?"

"Good gracious, what are you talking about at Seville? Even London and Paris know about San Plácido."

So she was duly informed that San Plácido, a convent founded only nine years ago at Madrid with the help and money of Don Geronimo de Villanueva, Marquess of Villalba and Protonotario or Secretary of State of Aragon—a name to remember—had fallen under the influence of the Illuminists, a sect maintaining that fornication among monks and nuns was no sin, if it were committed during the special state of grace which members of the Illuminist sect were able to attain. The nuns of San Plácido had become demonically possessed, and many acts of black magic and sorcery had been committed. It had been, for a while, quite fashionable to pay the nuns visits, because in their possessed state, they were supposed to be able to foretell the future. The Protonotario, a good friend of Olivares, had been highly compromised when the scandal was discovered and denounced to the Inquisition. But no one could touch him, because Olivares protected him.

"Even against the Inquisition?" Isabel inquired with a whisper.

Her informers nodded and exchanged knowing glances, conveying to Isabel the message that she had a lot to learn.

Well, San Plácido had then been closed down, and the nuns had been sent to other convents. But there was talk of reinstating them and reopening the convent so they could all look forward to renewed amusement. In the meantime, there were certain other pleasures easy enough to attain. For instance, there were a few confessors who were popular with many society ladies, because they loved to probe deeply into certain intimate details and because their guidance and advice was more titillating than spiritual.

As Isabel listened with increasing astonishment to these tales of debauchery, she started to have the uncomfortable feeling that someone was watching her, possibly with disapproval. Her eyes surveyed the room. But no, everywhere she saw groups, like hers, sitting on sofas and floor cushions or reclining in easy chairs, standing in small circles, talking, laughing, admiring small sculptures and paintings. Her glance searched for Pedro. He was listening reverently to Francisco de Rioja. The Countess Olivares was talking to Velázquez, and he was apparently describing something of importance to her, because she had lost her stiffness and gesticulated rapidly. The Count-Duke himself with a quizzical smile bent toward his critic Quevedo, and of the hundred or so guests present, everyone appeared similarly occupied. But where was Pepita?

Worried, Isabel stopped hearing the gossip and stood up. She had a better view now, and immediately she saw them, standing not more than a score of feet away, talking and staring at her. Pepita and Carlos de Queras. Of all people! How long had he been there, watching her like a falcon spotting his unsuspecting prey? Their eyes met, and he said something to Pepita and came straight across the room to bow to her.

As she curtsied to him, she sensed the surprise she caused to her new acquaintances. As a bachelor and future Grandee, Queras was considered an excellent catch, despite his temporarily reduced circumstances. Moreover, his father's renowned stinginess implied that his fortune would be in good shape once he could lay his hands on it. Almost every married lady could remember a single sister or cousin or otherwise deserving friend, and every unmarried woman had to fight for herself if she did not want to retire to a convent. Among females alone, Isabel's beauty had not caused any trouble, but when Carlos entered their circle, the whole relationship was thrown off balance.

"Why, Don Carlos," one of the ladies chirped, "fancy you back at Madrid. How long since we have last seen you at Court?"

He gave her an icy stare, and she shrank back.

"Doña Isabel," he said, "I did not know you had come to Madrid. We do have to renew our friendship. I am sure these ladies will not mind if I spirit you away for a few moments?" He smiled at them with a bow of his head, more mocking than sincere, and held out his right hand, palm up, to Isabel. Once again she accepted him, as there was no other choice, and walked away with him.

He had not changed. He was still haughty and smooth with

the same strange glint in his eyes, as if he were trying to say, I know something you do not know. Whenever she looked into his eyes, she felt uncomfortable. He did not, for all his ostensible admiration, really like her. He was not smitten with her, as her father had said, but he did seem to regard her as a pawn in his own personal chess game.

"How do you like Madrid?" he asked.

"I do not really know yet. We only arrived a week ago. This is my first time in company."

They stood near a window and looked down into the western court of the Alcázar, the *Patio de las Covachuelas*, as it was called. This was the courtyard open to the public, in contrast to the larger eastern patio which led to the Queen's apartments and was private. Even now, late at night, the *Patio de las Covachuelas* was full of life and bustle. Its arcades were occupied by booths, bookstalls, and jewellers' shops. Painters were exhibiting their work and doing a brisk business, since "art" seemed to be the watchword of Philip IV's government. A *covachuela* was literally a little cave, but the Spaniards had adapted it to mean audience chamber, and it was from the various state council chambers located on the ground floor that the courtyard had taken its name. The courtyard was lit by hundreds of torchlights, and for a second Isabel felt within her the beginning of a new feeling of belonging. She was in the center of Spanish life. She felt like reaching out to the crowds in the patio and laughing with the pure joy of being alive.

"For the first time out, you start at the top," Queras said sarcastically, and Isabel was reminded of his unwelcome presence. She looked back to the ladies she had just left and saw that Pepita had taken her place. She turned to Carlos.

His face was only slightly above hers; it was narrow with a small mouth, a fine straight nose and a long pointed chin. His eyes were dark under half-closed almost hairless lids, his hair dullish brown with some gray in it, receding from his forehead and falling straight and thin to the top of his collar. His body appeared frail, but he carried himself remarkably straight, perhaps to give himself more height. He was clean-shaven and powdered, and he used a heavy perfume.

Really, thought Isabel, he is presentable and not ugly. There is no reason for me to feel so hostile; I must overcome this aversion.

If she had felt more comfortable with him, she would have

asked: what do you want from me? But there was nothing natural about him, and she decided that she would have to accept his contrived ways.

"I am glad you think this is the top," she said. "I suppose if you live at Court, you must be a good judge of these matters."

"I do not live at Court. We have our own family palace at Madrid," Carlos replied.

"Oh, I did not know."

"There is no reason why you should have known."

Isabel started to play with her fan, at a loss what to say.

"I find Madrid rather boring," Carlos continued. "There are so few people here with whom I care to associate."

"I am afraid I don't understand."

"The true Grandees have left the Court." This remark she understood to mean that he belonged to the group contemptuous of Olivares. The true Grandees were those who had refused to collaborate with Olivares's plans for lifting Spain out of the economic morass, the true Grandees were the persons intriguing for the Count-Duke's downfall. Since she had taken an immediate liking to the Royal Favorite and since Pedro had told her beforehand that Olivares was anticlerical, liberal, and on the side of the New Christians, she now had good reason to be wary of Carlos.

"If you choose your friends among Grandees," she said with an effort at suppressing her pride, "I do not think I am the right company for you. After all, I am not of noble birth."

"Don't be foolish. You are a Valderocas. You know that sets you apart. Why else would you be received here?"

"Yes," she said, "the Count-Duke seems to appreciate certain commoners."

"So do I, and probably for the same reasons."

Isabel was stunned. His remark was as good as a slap. Oh, how she wished she could react accordingly. But as long as Queras and she were guests in the same room, guests of Spain's all-powerful statesman, there was no way to get out of her dilemma. Queras had her cornered, and he knew it.

"Why are *you* here tonight?" she asked lightly, as if she had not heard him.

"For political reasons."

"Then again you should not waste your time on me. I have nothing to do with politics."

"You . . . no, but she has . . ." His head made a slight motion toward the door, and Isabel, despite herself, felt awestruck when for the first time in her life she saw her monarchs: Philip IV, King of Spain, and his French wife, Queen Isabelle de Bourbon.

The Queen walked into the high hall at the hand of her husband, and everyone stood up. She was much prettier than Isabel had expected and at the same time extremely dignified. As the royal couple passed through the room toward the Countess, every man bent his knee, and every lady sank to the ground in a curtsy. Doña Iñéz de Zúniga curtsied, and Olivares bent his knee.

"Do they come often to such gatherings?" Isabel whispered, and a smile lifted the corners of Carlos's small mouth.

"He does, but she doesn't, usually," he whispered back, and somehow this exchange broke the stiff barrier that had lain between them.

"You have come tonight, because you knew she would be here?" Isabel asked boldly when the general conversation started again. "Did you not have to be invited?"

"No, this is their weekly reception, anyone who is anyone can come. I have come because I was told that she would be here, and second, because I knew you would be here."

"You could not have known that," Isabel said quickly. "You yourself were surprised to see me, you said so."

"That was just for the consumption of others. I have a reliable spy system."

She let the remark go unchallenged. It could be a lie. It could be the truth. Something else was more important, and now she dared ask outright.

"Don Carlos, what do you want from me?"

"Why, Doña Isabel, I thought you would have known that since our last meeting at Seville. I want to marry you, of course."

"Because of my money?" she hissed and now it felt as good as slapping him. But it left him completely unruffled.

"Partly," he said, "partly also for other reasons. I know more about you than you think, and I am confident we would get on remarkably well."

"I am just as convinced of the contrary," she said. Then with false sweetness dropping like poisoned honey from her tongue, she added, "I am confounded and deeply honored by your proposal, my Lord. I know it is meant as a courteous and chivalrous gesture which I must refuse, since I could never seriously aspire to marry into such old and noble a family as yours." She curtsied to him and picked up her skirts. He bowed to her, and she put her hatred for him in her eyes, before turning around and walking away.

Of all the important guests around whom circles of admirers were forming, the court painter Velázquez had been most kind to her, so she felt it was safest to join him. He was showing a portfolio of drawings by Tiziano Vecellio which he had just received from a friend in Italy. Among art lovers, original drawings by Titian were already valued sufficiently to elicit gasps of admiration followed by immediate offers for the whole collection as well as for particular sketches. Pedro was among the men eager to acquire the chalk drawings, but Velázquez refused; they were not for sale.

"My wife is very fond of Tiziano," Olivares said to Pedro. "I will see whether I cannot make him change his mind in private. Then, if he sells me the collection, maybe you and I can do a little art business on the side."

He had spoken in a subdued voice; the words were meant for Pedro alone to hear, but Isabel was close enough to catch them, and if Olivares's friendly tone surprised her, it also reminded her sharply that she had not made any headway in gaining the favor of his wife. While Pedro was doing his part, obviously getting along splendidly with the Count-Duke, she had not yet so much as said two words to Doña Inés. Glancing over her shoulder, she saw the Countess standing next to the Queen who was now seated in the high-backed chair, both of them looking at the man bending his knee before Her Majesty. The Countess's face was noncommittal, showing neither like nor dislike, but the Queen smiled graciously at Carlos. It was obvious that he had brought news of interest to her, for she turned to say something to the Countess, who thereupon walked away from them. Isabel quickly glanced around and realized that the Countess had been sent to get the King, for she was walking toward the opposite corner of the room, where Philip was chatting with Calderon de la Barca. That might be a moment to approach her hostess. But before she could figure out how to intercept Doña Inés and what to say to her, she felt the hand of Olivares on her arm.

"Doña Isabel, has anyone presented you to His Majesty?"

"No, Your Excellency."

"Very well then, nothing will give me more pleasure. Come along Don Pedro."

Thus, the three of them reached King Philip at the same time as the Countess.

Isabel had heard many descriptions of the King, and she had seen a copy of one of the portraits Velázquez had painted of his young sovereign, but she thought that both the descriptions and the painting had been flattering. True, the King was tall, with thin blond hair falling down in waves to the lobes of his ears. His eyes were the bluest of blue, and his long blond moustache was twirled gaily upward over his cheeks, but his soft almost colorless eyebrows and the outer parts of his eyelids were drawn downwards giving him the expression of a sad hound. His mouth was unpleasantly thick, and he had inherited the protruding heavy Habsburg jaw. He seemed bored and tired and not too pleased when Olivares presented the newcomers. He did not recall having invited Pedro's father to Court and the Count-Duke had to give him a lengthy explanation of exactly how Pedro fit into the glittering Court world, but when he learned that Isabel was not Pedro's wife, a spark of interest jumped into his somber features.

He nodded to Pedro. "Enchanted to make your acquaintance. Calderon here has many worthwhile ideas. I am sure he will not mind sharing them with you." With a nonchalant wave of his hand, he dismissed his minister, the poet, and Pedro, and with a slight bow to Isabel, he simply took her hand and led her away before the Countess could inform him that the Queen very much desired his company.

"My dear young lady," he said with a smile pulling his wide lips apart and a wicked gleam lighting up his dull eyes, "you were sent by heaven to delight the heart of your King. The Count says you just arrived from Seville. Do tell me what the people think of me down there. What do they know of their monarch? Am I a good King? Are they fond of me? At Madrid I meet nothing but flatterers. It worries me ever so much that I do not hear the truth about anything. You must be perfectly frank with me."

Isabel blushed. Philip had managed to direct her into an isolated corner of the large room. She was uncomfortable at being singled out, and she could feel the jealous glances of others like little darts penetrating her skin. The King's eyes swept over her figure, appreciatively, and she groped for words.

"Sire, you do me great honor," she mumbled. "I have led a sheltered life and not been much in contact with people, but in my father's house everyone always spoke very highly of

Your Majesty. My father said you were a great King and that he trusted you would turn out to be better than . . ." She stopped short of the blunder of telling him that his father, Philip III, had been no good.

"Better than who?" Philip asked, looking not the least bit tired now, but truly amused.

"Better than your grandfather," she said quickly.

Philip II was considered by all of Spain to have been the greatest King. His grandson was the exact opposite. Where the second Philip had been an energetic administrator who directed all foreign and domestic affairs himself, the fourth Philip was weak and listless, leaving the government entirely to his Favorite. And where his grandfather had been austere, Philip IV was a spendthrift.

"How is that?" Philip asked.

Astonished at her own audacity, Isabel began spinning a tale of the present King's great qualities, yet she was careful not to flatter him outright.

"His Majesty, your grandfather, was a most extraordinary ruler, but I have heard say that he wanted to do everything himself which is really most impossible for the sovereign of a land as big as Your Majesty's. My father thought that you were very wise to realize the importance of delegating certain powers to advisers, that it gives you a better and more detached view of the whole of your realms and that in the end your decisions would prove wiser for Spain."

Fernando had never held such an opinion in all his life, but since the Valderocases were now ready to cast their lot with the Royal Favorite, it would be foolish to tell the King that the people in general hated the rule by favorites.

Yet, there was another reason why Isabel and Pedro preferred this King to his predecessors: in matters of religion he was as lukewarm as others had been fanatical. Even his father, a weak king on most other accounts, had driven the Moriscos from the country in a last effort to purify Spain of insincere Catholics. The present King, though on one hand a willing slave of the Inquisition, was on the other an equally willing listener to the spokesmen of the Marranos of Portugal and was even now considering selling them certain privileges, if their offer was high enough. If any king could be persuaded to abolish the Inquisition, something which could only be done by royal decree, Philip IV was the best possible choice.

"You are very beautiful," Philip said, caressing her face

with his eyes, "and you have the voice of an angel. I am sure we must continue this conversation in a more leisurely setting. I see the Countess frowning at me. I suppose I will have to join my wife."

"I would very much like to be presented to Her Majesty," Isabel said quickly, for she could not bear the idea of being left standing alone for all to see that the King had left her because his wife summoned him. She was compromised enough for having been singled out by him.

Although she had discovered this evening that the King was only a man after all, and not even an attractive one, Isabel felt engulfed by the uncomfortable sensation that whatever step she took, she made matters worse for herself and for Pedro's cause. She had alienated the gossiping ladies because of Carlos de Queras, she had insulted Carlos, and finally she had drawn the attention of the King upon herself—a most dangerous situation. Gossip might have her in his bed this very night, and gossip of that sort would ban her from Court forever.

She curtsied to the Queen, sinking to the ground, and not daring to lift her face.

"This is Doña Isabel Valderocas," Philip said to the Queen. "I am thinking of making her brother special banking advisor to the Crown."

Carlos de Queras still stood next to the Queen. *"C'est la jeune fille en question,"* he said rapidly, and Isabel concluded that he usually spoke to the Queen in her native tongue, a sure way of pleasing her. The remark indicated that he had already talked about Isabel to Isabelle de Bourbon, and the Queen relaxed visibly and asked Isabel to be seated on a floor cushion at her side.

"Our cousin Carlos has told me that you are a friend of his, a young lady he greatly admires. I hope you will enjoy your stay at Madrid and that we shall have the pleasure of seeing you more often."

Calling Carlos a royal cousin was a pure formality she bestowed upon him somewhat prematurely; the Grandees alone had the right to be called cousins of the King. It was a way for the Queen to let her husband know that Carlos stood in her favor and also that Philip had better keep his hands off Isabel.

Philip was no dupe. He bowed slightly to his wife, and the corners of his thick lips curled upward. *"Amusez-vous bien,*

*Madame.''* He turned and left them without a word to Carlos, although he understood full well that it had been his wife's intention to obtain a favor from him for her protégé.

Carlos appeared disturbed and started to follow the King, but the Queen held him back.

"Never mind, dear cousin," she said with a mischievous smile, then she turned to Isabel.

"We were talking about the Retiro Park, where the Count-Duke is building a new palace. It should be ready this coming fall. At least I hope so, since it is about time we had a new place to go to. I hate the Escorial, and I hate Aranjuez. I wish we had something like Fontainebleau."

"I doubt there can ever be anything as delightful as a French palace in Spain," Carlos observed. "I have just returned from Paris, and believe me, I can hardly wait to return. The Louvre is being improved all the time, and His Majesty has also built a small new hunting palace, a pure delight. They call it Versailles."

The Queen sighed. "Then you will understand that after all these years at the Spanish Court, I am still not used to the stuffiness here, with the old black dragon breathing down my neck. I swear one of these days I will put a mouse under her skirt."

She had spoken fast, and Isabel was not sure she had heard correctly, but when Carlos emitted a short dry laugh, Isabel let out a little giggle herself.

The Queen had come to Madrid as a young girl of twelve in 1615 when she was married to Philip, then a crown prince of only ten years of age. It was a political match arranged by her mother Marie de Médicis. The marriage was supposed to ally the royal house of France, the Bourbons, to the royal house of Spain, the Habsburgs. After the assassination of her husband, King Henry IV, Marie de Médicis had ruled France more than shrewdly and had tried to keep France out of war with Spain. When her son Louis XIII came of age to rule, he chose to entrust France's fate to a favorite of his: the ascetic Cardinal Richelieu. For France, this proved to be a stroke of genius. Just as Olivares was determined to keep Spain on the pinnacle of glory, so Richelieu was determined to help France triumph over Spain. One of Richelieu's first ideas was another political match. If one sister of Louis XIII could be married to the King of Spain, he decided, another one could be married to the future King of England. Thus, Isabelle de Bourbon's younger sister Henriette had become the wife of

Charles Stuart and was now Queen of England. Since Charles
had first been engaged to a Spanish princess, the fact that he
had broken that engagement to marry a French one had
naturally contributed to the already existing friction between
England and Spain. The French Court, in the middle, with
one Bourbon princess Queen of Spain and another one
Queen of England, did all it could to further sabotage good
relations between those two countries. The Court of Madrid,
in turn, was mad at the Court of Paris and took revenge by
snubbing its French queen.

Isabelle de Bourbon was pretty, high-spirited, and full of
love for life. At first meek and unhappy because of the
constant effort of her entourage to belittle her, her miscarriages, her apparent failure to give Spain more than one
viable heir, the strict supervision of the Countess Olivares
over her Ladies-in-Waiting and over the education of her son
Balthasar Carlos and many other irritations, she had finally
reasoned that after all she was the Queen, and had started to
play a political role at Court, if only one of vengeance. She
had also overcome her disappointment at being unable to
hold the attention of her young husband, whose great sensuality demanded constant amorous adventures. Nor was she
any longer intimidated by Olivares. On the contrary, she
hated him and conspired with friends of the French Court and
with estranged Grandees to bring about his downfall. She had
never taken a lover, as some wicked tongues were insinuat-
ing, but she passionately loved the theater, the balls, and
pleasures of royalty.

For many lonely years she had craved the feeling of
belonging to someone, of being needed. That desire had been
fulfilled when in the fall of 1629, she had given birth to the
royal heir, Balthasar Carlos, a handsome healthy child whom
she truly worshiped. From the day of his birth, her political
ambitions had but one goal: to keep Spain and her colonies
and dependencies in good shape for her son. She dreaded the
wars with France, and she secretly accused Olivares of
squandering her son's inheritance by losing Spanish territory
and by causing dissatisfaction among the Spanish provinces.
Right now in the early summer of 1632, the French were
conquering bits and pieces of land in the north of Spain, and
the rich province of Catalonia had been completely antago-
nized by Olivares's high-handed treatment of the Catalan
Cortes. The Portuguese were also unhappy, and Isabelle de
Bourbon had begun to work more closely with the estranged

Grandees. One of her confidants, one of her agents of intrigue, was Carlos de Queras. To him she spoke freely. The black dragon breathing down her neck was the Countess Olivares, but since Philip had entirely succumbed to the magnetic personality of the Count-Duke, there was nothing the Queen could do but play gracious friend to the wife of the man she detested.

Isabel Valderocas knew some of these things. She knew the historical data, she knew the various relationships of the crowned houses of Europe, the ways in which the Habsburgs, the Bourbons, and the Stuarts were all in-laws; what she had not known until this moment was that the Queen could be a mischievous young woman desperately trying to derive some fun from her unhappy situation. In her official portraits she looked proud, cold, and bored, but when she talked, she sounded like a playful rogue.

"You think I would not dare?" the Queen now asked, joining in their laughter. "I will, too, and the Countess will squeak louder than the mouse I will put under her skirt."

"I hardly think your brother would approve," Carlos said softly.

"Oh, is the King of France becoming more dignified under the influence of this Richelieu?"

"Your Majesty, I am afraid your nostalgia for France makes you remember everything in the rosy shimmer of a fairy tale."

"You talked to him then? You talked to Louis? He does not want peace, does he? He has forgotten that we grew up together at Fontainebleau; worse he has forgotten that I am his sister. Even if he chooses to forget that he married a Spanish princess, that we are doubly allied by blood, how could he forget that we swore to keep together and help each other always? Did you give him the ring?"

"Yes, but His Majesty reminded me that he also has a sister who is Queen of England."

"Ha! Henriette! How dare he compare us. Henriette and he were never close." The Queen frowned and her glance fell on Isabel. "I trust you will not mention the mouse to anyone, will you?" she asked lightly.

"I am honored to be in Your Majesty's confidence," Isabel answered in French. "I would not dream of betraying it." Both young women looked at each other, and the Queen smiled.

"You are a dear, and one of these days I will have to talk to you quite seriously about Don Carlos, but I shall wait till he cannot hear me."

Queras immediately bowed to them, "Your Majesty, do not let my presence hinder you. I am humbly asking your permission to take leave."

So Isabel found herself alone with the Queen, a situation definitely more desirable than to be with the King. Carlos had hardly turned his back on them, when the Queen became serious.

"Carlos wishes to marry you," she said in a neutral voice. "Tell me why. Are you having a torrid romance? Or is it for your money?"

Again Isabel felt the blood shoot into her face. What did the Queen want from Carlos or from her? She had been extremely friendly with Carlos, treating him like an equal. Now, was she jealous? What had he told her?

"I met his Lordship in my parents' house at Seville this past spring," Isabel said truthfully. "We never exchanged more than a few words. I had not seen him again until tonight. I do not know why he wants to marry me. My family are not even *hidalgos*. His Lordship is the son of a Grandee; should he not marry someone more suitable?"

The Queen gave a scornful snort. "In this country nobility is sold to the highest bidder," she said. "With *limpieza* and money you can buy almost any title. But I am sure that this will occur to your brother. I wager it will be only a few weeks before the Count-Duke has found a title for you. Besides, Carlos can marry any Old Christian commoner without impairing his own standing. His father is a querulous monster, but the Grandees respect him. No, I suppose he must have fallen in love with you. Although I did not think I would ever see the day Carlos would fall in love."

"I cannot imagine that even now," Isabel could not help retorting.

"Why not? You are fair, you are young, you are lovely. His Majesty himself was drawn to you a short while ago." The Queen talked without a trace of irony or bitterness, quite as if Philip was not her husband.

"His Majesty was kind enough to inquire whether I had been presented to you," Isabel lied, and then she had the sudden inspiration of embroidering upon that lie. "He talked to me about His Highness, the Infante Balthasar. His pride for his son shines in his eyes. One can see that His Majesty adores you for having given him such a wonderful heir."

The Queen listened with incredulity. She was used to being treated with indifference, even by courtesans and similar parasites. Isabel's childish admiration softened her attitude toward the young woman. She knew that Carlos was a scheming, calculating man. He took the Queen's side, not out of respect for the Queen, but because he expected her to win in the end. If he got his hands on Isabel's stupendous wealth, would that be of any use to the Queen, or would he squander it on his own ambitious plans, whatever they were? Well aware of all this, the Queen was not sure she should play Doña Isabel into Carlos's hands.

"Tell me one thing," she asked. "Would you like to marry His Lordship?"

Isabel let her thick eyelashes fall over her eyes and remained silent.

"I see. You do not return his ardor. Why not? Do you have a lover? Or do you plan to enter a convent?"

It was always the same question. Love someone or become a nun. Or, if by bad luck you fell into the embrace of the king, love him *and* become a nun. Society abhorred an unattached woman. A woman needed protection either by a man ready to defend her honor with his sword or by the walls of a convent. Isabel yearned to be free, to be different.

She looked deeply into the Queen's eyes. This woman who like herself bore the most popular name for a Spanish girl—would she be able to understand if Isabel told her the truth? Was there a possible bridge between Isabelle the Queen and Isabel the commoner?

"Your Majesty, I do not know what I want. My father was kind enough to indulge in my whims and provide me with the best private teachers he could find. I sometimes wonder whether I would not have become happier if I had been taught no more than the most elementary reading and writing."

"No, you would not," the Queen said. "I know what you mean, for I experience every day the frustrations of being a woman. I am daughter of a king, sister of a king, and wife of a king, and yet I have no power at all. I can see mistakes, perceive errors, conceive of solutions . . . all for naught. My advice is not sought, and on the rare occasions I offer it, it is neither welcomed nor heeded."

Isabel's tête-à-tête with the Queen had not gone unnoticed. People started to look at them, and the Countess was coming straight toward them.

"My dear Countess," the Queen exclaimed with an exaggerated joy in her voice, "Doña Isabel is a refreshingly frank young lady. We will have to ask her to come to our next theatrical."

"With pleasure, Your Majesty," Doña Inés replied, and Isabel could not tell whether the Queen's friendship would make it easier or harder for her to get along with Olivares's wife.

Following closely behind the Countess, Carlos de Queras returned.

"Oh dear cousin," Isabelle de Bourbon now really seemed to take delight in the situation, "I do not think you have wooed the young lady long enough. But she is worth the effort, I think." She laughed out loud, a melodious silvery laughter, but Carlos smiled dourly, and Doña Inés frowned, so that Isabel needed to console herself. If she had lost a countess, she had gained a queen. Pedro would have to be satisfied with that.

The Queen's laughter also attracted her husband. Philip glanced suspiciously from Isabelle to Isabel without guessing why the two women had taken to each other. He would rather have seen them a little jealous of each other because of him.

Isabel thought it wise to escape his company and to avoid his eyes, even if that meant giving her attention back to Carlos. Like every well-dressed Spanish lady, Isabel carried a large lace handkerchief in her left hand. Now Carlos, according to proper Court custom, picked up one end of it and led Isabel away from the group crowding around the royal couple.

"I see you got along well with Her Majesty," he said softly, but there seemed to run an undercurrent of danger through his voice. "You are more clever than I thought. I am proud of you."

"Carlos, why me? There must be other heiresses. Why me?"

"Because I cannot stand simpering fools. I am not passionately in love with you, nor do I ask you to love me. You are cold by nature, or you would be married already. You want to be treated like a man. I will treat you like one. You are intelligent, you are ambitious, and you are rich."

"You do not need my money," she retorted readily, for she dreaded the logic of his words, and she wanted to end his speculations. "One day you will be richer than I am now. You can have any loan you want. My brother will be glad to advance to you any sum you may wish."

"I do not need a loan. I need a wife."

As she had gathered from the gossiping ladies, sex was the number one topic at Court, and who lay with whom the most often-played guessing game, so Isabel tried to chase him away by vulgarity.

"Do not tell *me* that. If you need wenching, perhaps one of these lovely ladies . . ." He interrupted her sharply.

"Stop it. You do not think like that, and I will ask you not to talk like that."

"Everyone else does."

"That is why I am not interested in everyone else. I need a wife for reasons I am not about to explain to you. I have decided that you are going to be my wife. If you were a Maid-of-Honor or a Lady-in-Waiting I would start right now to court you by putting on my hat and walking around with a moon face, but knowing your intelligence this shall not become necessary, I hope, even if Pedro does get ennobled."

"My Lord, Carlos, what are you talking about? You do not make one bit of sense to me."

"It is Court fashion," he explained impatiently, "that a gentleman falling in love wears the colors of his chosen lady on all official occasions and keeps his hat on even in the presence of Their Majesties to indicate that he is so much overcome by the love for the damsel that he forgets to observe normal behavior and etiquette. That is called *galant-ear en palacio*."

"How perfectly silly."

"Exactly my thoughts. You see we are more alike than you think."

Isabel was exasperated. He was compromising her in front of the Court. She was almost as good as betrothed to him. They could not hear the cutting tone in his voice, the dangerous quality in him that frightened her. They thought he was telling her sweet nothings, trying to seduce her, when every word he said repelled her more.

"Please, My Lord," she said trying to sound as firm as he did, "I do not care what you have decided. I do not want to become your wife, so you might just as well begin looking elsewhere. There are at least a dozen ladies right here who could find an eminently suitable wife for you. My answer to you is no."

"Your brother wants a title. You will discover one day, perhaps very soon, that he himself will ask you to become my wife. I will wait till then."

Isabel glared at him, thinking he could wait until the Holy Ghost materialized, but she dropped him a curtsy and sailed off again, wishing she could escape him for good. She ran straight into Olivares. The minister had been standing nearby, talking to Velázquez and at the same time observing her in a shrewd way.

"Doña Isabel," he said, and his voice reminded her of another voice with a much stronger Andalusian accent, "you seem flustered. Is His Lordship giving you a hard time?" Again she blushed, and she feared that her first evening at Court would surely end in a disaster if it dragged on much longer.

The Count-Duke nodded to the painter, giving him a sign to chat with Carlos de Queras, so that Olivares could have a moment alone with Isabel.

She smiled at him gratefully. "Your Excellency, I am confounded by your kindness. His Lordship knows me from Seville and has taken it to his head to tease me about becoming his wife."

Olivares chuckled. "Aha, I thought him impervious to female charms. You should be pleased to be able to change his mind."

"But I do not want to marry him," Isabel blurted out, "I do not even like him."

Olivares remained unperturbed. "I see. I take it you prefer His Majesty," he said with an amused quiver of his lips, indicating that she might have him if she wanted to.

"Your Excellency, please. I prefer HER Majesty."

He laughed, and people looked up and wondered how this common newcomer with the delicate face could be so spirited to provoke first the laughter of the Queen and now the deep resonant one of the Favorite.

"But my charming Doña Isabel, we were not talking about women. Let me put the question differently: who of the men present here tonight most appeals to you?" He seemed curious enough, she thought, as if he really cared, when it occurred to her that he was simply behaving as a perfect host, making her forget that one of his guests had bothered her.

"Well, whom do you like best? The brilliant Quevedo? The

serious Calderon? The sensitive Velázquez? My old friend
Rioja? It is just a game. Whom would you pick for an escort,
if you had the choice?"

She glanced at the men he mentioned, and then she turned
her face to him.

"I would choose you," she said.

"Oh, now you are being a flatterer."

"No," she said swiftly, "I am not. I admire you," she
added, safe in the knowledge that no one, but no one, would
ever believe such a conversation possible between an insignificant newcomer at Court and the most notorious misogynist
in Spain. "I admired you from the first moment I saw you,
and I think you like me."

"You remind me of my daughter," he said softly. "She was
taken away from us when she was about your age, and we
have never overcome our grief."

"I am sorry," Isabel said.

"It is all right. She used to bring out the best qualities in
people; she certainly brought out the best in me. And I think
in that way you may be like her. So, yes, I like you, too. Now
run along, and do not worry about Carlos de Queras."

She was relieved that he liked her, but his last words
reminded her of her father, who had spoken the same words
to her when she had first met Carlos, and a dark intuition told
her that her worries about Carlos were only just beginning.

A short while later, Their Majesties decided to retire to
their apartments, and after they left, everyone else was free
to depart as well.

# 16.

During their ride home, Isabel remained silent, but Pepita
could not restrain herself. She was filled to the brim with new
knowledge about life in the capital, and she immediately had
to tell Pedro and Isabel all the scandals she had picked up.
Pedro listened with amusement and seemed concerned only
when she mentioned the King. Her judgment of him was brief
and to the point, "He looks appalling."

"Nevertheless, be careful," he warned her, "or you will
have to take the veil."

"He would not dare touch me if you married me," Pepita said, much encouraged by all the loose talk she had been hearing. "But perhaps you want to wait until you get your title?"

"What title?"

"Is that not what we have come to Madrid for?"

"Is that what they are saying? That the Valderocases are finally ready to sell their independence for a title?" Pedro asked.

"Well, yes, isn't it true? Isn't the Court the world where we belong?" She made a sweeping motion encompassing the noisy street scenes around them. "Look at them, the scum, the thieves and whores, the beggars and scamps, the good-for-nothing common people. We do not belong with them."

"Pepita, what has gotten into you? Have you not known another world? We are merchants, working people: there are others like us."

"Oh yes, where are they? All the merchants I have ever met were Italians, or Frenchmen, or Genoese. Foreigners. Or perhaps Portuguese, which is worse, because they are New Christians and we have nothing to do with them. The rest of Father's friends were quality."

"Quality! And you think noblemen are good for anything? They think they were born to give orders because they never learned to obey. They never study, because they assume wisdom to be their natural heritage. They have nothing to do, so they intrigue and stab each others' backs, while openly practicing the most exaggerated forms of mutual courtesy. They outdo each other in vainglory; that is their daily occupation. No, Pepita, instead of swelling the ranks of the nobles, we should strive to encourage more Spaniards to regard work as a worthwhile pursuit and not as something degrading to be left to foreigners. Remember how we talked about this with Father and Rafael Cortes?"

But here Pepita held another trump. "Rafael Cortes joined the clergy, did he not? There you are, for all his inspired talk, he did not care to remain a nobody."

As Isabel listened to them, she felt a dagger being turned round and round in her heart. Would they never stop mentioning his name, when she was forbidden even to think about him? But they paid no attention to her.

"He is a traitor," Pedro said. "He hopes to jump into the highest level of Spanish society through the only door open to a poor boy who managed to get himself a university education. And do you know how he got that? By being my friend. I asked Father to pay for his studies."

"If it is the only door open to people like him, perhaps we should not judge him so harshly," Pepita said, looking at Isabel. But Isabel gave no sign of listening to them.

"No! he should have joined the Valderocas interest and worked for us," Pedro said firmly. "God knows, I offered it to him." Another thrust with the dagger, but Isabel still remained silent. Too many things had happened to her; she would have to sort them out in her mind before she could talk about them.

When they were back in the house and Pepita was running upstairs, eager to chat with Teresa, Pedro turned to Isabel with a whisper. "We will not discuss anything in the house. We have too many new servants; they may be unreliable. Find an excuse to leave Pepita between eleven and twelve tomorrow morning and meet me at Caietano's bookshop, quite accidentally."

"Agreed."

# 17.

The owner of the bookstore, a formidable old man of seventy with a mane of coarse white hair and green eyes under bristly white brows, was talking to Pedro when Isabel entered. He recognized her at once and excused himself to greet her with a bow.

"My Lady, the book we talked about has arrived."

Pedro joined them to ask in surprise, "You know each other?"

The old man looked at Pedro. "Not by name, but how could I forget a lady who is interested in Galileo Galilei?" He dropped his voice. "I received a shipment of books yesterday. I am afraid the author is going to be in trouble with the Inquisition in Italy."

"Señor Caietano, may I present my sister Isabel," Pedro said. "Isabel, you never told me you had ordered Galileo's work."

"I did not think it was important," Isabel said, and both the bookstore owner and Pedro chuckled.

"Every step you take is important to me," Pedro said.

"Point of honor," the old man added.

"Well, come upstairs and meet the others," Señor Caietano proposed and called out to a lad in the back room, "Juanito, mind the store."

If the invitation surprised Isabel, Caietano's tone of voice did even more so. Certainly, a Valderocas stood higher on the social ladder than a Madrid bookseller, but neither Pedro nor the old man seemed to be aware of it.

What happened next was still more perplexing.

The private apartments of Caietano and his family were on the second floor of the town house, above the bookstore. Isabel expected to be led into a small dark drawing room, the kind usually found in old buildings, with perhaps a faint smell of rancid oil and onions. Instead, she was ushered into a large clean room with whitewashed walls, black wrought iron ornaments, and a profusion of plants.

"Why, this looks just like a Córdoba patio," she exclaimed in delight.

"My wife is Córdobese," Señor Caietano said. "Angelita!"

Angelita came and looked small and frail next to her broad-shouldered husband. She wore a simple black dress, and a black scarf covered most of her gray hair. Her skin was like old leather, full of wrinkles, but her eyes were dark, brilliant, and alert. She greeted her guests not warmly, but with a reticence. Yet Pedro bowed to her, sweeping off his hat as if she were a duchess, so that Isabel felt compelled to curtsy to her, although she thought this was ridiculous and should be the other way around.

Señor Caietano seemed impatient with their formal greetings and motioned them through a side door into a smaller room.

There, around a long table sat six silent people, four men and two women, all fixing their eyes upon Pedro and Isabel.

It was a shock. Isabel was sure she heard no voices at all when she had entered the patio room; they must all have sat silently, like this. The confrontation was so unexpected that a shiver ran up her spine, and she grabbed Pedro's hand. He gave her a reassuring squeeze.

Señor Caietano introduced first Pedro and Isabel, then the others, "My oldest son Antonio, my second son Diego, my third son José. Our friend Lope Silva. My daughter Manuela. My daughter-in-law Serena. She is Antonio's wife." There were four empty chairs, and Caietano pointed to them, "Pray, take your seats."

Isabel sat down next to Serena, and Pedro sat next to her. Then Señora Caietano, Angelita, sat down on Pedro's left, and Caietano himself took the place of honor at the head of the table.

"Who is in the store?" Antonio asked.

"Juanito. I do not expect any customers. If he calls for help, you may go down." He turned to Pedro. "Juanito is my youngest son. He knows."

His voice assumed a brisker tone, "Well, let us not waste any time. I wanted Don Pedro Valderocas to hear your report, Lope. The situation is grave, and we will need both money and helping hands."

Lope Silva nodded. Then he spoke with a strong Portuguese accent, "To recapitulate, in 1628 we paid King Philip well over eighty thousand ducats for the right to leave for Spain. Many of us came here, but many left for France and for Flanders. It was to be expected that this mass exodus would frighten the government authorities, wherefore they, and especially the Inquisition in Portugal, have not stopped deluging His Majesty with urgent pleas to take away all civil rights from Portuguese New Christians. Since 1630, over a dozen of our best New Christian families have been thrown into the secret dungeons, and their belongings have been confiscated. So we want to submit a new petition to the King, representing to His Majesty that the New Christians are, after all, the only ones who maintain the commerce. We support Brazil and produce the machinery needed to obtain sugar for all of Europe. We maintain trade with Angola and the other colonies. We send countless ships to the East Indies. The custom duties of that merchandise alone is sufficient to maintain the royal navy. We are enriching his Kingdom. His Majesty must see that if he gives in to the demands of the Inquisition, not only we, but the whole of Spanish trade will be ruined. The only other wealthy people left in all of Spain are the Catalans, and the Catalans are determined not to contribute to any cause that is not Catalan. He still has gotten nowhere with their Cortes, and he never will. If he needs money, we alone are able to provide it. What is he going to do? Is he going to call a new *junta* to discuss our problems? The Church asks him no less than to exclude us from all trade and commerce. Does he not see it would be his own undoing?"

Lope Silva stopped and looked at each one sitting around the table. "What do you say? Shall we offer one hundred thousand ducats to Olivares? We have to act quickly. I am afraid that the King is considering handing all our petitions over to de Castro. If he does that, you know what is going to happen to all of us. Have any of you found out what Zapata advises him to do?"

Cardinal de Zapata was Inquisitor General for Castile and Aragon; de Castro held the same position for Portugal.

At this point Señor Caietano spoke up. "I have heard rumors that Zapata will be replaced shortly by Antonio de Sotomayor, the King's personal confessor."

"What is he like?" Lope Silva asked.

"Very old, very ambitious, and very eager to replace Zapata. Tremendous influence on the King."

"I have heard it said that he is Olivares's man," Pedro said, and everyone turned to look at him.

After two hundred years of religious persecution, suspicion dominated the conscience of every Spaniard. No one admitted openly to being a Marrano; a man had to be judged by his actions. Pedro Valderocas was known to be an Old Christian, yet by his actions he had gained entrance into New Christian circles. He had smuggled countless refugees out of Spain; he had donated money for bribes; he had been a friend in need to many a secret Judaizer. Before the meeting, Señor Caietano had said to his family and to the Portuguese merchant Lope Silva that he personally vouched for Pedro and for whomever Pedro brought to the meeting.

Pedro met their gaze steadily and continued, "I am in favor of waiting with the money offer until Sotomayor replaces Zapata. Otherwise, we run the risk that the King will take the money and might then be overruled by Sotomayor. It is certain that some action will be taken soon, because Sotomayor will want to assert his newly gained power. We must see to it that Philip keeps New Christians in business. We can convince him only by reminding him of the perpetual menace looming over the royal revenues. We must keep religion out of it."

"Keep religion out of it? But that is the whole point," Caietano's eldest son muttered. "The question of wealth and economics is a pretext as we all know. What we want is freedom from persecution and religious liberty for everyone. We must not forget that."

But old Caietano shook his head. "No, Antonio, Señor Valderocas is right. Let us keep our ideals and our faith in our hearts. Don Lope, I am afraid to tell you that your compatriots who have settled in Castile since 1628 have left the most rudimentary precautions in Portugal. As you all know, we will have a great *auto de fé* two weeks from now. Rumors have it that this will be the greatest Act of Faith ever celebrated in this city. Do you know who is going to figure most prominently in it?"

"No one knows ahead of time who the penitents are," the Portuguese answered.

"That is correct, and we do not know their crimes either, until the Inquisitors reveal accusations and punishment during the *auto*. But my sons and I have a very good guess. You see, there used to be a secret synagogue in the Calle de les Infantas. From one day to another all its members disappeared, as if swallowed by the ground. Most of them were Portuguese. They had invited me once to their services. I went, too, fool that I was, and had the raid been on that day, I would not be sitting here today. Nor would any of my sons, or my wife, or my daughter. We know that any day someone may remember my name under torture and that will be the end for all of us. Go tell your compatriots that Spain is no safer than Portugal when it comes to religion. Practice your trade, yes; practice your religion, no!"

"Is it not your religion, too?" Lope Silva whispered.

"We are good Catholics, and so are you," Caietano said, ignoring the plea in his guest's eyes. "You go tell that to your compatriots. Tell every single one of them. Let your mind be a businessman, your mouth a devout Catholic, and your heart be closed shut."

"I understand," Lope said.

"I hope the others do."

"There is something else we must try," Pedro said. "Sotomayor is now seventy-seven and we do not know how long he will be able to hold the position. There are five other Inquisitors on the Supreme Council of the Inquisition. But in addition, the King may name other representatives to the Suprema, clergymen or laymen, as he chooses. Well, we know that the King only chooses whomever Olivares tells him to choose, so we ought to try to get someone with a grasp on economics into the Suprema. As long as Olivares supports

Sotomayor, he could ask for a few concessions in return. Ideally, we need someone working for Sotomayor but spying for us."

"A spy in the Inquisition?" the Portuguese exclaimed.

"Rumors have it," Señor Caietano said, "that there is already a man who works for the same goals we do and who is closely connected with Olivares. Some say he is the leader of all our efforts; others think there is no coordination."

"Rumors, always rumors," Antonio muttered again.

"Most rumors are based on a grain of truth," Pedro said. "I, too, have heard that there is such a man. A sort of spy, if you will, but I do not know who he is."

"No one knows who he is," Antonio said, "and he may well be the invention of some desperate Marrano. I say we ought to petition the King, but I am willing to wait till after the *auto*. That should take the edge off His Majesty's Catholic fervor. Of course, if he gets a great share in the spoils of the heretics, he might be tempted to throw all his New Christians into the dungeons."

"You are too pessimistic," Pedro said. "Do you not know that the Suprema refused to divulge the sums it receives through confiscation? The King still pays all the inquisitorial salaries—at the same time he sees the Dominicans get richer and richer—do you think he likes that? No, all is not well between the Crown and the Inquisition, and for that matter, all is not well between the Church and the Inquisition."

"How is that?" several voices asked.

"The superiority of the Suprema is very galling to the bishops, since they argue that the Holy Office was founded to aid them not to form a competition. Rome and the Pope often side with the Church, but the Inquisition is a power in itself, not subject to the Pope. This is our hope for abolishing the Inquisition. The Spanish monarchs called this monster into being; they alone can kill it. And no harm would be done to the Church. The Church owes allegiance to the Pope; the Inquisition owes allegiance to the Spanish monarchy."

"Where do you get all this information?" Lope Silva asked.

"Some of it comes from the Count-Duke," Pedro said.

"In that case," Señor Caietano said, "I suggest that we follow Don Pedro's advice and present the Portuguese petition and the offer of one hundred thousand ducats to Olivares after Sotomayor becomes Inquisitor General. Don Lope will take that proposition back to Portugal. Can you raise the money on short notice?"

"We have pledges," Lope Silva said. "I do not know how much will come through. It depends upon whether there are any more confiscations in the meantime."

"Do not worry," Pedro said. "Raise what you can. I will come up with the difference."

At his words, a sigh of relief went through the Portuguese. Señor Caietano put his hand on Pedro's shoulder, "God bless you," he said.

Pedro stood up, "I am afraid we must leave now."

Manuela, Caietano's daughter, looked disappointed.

"I think my daughter would enjoy talking to Doña Isabel," the old man said. "She reads a lot, and they might discover a common interest."

Manuela was a slim olive-skinned girl with a perfectly oval face and the large sad eyes of a doe.

"I would love to stay," Isabel said, "but unfortunately I have an appointment. Let us make it another time." To Señor Caietano she added, "I do want to take the book. I read that Señor Galilei is pronouncing himself in favor of the Copernican system. I do not see why there should be trouble. Our astronomers have been accepting and teaching the Copernican theories at our universities for some time now."

"The Italians have not been as broad-minded," Señor Caietano said. "They tolerate the Jews but not modern astronomy. We tolerate modern astronomy, but not the Jews. Every country has its pet persecution."

# 18.

When Pedro and Isabel were finally in their carriage which had been waiting outside, Pedro told the coachman to drive out of town toward the Retiro Park. The day was getting hot, and the streets were dusty and smelled pungently of decaying garbage and excrement.

"There ought to be a way of keeping the streets clean," Isabel complained and breathed through her perfumed handkerchief.

"By having a dunghill in each patio?" Pedro asked.

"Well, I don't know, but I think people should not have to

empty their slop pails in the streets. Somehow, if all of it could be collected and driven out of town. . . ."

"For heaven's sake, Isabel, what a crazy idea. City streets always smell of garbage. Anyway, the odors strengthen our health. Everyone knows that. Now what do you think of Caietano?"

"He does not know who we really are, does he?"

"He must have a good idea."

"But Pedro, isn't it dangerous?"

Although the coach driver was a trusted Valderocas servant from Seville, and Alfonso, Pedro's footman, was more a friend than a servant, Pedro leaned to whisper into Isabel's ear. "He is their rabbi. He does for Madrid what Uncle Jaime does for Toledo."

"Heavens! Pedro, what are we getting into?"

"Are you afraid?"

She thought for a moment. "Afraid? No. I rather feel I am finally alive."

"Good," Pedro leaned back. "I saw you capture His Majesty's attention at the reception. What did he say?"

"Nothing much. Flatteries."

"He wants to see you in private?"

"He would like to."

"You know, Pepita is right. The King does not touch married women. As a rule that is. I have a hunch he likes virgins. Which makes you a good catch."

Isabel knew Pedro's remark was made in good faith, yet it reminded her that Rafael would forever stand between them, even if she never again laid eyes on the Dominican friar. She blushed.

"I am sorry," Pedro said, "I am a monster. My concept of honor must be completely addled."

"Life at Court is different," Isabel said. "I was much impressed with the women I met. They are so different, so free. I would like to be like them."

"No! You mean the courtesans? Their minds are like mills of promiscuity. They turn out nothing but dirty gossip. You will never be like that."

"What if I tried to seduce the Count-Duke?" she asked with an impish smile.

At that Pedro broke into laughter. "Haven't you heard his reputation? He is arrogant, vulgar, obscene . . . think of any damning quality, he has it."

"I like him," Isabel said.

"I do too."

"How far did you get with him?"

"I think we agree on what is necessary for Spain. I hope he will let me contact the right people abroad."

"He likes me," she said. "He told me so." She did not give him any further details of her talk with Olivares, and he looked at her skeptically.

"So you got somewhere with him, too," he said. "Yet, he is not a ladies' man. He may have seen that His Majesty took to you. . . ."

"I do not believe it," she interrupted. "I do not think he does that sort of thing, no matter how many lampoons make the rounds of the drawing rooms."

"But it is true that he protected Villanueva during the San Plácido scandal," Pedro said, "although the Protonotario of Aragon is one of the coarsest, vilest creatures I have ever met. It seems to me that if Olivares can be the friend and protector of so disgusting a character, he may be capable of the harmless task of finding a mistress for his royal employer."

Isabel thought of the stories she had heard from the courtesans, about Villanueva being found with his head in the lap of the abbess who was combing his hair for lice and about the lascivious activities of the entranced nuns. She had never heard so many obscene words and expressions as the giggling courtesans had dropped into her ears during the first lesson in Court scandals, and now she giggled herself.

"They say that Villanueva fancied himself becoming a cardinal," she told Pedro, "so he could help the Pope turn St. Peter into an Illuminist whorehouse."

"Isabel, watch your tongue!" He clapped his hand over her mouth.

She shook herself free and laughed. "That is not my idea," she told him. "It is part of a lampoon on Castilian Court customs."

All of a sudden the coach stopped rudely. They were jerked forward.

"What the devil?" Pedro exclaimed.

They were on the outskirts of the city, well on their way to the woods of Retiro, but the road was blocked by a train of carriages coming from the opposite direction, and a crowd was forming around the first one. Horses neighed, whips cracked, and ghastly cries filled the air. Without being told what to do, Pedro's footman Alfonso jumped down from his seat next to the coach driver and disappeared in the crowd. A few moments later he was back.

"It's the Count of Villaquemada," he reported. "A lad threw a stink egg in his path, and apparently his horses reared."

"Is anyone hurt?" Isabel asked.

"Yes, the lad. The Count himself cut his belly open."

"Cut his . . . oh my God. That is not possible."

Alfonso shrugged. "I saw it with my own eyes. It happened just now. The boy is dead."

Isabel leaned back and gasped. Pedro's mouth became a hard thin line, and he ordered the footman up on his seat. "Drive on," he yelled. As their coach started again, they heard Alfonso's voice screaming, and their own driver's whip cracking. "Out of the way, varmint! Make room, make room." The coach picked up speed as people were jumping aside right and left, to avoid being hit by the fast-trotting foursome. As the road got clearer, the horses kept up their speed, and soon they were rolling through the entrance to the vast park where Olivares was building a country retreat for the royal family.

Several hackneys and private carriages were standing in a clearing, and groups of drivers and pages were sitting about on the ground playing cards and rolling dice, while their masters were supervising the work on the pleasure palace or inspecting the progress of the landscaping.

Pedro told the men to wait for them, then handed Isabel out of the coach.

"Where are we going?" she asked.

"Just for a walk."

"Why did you drive off in such a hurry?"

"Because I do not want to get embroiled in the Count of Villaquemada's affairs. He is as ruthless as they come."

"But Pedro, he murdered the lad! Alfonso saw him. We have a witness."

Pedro gave a short dry laugh. "A witness for what? He is not going to be persecuted. The boy insulted him."

"But Pedro, to get killed for a stink egg!" The throwing of empty eggshells carefully filled with malodorous essences was a favorite pastime of mischievous youngsters, and one that even adults enjoyed during carnival festivities. To be killed for so popular a prank was a horrible punishment.

"The Count is notorious for the mistreatment of his

servants," Pedro explained. "He is said to favor flogging his chambermaids."

"But that is criminal! People get burned at the stake for less."

"He is not a criminal as long as he does not harm a person of quality. Look Isabel, forget about the incident. There isn't anything you or I can do about it. Every week people are being poisoned, stabbed to death, or shot here in Madrid, as well as in any other city of Spain. We cannot take it upon ourselves to fight all injustice. There is too much of it. What we can do is try to fight the most obvious part of organized injustice."

But Isabel was stubborn. An incident such as this disturbed her carefully arranged picture of Spanish society. She could not understand why one person should be executed for owning the wrong books, while a murderer went free.

"I can see that this is not a case of heresy and therefore does not fall under the jurisdiction of the Inquisition," she said, "but what about the secular courts? Can the family of the lad not sue his murderer? After all, he was not one of his servants."

"Oh, Isabel, sometimes you can be exasperating."

"And you are callous."

"No, I am practical. The Count of Villaquemada is a Familiar of the Inquisition."

"And so?"

"And so he can commit just about any murder he pleases, or any act of robbery or any other villainy. Members of the Holy Office cannot be persecuted in secular courts. They enjoy immunity for every crime except heresy. Now let us talk about the important things, while we are alone."

"Do you really believe that Olivares has a spy on the Suprema?" she asked.

"No, I do not think so. I think he has someone elsewhere in the administration of the Inquisition. A mere clerk in their archives would be invaluable. Someone who has access to the files on newly arrested persons."

"Do they keep accurate records of all the cases?"

"Of course. Once a person is apprehended by one tribunal, upon release, his name is made known to all the others. He will be watched until his death. How otherwise could we hear about convictions of second or third offenders."

Isabel shuddered.

Now Pedro spoke rapidly, telling her what he expected of

her. She was to cultivate a friendship with Caietano's daughter Manuela with whom she could discuss books and plays and practice her guitar, so that it would be possible for her to go in and out of the Caietano house without arousing suspicion. At the same time, Isabel must make friends in Court circles, preferably among the noblemen who were critical of Olivares. Since Pedro would soon pass for the Count-Duke's man, it would be most useful for Isabel to appear in the opposite camp. A marriage to Carlos de Queras would put her there without effort.

Isabel let herself be persuaded on all points but one. She was adamant in her refusal of Carlos as a husband.

"Can't you at least encourage him now and then?" Pedro asked. "If he escorts you around, you might meet his friends and possibly find someone more to your liking."

"Must I get married?"

"Of course, you must. What else can you do?"

"The ladies at Court are not all married."

"They are the daughters of Grandees or Titles who have the right to be at Court, because their fathers are courtiers."

"Not all of them." She intoned her words with an ironic inflection, giving them a single meaning.

"Those! They are no more than expensive whores," Pedro said. "You would not want to compete with them."

"Why not?"

"Isabel, remember who you are!"

His self-righteous exclamation brought her mounting anger to the seething point. "Pedro Valderocas Sanchez, don't act smug with me. You would marry me off to someone like Carlos de Queras, just to have a convenient spy in the other camp, as you put it. Would that not be selling my body and making me more of a whore than if I slept with a man who pleased me? Not only is your concept of honor addled, but every Spaniard's concept of honor is a travesty. In our world every man can do as he pleases, as long as he calls himself a fine Christian. Apart from that he can kill, steal, gamble, cheat his wife, beat his children, and commit every other sin in the decalogue. As long as he believes that Christ's blood was spilled for him, he will go to heaven, while his poor woman must lead a virtuous life and be content if he smiles at her occasionally. Well, I am not going to accept that! I will work with you, yes, for freedom, for justice, for religious liberty, for happiness, but I want my share!"

"Isabel, calm yourself. Not so loud. What if someone

should hear us? I promise I will not force you to marry anyone. But Isabel, be careful. Even if you think the way you do, you must not talk like that."

"All right, Pedro. I will be civil with Carlos. But never ask me to marry him."

# 19.

During the following two weeks, both Isabel and Pepita found themselves busier than they had ever been. In the mornings it was dressmakers or shopping, for dinner and supper they had company at home or they themselves were guests at the Alcázar apartments of courtiers or in the palaces of noblemen since word had quickly spread that Pedro Valderocas might become the personal banker of His Majesty.

Juana de Velázquez received them cordially. She loved to chat about Seville; she did not like Madrid and secretly wished her husband had never been discovered by His Majesty. Isabel and Pepita liked to keep her company because she was a good source of gossip. One day, while they were all three sitting on the floor cushions of Juana's *estrado*, Don Diego came in for a quick greeting. Happy that his wife had found friends she enjoyed, he sketched their faces and then generously let them have the chalk drawings. Coming from Velázquez, it was the highest compliment.

When they received an invitation to a ball given by the Count and Countess of Monterrey, Isabel was thrilled. She knew Their Majesties would be there, and she looked forward to renewing her friendship with the Queen. She even made up her mind that since it would help Pedro, she would at least pretend to be a coquette with Carlos de Quéras.

Yet, it was again King Philip's attention she attracted most. Of all the men at the ball, he was by far the most accomplished dancer, and when he led Isabel in a *gallarda*, an old-fashioned dance where the man kept his hat in his left hand, she had to admit that despite his ugliness, he possessed grace and charm. If he would only keep his mouth tightly closed, he would not be half-bad, she thought, because his teeth were yellowish, and his lips looked even thicker when he spoke. His skin had a sallow tone which was not alleviated by the drabness of his hair and moustache. But he evidently took himself to be irresistible, or perhaps he thought any woman should lay with him as a service to the Crown. Court dances were complicated and formal, more a rhythmic stepping and bowing. There was no opportunity for Philip to make her an assignation, and she skillfully avoided staying near him when the dance was over.

"I think His Majesty has a mind to summon you to his apartments," Carlos told her. "What answer will you give him?"

"What business is that of yours?" Isabel retorted with a mocking smile.

"I intend to marry a lady with an unsullied reputation," Carlos replied.

"Who said I was going to marry you?"

"I did."

She had a tart reply on her tongue but suppressed it when she remembered that she should not look upon him as a danger or a nuisance but as an adversary in a game. She had to coolly outmaneuver him.

"Well," she said, dimpling at him, "why don't you heed Her Majesty's advice then and pay me a more prolonged courtship?"

He took her word. The following night he came in a gorgeous gilt carriage drawn by eight horses to escort her to a private theatrical in Her Majesty's apartments. Despite the royal decree that all carriage mules were to be replaced by horses in order to stimulate Spanish horse breeding, few individuals could afford a coach and eight. But Isabel failed to find it as striking as Pepita who stood at the window admiring Carlos's arrival.

"No wonder he is in debt," Isabel muttered. "Why this ostentation; who does he think he is? The Duke of Osuna?"

But when she came home again, she was nevertheless impressed by her first solo appearance at Court.

"Imagine, the King himself played a part in the comedy," she reported. "Of course, he was the hero who won the leading lady, in more ways than one, I think. But do you know what? He is a good actor. Really."

On one score she was disappointed. She had not been able to speak to Olivares again. He was always preoccupied. Even while the play was going on, he had been reading dispatches and signing papers.

"What was the general gossip?" Pedro asked.

"Mostly the upcoming *auto de fé.* The King and the Queen and even baby Balthasar will attend. The *auto* is going to be held in honor of the Queen's recovery from confinement. Can you imagine! Although she has had nothing but miscarriages since the birth of Balthasar, and that was over two and a half years ago!"

"And we will all attend?" Pepita asked breathlessly. "My first *auto de fé!*" she exclaimed as if she had said, "My first ball."

Isabel and Pedro exchanged a glance. How could Pepita rejoice where they dreaded? For the first time, Isabel thought that Pedro would not be able to marry Pepita after all.

Every night when she went to bed, however late the hour, Isabel thought of Rafael. She no longer tried to force her mind in another direction, because she was afraid now of letting her memory of him fade. She had met many young men, but she thought most of them foppish and self-centered, vying for the Count-Duke's favor and not really interested in anything but their own superficial appearance. Rafael's description of life at Madrid, life at the Alcázar, had been accurate enough. It was as artificial as Quevedo's satires implied. Could she blame Rafael for seeking a more meaningful career?

She discussed the prospects of an ecclesiastic career for a commoner with Diego, Señor Caietano's second son, who was contemplating entering a religious order, mainly for the protection of his family. Although usually shy, Manuela violently opposed Diego's wish, and when the three of them drove for a promenade to the Retiro woods, the two Caietanos fought constantly.

Manuela wanted Diego to join the army, go abroad, and then defect to start life all over again as a Jew. To Diego, however, much as to Pedro, Judaism was something to be saved rather than practiced. He saw himself more in the role of dragon slayer, the dragon being the Inquisition, than in the part of Talmudic scholar. Manuela, as the well-read member of the Caietano family, was intensely concerned with the survival of Jewish studies, more than with the welfare of the Marranos. For her, spiritual values counted far more than economic considerations, and she declared she would gladly suffer for the sanctification of God's name. She had no use for Isabel's conviction that martyrs were simply people who got caught and did not find a way out. Manuela nursed a mystic wish to understand God, and she was an ardent believer in the Cabala and spent hours every day concentrating on the transposition of letters and numbers in order to gain a better insight into God's designs for mankind.

Isabel had tried to read the Zohar while staying with Uncle Jaime, but she had come to the private conclusion that the Cabala was nothing but superstition. Uncle Jaime had instructed her as much as he could in the faith of her ancestors, but whereas she had immediately accepted the teaching of God as an inseparable unity, she had rejected in her mind all ceremonies and requirements that went against her common sense. She hoped that one day a man would come who could do for religion what Copernicus had done for the understanding of the physical laws of the universe. Just as the great astronomer had proven all previous theories wrong, so a great philosopher would come and show that humanity's concept of God was wrong. After reading the Spanish translation of the Bible she had found in her father's library and kept for her own use, Isabel had concluded that the scriptures were simply stories, created by many writers, all leading to the same truth: that God was leaving mankind to itself to survive as well as it could. Neither were all the wicked punished, nor all the good rewarded, and God was never on anyone's side. King David had prospered despite his wicked deeds, while nameless men were slain despite their righteousness. She thought that each religious sect tried to recreate God in the image of its founders, and that if fish could talk, they might say that God was a fish, paradise a great water, and hell a dry sunny land.

Pedro had once said to her that one must be alive to serve God's purpose. If God had created men, then his purpose undoubtedly was for these men to live and multiply so that there would always be men alive. There was no purpose in men killing each other, especially over ideas generating from their own restricted human minds.

She did not explain these ideas to Diego and Manuela, but she encouraged Diego to undertake a career where he could do the most good for other people, since was it not preferable to save ten others, rather than only oneself?

"She is right, Manuela," Diego would agree. "Perhaps I am chosen to become the power to destroy the Inquisition from within."

"You are chosen only for what you choose yourself," Isabel said.

"Do you not believe that each man has a destiny?" Manuela inquired. "Don't you believe 'The Lord is my shepherd, I shall not want'?"

"It is a beautiful poem written by King David who mainly did what he himself wanted," Isabel replied dryly.

"Isabel is an Old Christian Judaizer," Diego reminded his sister. "She is on our side for intellectual reasons, for humanitarian reasons. . . ." Both Caietanos looked at Isabel, and Manuela was visibly uncomfortable. Fear was inbred in every Marrano, and if Isabel was not a Marrano, she was a possible future enemy.

Sensing her friend's uneasiness, Isabel hesitated but decided that her only allegiance was to Pedro and her Benahavel ancestors. If they had all taken years of trouble to pass for Old Christian, she was not going to let them down. The Caietanos talked too much.

"May I quote your father's words," she said to them. "Let your mouth be a devout Catholic, and your heart be closed shut."

"You are one of us, I know it, I feel it," Manuela said impulsively and flung her arms around Isabel to kiss her on both cheeks.

"Manuela, be careful of what you say," Isabel could not help warning her, but she returned her hug. "The rest of our family knows nothing about Pedro's and my feelings. Especially my cousin Pepita. She is as devout an Old Christian as the King himself, and please never forget it."

When they walked back to the clearing where the coaches were parked, Manuela was a few steps ahead, and suddenly Diego took Isabel's hand and held her back.

"I have to talk to you alone," he whispered.

"What about?"

He did not answer but pulled her hand to his lips.

"Doña Isabel," he said then, "I am madly in love with you. Ever since you first came to our house with your brother, I have thought of you. During that whole meeting, I did nothing but look at you and fall in love with you."

He looked at her with all the ardor of his nineteen years, pure adoration shining in his big brown eyes, a slight tremble in his voice.

Isabel was at a loss as to what to say. He meant no more to her than a child, her affection for him would never be different from what she gave Pasquito, her little Moor. Yet he was no young Court fop whom she could put off with a flirtatious joke. She did not want to hurt his pride or cast a shadow on her blossoming friendship with the Caietano family; nor did she want to tell him that she was twenty and too old for him. So she drew her hand away and cast down her eyes, mumbling, "I don't know what to say. . . ." which was the truth.

"Oh Isabel, I am sorry I startled you. I was overcome. But you see why I cannot join an order, not after I met you. You are not betrothed to anyone, are you?"

She smiled at him then and laid her hand on his arm.

"No, I am not betrothed. But neither am I used to such masculine ardor. You are taking advantage of an unchaperoned lady. What would you say if a stranger spoke like that to your sister?"

He seemed pleased that she should take him for a danger to her virtue and assured her that his intentions were most honorable.

"I shall speak to your brother and ask his permission to court you," he said.

"No," she retorted quickly. "He might not approve of it, and then if perchance I should fall in love with you, what would we do then? Let us just be friends."

"For as long as you wish."

And so Isabel's life in the capital fluctuated between frivolous entertainment among courtiers of loose morals and theosophical discussions with her Marrano friends; a conscious effort to discourage Diego's pure love and a wish to keep out of the King's way. She was also determined to refuse a marriage contract with Carlos de Queras. Yet, behind all this, there lurked her constant longing for Rafael. Her mind was tortured by pictures of Rafael lying with other women, and she hated herself for being obsessed by him. She told herself that she would be free of him, if she, in turn, could bring herself to make love to another man. However, she knew he could not be a boy like Diego, a cold appalling creature like Carlos, or a lecherous unattractive monarch. Where would she find a real man, a difficult man, a man who presented a challenge to her female instincts—a man like Olivares?

# 20.

During the week before the great *auto de fé,* visitors from all over the country were streaming into Madrid. The streets were so packed with people that the Inquisitors had to forbid the use of carriages, horses, or mules for the duration of the festivities, under penalty for common folk of a hundred lashes, and for gentlemen of forfeiture of the animal, one month in prison, and a heavy fine. The Inquisitors were the virtual rulers of the city. Had not the King conferred upon them the authority of police?

Town criers proclaimed at regular intervals that "The Holy Office of the Inquisition, for the glory and honor of God and exaltation of our holy Catholic Faith, will celebrate a public *auto de fé,* on Sunday the fourth of July at the Plaza Mayor of Madrid."

A procession of mounted Familiars and notaries, with drums and trumpets and clarions accompanying them, wound through the city behind the town crier, and not a soul in the capital and the surrounding villages remained ignorant of the event.

Moreover, Philip IV had ordered the city to construct a staging on the Plaza Mayor according to plans drawn by his chief architect. The Plaza itself was a beautiful square built by the previous monarch. It contained sixty-eight houses, all of them five stories high and of the same style, with a total of four hundred seventy-six balconies. There was room for fifty thousand spectators, and when there were bullfights, the owners of the houses and apartments could make a good deal of money by renting their windows and balconies. No such income could be made from the *auto de fé,* however, since the Inquisitors had the right to assign the balconies according to their choice. Since the solemnities would take up most of the day, under a burning July sun, a great canvas had been stretched over the whole plaza from roof to roof, submerging it in an eerie diffused light.

The royal balcony took up two stories, since it had an overhanging canopy. In the middle of the square, a fifty-foot-long scaffold had been erected, raised to the same height as the third-floor balcony prepared for the royal family in the center of one wing. On top of this sturdy wooden scaffold, two grandstands of rising rows of seats opposed each other. One was for members of the Council of the Inquisition and of the other Councils of Spain; the other was for the criminals to be sentenced during the Act of Faith. The rostrum of the Inquisitor General of Castile was elevated higher than the King's balcony. An altar had been erected in front of the Councils' seats, on a thick beautiful woolen carpet. Before it, a green cross would be placed on the eve of the celebration. Since the scaffold was almost two stories high, there was standing room under it, and two large pits opened in the center so that light and air could reach the ground. Between the pits, as on a bridge, were the elevated stands for two Inquisitors who would alternate in reading the sentences.

The erection of this complicated staging had taken over a month. Isabel, Pepita, and Pedro had come twice to watch the progress of the construction, and each time the stench of hundreds of sweating workers, added to the all-pervading odor of decaying garbage and refuse, had proven well-nigh unbearable. All three of them dreaded the idea of having to sit from early morning until late in the afternoon in the same place, surrounded by thousands and thousands of unwashed bodies. They could not afford to be squeamish, and the necessities of life were a topic neither unnatural nor taboo.

"We better not drink anything in the morning," Pedro said.

"But Pedro," Isabel said reasonably, "we may have to relieve ourselves. Surely that is permissible."

"I do not know," Pedro said. "Thanks to the Count-Duke, we will at least sit on a balcony, which is a great deal more than other common folk can expect, I warrant you. As to whether we will be able to move from our seats, I do not know."

"Pedro, are you saying that because of the holiness of this occasion, every Spaniard's bodily functions are suspended for the duration of the *auto!*"

"Well, it will be a good day for slop-men," Pedro said.

To be a slop-man was one of the lowest, most degrading jobs, but still it was a profitable one. The slop-man carried a covered pail and a special vessel. He made the rounds of taverns and public places, and for a fee, a person could relieve himself wherever he found himself, without inconvenience.

"Oh, I wish I could stay home," Isabel said. "Could I be sick? To tell the truth, I feel faint already."

Under Pedro's scornful glance, her fraudulent intentions withered quickly. Of course, she would have to attend.

# 21.

The procession of the Green Cross started in the evening on Saturday. Since it would pass through their street, right under their balconies, Pedro and Isabel had invited the whole Caietano family to spend the night at Valderocas House. Much as they loathed the terrible Act of Faith which would end in flaming death for men and women who had worshipped God according to their own conscience, neither the Valderocases, nor the Caietanos, nor the Portuguese merchant Lope Silva, nor any other secret Judaizer, reformer, or Protestant, dared refuse the contemplation of the holy spectacle. It was everyone's duty to see and be seen. A show of abhorrence would be heresy.

Even in their own house, quarters were cramped, for scores of servants, their own and their guests', helped fill windows and balconies as the dark sounds of the drums drew nearer.

The march was preceded by a hundred coal merchants, armed with pikes, who wore on their faces the proud satisfaction of men being rewarded for having furnished the wood for the *quemadero,* the burning place outside the city beyond the Puerta de Alcalá. They were followed by the Duke of Medina de las Torres, carrying the standard of the Inquisition. This great banner, made of crimson damask, was richly embroidered on one side with the royal arms and a green cross rising from the crown flanked by a sword and an olive branch, and on the other side with a shield showing the arms of San Pedro Martir. The gilt staff of the standard ended in a cross and from it hung cords with gold and silver tassels.

A crowd of other high nobles and Familiars followed the banner. Then came a white cross followed by thousands of monks of the various religious orders; then the local parish crosses and the parish clergy.

The green cross which gave the procession its name was

covered with black crepe and borne by the prior of the Dominican order. When the throngs of black friars passed beneath the balcony where Isabel was sitting between Pepita and Diego, she never once took her eyes off them. She stared at each one intensely. It seemed to her that she poured all of her strength into her eyes; no other part of her remained alive. There were hundreds of men, all in the same long black cloak with its hood resting on their backs, and from above she could see on every head the bare round spot shining white in the crown of hair around it. All monks wore a tonsure, only the size of the shaved spot varied according to their seniority in the orders.

She did not know what to hope, whether it would cause her more anguish to see him or more agony to ignore his whereabouts. She merely stared and waited.

When she finally saw him, near the end of the line of black friars, she thought that her heart would burst from receiving such a painful jolt. It was getting dark, but night had not yet fallen, and she saw him clearly. He was taller than all the others. He carried a torch and chanted the Miserere with the rest of them. She saw the beautiful shape of his face. His skin was whiter than she remembered it, and his eyes and hair that much darker. He looked straight ahead, and she feared he would not be able to see her. All windows and balconies were crowded with onlookers. Even if by chance he looked up, hers would be a face lost in the multitude. Yet, as he came nearer, she leaned forward, impulsively, holding on with both hands to the wrought-iron railing, never taking her eyes off his face. The procession came from her left, and when he reached Valderocas House, he was not farther than ten yards from her. He would get still nearer passing within a few feet of her balcony.

The air was vibrating with sounds, the deep pounding of the drums, the high notes of the clarions, the monotonous chanting of thousands of friars, and the hum of spectators. Pepita and Teresa had not ceased fanning themselves and keeping up a rapid chatter, Manuela was talking to Pedro, Señor Caietano and his third son José made comments under their breath. No one noticed that Isabel had not said a word.

Now, as she leaned forward, her mouth formed his name, but not the faintest sound came out. Then, just before he reached her balcony, his head moved; he looked up! The expression on his face never changed, his step never faltered, but for a few seconds their eyes locked, and his chanting stopped. Had he felt her presence? Or did he know that this was Valderocas House now and had he hoped to see her? Whatever had made him look up, Isabel knew that he had recognized her and that he, too, was hurt by the shock. When he had passed, she leaned back in her chair. She was relieved to have seen him at last, to be certain that he had joined the Dominican order as he had said he would. At the same time, she felt all her strength leaving her, all her hope deserting her.

Now Diego turned his face to her, and she heard his voice in her ear, "Doña Isabel, are you feeling all right? You look pale." She wondered whether he had noticed, but had there been anything to notice? He could not have seen her face, since she had leaned forward, and he could not know about Rafael.

She shook her head. "I am just bored," she mumbled. "Aren't you?"

"It is heaven just being near you," he replied, "but I could think of a better pastime for both of us."

She smiled at him, thinking that her heart was broken but that it did not matter to anyone. She was dead inside, but she would continue smiling.

That night, lights were extinguished early in the houses and palaces, and in the apartments of the Alcázar, for all of Madrid would have to be up much earlier than usual. The royal family would be expected to enter their balcony around eight in the morning, and they should, according to etiquette, be the last spectators to arrive. Some Dominicans would remain during the night around the altar bearing the green cross, and the coal merchants would stay outside the city to guard the *quemadero*.

## 22.

At daybreak, Pedro, Pepita, and Isabel walked the few blocks to the Plaza Mayor. At the entrance, Pedro had to show their invitations to a member of the German Guard, and an usher led them to the house which had been reserved for guests of His Excellency the Count-Duke of Olivares. The Favorite and his wife would be behind Their Majesties in the royal balcony. Already the air was stifling, for the canvas stretching over the plaza prevented any fresh breeze from coming in. The familiar Spanish odor of olive oil, onions, and garlic had been driven away by the smell of incense and wax candles.

When they entered the room assigned to them, Isabel recognized many faces from the dinner parties she had attended, and she felt that if there had been any doubts about her place in Madrid society, they were definitely dispelled when she was ushered to a seat in the front row of the balcony. There she was greeted warmly by Velázquez and his wife Juana, and by Pedro Calderon de la Barca, the famous young author she had met at Olivares's reception and seen again at the Queen's theatrical. She sat between Juana and the writer, while Pepita and Pedro were content with second-row seats behind Isabel.

The Plaza was rapidly filling with thousands of people, each one apparently knowing where he was going and what he was doing.

"I am amazed how well organized everything is. I suppose much credit is due to your husband," Isabel said to Juana, but the painter's wife shook her head.

"No, thank all the Saints, this show belongs to the Holy Office. Already Diego has almost no time for painting, what with preparations for the Buen Retiro and the perpetual Court festivities. He is working himself to death."

"What an audience," Calderon marveled. "What a place to give a Corpus Christi stage play." The playwright excelled in pieces about the miracle of the Eucharist.

"Have you watched many *autos de fè?*" Isabel asked him.

"Many? No. Public *autos* are expensive, you know. Only a few have been held in our lifetime."

"But isn't the Inquisition very busy?"

"Yes, there are many private *autos,* of course, only we do not hear much about those. But I do not think there has ever been an *auto* like today's. Except perhaps the one at Toledo in 1600 which King Philip III attended. And that was before we were born. But if you worry about heretics escaping their just punishment, you need not. The Inquisition has enough prisons in which to keep evil creatures from contaminating the true believers in the Holy Mother Church."

"God is gracious and compassionate," Isabel said. "What do you think will happen to the soul of a relapsed heretic when his body is burned?"

Calderon lifted an eyebrow and gave her a strange look.

"The soul will go straight to hell, where Satan is waiting to receive it."

Isabel wanted to ask, then God is powerless against Satan? when she received a strong kick in her left leg. Pedro sat close behind her and must have felt a warning was necessary. But she could not help carrying on her conversation. Calderon was considered a genius at a time when every educated man's highest endeavor consisted of poetic expression of exalted ideals. If she could learn his true thoughts on matters of faith, she would come as near to understanding the soul of Spain as would ever be possible.

"The relapsed heretics, they are mostly Jews, are they not?" she asked him.

"Truthfully not, for a Jew is a believer in Mosaic law, but one who had never been baptized. You may be glad to know that there are no such execrable people left in our country. The heretics of this *auto* are Judaizers, Marranos, just as evil as Jews, if not more so."

"But what do they actually do?" Isabel asked. "They are not necromancers, nor bigamists, and they are not perverts like the Illuminists. The Edict of Faith always tells us how we can recognize them by their Jewish customs, but what do they actually do?" She gave him an innocent look with her great luminous eyes and quite succeeded in convincing him that she was a well-sheltered ignorant female who needed instruction.

"Judaizers steal and crucify little children," he told her. "They wash themselves in human blood; they try to kill and ruin all Christians; they poison people and wells; and they desecrate hosts and crosses and crucifixes."

Isabel shuddered visibly, but for a different reason than Calderon suspected. She shuddered because Pedro's plan seemed utterly hopeless if men on the crest of Spanish intellect could seriously believe such blatant nonsense. She thought of the gentle Caietanos, of earnest Lope Silva, of Uncle Jaime, of Pablo Raíz and his wife, who was her own mother's cousin, and finally she thought of her own parents and her long line of Benahavel ancestors who had managed to escape the fury of misinformed masses by hiding their true identity under the Old Christian name of Valderoeas. There must be thousands of us, she thought, trembling with fear at being discovered and tortured into admitting the diabolical lies made up by horror-loving Inquisitors, and nobody will listen to or believe the truth. It is our God who is gracious and compassionate; it is our God who orders us to love our fellow men; it is our God who loves mankind so much that He even refrains from punishing the wicked. All we do is praise the everlasting God who created the heavens and the earth, while they and their three-fold God think of nothing but how they can better kill us. Why do they hate us so?

"I take it then you have never attended an *auto de fé*," Calderon said. "It is one of the most wonderfully awesome manifestations of our effort to insure the purity of our holy faith."

By and by, all the balconies filled, and everyone stood up as the King, the Queen, and little Infante Balthasar Carlos took their places. They stood again as Antonio Cardinal de Zapata, the Inquisitor General of Castile, arrived and slowly walked up to his high place in the center of the right-hand wing of the plaza. Again, the low throbbing of drums came rolling nearer, interspersed with the clear cries of trumpets, as the procession entered the plaza.

At its head was the band, then the crosses of the parish churches, shrouded in black, followed by an acolyte who rang a mournful sounding bell. Then, one by one, came the penitents, first those accused of minor crimes such as imposters and personators of officials of the Inquisition, then blasphemers, bigamists, Protestants, and repenting Judaizers. They all wore conical mitres and the dreaded sanbenitos, yellow robes reaching to the knees, transversed by a black cross. They were garments of shame which from this day on would hang in their parish churches with their names attached to them, so that forever after their families and descendants would be branded as relations of heretics and be excluded from entering the orders or becoming state employees or occupying any other position of honor. There were thirty-seven of these poor souls, each walking between two Familiars of the Inquisition and bearing a big burning yellow wax candle. Next came two porters of effigies. The effigies were carried on poles and also dressed with mitres and sanbenitos painted with flames indicating that the persons whose names and crimes were written on the effigies were to be burned. The second effigy was followed by a porter bearing a black box painted with flames. This meant that the person was not burned in absence but was a dead sinner whose bones were going to be burned with the effigy. The last ones in a row of sinners were seven relapsed Judaizers, each between two Dominican friars. They carried green crosses instead of wax candles, and their sanbenitos and mitres were painted with flames and little devils thrusting heretics into the fires of hell. All forty-four sinners were barefoot and seemed to walk with difficulty, their bodies emaciated and broken by torture, their spirits gripped by fear. Except for the seven to be burned alive, none of them knew what awaited them, whether lifelong prison, or twenty years as galley slaves, whether public scourging, or years of having to wear the garment of shame.

More Familiars of the Inquisition followed, then members of the Mendicant orders, then the standard of the Inquisition, and finally the Inquisitors themselves.

The procession slowly climbed the steps onto the scaffolding and marched under the King's balcony. Since Isabel sat only four balconies away from the royal family, and on the same floor, she had an excellent view of every member of the procession, and she turned white when she saw one of the relapsed heretics wearing a monstrous gag and an iron fork fitted to his chin and secured by a band around his neck and then down around his waist so that his head was kept up rigidly and he could neither speak nor bend over, and his eyes were bulging from the mere effort of still being alive.

"What is the matter with him?" she asked almost soundlessly.

"He must be an habitual blasphemer who would like to scream his heresies at us. They prevent him from talking, that is all," Calderon explained coolly without showing any emotion.

Suddenly, as they passed under the balcony of the King, another of the seven condemned let out a shout, "Long live the laws of Moses!" Quickly, the two black friars at his side pushed a smaller gag into his mouth and held it by a band around his neck.

Calderon gave Isabel a triumphant glance and made a gesture signifying: what did I tell you? But Isabel paid no more attention to him, for her eyes had started to search the long line of Dominicans for the tall figure she knew so well. But much as she tried, this time she did not see Rafael.

When finally everyone was in place, Cardinal Zapata came down to the altar ceremoniously and held up a cross to address the people.

"Raise your hands and let each one say that he swears by God and Santa Maria and this cross and the words of the holy gospels, that he will favor and defend and aid the Holy

Catholic faith and the Holy Inquisition, its ministers and officials and will manifest and make known each and every heretic, faultor, defender, and receiver of heretics and all disturbers and impeders of the Holy Office, and that he will not favor, or help or conceal them, but, as soon as he knows of them, he will denounce them to the Inquisitors; and if he does otherwise that God may treat him as those who knowingly perjure themselves. Let everyone say Amen!"

Everyone said Amen, but this general oath did not suffice, for the King was present, and just as his ancestors had been obliged to take a special oath at previous *autos,* so he now had to bind himself. The Inquisitor General walked to Philip's balcony with a missal and a cross. And the King stood up, laid his hand on the cross, and in the presence of his people, swore to protect and defend the Catholic faith as long as he lived and to aid and support the Inquisition on his faith and royal word of honor.

Oh God, thought Isabel, and this is the man whom we want to influence in the opposite direction. She wished she could see the face of the Count-Duke, or at least the face of her own brother, but they were all standing solemnly, and she dared not move her head.

Fray Antonio de Sotomayor, the King's elderly personal confessor, now took the pulpit and launched into a long sermon in which there was no mention of Christian love and compassion but much of lightning and thunder and hellfire for heinous unrepentant sinners and their silent accomplices. It was like the Edict of Faith and the Anathema all thrown into one. But as the midday sun was beating on the canvas, sweat started to form on their faces and to run down and leave marks in the layers of face powder, and the reiteration of well-known threats made no more impression on Isabel. All the fresh air seemed to be used up, and here and there a few ladies began to faint. Isabel felt nauseated, her bodice was getting tight, everything about her started to swim. Then her eyes fell on the victims in their grotesque attire, and her strength rallied. Things could be worse. She could be there with them, and she wondered, vaguely, absentmindedly, what would happen if she would get up, climb over the railing onto the scaffolding, and try to make her way to the bench of the condemned, proclaiming to one and all that she, too, was a Marrano and that by right she should be burned with them.

She would be restrained, of course. Her brother and

friends would claim that she had gone mad because of the heat, and they would send for a doctor to bleed her, the universal remedy for any abnormal behavior.

She made an effort to control herself, and she felt better when Juana Pacheco whispered to her, "My husband says there will be a break at two o'clock, and we will get some refreshments."

After the sermon, the reading of the sentences started, with all the details of the accusation, the efforts expanded by the Inquisitors to bring about repentance, including the tortures necessary to elicit a confession. Again, the lesser offenders came first, those who would be reconciled to the Church before the end of the *auto de fé* by solemnly abjuring their heresies.

By intermission time, all thirty-seven had heard their sentences, ranging from enforced wearing of the sanbenito to lifelong service as galley slaves. Two of the future galley slaves lost consciousness upon hearing the judgment, and Isabel as sister of a seafarer and co-owner of a merchant fleet wondered whether the strength of the royal navy depended upon such victims. She thought of the able well-fed crews of the Valderocas ships and understood why they always came in safely, while the royal vessels were often caught by English and Dutch privateers.

Refreshment rooms had been prepared under the scaffolding, and they were cooler than Isabel had expected, but there was a lot of noise from the footsteps above. Velázquez had seen the architectural plans and had been consulted on the layout of the refreshment halls. He therefore led his party swiftly around corners and through corridors to the place where snow-cooled drinks were served by Alcázar lackeys. Huge jars of snow were set in even bigger ones filled with freezing salts, and there was a choice of lemonade, cinnamon water, or cherry water.

"I wish I could spend the rest of the day down here," Isabel sighed, but a stern glance from her brother made her add, "although I would not want to miss the reconciliation ceremony." She would gladly have missed the whole remainder of the *auto de fé*, but such truth smacked dangerously of heresy. As Calderon raved on and on about the lofty beauty and magnificence of the ceremony, Isabel found herself tapping her foot impatiently under the protective layer of a dozen skirts. The fools, she thought, the stupid fools. Sipping her cool cherry water, she tried to plan an escape from the plaza, when the imposing figure of the Count-Duke entered. As usual, he was surrounded by a train of attendants and Court fops, a sort of human cloud that followed him wherever he went. What is he doing down here? she wondered. He certainly does not have to come for his own refreshments. The answer was simple. Olivares walked straight over to the big jars, grabbed a handful of snow, and rubbed it over his forehead, his cheeks, and around his neck. He then turned and walked decorously out of the room.

"By God, there goes an intelligent man," Pedro mumbled under his breath.

Isabel looked at him and when he smiled at her, she was relieved.

"That way, at least he keeps a cool head," Pedro added.

The second act of the nightmare began with the reading of the crimes committed by the principals accused. They were, indeed, as Señor Caietano had guessed, supporters of the secret synagogue which had been discovered in the Calle de las Infantas and had since been burned to the ground by order of the Inquisition. Among them were three women, one of them the owner of the house where the secret congregation had assembled. When Isabel heard the name of that woman, which was Isabel Nuñez Alvarez, she again had a sudden vision of herself sitting there with the accused, and she felt fear creeping into every fiber of her body, the horrible fear of being already marked for death. But when she forced herself to listen to the accusations, she found her fear changing into seething anger at the monstrous lies served to the believing public as proven truth.

It appeared that during their illicit assemblies, those heinous evildoers had flogged an effigy of Christ, had pierced and mistreated hosts stolen for this purpose from the parish churches, and their whole service had consisted of similar blasphemies. But the effigy—oh glory to God—had started to bleed and had cried out three times. This miracle, far from convincing the hardened criminals of the divinity of God's Son, had driven them to even more satanic frenzies. They had finally burned the effigy and the hosts with it, thus killing again the body and flesh of the Savior.

How can you believe such outrageous lies? Isabel wanted to scream in rage, but a glance to her right showed her the deeply absorbed features of Calderon who seemed to drink the words of the Inquisitor as if they were the waters of life. Did no one see through this fraud? Did no one understand that these people had done nothing worse than come together for a Passover meal, during which they had thanked their ancient God for ancient deeds, such as the delivery of their ancestors from Egyptian oppression? Oh Moses, where are you now? Come lead your oppressed people out of Spain! If there are saints in heaven, surely you must be one of them.

Had the sinners admitted their crimes? Not at first, said another Inquisitor, who now mounted the speaker's stand, but owing to the blessed inspiration of the Inquisitors who knew how to apply the exquisitely humane tortures invented and perfected for that purpose, confessions were obtained, and so, although their bodies would have to be burned, because their crimes were too great, the immortal souls of the sinners might yet be saved. For if at the last minute they would repent, which they had not yet done, they would be mercifully strangled before the fire could reach them, and they would be absolved of their sins. Moreover, since they would not be able to commit any new sins between the short time of the absolution and the garroting, their souls would then fly straight to heaven. But if they persisted in their erroneous ways, there was nothing left to do but to burn them alive, for the Church would have to abandon them and relax their sinful bodies to the secular arm of justice with the admonition not to spill their blood. Thus, the Great Catholic Church, the representative on earth of the merciful Son of God, would not be responsible for their death.

So it went on and on, in front of King and Court and clergy. For the purification of the faith, thousands of spectators were told in detail what they could expect if they were ever tempted to stray from the official dogma of the Holy Mother Church.

The last of the accused, Fray Domingo Romairón, was the worst heretic who had ever existed. He was so evil that instead of confessing his crimes, he had persisted in his heresies during seven years of imprisonment. The most terrible part was that he had been a monk, a man who had received high ecclesiastical honors. Indeed, it must be assumed that he was a helpmate of the devil who protected him during the tortures, how otherwise could he have withstood the rope, the water, and the fire without asking for mercy? Since the torture of heretics was one of the acts most pleasing to God, the crowds were duly informed of the various stages of his obstinacy. First, his hands had been bound behind him and by means of a rope running through a pulley, he had been raised to the ceiling, where he had been left hanging with weights tied to his feet, while the Inquisitors had asked him most gently to repent of his sins and to confess of his crimes. When he had persisted in calling to the God of Moses, which name he pleased to give the devil, he had been let down and pulled up in sudden jerks which should have been painful enough to make him admit his heresy. After an hour of this, the Inquisitors, in their mercy, had given him a respite and a chance of confessing alone in his cell to a Dominican friar.

Much to their distress, the Inquisitor continued, they had to apply the next torture where the man was laid with his back on a wooden trough with a bar running through it. This sometimes broke a criminal's backbone and with it his resistance. But not this time. He was then asked to swallow a quantity of water and his body was pressed together by screwing the sides of the trough closer. When he still refused to confess, a wet cloth was laid over his mouth and nose and a small stream of water was trickled into it until he sucked the cloth into his throat from where it was pulled out rapidly, drawing with it water and blood, but it was to no avail. The devil was with this man. He would not talk. The third and last torture, the singeing of his feet, had not helped either to induce this contumacious sinner to mend his ways. In former times, and even now in secular courts, other more effective means of torture were used, but the sensibilities of the Spanish Inquisition allowed no more than these three forms of torture, and so there remained no hope to save Fray Domingo Romairón's soul.

"And now to prove to all here assembled," the Inquisitor said, "that it is not too late for mercy, we will implore this Judaizer for the last time to repent his deeds, so that he may be absolved from his sins. If he confesses even now, he can still be united with the Holy Mother Church, the soul can still go to paradise, where the Father, the Son, and the Holy Ghost will accept him, as surely as Christ's blood was spilled on the cross." This was a last appeal to the man to let himself be strangled before he would be burned.

Hot and tense and in deathly silence, the crowds watched the hapless victim. He never moved. Two other men, who had confessed under torture but still not repented, were also given a last chance. Then two friars took off the gag and iron fork from the man called Jorge Quaresma who was a *letrado*, meaning a university graduate, but when he took the opportunity to defend his opinions, he was quickly gagged again.

There remained the official degradation of the former

monk. Four friars took off his penitential clothes to reveal underneath the attire of his order with all his ecclesiastical decorations. He was forced to kneel and slowly, one by one, divested of his garments. His hands, his tongue, and his tonsure were formally mutilated. Then he was dressed again in a hairshirt held by a rope and led to join the other condemned.

Now a notary of the Inquisition walked to the Inquisitor to bring him a box of crimson velvet with a golden fringe around it and a golden lock and key. From it the Inquisitor took the sentences of the seven Judaizers. They were relayed to the secular arm of justice who was asked to proceed with mercy and to avoid the effusion of blood.

The punishment was justified by a text of the New Testament, and the Inquisitor impressed upon his audience that Jesus Christ himself had said, "If a man abide not in me, he is cast forth as a branch and is withered, and men gather them and cast them into the fire, *and they are burned.*"

Thus, the four men and three women were cast out from human society, and between two Dominican friars, each was marched away from the plaza to the *quemadero*, where a dense crowd was awaiting their arrival. On their way, they would be hit and spit upon and covered with excrement thrown by the frenzied populace, and finally their bodies would burn until late in the night, and their ashes would be scattered over the fields, so that every trace of them would disappear from the face of the earth.

The two effigies and the box of bones followed the condemned. When finally the Plaza Mayor was delivered of their evil presence, the Inquisitor General could come down from his lofty throne and reconcile the thirty-seven penitents to their Holy Catholic Faith. While they knelt before him, he read a short catechism comprising the main dogmas, and to each question the penitents answered, "Yes, I believe." The abjuration formula was recited by the Secretary, and they repeated it word for word. Then the Inquisitor General personally exorcised them and while he prayed over them, the choir of the royal chapel began to chant the Miserere. Chaplains of the Inquisition struck the penitents with rods on the shoulders. There were more prayers and hymns and finally a general rejoicing, for the black shroud was removed from the great green cross. The mourning was over. Thirty-seven souls had been saved.

Or had they? Would their enforced wearing of the sanben-ito, their agonizing future as galley slaves, their public scourging, their prison life, would these punishments really convince the thirty-seven men, women, and youngsters that Christianity was the true daughter of a compassionate merci-ful God? This was a question Isabel would have loved to ask of Calderon.

If up to this moment there had been in her mind a lingering doubt about her identity, that doubt vanished forever. She looked at Calderon's satisfied noble face, at Velázquez's serious unperturbed features. They felt awe, as she did, and possibly even a certain trepidation which might cause them to become more observant in their faith, but they did not feel in their hearts the burning determination to set themselves apart from their fellowmen. They approved of the *auto de fé;* they thought it necessary and edifying. Isabel could not understand them. She thought that even if Pedro had never revealed to her that her ancestors were Jews, she would have felt the exact abhorrence, though perhaps not the fear which from now on would remain with her for the rest of her life—sometimes barely noticeable, like a dull pain, at other times leaping up and clawing at the pit of her stomach like a dreaded wild animal. No, it was not at all a question of ancestry. It was a question of choice. She was free to choose for herself to which side she would belong. She could still enter a religious order or marry a true Old Christian. She was free to accept the teaching that heretics were people inspired by the devil and that their painful death was pleasing to the Lord. Or, she could walk the difficult path of facing the truth which was as terrifying a venture as walking up Mount Sinai and facing the God of Moses.

She alone had that choice. Pepita, Calderon, Velázquez, Quevedo, all her other Old Christian compatriots, they did not have that choice. They were ignorant of the God of Moses. They did not know that Jews were people like everyone else, people who believed that God had created heaven and earth and that He wanted His creatures to love one another. But she knew. She had read the Old Testament and the New. And she remembered that Jesus had said of himself that he had been sent to the lost sheep of the House of Israel. So in the end, there remained no choice for her. There remained only the duty to help spread truth. Not by words, since this was impossible, but by her acts. She would help

Pedro with his project of influencing Olivares to obtain
religious liberty for Spain. As she saw it, this was not a
question of religion, it was a question of human decency.
Christianity, as she heard it preached, was based on the
premise of human sinfulness, whereas, in truth, all human
beings harbored within themselves the divine seeds of greatness. If all narrow-minded dogmas were abolished, if people
were taught to think for themselves and to discuss their
thoughts openly, perhaps the seeds would one day have a
chance to blossom.

## 23.

Screaming and laughter swept through the streets. The
serious part of the day was finished; the fun could begin.
Already street musicians and magicians were entertaining
raucous crowds. Practical jokes from throwing stink eggs to
chasing mistreated dogs and cats into throngs of idlers were
nothing more than common expressions of relief from the
solemnities of religion. The carnival season and the evenings
after the Corpus Christi festivities were similarly wild, and
the *auto de fé* was no exception. Hardly had the last drum
beat and clarion sound faded away, than bawdy songs filled
the air. Uncouth and shameless propositions were hurled at
passers-by, and one ingenious pimp was shaking a dice box
while openly praising the charms of his whores and calling out
their prices. "Two coins for a maidenhead, all slippery with
juice, try your luck, for a fuck, if you throw a deuce." Sure
enough, he found dupes to spend their money on his dice
which were as false as the advertised maidenhead.

Pedro and his two young women had to push and shove
their way through the packed streets, and all three sighed with
relief when they found themselves unharmed back in their
own apartments.

"Oh, but I swear I am glad to be home. A coach and eight
could not drag me outside," Pepita said.

"I am sorry to disappoint you," Pedro said, "but we are
expected around eleven o'clock in the gardens of Monterrey."

"Expected? By whom?"

"By His Excellency, the Count-Duke, who is giving a midnight supper in honor of Their Majesties."

"But how will we get there?" Pepita asked.

"On the wings of the Holy Ghost," Isabel remarked, but again she had gone too far for Pedro's sense of precaution and before she knew it, she had received a resounding slap.

"Go to your rooms and get ready," he said and turned away.

Pepita stared at Isabel with an open mouth. This was the first time she had witnessed Pedro strike anyone, and she expected Isabel's quick temper to flare up. But Isabel just shrugged.

"He must be tired," she said. "Let us do as he says and get ready."

# 24.

The town palace of the Counts of Monterrey was famous for its exceptionally well-planned garden, and it was here that Philip liked to relax in the company of friends.

To Philip IV, being King was a strenuous task. He hated to conform for hours on end to the picture of the devout and serious monarch the older generation expected to see. More than that, he hated the pomp and stiffness for which Spanish sovereigns had become renowned. If he had to show himself to his people, Philip preferred to do it in the role of horseman or sharpshooter or spectator at a bullfight. The tedious decorum of religious ceremonies bored him to distraction.

He was twenty-seven, married since the age of ten, expected to worry about a decaying economy, the growing national debt, the threatening loss of the last Spanish foothold in the Netherlands, the political intrigues of Cardinal Richelieu, the brewing discontent of the Catalans, and countless other crises as numerous as the flocks of sheep ravaging his countryside. None of these terrible situations were his making, and although he tried, he was unable to give them his undivided attention.

Not even the relative sterility of his marriage was his fault. God knew he tried. He was hot-blooded and had to make a constant effort to disguise his true passions. His lust was easily aroused, and when that happened, he could think of nothing else until he was satisfied. On occasion, he regretted what he called his sinfulness, but no sin frightened him until after he had committed it. His conscience never bothered him before, only after the act. It was true what they whispered; he did haunt the streets incognito—an easy enough undertaking when hardly a common man had ever seen him face to face, and after all, a young wench from the streets could be more fun and less trouble than a courtesan with an opportunity for jealousy and revenge. But a King could not continuously run away to satisfy his everpresent sexual appetite. And sometimes he had to try to enjoy himself in the company of understanding friends.

Philip's best and most understanding friend was Olivares. Contrary to the Queen's suspicions and to Court opinion, the Count-Duke had tried often and honestly to guide his monarch's interests into more dignified pursuits, but still Olivares had not forgotten his own past amorous adventures. He was immune now, his energy was in his brains, as he said, not in his *cojones,* but he could still remember how it felt to burst with desire, and he wanted to make life easier for Philip. He took upon himself the workload of government, and with it the blame for failures, securing for Philip the adoration of his subjects in whose eyes the monarchy was a divine institution, and a Habsburg King could do no wrong.

The Counts of Monterrey had been for several generations intimately allied to the Guzmáns, the family of Olivares. One Count of Monterrey had been Olivares's grandfather, another one was his father-in-law, and a third one had married his sister Leonor Guzmán. The Olivares couple were as much at home at the Monterrey palace as they were at their own apartments. Once, for the night of St. John, they had given a small dinner party here for Their Majesties to which no men were invited; therefore, all present, including the Queen, could exchange their stiff Court attire for comfortable gowns.

Olivares would always count on his sister to see to it that the Queen was properly amused, so that for a few hours she would forget her husband's neglect, and Philip was left free to court pretty young actresses and singers of a popular Madrid theater who were called to perform, since Queen Isabelle was passionately fond of stage plays.

The night of the *auto de fé* was beautiful, mild, and fragrant, a relief after the sticky air under the canvas of the

Plaza Mayor. The midnight supper was served in the formal dining room. It did not last very long, since everyone was anxious to enjoy the gardens. Comfortable armchairs and velvet-covered stools had been set out on the terrace, and here the King sprawled lazily and listened in a detached way to the conversation of his favorite people. Now and then, he would throw in a question, more to satisfy etiquette than his curiosity. A few words cast at Calderon were sufficient to elicit long and involved declamations during which Philip could pretend to listen, while figuring a way to break the resistance of a young lady who had caught his fancy but was fiercely guarded by an unattractive nobleman the Queen seemed to favor.

Isabel could feel the King's eyes on her, but she dared not return his glance. To her annoyance, Carlos de Queras constantly hovered about her like a lovelorn knight, and she knew that he wanted to prevent Philip from having a chance to talk to her alone.

Philip's head was covered with a handsome plumed hat, and the Grandees also wore their hats. Carlos was uncovered, because the right to wear his hat in the presence of the King would not pass on to him until his father's death.

Suddenly, Philip spoke up.

"How admirable you are, my dear Count, in the exercise of your self-possession. You have my permission to play by the rules of *galantear en palacio*."

There was giggling and laughter at the King's allusion to the rules of courting at Court, and there was speculation whether Carlos would now openly admit that he was too taken with Isabel to observe regular etiquette, or whether he would continue to treat her like his personal property without giving her the satisfaction of wearing her colors and forgetting to remove his hat in Their Majesties' presence.

When Carlos did not answer right away, all eyes turned to him, while Philip, happy to have found a passing amusement, continued to tease him. "If you think you are too noble to descend to such games, let me remind you that I am the one who confers titles around here."

Someone snickered, and Carlos still did not answer. He could not contradict his monarch, to do so was completely unthinkable; it would have spelled the end of Court life for every member of the Queras family. On the other hand, he was too proud to accept the humiliation gracefully.

Isabel, still violently disliking Carlos, rejoiced in his predicament as much as anyone, when it occurred to her that this was an unexpected chance to put Carlos in her debt. So she smiled languidly at Philip and said, "But Your Majesty, His Lordship and I are simply good friends, my heart belongs to someone else."

"Oh, and who is the lucky owner?"

"That, I cannot possibly reveal."

Philip never laughed in public, but he nodded vaguely, and Carlos was saved.

Isabel received a surprised glance from Olivares. He seemed astonished by the kindness of her move, or did he perceive its shrewdness?

Calderon, exploiting his growing friendship with the King, offered an easy revelation of Isabel's secret love.

"After having had the privilege of sitting next to Doña Isabel during the *auto de fé* and noticing how every word of the Inquisitors had her undivided attention, I think we may safely assume that the young lady's heart is engaged to Our Lord Jesus Christ, am I right?"

Swiftly, Isabel lowered her lashes, so no one caught the angry look in her eyes. Then she hid her face behind her fan. What was this preposterous fellow talking about? Was he trying to clear the way to the King's bed? If Philip thought she intended to enter a convent, he would not rest until he possessed her first. And Carlos, far from returning the favor and coming to her aid, viewed her with a speculating glance. It was Olivares who saved her.

"I did not know," he said, turning to Calderon, "that Your Grace was aspiring to a position as matchmaker between heaven and earth."

"That is a good title for a play," Philip joined in. "What about it Don Pedro Calderon?"

The poet realized at once, as did everyone else, that Isabel stood under the protection of both the King and his Favorite, and at least a dozen courtiers immediately made a mental note of inviting her to their next reception.

"Christianity, the successful matchmaker between heaven and earth," Calderon said, taking up the challenge. "We could show how previous religions have failed in bringing about a perfect union between the human soul and its maker. From the viewpoint of a religious historian, humanity can be divided into pagans, Jews, Moslems, heretics, and above all

Christians. To go on with the mental picture of a match-maker, we have to state that paganism has dismally failed in bringing mankind nearer to God. It is, in spite of its often misunderstood closeness to nature . . ."

Feeling that all eyes and ears were now riveted on Calderon, Isabel closed her fan and looked at the King. He caught her glance and gave her a small private smile. Then with a flick of his fingers, he called a lackey and had an extra stool placed next to his armchair. He continued to look steadily at Isabel, and she knew that he paid no attention whatsoever to Calderon's exposition of various forms of paganism groping through darkness of ignorance toward the bright light of knowledge emanating from the cross.

Down in the garden, the laughter of the Queen rang out clearly. She must have joined other couples who were losing and finding each other in the labyrinth of lover's lanes. Isabel hoped that this would turn the King's attention away from his project. But no, with an inviting gesture of his bejeweled hand, he told her to come sit at his side. She turned to Carlos.

"Your Lordship?"

Careful not to give Philip a second chance to tease him, Queras helped her out of her chair and led her to her new seat next to the King. He then bowed to take leave of her.

"Your servant, Doña Isabel."

Although her aversion to him had not weakened, she wished she could say, please take me home, because in a way, she felt safer with him than with the King. But she had to stay, of course, not only stay but listen to a long enthusiastic speech by Calderon, while feeling Philip's fingers surreptitiously caressing the nape of her neck.

Sexual passion and deep religious feeling intermingled to such a degree in the Spanish character that often one could not be distinguished from the other. Men venerated Saint Mary with a personal ardor closely resembling true courtship, women literally talked of Jesus as their bridegroom, and every Spaniard prided himself on being at once a passionate lover and an exceptionally fine Christian. Thus, while they were earnestly discussing the religious warmth and fervor of various Spanish poets, the cavaliers and ladies gathered around their monarch saw no reason to curb their indulgence in intimate caresses.

"As far as I am concerned," Calderon was saying, "the heathens will go to heaven, since it is probable that they would have recognized the Lord if they had but been given a chance. The sun cult of the Peruvians, for example, was a worthy effort to find the true God, and even Moslems, yes Moslems, can eventually be brought to declare for Christ. It is the Protestant so-called Reformation we must combat, since it is nothing but human error."

"What about the Jews?" Olivares interjected. "Is there any hope for them?"

The question was harmless, a mere point in a friendly debate. When Isabel quickly glanced around, she saw no one else looking up. Couples had formed and were more interested in each other than in abstract ideas. Only a momentary tensing of Philip's fingers on her neck told her that the King had listened after all, and that the subject did not leave him indifferent.

"The Jews are of malicious obduracy," Calderon answered at once. "They are the obstinate enemy occupying the last bulwark of the devil against the victorious advancement of Catholic leadership. Their religion is no error, such as Protestantism. Their religion is sheer blasphemy. I intend to elaborate on this in my next Corpus Christi play: hate of Jews must become second nature to every fine Christian. Listen to this:

> *Oh, qué maldita canalla!*
> *Muchos murieron quemados,*
> *Y tanto gusto me daba*
> *Verlos arder, que decía*
> *Atizándoles la llama:*
> *"Perros herejes, ministro*
> *Soy de la Inquisición Santa."**

The poet had raised his voice, and a look of annoyance passed over Olivares's features. Her new companion—terror —began to gnaw again at Isabel's heart. She wondered whether Olivares would be able to protect the Jews from the

---

*Oh, what cursed scum!
Many will burn to death,
And to see them burn,
Will give me such pleasure,
That, stirring the flames, I'll say:
"Heretical Dogs, I'm a Minister
Of the Holy Inquisition."

fury of the indoctrinated masses. Her eyes searched for Pedro, but she could see neither him nor her cousin. They must be somewhere in the garden. She also wondered how much influence the opposite camp would or could exert on the King. There were so many of them: the Grandees, the poets, the *letrados*, the Queen, the Cardinals, and the Inquisitors. Olivares alone was on the side of the New Christians. One man alone against a whole kingdom. How would he ever win?

Already there had been two attacks on Olivares's life; who said a third or fourth or fifth one could not succeed? The chances were stacked against him, and if his enemies triumphed over him, they would not leave a shred of goodness to his name. They would revile him and belittle his efforts and see to it that he was misunderstood and blamed and shamed more than if he had worn a sanbenito. She looked at him. His face had assumed the proud arrogant features known to the masses who had seen him riding through the streets of Madrid. But was that he. Or was it a mask he wore? The mask of a cruel self-assured overlord, hiding the loneliness and despair of a doomed idealist.

Suddenly Philip's finger left her neck, and he drew himself up in his chair.

"I want to stress that there are no Jews left in all of our realms," he said, "and we must not fall into the common error of tacitly assuming all New Christians to be Jews. As a father to my people, I must insist that all my children be treated with equal respect as fine Christians deserve to be treated. If there are any heretics among us, the Holy Office will not fail to rout them up, as we have witnessed today."

"How wise and good you are," Isabel murmured, and Philip's thick lips curled upward in pleasant anticipation.

"Shall we go for a walk?" he suggested.

His invitation was not as dangerous as Isabel feared. For as soon as he got up, so did everyone else, and there was a general exodus from the terrace toward the garden, where hundreds of torchlights illuminated the formal hedges and groves teeming with flirting couples and Court musicians. Isabel perceived the Countess Olivares surrounded by elderly Ladies-in-Waiting, and she made up her mind to change camps. By ceding her place to an eager if plain young courtesan, she put some distance between herself and Philip. Then she turned and walked quickly toward the circle of disapproving ladies who formed the court of the Queen's "Black Dragon of Morality."

She curtsied formally: "Your Ladyship."

The Countess nodded, "Doña Isabel."

"I do not know how to say this," Isabel began hesitantly, "but I am so deeply grateful for Your Ladyship's kind protection. I feel I need guidance and help, and there is nothing I could wish more than to be able to please Your Ladyship."

"Well?" said the Countess, seemingly evaluating in her mind the merits of Isabel's humility. "What do you want?" The other ladies continued their promenade, showing more tact than Isabel had come to expect of Madrid's female society.

"I want advice concerning His Majesty," Isabel said softly.

Inés de Zúñiga's plucked and painted eyebrows shot up, and the wings of her nostrils swelled.

"Whatever do you mean?"

"My brother is eager to serve His Excellency, the Count-Duke," Isabel said. "If I could, I would like to serve you, or Her Majesty. But I do not want to . . . to attract His Majesty's interest."

"It seems to me you have distinguished yourself by doing just that," the Countess said. "You should make up your mind about your future. Do you intend to find a husband? Or do you want to take the veil and vows?"

"I want to help my brother with his work."

"Women have no business meddling in men's affairs," the Countess said, echoing what her husband had openly advocated for years.

Isabel knew that if she could not break through the Countess's icy veneer now, today, she would never be able to do so. It was a gamble, as it had been when she had found herself alone with Rafael that far away noon in the Alcázar gardens of Seville. Again she grasped the opportunity.

"My brother says, as my father did, that your husband is the savior of Spain," she said putting urgency into her voice. "We must all help so that his greatness is recognized. His Excellency is strong, but he is also leaning on you. You are his best friend, his only confidant; are you not living proof of how important a woman is in a man's world?"

For a moment, the Countess stared at her, as if she was a ghost from the past, then her features softened. "You speak like my daughter, God bless her soul," she said. "There is a difference between helping a husband and helping a brother. If you want to remain at Court and avoid His Majesty's advances, it would be best for you to marry. Did I not hear that someone was courting you?"

"Carlos de Queras," Isabel said.

"Yes, indeed. Why don't you marry him?"

What a way to talk for a woman who was married to Olivares, Isabel thought. She had caught a whale and wanted her to be content with a miserable shrimp.

Seeing that Isabel was less than enthusiastic, Doña Inés smiled. "If you married him, I could arrange for you to become Lady-in-Waiting. Then, under my protection, you would be relatively safe from His Majesty." The Countess picked up her skirts, indicating that the interview was finished, and she was ready to join her friends who were waiting for her.

"Think about it, Doña Isabel."

Again Isabel curtsied. Then, for a moment, she wondered which way to turn. Wherever she looked, her eyes caught the sight of amorous couples, kissing and fondling each other and sighing sweet promises to be fulfilled at a later hour in various bedchambers of Madrid. Laughter and music filled the mild summer night, and there were lusty embraces and frivolous talk.

Suddenly, Isabel became disgusted with herself, disgusted with being a Spaniard. How could she belong to a people so immune to the suffering of others that they could deliver themselves wholeheartedly to the pleasures of life immediately after witnessing the terrors of violent death? How could they forget that at this very moment men were burning at the stake—nay, not how could they forget, but how could they rejoice in it, for was not this the purpose of the gathering at Monterrey? Had they not come here to proclaim their happiness at the death of heretics?

She turned away from the palace, away from the terrace and the torchlights. She walked to the opposite end of the garden, until she reached a high stone wall. Leaning against it, she took a deep breath. Finally, all was quiet; the music and voices had faded to a faint hum. She rested until a cracking of twigs, a rustling of shrubbery, and slow steps tightened her nerves like a bowstring. There were no torchlights in this spot, and there was no moon. She could not see who was coming, nor did she know whether it was a coincidence or whether someone had followed her. She stood perfectly still, and the footsteps stopped. A throaty Andalusian voice called her name.

"Doña Isabel, where are you?"

The voice, like a magic sponge, wiped off her rage and sorrow. Its husky inflection she had heard in her dreams, and now she almost thought she could see him, although it was very dark. She tried to call out to him, but she found her own voice would not obey her. Perhaps she had fallen asleep, and it was a dream after all.

"Doña Isabel, don't you know who I am?"

"Here," she finally said. "Here," and she heard his steps but was too weak to leave the wall.

"What a place to rest," he said. "Have you fled here from the attentions of your monarch? Or did the Countess frighten you? Come give me your hand."

She stretched out her hands, and he drew her in his arms and held her tightly. But as he bent down to kiss her, she remembered how disgusted she had been by the spectacle of fondling couples, and she disengaged herself from his hold. At the same time, she recalled the sight of him in the throng of black friars, and she clenched her fists in an attempt to keep her dignity. She also mastered her voice again and tried to make it cold and haughty. "Fray Rafael, what a coincidence to meet you here."

"No coincidence at all," he said. "I have observed and followed you all evening."

"You have?"

"Yes. Come along now."

It could only be a dream, walking through the night with Rafael, belonging to him, trusting him, knowing that she was meant for him, just as he was meant for her, loving him and knowing that he returned her love.

Following the path along the wall, they soon reached a side gate illuminated by torchlights. Here she got her first look at Rafael. He wore a short coat, riding breeches, and a hunting cap, much the same costume he had worn when she had last seen him at Seville. His face was pale. Did he spend all his time in the shade of chapels?

They walked through the gate and into the noisy, crowded city street. Rafael would have put his arm around her, if her skirt had not been too wide. There were still no carriages in

the streets, just crowds, singing and dancing and shrieking.
They crossed a few narrow filthy lanes, then turned into one
of the newer streets which was paved with cobblestones and
where all the buildings seemed to have been put up the day
before. Rafael walked slightly ahead of her, turning his head
to speak to her.

"What do you think of the Count-Duke?" he asked. "He
arouses violent dislike in most who meet him, but he has been
able to kindle the light of friendship and devotion in a few
others."

This cannot be true, Isabel thought. I cannot be walking
with him, listening to him, as if nothing had happened.

"I like him," she said. "Pedro and I think well of him."

"Most women detest him," Rafael said, "but I somehow
knew you would like him. Your father would have liked him,
too."

At the mention of her father, Isabel gave a start. Suddenly,
the dreamlike quality of their meeting was shattered, as she
realized that Rafael had broken all rules of etiquette by
neither calling on them, nor sending them a letter of condo-
lence when he apparently knew that her parents had died.

He sensed her shock and spoke rapidly and soothingly
before she did. "I am sorry, Isabel. I could not come. I could
not. I had to pretend that you did not exist."

"But why?"

He shook his head. "Later, later," he said.

He led her through a wrought-iron gate into a vast tiled
entrance hall. She did not know where they were going, but
as during her first meeting with him, she knew she would
follow him even to the ends of the earth. A curved staircase
led upstairs. They climbed to the third floor. He took out a
key and unlocked the dark oak door leading to a flat.

"This is the smallest apartment they have," he said when
they were inside and he had bolted the door. "The only one I
can afford."

Then, without waiting for an answer, he pulled her in his
arms so violently that for a second she was frightened. But
when she felt his lips on hers again, felt his strong thighs
against hers, felt his muscular body vibrate with desire, she let
herself go completely. She did not care who he was, friend or
enemy, she wanted him. When her fingers accidentally
touched his tonsure, she gave a sob. He pressed her even
harder against him.

"Isabel, I want you, I want you."

He pulled her through the small parlor to a room where a plain bed was the only piece of furniture.

Briefly, Isabel suspected that this was where Rafael might have brought other female guests. Indeed, if not as a love nest, why would a friar need an apartment?

After closing the shutters and lighting two wicks swimming in a cup of oil, he turned to help her unhook the stiff bodice of her gown, then he almost lifted her out of the wide skirt which could stand up by itself.

"Why do women have to wear this ridiculous complicated finery?" he muttered under his breath.

"To discourage love-sick monks," Isabel retorted instantly. "How often do you engage in this kind of activity?"

She had forgotten his spontaneous soundless laughter, but she was happy that she could make him laugh. There was something between this man and herself which she could not explain. There was a force drawing her into his arms, making her want him with every fiber of her body. No one else would ever affect her that way. There were other men she admired, as she admired Olivares; there were artists, poets, philosophers, with whom she sometimes wanted to be friends; there were men whom she sometimes disliked and sometimes vaguely liked, as for instance the King; and finally there was one man, Carlos de Queras, whom she loathed instinctively, even though perhaps groundlessly. But Rafael was the only man whose mere sight made her blood bubble with joy and anticipation. She was like the parched earth of Spain, waiting for an ancient rain god to come to her. If he wanted her, she would never be able to refuse him.

When he finally made love to her, all the intervening months were erased. Lying in his arms was all that mattered to her. Again, she enjoyed every caress, every movement of his body against hers. She had forgotten the intensity of her desire for him until she touched him again. Yet, when they collapsed together, and he sank down upon her, moaning, she had another stab of jealousy. The idea that he could lie like this with another woman was unbearable to her.

"Now, why did you have to pretend that I do not exist?" she asked when she felt that he had had sufficient time to recover.

"Because when I take on a task, I want to do it well. You know that I joined the order. I want to make a career of it. I have to be good if I want to advance. And I do want to advance and quickly."

She frowned. "I do not see what that has to do with me. You meet other women, do you not? Why else would you have this apartment?"

Again he laughed, but Isabel was determined not to let him see her inner confusion.

"Well," she asked, "what is so amusing?"

At this he stopped laughing and rolled over to lean on his elbow and stare into her eyes.

"Isabel, I have not made love to anyone since I left you at Seville. I do not claim any virtues that I do not possess. It is possible that I have been too busy to find a woman. It is also possible that I did not want to go through the trouble of finding one reliable enough not to chatter to all her friends that she had caught a monk by his tail. As for streetwalkers, it has never been my habit to pay a woman, and I do not intend to start doing so now. You do not have to believe me, if you choose not to. But each time I thought of you, that you were here in Madrid, I needed all my willpower to stop myself from going mad. I am telling you this now, because I do not think it will happen again."

"You mean, you do not love me anymore?" she inquired, instantly alarmed and no longer caring whether he noticed.

"I love you so much, you are a danger to my career."

"Then leave it," she whispered. "Others have. You can leave the order. We can live somewhere else. Oh Rafael, don't you see, it is all so easy as long as we love each other."

He shook his head.

"I joined the Dominicans because I had to. I have a purpose in life, a goal to pursue. I told you that before. If I had not seen you tonight, seen Carlos de Queras still courting you, seen His Majesty smiling his most significant smile at you and what is worse, touching you, I might have managed to stay out of your life. I followed you. I knew I would find you there. I was driven to the gardens of Monterrey, and I could not help myself. I had to see you."

"I hate Madrid," Isabel stated flatly. "I hate Court life. And I hate Carlos de Queras and all he stands for."

"That is a waste of emotion. I doubt he stands for anything," Rafael replied with a grin. "It is the King who has me worried. Has he given you an assignation?"

"No, and I hope it will never come to that."

"It will, sooner or later."

"Let us talk about you," Isabel suggested.

"On the contrary, let us talk about you. I have given you my accounts. If not the King, who is your current lover?"

"Rafael, I despise you."

"So it would seem," he said and covered her face and throat with kisses.

Isabel thought. She was a danger to his career, he had said. Well, that was mutual. He was a threat to her life as a Marrano. More than that, a deadly enemy. What would he do if he knew that while her body belonged to him, her soul belonged to *them*?

For after today, she could never again be a Christian. She would remain a heretic until she died. If he found out, what would he do? Denounce her to his superiors? Try to save her soul by torturing her into admitting her error? And then *relax* her body to the secular authorities who would burn her, after mercifully strangling her first, because she had confessed?

On the other hand, what if she could continue to meet him secretly, make him love her enough to leave the order and marry her? Could she really become his wife? The wife of a Christian fanatical enough to join the black friars? There had been instances of Jewish women converting Christian husbands to the faith of the children of Abraham. There was the case of an Old Christian merchant who had left the country with his Marrano wife and established himself at Hamburg where he was circumcised and admitted as a righteous proselyte into the House of Israel.

If Rafael committed a sin by loving her, she committed the same sin by loving him. Yet she was prepared to cling to him and make his career as hard for him as she could. If it were a career she could respect, she would love him enough to give him up, or so she reasoned, but it was a career she despised. If she could first seduce him into leaving the order, next seduce him into leaving the country, into moving to the Netherlands, next surround him with. . . . No, it was no use thinking that way. She, too, had a task to accomplish. She could not run away. It would upset all of Pedro's plans; it would destroy the good name of Valderocas and its usefulness.

Coming out of her musings, she found Rafael gazing at her.

"What were you thinking?" he asked.

"Why do you have this apartment?" she said, since it was the first thought that came to her mind.

"Still jealous?"

"No, curious."

"Curiosity is a dangerous habit."

"But often highly rewarding."

He continued to look at her, pensively.

"Isabel, can I trust you?"

"I will try never to lie to you," she said, on her guard, "so I cannot say yes, without knowing what you want from me."

"I had forgotten you were so damn clever," he said.

"Don Rafael, what do you want from me?"

He took her face in his hands.

"I want you to trust me," he said. "I want you to trust me implicitly, no matter what I do, no matter who I become, no matter what my title in the Church, no matter what you hear said about me, I want you to trust me. You must never doubt me or fear me. If you give me your full trust, if you will never question anything I do, if you will never again ask me to quit the order to marry you, if you will never try to interfere with my work, then we might be able to go on seeing each other from time to time. You say you will try never to lie to me. I do not want to lie to you either, but you may have questions which I must not answer, so I prefer you do not ask them."

As she looked into his eyes and listened to him, she longed to kiss him and swear eternal trust and loyalty, but how could she give him that precious gift, when she had already bestowed it upon her brother? For the first time, she understood what might have been her father's motive for keeping her ignorant. By preventing her from knowing who she was, he had protected her from inner torment and from the danger of betraying her people.

"I believe you when you say that you have not loved anyone since you left me," she said, carefully picking her words, "and I want to be able to believe you, whatever you choose to tell me. I can promise you this: I have not and will not let any other man make love to me. I love only you, and I will love you no matter what you do. I cannot help loving you."

She could see that it was not the answer he had expected.

"They will force you to marry eventually or to enter a convent," he said.

"Who is they?"

"The Court, the Countess Olivares, the Queen, all the wives who do not like to see an unattached female moving gracefully about their husbands."

"Do I move gracefully?"

"You do everything gracefully. Oh Isabel, I want to trust you. I want to go on seeing you. And yet, it is so impossible."

"It is not. I will come whenever you want me."

He stood up and put on his breeches and a silk shirt. "I will bring you home, and then I will come back here and change into my robes," he said.

"Yes, I wondered about that. Are you allowed out in secular attire?"

"There are a lot of things I am not allowed to do, and most of all I am not allowed to fall in love."

"But you have!" she said and it sounded triumphant.

"Yes, I have. But if they ever choose a husband for you, count on me to bow out of your life."

"That will not happen."

"The same applies if you enter a convent."

"You really convinced me in that respect," she said. "I do not care for the company of saints either."

"That is good. Now think it over and let me know your answer."

"What do you mean?"

"Can I trust you? Can I trust you the same way I want you to trust me? I do not ask you whether you love me. I know you do. I ask whether I can trust you, and you know it is not the same thing."

She knew, and suddenly she thought she understood perfectly. He had told her that she could trust him. By this he had meant that he would never harm her, that he would be loyal as far as she was concerned, no matter what else he did in the course of his work. He had meant that his work and his love were two different matters.

Well, she could promise the same, without hurting anyone. Of course, she would never betray him, just as she would never betray Pedro, and just as she would never betray Pepita. It was all a question of keeping one's love and one's beliefs and one's work meticulously separated into different compartments. She would not tell Pedro about her secret meetings with Rafael, nor would she tell Rafael that she, too, had an important task to accomplish—one diametrically opposed to his—and least of all would she ever let him guess that she was *one of them*.

She could probably trust him, as he said. But if he knew the truth, he would not love her anymore, even if he did not betray her. She remembered well—from having heard it so often—the story of the beautiful woman of Seville, the daughter of Diego de Susan, who had committed the error of trusting her lover. La Susana may have loved her *novio* as I love Rafael, Isabel thought, and trusted him as I want to trust Rafael, and yet, when all was said, he had betrayed her.

"How can you ask me to trust you like that, unfalteringly, when you admit that your work is more important to you than I am?" she asked finally. "If your work required it, you would refuse to see me, would you not, even if I needed you? Suppose I needed your help? Suppose I expected a child? What would you do?" He did not answer at once, and she got out of bed and started to get dressed.

He watched her, with a small smile on his lips.

"I will be careful," he said. "I do not think I have made any bastards so far, and I do not intend to. Apart from that, I don't see what help you could require. You are a wealthy young woman of impeccable lineage, and you have won the favor and good will of the most powerful couple in the country. I think you can look after yourself quite nicely. But I do understand your hesitation. You have every reason to doubt my word, since to you I am nothing but a cheating monk. I have no security to offer you. . . . No let me finish," he lifted his hand, seeing that she was about to interrupt him. "Except this: if you should ever get into a situation of life or death—no matter what that might be—please understand, if ever your life were threatened, you would be more important to me than my work."

She was dressed and walked to him. She had to tilt her head back to look into his eyes.

"I trust you," she said, "and I do want you to trust me."

Again he took her face in both his hands and kissed her on the forehead.

"Good. Now listen. This apartment is mine. I rented it under the name of Francisco Molina. Remember, Francisco Molina. I had to have it, because I need a place where I can rest and be myself, just be myself. A place where no one can order me around. Take last night, for example. Instead of guarding the green cross, I came here to sleep. You see, a cell in a monastery is sufficient for those who truly want to serve God. But that is not enough for me. I want . . ." he hesitated as if searching for the right word.

"You want power," she said. "You are filled with ambition and you want power. But why?"

"There you go again, asking questions I cannot answer."

"I am sorry."

"No, it's all right, I understand. Why do I want power? Perhaps for the same reasons Olivares wanted power. To do something for Spain."

She wanted to ask, but what? Then she checked herself quickly and suppressed the words. He did not wish to be questioned, and she would accept him unquestioningly.

Instead she said, "I hope for your sake that you will obtain the power you are seeking, and I hope for Spain that you will wield it wisely, if you ever get it."

"Thank you," he said and she glanced up swiftly to see whether he was smiling, but he looked serious. There seemed to be no doubt in his mind that he would reach whatever goal he had set for himself.

"When can I see you again?" she asked.

"I shall try to be here for a few hours every Monday and Thursday afternoon. Come whenever you can, during siesta time. If you do not find me here, leave at once. I would rather no one recognize you when you come. Also, if I am not here, do not come back. Wait until you hear from Francisco Molina. Do you understand?"

"Yes." She certainly did. If they were caught, someone would observe the place, and it could mean trouble for anyone who tried to enter.

"Good. Now, what will you tell Pedro when you get home?"

"That I had to flee from the ardor of a noble admirer, searched for him and Pepita everywhere, could not find them, and came home by myself."

"You will not mention that you saw me?"

"Rafael, I am not going to talk about you to anyone. If you want to be friends with Pedro, you will have to call on him."

"There was a time when Pedro and I were best friends. I would prefer not to see him anymore. According to the rules of honor, he would have to ask me to a duel if he found out about our love and with his swordsmanship that would be a quick end to my ambitions."

They passed to the first room, and Rafael lit a few more cotton wicks swimming in oil containers on the table. There was only one chair and a wall shelf with books, paper, a supply of goose quills, and ink. Rafael reached behind a row of impressive volumes and produced a jug and a glass.

"I suppose I might invest in a second glass and another chair," he remarked while pouring a fragrant dark red wine, "but I warn you, that is as far as my attempts at setting up housekeeping will go."

"May I look at your books?"

He handed her one of the small oil lamps, and she held it up to the two rows of leather-backed volumes.

Among the expected works of prominent Catholic scholars, of mystics like Juan de la Croce and Teresa de Avila, of the great theologian Thomas Aquinas, of the Dutch humanist Desiderius Erasmus, and of various contemporary poets, there was a book by Moses Maimonides. Maimonides, the twelfth-century Jewish philosopher from Córdoba, the great pole star in the firmament of Jewish knowledge! To read him now, why, merely to possess his works was heresy punishable by death at the stake! Unless . . . unless perhaps the owner of the work was a Catholic theologian studying his enemy in order to better attack him.

In any case, Isabel, as a good Old Christian, would never have heard of Maimonides. It would be perfectly safe for her to take out the book and to ask innocently, Oh, who is this? Already her hand went up to touch the book, when Rafael called her to the table, holding up the glass.

"Come let us drink to our good fortune."

She turned and smiled at him, remembering at the same time that she had promised not to ask any questions. She tossed her head back in the direction of the shelves.

"It is quite a company of saints you have collected."

"Every work requires tools," he replied, as he offered her the glass. "To what will you drink?"

She lifted it slightly. As the same old hope swelled in her heart, she proposed neither love nor trust, but challenge, "Let us defy the world."

She took a sip and handed him the glass. He took it and drank.

"Only you could have thought of that," he said. "I sometimes wonder whether you do not understand me too well for your own good."

"I do not understand you at all," she countered immediately, "and I have a hundred questions that I am never going to ask. Do not worry," she added when she saw his frown. "I said I am not going to ask anything."

"I am not sure. I have a feeling you will ask plenty, but come along now. Can you hide your face?"

She took a black lace mantilla from a pocket in her wide skirt and let it fall over her face. Most ladies carried a lace veil with them at all times, to cover their head should they enter a church.

Another walk and half an hour later Isabel knocked at the door of the Valderocas town palace.

Teresa, now head chambermaid, was waiting up for her. Isabel swept into the house and upstairs. To her relief, Pedro and Pepita had not yet arrived. Thank God, no involved explanations were necessary.

"When they come, please tell Doña Pepita that I left earlier because I did not feel well. I will try to sleep right away."

"At your service, Donã Isabel."

After Teresa had helped her out of her clothes, Isabel dismissed her, saying that she was too tired to have her hair brushed.

Left alone, however, she was not sleepy but bursting with excitement. She heard Pedro and Pepita come home an hour later; she heard Pepita stop in front of her door for a few moments before going to her own room, and then she tossed in her bed while faces formed and dissolved before her inner eyes: the long pale face of the King with thick lips and watery eyes, the massive black-bearded face of the Count-Duke, the cruel mouth of Carlos de Queras, and again and again the beautiful, soul-stirring, serious features of Rafael Cortes.

And behind it all there burned the seven fires, the fires she had not seen but could not escape, the fires which burned up all the trust that could possibly exist between a Marrano woman and a Dominican friar. Seven of her people burned to death by his people.

Oh God, when will it all end? Oh God, how long shall the wicked exult?

# 25.

A few days after the *auto de fé*, Fray Antonio de Sotomayor, personal confessor to the King, came to Olivares in the hope of gaining the Favorite's support for his bid to become Inquisitor General of Spain.

Cardinal Zapata had tried hard to wrest from King Philip the last remnants of control the Spanish monarchy could still exert over the monster it had created itself, and Olivares, against the power of the Church, did not hesitate to ask for concessions before offering his help to Sotomayor. In his typical fashion of dealing with state problems without consulting his King, the Count-Duke presented the situation to Sotomayor.

"The country is starving, the war with France and with the Netherlands is devouring all the revenues of the Crown, and the precious metals to be expected from the Indies are already pledged thrice over to foreign bankers who have advanced money to His Majesty. The only other possible source of income is the vast holdings of the Church."

Very old and desirous only of reaching the highest office in Spain as a reward for his long dedicated service to Church and country, Sotomayor had come prepared to reach a compromise, but the Count-Duke's bold insinuation was a frightening blow to him. He shook his head.

"If that is the price you ask, I cannot pay it. The holdings of the Church cannot be touched, the rights of the Church remain holy and superior to all other rights. May I suggest you go to the Grandees for higher contributions?"

"The Grandees are as jealous of their rights as the Church," Olivares replied. "And since they have to supply men and arms, they are doing their share."

"Excellency, what do you want me to do? Agree to the taxation of Church property? Even if I agreed, the Pope would not, nor would any of the bishops. Besides, it would be a measure contrary to my own judgment and conscience."

"Your Eminence," Olivares said, thus calling him by the title reserved for Cardinals, when "Your Illustrious Lordship" would have sufficed, "Your Eminence, we are not talking of prices here, the office of Inquisitor General is not for sale. It should be yours, because you are the man in whose integrity His Majesty puts all his trust. Are you not the intermediary between Almighty God and our monarch? Is it not in your power to reward the trust the crowned head of Spain deposits in you?"

"Church property cannot be taxed," the old man said. Olivares, who had no intention of taxing church property, congratulated himself upon having found such an opportune bargaining point.

"I suppose you are right," he said with a sigh. "We will have to find another source of revenue. Perhaps we could have recourse to the old law of King Ferdinand, whereby all confiscations made by the Inquisition go directly to the crown. I realize this somewhat modifies recent practices, but I do not think Your Eminence would actually oppose such a measure, if Your Eminence were Inquisitor General. . . ."

Olivares observed the old man fighting with himself: to go down in eternity as Grand Inquisitor of Spain was only slightly less glorious than to become Pope. At seventy-seven, after many years as the King's confessor, Sotomayor knew better than any other mortal how much Philip depended on Olivares. Sotomayor would become Inquisitor General by the grace of Olivares or not at all. But the old man was also a Dominican, and he approved of the Suprema's policy of not divulging even to the King the enormous sums received from the confiscation of New Christian property. So again he shook his head.

"That, too, is impossible," he said.

"Your Eminence, we must come to an understanding. As you well realize, our glorious country is run by two men: the King and the Inquisitor General. The King listens to me. I represent the worldly power. Do you wish to see as head of the Inquisition a man who acts for Rome, or do you wish to share with me in the government of our nation?"

"I must keep my honor, my integrity. . . ." the old man muttered.

"And your honor demands that Church property shall not be taxed and that the spoils of the confiscations shall not be shared with the Crown?"

"If you want to put it that way."

"Yes, I do," Olivares said. "Do you remember last year's junta composed of yourself, my own confessor Hernando de Salazar, the Bishop of Málaga, and the Duke of Villahermosa?"

"Concerning the money offered by the Portuguese Jews?"

"Exactly. His Majesty received a gift of 240,000 ducats from Portuguese New Christians"—Olivares stressed the word Christians—"for the right to leave Portugal. Most of them did not come to Spain, as we had hoped, but settled in the Netherlands. This must not go on."

"That was a way of getting money, though," Sotomayor pointed out, as Olivares had intended him to.

"Yes, indeed," said the Count-Duke. "Are you and I agreed then that the best source of income would be New Christians or Jews? If we could get more Jewish money, we could continue to exempt the Church from taxation."

"There is no stigma attached to Jewish money," Sotomayor agreed. "It is their faith we must combat."

Olivares nodded gravely, while inwardly rejoicing at his ability to lead the old friar into the trap he hoped to prepare for the whole Inquisition.

"Yet it so happens," he pointed out, "that they take their faith with them wherever they take their money. Italy, especially Venice, is full of wealthy Jews, despite the Inquisition in Italy. Do we Spaniards have to be more Christian than the Holy Father? Amsterdam is replacing Seville as the most important world harbor, and in Salonica they will soon pave the streets with gold. Or take Oran, our own Spanish fortress of Oran. Do you know that the fig trade of Oran is entirely in Jewish hands? And what is more, Jews control all the North African mints. The Kings of Morocco also use Jews as diplomats. But we have to persecute them!"

The affected bitterness in Olivares's voice did not escape Sotomayor. He was ambitious and concerned about his honor, but he was not a fool. He could never agree to giving up even one ducat of Church property to the state, since this would need his open approval and would be dragged through debates at the Royal Council and at the Supreme Council of the Inquisition and would cause repercussions as far away as Rome, with the possible result that he himself might be indicted. If, on the other hand, Olivares intended to rob some Jews of their money, so what? Sotomayor had confidence in the power of the Holy Office. The Inquisition would be able to halt any excess of philojudaism.

"You are a shrewd man, Count-Duke," he said. "You want to make the Jews pay for the wars we lead against heretics."

"Have we not always done so? Did we not reconquer Spain from the infidel with Jewish money? Did we not discover the New World with Jewish money? I seem to remember a Church theory saying that there must always be some Jews left on the face of the earth so that they may testify to Christ's identity when He returns to earth."

"That is true."

"Well then, if it is God's will that we cannot get rid of the Jews, why can we not use them? Let them work and make money, while we pray and spend it. Would that go against your honor, if you were Inquisitor General?"

"It would not."

"All right then. Under your rule as Inquisitor General, the

Spanish Church and most particularly the Order of the Dominican Friars whose most prominent member you are, shall get richer from confiscations of the properties of heretics, but not of Judaizers. There will be less and less Judaizers found in our country. Do we understand each other?"

"I am not sure."

"Most Judaizers are valuable taxpayers, and I expect that fewer and fewer of them will be persecuted. It is understood, of course, that the Inquisition has no power at all in the case of outright Jews who openly practice their own faith in their own houses of worship."

"Yes, but there are no Jews in Spain," Sotomayor objected.

"Your Eminence, you amaze me. Did we not just agree that we were going to use the wealth of the Jews in order to spare the wealth of the Church? Does it not follow that in order to get their money, we must have them here first? And did we not come to the conclusion that wherever they go, their faith goes with them?"

"Count-Duke?" Sotomayor's eyes were flashing.

"Yes?"

"Do you intend to invite Jews back to Spain?"

"With His Majesty's permission and provided the Inquisitor General washes his hands of the affair, in the well-established manner of Pontius Pilate. Yes, I do have the intention to invite Jews to settle at Madrid. Spain is on the brink of utter collapse. There is only Jewish money or Church money."

"It could mean your downfall," the old man warned, "if you dare repeal the expulsion order of 1492."

"Who said anything about that? We must be subtle. Some laws seem to pass into oblivion, or perhaps they die of old age."

"If I am Inquisitor General, I will do my holy duty of defending the faith at all times against all enemies," Sotomayor said and crossed himself. But he did not raise any further objection.

Immediately, Olivares followed his example and crossed himself.

"We will help each other carry the load of Spain," the Count-Duke said. "His Majesty will be pleased to know that you accept to guide the Holy Office in the right direction."

As soon as Fray Antonio de Sotomayor was confirmed in

his new position, Olivares undertook to find a trustworthy Dominican friar to serve as personal secretary to His Eminence. Thus, he himself set the stage for what he hoped would be the last act in the drama of the Spanish Inquisition.

# 26.

One morning Isabel sat chatting with Velázquez's wife Juana in the painter's apartment, when the usher announced the arrival of His Majesty. Philip had been looking for his friend in the studio, and, not finding him there, had decided to walk over to his private suite. Juana was flustered, her husband had ridden out early to the Retiro Park to check on the progress of the new pleasure palace. She did not expect him back till nightfall.

"Do you think he would mind if I showed my current portrait to a dear young friend of mine?" Philip asked.

"Why, Sire, you know you are always welcome at the studio."

"Fine, we will use the back entrance."

The Velázquez drawing room was connected to the studio by a private corridor. When Juana led the way, Philip turned to Isabel and held out his hand.

"You do want to see my portrait, don't you?"

His words and the accompanying gesture left no room for doubt that Isabel herself was the dear young friend and that this time there would be no easy way out. Juana opened the door to the empty studio. Philip stood gallantly aside to let Isabel enter first, then he turned to the painter's wife.

"Thank you for sharing your guest with me. I will remember your kindness."

The two women exchanged a glance, Juana's eyes pleading: What can I do? Isabel's eyes accusing: How dare you leave me alone with him? Then Juana curtsied and left. Philip shut the door. He had gotten her alone at last, away from the crowd of prying courtesans, away even from the swarms of servants, into the quiet privacy of Velázquez's atelier, where the only eyes staring at them were those of unfinished portraits.

Isabel walked toward the easel with the canvas depicting Philip in the costume of a hunter, holding a rifle, and looking down upon the viewer with an ever-so-slight expression of disdain, as if to say: I am superior to you not because I am the King, but because I know how to live, I know how to enjoy the beauty of art, of nature, of love, and of death.

She stopped ten feet from the portrait and stood still, trying to appear calm, while nervously awaiting his next move.

He walked around to stand in front of the painting and to look down on her, not with disdain but with speculation. Then slowly his hand caressed her hair and his fingertips gently slid over her cheeks and traced along her lips and over her chin down to her throat.

"How fair you are," he murmured. "How fair and how frightened. Stop trembling, Isabel. I am not going to rape you. That is not my style."

She felt the blood shoot into her face.

"Your Majesty, I assure you that never occurred to me. I . . . I do not know what gave you that impression."

For the first time in her life she heard him laugh outright.

"Then why do you look like a damsel in distress? Don't you think I know my reputation? Don't you realize that I too read the lampoons decrying my vile passions and deploring the victims of my lust who retire to convents after sharing my bed as a service to the Crown? I swear I cannot so much as look at a virgin that gossip doesn't pierce her maidenhead. Am I so repellent that no girl could possibly fall in love with me of her own accord?"

Embarrassed, Isabel looked down and twisted her lace handkerchief. She found him ugly, but his honesty touched her. Yet she knew without doubt that she would never let him make love to her; she belonged to Rafael. However, since it would scarce serve the Valderocas cause if she annoyed the King, she would somehow have to find a place for him in the assortment of her emotions.

"Well?" said Philip.

Slowly Isabel lifted her face until their eyes met. She saw that Philip wanted her, here, now, or as soon as possible, and she knew that his lust made him vulnerable. She had to be gentle in her refusal. She had to be a good actress to convince him—the superb amateur actor—that there truly was hope. She would have to play the part of the virtuous ingenue, until he would tire of the game and find another female to pursue.

As she thought of this, a warm, flirtatious smile played at the corners of her lips.

"On the contrary," she said, "you are attractive and that makes you dangerous. If girls fall in love with you easily, it is because you have all the advantages on your side. But how can you ever be sure they love you for yourself, and not because you are the King?"

He laughed again and pulled her in his arms. To her horror she discovered that she herself did not find it unpleasant to feel wanted by a King. His thick lips barely brushed over her eyebrows, down to the tip of her delicate nose, and to her surprise, he made no attempt to kiss her mouth.

"I fell in love with you the moment I saw you," he said, "and I will wait until you yourself forget that I am the King, provided you give me an even chance."

"And what would you consider an even chance?" she asked softly.

"That you do not run away each time I come near you, as you did that night in the Monterrey gardens. In matters of love, being a King is a drawback, believe me. My time is too limited to allow for assiduous courtship; neither can I spend hours trying to find out who my rivals are. I realize that you are not interested in my dear kinsman"—he gave the words an ironic twist—"Carlos de Queras, but I have not forgotten that you said your heart belonged to someone else. Yet, I see no one courting you seriously. Was Calderon right then, do you intend to take the veil?"

"No, Sire."

He gave an exaggerated sigh of relief.

"At least I will not have to climb convent walls."

Both of them laughed, and immediately Philip's arms tightened around her, but as soon as he felt her resistance, he freed her.

"Where have you laid your affections?" he asked.

"Nowhere, so far."

"I think you are lying, you little minx. Don't you know better than to lie to your King?"

"I thought I was supposed to forget who you are," she retorted. "Now you realize how impossible that is. You hold all the power, a word from you can destroy me, whereas I can do nothing to you."

"Oh yes, you can. You can reduce me to misery by cruelly refusing to let me convince you of my sincerity and of my love. Are you certain you do not love anyone else?"

"Of course I am sure."

"Did you like to dance with me?"

"Sire, you are the most accomplished dancer I have ever known," Isabel admitted truthfully.

"I am a much better lover, I warrant you."

"I would not know."

"Let me show you. I promise I will not hurt you. Please."

"No," Isabel said with a pout. "I enjoy your attentions, but I will not let you seduce me. I will never belong to a man who cannot be my husband."

"That brings us back to Queras. I hear he has proposed to you. I assure you, you will have more fun with me than with him. But I assume you would rather have a husband than fun."

"I do not want to marry and certainly not him."

"Udsdaggers, Doña Isabel, do not be childish. Who wants to be married? I was married at the age of ten, and no one asked me whether I wanted it or not. It is beyond my comprehension why that villain Carlos wants to be married, seeing that he does not even know how to court a woman. Well, I suppose I am jealous of him, because I see him around you so much. Let us talk about you. You can become a nun, a wife, or a whore; there is no other choice for a woman. Now you have been telling me that you want to be neither the first nor the second. What am I to infer from that?"

The longer he talked, the more Isabel took pleasure in her performance. Now she scowled, then she let a playful smile smooth away her frown, then she parted her lips seductively to let him see her pretty teeth.

"I have not made up my mind, Your Majesty, but I warrant you, you will be the first one to know whatever I decide."

"And I warrant you that no matter what you decide, you will belong to me first, unless you tell me now that my presence is disagreeable to you."

"Your presence disagreeable! Sire, how can you say such a thing? You know what an honor it is . . ." but he cut her short.

"Do not give me shams and lies. Tell me the truth."

She looked at his ugly face with the prominent lower jaw. He could not possibly think of himself as handsome, his attentive ears would catch the slightest wrong note. But he wanted to hear the truth.

"All right," she said. "The truth is that your attention flatters me, naturally, because you are the King. But in addition I find that as a man you fascinate me. You have charm, you have grace." To say that another person had grace was the highest form of compliment a Spaniard could bestow. Isabel hoped she herself had carried it off gracefully.

"One day I may regret not having taken you now, while I have the opportunity," Philip said, "but I want you to fall in love with me."

This time his arms went around her firmly and she forced herself to accept his kiss without turning her head away, but again she was surprised by his gentleness and bewildered by the reaction of her own body which seemed to respond to his desire naturally, in spite of the fact that her mind was appalled. Contrary to what Court gossip had made her expect of him, he released her after one thorough kiss.

"Convinced I am not a monster?" he asked.

She laughed lightly.

"Would that I never had a worse problem than being kissed by my sovereign," she said.

"What other problem can you possibly have?"

"How to remain at Court without being forced into either of the three categories you mentioned."

"Come to my apartment tonight, and we will figure out a way."

"That might put me into your third category, might it not?" She smiled, however, and walked casually away from him to gaze at the paintings in various stages of completion. The sketch of a dwarf playing with the young crown prince puzzled her; she could not understand Philip's strange predilection for the company of misshapen human bodies. True, every Court had its jester, but Philip surrounded himself with a gallery of deformed creatures whose sad faces were portrayed by Velázquez with cruel realism.

The King followed her.

"She is a most kind little woman," he said pointing to the dwarf. "She was like a scared bird when I bought her, but she turned out to have a fine mind in an abject body. My friends sometimes ask me why I employ dwarfs and humpbacks; they cannot stand to look at them. I tell them it is precisely because I worship beauty that I can feel how much they must suffer. The least I can do is give them a reason for dignity by employing them according to their mental capacities. I am supposed to be the father of my people; if I abandon them, who will protect them from the brutal mockeries of common ruffians?"

His words touched her heart, and now she looked at him with different eyes. All of a sudden Pedro's projects took on the golden shimmer of success, for if Philip was capable of imposing on the whole Court his conviction that spiritual beauty could reside in physical ugliness, he might also be strong enough to proclaim that regardless of religion, all men were brothers and that the Inquisition was an abomination more brutal than the mockeries of ruffians.

Philip pointed to the portfolio of Titian's sketches Velázquez had shown at the Olivares reception.

"Have you seen the Tiziano drawings?"

He opened the portfolio and took out the chalk sketches, one by one, explaining to her that some of them were preliminary sketches of details for paintings.

"Do you know that Tiziano lived in Venice all his life up to the age of ninety-nine, when he died not of old age but of plague? My great-grandfather, Emperor Charles, vied with the King of France for the privilege of making this artist his Court painter, but nothing could induce him to leave Venice."

Isabel particularly admired a sheet showing a rabbit in various poses.

"This must be a sketch for one of his famous paintings: the Virgin with the Rabbit," Philip said.

Listening to him, Isabel realized that he was trying to woo her by displaying his knowledge of art, by impressing on her that he was a fine, sensitive being and not the vulgar lecher of common gossip.

"I wish Don Diego would sell one of these drawings," she said. "My brother tried to buy one; and I think His Excellency, the Count-Duke, did, but Señor Velázquez will not sell."

"Do you collect art?"

"Chalk drawings, maps, and old manuscripts are my favorite items."

"The next time we go to the Escorial you must accompany us. I will show you the library of precious volumes my grandfather put together. I have been told there is no finer in Europe."

Isabel had all but forgotten that Juana must wonder what was happening to her, and she reminded Philip that it might be time to rejoin their hostess.

"You are too worried about gossip," Philip said. "If you

had lived with it as long as I have, you would not pay any attention to it."

Isabel smiled, because Philip talked as if he were much older than she, when, in reality, only seven years separated them. But then, she thought, perhaps a man of twenty-seven felt old if he had been married since the age of ten.

"Well, let us go back, since you say we must." He opened the door for her and briefly brushed her cheek with his lips.

He stayed for a few minutes of small talk with Juana and told her he would be back in the evening.

As soon as he had left, Juana started to fret.

"I swear I did not know he was coming. He never does that when the servants tell him that Diego is not here. I cannot understand what got into him."

"Perhaps the other door to the atelier was locked," Isabel said.

"It always is when Diego leaves."

"Well then, why could he not come through here and look at the painting?"

"You mean nothing happened?" Juana asked with incredulity ringing through her voice.

"Nothing worth repeating," Isabel assured her. "He talked about his great-grandfather and about Tiziano, and he explained the paintings to me."

"Is that all?" Juana said. But Isabel was not sure whether the sigh she heard was one of relief or of disappointment.

# 27.

Isabel did not mention her meeting with Philip to anyone, because it confused her that the King's embrace should have struck a responsive chord in her body, when her common sense found him so ugly. Was it normal to respond so easily to a man's lust? Yes, she concluded, it must be, for otherwise there would be no point to the way Spanish fathers and husbands treated their women, locking them up, and never allowing them to be alone with a man. She also realized how extremely fortunate she was that Pedro had not hired a duenna for her and Pepita after her mother's death.

During her next visit to Rafael's apartment, when they sprawled, happy and exhausted, on the fine white linen sheets she had brought from Valderocas House, she tried to find out how a man felt about the pretty women he met.

"Have you known many girls before me?"

"Many, but none gave me as much pleasure."

"Why not?"

"I was not in love with them."

"But still you did the same things with them that you do with me?"

"But I did not enjoy it as much."

"Then you can make love without loving?"

"Of course."

"If a desirable girl dropped in your lap, would you make love to her, if she wanted to, and still love me none the less?"

"If the circumstances were right, I think I could."

"Yet you do love me?"

He grinned. "What is this? A first inquisitorial interrogation?"

"I only wanted to know."

He stared at her for a minute, and there was a wicked glitter dancing in the deep of his eyes, then he rolled on his back and drew her on top of him.

"Come now, show me what you can do."

As she slid onto him, his mouth reached for her erect pink nipples, and she let out a cry of triumph and wild abandon. When she started to rock back and forth, she had a brief vision of herself as a man who raped a resisting young maiden, and she thought the King was a fool if he expected her to submit to him voluntarily. Then the vision was gone, and she thought of the thickset body of the old chief minister, the whale Doña Iñéz had caught. Then that too was gone. She thought, but I, I have caught an archangel, Rafael.

"Rafael, Rafael," she panted as her breathing came faster and harder. Then Rafael arched up against her and she fell down upon him, drinking in the lusty smell of his skin and moaning with pleasure. Suddenly, he pulled away from her, shaking and white. "Hold me," he sobbed, guiding her hand to catch the spilling seed of life.

"I am sorry," he said, after they had lain still with their eyes closed. "It doesn't work this way. I have no control." Now she understood how careful he had been for her sake, never letting himself go completely. She loved him so much she wanted to tell him—everything. Yet, she knew she could

never do so. He was a Dominican friar, the enemy of every
Marrano.

Before she left, she looked at his books again. She thought
she would take up the Maimonides and at least glance at it
without saying anything, just one glimpse; but when she
looked for it, the volume was gone. She could not find it
anywhere.

# 28.

Toward the end of September, Pedro took Isabel to what he
termed a special meeting in the cellar of the Caietano house.
All the Caietanos were there, even Diego, who lately traveled
a good deal and seemed resigned to the fact that she did not
return his love, and the Portuguese merchant Lope Silva, and
two bearded men who had come from Salonica on a Valderocas ship to Seville from where Pedro himself had escorted
them to Madrid.

Thus, for the first time in her life, Isabel met with authentic
Jews. Not Marranos, but true, practicing Jews, who knew
Hebrew, who had not forgotten the prayers, who had been
born Jews and had never hidden their identity. And there, in
the secrecy of the Caietano cellar, they chanted the service of
Rosh Hashana, the beginning of a new year on the Hebrew
calendar. They had brought no prayer book, nor the traditional ram's horn, the shofar which was sounded in the
synagogues of Salonica, Amsterdam, Oran, and every other
place where Jews were allowed to assemble and pray. But
they interrupted their chanting now and then to explain in
Spanish that this was the moment for sounding the shofar, the
instrument used in ancient times to call the Jews together and
remind them that they were a people chosen to serve God. It
would have been too dangerous to carry any baggage containing Hebrew books or ceremonial objects. Every arriving
traveler was searched by customs officers who were paid
members of the Inquisition, and these two had been searched
closely, for they came from a pagan country. But they had
shown letters of invitation signed by Gaspar de Guzmán,
Count of Olivares, Duke of Sanlúcar.

Their brains, however, could not be searched, and in their

minds they carried gifts more precious than ram's horns, or prayer shawls, or seven-armed candelabras, or even Torah scrolls: they carried the knowledge of what a practicing Jew must do to remain a Jew—a knowledge that had worn thin in Spain over the past one hundred years.

They intoned Kadosh, Kadosh, Kadosh: Holy, Holy, Holy is the Lord of Hosts, and to their listeners who had forgotten the Hebrew tongue, they explained what the Lord required of every Jew: "Only to do justly, and to love mercy, and to walk humbly with thy God."

There was spoken during this service not a word of bitterness, not a word of hatred. It was as if persecution and Inquisition did not exist, only a world full of human beings who deserved to be loved.

Isabel, who loved Pedro and Pepita and Pasquito and Uncle Jaime—but, above all, Rafael—wished God would grant her the power to convince every single Dominican friar that her people neither scourged crucifixes, nor martyred little children, nor planned to poison wells.

Ten days later they chanted another service deep in the ground under the old Jewish quarter of Toledo, for Pedro had insisted that they spend Yom Kippur, the Day of Atonement, with Uncle Jaime. This was the day Spanish crypto-Jews had come to call the Day of Purity. Diego Caietano came with them, and Pedro wanted to invite Manuela also, but both the bookstore owner and his wife had sternly opposed their daughter's going. Their ideas of what a young lady could do or not do were as strict as any Spaniard's, and they would not let her spend a night away from home unless they went with her. Since they could not come, she too had to stay home. Isabel was glad they refused; Manuela was sometimes fanatically ready to suffer for her faith, and Isabel feared that Pepita might become suspicious.

Once again, she mentioned her fears to Pedro, begging him to marry Pepita and confide in her, but he would not. So Pepita came with them, blissfully ignorant that she was living in the midst of a group of heretics. The most remarkable fact was perhaps that indeed, outwardly, they all behaved like fine Catholics. Even their two visitors never betrayed by a word or a gesture that they were anything else. Upon Pedro's insistence, they had shed the traditional Jewish costume they wore in Turkey, particularly the tall red hats, and had accepted the clothes he had brought with him on board ship when he had gone to pick them up. They were the first Jews Pedro had contacted with Olivares's permission, and the chief minister was not yet ready to flaunt his boldness in the face of the Inquisition. Officially, the Old Christian Pedro Valderocas was taking two merchants to look at the Toledo silk industry in order for them to judge whether the products of the Toledo silkworms could compete with the finest oriental silks and were worth exporting.

At Toledo there were long discussions in the middle of night, held in the underground meeting place. The visitors said that the Spanish Jews living in exile in Turkey still had their hearts at Toledo, and that some of them had kept the keys to the houses their ancestors had left behind when they were expelled from Spain in 1492.

"If you were given the right to reside on the outskirts of Madrid and build your own synagogue, would you come back to Spain?" Pedro asked them.

The visitors said they themselves would not; they preferred to live among Moslems who at least never accused them of deicide, but they knew that many other Sephardim were dreaming of returning to the country of their ancestors. If Olivares wanted Jews to settle in Spain, he would have no trouble finding them, provided he gave them letters of safe-conduct and guaranteed immunity from the Inquisition. It would be best if an Old Christian were sent to contact the Jews, so that the undertaking would not look like a one-sided Marrano plot.

"I am an Old Christian," Pedro said. "The Valderocases have been Old Christians since time immemorial. Would that make me a suitable envoy?"

"Would all the good Old Christians had as much under-standing of our faith as you do," Pablo Raíz said with a twinkle in his eyes.

"Are there more Old Christians of your trademark in Castile?" one of the visitors wanted to know.

"Don Jaime and myself are the only ones I know of," Pedro said, "and the only other member of our family who thinks as we do is my sister Isabel."

"Except for you, Valderocas, and for Olivares, every other Old Christian is against us?"

"Olivares thinks not; he thinks that times are changing, and he is willing to try."

"How will he sneak his ideas past the Suprema?"

"By convincing them it is a purely economic measure."

During the Day of Atonement, the men walked from one

silkworm owner to another, accepting no refreshments anywhere, pretending they had just eaten, and for their midday
meal, Uncle Jaime had instructed the servants to prepare
baskets with food which they took with them on a walk
outside the city walls where they deposited the food in a
secluded spot. The men went alone, while Isabel stayed home
with Pepita, where she could not abstain from food, as she
had wanted to. She said to Pepita, "Let us prepare a festive
meal and have a party tonight, and cook the things Mother
used to cook," and to her surprise Pepita answered, "Then
we better not eat now, remember Mother said it was good to
fast before a feast?"

They looked at each other, and both broke into tears. Up to
that moment, they had run away from their grief into the
whirl of social events in Madrid. Now in the quiet of Jaime's
house, their sorrow caught up with them, and they hugged
each other and cried together.

Before they returned to Madrid, Isabel asked her uncle to
lead her once more, alone, to the Valderocas treasure
chamber. Pedro would often travel abroad, and if anything
happened to him, she would be the only one to know about
the treasure, and she wanted to be sure she could find it. He
agreed, and this time he let her open the hinged door herself.
When they were inside, he showed her two small silver oil
cups which were to be used on Friday nights when a wick was
lighted in each to burn as a Sabbath light.

"I asked our visitors for the exact words of the blessing,"
Uncle Jaime said. "Now I can teach them to you."

So Isabel learned the ancient Hebrew words for: Blessed
art Thou, Oh Lord our God, King of the Universe, who hast
sanctified us by Thy commandments, and commanded us to
kindle the Sabbath lights.

"May I have the cups?" she asked him.

"No, it would be too dangerous. There is a shield of David
on them. Do not light candles either, child. Just light a flame
in your heart and say the blessing in your mind."

"Uncle Jaime?"

"Yes?"

"Do we Jews have a confessor?"

"No. We have God. Yesterday was the Day of Atonement,
the day we ask God to forgive our sins—that is sins committed against Him—and there are many, for here in Spain we
have forgotten most of His laws. Why do you want a
confessor?"

"Because I am confused. I see Christians murder in the name of Christ, but in other times, Christians, too, have been murdered. I do not want a confessor so much as someone to talk to. All this killing seems to be done from ignorance. Apart from the divinity of Christ, our faith, from all you have taught me, is really not that different. If Jesus was a Jew, reared in Judaism who preached to Jews, why would we have killed him?"

"We have not killed him."

"But the gospels say so. It says there that the Jews screamed 'May His blood come over us and over our children.' "

"Assuming the gospels are correct in every word," Jaime said, "why would the screams of a few fanatics entitle the rest of the world to take this as an order from God to kill all the descendants of Jesus' people? This never made sense to me. Do you know that at the time Jesus lived, your ancestors and mine were probably already living here in Spain? I am sure the Benahavels were here before the Valderocases ever set foot in this land."

"I never thought of it that way," Isabel nodded, "but there is something else. We grow up learning that it was Christ who introduced love and compassion into the world, that Mosaic Law knows only the harshness of an eye for an eye and a tooth for a tooth, when, in reality, the Prophets and the Psalms are full of love and compassion and mercy. Why, there is not a word in the Sermon on the Mount that cannot be found in the Bible, in our Bible."

Jaime could not help smiling at her eagerness.

"I know," he said.

"But if we can see that," Isabel went on earnestly, "why can't they? People like the Dominican friars. And if they cannot see it, why can't we explain it to them? Why do they hate us so? Why do they invent lies about us in order to burn us alive. Why?"

"Because they do not want to face the truth."

"What truth?"

"That Jesus is not the Messiah as foretold by Isaiah. The wolf does not dwell with the lamb, the leopard does not lie down with the kid, and the calf and the young lion are still enemies. They are still hurting and destroying everywhere. So if we go by Isaiah, the condition of the world since Jesus' advent does not justify the claim that He is the Messiah. If they studied the scriptures, studied them well, they would begin to have doubts. Child, we have never reviled Jesus, as they think we did. On the contrary, our great Moses Maimonides himself has acknowledged him as one who prepared the way for the Messianic Kingdom. Whoever read Maimonides would understand that. We are willing to accept Jesus as a gifted and exalted teacher, even as a prophet, but we cannot, in all honesty, adore him as a God become flesh."

"I wish I could talk to Mother. Life is so difficult, Uncle Jaime. What if I fell in love with a true Christian? Not all Christians are Inquisitors. We cannot condemn all of them for the terror perpetrated by a few, can we?"

He lifted the oil lamp he was carrying to her face and looked at her for a long time.

"Isabel, if you fall in love, remember the fate of the beautiful Susana. Whoever he be, love him if you must, but never, never trust him. Not if he is an Old Christian."

She found that she still held the small silver container in her hand. Now she placed it back among the collection of ceremonial objects. Then she closed the door herself and led the way up and down through musty corridors back to Jaime's house.

# 29.

Upon her return to Madrid, Isabel was told by Teresa that a flat parcel addressed to her had been delivered by a lackey wearing the royal livery. She opened it in front of Pedro and Pepita. It held, in a beautiful frame and behind glass, the chalk sketches of the rabbit by Titian. There was a note, too, speaking of admiration, love, and devotion, signed Felipe de Habsburg.

"Who is he?" asked Pepita.

"If I were not so dumbfounded, I would say he was the King," Pedro said.

"But the King signs himself Yo El Rey," Pepita pointed out.

Both she and Pedro stared at Isabel who had not yet said a word. As Isabel looked at the drawings, she remembered every detail of her meeting with Philip, and she was more confused than ever. Now she would be forced to explain to

Pedro and Pepita what she would have preferred to keep secret.

"Is it the King?" Pepita asked with excitement dancing all over her face. "Is the King in love with you?"

"Udsdaggers," said Isabel, using the King's favorite exclamation, "who gave you that idea? As you said yourself, it isn't signed by the King. So it cannot be the King."

"It is! It is! Oh, Isabel, how exciting. What are you going to do?"

"Yes, how are you going to thank him?" Pedro asked, "or is he thanking you?"

All of a sudden, she was angry at their curiosity, their insistence on sharing her adventure with them, and she made up her mind to tell them nothing at all.

"The man has a name," she said, "or he would not have signed it. So it seems to me that sometimes he wants to be a human being; a friend, perhaps, who can give gifts to people he likes. I think Felipe de Habsburg is a kind man, and I shall thank him at the proper opportunity."

"Eh, I think she is defending him," Pepita remarked, "I think she is in love with him."

"Flimflam."

"I think she does not realize the value of this gift," Pedro said.

"I'll warrant you that I do," Isabel snapped. "It will hang in my room."

# 30.

Uncomfortably shifting his weight from one side to the other, by crossing his legs now this way and now that, Philip sat on a satin-covered armchair in his bedroom and listened morosely to a lecture delivered by his friend and Favorite, the Count-Duke of Olivares. But he found it impossible to concentrate for a long time on a subject he dreaded.

"All right, all right. So there is no money in my treasury. See that you do something about it," he interrupted, "I cannot be blamed for that too. I have been doing more than enough. I went to Catalonia, I consented to listen to the imbecile demands of Barcelona, I practically humiliated

myself before the Cortes of Aragon. Enough is enough. You
have my confidence, I give you the power to do whatever you
deem necessary. I will sign whatever I have to sign, but,
udsdaggers, spare me the details."

"Sire, I cannot in this matter keep my own counsel,"
Olivares said soothingly. "I am afraid I will have to keep Your
Majesty's attention for a longer time than usual. It is a matter
of urgency as well as delicacy, and seeing that your royal
timetable shows no engagement for tonight . . ."

"I am sorry, Count; I am helpless in these matters, do
make it short."

Gaspar de Guzmán knew only too well in what matters his
monarch was helpless, and he had timed his arrival to
coincide with Philip's need to disappear in the streets of the
more disreputable part of town. Now he glanced down on his
young King disapprovingly, and suppressing an ironic smile,
he went on to depict in grisly colors the terrors lurking for the
Spanish crown in the shadows of poverty and indebtedness
that were growing higher than the Pyrenees and more dangerous than Vesuvius and Aetna.

"Devalue the currency," Philip proposed, resorting to
what had been his father's favorite remedy for similar problems, but the Count-Duke shook his head.

"You have pledged solemnly yourself not to repeat that for
the next twenty years," he said, although he was the first one
to realize that this promise would never be kept. "No, I am
afraid we will have to tax Church property."

"Impossible," Philip said at once. "I am a miserable sinner,
and I know God punishes my nation for my own sins, but I
cannot subscribe to so blasphemous a measure. Never."

His spontaneous and firm answer reinforced the Count-
Duke's suspicion that Sotomayor did more than just hear the
daily confession of the King's carnal sins.

"Yet, that is where the money is," Olivares said. "There
and in Catalonia, of course, and one day I swear I shall bring
those proud Catalans to their knees, and they shall contribute
their fair share. However, that may take years, and in the
meantime, we must defend Spain against her enemies, and
not only Spain but our Holy Catholic faith, and how shall we
pay for the troops and the arms?"

"What about the confiscations made by the Holy Office,"
Philip asked. "They must have scooped up a fat lot from those
base miscreants who figured in the *auto*. How much was it?"

"They refuse to divulge the sums they take. I am afraid the

Dukes of Lerma and Uceda allowed the Inquisition that practice."

"Can you not change that?"

"Your Majesty can."

"I? Meddle in the affairs of the Holy Office? Count . . . dammit . . . let's talk about this some other time. I'm in a hurry now." He reached for a bell-pull, but Olivares laid his hand on Philip's arm.

"Sire, I have thought of a solution."

*"Hombre,* come out with it. Do you have to display your sense of drama with me?"

Olivares chuckled.

"As a matter of fact, I hold a sort of down-payment from some people who would be much delighted to serve Your Majesty."

"What? What's that?"

"A hundred thousand ducats, in gold."

Philip jumped up and put his slender hand on the Count-Duke's heavy shoulder, "Old friend, and there is more where that came from?"

"Much more."

"How soon can we get it?"

"It is not a matter of getting it but of getting the people who produce it. They are not in Spain."

"Who are they?" Philip asked, and a cloud of suspicion passed over his eager face.

"They are a group of people who monopolize the Mediterranean trade and much of the trade with the New World. They own and operate the North African mints, and they make Amsterdam more important than Seville."

"Why would they want to settle in Spain? We have enough foreigners. You yourself have repeatedly harped on that theme."

"They are not really foreigners. They love Spain despite . . ." Olivares stopped short, for he did not dare pronounce what he thought, despite the injustices their forefathers had suffered in Spain.

Suddenly, Philip caught on, and his face fell. Another of his minister's ambitious plans. Would any of them ever be realized?

Since his early youth, Philip had found in Olivares a strong hero and father figure. The Count-Duke had won his trust and admiration, but sometimes Olivares's bold ideas frightened Philip's basically conservative Habsburg mind. In mat-

ters of religion, Philip had the troubled conscience of an
habitual sinner inclined to listen to the advice of his confessor.

"What does our new Inquisitor General think about this?"
he asked, causing Olivares to wonder for the hundredth time
why the Lord saw fit to grace the throne of Spain with
indecisive weaklings. He thought it wise to remind the King
that after all the Inquisition depended at least partially on the
good will of the Crown.

"The laws of Spain are made by the King," he said, "and
the Inquisitor General is named and dismissed by the King.
Surely Your Majesty will not let that royal prerogative be
taken over by Rome?"

"Even I am subject to the Holy Office," Philip answered.
"Not so much as a dust speck of suspicion must ever blemish
the Crown of Spain."

Philip hated this kind of mental effort. He longed to get out
of the stuffiness of the Alcázar into the freedom of the streets;
he could not stand it anymore, it was all so pointless. He was
a man of flesh and blood, not a puppet to be manipulated by
power-greedy ministers and churchmen. Oh, he was so weary
of it all. None of it had the eternal value of art, the beauty of
poetry, the charm of a well-executed dance, the breathless
vitality of a great hunt, the incomparable satisfaction of a
perfect embrace. The problems of government—may the
devil get them. One day he would die and that would be the
end, and they all would die with him, or before him or after
him, but die they must. So who dared keep him from living
while he could still enjoy himself? All kingdoms crumbled in
the end, and their rulers were forgotten, but the creations of a
genius lived forever. What was the most glorious achievement
of his grandfather, the much-praised Philip II, if not the
Escorial, that grandiose monument to the glory of God and
the best in man?

If he had to be a king, he wanted to be a king of artists.

And, of course, he wanted a chance to be himself. And he
wanted that chance right now. He would demand it, and he
would have it. Forget the problems of state.

But the stern glance of his mentor reminded him of his duty
to attempt royal self-control, wherefore he made an effort to
sound wise and composed.

"Surely, Count, you must know that the purity of the faith
is my greatest endeavor. I have shown many times that I am
willing to treat our New Christians as if there were no

difference between them and Old Christians. The faith is what counts, not the ancestry. I have refrained from calling them Jews, or Hebrews, or People of the Nation; I have never implied that they belong to a different people or race; and I truly do not believe they do. You have been my tutor during my years as crown prince. You know I have studied history sufficiently to realize that these people are Spaniards, and I have repudiated the notorious Green Book of Aragon according to which hardly a nobleman could claim to have pure blood. I am sure if I searched hard enough, I could find some traces of Jewish blood in my own veins! To tell you the truth, and I would confide it to no one but you, the whole subject bores me out of my skin. But my studies have also convinced me that the Inquisition has been a great pillar of Spain's power and is necessary and indispensable to keep the people in line. So I play my part, as I play all parts required of me. I am a good father to my people, I confess my sins, and I ask for advice from individuals whom I believe inspired by God. But enough is enough!" His voice had lost its initial ceremonious tone as his anger was mounting, "I don't know yet what you want from me. If it is new privileges for the *conversos,* that is fine with me. We can't very well take their money and give nothing in return, for that would go against my ethical beliefs. But if you ask me to tax Church property, I warn you, my holy Catholic upbringing says no. A Habsburg cannot curtail the rights of the Church. And as far as those people you talk about, it better be a proposition agreeable to the Holy Office."

"In Rome, right under the nose of His Holiness, they have a synagogue and a place where the Jews live," Olivares said. "And the Italian Inquisition can do nothing about it. But Spain, I am afraid, is ruled by her Inquisitors and not by her monarch."

"So that is what you want," Philip said. "Abolish the expulsion order and invite the Jews back into Spain. *Hombre!* The Holy Office will ask for your head or rather for your precious soul."

"And will you give it to them?" Olivares asked.

The King gave a snort.

"Your Majesty," Olivares began earnestly, "I beg you to consider the welfare of our countrymen. A third of the population roams the countryside as beggars and bandits. We have to feed them, resettle them, create work for them through commerce and industry. For that we need money.

And to get money we need more freedom. The world is full of men who are not Catholic but who do have money. And who used to be Spaniards. To attract them back to Spain we need religious liberty. I am not jesting, Sire, and if you are dissatisfied with my advice, I will most humbly throw myself at your feet and implore you to relieve me of my duties. I am getting old and sick under the load of government problems. You are no longer the youngster who needed help; you can take over. I will send for all the files and documents, and I will lay them into your hands, knowing you will devote every minute of your time to studying them and making decisions wiser than those I propose." Olivares actually bent one knee to the ground and stayed in this for him uncomfortable position until Philip pulled him up.

"Do not let me hear that nonsense again," the King said. "The mere thought of your mountains of paper work frightens the devil out of me. And now forgive me, but I really must leave."

"Then I beg you to grant me a short vacation," Olivares insisted.

"Not a minute," Philip said. "You convinced me that our situation does not permit any waste of time. I order you to contact members of the Royal Council and some of our foremost theologians. If you can convince them of the wisdom of your plans, you may go ahead. I wish you success."

With that he rang the bell and asked for his walking-clothes.

Olivares wanted to leave, but now that Philip had his mind on more pleasant matters, he insisted the Count-Duke stay until the servants had finished dressing him.

"You know that blond Valderocas girl? I am crazy about her."

"I am not going to help you with that," Olivares said.

"Hoho, the first time I see you interested. I have never quite believed the rumors that you are the passionate lover Manlio in Rioja's poetry. Have I caught you at last?"

"You misunderstand. I am—for political reasons—interested in the young lady's brother. As a matter of fact, he is going to be the envoy to the places we just discussed. He is a fine trustworthy Old Christian, yet a man who understands our problems. By his connections as master trader, he is uniquely qualified to contact the people I have in mind."

"So?"

"He is also, due to his parents' death, the protector of his sister's honor."

"The King is sacred," Philip retorted, alluding to the current success by a new young playwright, Francisco de Rojas Zorrilla. In his play, a simple worker killed a courtier who had molested his wife, after sparing him first because he thought the man was the King. Philip himself planned to play the part of the wronged husband in a private Court theatrical, and he had already studied his lines.

*"No hay de permitir me agravio, del rey abajo ninguno,"* he declaimed, while his servant was buttoning his short coat.

"True, yet I would hate to lose my chief negotiator and in addition have him remove his wealth and his banks and his fleet and put them at the service of the Bourbons or the Stuarts."

Philip was dressed now and in high spirits.

"You have my royal word of honor that I will woo the young lady with delicacy and patience," he said as he strode to the door, followed by two hunting dogs who up until that moment had lain at the foot of his bed.

"I would prefer you did not woo her at all," Olivares muttered.

Philip wagged his finger at him. "Manlio, Manlio, I suspect . . ." Then he was gone and Olivares, shaking his head, went back to his office to ponder over the reports from the front.

# 31.

For his nighttime tours of the city, Philip used a plain unmarked coach covered with gray-green oilcloth. Under his reign, Madrid had acquired the reputation of a city where strangers were welcome, nightly pleasures abundant, food and drink better than anywhere in Europe, and pretty whores available at every street corner. After sundown, the crowds in the *tascas* and brothels were as thick as the everpresent swarms of flies and as anonymous as the rats feasting on the piles of refuse alongside the houses. Face masks were commonly worn by men and veils by women. A simply dressed tall blond man attracted no attention among people who had never seen a Habsburg face to face, nor viewed his jutting jaw on Velázquez's portraits.

Philip's favorite place was the Casa del Celestina, otherwise known as Juliana's. The name Celestina had been borrowed by the owner, the fox-faced Juliana, from a famous novel published over a century earlier but still much read throughout Spain. The protagonist of that story was a procuress well worthy of imitation, or so Juliana thought when she kept what she called pleasure quarters for cavaliers and servants, noblemen and thieves, high dignitaries and successful criminals. Like her model Celestina, whose only flaw was her sorry demise at the hands of a murderer, Juliana had gained entrance into the palaces of the nobles, the homes of the well-to-do, and the hovels of tinkers and slop-men. She kept records on prospective employees from the age of ten to the age of thirty. She knew who needed an abortion, who had gotten into trouble with her master, who wanted to escape a wronged father's wrath. She offered compassion and help, and if the girl's youth, or freshness, or beauty warranted it, she offered a sensible income.

If Señor Vicente, he of the pathetic eyes and the prominent chin, was her favorite customer, because he came often and paid well, he was also the most demanding one, his taste running to ripe young beauties with dark hair and full breasts. Juliana made sure to have a new one on hand every week and to keep the best room in readiness, for unless he picked up what he wanted over a drink at a *tasca*, Señor Vicente arrived at Celestina's overexcited from reaching under too many skirts on his way and in no mood to wait his turn. Sometimes he would come in with a girl and just use the room, for which he paid as handsomely as if she had furnished him with enough lust slaves for an orgy. On other nights, he would request a frightened twelve-year-old virgin so that he could perfect himself in overcoming shyness. That desire too, Juliana strove to fulfill; she gave lessons in coyness to her promising younger students, and she had developed a special method for replacing missing maidenheads.

Tonight Juliana was particularly pleased when she heard his lusty voice in the patio shouting his usual *"¡Hola! ¿Qué tal?"* for she had gotten a very young Moorish slave girl, barely eleven, with pretty uptilted breasts, a flawless skin, and a voice so low and caressing it sent visions of profit into Juliana's scheming mind. The poor girl had run away from her master, the vicious Count of Villaquemada. Juliana presented her with pride to Señor Vicente. But he brushed her aside.

"Udsdaggers, old girl, are you running a nursery now? And a Moor yet! Off with her!"

The frightened girl took off in a trice. Then Philip, in his disguise as Señor Vicente, gave his detailed instructions to be followed on the spot or he would find a more compliant hostess.

"I want a fair girl, about that high, with hair the color of dark honey, emerald eyes, a voice like an angel, and the softness of a kitten."

"I hope you don't expect to be the first one in the bargain," Juliana countered sarcastically. In her mind, she immediately reduced the matter to a somewhat clear-eyed lass, for she had enough wigs to make every girl in her establishment a blonde to suit the usual taste of her customers for nordic beauties.

While he waited in his room, sprawled on red satin sheets, and stared at the ceiling and walls covered with scenes from Greek mythology, his mind wandered. Soon all the maidens submitting to the god Zeus in his various incarnations as bird or beast or rain, took the form and face of Isabel Valderocas, and Philip himself was the god who had to possess her.

When the door finally opened and a young lady walked in, wearing a soft green gown cut low enough to reveal her shapely bosom and slit open in front to let him glimpse her slim legs, he propped himself up on one elbow. Slowly, she covered her face with her emerald lace fan, and even more slowly she turned around to let him see her long blond hair falling in waves to her shoulders. Then she dropped her gown for him to admire her umblemished back and he jumped up from the bed, seeing only the green and the softness of her gestures and the long blond hair, and he seized her brusquely, threw her on the bed and crushed down on her with all his weight. He closed his eyes and tore into her, pouring into her all his accumulated energy, and his mind said only Isabel, Isabel, Isabel.

He sent her away without opening his eyes, and thus he never knew that hers were as coal black as those of the young actress La Calderona who had given him the beautiful child Don Juan of Austria, before retiring to become the abbess of a convent.

Now that his desire was appeased, he could think again, and in his mind he compared the more memorable of his paramours. There had been a few worthy of becoming an official royal mistress, but he had always tired of them. La Calderona had been the only woman he had really loved. He had begged her, even after the birth of their son, to remain his mistress forever, but she had pleaded with him to let her go. She said she had done all she could do for him. Apparently, she, too, had lain with him only because he was the King. She had considered it her sacred duty to satisfy her monarch's desire. After the birth of their son, whom he had officially recognized and to whom he had given the illustrious name of Don Juan of Austria, she had refused to return to him.

So perhaps Isabel Valderocas was right. He could never be sure of any woman's love. Not as Philip the King. But what as Señor Vicente? No, that was no better. Señor Vicente paid for his pleasures, just as Philip did.

Isabel Valderocas. He repeated her name in his mind. She was wealthy enough not to need money. She was too intelligent to think it her duty to lay with him. And she really did not seem overawed by the sacredness of his person. Perhaps, if he were patient . . .

# 32.

For many years there had existed at the east gate of the capital, behind the monastery of San Geronimo, a beautiful informal park with a modest suite of apartments used by the royal family as an occasional retreat or guest house. When the Queen complained that the old Alcázar was too drafty and ugly, the Escorial too austere, and the climate of Aranjuez too unhealthy, the Countess Olivares had suggested to her husband that they might think about making the Retiro more enjoyable for the royal couple. Olivares agreed and the Buen Retiro Palace became the Count-Duke's personal gift to his monarch.

Inés de Zúñiga began the transformation by ordering the construction of an aviary where she kept a collection of rare hens and roosters. Her Majesty was delighted, as she was with any new addition to the attractions of the park, but when foreign ambassadors dropped by and reported back to their sovereigns, all of Europe started to snicker at what was called the Olivares chicken coop. Richelieu himself speculated in front of the Spanish ambassador as to the intriguing possibility that Olivares might after all be a hen-pecked man, a suggestion that soon trickled back to Madrid via the British diplomatic pouch. Court gossip formed the larger part of European diplomacy.

Whereupon, in an honest endeavor to please his King and to show the world that no sovereign was more splendid than Philip IV and none more worthy of a magnificent palace, Olivares used his own wealth to create a setting so perfect that it would become the envy of other royal capitals. He began by secretly buying up the grounds surrounding the existing park. Then he had hundreds of gardeners tailor them into a shape he personally designed. No one paid much attention to what was going on in those woods, until one day an army of constructors, engineers, bricklayers, cabinet makers, weavers, painters, and decorators appeared to build a well-proportioned baroque palace, with a central court where clipped hedges and ornate fountains invited guests to walk about and perhaps venture beyond the formal gardens into a park abounding with grottos, cascades, lakes, hermitages, and aviaries. Now, the foreign ambassadors wrote home that Spain might not be as poor and exhausted as they had suspected, if she was still capable of paying for such a fairy-tale marvel.

There was much vicious gossip though, spread by the Count-Duke's enemies, who accused him of pressing the Grandees into making him precious gifts of art for his folly. But, in truth, those who could afford it vied with each other as to who could make the most ostentatious contribution to the furnishings of the palace. Apart from that, the money for all these splendid extravagancies came out of the Count-Duke's personal pocket.

The most talked-about innovation was the great square theater lake where miniature galleons were used for pleasure rides or to lend authenticity to outdoor presentations of stage plays which, thanks to Cosme Loti's ingenuity in using the latest technical inventions, became more admirable for their complicated scenery than for their dramatic value.

The building itself was yet to be finished, when, in October 1632, Olivares decided that it was time to present the King with the golden key to his future home, and the world was invited to a peek preview of the newest stage for royal amusements.

The true reason for Olivares's wish to create a joyful event was the poor turn matters of state had taken since the frustrating trip to Aragon in a futile attempt to unite the provinces. The King had undertaken that journey in the company not only of Olivares, from whom he was inseparable, but also of both his younger brothers, the Infante Carlos and the Cardinal Infante Ferdinand. On the way home, after three months of useless bargaining with the stubborn Cortes of Valencia, Aragòn, and Catalonia, disaster had struck. The Infante Carlos, a soft, compliant, and slightly mysterious young man and after baby Balthasar the closest heir in order of succession to the throne, had contracted what seemed to be an ordinary ague. But toward the end of July, he broke out in spots and died in agony.

It was a case of typhus, but the Count-Duke's detractors did not hesitate to spread the rumor that Olivares had planned to decimate the King's brothers by slowly poisoning them, since they might have some influence over His Majesty. There were rumors, too, that Olivares and the Cardinal Infante Ferdinand hated each other bitterly, because Olivares supposedly had forced the Infante into ecclesiastical garb. The Count-Duke, however, understood Ferdinand's wish to become a military hero, but when he had finally agreed to offer him the post of supreme commander of the Spanish armies in the Netherlands, the bad tongues immediately accused him of wanting the Infante to die in battle. So now Olivares had to beseech Ferdinand to wait at least another year. He could not allow him to leave Madrid so soon after the death of his brother.

Another point of much grumbling and discontent throughout Spain was the universal tax on salt, from which neither the Grandees nor the clergy were excluded. The tax had been designed by Olivares as a means to squeeze some money out of the rich as well as out of the poor, especially since the rich had to nourish their thousands of servants at an exorbitant salt price. Olivares had even induced Philip to sign a royal decree ordering the civilian population to supply the soldiers quartered in their villages with candles, vinegar, and salt, thus saving the royal treasury the tremendous expense of providing the troops with this most essential part of their diet.

But the great war, although largely fought in the plains of

Germany and far from the Spanish motherland, continued to devour all Spanish resources like an insatiable monster, and the Count-Duke was nearly at the end of his wits. Only by superb diplomacy was he able to keep England neutral, but even the easily duped Charles Stuart would finally be wise to the Spaniard's tricks. Already Hopton, the English Ambassador at Madrid, was pressing Olivares mercilessly as to his true intentions. Then, what would he do to save Spain? Would he be able to remain the sturdy pillar against which Philip could lean?

Moodily, he joined his wife who was giving the last instructions for the opening ceremonies of the new palace. He nodded absentmindedly when she told him that at the ball scented purses filled with ducats, gold flasks with perfumes, and brocade dress lengths would be presented to the ladies.

"What is wrong?" she asked, with concern in her voice.

"Nothing in particular," he sighed.

They looked at each other, and the Countess smiled reassuringly. She had been his helpmate for so many years, after an ostentatious and ardent courtship prompted not by her beauty—she had none—but by her standing at Court, that they understood and trusted each other. They often guessed each other's thoughts and motives.

"Do the Valderocases have good places for the cane tourney and the bullfight?" he asked her.

"So it is money trouble again," the Countess said. "I will do my best."

Gratefully, he placed a kiss on the back of her hand.

# 33.

Riding into the theater square at the side of Olivares, Philip IV, King of Spain, looked more resplendent than any of his courtiers and more impressive than his handsomer brother the Cardinal Infante. He wore a chestnut-brown velvet coat with rich embroideries and a matching beret decorated with a blue and white featherbushel. In his hands, he carried a shield gleaming in the warm October sun and a smartly decorated lance. The choice of colors was most becoming. The brown reflected onto his face, softening its usual pallor; the gilt embroidery helped to create the impression that his hair was not dirty blond but golden; and the blue and white feathers cast a nuance of perky freshness over his long pathetic features.

"Seen like this, he does not look so bad," Pepita whispered to Isabel when they had taken their reserved seats in the grandstand to watch the King and his Favorite, both intrepid horsemen, lead their prancing chargers through the difficult figures of the *parejas.*

Isabel's eyes, however, were not on Philip but on the Count-Duke. In spite of his more advanced age and heavier weight, he rode every bit as well as the King.

Since her return from Toledo, Isabel had not seen Philip in private and had not yet thanked him for the gift he had sent to her. Now she feared that the hour of reckoning drew nearer, that Philip would definitely attempt to single her out during the ball which was to follow the tourneys and the bullfight. She wondered whether she would be able to approach the Count-Duke and possibly ask him for advice.

"Don Carlos de Queras is coming," Pepita whispered in her ear. Isabel answered with an angry look. Carlos, when compared to Philip, was just a nuisance, not unlike a mosquito. Since Pedro was not sitting with them, she would be able to indulge in the pleasure of impoliteness, should Carlos try to annoy her.

Carlos, however, had found a new stratagem to corner her. Sweeping off his hat and bowing deeply to Pepita, he inquired whether he might have the honor of introducing her to a Lady-in-Waiting who had taken an interest in Pepita and invited her to sit with the other Ladies-in-Waiting. Such an offer was impossible to refuse. Pepita left with Carlos, who then came back to take the empty seat at Isabel's side.

"Seeing that you are carving yourself a little niche in the King's affections," Carlos whispered, "I suppose I shall have to consider courting you with the due attentions. I wish I could be as ostentatious as our dear Count-Duke was when he set out to win the black dragon, but knowing my sorry state of finances, you will understand that such courtship is out of the question. Unless Don Pedro wishes to pay for it."

The only thing Isabel knew was that several pairs of eyes were fixed on her, and so she smiled meekly.

"What do you mean by that remark?"

"What remark?"

"About the King."

"Yes, what about him?"

"I am asking you."

There was again that nasty glitter in his eyes. "And I am asking you," he said. "It seems His Majesty sends you expensive presents. Very unlike his usual behavior with courtesans."

Isabel frowned. Had Velázquez's wife been talking? More likely the servants, the eternal scourge of every grand household. Many a servant got paid twice, by his own master and by the party for whom he spied on his master. Did Carlos keep informers among the Valderocas personnel? Or were they simply proud that their mistress had received a royal gift and had they tattled out of presumptuousness? At any rate, it would do her no good to deny it. Juana might already have talked about her meeting with the King.

"And if he does," she said, *"he* can afford it."

As before on similar occasions, Carlos remained impervious to her barb.

"I suggest you listen to me," he said quietly, but he was interrupted by the orange-man walking around between the rows with his baskets of oranges and other fruits. Impatiently, Carlos waved him away.

By now the first part of the quadrille was finished, and the riders took up their places for the cane tourney. Isabel had never seen a tourney and watched with interest when Philip lowered his lance before the Queen, and she threw him a white and blue lace handkerchief. Then, perplexed, she looked at the lace in her own hand. It had the same color combination, indeed, it was identical to the one the Queen had just given her husband.

"One would think he was wearing your colors," Carlos said.

And he is, too, Isabel thought, because the lace handkerchief had been brought to her in a pretty box by a delivery boy who did not know the sender. There had been no letter, and a lace handkerchief not being an expensive gift, Isabel had been unsure as to the identity of the sender. But she had liked it, and since there was a blue and white gown among her dresses, she had chosen that one to wear to the tourney.

"A coincidence," she said to Carlos, but she smiled when Philip waved the scarf to the cheering crowds. Whereas up to now she had secretly hoped Olivares would win the tourney, she felt it would be disloyal to wish for the defeat of a man who wore her colors. There was no reason to be concerned,

however, for the King's team of four threw their canes very
accurately upon the shields of their opponents, thus forcing
them to retreat.

Following this portrayal of a tournament of old, there came
the *juego de sortija,* a game where the participants had to
unhook a ring from its place by spearing it onto the tip of their
lance, while galloping at great speed past a statue holding the
ring. In this game, too, Philip won easily, not because the
others were cheating and letting him win, but because riding,
hunting, and spear throwing were sports he had practiced
since early childhood with the earnest endeavor of becoming
a champion. The only man who could beat him was the
Cardinal Infante Ferdinand, but a high Prince of the Church
could not ride in a public tourney, and so the young man had
to sit gloomily in the company of prelates and priests and
hope that the Count-Duke would make true his promise and
send him to Flanders at the head of an army. Although the
King won all the prizes, Olivares distinguished himself by
finishing second.

"Isn't the Count-Duke marvelous," Isabel said to Carlos.
"He is old and heavy and overloaded with work, and yet he
performs like a young man. How is it that you are not riding
in the tourney?"

"I hate sweating for the benefit of the public. Do you not
see the ridiculous emptiness of these games? If the King is
such a good shot and swordsman, why doesn't he lead his
troops in the field? We need military victories, not play
victories. There go the men who ruin Spain, while Richelieu
leads France to greatness."

"Why are you here, if you don't like it?" Isabel asked
acidly.

By now people were shouting and laughing and talking and
cheering, and no one watched them anymore. For all conver-
sational purposes they were as alone as if they had been on a
deserted island.

"Listen to me," Carlos said. "You and your brother think
that the Count-Duke will remain in power forever. Many
other *letrados* make the same mistake, although some, like
Quevedo, see the truth and try to warn the people. The
country is boiling over with discontent. Mark my word,
before long we will be fighting in Catalonia, because the
French are planning most effectively to take that province
away from us. And in Portugal there is a strong group trying
to talk the Duke of Braganza into leaving Spain and declaring

himself King of Portugal. That may take years, but I tell you it will come. I myself am in close touch with the Duke of Medina Sidonia. He is as unhappy about the situation as I am. My family owns almost as much land as the Guzmáns, and we were promised a duchy by Philip III for the great services my family has rendered to the Spanish monarchs since the time of the Catholic Kings. We are discontent, I tell you. We are discontent. You know that Medina Sidonia is the head of the Guzmáns, but the Count-Duke has tried repeatedly to accumulate greater wealth and prestige in the hands of the younger branch of the family, which is why he chose a member of that branch as a husband for his daughter, the one who died in childbirth. He made that son-in-law a duke. The Duke of Medina de las Torres. Ha! What a fraud. I told you before, there is not a true Grandee left at Court; sooner or later the Count-Duke will be defeated, and we will take over. By marrying me, you will be in the right camp. By becoming the King's harlot, you will end up in a convent, and by marrying one of Olivares's creatures—in case you had considered that—you will be choosing misery and shame, for when he goes, none of his creatures will remain."

He had spoken in a quiet passionless voice, convinced of the truth of his ideas—preposterous though they sounded. If there had not been his uncanny glance, Isabel might have thought him reasonable, if slightly eccentric. It was not his fault, she told herself, if his eyes had heavy lids without lashes, thus resembling those of a reptile; it was not his fault if he had a small mouth, although the ugly twist to it was of his own making, and it was not his fault if his chin was pointed and long. After all, the King had an ugly face, with a chin much worse than Queras's and with a large, flat, loosely dangling lower lip. No, it was not his lack of handsome features, it was something else that made Carlos repugnant. She had thought Philip physically repulsive, but after letting him kiss her, she had come to like him. Such a change of attitude would not be possible with Queras. There was something dangerous about him, and whereas once she had thought she would rather be alone with him than with Philip, she was now convinced of the contrary.

"I still do not understand why you want to marry me," she said to him. "Why do you want to save me?"

"You want me to lay my cards on the table? Well then. You, your brother, and your cousin are the only heirs to the Valderocas wealth. When you marry a Grandee, you will be expected to bring a very large dowry. Combined with the Queras wealth, of which I am the only heir, it would make us easily one of the richest couples in Spain."

"Is there not a Grandee's daughter you could marry?" she inquired. "There must be someone besides me."

"The Grandees who have pretty daughters also have many other children which decreases the daughter's share of the inheritance. Furthermore, a Grandee does not have to pay the high price of admission to our class. A son of a Grandee is no more than a normal match for the daughter of a Grandee. You are low-born, not even the daughter of an *hidalgo*. By marrying me, you would become a Countess and, as soon as Olivares is gone, a Duchess."

"Oh?" she said. "Is a duchy what Her Majesty promised you in exchange for Olivares's head?" He gave his mouth the usual ugly twist but refused her the satisfaction of answering her remark.

"It is unfortunate, to say the least, that I should have to talk to you at all," he said, "and highly improper, too. It is not up to a young woman to decide whom she wants to marry, but since your brother entertains that crazy notion . . ."

"Leave Pedro out of it," she said harshly. "My father was of the same opinion. Why do you think I am not married? Even when my parents were alive, I had the right to make my own choice. Much more so now. And that choice does not happen to fall on you." In her mind she added that she would rather be the Count-Duke's whore than Carlos's wife, but knowing his hatred for Olivares, she kept silent. Then she had another idea.

"You should not be offended that I refuse," she said. "It cannot hurt you, since you are not in love with me. Why don't you marry a woman with whom you are in love?"

"There is no woman I am in love with," he said coolly.

"And how do you expect to find one who will love you?"

"I do not."

"Then why marry at all?"

He gave her a strange discomforting look, and she did not know what to make of him. The mere idea of being married to him made her shudder.

The cane tourney was followed by a bullfight. Several bulls were let simultaneously into the arena to be encountered there by cavaliers on horseback with lances. Each fighter had twelve attendants on foot armed with swords who actually killed the animals after their masters had made an impressive show of their courage. There was sudden quiet, because the spectacle of death gripped the Spaniards more than the equestrian derring-do of their monarch. Philip himself, almost a year ago today, had shown his own enthusiasm for the art by killing a dangerous unmanageable bull with one masterly shot from his seat in the balcony of the Plaza Mayor. Bullfights were held three times a year at the Plaza Mayor, but this was the first such spectacle in the court of the Buen Retiro, and the fighters were anxious to please the high-born spectators and make this the most memorable event of the day.

After the first batch of bulls had been killed in the allotted time, the arena was cleared of men and carcasses, new sand was thrown to cover the traces of blood, and the drums and clarions announced a special attraction. Into the hushed silence walked a young Moor, a handsome lad in a brilliant red and silver livery shining in the sun. He slowly turned and bowed in all directions. Then he knelt in the center of the arena, holding a long spear firmly in his hands, and waited for the bull, alone, without any helpers.

When the animal came charging in, a formidable mass of black fury, a gasp went through the crowd, but the Moor did not budge; he knelt sturdily, holding up his spear toward the bull, piercing the animal so skillfully through the chest that the weapon was pushed by the animal's own weight through its body and came out in the back. When everyone realized that the Moor was unharmed and the bull dead, there was no end to the shouting, clapping, laughing, and olés. No one had ever seen anything like it. The crowds chanted:

*El rey de los Moros*
*El rey de los toros*

and many of the common folk, the footmen, and servants, jumped into the arena to carry the young matador on their shoulders.

"Excellent, really excellent," Carlos said softly. Isabel was surprised that he had been gripped by the spectacle just like the others.

"I didn't think you'd like bullfights," she said to him, a faint trace of annoyance in her voice.

"I would not know why," he answered. "I am as Spanish as anyone else around here, I wager you, and perhaps more so."

Isabel made a grimace and wished she did not have to talk

to Carlos anymore, unless she could call him by the satirist
Quevedo's favorite derogatory term: obnoxious whoreson.
But, of course, Carlos was unruffled. She could not really do
anything to hurt him, unless she could find some weakness.
So far she had discovered none, unless it was his temporary
poverty, and even that she was not sure was true. He might
simply be as stingy as his father and only pretend to be in
reduced circumstances.

"A few years ago, I saw a bullfight at Valladolid in a most
interesting arena," Carlos said casually. "It has a trap door
which can be opened when a bull gets too dangerous, and
when the animal rushes through that door, it falls onto a
lubricated wooden slide board and slides into the river where
the fight continues. Some fighters stand on barges and throw
spears; others—courageous swimmers—fight with swords."

"How perfectly horrible."

"Horrible? It was the most sensational fight I ever saw,
apart from today's performance. That young man was extraordinary. What courage! What grace! Would you like to
meet him?"

"Do you know him?"

"No, but I intend to. I will become his patron."

"Perhaps he already has a patron," Isabel said. "You make
a habit of claiming people for yourself."

"I make a habit of getting what I want."

"Well, not from me," she said.

He gave her a piercing look. "I will, especially since I am
patient and have plenty of time. A year, two, three, if
necessary. I will always be around, watching, waiting . . ."

"I might marry someone else, you know."

"I will see to it that you do not. But I don't think that will
become necessary. You do not seem anxious to find a
husband."

"Well I might give myself to the Count-Duke or to the
King."

His sneer intensified. "Don't be vulgar. Let us talk of
something else, since we cannot agree on bullfighting. What
did you think of Galileo Galilei? Do you really understand
what he is saying?"

She was startled. "Who told you I was reading Galileo?"

"Your cousin did. Do not look frightened. I approve.
Astronomy is becoming rather fashionable."

Pepita! He was talking to Pepita! So that is who had told

him about the King's gift. When did he see Pepita? This was grave; this was dangerous. She had to tell Pedro.

"Women are not supposed to have brains," he continued, "nor aspire to any kind of education. But I, on the contrary, think that it is an asset. If you marry me, I would encourage you to continue your studies, and if you wished, we could play host to the most brilliant writers and philosophers of Spain. Does that appeal to you?"

"Your Lordship, do you not see that I can have all these things without becoming your wife?" She was growing impatient with him. Was this his way of courting her? Promising intellectual companionship? Making it clear to her that he would not treat her as a piece of chattel—as by law he could—but as an intelligent human being? His words sounded reasonable, but his features remained ugly. His eyes always appeared to be half-closed and his head thrown back so that he seemed to look down his straight thin nose. But, no matter where he looked, his glance remained cold, excluding any possibility of friendship or mutual trust.

The attractions in the arena were over, and the crowds rose and started to move out of the rows to walk about the gardens and toward the theater lake, admiring, praising, and speculating as to the expenses involved in the creation of the palace. Anxious to get away from her escort, Isabel cast furtive glances at the people around her, but just as she spotted Velázquez, Quevedo, and her brother, she heard Carlos's voice introducing a friend of his, the Count of Villaquemada. When she heard his name, and even before her eyes had focused on the broad sallow face with the black stiletto beard and bushy black hair, the memory of a street urchin slain in fury because of a stink egg struck her with the force of lightning, and she could barely keep herself from recoiling when the Count swept off his hat and bowed to her. Murderer, she thought when she curtsied, murderer, but what she saw was a bland fusion of mediocre features, fat jowls, a moderately fleshy nose, indifferent dullish brown eyes, thin colorless lips, nothing to indicate that here was a killer, a torturer, who regularly abused his servants and kept his wife locked up in a country estate far from Madrid.

"So this is the intended Lady de Queras," Villaquemada said with a meaningful glance at Carlos. "Congratulations."

"Not yet, *hombre*, not yet," Carlos said quickly. "I have not even started to court her according to the rules."

"Sorry, my misunderstanding. Well, nevertheless, count me as your friend," Villaquemada said to Isabel.

"And he can be a powerful friend, indeed," Carlos added.

Isabel said nothing. Her face remained politely immobile, an expression taking all her willpower, because despite her progress in the necessary art of dissimulation, she was afraid of betraying her distaste for the company of so brutal a knave.

"If there is one thing I appreciate, it is a woman who keeps her mouth shut when men are talking," Villaquemada said with a rakish blink. "It is the only characteristic I have in common with our illustrious Count-Duke, who even now seems to expect us to queue with the rest of his worshippers. What do you say, Carlos, shall we oblige him?" He pointed with his head slightly in the direction behind Isabel. When she turned around, she saw a reception line forming before a beaming Olivares, who stood next to his wife and looked utterly delighted by the compliments coming from the arbiters of Madrid's society.

"Yes, please let us join them," Isabel suggested.

"Not I," said Carlos. "I disapprove of every *maravedí* spent on this folly. You two may go if you wish."

"Did you think I was serious?" Villaquemada asked in a voice vibrating from suppressed laughter. *"Válgame Dios,* I cannot stand the man, smug and proud while secretly killing the flower of our royal manhood."

"What do you mean?" Queras asked quickly. "What has happened?"

"Haven't you heard? He will send the Cardinal Infante abroad at the head of fourteen thousand men. More than one of us suspects that he will have him killed in battle, not like King David for the love of a woman, but for the love of a man."

"I do not understand," Carlos said.

"He loves the King," Villaquemada explained. "He wants to dominate him completely; he cannot stand a rival. First he poisoned the Infante, now he wants to eliminate the Cardinal Infante. It would not surprise me if he even tried to poison the Queen."

Carlos blanched. "Is that your own speculation?" he asked almost inaudibly.

"No, many others think as I do."

Isabel had heard enough. She did not believe one word.

She had listened to enough gossip to know that this particular brand of viciousness was born of ill will and envy. But while she still wondered how she could shake her unwelcome suitors, Villaquemada yawned.

"I find this place depressing. May I invite you to share my coach for a leisurely promenade in the Prado?"

"With pleasure," Carlos accepted and held out his hand to Isabel.

She curtsied formally. "Your invitation honors me," she mumbled. "I am afraid, though, I have a previous engagement." It was the very least she could say, when, according to etiquette, an overwhelming statement of deep gratitude was in order.

"You do not know what you are saying, Doña Isabel," Carlos said. "Your engagement would have to be with someone nobler than we are, and I really do not see whom that could be."

"Oh, do you not?" Isabel retorted with a sly smile, tilting the corners of her mouth. "What about His Majesty, would you consider him noble enough?" And she swirled around and left before they had time to recover from their surprise.

# 34.

"What was that?" Villaquemada asked. "How can she have an engagement with Philip—at this time of day?" He looked at Carlos accusingly. "I thought you were about to sign the marriage contract. How much longer are you going to dawdle? She will escape you in the end."

"She will not. Of course, she has no engagement with the King. She is afraid of me, she does not understand me. She does not know what I want."

"Can you blame her for that? If you want your plans to succeed, you must show more ardor. Remember what is at stake. She is by far your best choice."

His words had a strange effect on Carlos.

"Enrique, do you think our plans will work?" he asked with an urgency as if his life depended on the answer.

"You know they will, eventually. It may take a few years,

but we have time. You need more money. So you will have to
escort my lady Valderocas to the ball. How much does it cost
nowadays?"

"What?"

"*Galantear en palacio.*"

"I will not make such a fool of myself."

"If you must, you must. I will advance you the funds if
necessary."

# 35.

In the meantime, Isabel had joined Pedro just before he
reached the Olivares couple, and this time both the Count-
Duke and Doña Inés smiled warmly when she curtsied to
them.

"We hope to have the pleasure of seeing you at the ball
tonight," the Countess said.

"I have good news for you, Pedro. Present yourself at my
audience chamber tomorrow at eleven," Olivares said.

As soon as they were a few steps away, Isabel repeated to
Pedro every word of her conversation with Carlos and
Villaquemada, but what she considered the worst she kept for
last.

"Imagine Pepita tattling to Carlos! When does she see
him?"

"The sneaky whoreson," Pedro muttered. "Is he courting
her, too?"

"Well, he calculates that each one of us is worth one-third
of our combined wealth. Perhaps he thinks if he cannot marry
me, he can marry her."

"I have a mind to send both of you back to Toledo," Pedro
said. "That would solve a good many problems, especially
since I expect to be gone during the coming year."

"Gone where?"

"Olivares will send me to Amsterdam, to Salonica, and to
Venice, and later on perhaps to Oran. Unless you want to live
in a convent until my return, you will have to stay with Uncle
Jaime."

"Why can I not stay in Madrid? There are many unmarried

society women at Court," Isabel said. "I do not want to leave Madrid."

"Why not? You cannot help me when I am not here. On the contrary, it would lower your value if you stayed alone. Your reputation must remain spotless, because I am responsible for it. We cannot afford to have you gossipped about. It is too dangerous. On one side Queras and the barbarous Villaquemada, on the other, the King. What would you do if he came to visit you at night during my absence? Throw him out and create a scandal? Or admit him and ruin yourself?"

His words fell on her like a hail of stones, each new one more painful than the last. She did not want to leave Madrid; she wanted, above all, to continue her meetings with Rafael.

"When do you think you will leave?" she asked quietly.

"For abroad? I think early next spring."

She gave a sigh of relief. This was a reprieve, for spring was far away; they were only in October. Anything could happen before spring.

"But there is something else," Pedro continued, "something which makes it imperative for me to leave for Seville in a few days. I have some merchandise that must be shipped as soon as possible. It would be most convenient if you could move to Toledo at the same time. That would explain why we leave Madrid with many coaches and a train of servants."

"But I do not want to leave," Isabel rebelled. "Not now, not right away, please, Pedro."

His eyes narrowed. "You must! I need your help with this particular merchandise . . . Sarita."

He pronounced the diminutive of her Hebrew name in a barely audible voice, but its effect was miraculous. A wave of understanding, love, and compassion welled up from the bottom of her heart and swept away her fear and bitterness. This was a matter of survival, this was her work, the fight against the Inquisition, the deadly game in which she had to win or lose her life.

"All right," she said. "We will move whenever you say."

"It is not forever," Pedro said. "We will always come back here."

"*Sólo Madrid es Corte,*" Isabel said, repeating a popular expression.

"Yes, and that makes it the most important place for us. Besides, it may solve your problem with Carlos. He might find another victim, if you disappear for a while."

"I doubt that. He has his mind firmly set upon our money. But it would cool off Philip."

"So he does need cooling off?"

"I am afraid so." She finally told him about her meeting with Philip. "But it was harmless," she concluded, "just a kiss."

"I suppose you know how to shift for yourself," Pedro said. "But Pepita worries me. That lady has gone too far . . ."

"There she comes now," Isabel said.

Indeed, Pepita was hurrying toward them lifting her skirt in front of her, an impish smile dancing all over her pretty face, her complicated hairdo coming apart at the ends, the very picture of a carefree soul.

No sooner were they sitting in their coach and rolling back toward the city, than both Pedro and Isabel interrogated their cousin sternly about her talks with Carlos. Her innocence was disarming.

"Really, I think you are doing him an injustice," she said. "He is shy, he is in love with Isabel, he is afraid she will reject him because he is not handsome enough and because he cannot court her with as much flamboyance as he thinks she deserves. He also fears that she might be attracted to His Majesty, and how can he compete with a man who sends her Tiziano drawings."

"What a fib! I never thought Carlos could act," Isabel exclaimed. "How can you believe such flimflam, Pepita?"

"You once said that Felipe de Habsburg was a kind man," Pepita retorted. "I have as much right to claim that Carlos de Queras is kind. He has never shown me but kindness, and he brings presents to Pasquito."

"He what?" Pedro interrupted aghast. "That is preposterous. Is he bribing our servants?"

"Oh no," Pepita said, "nothing like that. I think he likes him. He brings him little things, like a bullfighter's cape, or the statue of a bull, things like that, and he talks to him about bullfighting. He is quite different when he talks to the boy. He asked me once whether we would sell him, but, of course, I said no."

"When does he come?" Pedro asked. "I thought he was courting Isabel, yet she does not know of these visits."

"Well he came only four or five times, and really with dozens of people calling on us every day, I never thought twice about it."

Pepita's answer made sense. Valderocas House had become a magnet drawing Court idlers. There was a steady stream of visitors. They came to sit in the cool shade of the patio, to drink a glass of almond water or a cup of chocolate, and to exchange the latest news of the day. Often several visitors lingered around together, and whoever was home, Pedro, or Isabel, or Pepita would act as host. The task most often fell to Pepita. In Madrid this was the normal way of passing the days. What was not normal was Carlos's bringing presents to one of their Moorish slaves.

"Why would he want to buy the boy?" Isabel mused. "Does he want to have him trained as a bullfighter?"

"That does it!" Pedro said. "You are moving back to Toledo a week from now. You can start packing your things."

"Oh, and what about you?" Pepita asked.

"I will go to Seville on business, and next year I am going to be traveling abroad."

"You want to be free to court Manuela Caietano," Pepita said in a toneless voice. "I knew it all the time. You are in love with Manuela, do not deny it."

Surprised, Isabel looked from one to the other. She had been so absorbed by her own problems, above all by her constant thoughts of Rafael, that she had apparently missed some important activities around her.

"I am not in love with Manuela," Pedro said. "Who put that notion into your head?"

"I saw you with her at the promenade of the Prado; you were walking up and down and talking to her."

Pedro shrugged his shoulders, "You are silly. Manuela had a message for me from her brother Diego who was supposed to meet me there."

"Is that true?" Pepita asked softly. "You are not in love with her?"

"Of course not. If I ever fall in love with anyone but you, I will tell you. In the meanwhile, I want you to go live at Uncle Jaime's, because I want you to be well protected while I am gone."

"Oh, Pedro," Pepita said and Isabel could hear the unspoken question: When are you going to marry me?

But Pedro was not anxious to marry.

# 36.

The Palace of the Buen Retiro was still unfinished and unfurnished; even the doors had not yet been installed. Invited to roam through the long narrow halls, some of the guests walked up and down the marble staircases, and over the terraces into the newly planted gardens. But most of them stayed in the great ballroom.

For two hours, Isabel had not stopped dancing. Her partners had included the Count-Duke, the Duke of Medina de las Torres, Don Luís de Haro, the Count of Monterrey, the infamous Protonotario of Aragon, who in Isabel's mind was firmly etched as the man whose head had been deloused by the Abbess of San Plácido and who had subsequently been protected from the Inquisition by Olivares, and a score of others. None of the popular Court dances allowed a couple to exchange more than a few words, be it the *almaña,* the *gallarda,* the *pavanilla,* the *pie de gibado,* the *Rey Don Alonso,* or the *galería de amor.* All of them required a precise knowledge of many graceful steps, curtsies, and bows; indeed, every movement was prescribed, and a dancer did not come closer than a yard to his leading lady. Nevertheless, when during one of the figures the King was her partner, he conveyed the reproach that she was not keeping her part of the bargain. His face never showed any emotion in public. He had learned to hide his passion behind a mask of indifference, and his lips hardly moved when he talked to her. But when she sank into her final curtsy, he held out his hand and completely against Court ceremonial led her out onto a terrace. Other couples discreetly vanished when they saw who was coming.

"You have been avoiding me, Isabel. How can you be so cruel? You know I am a prisoner of the Old Burgundian Court ceremonial. I am not half as free as my brother-in-law Louis of France and not a tenth as free as my sometime friend Charles of England. Yet, I have made a greater effort than they to give the people at my Court an amount of licence impossible anywhere else. As a young woman, you should be the first to appreciate how much I have liberated you from the censorship of former times. You can move about freely, you can exchange pleasantries with gallants, and you can express your feelings, whereas I must be the incarnation of dignity. I daresay no one ever heard me laugh in public, since royal etiquette allows me to show neither joy nor sorrow. Must I be punished too by eternal solitude? I would like to court you, Isabel; I would like to spoil you; I would like to flaunt my love for you in the face of the world. Would that make me a worthier man in your eyes?"

"Sire, of course not. You must not speak to me like this. We all admire you; we all love you."

"That is not the kind of love I am yearning for." He sighed. "I was thinking of you during the games today. I won them all for you. You know that, do you not?"

Isabel nodded, and out of a pocket in her farthingale, she pulled the blue and white scarf and started to play with it.

"Why do you not wear it tonight?" he asked.

"I would not dare. But as you see, I still have it, and I wore it to the tournament." She hesitated a moment, "Your Majesty, there is something I want to tell you . . ."

"Yes?" Immediately his blue eyes looked alert.

"I will be leaving Madrid soon."

"Why? Where are you going?"

"Back to Toledo."

"Why?" he repeated. "Why? Has anything unpleasant happened to you?"

"No, I want to think. Madrid is so busy. I am not myself anymore. I hardly have time to open a book."

"So you will enter a convent, after all," Philip said dully.

"No, I will not. As a matter of fact, I will come back to Madrid, after I have found the answers I am seeking."

"Come with me tonight," he whispered. "I will give you all the answers. I want you, Isabel, I want you . . ." Rafael had said these same words, and she had heard him and answered his desire, but for a fleeting moment she wished she had never met him. Philip's eyes were pleading and honest, and she thought that if she did not love Rafael so exclusively, she would give in to Philip and perhaps she would become the kind of mistress kings worshipped and listened to. She was prettier and a hundred times smarter than any courtesan, and younger than the Queen.

"I will not leave until you promise to meet me in private," he said.

"I could play false," she pointed out. "I could accept an assignation and then not come. . . ."

"If you do that to me, I will have you dragged to the Alcázar in my speediest carriage, and I will give the lampoon writers enough material for the next ten years," Philip said with a deep tone of anger running through his voice. "But tell me," he added in a more concerned tone, "who is bothering you? Are you afraid of me? Say yes, and I will not speak to you anymore, not single you out anymore, just adore you from afar. Do not go away because of me."

Impulsively, she reached out and touched his hand, saying softly, "Felipe . . ." then realizing she was committing the lese majesty of touching the royal person, she pulled back her hand and looked at him timidly.

Immediately, he caught her hand and brought it slowly to his lips.

"Isabel, is there hope for me?"

"For Your Majesty? I think not. For Felipe? Perhaps . . . I do not know. I really do not know. Will you let me go to live at my uncle's house at Toledo for a year or so?"

"To forget me and come back married?"

"If I promise not to marry or to enter a convent, will you let me go?" She made it deliberately sound as if her departure actually depended on Philip's approval, because she felt her best weapon was an appeal to his basic goodness.

"Let me have just one hour alone with you," he pressed, "and you will change your mind. I will make you very happy, I warrant you. I will not hurt you. I beg you, Isabel."

"That is exactly what I am afraid of, Sire, that I will change my mind. What if I should fall in love with you?"

"Nothing would please me more."

"Until you tired of me," she said with a pout. She folded the pretty square of lace and put it back in her pocket. "No, I think it is far better if I do not see you anymore before I leave Madrid, unless . . ."

"Unless what?"

She turned her head aside to avoid his eyes, but he cupped his hand under her chin and forced her to look at him.

"You may regret having given me the drawing," she said. "You may feel I do not deserve it. It hangs in my room. I look at it every morning when I get up, and I have not even thanked you for it."

"Take it with you to Toledo then," he said. "I never expect payments for the presents I give. I wish you a good trip."

Now I have insulted him, she thought frantically, but she curtsied deeply to hide her confusion.

He left the terrace abruptly to join the dancers in the gallery and at the door almost collided with the Count-Duke.

"Doña Isabel," Olivares exclaimed with a big smile, "what are you doing out here?" Then as he stood next to her, he whispered, "The Countess thought you might be in trouble."

"Oh, Your Excellency, I may well be. I am afraid I have offended His Majesty."

"No pretty wench ever offended His Majesty, but what happened?"

"I told him I was leaving for Toledo, and I refused his advances too clumsily."

"You could not be clumsy if you tried, and His Majesty will know how to console himself, I warrant you. Are you going to miss Madrid?"

"I am going to miss you," she said.

"Oh, not content with breaking your sovereign's heart, you now make a grab for mine?"

"Do not tease me. I watched you at the tournament. You were splendid."

"Thank you, dear. I approve of your going to Toledo. I think it will be best for you and for us if you stayed with your uncle while Don Pedro travels."

"Why for you?"

"If I send your brother on a mission, the Countess and I would feel morally responsible if anything happened to you during his absence. I will be relieved to know you are safely out of reach of a certain party."

"Thank you, Your Excellency."

"I noticed this morning that you were escorted by his Lordship the Count of Villaquemada. Since when does he figure among your friends?" His voice was beautiful and caressing as always; Isabel could not discern any more than polite curiosity.

"Don Carlos de Queras introduced him to me. I cannot say I was pleased about it."

"Oh, but you are wrong there. The Count of Villaquemada is not a man to be underestimated. He is the devil's advocate in person, a man to be watched. What did he talk about?"

Suddenly Isabel had the impression that this subject was the real reason for the Count-Duke's conversation with her, that he was trying to use her as if she were his spy, a part she was only too happy to play.

"He is full of vicious gossip," she said, boldly cutting through all pretenses, "and he acts as if he had a trustworthy informer inside the palace."

Olivares gave her a sharp glance. His onyx eyes sparkled in the shine of the torchlights, and his darkly handsome face showed a mixture of cunning and irony. "Never mind the gossip, I have heard the worst. What interests me are his actions. Has he traveled recently? He owns land in Aragon; has he been there?"

"That I do not know. But Carlos de Queras has been traveling. He mentioned that he is in contact with the Duke of Medina Sidonia. I think he is the one who intrigues."

"Yes, Queras fancies himself in the role of my worst enemy," Olivares said pensively. "It would greatly oblige me if you kept up your friendship with him. I do not want him to see us together, so we will return to the ballroom by separate ways. Also, I would not want to spoil my reputation as the great Spanish misogynist. Now, do not misunderstand me," he said when he saw a little smile pulling at Isabel's lips, "I really think women are incapable of rational thinking and their political opinions are not worth a fig. Normally, I would not dream of trusting a woman to help me. However, there comes a moment when an exception is needed to confirm a rule. So if during your brother's absence and while you are at Toledo, you should have any traffic with Carlos or his precious friend, I would be happy to receive a word from you. No one will believe you, if you tried to tell anyone that I asked you to be interested in politics, but it does seem to be a good topic for you and Carlos to talk about. Do you understand me?"

"I think I do."

"Good. Perhaps you shall marry Carlos, after all."

"No, not that."

"Think of yourself behind a puppet stage where I pull all the strings. There, I give you the little future Grandee, for you to manipulate as you see fit." He took both her hands and pressed them briefly, before turning around and walking down a few steps into the garden.

Isabel went back to the ballroom.

# 37.

It was no use trying to be brave about it, she could not hide it from him as she had wanted to. The minute she came through the door her face betrayed her, and her eyes filled with tears as she threw herself into his arms.

"What is it, my love? Don't cry. What happened?"

But she could not speak. She had controlled herself too much since Pedro first told her that she would move to Toledo; she had accumulated her anguish to a point where it was spilling over. He sat down and pulled her down on his knees, holding her like a child and rocking her soothingly.

"You cannot come anymore?" he asked gently. "Is that it?"

She nodded. "Oh Rafael, Rafael, why can we not elope? Let us go away from here. I want to be your wife. I want to have your children. You are more important to me than anyone. How can I bear being separated from you?"

"You will bear it, and I will bear it," he said quietly. "We are not ordinary people, you and I, we will always belong to each other. But tell me what happened. Are you going to be married?"

"Rafael! I am never going to marry. I belong to you. I have to stay in Toledo for a year with Uncle Jaime, because Pedro will be traveling again, and he will not leave Pepita and me alone at Madrid."

"Is that all?" Rafael said with a deep breath that changed into a grin as he exhaled. "A year at Toledo? I expected worse. A year is nothing."

"Nothing?"

"Isabel, you have to learn that there are several ways of looking at a situation. We meet here once or twice a week for a total of four hours at the most. Suppose you stayed away a little more than a year, sixty weeks for instance, that would make it two hundred forty hours, an amount of time that could be squeezed into ten days. That is nothing to be hysterical about."

She looked at him in amazement.

"And what about the rest of the time? I shall miss you."

"I shall miss you, too. But we knew that this could not last forever. Be happy that we have been able to know each other so well. Be sensible."

Today she was not ready to be sensible about anything. Getting up from his lap, she spoke sharply. "Been able to know each other, you say. Rafael Cortes, I still do not know the first thing about you. You never let me share your thoughts. I do not even know what your real goal is. You never confide in me!"

"And what about you? Do you confide in me anything more precious than stale palace gossip? Do you share your thoughts with me?"

"Why should I, pray? A thought for a thought."

"You love me," he said quietly, "but you do not trust me, do you?"

"What about you, do you trust me?" she asked in quick defiance.

"Only to a certain extent."

"And why is that?"

"Because you still want me to leave the order and marry you. But I can never do that; I am married to my work."

"Yes, to Santa Maria," Isabel snapped with flashing eyes, and before she realized what she was saying, she added heresy to blasphemy. "Why don't you go to bed with her?" she hissed. "There is a thought for you!"

In a trice he was beside her, clapping his hand over her mouth and shaking her harshly. "You don't know what you are saying."

But she was exhausted and angry. Her whole life consisted of dissimulation. Something within her cried to be let out and for once she was not going to suppress it.

"I do know what I am saying. And I will not take it back. What are you going to do about it, Fray Rafael? Make me wear a sanbenito?"

His face went perfectly still and white, and they both stood tensely waiting, like two wild animals, neither daring to be the first one to attack.

Finally, he turned away.

"Leave me alone," he said. "Go now, and don't come back."

Don't come back. That was all she heard. Don't come back. She took a step forward, her hands went up in the air trying to find some support, but there was none, and she fell into darkness.

Her head still spun when she awoke to find Rafael bending over her.

"Isabel, Isabel, are you all right?" he asked anxiously.

"I feel sick," she replied slowly, for her tongue could barely move. "What happened?"

"You fainted, darling. Here, you were laced too tightly."

She was lying on the bed, and he had opened her dress and was unhooking the bodice. She remembered then, and tried to sit up, but once more she felt nauseated and had to lie down.

"Here, drink some wine; it will make you feel better."

His concern, his gentleness, his graceful movements, it was all too much to leave or to forget, and tears were streaming down her temples and into her hair.

"You foolish girl," he said. "You are trying so hard to understand where wiser men have failed. Come now, drink some wine."

Obediently, she raised her head and he brought the glass to her lips.

"Why did you try to hurt me?" he asked her.

She pressed her lips together and her mouth became a thin hard line, very much like Pedro's when he was angry.

"I think you still do not understand," he said and shook his head. "It is not your blasphemy that hurt me, it is your lack of trust. Do you think I would ever betray you?"

"Do you not think heretics should be punished?" she asked. "As a friar who walked in the procession of the green cross, are you not sworn to purify the faith?"

"What does a lover's quarrel have to do with the faith?" he asked her. "Go ahead, say your litany of profanities, if it makes you feel better. There is only one thing I want you to promise me."

"What is that?"

"That you will never lose control of yourself in front of anyone else. I will not have a minute's peace of mind if I have to suspect that you may curse the saints because something displeases you. I want you to swear."

"Do not ask me to swear by anything. I do not believe in elaborate oaths. If you ever hear me use one, you can be certain I am telling a lie. The bigger the oath, the bigger the lie!"

"Just promise me then that you will watch your tongue and censor your speech."

"I promise," she said.

He bent over her to place a kiss on her forehead, on the tip of her nose, and then as his lips touched hers, her arms went around his neck and she pulled him down, and the world was shut out.

She was to meet him once more before her departure, but on that same morning, a letter was delivered to her from one Francisco Molina. When she tore it open, there was a harmless note from a perfume dealer saying that the Italian merchandise she had ordered had not yet arrived, but that he was going personally to Rome and would bring her back what she wanted. He had to leave immediately and would inform her later of his return.

It was possible that he was being sent to Rome, she thought, and by coincidence it had happened now. But, she was more inclined to believe that he wanted to spare her the difficult moment of separation; and she doubted and fretted while preparing for her trip to Toledo.

# 38.

They went with a train of eight coaches this time, each drawn by six horses. That was an expensive way of traveling and one most people tried to avoid by using mules once they had left the city. Pedro, however, was anxious to conform to the terms of the royal pragmatica of 1628 that forbade the use of mules for coaches in order to stimulate Spanish horse breeding. His cargo was illegal enough. In the disguise of servants, he brought a dozen men and women whose defiance of official dogma had brought them into the dungeons of the Inquisition.

Someone, Pedro knew not who—perhaps that mysterious leader of Marranos—had apparently convinced Olivares that it would be preferable if these New Christians were permitted to escape to Amsterdam. Olivares, in turn, had pressured Sotomayor into handing over the files on these persons. From the dungeons of Toledo, where they had been held *sin comunicacion* since the time of their arrest, they had been brought to Madrid. After sparing no effort to convince the prisoners that he honestly intended to change the attitude of Spain toward the fate of the Marranos, Olivares had charged Pedro Valderocas with the task of assuring safe-conduct to these persons from Madrid to Seville where they were to embark on a Valderocas galleon officially bound for Mexico.

After one month in the secret prison, the refugees, seven men and five women, traveled in complete silence. One of the women was young, about Isabel's age, and she carried in her arms a tiny infant whom she never put down for a minute, unless it was into the arms of her husband.

Toward night, when they stopped in an open field, the young woman chose a spot removed from the others to prepare a place to lie down for herself and her child. Isabel walked over to help her.

"Let me hold your baby, while you get ready. It will be easier for you."

The girl shook her head and clutched the child even closer to her bosom, but Isabel got a brief look at the infant's face, and what she saw frightened her. He looked grotesquely shrunken and old, unlike any infant she had ever seen.

The men were busy with the horses, and Pepita was chatting with Teresa, so Isabel went to the coach containing the food and prepared a tray with bread, fresh grapes, cheese, and chocolate. Then, thinking of the baby, she took a bowl and soaked a few biscuits in water. She took the tray to the young mother and sat down next to her.

"Do not be afraid of me. I know who you are," she said. "Don Pedro is my brother. He will take you to Amsterdam, and there nothing bad will happen anymore. You must keep strong for the voyage, and you must eat so you have milk for your baby."

The girl looked at her with enormous dark sad eyes and said nothing.

"Please, eat something," Isabel said.

The girl swallowed. She opened her mouth as if to speak, but no sound came out and she closed it again.

"Please, for your baby," Isabel said.

The girl swallowed again. "He is not my baby," she finally said in a toneless voice.

Isabel said nothing. For a while they sat side by side, the girl leaning her back against a rock, Isabel with her arms around her knees, both staring into the fast-approaching night. Then, after a long silence, the young woman began to talk, very softly, as if it were an old story half-forgotten and not a recent experience.

"The mother was lying there, on a heap of straw, in the dark, in the cold, with the naked child in her arms . . . Have mercy, God have mercy, she said all the time, God have mercy. She had . . ." the girl's voice broke, and she needed time before she could go on, "She had given birth down there, on the floor, in the dark, and they had left her the child, and he was still alive after four months. But she was very weak and afraid she would die. She had asked for an audience and begged to be removed to a more suitable cell, but they told her to discharge her conscience and save her soul. Save her soul, when all she thought was to save her baby."

Isabel listened in silence.

"I asked her if she could not invent a confession," the young woman continued, "but she did not know what she was accused of. You see, they never told her. I was put in with her. I do not know why. Perhaps they ran out of room. Before I came, she had not seen another human being, except for the warden who brought us the food and took out the slop-pail, and even me she could not see, only feel, because it was pitch dark most of the time, and I myself could only get a glimpse of her when the warden came."

"How long were you there?" Isabel asked.

"For about a month. She had no milk, and she was chewing the stale bread they gave us, and then she would put it in the baby's mouth so he could swallow, and it is a miracle how she kept him alive. But she had given up hope of ever getting out, and when the warden came and told me to get up and out, she wrapped the child in the old petticoat she used for his blanket, and she begged me to take him along, no matter where, just out of there. I carried him like a bundle under my arm. He weighs hardly anything, and he never cries. He is much too weak."

Isabel clenched her teeth to fight back her tears, but she kept seeing the woman lying weak and exhausted on the foul straw, her misery unspeakable, unthinkable . . . Did a man not have to be a devil to ignore her simple plea for better quarters, to tell her to save her soul when she begged for an audience? Who were the men responsible for such suffering? Who? Dominican friars, of course. Did Rafael know? He must know. Was he then a willing instrument of such organized terror? Could she still love him after hearing such a story?

"God chose you to save this little boy," Isabel said. "You must think of that now and eat and feed him well and take good care of him. Perhaps his mother, too, will get out one day, as you did."

"There is no God," the girl said, "or he would have heard the mother when she implored him for mercy."

"If there is no God, then you have no one to rely on but yourself," Isabel said. "If there is no God, then the religious fervor of Spain is nothing but human folly, a folly we must combat. If there is no God, He cannot be against us, and therefore we have a chance to win. You must help us, you and your husband, and your friends, and this little one when he grows up. Then, one day, there will be no more Inquisition. We must work together and we must conserve our strength, build up our strength. Therefore you must eat, for by accepting to be saved and by accepting to save this child, you have committed yourself to the cause of justice, to the cause of liberty. How can you help us if you let yourself and your child die of hunger?" Isabel had spoken firmly and for the first time, there seemed to be a bond between her and the girl.

"I do not understand you," the young woman said. "Why are you doing this for us? Why do you expose yourself to the danger of incurring the wrath of the Holy Office?"

"Because there are hundreds of people wasting away in dark holes like his mother, without hope; because there are thousands of others who live in eternal fear as you did; and because someone is needed to rally the oppressed and give them hope and strength. If the righteous do not stand up and fight, the wicked will exult forever."

"But I was told you are Old Christians," the girl said.

"So is Olivares, yet he saved you. What is your name?"

"Beatriz."

"And the baby's?"

"I do not know."

"Oh, but you must give him a name."

"You think so?"

"Absolutely. He is going to live. I know it."

"Let us try to feed him first. But he throws up everything containing milk," Beatriz said.

"I brought some soaked biscuits."

Beatriz placed a small amount of the mixture on her finger and pushed it into the tiny mouth. He swallowed. She repeated this, alternating with drops of water which she poured from a spoon into his tiny mouth.

Torchlights had been lit, and a campfire was burning. Against its flickering shine, they could see the dark silhouette of a woman coming toward them.

"That is my cousin," Isabel whispered. "She does not know anything; only Pedro and I do. She thinks you are a servant Pedro is taking to someone at Seville."

"*¡Hola! ¿Qué tal?* How is the baby doing? Can I help you with anything?" Pepita said gaily as she peered down at the infant who had fallen asleep following the last of his meal.

Again Beatriz clutched the little bundle closer in her arms, but her voice was remarkably controlled when she answered, "Thank you, everything is just fine. The fresh air seems to be very good for my son."

"What is his name?" Pepita asked.

Isabel looked anxiously at Beatriz and held her breath, but the girl hesitated only an imperceptible moment.

"Pedro," she said calmly.

"What a coincidence. It is the name I like best," Pepita said. "Well, if you do not need anything, I think I will walk around awhile. I am all stiff from sitting in the coach all day. I hate traveling. It is a real torture, don't you think?"

"My little Pedro loves it. The swaying motion of the coach puts him to sleep."

"Good night then. Sleep well," Pepita said and walked back to the campfire.

Soon the sound of guitars and singing drifted into the night. The real servants were having a good time, and the pretend ones had to keep up with them.

Two days later, they arrived at Toledo where Beatriz and her husband Duarte Perez were given quarters in the house of Pablo Raíz until the group left for Seville.

On the eve before their departure, Duarte Perez came to call on Isabel at Uncle Jaime's, and when he said he had to talk to her alone, she led him to the library and closed the door.

"I cannot thank you enough for what you have done for Beatriz," he said, as he took a flat box from his coat pocket. "I beg you most humbly to accept this token of my gratitude."

"It is beautiful," Isabel said when she opened the box and saw a flawless pearl necklace on a lining of dark blue velvet. "It is beautiful, but I cannot accept it. It is much too precious; you must give it to your wife."

"Beatriz has all the jewels she needs. You have given her something more valuable than this; you have given her hope and courage. It was hard for her to come back to Toledo. She was convinced at first that our freedom was a mistake, that we would be brought back to the dungeon. The first days when we were free I thought she would go mad, but that night in the field when I saw her let you hold the child, I knew the worst was over. You would offend me deeply if you refused my gift."

He looked at her, and she noticed for the first time that his eyes were dark and deep-set like Rafael's. But his face was rugged and square, a solid reliable face under a shock of prematurely gray, almost white hair. He was as tall as Rafael, but broad-shouldered and heavier. When she compared the two, she realized that Rafael had become the yardstick by which she tended to measure every man she met, and she was ashamed.

"Thank you, Don Duarte. I shall always treasure this gift. And I hope Beatriz will be happy at Amsterdam. My best wishes go with both of you and little Pedro."

"Pedro," he said, "I hope he grows up to become as courageous as the man for whom he was so quickly named. Both Beatriz and I admire your brother very much, and we shall endeavor to work for him in whatever way we can. Perhaps we shall see each other again one day."

"*Si Dios quiere,* if God wills it," Isabel said.

Duarte shook his head and a sadly amused smile ran along his lips. "Here is one heretic who is not a Judaizer," he said. "I am an atheist."

"Happily your wife shares your conviction," Isabel said. "Without counting on divine help, you will have to work that much harder for the welfare of your fellow human beings."

"And you," he asked, "when you help others as you are doing, do you count on divine help? Why do you expose yourself to danger? Does your God order you to do that?"

"I do not know," she said. "There is that innate feeling that to hurt people is evil, but to alleviate suffering is good."

"So, like Eve, you have eaten from the tree of knowledge of good and evil," Duarte said. "Have they not told you that this is the sure way to arouse your God's wrath?"

"But how can you be sure He does not exist?" Isabel asked. "How can you be sure you are right, and everyone else is wrong?"

"The same way you know that saving a heretic from the stake is good, when the whole world tells you that, on the contrary, burning him is most pleasing to God. But perhaps your God is different from their God. In this world there is a profusion of Gods: Jahweh, Christ, and Allah are the ones we know. But I am a seafaring merchant and have traveled to the Orient. There you have countries teeming with countless deities. Does not the mere fact that one has a choice indicate that all of them are man-made?"

"You are an interesting man, Don Duarte. It is comforting to know that the *conversos* are not the only ones who think."

He gave her a sharp look.

"Sorry to disappoint you again, but we are *conversos*, Marranos, if you wish."

She frowned. "I do not understand."

"It is very simple," he said. "Our ancestors were Jews. They converted and became New Christians. To me, Christian hypocrisy does not appeal, neither, however, does the bulk of Mosaic law."

"Then you will get into conflict everywhere," Isabel said, "even in Amsterdam. As you said yourself, there are many religions, the choice is yours. But nowhere will they tolerate a godless man. You must conform, at least outwardly, if you want any kind of security for Beatriz and yourself."

"Is that what you do? Conform outwardly? No, do not answer. I know you do, otherwise you could not live here. But are you happy that way? Has your God ever spoken to you? Do you know He exists anywhere but in your own mind? Is he a God of wrath? Then why does he not strike the wicked? Is he a God of compassion? Then why does he not hear the tortured victims of inquisitorial terror?"

He spoke in a low, urgent voice, and what he said made sense. It made far more sense than Rafael dedicating himself to the Dominican friars just because they were politically influential; it made more sense than Calderon's unquestioning faith in Roman Catholic doctrine; and it made more sense even than the stubborn adherence to snatches of her own ancestral religion, as practiced by Uncle Jaime, the Raízes, and the Caietanos.

Yet, Duarte admitted to being a Marrano. What did that make him? A Jewish atheist?

"Forgive me, Doña Isabel, for arguing with you. It was ill-bred and inconsiderate of me, when I should thank you on my knees for making Beatriz smile again."

"There is nothing to forgive," she said. "I only wish it were possible to discuss your ideas in public. You are a philosopher."

"Not really. You are a good listener."

She gave him her hand and he took it and bent over it.

"Good-bye, Doña Isabel. May your God bless you."

"Farewell, Don Duarte. Take good care of Beatriz and little Pedro."

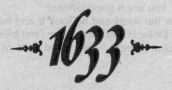

## 1.

The Reina was gliding through the Zuider Zee toward the harbor of Amsterdam. A fresh wind billowed her sails; crew and passengers alike had forgotten the storms of the Atlantic and looked forward impatiently to the moment when they would set foot on land that did not belong to Spain.

Pedro and Isabel stood at the bow and watched the landscape fly past them, lush green pastures and dark fertile soil, dotted by hundreds of windmills. For Pedro, this was the second trip to the rebellious Netherlands within less than a year. First, he had taken Duarte and Beatriz Perez and their fellow refugees to Amsterdam, where he had spent part of the winter. He had come back to Spain by land, expecting to find Isabel and Pepita with Uncle Jaime.

At Toledo, Pepita had greeted him with the startling news that Isabel had left to take up temporary residence at a convent in Andalusia. Uncle Jaime confirmed this. It was a very normal thing for a young lady to do. Many daughters of good families retired to convents now and then. She would return when she had her fill of solitude. But as soon as Pepita left them alone, Jaime explained that Isabel had learned from Diego Caietano that another group of secret Jews was preparing to leave the country, and she had begged Jaime to let her go to Seville where she would wait in her father's house for Pedro and the new refugees to arrive. She was determined to go to Holland with them. She wanted to meet real Jews, and she wanted to taste the spirit of freedom. Jaime had asked Pedro to take her along. If she wanted to stay abroad, they could always tell their acquaintances that she had retired to a convent permanently.

Isabel had been elated when Pedro consented. The adventure took her mind away from Rafael, besides making her a closer partner in Pedro's work.

"Everything looks so different from Spain," she said to Pedro. "Fresher, crisper. Why, even the sky seems bluer, and the clouds whiter."

"A country rich in good earth," Pedro said. "That is why the Spanish monarchs do not want to give it up. Our troops are still fighting to retain control of the southern provinces, but the seven United Provinces will eventually win, I am sure, and they will bring all the remaining Spanish possessions under their banner."

"How did Spain ever come to possess these lands?" Isabel asked.

"Isabel! Should you forget your history? I cannot believe that is possible."

"Well, I suppose I have."

"The Catholic Kings had many children of whom only one survived, the one we call mad Juana la Loca. Juana married Philip the Fair, a Habsburg and the first of our Philips. He was the son of Emperor Maximilian and of Mary of Burgundy. He inherited the Low Countries from his mother."

"Now I remember," said Isabel. "The son of Philip the Fair and Juana la Loca was Charles I of Spain, who became Holy Roman Emperor and was called by the rest of the world Charles V."

"That is right," continued Pedro. "But he, like his father Philip the Fair, had grown up in the Low Countries and was attached to the Dutch and understood their mentality. He was able to unite all of the realms of the Habsburgs under his sceptre. His son, our Philip II, inherited Spain and the Netherlands, Sicily and Naples, as well as all the territories in the New World, but not the German and Austrian lands of the Habsburgs. Now Philip II, as you know, was very Spanish and very Catholic. When Calvinist preachers came to convert the local population of the Low Countries, instead of treating the affair with mildness and tolerance, he sent the Duke of Alba to crush the heresy."

"So if Philip II had tolerated religious liberty, the Nether-lands would still be Spanish?" Isabel asked.

"Possibly. Religious fanaticism has done more harm to mankind than the black death."

"What if someone sees us at Amsterdam and reports us to the Inquisition?"

"We have the excuse of spying for the Count-Duke. I hope he would protect us."

"But Amsterdam is not the capital of the United Provinces, is it?"

"No. The Stadtholder and Admiral General of the Union, Fredrick Henry, resides at The Hague where he entertains a fashionable Court. Like our own monarch, he enjoys painting and architecture. I brought a few canvases, just in case the leader of a republic appreciates Old Masters as much as a king."

The head of the young republic might be The Hague, a pleasant town of palaces and parks behind the dunes of the North Sea shore, but the heartbeat of the United Provinces could only be felt at Amsterdam, the rapidly growing harbor city whose comfortable merchants were pushing their way into economic world supremacy.

The Spanish and Portuguese refugees, attracted by the promise of religious freedom, contributed heavily to the wealth of the country. They lived in a handsome residential quarter in the south of the city around Breestraat, where they continued their own way of life, speaking Spanish and Portuguese, attending three synagogues which varied in their degree of orthodoxy, building schools for their children, encouraging adult learning, marrying among themselves, and making themselves well liked by the Christian community. There had been an initial problem. At first, they had been accused of secret papism, but when the Calvinists understood that they were Jews and had suffered more at the hands of the Inquisition than the Protestants, they were allowed to live in peace. Now harmony reigned between the Christian and Jewish communities. The Jews maintained active commercial relations with their coreligionists in Morocco, Venice, Tur-key, and the West Indies; they helped establish important industries; they were among the founders of the famous East India Company, and the wealth of a few was legendary. But they were not only merchants. They were scholars, physi-cians, soldiers, poets, attorneys, and diplomats. A few of them had been burnt in effigy in their home cities on the

Iberian peninsula, but none of them was disturbed by that small matter—as long as they prospered in Holland, the Inquisition in Spain and Portugal was welcome to their effigies.

During his previous visits to Amsterdam, Pedro had befriended an influential art dealer, Hendrik van Uylenburch, of an old aristocratic Dutch family. He was a member of the liberal Mennonite sect, but he lived in a town house among the Jews of Breestraat. He helped upcoming young artists, especially one young man for whom he had built a studio in the attic of his house. Pedro had seen the young man's paintings and had told Isabel he intended to buy one or two. He was convinced the painter was as good as their friend Velázquez and perhaps better than the current King of European artists, Peter Paul Rubens.

"What is his name?" Isabel asked.

"Rembrandt van Rijn."

They entered the harbor. It was much busier than the one at Seville; the vessels were so numerous they almost hid the water, and their masts gave the impression of a forest. Isabel wondered how they would ever be able to weigh anchor near the wharf, but Pedro took the wheel and piloted them swiftly and efficiently through the jungle of small and large boats. Soon they walked down the gangplank onto soil not belonging to Spain.

Duarte Perez had come to the wharf to welcome them, and with him were two important members of the Spanish-Portuguese community. One, round of face and with a kind smile, was Menasseh ben Israel, rabbi of Neveh Shalom, writer, orator, and founder of the first local Hebrew printing press. He was a man keenly interested in the fate of the Marranos, since his own father had escaped from Spain after having been imprisoned by the Inquisition. The second one, handsome and dark-bearded, was Isaac Aboab da Fonseca, a profound Talmudic scholar and rabbi of Beth Israel.

The two religious leaders had come to welcome the refugees and to offer them their help and spiritual guidance. Indeed, the group had hardly set foot on shore, when Menasseh was already inviting them to his synagogue and encouraging them to throw off the cloak of ambiguity and openly adhere to the faith of their fathers. He strongly recommended Dr. Ephraim Bueno as the man to see about the circumcision, and he assured them that as Jews they were safer in Amsterdam than in Jerusalem.

Duarte Perez insisted that Pedro and Isabel stay with him and Beatriz at his own town house, a few blocks down from the Uylenburchs and the Menasseh ben Israels. So Pedro and Isabel temporarily took leave of their travelmates and the two rabbis and climbed into Duarte's carriage.

The first impression Isabel had of this foreign city was that, unlike the often flimsy structures of Madrid, the red brick town houses with sandstone decorations and high elaborate gables looked sturdy and sedate. Next she noticed the cleanliness. Perhaps it was the abundance of water and the presence of the canal network that could swallow the garbage, debris and excrement that lay festering in the streets in Spanish cities, or perhaps the cooler climate did not encourage the development of the all-pervading stench of decay to which a Spaniard's nose was accustomed from childhood. Whatever the reason, Isabel thought the city looked clean and smelled clean, and she was more than ready to admire anything Dutch.

As she soon discovered, there was much to admire, for the Dutch were everything the Spaniards were not. They were industrious where the Spaniards abhorred work; they were easygoing where the Spaniards were fanatical; they had a well-established community of prosperous burghers, where Spanish society knew only high-born parasites and low-born poor; but most of all the Dutch were tolerant, whereas the Spaniards were narrow-minded. This Dutch temperament was catching. The Spanish and Portuguese newcomers had adjusted easily into the life of the larger community. In spite of keeping their language and practicing their own religion, they had adopted Dutch dress, manners, and outlook on life much faster and more easily than another group of immigrants coming from the east.

It was a few days after their arrival that Isabel first saw men who looked different from anyone else she had ever known. They wore heavy coats down to their ankles, long untrimmed beards, and high red fur caps, all garments somewhat out of place in the moderate spring climate.

"Who are they?" she asked, when she was riding through town on a sight-seeing barge trip with Beatriz, Duarte, and Pedro.

"You will not believe me," Duarte said, "but they are Jews."

"Jews? Why do they dress in so unusual a fashion?"

"Because that is the dress they are required to wear in Poland."

"I did not know there were Jews in Poland. When did they get there? And what are they doing here?"

"The same as ourselves. They fled from persecution."

"You mean they went from Spain to Poland and now they come here?"

"No, Doña Isabel. They were never in Spain. They are Ashkenazim."

"What does that mean?"

"It is a Hebrew word meaning German. Just as we are called Sephardim, that is, Spanish Jews. They are Jews from Germany, from Poland, from Russia. They do not speak Spanish but their own language which is much like German."

"And you are sure they are Jews?"

"Very much so. They have their own synagogue here at Amsterdam. They are much more observant than we are, and I do not think they want to mix with us."

"Are there many of them?"

"As of now we Sephardim are superior in number, but more and more Ashkenazim are arriving with every new wave of persecution."

"Do they have the Inquisition in Poland?"

"No, that particular atrocity is the proud achievement of Spain. They are being sporadically hunted down and killed by the local populace."

Isabel said nothing more, but a thought was clearly written on her face. Suddenly, she was not so certain she wanted to be a Jewess.

A dinner invitation came for all four of them from Menasseh ben Israel. Beatriz said she could not go, because she was in her seventh month of pregnancy and did not care to show herself in company.

"You will be the only woman there," she warned Isabel, "since they all adhere to the old Spanish custom of keeping the women apart. I am surprised they invited me, but I think they would be shocked if I came. The Dutch are not strict at all."

Isabel went nevertheless, and she did not regret her decision.

The rabbi was a pleasant man, combining personal charm with depth of feeling and intellectual brilliance. He was of medium stature, had strikingly trusting large brown eyes in a roundish face, framed by short, wavy brown hair. His moustache and beard were well trimmed and neat. He proudly presented his children, Gracia, Joseph, and Samuel, in whom, he said, ran the blood of King David, for his wife was Rachel Abrabanel, daughter of Don Joseph Abrabanel, who claimed to be a descendant of the famous Isaac Abrabanel, philosopher, statesman, and treasurer to Queen Isabel the Catholic.

"And the Abrabanels, you see, are direct descendants from King David," the rabbi triumphantly finished the presentation of his family.

"I thought all Sephardim descended from King David," Pedro said with a grin.

"In a way you are right. Indeed, we believe that the Jews who went to Sepharad were mostly from the tribe of Judah which is the tribe of Jesse and David, his son. But the Abrabanels specifically descend from King David himself."

The three little descendants of the ancient royal house of Israel were permitted to show off their learning by reciting and translating passages from the Pentateuch before their mother hustled them off to bed. They were handsome and intelligent children, justifying Menasseh's inordinate pride.

Except for Menasseh's wife, Rachel, there were no other women, so Isabel sat at the place of honor to the right of her host.

The dinner was plentiful and lasted a long time, and there were animated discussions between the many courses. The guests, three of whom were distinguished physicians, kept up an incessant flow of conversation, turning for the most part around the first volume of a work their host had published a few months earlier. The book was called the *Conciliador,* and in it Menasseh made what was considered a successful attempt to reconcile the passages of the Scriptures which might appear to contradict each other.

"How did you get the idea for such a book?" Pedro asked. "Did you find there was a demand for it? Is our age more skeptical than former generations?"

"One of my objectives was to reach the Marranos who are on the verge of rediscovering their Judaism but somehow hang indecisively in the air—not professing Christianity nor accepting Judaism."

"You can count me among those," Duarte Perez said.

"Yet, while I admire the tremendous effort that has gone into your work, I think it raises more questions than it solves."

The three rabbis at the table, Saul Levi Mortara of Beth Jaacob, Aboab da Fonseca of Beth Israel, and Menasseh ben Israel of Neve Shalom, turned toward Duarte such angry looks that any outsider could feel immediately this was not their first discussion on the subject.

"It is a good thing you are not a philosopher, Don Duarte, and do not spread your heresies other than by word of mouth, or we would be forced to excommunicate you," Mortara said sternly; the two others nodded consent.

"Excommunicate . . . heresy? What do you mean by that?" Pedro asked in bewilderment. "I thought those were Old Christian words."

"Duarte has expressed disbelief in life after death. He thinks that when a man dies, his soul dies with him, that there cannot be a part of him living on that returns to the eternal source from whence the human soul comes. Nor does he believe that God rewards virtue or punishes evil. In sum, he does not seem to believe in the existence of God," Fonseca explained. "And that is what we call heresy."

"Of course, God exists," Pedro said, "or you would not have the Torah. But I do not find immortality of the soul to be a dogma contained in the Pentateuch. Is it not possible to let every individual decide for himself what he wants to believe regarding his personal immortality?"

Ephraim Bueno, a physician famous enough to be called by gentiles who named him Dr. Bonus, had been listening with growing amusement.

"If you were bodily sick and wondered how to cure yourself, would you call a rabbi? or a tailor? or a lawyer? Of course not. You would call a doctor and heed his advice, because the man presumably spent years learning his profession. Then why, when you have doubts about the fate of your soul, do you trust in your unlearned judgment? You may do so, if you wish, and mistreat your soul, just as a sick man may try out all kinds of incorrect medications, but you should not go about spreading your errors. There are laws against medical charlatans—not that they are often applied—and there should be laws against religious charlatans. That is why we have to exclude from our religious community anyone who preaches false opinions—the term being heretical opinions—lest they contaminate others. Our friend Duarte Perez in whose judgment we trust when it comes to shipping and trade, would do well to confine his opinions to those matters which he knows best. But if he ever tried to spread his preposterous atheism, we would have to take steps to prevent him from doing so. Unfortunately, excommunication, which means pronouncing the Great Ban and bodily removing him from our tight-knit community, would be the most effective means of stopping him."

Duarte, like Pedro, had listened respectfully, but in the end he smiled.

"The more you try to restrain me by menaces, the more obstinately will I try to resist your reasoning. There are others who feel as I do. As long as men are dominated by fear, they will act with hatred, anger, and guile. Only complete freedom from fear will permit man to deploy his capacity for living and acting without injury to himself or to his fellowmen. Apart from the Ten Commandments, all religious laws are ludicrous. What wrong do I do to my neighbor by believing that when I die, I die completely, that nothing awaits me beyond death? And if my beliefs do not hurt anyone, why should they be considered criminal by you or anyone else?"

"You do accept the divinity of the Ten Commandments, though," Menasseh said, in an effort to smooth a controversy over which he did not want to preside at his own dinner table. "So you are not a godless person."

Duarte shot a quick look at Isabel, and she realized he remembered her words that he would be in trouble if he came to be considered a godless man.

"I am willing to believe that the Ten Commandments were written by the man we call Moses," Duarte said. "Moses being as good a name as any other, I do not wish to argue about that. The man Moses believed himself to be directly inspired and protected by God. He therefore lived and acted in a perfect security which no one else has been able to attain. It is this freedom from fear which enabled him to stand up to Pharaoh and also to compose the commandments. If they were followed to the letter, they would permit mankind to live in the same exalted state of liberty Moses achieved for himself."

"There now!" Menasseh interjected with an audible sigh of relief. "This is what I have been preaching. Only within the framework of Mosaic law can we achieve freedom and happiness."

"No," said Duarte. "I was speaking only of the Ten Commandments, not of the bulk of Mosaic law. And if the first three commandments were missing, the other seven would not lose their value. The first three are only there because Moses needed a higher authority than himself to enforce his laws. The populace is never won over by common sense but only by fear of the supernatural. The more supernatural powers one can conjure, the firmer one's capability of imposing laws and taboos."

Before Rabbi Mortara could launch into a biting reply, Rachel stood up and proposed that they move into the adjoining room.

"And excuse me for interrupting, but I heard Doña Isabel expressing great interest in seeing your printing press. Perhaps you could give Don Pedro and her a quick tour of the shop?"

Her husband immediately took her hint.

"Would you like to come with us Duarte?" he asked the Portuguese, and Duarte laughed.

"I know I cannot be trusted in the company of Rabbi Mortara and Rabbi Fonseca, so I will come along," he said.

Rabbi Aboab da Fonseca was sometimes working with Menasseh as proofreader, but most of the time Menasseh himself was author, editor, publisher, proofreader, typesetter, printer, and bookseller for his printing house.

"I hear you have finally taken a helper," Duarte said to him as they entered the large ground-floor room where the printing press stood. "How is he doing?"

"Much better than I expected. He does the typesetting for the Hebrew texts. The Polish Jews know their Hebrew much better than the Sephardim."

"He is an Ashkenazi?" Isabel asked, remembering the strangely dressed people in the streets.

"Yes, and here he is, still hard at work." They had spoken Spanish, but now their host called out in Dutch, "Judah, I would like you to meet new friends of mine from Spain."

The young man turned from the long table where he had been laying out sheets fresh from the press. What Isabel saw was a handsome, frail-looking young Jew, with curly hair framing his face, broad slavic cheekbones, slightly protruding lips, and a care-worn expression around his eyes. He had a beard and wore a small skullcap. His name was Judah Leib, and he spoke Yiddish, Polish, Hebrew, and Dutch. There was

an aura of sadness about him which strongly appealed to
Isabel. He reminded her of the victims she had seen at the
*auto de fé*, and something inside her said YES, he is my
brother, indeed.

"We have a young painter living across the street who has
been begging Judah to sit for him, but Judah does not believe
in portrait painting. Still, I am trying to convince him that it is
not sinful to pose as a model," Menasseh told them.

"Are you talking of Minheer van Rijn?" Pedro asked.

"Yes, Rembrandt. Do you know him?"

"I met him during my last visit to Amsterdam. As a matter of fact, I intend to trade some paintings with Minheer
van Uylenburch who is his patron, I believe. I would like
him to paint a portrait of Isabel. Do you think he would
consent?"

"He would be only too happy, I can assure you."

The walls in the printing shop were decorated with illustra-
tions from books published by Manoel Dias Soeiro,
Menasseh's Spanish name which he kept for business purposes. A large woodcut showed the figure of a pilgrim with
staff and bundle and the motto *Peregrinando Quaerimus*,
Menasseh's printer's mark.

"By our wanderings we seek," Isabel translated pensively.
"That is how I feel and why I have come here. But truly, what
do we seek?"

"God," Menasseh said.

"Truth," Duarte Perez said.

"Peace," Pedro said.

And peace was the topic when they returned to Rachel
Abrabanel's drawing room. War had been raging for fifteen
years now, and the end was not in sight. Sometimes the
Protestants won and sometimes the Catholics, but no one
really knew anymore what the fighting was about, because the
French who were Catholic and therefore presumably should
ally themselves with the Holy Roman Emperor and the King
of Spain, on the contrary, gave support to the Protestants,
whereas Protestant England, instead of supporting the
Dutch, tacitly supported the Spanish cause, because she
wanted to counteract Amsterdam's bid for maritime supremacy.

"When are you coming here permanently?" Fonseca asked
Pedro. "You should direct all of your galleons to Amsterdam
and escape as long as you are still in favor with Olivares and

free of suspicion. A new company has been formed here, the Dutch West India company. You could buy up a majority of shares and control the trade with the New World."

"No," said Pedro. "I want Spain to control the trade with the New World. I want maritime supremacy for Spain."

A silence fell over the heads of the Amsterdam Sephardic community when they heard these unbelievable words.

"This is what I have come for," Pedro continued, "and I might as well tell you now, I want you to come back to Spain."

He rose quietly from his seat, and never had Isabel admired him more than when she saw him proudly defying the stares of his aghast audience.

"I realize that you may think me preposterous, but I am a true Spaniard, and it hurts me to see our country fall into decadence, for this is, indeed, what is happening. The world talks about our victories and defeats and still assumes that we are a great power, when, in reality, we are sinking into poverty and insignificance. Olivares has tried his best to hold up the crumbling edifice of our economy, but he is doomed to failure unless experts come to his aid. What makes the Republic of the United Provinces great is the affluence of her burghers. We do not have any burghers in Spain; we have only the very rich and the very poor. The expulsion law of 1492 was the greatest folly any monarch could have committed. Under the guidance of the Count-Duke, even our nonpolitical Philip seems to understand this. At any rate, he has given Olivares a free hand with the councils and the clergy. Olivares himself has sent me here to contact the influential Jews of Amsterdam and to propose to you to come back to settle in Madrid, where you will be given a new part of town to live in and the right to build your own synagogue. Duarte Perez can testify to the fact that the Count-Duke interfered with inquisitorial procedure on his behalf and that he was permitted to leave Spain with part of his wealth intact. This should be proof of the Count-Duke's good intentions.

"It may be completely immaterial to you what happens to Spain. Indeed, you may rejoice in her downfall, since Spain made you suffer. But please consider that what I propose means religious liberty. It means synagogues in Spain. Might that not lead to Protestant churches? To mosques? To complete personal freedom? Imagine, freedom to worship, freedom to speak, safety from persecution! Is that not worth fighting for? Not fighting on the battlefield, as we have done in vain for scores of years, but fighting by political and economic means. I am not interested in getting Jews into Spain for the sake of their wealth—that is an official mantle for my policies. I want to bring about an end to the Inquisition. I have Olivares on my side. If you help me, how can we fail?"

They knew that Duarte had been liberated with the Count-Duke's help. Nevertheless, Pedro's words left them spell-bound. Even Rachel looked up from her embroidery.

"Of course, you will come back under your new names. You will not be Marranos anymore, you will be Jews and as such completely outside the sphere of competence of the Inquisition."

They remained silent, until at long last Menasseh answered. His voice was cold and firm. "None of us will ever return to Spain! Spain means no more to us than any other country save the Holy Land. We have a good life in Holland. The Dutch have accepted us and treat us well."

*"Ubi bene, ibi patria?"* Pedro asked with a slight sting of irony.

"Spain does not want us," Fonseca countered. "Spain despises us. Why should we help her? If what you say is true, if Spain is on the brink of economic disaster, she gets no more than she deserves. I owe Spain no loyalty. Let Spain break down completely. Then freedom will come without our help."

"My feelings exactly," said Mortara.

"What about you Duarte?"

"One month in the dungeon of Toledo cured me of any sentiments, patriotic or religious."

"Dr. Bueno?" Pedro turned to the physician. "If there were a Jewish community in Madrid and they needed a good physician, would you come?"

Ephraim Bueno shook his head. "In Holland I am someone. My father was called to the deathbed of Prince Maurice of Nassau, because the gentile physicians thought he might still know of a cure when they despaired. There are many important Christians among my patients. I am respected for my knowledge and skill. Why should I give that up to go to a country where I would need a pass of safe-conduct whenever I ventured outside my street? Why should I let myself be treated like a bearer of pestilence, when I can be treated like a nobleman?"

"The Spaniards need to be educated," Pedro said. "Your forefathers have lived in Spain for perhaps a thousand years. The Inquisition is not yet two hundred years old. Must we really give up hope without fighting back? If your coming to Spain would help abolish the Holy Office, could you hope for a greater achievement than that?"

"Let them abolish the Office they call Holy first, then we will come," Menasseh said. "There are other parts on this earth where Jews are needed. Personally, I am more interested in getting Jews readmitted to England. My efforts will be directed that way."

"May I approach the other members of your community?" Pedro asked. "Perchance some of them are homesick for Spain."

"You are free to speak to any former Marrano," Rabbi Mortara said. "I doubt you will find any buyers for your ideas."

"You should go to Oran," Menasseh proposed. "I will put you in touch with Josef Pallache who is Consul of Morocco. His father Samuel was one of the founders of our first congregation here."

"Does the King of Morocco send a Jew as his Consul to Amsterdam?" Pedro asked.

"The Kings of Morocco have traditionally been tolerant. I think the Moroccan rulers might also welcome closer ties between Spain and Morocco. You should direct your efforts toward North Africa."

"Or go to Venice or to Salonica," Rabbi Mortara proposed.

"I still say abandon your plans and come yourself to Amsterdam," Duarte said. "The Spaniards are stiff-necked fanatics, and you will not change them."

# 2.

The house of Hendrik van Uylenburch was a center for art lovers. People came to meet, chat, and swap, and there was always some young artist on hand to give lessons in drawing and oil painting. On the top floor, under the roof, was a large atelier Uylenburch had given his favorite protégé, promising Rembrandt van Rijn.

When Pedro took Isabel for the first time to the Uylenburchs, joy and laughter filled the big house. They were celebrating Rembrandt's betrothal to Hendrik's cousin, pretty young Saskia van Uylenburch. Isabel felt instantly drawn to the young lady, because she had Pepita's impish charm, although she did not otherwise resemble Pepita. Indeed, for Spanish tastes, Saskia was heavy, even fat, but among Dutch women, she passed for a great beauty. She had a full face with the round chin and dimples of a cupid, a mischievous smile on full, sensuously curved lips, and tawny hair pulled back from her face except for a few tendrils on each side of her forehead. Around her neck she wore a precious pearl choker which she never removed. Isabel saw her with it no matter whether she was dressed simply or for special occasions.

Isabel spent many hours in Saskia's company, since the art dealer and Pedro got along well and found much to discuss. She asked Saskia how a young woman of a prosperous Dutch family grew up, what she learned, what she thought, what she expected from life. Her hopes, Isabel thought, were modest. She wanted to be a good wife to the plain-looking young painter whom she adored.

Pedro had asked Rembrandt to sketch his sister, and one day Isabel climbed up to the studio. After being accustomed to the noble face of her friend Velázquez, Isabel found Rembrandt's looks lacking in quality. His features were coarse, his nose bulbous, and his hair hung about in wild unbecoming frizzles. Even his moustache was in need of a trim.

His studio was a spacious room with a large window in the inclined ceiling, plain, whitewashed walls, and a heavy wooden door around whose frame the plaster had started to peel off. The floor consisted of paint-besplattered oak boards, and a long table held palettes, brushes, paint knives, containers with prepared paint, others with oil, and bowls with ground ingredients for mixing colors. Several easels stood in the middle of the room around a forlorn-looking armchair. Compared to Velázquez's palatial atelier, this was crude and primitive.

The biggest easel held the painting Rembrandt was currently working on, a *Descent from the Cross,* ordered by the Stadtholder. Isabel had seen hundreds of paintings. To be able to distinguish between good art and bad was a desirable social grace at the Spanish Court.

Now she saw her first Rembrandt painting, and she experienced the same pang of recognition Pedro had known when he had seen his first Rembrandt. Here was a man touched by genius.

The artist was observing her all the time. Now he bade her sit in the armchair, and with rapid concise movements, he drew a series of chalk sketches of her face—one showing the haughty expression she no doubt had displayed upon entering the atelier, then her wide-eyed wondering, finally, the quiet dignity of a person who feels she is in the place and among the company she deserves. He showed them to her with laughing eyes.

"Which one is you?"

Without a moment's hesitation, she pointed to the last one, but Rembrandt shook his head.

"I am not satisfied that any of these faces is truly yours. You are hiding something inside you. You are not happy."

No, of course not, she wanted to shout. How can I be happy, when life is so confusing? I am in love with a man who is the enemy of my people, yet I yearn for him because he is a part of me. I do not even know where he is, or whether I will ever see him again, yet I must not mention his existence. How can I be happy, if I have to tear my most intense feeling out of my heart?

But she smiled and said, "In your eyes, Minheer van Rijn, no woman can ever be as pretty or as happy as Saskia. Right now, you should paint no one but her."

"No, you must come back and sit for me, and we will talk, and perhaps I will say something that touches your heart, and your portrait will be alive and perfect."

She resented his perspicacity, and she told Pedro she did not want to be painted by Rembrandt.

# 3.

While Pedro absented himself to travel to Hamburg and Frankfurt to contact the few Spanish Jews who had ventured that far, Isabel remained with Duarte and Beatriz and seriously questioned herself whether she wanted to return to Spain. To stay in Holland would mean a separation from Pedro, who was determined to return to Spain and remain a Spaniard. But it would also mean that she could live free from fear, that she could express her ideas openly, that she could own and read the books of heretics, and that, at last, she would escape the web of secrets, intrigues, half-truths, and outright lies that had caught her in Spain.

Yet by remaining in Holland she would endanger Pedro and their whole enterprise. No, she would have to go back. But at least she could enjoy her freedom of speech while it lasted.

Beatriz had given birth to a girl, a fat little nine-pound baby who had taken almost all the strength out of her slender mother. So, while Beatriz rested, Duarte and Isabel talked.

One evening, Duarte told Isabel about Uriel Acosta, a man whom she had never met, because he had been excommunicated from the Jewish community and lived in seclusion. According to Duarte, Uriel was the most brilliant philosopher alive.

Uriel Acosta was the descendant of a noble Portuguese family. His father had been a believing devout Old Christian, and Uriel had received the best possible Catholic education. Uriel, however, was a thinker, a man capable of drawing conclusions, and after comparing the spirit and message of the Bible with life as he witnessed it every day, he thought that Christianity was a distortion of every divine commandment revealed in the Bible. Seeing the cruel persecution of Judaizers, his sensibilities revolted against the religion of his fathers, and he tried to find understanding in the ancient religion of Mosaic laws. After his father's death, he converted his mother and brothers to his beliefs, and the family fled to

Amsterdam, where they officially embraced Judaism. Great was his surprise when he found that Judaism, far from being the liberating religion of personal freedom, was a maze of rabbinical explanations and prescriptions ruling the most minute and intimate human functions. Incensed, he composed eleven theses attacking rabbinic Judaism as a fraud without any biblical justification. Warned repeatedly by the rabbis and elders of the community, he nevertheless continued to defend his ideas and published a voluminous work expounding his theories. He finally crowned them by a complete denial of the immortality of the individual. This was more than the Jewish or Christian burghers of Amsterdam could tolerate. He was arrested, fined, and deprived of his books. Finally, he was solemnly excommunicated by the Jews in a ceremony not unlike the great Anathema pronounced once a year by the Spanish Catholic Church. All the curses of Sodom and Gomorrah were called upon his head, and, being a sensitive soul, he recanted.

"What happened then?" Isabel asked while a shiver ran up her spine.

"Nothing at all," Duarte said. "He is not received by anyone, no woman wants to marry him. He is the virtual *bête noire* of the community. I may be the only friend he has. He mistrusts everyone else. But his mind does not stop working, and he is now writing another book. He might become the founder of a new religion. According to him, revealed religion is in direct opposition to the laws of nature, and the only fruits of revealed religion are hatred and superstition. Think about that. Think carefully!"

She did and, indeed, the only other result of revealed religion coming to her mind was that of national unity.

But Duarte disagreed with her.

"That has been the fallacy of the Catholic kings," he pointed out. "Where is the national unity of Spain? The Count-Duke is desperately trying to impose a Union of Arms, and he cannot even get Catalan Old Christians to get along with Castilian Old Christians. No, if there has to be religion, and it may well be that humanity cannot get along without that notion, it should be a religion of nature and of reason. Reason alone bids us love our fellowman. The instinct of self-preservation tells us to form commonwealth communities."

"And what about God?"

"God gave us the powers of reasoning. He is still waiting for us to use them. You see, time never runs out on God, it only runs out on the individual. Thousands of years are but a day in the sight of the Lord. So one day, perhaps ten thousand years from now, we shall begin to use our reason, and we shall not know war anymore, nor strife, nor ridiculous narrow-minded rules dreamed up by old men who had nothing better to do. That to me would signify that the Messiah has arrived."

"Duarte, you are not an atheist, and you should not call yourself one. You are a Jew, and you must try to understand the human frailties of the old Talmudists."

"But if I am to believe, as I am perfectly willing to, that God remembers that we are dust, that we flourish as a flower of the field, that our days are as grass, how can I believe at the same time that a ritual means anything? For the wind passeth over it, and it is gone, and the place thereof knoweth it no more. . . . You see, Uriel Acosta and I are not unbelievers out of ignorance. We practically know the Scriptures by heart; we are unbelievers in human eyes, because we recognize that God is so far beyond human understanding as to be nonexistent. He is everything—we are nothing. We cannot relate to Him in any way. If He created us, He created us as He did the sun and the stars and the moon and the clouds and the waters and the beasts.

"It all took more than six days and perhaps we are still an unfinished product, since our reasoning is certainly poor and faulty. God is not dependent upon us, nor upon our prayers, nor upon our gratitude. Just as animal sacrifices meant nothing to Him, so He does not ask for a blessing each time we eat. He does not demand our thanks when we are happy, He does not want to save us, for we do not need to be saved. He does not die for us, because we are not in need of redemption. Ever since our creation, we have despised the only gift that sets us apart from the rest of creation, namely our power of reasoning. So if we want to persist in giving God our feeble human qualities, all He should feel for us is contempt. This is why I say we should get along without God. The force of creation, the prime mover as the Greeks called Him, is so far beyond our grasp, that even trying to find attributes for Him is an insult. We cannot call Him compassionate nor angry, for these are human qualities, we cannot call Him a father, we cannot even call Him HIM, for how can

He be a male, instead of being an abstraction? I say let us stop wasting our short life speculating about God, and let us concentrate on knowing and appreciating each other. Official religion is man-made nonsense cluttering up our existence."

"But what if you are wrong?"

"Is it not much more terrifying to think that I may be right?"

"Are these your own ideas, or Uriel Acosta's?"

"They have been my own for a long time now, but Uriel expresses them much better than I can."

"Oh Duarte, I am afraid." Isabel looked at Beatriz's pale face, at little Hannah sleeping in her cradle, at young Pedro who at one year of age was still too weak to pull himself into a sitting position; she was sick with fear for all of them.

"Beatriz, you must keep your husband from spreading his ideas. He would be a heretic at any time and for any religion."

"What if he is right?" Beatriz asked softly.

"Would you rather have him be right and dead?"

"In Holland they do not kill us for our opinions," Duarte reminded her.

"They may not kill you, but look what they did to your friend Uriel. They certainly will not hesitate to throw stones into your windows, or spit upon your children, or make life too miserable to endure."

"I have thought of that," Duarte said. "If that happens, I shall move to the New World."

"But the Inquisition would get you there."

"Not in the Dutch colonies and not in the English colonies."

"The English colonies! Are the Dutch traders not at war with the English traders?"

"Look, my dear, I am Duarte Perez, a man without a country, a man without a religion. I am at war with no one. I am wealthy enough to be welcome anywhere. I want to be left in peace, and I will live in peace with my fellowmen."

"Then why can you not live in peace here? Why do you have to stir up controversy?"

"Because I love my fellowmen too much to see them destroy one of the finest philosophers we ever had."

"Uriel Acosta?"
"Uriel Acosta."

After this talk with Duarte Perez, Isabel knew with certainty that she did not want to remain in Holland. She would go back to Spain without regret.

# 1.

More than a year of absence from the capital did not make much difference with regard to politics and gossip. The general situation had not changed at all. Olivares was still the man in supreme power, Quevedo still wrote his biting satires, Calderon still composed his high-minded allegorical plays, the Buen Retiro was still being finished, and who slept with whom was still the most fascinating topic.

The news bulletins bore such exciting details as the story of a newly arrived confessor for a convent who had seduced some two dozen young nuns right in the confessional before the mother superior caught him *in flagrante,* or the one about the village priest who had deflowered every young girl who had confessed her first monthly flow, or the one of the wronged wife who had killed her husband with a dagger after discovering him in the act of the *pecado nefando,* the "abominable sin" with another woman.

Isabel and Pedro had come back by way of land, stopping over at Antwerp and at Paris. Isabel had stayed at Madrid, and Pedro had gone to Toledo to pick up Pepita, to whom he explained that Isabel, tired of convent life, had returned to Madrid alone. Pepita accepted this explanation, although her lively and natural curiosity about life at the convent forced Isabel to make up stories about nonexistent events.

Before the beginning of Lent, the three Valderocases gave

a magnificent reception, reminiscent of the Valderocas receptions at Seville. Pepita, for a short while, cherished the hope that Pedro would finally announce his engagement to her, but he did not. Isabel hoped she would hear from Rafael Cortes or that he would even come to the reception, on this, the second anniversary of their meeting, but he did not.

Something else happened, however, something important enough to lift the name Valderocas once again sky-high in the eyes of the Madrileños. Both the Count-Duke and the Countess of Olivares attended the reception. And with them came His Majesty, King Philip IV of Spain. Neither the Favorite nor his wife, much less the King, had been invited. To extend an invitation to them would have been much too presumptuous on the part of a common man. Their coming bestowed upon the Valderocases an indelible mark of distinction, and during the following months, they received more invitations by Court-conscious families than they could possibly accept.

Isabel blanched when she saw Philip, but here, in her own house, he did not single her out. He spoke mostly to Pedro, and she thought his infatuation had passed. Only when he left, he found the opportunity to draw her up from her curtsy, bend toward her, and murmur softly, "You are the only woman for whom I have ever waited patiently. I still want you."

After Easter, Olivares invited them to a reception in honor of the Inquisitor General, Fray Antonio de Sotomayor.

"In honor of Sotomayor? What do you suppose is going on?" Isabel asked.

"A head count of all his supporters," Pedro suggested. "He has won over a few royal council members and has talked to members of the Suprema. I think he is ready for action."

"What action?"

"To call some Jews to Madrid."

"Outright?"

"Yes. I have been selected, with His Majesty's approval, to carry invitations to Oran and Salonica. But this is still tentative. The date has not been set."

"Oh Pedro, I cannot believe it. You mean he is really winning support for our ideas? We will have a synagogue at Madrid? And a Jewish quarter?"

"Hush. It is all in the planning stage. As soon as the papal nuncio hears about it, all hell's furies will dance. Cardinal Monti is not one to be afraid of accusing the King himself. Actually, he would please himself in the role of Nathan lecturing King David. We must avoid informing him until the very last minute; preferably facing him with a *fait accompli*. I think tonight there will be some general information gathering. I hope Calderon is in one of his milder moods. Another '*perros herejes*' poem could spoil the evening."

Well over two hundred guests attended the reception, few of whom knew what was going on. The general talk centered around the high cost of living and the urgent necessity to fill the royal coffers. Silver was getting exceedingly rare, the American mines were running dry, and new means of bringing wealth into the country had to be found.

When His Eminence arrived, a line formed, and the Count-Duke himself presented each guest with a few appropriate words. Just as Olivares was constantly surrounded by a train of secretaries and servants, so the High Prince of the Church was followed by a silent group of Dominican friars who kept respectfully three steps behind him, no matter where he walked or stood.

It was a strange feeling to curtsy deeply to a man who was the acknowledged head of a nation's most terrifying institution. What would Duarte Perez think, if he could see her thus, Isabel asked herself, or Menasseh ben Israel, or Uriel Acosta? She caught a glimpse of the old Inquisitor's face. He looked neither kind nor evil, just old and a bit self-righteous perhaps. The murders he had ordered left no imprint on his face.

Suddenly, her glance fell behind him, upon the tall figure of one of his monks, and she met the intent gaze of two deep-set eyes burning in a face she knew so well. It gave her a violent jolt of recognition. Her knees grew so weak she could hardly remain standing. Her lips opened slightly, but she had forgotten what she was going to say. Olivares noticed the change in her features and turned to Sotomayor to mention that she seemed overcome with the honor of being presented to him. She remembered where she was, forced a smile to her face, curtsied again, and moved on. But Olivares turned swiftly around before he presented the next guest to His Eminence.

She kept herself at the far end of the room. She had to avoid coming near him, because it was impossible to remain indifferent in his presence. He was like a part of her that she wanted so desperately she felt like rushing forward and throwing her arms around him. This was how the King must feel when he lusted after a girl, but this was also how a mother must feel when she was reunited with a son whom she had believed lost. It was a feeling of overwhelming desire, at the same time of absolute purity. One day she would perhaps make love to someone else, she would marry someone else, she would possibly even be happy with someone else, but this man was the only man whose mere sight would always be enough to call forth a fiery storm within herself.

She stood with a group of ladies. They chatted of dresses and jewelry, while nibbling scented pellets of red unglazed clay—Quevedo called them dried mud—which were supposed to give one a fashionable melancholy pallor. She did not listen to their chatter, and she refused the clay. She was pondering how she could leave the palace gracefully, when one of the Count-Duke's pages informed her that His Excellency wished to speak to her.

A speculative smile hovered around Olivares's lips when he made the presentations. "Doña Isabel, you may recall Fray Rafael Cortes. I had once sent him as my personal messenger to your father. He is now the private secretary of His Eminence, the Inquisitor General."

"Of course, I remember," Isabel said and curtsied.

"May I add that Fray Rafael is decidedly marked for a brilliant career? It is a pity he has not yet reached the necessary age to become an Inquisitor. But this, of course, is a self-correcting fault. I understand the Holy Father himself was favorably impressed when Fray Rafael recently accompanied the Archbishop of Córdoba on a special mission to Rome. Well, there you are, I thought you should meet your famous fellow Sevillano."

Isabel gave a nod of gratitude. "You are very kind to me, Your Excellency."

The Royal Favorite again smiled inscrutably, as if he knew something they did not know about each other.

"Is it really you?" she asked softly, when Olivares had left them. "I cannot believe it. Private secretary to His Eminence, on your way to becoming a powerful man. How did you accomplish it?"

He lifted one eyebrow and one corner of his mouth in a quizzical, mocking smile.

"Have you forgotten my resourcefulness? I always get what I want: the best bargain and the prettiest wench." He could not keep from breaking into a quick grin, and she knew he was teasing her to keep them both from betraying their true feelings.

"Oh, Rafael . . ."

"Careful," he warned. "You cannot go to pieces over His Eminence's secretary in the middle of a reception. Smile politely, and I will tell you all you want to know."

"Since when are you back in Madrid?"

"I came back a fortnight ago."

"Do you still have the apartment?"

"No. I am looking for a new one."

"Were you in Rome all this time, since we last saw each other?"

"Goodness, you are as curious as ever! Yes, I was in Rome all this time, with one interruption. I came back here once last summer, but no one knew where you were. In some convent in Andalusia, they said. I did not have time to search for you. I had to go back to Italy."

"Will you stay in Madrid now?" Excitement started to flush her cheeks. Her eyes sparkled.

"Yes. Will you?"

"Yes."

They looked at each other, and a warm happy feeling of anticipation spread through her body. Forgotten were Duarte and Menasseh and Beatriz and the dungeon-born baby. She would again become the mistress of a Dominican friar, and it was at once the most incredible and the most normal thing to do.

"Be careful. Your brother is approaching," Rafael said rapidly while hardly moving his lips. Immediately, Isabel forced an innocuous smile on her face.

Rafael stretched out his hand, "Pedro, what a pleasure to see you!"

But Pedro ignored the gesture.

"Fray Rafael, congratulations upon the swift progress of your career," he said stiffly. "I am surprised you are allowed to leave the side of His Eminence to court young ladies."

"The spiritual conversation between a Dominican padre and Doña Isabel Valderocas can hardly be called courting," Rafael replied. "I suggest you relax your vigilance."

"Fray Rafael was telling me about Rome," Isabel said to

Pedro. "I find his description of St. Peter's fascinating. Fray Rafael, we will be delighted to have you to dinner one of these days. Do let us know when you are free."

He smiled pleasantly.

"I am afraid my time is much taken right now, but I thank you most sincerely. It was a pleasure to meet you again."

He turned to resume his place among the shadows behind the old Inquisitor General, and Isabel glared at Pedro, furious that he had interrupted them before they could agree on a place to meet.

They were hardly in their coach before Pedro gave vent to his feelings.

"I forbid you to invite that man. He is not going to be received in our house."

"But Pedro," Pepita said, "you are too harsh with Isabel. She did nothing wrong. Why can she not be friends with him? The fact that he is a padre now should prevent any shade of scandal."

"Who asked you anything, Pepita? You do not know the first thing about men. And that particular man, I happen to know well enough. I would not trust him around my own mother. He is the worst wencher I ever saw, and the frock does not make the least bit of difference. And so you are not to receive him either, Pepita, in my absence. Carlos de Queras, yes, Rafael Cortes, no! By the way, what happened to Carlos? I have not seen him around."

"I think he is abroad," Pepita said. "But to come back to Fray Rafael, in Seville you invited him to ride through town with us, and even Father did not object."

"Because he was a plain bachelor then, not a good prospect by any means, but a *letrado,* a man who could have been an acceptable husband to either one of you. A man who could have honorable intentions. How can a priest have honorable intentions?"

Isabel knew that the whole dramatic act about honorable intentions was being played for Pepita's benefit. The truth was that Pedro could not forgive Rafael for having joined the Dominicans who to Pedro were the worst enemies of Spain. If she wanted to be honest with herself, Isabel had to admit that she, too, should feel hatred for Rafael and men like him. They were torturers of innocent beings; they kept dungeons where babies could be born and die without anyone caring;

they tore children from their parents' arms; and they condemned youngsters to live as galley slaves; they crushed people's bones and burned the soles of their feet. So how could she be angry with Pedro for detesting Rafael? She, too, should abhor him.

As for the accusation that Rafael was a wencher, that, of course, was meant for her ears. Pedro wanted to put her on guard against Rafael's guiles. It was much much too late for that.

## 2.

To find a small apartment was no easy matter, because Madrid's housing situation suffered from many complex habits, rules, and regulations that restricted supply. The houses and palaces of the rich had several floors, each comprising fifteen or more rooms completely furnished for different seasons. During the winter months, families would live on the top floor, the warmest one, and in summer they would move to the cool street floor. Each of the great households had hundreds of servants. It was, indeed, against law and custom to ever dismiss a servant for a reason other than a serious crime. When a man died, his family inherited his servants, and the domestics stayed with the same family for generation after generation until they died of old age. Under these circumstances, it was impossible for anyone, however wealthy, to lodge all his servants under the same roof. Instead, they were paid small wages which covered the cost of a modest room in another part of the city. All their food came from their master's pantry, which they raided faithfully every night before retiring to their own lodgings. In the morning, the servants in charge of shopping went to buy new provisions for the entire household, and by nightfall everything again disappeared.

There was a law requiring all owners of multistory buildings to put either one complete floor at the disposal of the Court or to pay an exorbitant tax. Consequently, many parts of town consisted simply of small lanes of one-story houses. Here the servants lived, in a maze of narrow streets where refuse piled high and mud was knee-deep. Farther out were walled yards where the rich kept their coaches, calashes, sedan-chairs and litters, and the endless stables for their horses and mules. Very few town houses had courtyards big enough to accommodate even a small carriage, and thus animals and vehicles were kept outside the city proper. Attached to the stables were small flats for the grooms and their families.

In all of Madrid there were few streets where a stranger might find an inexpensive yet decent apartment. Those were the streets of the better class of tradesmen, of pastry shops and wig makers, of silversmiths and tailors, of leather craftsmen and booksellers. It was in one of those streets that an enterprising Portuguese had converted three adjoining houses into one apartment building, and here Rafael rented a tiny flat for Señor and Señora Francisco Molina, mapmakers for the Valderocas shipping company.

Rafael would have preferred a more fictitious employer, but Isabel convinced him that it would be best if their household appear as respectable as possible to avoid any suspicion, and that since she was in charge of all correspondence and inquiries concerning the business, she would be the one to answer any questions concerning the identity of a person claiming to be a mapmaker for Valderocas. Besides, as long as they paid their rent on time and appeared now and then at the flat, no one would doubt that they spent the remainder of their days or nights at their employer's. And besides, mapmakers were likely to travel a great deal, were they not?

They tried to meet as often as they could, although Rafael rarely knew ahead of time when he could be free. They both had a key to the apartment, and they could leave notes for each other.

Isabel finally felt that she had reached the pinnacle of personal freedom. She came and went through Madrid as she pleased, a minor celebrity, and no less than two dukes asked her to become their mistress. She refused pleasantly, saying she intended to remain a virgin. Then someone started the rumor—delightful in her opinion—that she had become the concubine of the Count-Duke. But since they were never seen together and the Countess continued to receive and favor her, this bit of idle tattle disappeared like a trickle of water on sand.

At first appalled by his sister's complete reversal of attitudes, Pedro had to admit that she was successful in all her undertakings. Madrid was bored with demure, well-behaved females: a woman who was young and beautiful and obviously neither a wife, a nun, nor anyone's mistress, was an exciting novelty. People were anxious to learn how it felt to be above the laws of female honor, and many women confided to Isabel all the secrets and gossip they knew, in exchange for some advice on how to escape their own society-imposed prison. Whatever gossip she heard, as well as all the fruits of her eavesdropping in the various drawing rooms, Isabel reported faithfully to Pedro.

She never grew reckless to the point of going out during the evening. Unless there was a dinner she attended with Pedro and Pepita, she stayed at Valderocas House, and she did most of the Valderocas work at night in her room or in the library. This was the Isabel only Pedro knew: the woman who patiently verified accounts, payrolls, and bills of sale, who composed letters to be copied by Pedro's secretaries, who watched that not one ducat of Valderocas money was wasted. He appreciated her more and more as an indispensable partner, as his only friend. He did not know that on the days when he imagined her at the matinee of a theater, she was really giving herself to a man he despised.

If Isabel was happier than she had ever been, she had to admit to herself that she loved to live dangerously. All parts of her life fit together so well, a change in one would upset the harmony of the whole. Her moments with Rafael were so brief that there was little opportunity for discussion, let alone misunderstandings or quarrels. They never stopped delighting in each other's caresses and thought of themselves as accomplices in sin.

One day she asked him what was meant by *pecado nefando*, the nefarious sin that sounded so mysterious and terrible. What could be so abominable as to merit the death penalty, yet so tempting that lovers would continue to do it?

She was warm and soft in his arms, and he looked at her and slowly turned her around so that she lay on her side and her back fit snugly against his chest. While he caressed her breasts, he murmured into her ear and told her what he would do, and why it would be wonderful for him, because he would be able to let himself go deep within her body without any danger of getting her with child—this being the meaning of sin against nature—and he asked her whether she thought she could bear it. For an answer, she reached down and guided his hard phallus, and when he entered, she clenched her teeth, for she disliked this sensation. But she let him have his way until he broke down sobbing with pleasure.

When it was over, he pulled her around so she faced him again, and he saw tears in her eyes.

"You did not like it?"

She shook her head.

"I am sorry. We will not do it again."

"But you liked it," she said. "I could feel you go mad with pleasure."

"I am not certain," he said. "My body liked it, but my spirit feels ashamed."

"But it was not the first time you did it?"

"Yes, it was." He remained pensive. "The sin of Sodom—I always lusted for it, but I never dared," he said after they lay still for a while. "Will you love me any less?"

"Love you less?" she exclaimed. "When there is finally something you have done with no one but me?"

He gave his silent laughter and covered her face with kisses.

"I adore you more than you will ever know. I wish you could stay with me always, follow me wherever I have to go. I will never grow tired of you."

The words she wanted to hear! Other words jumped into her mouth, the words to answer his. This was the right moment, she knew it. But then, calling upon all her will-power, she swallowed those words, and she forced herself to tease him.

"The Cardinal's Mistress—Comedy in three acts by Lope de Vega," she said. "Or do you think we should engage Calderon to compose a Corpus Christi play about the temptations of Pope Rafael?"

He looked at her and frowned.

"You have changed during our separation. Once you would have asked me to give up the priesthood if I really loved you. I wonder whether you are beginning to understand me."

She turned away from him brusquely.

"Let us not talk about that."

"Oh!" He sounded disappointed. "So you still hope I will marry you. I should send you away and not see you anymore. You must not sacrifice your life for me. You should marry a man you can be proud of. Why does Pedro let you out and about by yourself? Where is his sense of honor?"

"Rafael, really I do not know what you are talking about. I love you, and you say you love me. I detest your being in the orders. And you dislike the fact that from the innocent well-protected virgin you seduced, I have turned into a pseudo-courtesan who is the talk of Madrid. You yourself keep telling me that I am a sensual woman, and I know I am. Just looking at you, even just thinking about you when I am alone, makes me dizzy with desire. And do not think I am completely indifferent to the way other men look at me. I enjoy feeling wanted, but I will belong only to you. If you want us to stay together always, let us go away together. I do not even ask you to marry me. You know I am content to be with you, whichever way you wish. You have studied at the Casa de Contratacion. People like you can make their fortune anywhere in the world. There is more than one way to become rich and famous."

"I do not want to be rich and famous."

"Yes, I know. You want power. But power for what? Power is just a word, unless it is used for something. What do you really want?" She asked him seriously and with exasperation in her voice, because he never spoke to her of his work. She did not know what being secretary to Sotomayor involved. She only knew that as a Dominican friar and active member of the Spanish Inquisition, he already must hold power enough to cause the arrest and torture and perhaps condemnation to death of any human being who somehow offended him or stood in his way. Why did he want this power? Why did he not go after a bishopric which would bring him money or after a similar sinecure? Why did he not try to be nominated for one of the four orders of knights, which assured standing at Court and a good income . . . or had he tried this? He never talked about these things. What did he want? He was already completely invulnerable. The law could not touch him. If she or any other normal mortal accused him of anything, including murder, the accuser would land in a dungeon, whereas the Inquisition would always protect Rafael Cortes.

"Remember how you asked me to trust you?" she reminded him. "Well, I trust you, but I have come to think that love—after all—may be more important than trust. I would love you no matter what you did. You could murder, and I would take your word that it was necessary. I would always stand by you and love you, but you will not even tell me what you want from life."

He did not answer her. He looked at her gravely, and it occurred to her that she did hold at least one power over him. He wanted her badly enough to have agreed to the dangerous arrangement of meeting her regularly at this apartment, of wearing a simple silk shirt and tight breeches under his long white robe and black cloak, in order to be able to switch his outfits quickly in an empty courtyard or in a private house of the poor section of town where a few silver coins closed anyone's mouth. He wanted her badly, not only to satisfy his sexual appetite, but because she was more alluring to him than any woman he had known. He was in love with her and could not help it. He had contacted her the next day after the reception, saying it was impossible for him to be in the same town with her and not make love to her. And so they had been meeting again as often as possible to make love.

Once she had called his penis Machiavelli, for she said it had its own life, wily and unscrupulous, and it obviously placed expediency over morality. The works of the Italian author Machiavelli were much read in Spain, since it was generally assumed that his main work, *The Prince,* was based on the life and politics of the crafty Ferdinand of Aragon, husband of Isabel the Catholic, who had expelled the Jews from Spain. Rafael had laughed his silent laughter and suggested that Machiavelli could always be trusted to force his way into the castle of the Queen, whereupon Isabel had slanted her eyes and parted her lips and whispered huskily that the Queen would be on her guard. They had mutually embroidered their story of the resistance and possible rape of the Queen until their bodies had strained together in ecstasy.

Rich in vulgar expressions, Spanish common speech fairly bristled with references to people's genitalia and speculation as to their possible inadequacy or incompetence, but both Rafael and Isabel were reluctant to use these terms, even the picturesque ones, and so their love life had become the story of harmony between Machiavelli and the Queen.

Now Isabel was lying on her side, leaning on one elbow and looking intently at his face. He was lying flat on his back, both hands under his head and he looked at the ceiling. He had heard her questions, but he was trying to put her off.

"You see what a treacherous fellow he is, this Machiavelli," he said. "He cannot be trusted, for now he has forsaken the Queen for the whore of Sodom."

Isabel did not smile. She did not want fancy jokes. She wanted an answer. Her voice was in his ear, soft, insistent:

"Rafael, what do you want? What do you really want? Please trust me."

He did not look at her, he did not change his position. He simply spoke the most incredible words she had ever heard.

"I want to be Inquisitor General of Spain."

There was nothing more she could ask; there was nothing she could answer. There was nothing, absolutely nothing she could say to such a stunning statement.

She left the bed and walked to the stand with the water basin to wash herself. Then she dressed slowly, avoiding looking at him. She would leave, she thought dully, and never come back, because if this were his true desire, nothing could ever be the same between them.

When she was ready, she walked to the door. She did not even look back at him who was still lying on the bed in the same position.

But when she opened the door, he jumped up, pulled her back, slammed the bolt shut, picked her up in his arms, and threw her back on the bed. His mouth, his whole body came crushing down on hers . . . and nothing had changed.


# 3.


Pasquito had grown considerably during the two years since their coming to Madrid. The small, plump boy of eleven had become a svelte, handsome lad of thirteen. He had to remain a slave if he wanted to stay in Spain, since no free Moriscos were allowed by law. Isabel had intermittently continued to teach him reading, writing, arithmetic, and especially her own evaluation of history, and when she had come back from Amsterdam—officially from a convent in Andalusia—she had made a pact with him. If he would continue to study under her direction, she would provide him with enough money at the age of sixteen to sail to a part of the world where he would be able to live as a free man. She talked to him about Amsterdam, telling him she had met people who had visited that place, but when he looked at her with his dark intelligent eyes, she thought he guessed that she had been there herself, and she regretted not having taken him along. She loved him like a younger brother, the way she loved Pepita; it made no difference that he was legally her slave.

The problems with Pasquito began the same day Rafael told her of his intention to become Inquisitor General.

Rafael had kept her much longer than usual, and she came home tired but happy in her knowledge that they would always love and desire each other, even if he succeeded in his goal. To her dismay, when she walked into the patio, she found Carlos de Queras talking to Pepita, and with them the insufferable Count of Villaquemada.

The men were sitting in comfortable armchairs on thick Moroccan rugs which the servants laid out every morning after washing the patio tiles with cold water. Pepita hovered on a pile of velvet cushions. The air smelled of roses; lackeys served almond water and clay pellets; others waved great fans to keep flies away; and Pasquito stood calmly in front of the visitors who were commenting on his looks as if he were an inanimate object.

*"Hola,"* Isabel greeted them. "What is going on here?"

The two men jumped up and bowed to her with much gesturing of their plumed hats.

"Carlos was telling your charming cousin how much he admired your Moor," the Count of Villaquemada said. "He thinks he could make something out of him. Turn around lad!"

Pasquito shot him a glance full of hatred but obeyed.

"I would like to buy him," Carlos said. "Perhaps now that his mistress has arrived, we can conclude a deal. Doña Pepita always told me he was not hers to dispose of."

"Please excuse me for a moment," Isabel said. "Come along Pasquito."

The boy followed her across the courtyard and upstairs where she took him to her room.

"What is this, I hear?" she asked him. "Do you wish to go with His Lordship and become his servant?"

"Oh no, Doña Isabel, please do not sell me. And please do not give me away. I don't want to leave you. I swear I will run away and become a vagabond if you force me to go with him. I cannot stand him. He keeps pinching me and touching me. It is horrible. Please Doña Isabel, do not send me away."

"Of course not," Isabel said.

But he was still afraid. "The Count said Don Pedro would have to give me to His Lordship if he found out that His Lordship wanted to buy me. That is not true, is it?"

"In a way it is," Isabel answered. For, indeed, it was customary for gentlemen and ladies of means to offer as a present anything a friend or visitor might admire, however valuable the object. Good breeding, of course, required one to refuse the gift immediately, and sometimes friends would spend days sending and returning a gift, until etiquette was satisfied, and the object would remain with the original owner. In this case, Isabel was sure, however, that Carlos, once he laid hands on Pasquito would not return the boy. He would send a valuable replacement, perhaps a horse, or a passel of hunting dogs, or a rare statue, but it was clear that his mind was set on owning the young Moor, and Isabel was furious that he should be so insistent.

Pasquito looked at her, and she could read horror in his face, so she smiled to reassure him.

"You may remain here in my room," she told him. "And you will never leave my service, until you, yourself, desire it."

"Thank you, thank you," Pasquito said, and he dropped on the floor to kiss the seam of her dress, but she pulled him up and took him in her arms and hugged him.

She left him upstairs and went to join the others in the patio.

"Pasquito wishes to remain in my service," she told them, "and therefore he is not for sale."

"Am I to understand that you ask your slave for permission to sell him?" Villaquemada asked with condescending surprise. "That is a very bad practice. Take my advice and treat your slaves like the dogs they are. If not, they will come to despise you and show nothing but disrespect. Especially Moors."

"Moors are people like other people," Isabel said.

"As a fine Old Christian, I beg to differ," Villaquemada objected. "Moors may be a shade better than Jews, but they are all *perros herejes.*"

"I agree," Carlos said. "What about you, Doña Pepita? Would you feel a Morisco to be as good as you are in the sight of God and your fellow Old Christians?"

"What a question," Pepita said. "I am a Valderocas and

that is as good as being a duchess. How dare you insinuate a comparison between me and a Morisco?"

"Well said," Villaquemada applauded. "You should put a little more sense into your cousin, and you might both end up being real duchesses."

They went on discussing at length the differences between an Old Christian of pure lineage and any other naturally inferior human being. Isabel did not participate in their conversation, and after a while they rose and left.

At Valderocas House dinner was served at ten o'clock. Afterwards, the servants would clear the table and retire to their own quarters. The only ones to stay through the night were Pedro's personal footman Alfonso; Pepita's maid and confidante, Teresa; a young Moorish girl named Maria, whom Isabel was training as her own chambermaid; Isabel's slave Pasquito; an old doorman who had already served their parents at Seville; and half a dozen general servants and bodyguards who had been with them for many years and who, if necessary, would defend their masters' lives with their own. Except for Maria, whom Isabel had picked up one day as a half-starved beggar in front of the Caietano bookstore, all sleep-in domestics were reliable persons. Maria still had to prove herself.

That night after dinner, Pedro asked Isabel and Pepita to join him in the library, since he had news of importance. It seemed that Olivares had decided to send him as a special envoy to various countries around the Mediterranean.

"That poses the same question as before," Pedro said. "What are you going to do during my absence?"

"We are going to stay right here at Valderocas House," Isabel said. "I see no point in our moving to Toledo whenever you go abroad. Times have changed. We are well enough protected from physical harm. No one is going to break into the house with all the servants around, and it is perfectly safe for us to remain here."

"But you will not be invited anywhere," Pedro objected. "You will be snubbed by the Court. Besides, it will give me a bad name to have neglected my duties as your protector. Things are more complicated than you think."

Pepita was quietly stitching on her embroidery. "I have thought that perhaps I could get married," she now said without looking up and in a strangely impersonal voice.

"What?" Pedro and Isabel exclaimed in unison.

"The Count of Villaquemada and Carlos de Queras told me they knew of a certain nobleman who is looking for a good match. He needs money, and he offers a title. I would live at court and be made Lady-in-Waiting to the Queen. But, of course, it would require a considerable dowry, and I do not know how much you are willing to give me."

Isabel stared at Pepita with a half-open mouth. She did not understand what was the matter with her cousin. Her words were preposterous, but Pepita obviously thought she was talking sensibly.

Pedro quickly gathered his wits. "Is that the kind of stink egg those two varmints have been hatching? And who is the debt-ridden nobleman fishing for my money? Do you know him? Do you love him, perhaps?"

"I do not know who he is, and it does not matter in the least," Pepita answered with the same detached voice. "I have had a lot of time to think while you were both abroad, and now that I know you were together, while Isabel left me at Toledo with the lie about the convent, everything appears in a different light."

"Who told you that?" Pedro gasped and jumped up from his seat to close the door leading from the library to the patio.

"Carlos saw you in Paris."

"A curse on his distempered brain! And so now he wants to blackmail us into letting you marry him."

"Oh no! He still wants to marry Isabel."

"And for you he only acts as marriage broker. How very disinterested of him. How much does he want to be paid for his services?"

"I can tell you that," Isabel broke in. "He wants nothing but Pasquito. Is that not true, Pepita?"

"So what if he does," Pepita said. "Is it not a cheap enough price to pay? He's only a Moor."

Suddenly, there was deathly silence in the room. Isabel stared at Pepita, then at Pedro, and Pepita, who obviously had expected a violent protest, finally looked up from her needlework and into Pedro's face.

His features were eerily dangerous: his downward slanted eyes narrowed with contempt, his mouth had become a thin, hard line, his nostrils inflated with barely contained rage. He took two steps towards Pepita, and while Isabel gave out a scream, "Pedro, no!" he grabbed Pepita by the front of her dress, pulled her up with one jerk and with his free left hand slapped her face so hard that she staggered and fell to the floor.

"Stop it, Pedro, for God's sake, stop it!" Isabel screamed. She tried to hold him, but he shook her off.

"So he's only a Moor," he yelled with slashing fury. "And who do you think you are? A Valderocas perhaps? Go marry your nobleman! See how much he would like to marry a poor Morisco. Isabel! You tell her!"

He turned around and left the room, slamming the door as he went.

Isabel rushed over to help Pepita whose face had started to swell. She led the shaking girl to an armchair. Then she was at a loss as to what to do. There could be no doubt that Pedro was deeply hurt, more than he himself realized, or he would not have lost his self-control over a matter that could have been settled by the simple refusal of a large dowry. After all, he had never objected to Pepita's marrying someone else. If he had been as indifferent to her as he pretended, he would not have gotten angry at all.

And what did he expect his sister to do?

Pepita looked up at Isabel who stood bending over her and softly touched her swollen cheek.

"What did he mean?" she asked dully. "I am your cousin. Why does he call me a Morisco?"

"Because that is what you are," Isabel whispered. "You are a Moor. The same as Pasquito."

"I don't believe it! Mother would not have brought me up like her own daughter. Father would not have spoiled me. They wouldn't . . ." Her voice broke, and she sobbed and sobbed and could not go on.

"Yes, they would," Isabel said softly. "They would take a little Morisco baby who had lost her parents and bring her up as their own, because they found her to be sweet and innocent and worthy of love."

"How do you know?" Pepita asked. "It is not true! It is not true. I am I. I am Pepita Valderocas!"

"What Pedro said, however cruelly, was correct. You can ask Uncle Jaime. Oh, Pepita, I am sorry that you should learn the truth like this. We should have told you; I know we should have. But you must understand that it doesn't make any difference. We love you, but Mother did not want you to know."

"Then she should not have told you and Pedro," Pepita said.

"We would have found out. There was no place for you in our family tree. We know the Valderocas ancestry."

"Yes. And I should have guessed," Pepita said in a toneless voice. "I was the only stupid one who did not like to study, who was not interested in family trees and *limpieza* documents, who simply thought she was somehow a member of a fine Old Christian family, when in reality she was only the daughter of a slave. Oh my God, Oh Santa Maria. . . ." She bent over and hid her face in her hands, and Isabel tiptoed out of the room in search of Pedro. She felt that he owed Pepita an apology, or at least a more detailed explanation.

But Pedro had left the house without telling anyone where he was going. Isabel went back to the library to see what she could do for Pepita. Only Pepita did not want to see her or talk to her and had locked herself into her own room. There was really nothing Isabel could do to repair the damage of Pedro's outburst, except to tell Pepita the whole truth about the Valderocas family, a matter too grave and dangerous for her to undertake without Pedro's consent. She went several times to knock at Pepita's door, "Please dear, let me come in. Let me explain to you. Pedro did not mean what he said. He loves you. You hurt his feelings by saying you wanted to marry someone else. I swear that is true, please open the door." But there was no answer from inside, and Isabel dared not continue to make a spectacle of herself in front of Teresa and Maria. She hoped the servants had not heard Pedro's shouting, but if they had, it would be a test of their loyalty to see whether they prattled to the others who came in the morning.

After she went to bed, she lay awake for a long time, listening to every noise in the house, ready to jump up in case Pedro came back. She was worried about the news that Carlos had seen them in Paris, and very angry with Pedro, for leaving her to cope with the problems he had created. The dangers inherent in her secret life with Rafael were suddenly like dust specks in the sun compared to the rocks Pedro had hurled at the mosaic of their life. Finally, toward morning, she fell asleep.

She awoke from the clamor of the arriving servants and dressed hastily without calling for Maria. She hurried to Pepita's room. The door was unlocked. She walked in.

Everything was neat, as usual; the bed was made, there were fresh flowers in all the vases, and Pepita's large embroidery frame with the half-finished tablecloth stood in front of the window. Isabel went to the breakfast room and crossed Teresa on her way down.

"Where is Doña Pepita?"

"I do not know, Señora."

The place settings at the breakfast table had not yet been touched. Apparently, neither Pedro nor Pepita had had any breakfast.

Isabel walked out into the patio. It smelled of freshly watered plants and of almond cakes, since at that moment several porter boys walked by balancing baskets full of pastry on their heads. The steward stood at the entrance to the kitchen and counted the number of baskets. Every servant Isabel passed greeted her with a bow and, "Good morning, Señora," but none had seen Doña Pepita. She made a complete tour of the house and finally went back to Pepita's room, where she found Teresa.

"When did you make the room?" she asked.

"I did not make it. I have come in just now for the first time today."

"Teresa!"

"Yes, Señora?"

"Where is Pepita?"

"I do not know."

"When did you last see her?"

"Last night, after she came up from the library. She sent me to my room. She said she did not need me anymore." Teresa was sharing a room with Maria.

Isabel stared at the girl, then she experienced a terrible intuition. The bed had not been slept in. Pepita had left the house.

Why? What was she planning to do? Kill herself? Confess to a priest? Throw herself upon the mercy of the Church? Enter a convent? No, that she could not do. She would need a *limpieza* document to join an order of nuns. Where was she? Where could she go? Had she packed a travel bag? That would be a clue. Frantically, Isabel pulled open every drawer, every wardrobe door, but nothing was missing.

"Teresa! Count her dresses. Which one is she wearing? Is her jewelry here? Teresa! Please hurry! Do not stare at me. Don't you understand? She is gone. Pepita is gone. We must find her immediately."

Teresa let out a scream and ran out of the room, but Isabel quickly caught up with her and pulled her back inside and closed the door.

"Teresa, this is important. What did you hear last night? You and the others. Why do you think Pepita is gone?"

The young woman looked at her with frightened eyes.

"You must tell me the truth. You and Pepita were good friends. She talked a great deal to you while I was gone. What was she saying?"

"She loves Don Pedro, but she felt sure he would never marry her."

"Why not?"

"Because he could make a better match at Court. She thought he loved her but did not want to marry her, because he could marry the daughter of a Grandee."

"Did she tell you that she planned to marry a nobleman?"

"Only recently, since we came back to Madrid. She said she might as well be married and live at Court. She was very bored at Toledo; she did not want to go back there."

"Do you know what happened last night?"

"Don Pedro got mad and left."

"Did any of you hear what he said?"

"No, Señora."

"Teresa, think well. I know our walls have ears. If you want to save your mistress, you must talk now, or it may be too late. What did Alfonso tell you?"

The maid blushed, and Isabel knew her guess had scored. She had long suspected that Teresa and Alfonso were carrying on their own affair. Now she held their destiny in her hand.

"Well?" she asked.

"Alfonso says Don Pedro wants Pepita for himself, without having to marry her, and . . ." The girl stopped.

"And what?"

"And that he accused her of having Moorish blood so she would not be able to marry anyone else."

"That is exactly what he did. It is not true, of course. He was very jealous. He said the first thing that came into his mind. He wanted to hurt her, because she had hurt him. Now Teresa, I want to tell you a secret. Don Pedro is going to marry Doña Pepita, just as soon as we are going to find her. He told me so himself, because Doña Pepita is a Valderocas, and for a Valderocas, the best possible match is his first cousin. Now swear by Santa Maria that you are not going to tell that to anyone."

Teresa swore, and Isabel hoped she would hasten to find Alfonso to tell him the secret, and that within an hour all live-in servants would be informed that whatever had happened was a lovers' quarrel. Then, if Pepita could not be found right away, Isabel would announce that she had taken refuge with Uncle Jaime.

"I must go out and find Doña Pepita, before she does anything rash. You see, I am afraid she may want to get married, just to get even with Don Pedro." Isabel forced herself to sound reassuring, as if it were merely a matter of riding around the corner to find her cousin. The first rule in any emergency was to keep the servants calm. "Now, you go and ask for Alfonso. I will be in the breakfast room."

She went downstairs, and since she did not think she could swallow any food but, on the other hand, wanted to appear nonchalant, she asked for a glass of coffee, a brew Pedro had adopted as his daily breakfast drink. While she waited, she interrogated Alfonso.

"Where do you suppose Don Pedro can be found at this hour?"

"I do not know, Señora."

"Well, you do know that he quarreled with Doña Pepita. What you do not know is the true reason behind that quarrel. I expect you to go out right now and find Don Pedro."

"I would not know where to look."

"Alfonso, Don Pedro has been out all night and will hardly be found in the audience chamber of the Count-Duke, or I would go and find him myself. You have accompanied him many times to places where unmarried gentleman try their luck. Please go and make the rounds of those places. Be off."

He bowed and turned without a word, but at the door he bumped into Pedro who had heard Isabel's last words, and came in looking tired and unkempt, but otherwise satisfied with himself.

"What is the hurry, at nine in the morning? Mmm, I smell coffee. How considerate of you to have some ready for me."

He let himself drop on the wooden bench running along the wall and stretched his legs.

"Alfonso!"

The servant helped him out of his boots and Pedro yawned.

"You could have found me at the Casa Celestina, otherwise

known as Juliana's," he said to Alfonso. "And my luck was so good that I am ready for a good ten hours' sleep. But first, see that I get a good meal. I don't know whether I am more sleepy or more hungry."

Alfonso left and Isabel swiftly got up and walked over to Pedro. A whiff of his breath sent her into a cold fury. To get drunk was the worst, the very worst offense a well-bred Spaniard could commit. To be called a drunkard was as bad as to be called an infidel.

"Guess who I met," Pedro said. "An erstwhile admirer of yours, Señor Vicente. Of course, I pretended not to recognize him."

"I don't know what you are talking about," Isabel said, and she was ready to cry. What the devil was she supposed to do? She considered for a moment calling him by his true name, Benahavel, to shake him up, but then she thought he might be too drunk for that. She left him instead and whispered to Alfonso that his master's state was a disgrace and that Alfonso himself was responsible for that.

"How could you let him go out alone?" she said. "Now I count on you that absolutely no one sees him like this. And do not tell him a word about Doña Pepita. His quarrel with her started all this. Your master drunk! Alfonso, you ought to be ashamed!" She did not need to scold him. To have a drunk master reflected shame enough upon a servant.

Before going to her room to get dressed, she ordered the Valderocas town coach and four to be brought from the stables. When she came down, Alfonso told her that he had put Pedro to bed and that he was snoring.

"Keep him here until I come back," she said.

The most logical places to look first were the churches. She spent well over two hours peering at every kneeling woman but to no avail. In front of every church she was greeted by scores of beggars, cripples, blind men, and haggard children. They followed her and tried to touch her, and she felt as if she were drowning in a sea of filthy rags and flea-bitten, stenchy bodies. Voices described the worst miseries imaginable, and she threw them handfuls of coins before escaping again into the safety of her coach until they arrived at the next church.

She had no idea where she herself would have gone if she had wanted to run away from home. She tried to put herself into Pepita's place, and it occurred to her that if Pepita had indeed believed that she was a Moor, she might do either of three things: She might try to kill herself because she could not bear the shame; she might try to denounce herself to the Inquisition; or she might try somehow to contact other Moors. Isabel thought that she herself would do the last of these things. If she were a Moor, she would try to discover who her own people were, just as she had tried to discover what Judaism meant when she had found out that she was a descendant of Jews. She had to consider, however, that Pepita was of a different mentality and had never seemed to possess an inquiring mind. It was hard to be certain about what Pepita might do.

Then she thought of the Caietanos, and she sighed in relief. At least she had friends. She was lucky to find Señor Caietano alone at the store. She told him briefly that Pepita had found out something they had kept secret from her, namely that she was of Moorish blood, and that she had left the house during the night, before they could give her any further explanation.

"Does she know anything else?" the old man asked immediately.

"Nothing."

"Even so, it is extremely dangerous. If she confesses, her name is bound to be sent to the Inquisition. And then you will be called, and you know what that means."

"That we have been sheltering an infidel and passed her off as Old Christian."

"Yes. And that will be the end of your unblemished name. Will she realize that?"

"I do not know."

"Where is Pedro?"

"Waiting for an audience with the Count-Duke." She would have rather bitten her tongue than admit that he was drunk at home.

"Do you think she would go to Don Jaime?"

Isabel shook her head. "I do not think she would want to go to any friends or family. She is probably sick with shame."

"You must find her at any cost. If she falls in the wrong hands . . . Do you realize our whole group could be discovered? If the Inquisition has her, you and Pedro must disappear from Spain, or so much effort will have been spent in vain. I will try to get word to the leader of our group."

"Then you finally know who he is?" Isabel asked.

"No, I do not."

"Then how can you?"

"Look, you did not know this, but Pedro passes on information to me, and I am in touch with another man, whom I see from time to time, who, in turn, is in contact with a man who coordinates all of our efforts."

"But do you not think it would be better if we waited? After all, the name Valderocas would come immediately to the man's attention, if she was picked up."

"Not if she was picked up at Seville, or at Valladolid, or who knows where she might go."

"But what if she does not turn herself in? Then you would have alerted a lot of people to the fact that there might eventually be some blemish on our name. Valderocas is one of the finest Old Christian names in Spain."

The tall old man looked at her for a long time with his green eyes under white bristly brows, and then he nodded.

"You are right, little Isabel, you are perfectly correct. We will not tell anyone. We will take that chance. In the meantime, you must search for her."

"How? Where?"

"Among the *pícaros*."

"The scum? Oh, my God, how will I do that?"

"Not you. Pedro will have to do that. The earlier the better. Tell him to read his friend Quevedo. *El Buscon* would be a good book to know. To prepare himself."

"But that is a satire. Those people do not really exist."

"No? Not for you perhaps. Believe me, there are only too many of them in Spain. But Pedro is a man who can take care of himself. He is going to find her. Send him to me when he returns from the Alcázar. I will give him some ideas."

He squeezed her cheek, "Do not look so scared; trust in God."

She smiled wanly and thought to her amazement that she would give a fortune if this moment she could talk to Duarte Perez.

# 4.

Shortly before Isabel returned home Pedro was summoned by the Count-Duke.

Alfonso, just as anxious as Isabel to have Pedro seen by others only in grand condition, splashed cold water over his master and rubbed him off vigorously. He, like everyone else, assumed that Pedro desired a title of nobility, and since the servant's standing would rise in accordance with his master's increased importance, Alfonso intended for Pedro to be in the best frame of mind when he went to see the Count-Duke. Therefore, Alfonso assured him that Doña Isabel had everything at home well under control, and he did not judge it necessary to inform Pedro just then of Pepita's disappearance.

# 5.

For Olivares, this morning was a moment of triumph. Proudly he handed to Pedro a sheaf of papers which in his eyes were already transforming the fate of Spain. They were royal licenses granting individual Jews admission to Spain by order of King Philip IV.

"Have every community select their own spokesmen and fill in the names accordingly," Olivares instructed Pedro. "Our main objective now is speed. I want to see at least a dozen Jews at Court before the end of the year. You must leave immediately to contact as many Jewish communities as possible in North Africa and the Levant. I feel I have made great progress with members of the Royal Council and with our best theologians, and I do not expect too many obstacles to our starting a Jewish community right here in Madrid. This should also encourage more *conversos* to have confidence in my government and stop them from leaving for the rebellious Netherlands."

"I am afraid they will still pressure for a formal removal of the expulsion law," Pedro said.

"Time will take care of that. Do you realize that these documents represent an official invitation to admit heretics to the service of the King? I do not see the Kings of France or England do as much."

"There is no Inquisition in France or England," Pedro reminded him.

"I am doing my best," Olivares said curtly.

Pedro nodded. Yet, once more he underlined his impartiality.

"Anyone as concerned as I am about the economy of Spain will appreciate the wisdom of your decision. This is not at all a question of religion; it is purely a question of politics and finance." It would never do to let Olivares guess that his one and only goal was to obtain complete religious liberty for Spain.

"Sometimes I think you are the only Old Christian with a head on his shoulders," Olivares muttered. "You must leave on your mission immediately."

"Your Excellency, there are certain Valderocas affairs I have to set in order. It will take a few days."

"I would not say this to anyone else, and I will deny publicly such a thought could enter my brain," Olivares said, "but I am willing to give credence to the rumors that your sister is a highly capable and shrewd woman. Leave your affairs in her hands."

"But Your Excellency . . ."

"No more of that. You will leave Madrid today, proceed directly to Barcelona, from where a royal galley will take you to Venice, Salonica, and finally Oran."

"I prefer traveling on my own ship," Pedro said.

"Why? What is wrong with a royal galley? You should be honored."

"I prefer safety to honor, Your Excellency."

For a moment, it looked as if Olivares would take this as a personal affront. His face grew red, and the veins on his temples swelled, but Pedro held his glance, and the approaching fit of bad humor subsided.

"How, then, do you propose to travel?" he asked.

"From Seville directly to Oran, from there to Venice and

Salonica. Then, on my way back, I should be able to pick up
the spokesmen from Oran who will have had plenty of time to
get ready, and so I can bring you your first Jews when I return
to Madrid."

At that Olivares's frown dissolved into a grin.

"Agreed. Provided you leave today for Seville. I must insist
on that. You must depart without delay."

Pedro had heard that the Count-Duke on occasion fell into
extremes of superstition, and he suspected this might be one
of those occasions. Perhaps he had made a vow that if the
King signed the royal licenses, he would get them out of
Madrid and on their way that same day, or perhaps he was
afraid Philip might change his mind. The documents were
precious, indeed, the first sign that after almost a century and
a half of religious persecution, one man had dared challenge
the supreme policy of his country. It might be best to follow
the Count-Duke's orders.

"I will give you two dozen of my best guards; they will ride
to Seville with you and your men. You will set out tonight on
horseback. No mules. I want to get you on your ship as soon
as possible. Is there a vessel ready to go?"

"Always, Your Excellency."

Two dozen guards, Pedro thought, did Olivares fear for
Pedro's life? Or was it to make sure he left right away and did
not tarry?

"Do you know, Don Pedro, that you are the only resourceful man around me who has never asked for any favor?"

"I am happy enough to serve Your Excellency."

"I will remember that. The guards will be waiting for you at
six o'clock on the palace square in front of the royal mews.
Good-bye, Don Pedro, and God be with you."

"Your Excellency," Pedro bowed and left, the roll of
documents in his hand.

# 6.

As soon as she learned that Pedro had gone to the Alcázar, Isabel asked to be driven to the main gate where she waited for him. When she saw him, she alighted from the coach and rushed to meet him.

"Have I news for you!" he said when she reached him.

"You found Pepita?" she exclaimed still breathless from nervous anxiety.

"Pepita?" he asked with a mien so perplexed that she realized he still did not know what had happened.

She told him as fast as she could what she had said to Pepita, what she had explained to the servants, and her brief talk with Caietano following the fruitless search for Pepita.

He was utterly stunned. Never for a minute had he considered that Pepita might actually believe him. In truth, his scorn had been directed at Villaquemada and Queras for filling Pepita's mind with their own foul ideas. But he had felt let down by Pepita, in much the same way he had felt let down when Rafael joined the black friars, a deed he would never be able to forgive. As for Pepita, he had reasoned with himself on his way to see the Count-Duke, that she had acted like a spoiled child and had earned the good slap he had administered.

"You should not have told her," he said to Isabel. "You should have told her I was crazy or drunk or something. You were not hurt. You had no reason to be angry, and you should have arranged things."

His accusation left her speechless. He blamed her.

She looked at Pedro, and she saw, under the handsome beard, the face of a mischievous boy who had been caught by strict old Don Fernando Valderocas Dominguez and who tried to put the blame on his sister. And she saw her mother taking the boy in her arms and protecting him, and she saw Pedro's face go desolate after her parents' death and his shoulders sag under too much responsibility, and then she remembered the return of his boundless energy and joy when she had joined forces with him against the hostility of the

285

world. And thus, all at once, she understood that Pedro could find courage and strength only in the love of his family. He had counted first on his parents, then on his sister for trust and moral support, but unconsciously he had also drawn on Pepita's love, and what he had taken to be Pepita's betrayal had come as a severe jolt.

They sat in the coach next to each other and slowly Pedro began to realize himself the grave implications of Pepita's flight.

"You must find her," he said, "I am leaving tonight for Seville."

"No, you are not! You are going to find her."

He shook his head, put a finger to his mouth, and let her see one of the documents.

She agreed that he had to leave immediately. She also accepted the fact that she was to blame for Pepita's disappearance. But she saw the matter in another light. Never again would she wait for Pedro's consent to act on behalf of the Valderocases or the Benahavels. Never again would she rely on any judgment but her own. If she had told Pepita the truth a long time ago, the whole truth about the Benahavels, their life would have been so much simpler.

"I am counting on you to find her," Pedro said.

Isabel nodded. She knew that already. "On your way to Seville, stop and tell Uncle Jaime to get in touch with me if he has any ideas where we might look for her."

"Perhaps she has gone there," Pedro said hopefully. "Oh Isabel, I love her. I should have married her. Oh Isabel, you must find her."

"Yes," she said. "I will find her, and you will marry her. But you will have to send back word to the house that she went to Toledo and from there to a convent. That way I can keep the rumors down while I look for her."

"I will do that."

"And Pedro, leave Alfonso here."

"Why?"

"Because I may need him. Also, he is in love with Teresa. If we double his salary and give him a fancy title like major-domo and if we provide a dowry for Teresa, they could get married. And then they would do anything for us."

"All right. Yes. If only you find Pepita."

"Do not worry, I will."

# 7.

A week went by during which Isabel walked through every street and alley in Madrid. Dressed as a servant, inquiring in practically every household whether a new maid had been hired, standing in line at the convents where free soup was being given out at noon and at night, carrying with her the small frame with the Velázquez sketch of Pepita, accosting thousands of strangers, men, women, and children. But no one had seen any women resembling Pepita. Isabel had made up a story that she and Pepita were sisters from Seville looking for work in the capital and that they had become separated on the road. But no one was much interested in her plight.

She changed her clothes at the apartment, and one morning, just as she was putting soot on her face, Rafael arrived.

"Hello, my beloved queen, is that your new disguise? For the wife of a mapmaker, it seems somewhat vulgar."

"Rafael! What are you doing here so early?"

"And you? What has happened? You have missed two afternoons."

He pulled her to the window and stared in bewilderment at her mended brown dress, the oily spots on her scarf, her sooty face, and with his finger touched the dark rings under her eyes. They had not been put there with make-up.

"My skin crawls, just to look at you," he said. "Would you care to give me an explanation?"

"Yes. I am trying to look like a female *pícaro,* and I am scared to death."

"Like a *pícara!* But why? Have you been reading too much lately? Are you perhaps as fascinated by female vagabonds as Don Quixote was by knights errant?"

"Oh, please do not joke, Rafael. I am so afraid."

"Of what?"

She was already exhausted, and the confrontation with Rafael was more than she could take. She simply slumped on the edge of the bed and let out a sigh of despair.

"Now, please take one thing at a time," he said. "Why are

you scared? In Spain, to my way of thinking, there is only one reason to be that afraid. So what have you done?"

She looked up at him, and fear, that ugly animal, again gnawed at her stomach, just as it had during the *auto de fé*. His deep-set eyes were somber enough to scare any sinner.

"Nothing," she said. "Pepita has run away, and I am looking for her."

"In that outfit?"

She realized that she would never be capable of inventing a lie complicated enough to explain all her fear, her strange disguise, and her behavior. The time had come to test their mutual trust. Isabel told him exactly what had happened up to her own part in it.

"So then?"

"So then she ran away."

He looked at her and frowned. "You are leaving out something. She would not run away because of that. She knows Pedro, probably better than I do. She would not take anything like that at face value. Calling somebody a Moor, why it is a most common insult. And then you were there to explain it to her."

"Explain what?"

"That he was jealous. That it really showed he cared for her."

She looked up at him, and she was ready to cry.

"But I didn't," she said with a small voice. "I guess I don't always make the right decisions."

She could see that the truth dawned on him.

"Isabel, did you tell her that she is a Moor?" He pulled her up and stared at her so intently that she closed her eyes. He let go of her.

"So it is true," he said. "And it is the reason why he has not married her. I always wondered. And you are the one who had to tell her. Good Lord, how could you do such a thing?"

Condemned. She was condemned. Even he condemned her.

He shook her rudely. "To spite God, how could you get us into such a predicament?"

Us? Had he said us?

"So, she is not an Old Christian like you. She is not your cousin," he continued. "She is a Moor. Is that all now?"

"That is all. Except that Pedro has left on a mission for the Count-Duke."

"He left, knowing that Pepita has run away? And he left you here, alone?"

At his questions, her loyalty to Pedro took the upper hand.

"No, he does not really know that she is missing."

"The devil he doesn't. You can't fob me off with that tale. He is counting on you to find her. He is always counting on someone else."

"If she confessed, would the Inquisition have arrested her by now?"

"That is the first thing I have to find out. Whether there have been any arrests in Madrid. If she denounced herself, she would probably have done so right away."

"Will they come for me then? And if so, what will happen to me? What is the punishment for passing off a Moor as Old Christian?"

He looked at her askance, and a cloud passed over his face.

"Do not even think like that. Pepita *is* an Old Christian, and nothing will happen as long as I have a breath in my body. Now listen carefully. Stay right here and do not move or show yourself until I return. Then I will tell you what to do. Who else knows that she disappeared? Now please Isabel, trust me and do not lie to me. I must know."

"The servants knew, but I told them I got a message that she is with Uncle Jaime. Alfonso and Teresa alone know that she is still missing."

"Do they know why?"

"They think she is a true Valderocas, but they heard Pedro accuse her of being a Morisco. They think he did it to insult her."

"And that is the best story to stick to, no matter what happens," he said. "How loyal are they?"

"You know better than that," she said bitterly, "before the Holy Office there is no loyalty other than to our Holy Faith."

"Oh God, Isabel, who else knows?"

She hesitated long enough for him to realize that she was conscious all the time of his position as secretary to the Inquisitor General. What she was actually doing was denouncing all her accomplices without even having the excuse of being tortured into doing it. She was again sitting on the edge of the bed, and now he knelt down and took both her hands into his and looked into her eyes. He made his throaty Andalusian voice as smooth as if he wanted to seduce her again. "Isabel, you must tell me all you know. Remember, you promised to trust me implicitly."

"About Pepita, you mean? I do not know too much. Just what my mother told me before she died."

"No, no. Forget all that. Pepita is a true Valderocas. Old Christian as she can be. With whom have you talked at Madrid?"

Names. He wanted names.

"Just one person," she said, "an old man. I know he would not talk."

"And your Uncle Jaime knows?"

"Yes, of course."

"About the old man. Who is he? You said yourself that no one is loyal before the Holy Office. How do you know he can be trusted?"

"Why do you have to know his name?"

"Because I am going to risk my career and my life to find out whether Pepita has been arrested or whether there have been any charges against her or you or Pedro, and I want to make absolutely sure I am not going to trip over a Señor Unknown. If your old man by sheer coincidence was arrested on another charge, I would prefer to get him out myself before he can implicate you."

Here was her chance to take fate into her own hands. She vaguely heard Pedro's warning, "Do not trust him," and Uncle Jaime's advice, "Love him if you must but do not trust him," but life without even a grain of trust did not seem worth living.

"He is a bookseller," she said, "the father of a friend of mine, Señor Caietano."

"Oh, all right," his voice sounded relieved.

"You know him?" she asked.

"Not really. I bought a few books from him now and then. You must realize, however, that booksellers are people more liable to come in contact with the Inquisition than men of other trades. The Inquisition censors all books, imported, printed, or sold in Spain."

"And you think you can find out about Pepita?"

"If she has been arrested or charged with anything, I will find out where she is. In the meantime, you must stay here."

He took her in his arms and swiftly pressed his mouth to hers, then he was gone.

She waited, it seemed forever. She peered into the street from behind the louvered shutters. She watched water sellers,

mule teams, vegetable men, boys with baskets, street musicians, beggars who pretended to be blind or crippled, a gang
of gypsies dancing on stilts and attracting attention while their
youngsters stole right and left. *Pícaros*, all of them?

No, *pícaros* were vagabonds and swindlers out of choice,
not out of necessity. A life of begging and stealing appeared
more attractive to them than a life of work. Although, God
knew, they worked hard enough at being ne'er-do-wells. They
were a sharp-witted lot, the true *pícaros;* their mothers were
whores and their fathers were hangmen; he who joined them
without experience was exploited mercilessly. Did Pepita
know this? Where was Pepita? Beaten senseless and robbed
of whatever she had taken with her? Suffering in a dark
dungeon? Learning to earn her daily bread by selling her
body? Oh God, please do not let Rafael find her, Isabel
prayed. She would rather go out and search herself.

Rafael came back after dark. The only inquisitorial arrests
that week had been a couple of men accusing each other of
sodomy. There were no unaccounted murder victims either,
nor was Pepita among the dozen harlots thrown into the city
jail. He did not know whether to feel elated or dejected.

"I do not want you to go on searching for her the way you
have been doing. You might come to harm."

"I must, Rafael. I will find no peace otherwise."

"I wish I could go with you, but most unfortunately I am
being sent to Córdoba."

"What for?"

"To go over some matters with the Archbishop. You know
that I had accompanied him to Rome last year."

"Yes."

"I might have to go again, but not before next year."

"And to Córdoba?"

"Tomorrow. I will be away for a month at least."

"Oh Rafael!" She threw herself in his arms and clung to
him. "Be careful," she begged.

"What do you mean?"

"Do not get yourself into trouble because of Pepita or me.
And don't worry. I will take care of myself."

"I despise the thought of you being alone in Madrid. I
always thought of you as being someone entirely invulnerable. This thing with Pepita comes as a bad surprise."

"You think I should not have told you?"

"No, I think you should not have told her. I think your

mother should not have told you. Too many families labor at
their own downfall. Talk to no one. Confide in no one. Trust
no one."

He almost sounded like Pedro or Uncle Jaime.

"Trust no one but you?" she asked.

"Me, yes. But I will not always be with you. You know
that. You must learn to keep your own counsel."

"Let us keep this apartment forever," she said. "I will
come here to think about you, even next year when you go to
Rome."

"Until you get married."

"Why do you keep saying that?"

He gave her a strange, sad look, as if he could see the
future and perceived misery.

Why, oh why did he crave the most blood-stained office on
earth?

# 8.

In the meantime, Alfonso and Teresa had gone about their
own discreet inquiries and come up with a few ideas which
they submitted to Isabel. Alfonso, red-faced and embarrassed, told her of a certain Juliana, mistress of a place called
La Casa de Celestina, who had the reputation of helping
young ladies in distress. But it might take a lot of cash to
make her talk. Teresa suggested a fortune-teller who—also
for a good many ducats—could fall into a trance and converse
with the spirits of the deceased and thereby discover whether
a person was dead or alive. Another possible source of
information was an astrologer, renowned for having cast
horoscopes for members of the royal family. If Isabel knew
Pepita's birthdate, he might be able to tell what had happened to her.

Isabel's common sense told her to try Juliana first.

Dressed well, but not too fashionably, with a veil completely hiding her face, she took a sedan chair for hire to the
entrance gate of Celestina's Casa. At first, she had considered
asking the porters to leave her at the corner of the street, but
then she was glad she had not, for the narrow lane stank
fresh garbage debris and excrement thrown from the houses

with the mere warning, *"Agua va!"* If she had walked, she would have been splattered with filth.

The men leered at her when she paid them.

The doorman, a heavy ruffian with a face like a battlefield, opened the wrought-iron gate and stared at her in such a way that she wondered whether she had landed by mistake in the fortress of a chief of the criminal brotherhood, the *germanía*. It was past five o'clock, a most civil hour for one lady to call upon another, so why was he suspicious?

"You want to talk to Doña Juliana, eh? Take off the veil."

"I beg your pardon?"

Without further ado he pulled the front of her veil and threw it back. Frightened, she took a step away from him. He grinned lewdly. His two front teeth were missing. Apparently, she passed inspection, for he turned and called over his shoulder, "Cojuelo!"

The next rogue limped and wore an eye patch, but at least his remaining eye neither glared nor leered, and she followed him into a long, narrow hallway. Half-way down the corridor three steps led into a courtyard with a marble fountain, statues, and climbing bougainvillea. Many thick cushions were distributed at random on the mosaic floor. Cojuelo pointed to one of them, and she took that as an invitation to be seated.

Preferring to stay upright, she walked around and looked at the statues, all nudes in suggestive poses.

"None of them are as pretty as you, my dear," said a well-modulated throaty voice. She swirled around and saw a woman of about fifty with tawny, silver-streaked hair, highly inflated nostrils, and slanted hazel eyes heavily lined with kohl. These, and her pointed chin, made her look like a fox.

"Doña Juliana?" Isabel asked.

"Yes?"

"I am . . ." Juliana lifted a slim brown hand and interrupted.

"Do not tell me who you are, just tell me what you want." She led Isabel to a mattress covered with Moorish embroidery. "Sit down. Now what is your trouble?"

"I am looking for a girl."

"What kind of girl?" Juliana sounded friendly. Isabel sank down gracefully on the mattress, and Juliana sat on a cushion opposite her and fanned herself lightly, very much like a lady of quality.

"The girl is my cousin. She ran away from home."

"Why?"

What would Pepita tell people? Possibly the exact contrary of the truth.

"She was supposed to marry a titled old man she did not like," Isabel said.

"So you have money?"

"Oh, yes."

"What a pity."

Isabel's face turned into a polite question mark.

"I would have liked you to work for me," Juliana explained.

"I am sorry," Isabel said, "but I will certainly pay you for your time and effort. Would you look at this sketch and tell me whether you have seen the girl?"

Isabel stood up, and immediately Juliana leaped nimbly to her feet. When Isabel showed her the Velázquez sketch, Juliana shook her head.

"No," she said, "she has not come here. At least not yet."

"Thank you," Isabel said and turned to leave.

"No wait," Juliana held her back and removed Isabel's veil. "Your hair, it is beautiful. High cheekbones . . . the finest, whitest skin I have ever seen . . ." She seemed to talk to herself. "Wait, perhaps I could still help you. I know everything that goes on in this town, everything worth knowing, that is. If your cousin is staying in Madrid, my boys will find her sooner or later. When it comes to finding a lost girl as pretty as this one," she pointed to the drawing, "no one can help you more than Juliana. At any rate," she moved closer to Isabel and almost whispered, "I would like you to meet a special friend of mine; you are everything his heart desires. You will stay here until he comes."

"Thank you very much," Isabel said taking a step away from her, "I really cannot impose myself any longer. . . ."

But Juliana laughed, "No imposition, sweet-face!" Then she clapped her hands sharply, and out of nowhere three old ghastly, garish females pounced upon Isabel and pulled her away.

"To Señor Vicente's room," Juliana ordered, and when Isabel tried to free herself, their grip on her arms tightened.

"Better come along, dear, or you will be black and blue."

Suddenly frightened, Isabel let out a shrill shriek, but that only brought the scar-faced ruffian along, and one look at his square massive body shocked her into docility. They took her to an upstairs room with a four-poster bed boasting red satin sheets and matching curtains. In no time at all, they had stripped her of all her clothes. Juliana stood in the doorway, supervising the operations. When they handed her the skirt, she lifted it, as if to weigh it.

"You should not walk around with all that money," she said, giving off clucking sounds of disapproval. Then she sat and calmly began to count the ducats she extracted from Isabel's pockets. From time to time, she looked up to comment upon her figure.

"They should have put an iron corset on you when you were younger," she said. "That would have kept your breasts small. But otherwise you are slim, almost lean. I get too many foreigners these days, all fat like upholstery. Here, put this on." Juliana threw her a long blue cape which her three tormentors draped around her shoulders. Then the limping fellow came and brought a wooden box into which Juliana put the money.

"Two hundred ducats," she said. "That is enough to keep a man alive for a couple of years, and comfortably at that."

"Perhaps you should ask a ransom for her, instead of throwing her to that pig Vicente," a grumbling voice suggested, and Isabel realized that all this time the heavy ruffian had stood just outside the door.

"There is nobody who would pay for me," Isabel heard her own voice, clear and bitter with contempt. "That money is all I have. And that story about my cousin was a lie. I really came for something else."

"Oh, a quick-wit, eh?" Juliana said.

"I will explain it to you," Isabel offered, not sure yet what tale to invent.

"You'll do your explaining later," Juliana said. "Tomorrow will be early enough. Just let me know one thing. Are you going to be a shrew or an experienced little pinch-prick? I'd like to warn my customers."

"You want me to examine her?" the oldest of the three witches asked. Isabel looked at her with horror. She had bloodshot eyes, a long nose almost touched her upper lip, her wrinkled skin was blotchy, and the rims of her clawlike fingernails were in mourning.

"Don't you dare touch me," Isabel spat. "Can you look into my eyes? They are blue and mean, and there will be no hand to protect you!"

The woman crossed herself and fled in terror. In some parts

of Spain, blue eyes were considered bad luck, but Isabel had suggested that she possessed the evil eye, against which only the wearing of a charm in the form of a hand could protect. People afflicted with the evil eye would protect their friends against any danger by offering them charms or by giving them a special blessing before looking them in the eye, lest they hurt them inadvertently.

"Evil eye, my ass!" Juliana said, but Isabel saw that she put her hand on her flat bosom and she suspected that the latter-day Celestina wore all kinds of charms under her dress.

"As you like," Isabel said, "but no examination will be necessary. I am not a virgin, and I know my way around men."

"For Vicente we might have to fix that," Juliana said, "but perhaps you know already how to do it yourself?"

"I know everything," Isabel assured her haughtily. "I told you I came for a good reason. I am sure you and I can do some business, if you but give me a chance to talk to you alone."

Up to that moment, the house had been quiet, and Isabel had thought herself alone with the four women and the two men. Now there were other sounds coming to her, snatches of songs, laughter, giggling—apparently the household was waking up from its siesta.

"Till later then," Juliana said with a gurgling laugh. She gave a sign to the two remaining women, and in a trice the room was empty, the door snapped shut, a key was turned, and Isabel was alone.

A sharp bite on her buttocks made her jump. She flung the cape away and shook herself. It was preferable to stay naked than in a flea-bag.

For the first time she looked at her prison cell. Besides the four-poster, there was a narrow marble-top table leaning against one wall and above it a gilt-framed mirror flanked by gilt wall sconces with twisted yellow wax candles. Two chairs with carved backs but no arms completed the furniture. The most remarkable thing about the room was its ceiling and wall paintings. They represented a park with hedges and trees and grottos inhabited by sensual beings from Greek mythology. Playful nymphs were spied upon by hideously grinning satyrs whose phalli were drawn by the artist with a consuming love for detail. Priapus himself sat on a tree stump, legs spread open toward his worshippers, especially a half-dressed young shepherdess about to place a kiss on the rosy tip of his gigantic erection. Further down, on the border of a lake, Leda embraced the inevitable swan, but here the artist's imagination had failed. He had obviously never studied a swan's reproductive organs, and there was nothing but an abundance of white feathers and Leda's shapely legs encircling the bird. A bull's penis, on the other hand, as well as his *cojones,* were only too familiar to most Spaniards. Therefore the rape of Europa could be shown satisfactorily, although why Europa should gaze lovingly at the deadly horns of such an animal would be a mystery to most *aficionados.* Danaë— completely contrary to legend—had been taken out of her brazen tower, while Zeus, in his form as a golden rain, fell lovingly upon her half-parted lips, her nipples, and her curly pubic hair. Aphrodite herself looked with desire upon her father Zeus, while at the same time giving herself to her brother Hermes and promising an identical pleasure to her brother Dionysus, waiting in line.

In spite of her embarrassing plight, Isabel was amused by the frescoes. From a purely artistic viewpoint, they were below the work of a Velázquez or a Rubens, but for sexual inventiveness, they surpassed anything she had ever seen, and she wondered whether Rafael would appreciate them. The thought of Rafael brought her sharply back to reality. She knew it would be in vain, but nevertheless she tried the door. Made of heavy oak and locked! The window? Large enough, but well guarded by picturesque iron grilles. She was trapped, no doubt about it. She was a stupid, naked girl locked in the luxurious chamber of a whorehouse. No longer the intelligent Isabel Valderocas, haughty heiress to a shipping fortune, brilliant manager of a banking and trading house, protégée of the most important couple in Spain—no, she was the dupe of a common gang of *pícaros.* What good were the novels depicting the perfidy of those people? What good was the fact that she had read the classical century-old play *La Celestina,* that through Quevedo's books she knew all about vagabonds and thieves and pimps and the criminal brotherhood called *germanía?*

Should she disclose who she was? No! The scandal would be all over Madrid within a few hours. No one, but no one, must ever know she was here. But how the devil was she going to escape?

She went to the bed and inspected the crimson sheets. The upper one looked doubtfully clean, the bottom sheet had some spots on it. All right, the upper sheet then. She pulled it off and shook it and went over it inch by inch. When she could detect neither crawling nor jumping insects, she folded the sheet and wrapped it twice around her, tucking in the top. The flea-ridden blue cape she kicked into a corner.

Then she walked to the window. The courtyard with the marble fountain was filling with women, young girls, old women, big women, small women. Two of them were dressed in transparent veils. There were rugs on the tile floor now, covered by more cushions and more mattresses, and they sat crosslegged like well-bred Spanish ladies, or lay half-reclining like Roman temple goddesses. A dozen dogs leaped and chased each other and barked, and in a corner a blind gypsy played a guitar.

Isabel closed the shutters, so she could see without being seen. Juliana walked among the girls, jesting and laughing and pointing up to Isabel's window. Was she telling everyone she had caught a rare bird for Señor Vicente?

Vicente, she thought she had heard that name before, but could not recall when or where. Some unknown turbulence kept churning within her—fear? No, that would be absurd. As Rafael had said, the only reason to be deathly afraid was the Inquisition. Being caught in a whorehouse—objectively seen—was rather funny; but a devilish nuisance too.

She planned her escape. When the door would open to let in whoever was coming, she would be standing there. She would push him aside and run like a devil from holy water. Then they would be behind her, trying to catch her, but she would make a raging pest of herself, and they would be glad to be rid of her and throw her out into the street. This seemed the only way she could escape. She must keep the blue cape ready, however, for she could not run with the red sheet around her. But there still was enough time, she would hear them coming.

Night was falling. Torchlights were lit in the patio. The first men arrived, joked with Juliana, went from girl to girl, pinched exposed nipples, lifted skirts, pulled the lass of their choice up from her cushion and disappeared in the hallway. Others stayed outside, let themselves fall down on a mattress next to a girl and hollered for service. Youngsters resembling seasoned demons brought trays laden with appetizers and drinks. Isabel could recognize onions and garlic and cheese on the plates. How could anyone possibly eat that and then make love?

Hours dragged on endlessly. Isabel was still alone. No one came to bother her; no one opened the door. They had forgotten she existed. But she never left the window. She had carried one of the chairs to it and was sitting, her nose glued to the louvered shutters.

All of a sudden a wave of hilarious shrieks came from below. A customer had brought a bitch in heat. The dogs were yelping and going wild.

"Hey girls," the owner of the bitch shouted, "Look at that dozen pricks, all for one hot cunt. Why don't you take pity on your beasts and oblige them. I'll pay for the whole lot of them."

In the meantime, the strongest of the dogs was panting on top of the bitch to the accompaniment of clapping and shouts of *olé*.

"Now you frightened her," the owner complained. "See, they can't get away from each other." That called for a new wave of laughter.

"You'd like that to happen to you, I wager," a fat harlot shouted.

He took up the challenge. "If you can do that to me, I'll pay you double."

New customers arrived.

"Sorry gentlemen, you'll have to wait," Juliana said. "There are no more rooms."

There was her room, Isabel thought. Perhaps Vicente would not show up—whoever he was.

But Juliana would see to that. Right under Isabel's window she gave her instructions, doubtless so that her prisoner could hear her.

"You two, go, run through all the *tascas*. If you see Señor Vicente, you know, the tall one with the mask, tell him Juliana has a special treat for him."

There had never been a feeling like this for her. Her armpits were wet with nervous sweat, her hands trembled, her whole body felt taut like the string of a guitar.

The clients who could not get rooms went about their business right there in the patio: "Here, pinch-prick, stuff a cushion under your ass, it's more comfortable that way."—"I want the two of you, sucking one and fucking the other."—"Eh that costs double!"—"Never mind, feel that bag? That's ducats, but my *cojones* are just as full."

And there was the familiar slop-man, walking around with his chamber pot for hire.

Had Pedro really come to a place like this? Pedro! Hadn't he mentioned a Señor Vicente?

Into the patio walked Juliana, leading the way. She was followed by a well-built man wearing an elegant plumed hat, a court collar, and a full vizard. His silhouette against the torchlights seemed slightly familiar. He held himself very straight and walked gracefully.

"Udsdaggers, old girl, she better be all you say, or I'll have you whipped for dragging me away from your competition."

That voice! Resonant like an actor's. That walk! Harmonious like an accomplished dancer's. It couldn't be, it just couldn't be. . . .

Finally, the key was turned in the lock, the door opened. Isabel stood motionless behind the chair, gripping its back with both hands, incapable of walking even one step. She had a brief glimpse of Juliana lifting an oil lamp and lighting the way for one of her boys who came with a long taper to light the candles in the wall sconces.

"Here she is, all beautiful and frightened, aren't you dear?" Juliana said with poorly hidden irony flitting through her voice. "A challenge only you can appreciate." The last words were addressed to the strangely familiar looking man with the face mask.

"Leave us alone," the man said. Again the door fell shut. He pushed a bolt.

Isabel did not move. She was almost sure now of his identity, and she wondered, apprehensively, what he would do next.

"Come here, let me look at you."

He walked over to her and softly put his hands on hers, by his touch loosening her grip on the chair, then he pulled her to the light. But as soon as he got a look at her face, he dropped her hands and stood paralyzed. She thought she could see the expression of horrified surprise under the black silk mask, and since she had recognized him, she did the only sensible thing a Spanish lady could do in the presence of her monarch. She sank into a deep curtsy.

"Your Majesty."

He held out his right hand to her and drew her up, while at the same time removing his hat and his vizard. His face, if anything, showed incomprehension. His mouth hung slightly open, his moist lower lip looked thicker than ever, his blue eyes were bewildered as if he dared not believe what he saw.

They looked into each other's eyes for a moment and again

he dropped her hand. His glance swept over her quaint costume, her bare feet, her red-golden hair falling in loose waves to her shoulders.

"Is it really you? What happened? What are you doing here?"

"I was carried off against my will. They took everything I had."

"Who?"

"The owners of this place, I suppose."

"But how? Why?"

"I don't know. Sire . . ."

"Stop. Don't call me that here. Here I am known as Señor Vicente."

An idea came to her. He probably did not much relish their mutual encounter in a place like this. After all, she did know the Queen and the Countess Olivares, in fact the whole of Court society. This meeting could furnish some saucy material for Quevedo. And on another score, he would obviously be embarrassed if she should disclose his true identity to their common hostess Juliana. He did take the pains of coming masked, so he did not want to be recognized. If she betrayed him here, he would not dare come back—which would mean a disappointment to him, since he obviously enjoyed the place as a regular customer.

If he had in any way been drunk with wine or desire, the unexpected confrontation sobered him quickly.

"Since when are you here? What have they done to you?"

"Nothing, except robbed me of all my clothes and two hundred ducats. You see, I was on a shopping trip. Oh, I suppose I could have saved myself by telling them who I am, but Sire, how could I do that? They must not know who I am. The gossip would ruin our name."

"Nobody touched you?"

"Oh no. No one even came up here after some ghastly creatures undressed me and left me here in order to sell me to Señor Vicente." She could not help a mocking lilt when she pronounced his fictitious name, and an amused glitter leaped up in his eyes.

"I told you once before what I think of gossip," he said, "but this time I must agree with you. We should try to avoid it. As for Juliana, she outdid herself."

"What do you mean, Sire?"

"Please!"

"Señor Vicente."

"That's better. I must have described you so often, she recognized the original of my desire when she saw you. So you were lured here under a pretext and she kept you here, locked up since . . . ?"

"Since six o'clock."

"This afternoon?"

"Yes."

"You are lucky I came tonight. I don't come often, you know." To judge by the boyish smile spreading over his long face, he apparently decided to treat this as a comic episode, and he allowed himself a chuckle of relief. "What would you have done if Señor Vicente had turned out to be a *pícaresque* cutthroat?"

"I was prepared to bribe whomever came up here to take me home. Will you take me home, Señor Vicente?"

"Well now," he said, "you know, of course, that you don't have to bribe me. As a matter of fact, I think we understand our mutual situation only too well. On the other hand, how long has it been since you have granted me the joy of your company? You know how I feel about you."

He looked around, saw the chair leaning against the wall at the place where poor Europa was giving in, and started to remove his outer clothes, hanging up his hat and his sword, throwing off his cape and the vest with the curved collar.

"Do you mind if I make myself comfortable for a while? I am rather tired of protocol and Court ceremonies. That is why I come here where no one knows me."

He stood in front of her in nothing but his slim tight breeches. His body was handsome, the body of a man spending a great amount of time on vigorous outdoor sports. She appeared small and frail in her makeshift finery, and he softly placed his hands on her shoulders.

"Isabel," he whispered, "do you remember who I am?"

For a second she was confused. What did he mean? Then she remembered his words on that far-away day in Velázquez's studio when he had said he would wait till she forgot that he was the King. On the other hand, could he ever expect to be Señor Vicente for her? Would that not place her on the same level as all the other girls of this place? Who did he want to be?

"Felipe?" she asked, pronouncing the Spanish version of his name as lovingly as if she had called him sweetheart.

"I am still in love with you," he said. "I still want you more than any other woman."

She lowered her thick long lashes. What could she say to that?

"Don't you feel anything when I touch you?" His hands were sliding down her arms, up again, along the decolleté of the red satin sheet, that thin protection, so easily undone.

"Look at me."

She looked at him with a timid smile. He bent down to kiss her, tenderly, almost chastely; then, when she did not move away, he took her in his arms. His breath smelled faintly of garlic, and she was afraid he would want to explore her mouth with his tongue. She dreaded it, but instead he started to kiss her throat, her neck, behind her ears, while his hands slid expertly over her body, still outside the satin sheet.

She began to feel it then, a delicious swelling, a wetness seeping down her thighs, her body responding as easily as if she had always desired to have Felipe de Habsburg for a lover. His left hand encircled her waist, holding her tightly, while his right slowly pulled out the top of the sheet and slid down to stroke her breasts in a gently caressing motion all around her nipples, but without touching them.

"I will not wait another two years for such an opportunity," he whispered. "I want you now. You need not be afraid of me. No one will ever know. And I will be careful, I will not hurt you." He buried his face between her breasts, and she could feel his lips and the tip of his tongue on her skin.

His avid hands, now all over her body, had pulled away the sheet completely, and one hand slid down between her thighs. Suddenly he stopped.

"But you want me," he said, as if surprised. "You do want me. Come." He made an attempt to pull her to the bed, but she resisted.

"Not here," she said imploringly. "I could never face you again if we do not leave this place first."

"Why not here?" he asked. "It is perfect. No one knows us, no one will disturb us."

A new wave of coarse laughter came up from the patio. Isabel shook herself in disgust.

"You are right," he said. "Let us escape this place. Just tell me the three words I want to hear, and I will take you home and give you time to forget you ever saw this place. I promise I will take you home now, if you promise that you will come and be mine when I call you."

She smiled at him and nodded and swiftly picked up the sheet and wrapped it around herself like a cape.

A frown came into his face, and she feared he would change his mind. Then he took two rapid steps to the door, pulled back the bolt, and opened it brusquely. Juliana almost tumbled into the room.

"Eavesdropping, eh? A pox on your bawdy curiosity! Go get the girl's clothes and her two hundred ducats, or this is the last you've seen of me!" Señor Vicente completely lacked the royal qualities of forbearance and patience, and apparently he got along well without them, for Juliana sounded intimidated, despite her protests.

"I only wanted to make sure everything was all right. And by my troth, I dare swear I don't know anything about two hundred ducats."

"Udsdaggers, old whore, d'you want an army of catchpoles to descend on your stinking place, or d'you want to stay in business?"

Juliana threw a glance of baffled hatred at Isabel and crossed herself, mumbling something about evil eyes and she-devils.

Isabel dressed as quickly as she could, conscious that Philip never took his eyes off her. When she put on her veil, she left one eye free, in the manner of professional streetwalkers.

They made a grand exit. Before the choice of losing her best customer or keeping a small cash profit, Juliana's business sense took over, and she swallowed her pride to the point of grudgingly admiring Isabel's talent.

"If I had known you're one of us, I wouldn't have played that trick on you. I hope you take it as the prank it was meant to be."

As soon as they stepped out into the street, Isabel pulled her veil to completely cover her face. Philip was wearing his full mask. A coach drawn by four mules was waiting for them.

"So you are a maid then," he said to her, loud enough for the ears of his coachdriver, "and where do you live, my dear?"

"Calle Santiago."

"Calle Santiago," he said to the driver.

Inside the coach, behind drawn curtains, Isabel lay in his arms.

"You still have not told me what I want to hear," he whispered in her ear.

"How can I admit it?" she whispered back, "I don't want to fall in love with you."

"But why not?"

"Because you would never be faithful."

"Again, I should have taken you when I had a chance."

"Then I would have despised you. Instead I love you."

"No," he said, "you don't love me yet. But you want me. That's what I wanted to hear. And that makes you so much more precious to me."

So he really feared that most girls only let him have his way because he was the King. What a pity, for he was perceptive and pleasant to be with. Actually, it would have been easy to let him make love to her; if the place had not been so horrid, she would not have been able to remain virtuous. Strangely enough, the response of her body was completely separated from her other feelings; she could easily visualize herself in the ultimate embrace with the King without losing any of her love for Rafael.

His hand went under her skirt. "Let me touch you once more," he begged. She was not in any position to act self-righteously. He was kind enough—or diplomatic enough —to take her home when he could have taken her to the palace.

"Tell me," he said again. But although at that moment it would have been the pure truth, she could not bring herself to say "I want you," for fear it might prove too strong an aphrodisiac. He touched her softly, proving to himself that he still excited her, and he started to kiss her with wild abandon. When the coach stopped at the corner of Calle Santiago, they were a few yards from Valderocas House.

She pulled herself away from him and sat up straight, before the groom opened the door and helped her out. Her face was veiled again, and Philip too had pulled his mask back in place.

During the summer months, night was the only time to cool off, so the streets were more crowded than during the daylight hours. She had to fend off compliments while walking the few steps to the entrance gate of her house. The door was opened immediately. Alfonso and Teresa had been waiting for her, anxiously.

But before she entered the security of her own home, she turned around to look back at the coach. He was still there, leaning out of the window, and she waved briefly.

# 9.

Since she did not know Pepita's birthdate, Isabel judged a visit to the astrologer unnecessary, but she wanted to try the fortune-teller. Not about to repeat her colossal mistake, she took the biggest Valderocas town coach with the decorative golden V that looked like a coat of arms, and she also took Alfonso and several other footmen, instructing them to wait for her outside the narrow house and to come in after her if she was not back outside within the hour.

The fortune-teller, La Cofrada, was a woman of indefinite age dressed in black and reeking of rancid olive oil. She occupied one obscure room above a cook-shop where she apparently lived, slept, ate, and went about her business. The main decorations, as far as Isabel could see, were bones—relics or remainders of what went into the shop's meat pies, it was difficult to tell—but there was also a shelf with glass phials of many colors and little containers of clay holding powders and lotions and unguents. An assortment of herbs and roots was hanging from the ceiling, and a half-dozen live cats lay around sleepily on a mattress.

Isabel, upon seeing the place, had little hope of success; nevertheless she stated her business. She showed the sketch of Pepita and told more or less the same story she had told Juliana, adding that she wanted to find out whether Pepita, whom she called her sister, was still among the living.

La Cofrada contemplated the drawing for a long time, then she pointed to a greasy cushion on the floor.

"Sit down. I have a question first."

Isabel sat on the cushion.

"If you do not tell me the truth, I cannot help you," La Cofrada said.

"What do you have to know?" Isabel asked.

"That girl, she is not your sister."

An astute remark. La Cofrada had intuition and perhaps a knowledge of human frailty.

"Yes," Isabel admitted.

"Then why did you lie to me?"

"I wanted to test you."

"Are you satisfied?"

"Yes."

La Cofrada looked at Isabel's clothes, then went to the window to throw a glance at her coach.

"If I fall into a deep sleep, I will not be able to work for several days; it tires me very much. That means I will not be able to see other clients."

"How much?" Isabel asked.

"Twenty ducats."

"Ten," Isabel said. She hated to haggle, but she knew the woman would otherwise regret not having asked for more.

"Eighteen."

"Fifteen, and I will recommend you to my friends at Court if we get results." She gave her the money and watched her deposit it in a leather box among the bones.

After chasing the cats from the mattress, La Cofrada chose a human skull from her collection of bones, stretched out on the mattress, placed the skull on her breast, and folded her hands over it.

"Do not be scared if you hear voices different from mine," she said. "The spirits will talk directly through me to you. And do not accuse me afterwards of anything they said. I will not remember anything when I come out of the sleep."

She breathed deeply several times, then she started to sigh and groan. She opened her mouth, her breathing became shallow, and a deep voice said, "What do you want to know?"

Startled, Isabel turned around, but she was alone with the woman, the voice must have come from her.

"I want to find a young woman named Pepita Valderocas," Isabel said.

"I do not know her," the voice answered.

"Could you please find out whether she is dead or alive?" Isabel asked, politely but also timidly.

"Wait then," the voice said.

For several minutes there was nothing but La Cofrada's shallow breathing. Then the voice spoke again.

"She is not known among the spirits of the dead."

Angered by the voice's apparent ignorance and fearing she had made a fool of herself, Isabel spoke up more boldly.

"And who are you?" she asked, raising her own tone of voice.

It was a mistake.

"How dare you ask me, insulting mortal, searcher of Moors," the voice roared. "Out of here, infidel, go to Granada!"

Frightened, Isabel jumped up, the cats mewed, and their hair bristled as if a dog were around, but La Cofrada lay on her mattress showing no signs of life, except for her shallow breathing. Isabel picked up her fallen courage. "Why to Granada?" she inquired more placidly. But there was no further answer. She went to touch the woman's folded hands. They felt cold.

"Wake up," she said, for the fortune-teller looked waxen and ready to die. "Please wake up. I will pay you twenty ducats. Please wake up."

The woman did not move. Resolutely, Isabel took away the skull, whereupon La Cofrada began to breathe deeply as in the beginning, then she moaned and opened her eyes.

She looked drowsy. Slowly she sat up.

"Oh, you," she said. "Why did you wake me up? Was something wrong? Was there no spirit? Sometimes one has to wait, you know." She glanced at the wooden box.

"Your spirit insulted me," Isabel said, just in case it was all a sham. "He was very rude, and I do not think I can recommend you to my friends."

The woman touched her forehead.

"I am sorry," she said. "I suppose you want your money back, but I assure you I am completely exhausted. I swear by the Holy Virgin that it is not my fault."

"Well, anyway, you may keep your fifteen ducats," Isabel said.

La Cofrada said nothing. Apparently, she really had not heard Isabel's offer of twenty, or was it all part of a clever deception, her way of maintaining her reputation?

"Come to think of it, I will pay you the twenty ducats you originally asked for, so then if I ever decide to come again the spirits may be more polite."

"The spirits have nothing to do with money," La Cofrada said. "Money means nothing to them."

Nevertheless, Isabel handed her another five ducats which she added to those already in the box.

Glad to escape the gloomy bone collection and the stench of rancid oil and cat urine, Isabel hurried back to the coach, but for the remainder of the day she stayed home and pondered over the words that somehow had come out of La Cofrada's mouth. "Searcher of Moors, infidel, go to Granada." How could the woman know that Pepita was a Moor, unless the drawing reminded her of someone with Moorish blood. She had looked at it for a long time, perhaps the thought that Pepita looked Moorish had crossed her brain. Granada had been the last stronghold of the Moors in Spain. Granada and Moors went together. And anyone looking for a Moor and taking an abnormal interest in a Moor, might be termed an infidel. So everything could be explained logically. And yet, there was something uncanny about her experience.

That afternoon Carlos de Queras came to call upon her, accompanied by the Count of Villaquemada, but Isabel asked her maid Maria to present her excuses. She did not feel well enough to receive anyone. A royal lacky brought an invitation to join Their Majesties for dinner and a private theatrical, but she sent a note that she feared she was coming down with a quartan ague and would not be able to attend.

All other visitors and invitations were fobbed off with the same story.

Meanwhile, she thought and thought and rethought. Whether or not La Cofrada was truly a mouthpiece through which the spirits of the deceased could talk, what she had said made sense. If Pepita were neither dead nor in the claws of the Inquisition, she might, indeed, have gone to Granada. There might not be any Moors left at Granada, but if Pepita wanted to try to get in contact with any remaining Moorish communities, she would certainly go to Andalusia, and not to the towns where she might be known, like Sevilla or Córdoba, but more likely to the city of which she had sung so often but which she had never visited.

It was not in Isabel's character to hesitate over decisions, not for her to wonder, to waver, to hang in doubt. It never took her long to make up her mind, and by nightfall she had resolved to go to Granada in search of her cousin.

# 10.

The beginning of August was the hottest season in Spain. Thirsty for the rains that never came, the Manzanares, torrential in winter and spring, had dried up and become a mere brook so shallow that visitors to Madrid were joking the

Madrileños would do well to sell their imposing Segovia bridge in exchange for some water. Even the liquid refuse thrown daily into the streets was soaked up quickly, and there was dust everywhere, seeping into the houses, settling on the furniture, invading noses and lungs. No one went outside without using at least a half-mask over nose and mouth, and all those who could afford it added huge spectacles surrounded by veils. After sleeping all day, people left their homes toward nine in the evening in search of the fresh breeze from the Sierra Guadarrama, and at night friends visited each other and chatted in front of their houses until four or five in the morning.

Señor Caietano strongly opposed Isabel's plan to travel, but since she was not his daughter, he could not prevent her from doing what she wanted. He insisted, however, that she take his third son José along, as one of her attendants. José was twenty now, well-built and agile like a bullfighter and blessed with a special knack for getting along with vagabonds and ne'er-do-wells. He had attended the University of Alcalá, but he was passionately interested in the ways of the common people. He was writing a book on a hypothetical revolt by the *pícaros*. His previous claim to fame was the publication of a *pícaro* dictionary much praised by dramatic authors who liked to add authentic touches to their plays about *pícaros*. His dictionary also contained a chapter on the manners and morals of the *germanía*, the official crime organization of Spain, whose members were not mere pickpockets and swindlers, but seasoned criminals who had to qualify to belong by either having served a sentence as galley slaves, having been flogged in public, or having escaped a death sentence. Members of the *germanía* were assassins for hire, armed robbers, and relapsed thieves. Señor Caietano felt that in José's company, Isabel would be well protected.

They decided upon the excuse that she would go on a pilgrimage, Santa Maria having appeared to her in a dream and ordered her to visit certain shrines.

Preparations were quickly completed. She traveled in a litter covered with oilcloth and carried by four mules. They took another sixteen mules along, eight armed footmen, two mule-drivers, her maid Maria, and Pasquito.

Alfonso and Teresa stayed behind in charge of Valderocas House.

They set out for Toledo early one morning, right after dawn. From Toledo, where Isabel had stopped to talk things over with Uncle Jaime, they traveled to Ciudad Real. The road was dusty but otherwise smooth, and apart from a few clergymen riding on mules and holding black parasols over their heads, they encountered no one except the inevitable flocks of sheep and now and then a local peasant. South of Ciudad Real the road began to climb. They were nearing the eastern spur of the Sierra Morena, the great mountain chain in the south of Spain. Unlike the wooded Sierra Guadarrama, these mountains had arid slopes and naked brown rocks—an eery landscape where Isabel expected at any moment to come upon the knight of the woeful countenance.

Twice they had to stop to spend the night between Ciudad Real and the mountain pass of Despeñaperros. Each time they found a miserable inn consisting of nothing but two interconnected rooms, one for the humans and one for the animals, although judging from the odors and the filth, the human side was hardly distinguishable from the animal side. The mountain pass was difficult. They had to follow tortuous valleys, and it took hours to advance a mile.

Having nothing else to do, Isabel talked a lot to Maria, and finally the girl lost her shyness and chatted pleasantly, instead of repeating her eternal, "Yes, Señora, no, Señora, thank you, Señora."

But when they finally reached the highest point of the pass, and Isabel told Maria that they were now descending toward Andalusia and that soon they would be at Jaén, the gateway to the old Moorish kingdom of Granada, Maria gave a gasp and became white in her face.

"Jaén," she said. "I did not know we would go to Jaén."

"And why not?" Isabel asked.

The girl bit her lip. "Jaén, that is a dreadful place."

"Why?"

"I come from Jaén."

"And so?"

"Jaén, no! no!" The girl was almost shaking. She obviously had memories of Jaén as a place in hell.

Isabel thought for a moment. Maria was sixteen, perhaps seventeen. She had picked her up one day in front of Caietano's, begging for a few reales to buy herself something to eat. Isabel had pitied her and taken her to Valderocas House. Since then, Maria had been a self-sufficient shadow, combing and brushing her mistress's hair, laying out her clothes, picking up her room, and helping Teresa, with whom she shared a small bedroom. Up until this voyage, Isabel had never really spoken to her. She did not know anything about the girl, except that she had Moorish ancestry, because Maria herself had told her that.

"What happened at Jaén?" Isabel asked.

"No, no!"

"Maria, the day I found you in the street, all thin and hungry, you looked to me like a girl who could be trusted. Now, if you do not tell me about Jaén, I will feel that you have betrayed my trust in you. You know I will protect you, no matter what happens."

"I cannot tell you," Maria whispered.

"All right. If that is how you feel, I cannot keep you any longer in my service."

For a moment, Maria fought with herself, then, with a toneless voice, she said, "There is a witch at Jaén."

"A witch? I cannot believe that."

"She took me in because my parents had died, when I was nine. She does terrible things. I cannot tell you, terrible. I finally ran away because I could not stay with her any longer. She says she is a holy woman, but at night, she flies away and kills little children and she serves the devil."

"How do you know?" Isabel asked, trying to remain serious and not to show her skepticism.

"I know. She wanted me to come with her. But I ran away."

"Why did you not denounce her to a priest?"

"Because the priest is her friend."

"The priest of Jaén is the friend of a witch?"

Maria looked at her with terrified eyes, and Isabel could see that Maria was frightened to death.

The information was intriguing. Of course, all Spanish villages had at least one local saint and one local witch. What was strange was to have the two combined in the same person. The woman who pretended to be a saint, while at night paying homage to Satan. It was too fantastic to be true. She would have to tell José, it might even inspire him to add a chapter to his book on *pícaros*.

An ancient town at the bottom of a mountain that jutted into the sky like a warrior and was crowned by an old castle built hundreds of years ago, Jaén used to guard the entrance to the fruitful kingdom of Granada. From the castle the *reconquistadores* could be seen for miles away and the kingdom alerted to the attackers. The town itself comprised old houses with whitewashed walls and purple tile roofs, a few aristocratic mansions whose owners did not care to reside here in the heat of summer, a small monastery, a convent, the Alcalde's house, several inns, and a glorious honey-brown cathedral whose original gothic architecture was in the process of being improved by baroque adornments.

Contrary to Isabel's expectations, the town was not an abandoned nest, but swarming with visitors celebrating an event in the life of some local patron saint. And there was to be a great procession and a play by a visiting troop of actors.

"What are we going to do? The inns must be full, where are we going to stay?" Isabel asked of José Caietano.

"No problem at all," said he. "Leave it to me, and we will be treated like royalty."

Isabel and Maria stayed in the litter and peered out from behind the curtains at the gaping crowd which soon formed around them. The footmen surrounded the litter as if they were guarding a king, for José had already given them his instructions. Ten minutes later he came back.

"The Alcalde of Jaén will be most honored to receive the Duchess de Miraflores in his own home."

"Duchess?"

"Yes, you are on a special pilgrimage to beg of all saints to grant the Duke and you the blessing of an heir."

"José!"

"It was the most respectable explanation I could think of. They are thrilled to the marrow of their bones to have such a fine personage grace their festivities."

"But what if the real Duke or Count or whoever owns this countryside shows up. Wouldn't they find out that there was no such title as Duke de Miraflores?"

"His Majesty can create a Duke with a flick of his finger. You will have to be outraged at the ignorance of whoever does not recognize the Duchess de Miraflores."

Isabel looked at Maria. "How does it feel to be the personal maid of a Duchess?"

Maria smiled warily. She was still afraid.

The Alcalde, Don Ricardo Lozado, had a pointed nose, bad breath, and a disconcerting way of constantly rubbing his hands. If he were honored to receive a Duchess, he was also visibly at a loss as to how to behave. It was not hard to guess that here was a country squire of the old Spanish school; he probably had never eaten at the same table with a woman, and Isabel's arrival upset whatever plans he had made for that evening. He was relieved when she assured him that the Duke and she never took their meals together, and that she would much prefer to retire to the ladies' quarters.

Maria held herself close to Isabel, just one step behind her, as if she expected at any moment to have to hang on to her mistress's skirt for dear life.

They were received in the ladies' sitting room by Doña Ana, a slim, tall beauty who did not look a day older than eighteen. It turned out that she was not Señor Lozado's daughter, as Isabel had thought, but his wife. She curtsied deeply to Isabel, then asked whether she would like her to send for a chair.

"But of course not, my dear," Isabel said and sank down, cross-legged, onto one of the richly embroidered cushions on the *estrado*. "I am much more comfortable like this."

"I thought that at Court all ladies sat on chairs," Doña Ana said.

"They would not dream of it," Isabel replied. "Why, even the Queen sits on the floor, and except for formal occasions, all the Court ladies prefer their floor cushions."

"I am afraid that Your Ladyship will find we are not prepared to receive Grandees. I beg you to forgive me if I make mistakes." She looked questioningly at Maria, who was still standing up.

"This is my personal maid," Isabel explained. "She never leaves my side."

"Of course, my Lady, please be seated, Señorita."

Maria sat on another cushion.

They talked about the inconvenience of travel and about the upcoming festivities, but all the while Doña Ana was casting furtive glances at Maria.

"I heard that you have a holy woman at Jaén," Isabel said finally. "Perhaps I should visit her. I am on a special pilgrimage."

Doña Ana blushed, and Isabel could have sworn she looked disturbed. She did not answer but instead rose and excused herself, saying she needed to give orders to the cook. As soon as she had left the room, Isabel and Maria looked at each other.

"What is the matter with her?" Isabel whispered. "Do you know her?"

Maria nodded. "She is an orphan," she whispered back, "one of the girls Angéla de Jesus took in, like me. An Old Christian though. She was in love with a young man from a good family. But then the priest got her, and then Angela fixed her up, and later they probably sold her to the Alcalde who used to have an old hag for a wife."

"Good God! Do you think she recognized you?"

"I think so. I was thirteen when I ran away. So it was only three years ago."

"What do you mean the priest got her?"

"Like he gets everyone," Maria hissed. "He takes all the girls he wants when they come to confession. Later, Angela fixes them up so they are like no man ever touched them."

Isabel slapped her forehead with the palm of her hand. "Many bad years and many boils and tumors plague them!" she muttered a common curse. Then she thought for a moment. "Do you think she likes to be married to the Alcalde?" she whispered into Maria's ear.

"That stinking old goat! She must hate every minute of it. But what can she do?"

Doña Ana walked back into the room. She had put white and red paint on her face, a little awkwardly. Was it an attempt to be fashionable for the Duchess, or to hide traces of tears?

"Doña Ana, I wonder if I could ask a special favor from you? It has to do with my pilgrimage, and it is a rather delicate matter . . ." She motioned Maria to get up and leave the room. Maria went, hesitantly, but she did pull the door shut.

"Ana," Isabel said as soon as they were alone, "I have come to help you. I have heard who you are and what happened to you, and I will help you to escape, if you want to leave Jaén. You can come with me to Madrid, where women can live comfortably without a husband, or you can live in a convent, if that is what you prefer. The only thing you have to do is make up your mind quickly."

The girl stared at her with bewildered eyes, and the thought flashed through Isabel's mind that she might suspect this to be a trap. So she went on talking swiftly. "A friend of yours told me how unhappy you are. I know you must wonder what this is to me, so I will tell you a secret. I am not a Duchess. That was an excuse to come here and talk to you. And I do not do this out of sympathy for unhappy wives, but because I want something from you in return."

But now Ana had had time to assemble her wits and as a girl who had seen more than one appalling side of life, she was quick to grasp her opportunity.

"Anything at all, so long as you help me to leave here."

"Oh, it is not much. The only thing I ask you is to look carefully at this picture and tell me whether any woman like this has recently come through Jaén."

She showed her the sketch of Pepita and described her cousin. But Ana shook her head.

"I am sorry. I am never allowed outside the house. I have not seen anyone since I was married."

"You mean they keep you a prisoner?"

"Wives are not supposed to go out, except to mass."

"To hear the inspired sermon of the special priest of Jaén?"

"Have you heard about him, too?" Ana asked.

"Yes. Do you think he or Sor Angela would have seen this girl, if she has come through Jaén?"

"She probably would. Oh, I wish I could be more helpful."

"Tell me one more thing, and I will be satisfied. Why doesn't anyone denounce this clergyman?"

"Because everyone is afraid of Sor Angela. She can put curses on people."

"Then how did she get the reputation of being a holy woman?"

"Oh, she is a saint all right. A saint of thieves and robbers and cutthroats. She does miracles for those who share their profits with her, and she curses those who do not accede to her wishes. Are you really going to take me with you? How will you be able to do it? I am never unchaperoned for a minute. I cannot leave the house unnoticed."

"I daresay you will be able to watch the procession with the Duchess de Miraflores. And if in the middle of all the speeches and sermons I should feel faint, you as my hostess will be obliged to accompany me. As a matter of fact, you will be around me most of the time. Today is Friday. Tomorrow I will have to visit the famous holy woman and the priest to find out whether they have seen my cousin, and Sunday, in the height of confusion, we will leave. Do not worry, everything will go well."

"Do not go alone to see the priest," Ana said.

"I hardly think a Duchess will be assaulted, do you?" Isabel asked with a grin, and slowly her confidence spread to Ana who impulsively opened her arms and pulled Isabel close to her.

"If you take me to Madrid, I swear I will be your friend forever, and I will be a good servant to you."

The holy woman lived on the outskirts of Jaén in a house built of clay bricks. Her property was completely surrounded by a high mud wall. She had several servants, all young peasant girls, none as pretty as Ana or Maria, but all looking lifeless, like sleepwalkers. Suddenly, Isabel remembered Maria's remark about Angela flying out at night to kill little children. Where did she get that story? What was going on at night behind these walls?

Sor Angela was about fifty. She had a hawkish nose, swarthy skin, a wart on her cheek, and her hands were very skinny. For a greeting, she turned them palms up, so that Isabel would immediately see the stigmata. Probably self-imposed wounds, Isabel thought.

She received Isabel seated like a queen in a high-backed chair, and she pointed to a tabouret. But when Isabel informed her that she was the Duchess de Miraflores and accustomed to sitting in chairs, Sor Angela asked one of her girl attendants to bring in another chair for her guest.

After Isabel told her the purpose of her pilgrimage, Sor Angela advised her to leave a special donation at the side altar of Santa Maria la Coronada in the church of Jaén, to recite nine Ave Marias—one for each month of hoped-for pregnancy—and to confess all her sins, committed and imagined, to Father Cuevas. Isabel thanked her profusely then, as an afterthought, broached the subject of Pepita, whom she termed this time a run-away niece on her husband's side of the family.

When she handed her the sketch, it seemed for a moment that there was a flicker of recognition in Angela's eyes, but then the woman denied having seen Pepita.

"If she is a Moor, you might find her at Granada," she said.

"She is not a Moor," Isabel said indignantly.

"No? On the drawing she looks like one," the woman said.

Before Isabel was permitted to leave she had to purchase a floor-length chain of beads threaded by the saint herself, as well as a small relic—the finger bone of a martyred child—for more money than she cared to spend. If Angela de Jesus was no saint and no witch, at least she was a shrewd business woman.

Maria had stayed with Doña Ana at the Alcalde's house, because she vehemently refused to go near Angela's house or the house of the priest. So Isabel invited José to accompany her, and she asked him to break into the priest's house, should he hear her yell for help. The obligation of going to confession to a priest's private abode was utterly archaic.

"You would think we were living a hundred years ago,"

Isabel complained angrily. "By now every church should be equipped with a confessional. I wonder where he receives his potential penitents, in his bedroom, perhaps?"

Without giving José time for an answer, she told him all about Doña Ana and asked him to work out the details of their flight. He looked at her strangely and shook his head.

"What is the matter, do you not agree?"

"I am amazed at you. You are quite a woman, Duchess. No wonder my brother is in love with you."

"Your brother? Oh, Diego . . ." She had all but forgotten Diego Caietano's existence.

José laughed. He had beautiful teeth and an infectious way of showing them. Isabel could not help joining in his mirth.

"Poor Diego," he said, "the poet of the family."

"I thought you were the writer," she said.

"The writer, yes, but not of poetry. I am an extremely practical man. I never reach for fruits that hang too high."

"But you will help me save Doña Ana."

"And I will save you from the clutches of the priest. Have you any reason to suspect you might yell?"

"Yes. But there is still another job for you. If you can manage it, that is."

"Are you appealing to my pride?"

"José, I want you to find out how the local saint spends her nights."

"She might be digging up bones to sell."

"Perhaps. But you are the expert on *pícaros*. If you were a thief and wanted to rob her place, you would find a way to get inside, would you not?"

He grinned, "You and I, we would make a good pair of *pícaros*."

"We might have to yet, at Granada."

The priest's housekeeper was old, toothless, and half-deaf, so that José had to scream that the Duchess de Miraflores was on a pilgrimage and desired to speak to Father Cuevas.

Of medium height, fleshy but not fat, with just the beginning of a double chin and a yellowish tinge to his moist-looking skin, the priest exuded an air of wine and garlic, and his eyes swept over Isabel with the assurance of a man who knew all about women.

She explained to him why she had come, that according to Sor Angela, a prayer from him might help to incline heaven to grant her an heir for the illustrious family of the Miraflores.

She thought she would get to her true mission of asking about Pepita after she had had a few words with him.

He stared at her intently and she felt uncomfortable, but finally he bade her sit down on a cushion and when she did, he sat himself on a tabouret at her side.

"What we need is not a prayer so much as an understanding," he murmured, bending toward her. "Thanks to my blessed communion with Sor Angela, I am able to enter at times into a special state of grace during which nothing is impossible for me, because then God works wonders through my body." He went on to describe in detail how he and she should kneel together to implore God to let his special grace rain on them like gentle drops of a spring shower (Zeus descending on Danaë?) and that once he attained that blessed state he would be able to pass it on to her by releasing it into her body. She would be cured of her barrenness, provided she let him make her body receptive to all this holiness by letting him touch her and caress her.

A madman, thought Isabel, clearly a madman. For once she agreed with the Inquisition, the Illuminists ought to be punished. She got up quickly and backed away from him toward the door.

"I thank you so much. It is something the Duke and I will have to consider," she said in as much a formal tone of voice as she could muster, but he jumped up and pushed her so that she stood cornered with her back against the wall. With incredible force he held her arms flat against her sides while pressing his body heavily to hers.

"The Duke should not let you out of his sight," he said breathing heavily. "He should fuck you and fuck you, but I will gladly do it for him. Perhaps he doesn't know how. Let me give you a lesson. You can teach it to him later."

He went on murmuring obscenities into her ear, perfectly safe in the knowledge that no woman in her right mind would dare denounce a priest. Isabel had heard of similar cases, the titillating confessors of the Madrid courtesans were nothing but refined versions of this country profligate.

It flashed through her mind that she should yell now, but when she felt his mouth on hers, she did something else. Her tongue darted out swiftly while she closed her eyes and kissed him back. He was so astonished at her lack of resistance that he loosened his grip on her arms. Just as his hands came up to search for her breasts, she pulled up her knee so suddenly that she sent him reeling back moaning with pain. In the same instant, she was out of the door. In the hallway, she almost ran over the housekeeper, and she reached the street with her veil flying behind her.

The footmen jumped to attention, José opened the door to her litter, and five minutes later she was back at the Alcalde's house, where she spent the next hour complaining of a toothache that required her to rinse her mouth thoroughly and keep wet compresses on her face. She would have liked to leave Jaén right then, but that would have demanded a complicated explanation, and so she decided to stay with her original plan.

José came to talk to her early next morning and to take her to morning mass. The pilgrimage was truly a marvelous excuse, anything seemed possible under the guise of religious fervor. While they walked slowly to the Cathedral, José told her what he had been able to observe.

"It was pretty dark when I reached her house, but as soon as I started to climb the wall, about half a dozen dogs began to bark, and I had to retreat quickly. I went back to town and with my usual luck found one of the innkeepers only too happy to sell me his mutton bones, for a considerable sum I might add, after I told him it was for a practical joke. Armed with those bones, I returned. They made the curs tender as little pups. There was more than enough to keep them that way, until I got into the house. I kept half of the bones for later. One of the window shutters was loose. I slipped inside and found myself in a kind of storage room, full of bags and skins and jugs and jars. By then I had become pretty used to the darkness, and I could distinguish a few things and find the door. It was locked. I was about to climb out again when I heard footsteps and the sound of keys. So I made myself round and small next to all the bags, and I thought that might be the end of me—man attacks local saint, a definite case for the Inquisition. Well, it did not come to that. Whoever came in, barefoot, took only a couple of jars and left. The door remained half-open. I followed the person, and when I reached the door, I was looking straight into the saint's parlor. It was a sight to behold—full of candles, and in the middle of the floor on a thick round cushion Sor Angela sat without a stitch of clothing."

"You are joking," Isabel said with a gasp.

"Not at all. Around her twelve girls were kneeling, mostly the ones you saw at her place, I presume."

"Naked?"

"On my oath."

"What happened next?"

"Well, she got up and knelt in front of each girl, holding up a jar from which the girls took some sort of unguent that they rubbed all over their bodies."

"My God, what then?"

"After they were all finished with the rubbing, there was a quaint odor wafting over to where I stood. It almost took my breath away it was so strong. I was not surprised to see the girls, one by one, fall like dead persons to the floor. When they were all stretched out, Angela got up from her cushion and touched them in various places and stroked them and told them things."

"What things?"

"Forgive me, Doña Isabel, but that I would rather not repeat."

"Well, tell me at least the nature of her talk. Did she threaten them?"

"No, I think the first idea was to make them believe they were—er—giving themselves to the devil, and the next was to tell them they were flying away with her in search of newborn unbaptized infants whom they had to kill in order to prepare their special salve."

By now Isabel was beyond the stage of exclamations.

"After she had finished that task, she rubbed the salve on herself and sat herself astride that round cushion until she fell forward into the same state of trance. I stayed for a long time; it seemed interminable. I even ventured across the hallway into the room where they lay, but they were in a heavy sleep. So finally I left, since I was afraid they might not wake up till morning, and then I would have a hard time getting away. So I left the way I came, through the window, and the whelps were again very happy with their bones."

"So she is a witch," Isabel said.

"Yes, there can be no doubt. But I wonder what they get out of it?"

"Do you suppose that ointment makes them feel good? They might get exciting dreams. Perhaps they want to do it again and again?"

"Yes, she herself looked rather satisfied in her sleep, and two of the girls grinned. The others looked sullen or dumb."

"Do you think the Inquisition will get her eventually?"

"If anyone else climbs in there, the way I did they will be reported, I suppose. But generally the Inquisitors hold that such persons are mentally deranged. We haven't burned any witches in Spain, although I understand they do in most other countries."

"We have too many Jews to burn," Isabel said grimly.

José looked at her with sudden apprehension, and Isabel noticed for the first time how brilliantly green his eyes were, and she smiled at him wistfully, thinking how the world was full of handsome men, men like José and Diego Caietano, or the virile and profound Duarte Perez, and how she had fallen for a Dominican friar whose highest goal was the bloodiest office of Spain.

"But where does she get all those bones she sells?" Isabel asked.

"I have a hunch they are chicken or lamb bones. No one would know the difference."

"This is terrible, José. Someone ought to denounce her."

"After I left her, I did a bit of gambling at the inn. The men hanging around that place were all convinced she is the holiest of holy women."

"Does she bless their dice?"

"Who knows?"

The Cathedral was dark and empty, except for the side altar of Santa Maria la Coronada, where a few young women were on their knees praying fervently. As they passed by, Isabel wrinkled her nose. She looked at the women and then at José, and he gave an imperceptible nod. Then suddenly Isabel understood. The priest would have a good time during the coming week. Twelve poor souls with too many distressing adventures to confess.

They stayed for mass, and Isabel was thankful that another priest officiated. It would have been unbearable to observe the devil in person making a mockery of what after all was a holy ceremony for most of her compatriots.

On their way back to the Alcalde's house, José explained his plan to escape from Jaén. It should be done during the siesta, when everyone was sleeping. Santa Maria would have ordered them to leave immediately, and who dare disobey her?

The procession started at eleven. Tapestry was hanging from every window, a band of clarions and drums preceded the lines of priests and monks carrying crosses, large wooden figures representing various saints followed, then a sedan chair with Sor Angela, then a group of barefoot nuns, and finally the notables of the town and the local Familiars of the

Inquisition, led by Doña Ana's husband Ricardo Lozado, Alcalde of Jaén.

Isabel and Maria sat with Doña Ana on a balcony overlooking the place in front of the Cathedral. They enjoyed a semblance of shade from a blue canopy that matched their carpet and cushions, and while they watched, they chewed ripe olives and threw the pits over the railing into the passing procession. At noon the speeches began. Sweat was pouring from every face; the sun became unbearable. If she were to faint, Isabel thought, she might as well do it now.

"I feel I am about to faint," she informed Ana.

"Wait until the spectacle. It will be less conspicuous."

The play was a plagiarized version of one of Calderon's Corpus Christi plays, probably fabricated by one of the actors who tried to earn an additional income as author. This was a common vice among theater people; they took one or more famous plays, mixed up the characters of one with the action of another, and passed off the end result as their own effort. Doña Ana moaned that the story was incredibly silly and boring, but for Isabel who recognized which line had been stolen where, it held the fascination of a parody. She promptly forgot to faint. At Madrid the actors would have been pelted with foul eggs and putrid vegetables, but the less discriminating Jaén populace treated them to a rousing *olé*.

During the banquet for the notables, the ladies were left to their own devices. Doña Ana, who had set her heart on leaving, did not hesitate to sacrifice her long brown hair to achieve a successful flight. She cut it off boldly, painted the remaining stubble red, added freckles and blemishes to her flawless skin, and slipped into one of Pasquito's shirts and the only spare pair of breeches he had brought. José had informed the men and Pasquito that they would leave Jaén with one extra mule driver, a young lady in disguise. To the loyal Valderocas servants, smuggling a girl was a welcome adventure, and Pasquito had offered his spare clothes.

They left Jaén during the siesta. The road leading south was smooth, and they advanced quickly. To travel even faster Isabel left the litter and rode with Ana and Maria at the head of their mule caravan. They rode through endless olive groves, for this was the heart of Spain's olive district. But the air was hot and still, and there was not one sound except for the eternal song of the cicadas.

The heat and the even pace of the mule made Isabel sleepy. If only she were back at Madrid. If only she had not talked to

Pepita, making her run away. Doubts began to nag her. Would she ever find her cousin? Was not this whole trip outrageously stupid? What if Pepita was still in Madrid? What if she had never come south?

To keep awake and to pass the time, she asked the two girls to ride a little faster so that they could talk without being overheard. When they had put some distance between themselves and the troop of men, Isabel mentioned that she had been to see the priest of Jaén.

"What happened?" Maria asked so quickly that Ana gave her again a sharp glance.

"I escaped with my virtue intact."

"That is because you were a Duchess and had a place to escape to," Maria said bitterly.

"The Duchess did not impress him," Isabel said. "I kicked him good and hard."

"I tried that once," Ana said, "but I had no place to go, except to Sor Angela. She gave me something to make me unconscious. When I woke up, he was crushing me under his weight and raping me. To teach me something to confess, he said. After that I did not fight him anymore. I would rather know what happened than have him use me when I was unconscious."

"How old were you when this happened?" Isabel asked.

"Fifteen."

"And I was thirteen," Maria said. "It was three years ago, wasn't it?"

"So you are the little witch who ran away?" Ana asked. "I thought I had seen you there."

"I ran away shortly after you arrived."

"Then you do not know all the things she made us do since that time. Believe me, she has perfected her witchcraft during the years after you left."

"Did she repair you to marry you to the Alcalde?" Maria asked.

Ana grew red and nodded. "That was a year ago. But honestly I do not know what was worse, staying at her house and getting those dreams, or sharing a bed with the stinking old Alcalde."

"What dreams?" Maria asked again.

"Remember how she asked us to go along when she flew away at night?"

"That is why I left. I was scared she would force me."

"Well, the first time she did it was right after you left. She called all the girls and made them undress. But I was hiding in the storage room under an empty bag. I wanted to see what she was doing. Well, she made them all unconscious with her witch's ointment, and she stayed there with them all the time until morning. They flew nowhere. It was all something she put in their minds while they were sleeping. But you should have heard them the next day. They swore to me they had flown away with her and killed little children and made love to Satan himself in an empty field.''

"Why did you not run away then?" Isabel asked.

"I did. But the priest wanted me back, and they sent out a search party and found me and brought me back. After that, I was watched closely all the time. She fixed a room for me, where the priest came to take me whenever he chose."

"And those dreams?" Maria reminded her.

"Yes, she finally got me to go to those witch parties."

"What do you mean?"

"I usually dreamt I was flying with her and the others, naked, up to the castle where we would meet other witches and from there we would fly to people's houses and cast spells over them and kill some and hurt others."

"So it was always just dreams?" Maria asked.

"No, a few times we really left at night, and she would take us to a field on the side of a hill, where we met the devil."

"The devil! What did he look like?" Maria asked.

"He wore an animal mask and horns and he had goat skins all over him, and in back, under his tail, there was a face which we had to kiss. After that, each one of us had to slide onto his—thing—to become his brides."

"All of you?" Maria said with doubt in her voice.

"Yes, but I think it was not real. It felt cold and hard and it hurt. It did not feel human."

Isabel listened with horrified fascination. Did Rafael know about things like this? Here was a field of activity for the Inquisition. She would tell him. The witch and the priest should be brought before an inquisitorial tribunal. She had no doubt that the masked devil was none other than the priest in disguise. Or perhaps she should think the other way round. A devilish person had taken the disguise of a priest.

"When we get to Madrid, I want you to bring charges against Angela and Cuevas," she said to the girls. "I think if you denounce them and the other girls are called as witnesses, you might be able to rid Jaén of this terror."

"Go to the Inquisition? Never!" Ana exclaimed immediately. "Don't you realize that we would be judged as sinful as they are, because we participated? The least they would make us do is wear a sanbenito. I would rather kill myself first."

Maria agreed. She would rather be a respected Old Christian whore, she said, than a virtuous heretic.

"Wear a sanbenito, me? I would rather yet return to Jaén," she said.

This was what the Inquisition had accomplished, Isabel thought with anguish. Young girls who would not kill themselves to protect their virtue would gladly do so to protect the illusion of an unblemished name.

But could she blame the young women? They were not concerned about such abstract notions as good or evil; they were worried about their own survival in the most undisturbed way. Now that they had escaped the horrors of their childhood, they were not eager to burden themselves with further dangers.

At length, her thoughts went back to Pepita. Her cousin had led a life even more sheltered than Isabel's, since Isabel had at least ventured now and then into the world of crude reality, whereas Pepita would be a much easier prey to countless villains.

By nightfall, they were some thirty miles south of Jaén. José proposed that they camp in the open and that Ana should sleep near him, so that he could pretend that she was his servant, should they be overtaken by the Alcalde's men.

His suspicion was justified. Shortly after midnight, when Isabel and Maria slept next to each other on a blanket, and Ana on a man's cape with a hat over her face, two mounted guardsmen from Jaén came upon their camp. Isabel woke up from José's voice.

"Welcome, would you like to share our campsite?"

"We come for Señora de Lozado," one guardsman answered.

"You have the wrong party," José answered smoothly. "We are with the Duchess de Miraflores."

"That is the right party then," the other one said. "The Alcalde sent us to inspect every person of Her Ladyship's entourage. His wife was carried off. It is a grave affront to his honor."

"I am sorry to hear that. The Duchess held the Alcalde in the highest esteem. I swear she would be the first one to see his honor satisfied. However, I am afraid I will have to consider it an affront to Her Ladyship's honor if you suggest that one of our men could be the perpetrator of so heinous a crime."

"The Alcalde insists we have a look at the ladies in your party."

Isabel had heard part of their exchange and now came over.

"What is this?" she asked José in her most arrogant voice. "Who are these men?"

He explained what they wanted.

"They are lucky the Duke is not here, or they would be less their heads by now. I shall report this to His Majesty. After all, my husband is his cousin. I vow the Alcalde of Jaén will be sorry." Turning to the men directly, she added, "There are no women with us except my personal maid."

A few men had awoken and came to form a circle around the two guardsmen. The two looked fierce, their pistols gleamed in the moonlight.

Isabel hesitated. Her men were armed, too. They would kill these two without scruples if ordered to do so but that was inviting more trouble than they cared for. It would be much better and simpler to satisfy the men.

"José, you handle this," she said. "I do not wish to be further disturbed." She turned and left.

"I am afraid the Alcalde is going to be in trouble," José said to the guardsmen with just the right touch of concern. "No use getting yourselves in trouble too, is there? Better clear out of here, eh?"

"We will stay here till morning," one said. "Then we will watch you leave, so we will be able to see who is with you. And do not think you can finish us off," he added ominously. "If we do not get back to Jaén tomorrow, the whole town will come after you."

"I am glad you see it my way," José said. "I offered you to share my campsite from the beginning. Just one bit of advice, don't bother my men. We have a long journey ahead of us, and we need our rest. If you cause trouble, the devil's going to be your paymaster."

The two took their horses and led them a short distance away where they settled for the night.

José told Isabel that it would be best if they all filed casually past the men in the morning. They would be satisfied and report to the Alcalde that Ana was not with her. After all, the vindication of the Alcalde's honor could only be achieved by Ana's death.

He went to stretch out close to Ana. She shook with fright.

"They cannot do anything," he whispered. "And even if they should recognize you, which I doubt, they would have to look at you closely, and then they would have to ride back and report to the Alcalde. That will give us time to reach Granada. There is no danger at all that you will have to go back. Go to sleep. I will watch over you. And I will personally kill anyone who wants to take you back."

She started to cry, softly without making a sound, but he realized that something was wrong and reached out to touch her. "Still afraid?"

She calmed down. He left his hand on hers and at length she was breathing evenly.

José did not sleep. At dawn he woke up everyone, and they had a brief breakfast, a piece of bread and some lukewarm chocolate. He told Ana to keep her hat on. When Isabel and Maria joined the men, under the watchful eyes of the two guardsmen from Jaén, José suddenly pulled Ana's hat off and flung it to the ground.

"Eh boy, mind your manners! Who the hell do you think you are? A Grandee perhaps? Varmint, I'll skin you yet. Off with you, look after the mules." He gave her a rude push in the direction of the animals. The guardsmen never saw her face, only the short shaggy red hair.

Ana stumbled off to adjust saddlebags, and two other men joined her.

Now the bigger of the two guardsmen dismounted and came to José bowing humbly.

"What do you want now?" José demanded.

"With your permission, Your Lordship, we would like to take a look at the litter. We have seen your men, and we have seen the two ladies, and the only place we have not seen is inside the litter."

"Search the litter? By God, I ought to run my dagger through you! Why don't you search all the beds of Jaén? Many a proud man lives in cuckold's town. It seems to me your Alcalde may have taken up residence there."

At his words Isabel drew near.

"What is it, José? What? Those men are still here?" Suddenly, she started to laugh. "How funny it all is. Imagine when I tell His Majesty about this. I think I have finally found a way to make him laugh. I will tell him how the Duchess de Miraflores was practically waylaid by two uniformed sots of Jaén. Find out their names; we ought to remember this well."

She turned away, then changed her mind and turned back. "I am ready to leave. You may see me to the litter." She motioned for Maria to follow her, and both ladies climbed into the litter.

The guardsmen followed on their heels and satisfied themselves that the litter contained no hidden person.

Men and mules were ready to leave and took off. José stayed behind.

"Your names?" he asked sternly.

Their long faces showed that the two guardsmen had no desire to be in the bad graces of a personage at Court, and they also had doubts as to the correctness of their behavior. None of them was willing and ready to go to jail for the love of his Alcalde.

"Our apologies, Your Lordship. It is not our fault. We only stayed in the course of our duty. I am a poor man, I have seven children. I do not want trouble. Please, Your Lordship . . ."

José inflated his nostrils with contempt.

"Just clear out and thank the Lord that the Duke was not here. And tell your master he will hear from us yet. And no pleasant things either. We take this slander as an insult to our honor. We will send him a written challenge."

Happy to escape what to them now seemed like well-founded wrath, they galloped fast in the direction of Jaén.

The remainder of that day passed without incident, and in the evening of the following day they reached Granada.

# 11.

At first Isabel was disappointed. She had expected to see the so-called eternal snow on the crest of the Sierra Nevada, but in August even the highest peaks lay bare in the last rays of the setting sun. As if to compensate for the lack of majestic whiteness, a golden haze, emanating from the Alhambra, spread back over the sparse vegetation on the mountain slopes to melt into the blue of the sky. Built on steep hills separated by valleys and ravines, the town was nothing but a maze of narrow alleys with small whitewashed tile-roofed houses. One of the hills was crowned by Spain's most famous

Moorish palace and by the Renaissance palace of Emperor Charles V who had had no compunction about imposing his own austere taste upon the sensuality of past generations of Moorish kings.

From the Albaícin, the old quarter facing the North side of the Alhambra, Isabel and her attendants admired the sturdy walls and towers shimmering reddish in the sunset. Suddenly, Isabel was gripped by a violent feeling of belonging. Here was Spain. Here was the ancient soul of Andalusia, the birthplace of so many Spanish customs, the lovely abode where Pepita's and Pasquito's ancestors had lived in glory for so many centuries.

Since so few people were traveling to southern Spain in the heat of summer, they easily found an inn with enough rooms for all of them. Before retiring for the night, Isabel called all her men for a strategy meeting. They were given leave to roam through the city, provided they reported every morning at ten and every afternoon at five to José, who would tell them whether they were needed or not. Pasquito was to sleep in José's room and stay with José and Isabel during the day. Maria and Ana shared another room, and Isabel took a room for herself. The footmen and muleteers were sent to the dormitory for servants. There were twenty beds there, and Isabel had the choice of paying for the ten unused beds or of taking a chance that another party of travelers might lodge there with her men. Knowing that the ruse of the innkeeper would be to find some neighbors to pose as fictitious travelers if no real ones materialized, Isabel said she would pay for the difference. Then she asked Ana and Maria to join her for supper in her room and went to sleep early, after persuading Ana to wash her hair and face and think about buying a wig and new clothes.

The innkeeper's rooster woke her up much earlier than usual, but she had slept long enough to feel refreshed and strangely happy. She had dreamt of Rafael and of finding fulfillment in his embraces, and she took this to be a good omen. Stretching lazily, she smiled at her fading dream, then she folded her hands under her head and began to think carefully about her task of finding Pepita. What could Pepita do to earn a living? She could embroider, of course; she would have no difficulty finding a place as needleworker to a rich lady, but would she want to do that? The proud woman who called herself a Valderocas? Would she want to be reminded every day of the life she had left: the life of mistress of a great household? No, Pepita could certainly not bear a life of servitude. What else could she do? Why, dance with castanets and sing. She might join a theater company.

José came to call upon Isabel at nine o'clock. Isabel wore a loose-fitting gown, since both Ana and Maria were still sleeping, and she was waiting for Maria to help her get dressed. Etiquette did not permit her to receive a young man in such casual attire. Moreover, her feet were showing. For a lady of quality to let a man see her feet was the most special favor she could bestow upon him. She remembered clearly how Philip had stared at her bare feet when he had first beheld her at Juliana's. José had knocked and called her name. Now, with a wild desire to shuck all etiquette to the devil, she went to open the door.

"Come in."

He was startled when he saw her, but he came in and closed the door. When she looked at him questioningly, he bit his lip to refrain from laughing.

"What is the matter?"

"You are the matter. You are impossible. How could my father know you so well?"

"Your father?"

"He warned me that I would find you eccentric and devil-may-care, and he told me to treat you strictly like a brother. I suppose Diego must have talked to him about you."

"Flimflam! Diego never saw me like this. Your father knows my reading tastes because I discuss books with him, so he knows I have a head on my shoulders, about which I care more, I warrant you, than about my feet."

"Yes, but have you not considered that you might be too much of a temptation for a less serious-minded human being? Diego fell in love with you with much less opportunity than I have."

She let her thick lashes drop. "I am sorry," she said. "I shall try to mend my ways."

"Oh no, please stay as you are. I love you!"

"José, have you taken leave of your senses?"

"If I had, you would be in my arms right now. But I know very well that I am no match for you, and I am not going to eat my heart out over you, the way Diego does."

"He is not eating his heart out."

"Why do you think he is working with your brother for the Count-Duke? He wants to impress Pedro so much that he will win his consent to marry you."

"That is foolish. Pedro has nothing to say in this matter. It is my choice."

"And have you chosen?"

"No. And mark my words, I will not marry. To my knowledge, being a wife carries nothing but disadvantages. A wife cannot go out of doors for a ride except twice a year with her husband, if that much. She has to spend her life between her room, her balcony, and her church. And a well-to-do woman does not go to a public church. Oh no, that would expose her to the eyes of strangers. She has a private chapel in her own home."

"But all these conditions are the same for an unmarried lady. Much worse. Manuela never goes anywhere, except sometimes to visit you, and then one of us accompanies her to the house and picks her up. Manuela has never been alone in the street, as far as I know, much less alone with a man."

"And I suppose if you ever found her talking to a man, you would kill the poor gallant with your own hands?"

"I don't know. It depends."

"José, you aren't serious."

"I assure you I am."

"But then . . ." She stopped, thinking then he must take her for no better than a whore. Was that why he called her sweetheart, instead of Doña Isabel? Had she made such great strides away from the rules of society in her unquenchable zest for life? How could she feel so Spanish when contemplating Granada and so foreign when she was required to conform to her native customs? She had seen how sensibly the Dutch people lived in Minheer Uylenburch's house. There was no constant separation of the sexes. Men and women shared the same table, sat on the same chairs, and had ample occasion to talk to one another. And the French were even more delightfully free. The ladies she had met in Paris took themselves to be at least as important as men, if not more so.

"But then, you are completely different from any woman I have ever known, and so you should not be measured with the same yardstick, Doña Isabel," José said softly, and there was no disrespect in his voice.

She wondered what Rafael would think of her if he saw her

alone with José, but then she thought the devil with it, she was as she was, and she would not permit anyone to sit in judgment over her.

"I think your father's advice was excellent," she said sternly. "Just pretend I am your brother, and we will get along splendidly."

"My little brother," he said mockingly, for he towered over her by a head.

"Your big brother," she reminded him. "I am two years older than you are."

At that they both grinned, and then they sat down to make plans for finding Pepita.

For three days and nights they explored every street, every nook, almost every patio of Granada. They showed Pepita's picture to pastry cooks, convent doorkeepers, market-place vendors, town criers, water sellers, and even street urchins. At night they followed the sounds of guitar music and castanets, but no one had ever met Pepita.

On the morning of the fourth day, Isabel was becoming discouraged. She had seen so much poverty, filth, hunger, and squalor that she asked José to take her to visit the Alhambra. She also asked Maria and Ana to join her, but they were working on several dress lengths Isabel had bought for Ana, and they wanted to finish their sewing before they would have to move on. The Alhambra to them was just another castle, and Maria assured Ana that from the outside it certainly looked less inviting than the royal Alcázar of Madrid.

Since the Catholic Kings had taken over the palace from the Moors and proclaimed in it the infamous order expelling the Jews from all their realms, the Alhambra had been the property of the Kings of Spain. Emperor Charles had loved it so much that he had built his own palace onto one of its walls. Now the whole complex belonged to his great-grandson Philip IV. The huge intricately carved door to the courtyards was open to visitors, as was the King's court of the Alcázar in Madrid. José and Isabel could visit the Court of Myrtles and the Court of Lions, all other halls and rooms were closed and could not be visited since the King was not in residence.

The Court of the Lions was the most exquisite patio Isabel had ever seen. In the middle of a rectangular yard, surrounded by finely chiseled columns and arches, was a fountain of twelve water-spewing stone lions. She stayed for a long time admiring the perfect symmetry of the details, and she regretted not being able to take at least a peek behind the wooden doors.

"What a shame that all this beauty is wasted now," she said to José. "I wish I could tell His Majesty to spend at least a few months here with the Court. I don't think I could ever tire of living in a place as gorgeous as this. There has never been an architect like the forgotton Moor who designed this. Even Herrera cannot touch him. I would take this over the Escorial any day."

"Somehow I seem to recall that my father once said the Alhambra was a Jewish idea," José said. "Some Jew had been minister of the Caliph and had proposed the building of this palace, and the twelve lions are supposed to be the twelve tribes of the ancient Hebrews."

"I suppose it is heresy to mention that," Isabel said.

They were joined by an old man in royal livery who introduced himself as the chief usher of the palace, Don Enrique Pajarero Navarro.

"Doña Isabel Valderocas Sanchez is a friend of Her Majesty," José said. "She is very desirous of seeing the palace in order to encourage Her Majesty to spend a vacation here."

"Oh, what a pleasure, My Lady, what a pleasure indeed," the old man bowed courteously and ceremoniously. "But you should have notified us of your arrival. We would have made arrangements to show you the palace, if Her Majesty had sent a courier, it could have been arranged."

"Is there nothing you could show us?" Isabel inquired, "at least one room?"

"No, everything is locked. It is a great responsibility, you understand, a great responsibility. You cannot imagine how we have to watch the men who come to work here, most of the furniture has already disappeared. Well, perhaps I could let you see the Hall of the Throne. You know, where the Catholic Kings signed the order expelling the Jews from our great and wonderful Christian Kingdom."

"That would be kind of you," Isabel said. She eyed the old man curiously, had she detected any irony in his voice?

"There are workers in there now, repairing a few cracks in the plaster carvings on the wall."

He beckoned them to follow him, and he pushed the door open and let them walk into a large empty hall with arched windows and the most fantastic delicate designs carved into every inch of wall space: flowers, fruits, stars, coats of arms, and Arabic lettering, all interwoven to look like a giant tapestry, like a poem in stone, like the entrance hall to paradise. When Isabel let her head fall back to look at the ceiling, she saw a dome of small symmetrical stalactites, seemingly reaching up toward endless skies.

Tears came to her eyes. "It is magnificent," she whispered. "And to think that no one is able to enjoy it. I could spend days just looking at this room."

"That is what a young lady said to whom I showed this recently. She had come up here, and she sat in the Court of Myrtles, by the reflecting pool. She just sat and looked, for a whole day. Poor thing, she seemed so unhappy. So I finally talked to her, and I let her see this throne room."

"Who was she?" Isabel asked with a ghostly shiver of premonition spreading over her.

"I do not know. She was planning to leave Granada with a gang of gypsies, she said. But she did not sound like a gypsy, more like a lady of quality. Pasquita, her name was, Pasquita."

"Pasquita! She would not by any chance look like this?" From the deep pocket in her skirt Isabel pulled out the small frame with the sketch of Pepita which she carried on her at all times. It would be so like Pepita to give herself the name of the boy whom she had insulted because he was a Moor.

He took the frame and looked at the drawing.

"Why yes, there is a resemblance. Yes, yes, that is the woman. Who is she?"

"A cousin of mine who ran away from home. Oh, I must find her. I simply must. She ran away because of a misunderstanding. I have been searching for her. There is no reason for her to be unhappy. Oh, please Your Grace, do you know where she went?" She turned to José, "Now, why would she go with a gang of gypsies?"

"That is quite common, I hear," the old man said. "Becoming more so as things get worse. Many young people roam the country like gypsies."

"Did she say where they stayed, the gang? Where they were going?"

"Hmm . . . The mountains of Ronda, I think. She mentioned something about Ronda."

"And when did you last see her?"

"Oh, about a week ago, I would say."

"José, how fast do you think these gypsies travel? And by what road? We must leave immediately."

"They do not travel quickly," Don Enrique answered. "They stop at every hamlet to give performances and steal what they can. I would venture to say they are not farther from here than a day's journey."

"I don't know how to thank you," Isabel said.

"Tell Her Majesty Granada is best in the spring. If only I could see this place once as a Royal Palace, for a few weeks even, I would feel richly rewarded, believe me."

Isabel could not get down to the city streets quickly enough.

"We must be ready to leave at five o'clock when the rest of the men report," she said to José. "In the meantime, you must find out which road they have taken."

At five José reported that he had talked to the common townfolk, the tradesmen, waterseller, and blacksmiths, and that according to most of them the gang had taken the road straight west to Santafé, from where they would keep on a west southwesterly course across the hill country to Antequera. From there they would probably turn southwest to the wild mountains of the Serranía de Ronda.

"But why would Pepita want to go to Ronda?"

"Ronda is a very old city," José told her. "The access to it is difficult, and people say the town was never quite cleared of Moors, because all they have to do is take refuge in the impenetrable mountains until their persecutors leave, and then they can return."

"Not in the day and age of the Inquisition," Isabel objected. "No one can hide from them."

"It is probably just talk," José admitted. "But Pepita may have heard it, too. You see, she did come to Granada, which you thought was the logical choice. At any rate, we must intercept the gang before they get anywhere near Ronda. I would not want to brave the Serranía with only ten men. The place is a *germanía* stronghold, I am sure."

They left in great haste and traveled all evening and most of the night. At Santafé, they learned that the gypsies had passed through, and at Loja, where they arrived the next night, the peasants were cursing and swearing. It seemed the gypsies had put on a dance performance and while everyone was watching, others had looted the homes.

"I do not know what they could find to steal in this forsaken dustbin," Isabel said with a disgusted look at the small desolate stone houses with doorways which were gaping black holes giving out an odor of old sweat and excrement. "I swear I cannot imagine Pepita with them."

"If she is not, I suggest we go back to Madrid," José told her. "We cannot continue like this, or we will turn into gypsies ourselves."

They had hardly stopped when the litter was surrounded by dozens of half-naked children with scaly crusts on their faces and swarms of flies like halos around their heads. They were so thin Isabel could not stand looking at them.

She pressed a handkerchief to her nose. Then, when she had fought her nausea, she gave the order to go on.

"We will camp in an open field."

They traveled for several more hours until the men began to grumble they were tired. The moon was full. Isabel would have liked to travel on, but José persuaded her to camp in a field littered with boulders and rocks. After their dinner of dried cold beef, olives, and tomatoes—the latter having become a staple food since they had first been imported from the New World—everyone was exhausted enough to fall asleep quickly, except for the two men José always assigned as guards.

But Isabel rested only lightly in a slumber made up of the song of the cicadas, the silvery moonlight, and thoughts of Rafael. Suddenly she awoke, certain that she had heard Pepita's voice. She listened intently. No, it must have been a dream. Yet, after a while, she felt a light breeze on her face and at the same time there came snatches of music from far away. Softly she got up and went to wake José. She found him sleeping with his hand on Ana's hand. She touched his shoulder.

"Yes, what is it?"

"I think we are near the gypsy camp. Come."

"No, I will go alone. You stay here."

"Why?"

"Because I will not take a young woman in the middle of night into a camp of wild men."

"All right, then I will be a man." She went to Pasquito's saddlebag and extracted from it the same spare breeches and shirt Ana had worn during her flight from Jaén. Without the slightest twitch of conscience she changed her clothes, pinned up her hair, and borrowed a sloping hat from one of the sleeping men.

"There now!" She mounted a mule and José, muted by her

lack of qualms, followed her on another mule. The guards were informed of their plan to ride over to the gypsy camp.

"Now we are in the undesirable position of the two sots of Jaén," José muttered. "Let us hope the gypsies are as understanding as we were."

"Holy Ghost! You are right. We cannot simply come upon them like this. What if they shoot us?"

They followed the dirt road until they came to the foot of a hill.

"Stay here and keep the animals," José whispered. "I think they are just on the other side of this mound." He slunk away and was soon out of sight. She waited for a long time, listening to snatches of voices, to laughter and guitar music, but much as she tried, she could not hear any voice resembling Pepita's. Finally, José came back.

"They have a covered wagon," he reported, "and a dozen mules and some fine horses. There are not more than ten men, I would think, but at least as many women."

"Is Pepita with them?"

"Honestly, I could not tell."

"I want to see them for myself."

"Climb up the side of this hill. You will come to a large boulder. You can stand behind it without being seen and look straight down into their camp."

Isabel was excited. All her fatigue was gone. She wanted to hug José for being so patient and letting her follow her own code of behavior, but, of course, he would not understand. He would think she was falling in love with him. She slid down from her mule and started to climb the hill. When she came to the rock, she leaned against it in the shade. The camp was about fifty feet away from her. She could make out the people clearly, but they all looked alike: dun faces and bodies sitting and lying on the ground in groups of two or three or four. Impossible to distinguish one from the other. Suddenly, a feeling of recklessness overcame her, such as she had never experienced before. The whole situation was so unreal, so truly impossible that she was half-ready to believe it was a bad dream after all. Without considering that José was standing by the road holding the mules and might be discovered, she let out one loud cry.

"Pepita!" She held the last vowel and it rang hauntingly through the night.

Everyone in the camp jumped up. She had even aroused the sleepers. She watched them stand still, to listen for further sounds, but she made none. Then the men huddled together and dispersed in various directions. Her shout had come so unexpectedly that they could not decide from where. Nevertheless, a few men started walking in the direction of José. A short while later she saw them come back escorting José and both mules to their camp. She watched as they all formed a circle around him, and then she saw in the distance a lonely figure walking slowly toward the huddle. In a few leaps she was down the hill and past the others, almost flying toward the girl who was coming, seemingly out of nowhere, to join the camp.

"Pepita," she was crying, "Pepita!"

"Isabel! You!"

They tried to see each other's faces in the fallow light of the moon, and they kissed each other and clung to each other, completely oblivious to their spectators.

"You came to find me?" Pepita asked weakly, as if unable to believe it.

"Why else would I be here?"

"Is that Pedro?"

"No, that is José Caietano. Pedro is abroad. Oh Pepita! How could you? How could you?"

Pepita was shaken by violent sobs, and all the gypsies started to talk at once, then one of them, a big fierce-looking man with a long twirled black moustache grabbed Isabel's arm and addressed Pepita.

"Pasquita! You are not one of us, but you are a good helper, and you may stay with us and go to Ronda. We will forgo the remainder of the trial period. You may live with us and you will be treated as one of us. You do not have to go back to your former life if you don't want to. One word from you, and I will personally send these two fellows to hell."

He apparently mistook her for a boy, Isabel thought with surprise, until she remembered that she wore Pasquito's clothes.

"No, Zamoro, it is all right. I think I will go back with them."

"As you wish. I hate to see you go, though. You would make a good gypsy."

"Thank you, Zamoro."

"Come to think of it, I am not sure I should let you go. How do you know they won't force you again to marry that brute?"

So Pepita had indeed told that kind of story.

"They would not do that twice," Pepita said sweetly.

"Well, if they do, you come straight to the Serranía and ask for Zamoro."

The moon was shining on his swarthy face, and his eyes were gleaming savagely. Isabel would have been scared of him, had she encountered him alone somewhere, but Pepita looked at him gently, and presently a wistful smile came over his face, and he bent forward and whispered something into Pepita's ear. Then he turned and left abruptly, giving an order to let them go.

No one else seemed especially upset about Pepita's departure, although a few other men mumbled, "Farewell Pasquita." They did not offer to return the mules they had taken from José, and the three of them walked off into the night.

"Will they come after us to visit our camp?" José asked when they were out of earshot.

Pepita did not answer.

"We better move on toward home right away," Isabel suggested.

"Yes, but we cannot go back through Jaén," José said.

"We can go back to Loja and from there to Lucena," Isabel said. "From Lucena it's not far to Córdoba, and from there we take the road to Toledo."

"How do you know we can get from Loja to Lucena?" José asked.

"Oh, I am a good reader of maps," Isabel replied vaguely.

"How did you find me?" Pepita asked. "I don't understand."

"I don't understand it myself," Isabel said. "I only know that Pedro would have killed me if I had not found you."

"Isabel, Isabel," Pepita sobbed, "will Pedro forgive me?"

"Flimflam," Isabel retorted irritably. "What kind of talk is that for a Valderocas?"

"But you said I was not a . . ."

"Pepita Valderocas!" Isabel interrupted tartly. "It took us a long time to find you, and I do not even know how I am going to present you to the others who came with us. It is hardly suitable for the future wife of Pedro Valderocas to have been fished out of a gypsy camp. So whatever you say, from now on, do keep in mind that the name Valderocas obligates as much as the name of a Grandee."

José whistled softly.

"What now?" Isabel snapped.

"What a sharp tongue you have."

"No, she is right," Pepita said. She was walking between José and Isabel, but now she stopped. "I am so tired, I think I have to rest for a moment."

"What if those gypsies come to steal our mules?" Isabel asked.

"I am hungry too," Pepita said. "Could we sit down for just a moment?"

"Why don't you two sit down here, and I will go and get the litter?" José proposed. "I want to move on tonight, at least out of the way of the gypsies."

The girls sank down on the ground, and José started to run toward their camp. As soon as he disappeared in the night, Isabel's attitude changed.

"Pepita, I was so worried about you, you cannot imagine. Why did you do this to us? Why did you run away?"

"But you didn't want me anymore."

"Who said that?"

"You said I was a Moor."

Isabel thought it over quickly. Rafael would want her to deny this; Rafael would want her to tell Pepita that it was not true. Rafael wanted them to be Old Christians; he wanted them to be safe. But what good were lies? If she wanted Pedro and Pepita to marry, she must bring them together first. Pepita waited; did she hope to hear a denial?

"What difference does that make?" Isabel said slowly.

Pepita started to cry. Her head hung forward. She hid her face in her hands and cried soundlessly.

"I was afraid you might have gone to tell a priest or to tell the Inquisition," Isabel said.

At that Pepita stopped and looked up. "You know I would never do that. They would have harmed you and Pedro. How could you even think such a thing? I would rather die than hurt you or Pedro."

At this answer, tears welled up in Isabel's eyes, and she took Pepita in her arms and hugged her. "Is that true, Pepita? Would you rather die than see Pedro harmed?"

Pepita nodded. "Sometimes, when I was younger," she said slowly, "when we went with Father to hear the Edict of Faith and the Anathema, I used to ask myself what I would do if Father or Pedro were secret Judaizers, or other heretics, and at night in my bed I used to dream up a whole story like this, how I would save them and how everyone would love me for it. Isn't it strange how the opposite came true?"

"What do you mean the opposite?"

"Well, I am the heretic, and you are saving me."

"You are no heretic. You must not even say that!"

"Oh yes, I am. I went to Granada, and I thought a lot there, and I looked at the Alhambra—you should see how beautiful it is—and I thought to myself, I should be proud to be a Moor. I was going to Ronda. I have heard there are Moors at Ronda. . . . You know, Isabel, I will never be the same anymore. Only I missed you so much, you do not know how much I missed you, and Pedro. I was miserable without you, and now I don't know what to do. I am not sure I am going back with you. I may yet go with Zamoro. I just had to talk to you. I was thinking of you when I heard your voice. I thought I was going mad, but then I saw you, and now I don't know whether I am dreaming or not."

"Does it mean a lot to you, being a Moor? Pedro is very angry with me for having told you. Even now, if he could hear me, he would be wroth, and now you tell me you are proud of it. Why would you want to be proud of it?"

"Because it makes me more myself. I am no longer just a poor relation. I am myself."

"Pepita, Pedro needs you. He needs you desperately."

"How?"

"The dream you used to make up, that dream is true. Father was a heretic, and Mother, and Pedro, and I am, too. We are all heretics, and you were the only fine Christian in our family."

"I don't understand."

"Neither did I, at first. But you will, if you want to. You see, everything really depends on you now. If you want to, you can be one of us, you can help Pedro, you can finally marry him . . . but you must realize that we live in constant danger."

"Why did you never tell me? Didn't you trust me?"

"I did not tell you because I only learned everything after Father and Mother died, and then I swore I would never tell anyone. But I already broke my oath once by telling you that you are a descendant of Moriscos, now I break it a second time by telling you that we are . . ."

She stopped and Pepita said, "New Christians?"

"Yes. Marranos."

"Oh Isabel!"

They remained quiet, huddled together, and then they saw the whole mule train coming for them, and they got into the litter and Ana and Maria had to ride on mules, because there was only room for two in the litter.

Pepita said nothing, so that Isabel began to fear that her cousin was sick. She had never known her to be silent for any length of time. But presently, Pepita's head sank on Isabel's shoulder and she fell asleep.

They stopped later, after backtracking to Loja and from there swinging northward in the direction of Lucena. Pepita did not wake up, and Isabel let her sleep in the litter. She herself stretched out on a blanket in front.

When she woke up from the sun on her face, she peeked into the litter, and she hardly recognized her cousin. Pepita's face had grown terribly thin, her skin was brown like a gypsy's, she looked lean and dirty like a hungry vagabond.

Isabel brought her the usual breakfast, strong sweet chocolate and biscuits, and she gulped it down faster than a starved animal.

"Do you think I could have some more?"

"Why, of course, have all you want."

She smiled timidly at Isabel, and thick round tears were rolling down her cheeks again.

"My God, Pepita, have they not given you anything to eat?"

"They don't have anything to eat. Oh Isabel, I have learned so much, you wouldn't believe it. Our countrymen are starving, literally dying of hunger. They are poor and filthy and sick and ignorant, but they are hungry first. And when you are hungry like that, you don't care about anything but filling your stomach. That is why I was glad when I met Zamoro. It was at Jaén. . . ."

"Jaén," Isabel interrupted, alarmed. "What happened there? What were you doing there?"

"Nothing much. I had gotten a ride down there with some peasants, but I did not want to stay with them, so I fell asleep in the Cathedral. It seemed like a good place for a siesta; I was so tired. Some priest found me there and sent me to some holy woman, but one look at her gave me the vapors, so I sneaked away after dinner. That is when I came upon the gypsies, that is, I ran so fast I stumbled and someone caught me, and it was Zamoro."

"Were you not scared of him?"

"I was at first. But he was very kind. He told me to beware of the people of Jaén, and when I said I was a runaway, he took me to the other gypsies. They said they would give me a month to prove myself, then if I did everything right, I could live with them."

"What did you have to do?"

"Oh, nothing much. Sing and dance to attract crowds where we stopped."

"While the others went to steal?"

"We had to live somehow."

"Why not work?"

"What kind of work? There is no work. There are thousands more servants than people to serve, and gypsies dare not settle down and cultivate the soil. Do you know that officially they have been expelled from Spain? Just like the Jews and the Moriscos. The difference is that the gypsies will simply not go. They stay around, moving from one town to the next, always free, here today, gone tomorrow."

"And Zamoro?"

"What about him?"

"Was there anything between you and him?"

"No, but if you had not come to save me, there might have been. He is terribly ruthless, but he was tender with me. He was the only human being who cared about me, since I left Madrid."

"And just because of that you might have given yourself to him and lost your honor?"

"Oh Isabel, what is honor when you are hungry? Hungry for food, hungry for shelter, hungry for affection. After all I've seen, I am so tired of all this talk about honor. That is good for stage plays, not for real life."

"But Pepita, your honor is Pedro's honor. Imagine what he would do to you if he thought you had dragged his honor in the mud."

"I am sorry, Isabel. I am not living by that code anymore. I have yearned for years to be Pedro's wife, and I have kept myself pure for him. If he thinks that my contact with the gypsies has sullied his honor, I will simply have to leave again. I have grown up, and that is why you do not have to pretend that Pedro wants to marry me. I will survive if he does not."

"But he does! He does! He is lost without you. It is only that he never dared," she lowered her voice, although they were sitting apart from the others. "You know why."

"Doesn't he know I love him more than myself?"

"How could he? You were always so pious. You went to mass every day, you even enjoyed the *auto de fé*. You were such a perfect self-righteous Old Christian. . . ." Her voice trailed off.

"But Isabel, I only did what I thought was expected of me. I tried to please all of you. I asked Mother how a young lady should behave, and I tried so hard. I learned to sit for hours with Mother and her friends, although their talk bored me. I learned to embroider and sew and to supervise the household. Only once in a while, when I could not stand it anymore, I sneaked away to be by myself. You did not know that, did you? As for the *auto de fé*, I abhorred every minute of it, but I heard Calderon praise it, and I saw how everyone was expected to enjoy it. I always felt I was different and alone, and I had to hide my true feelings. I tried to copy the people of quality, at least copy their talk so no one would guess that I was a monster and a sinner underneath. When you told me I was a Moor, all my dissimulation came crashing down on me, and I finally knew I could never be one of you. I had to leave."

"I still do not understand why you said you wanted to marry a nobleman," Isabel said.

"Because I thought Pedro would be happy to get rid of me gracefully."

"Oh God, if only he could hear you." Isabel remembered how deeply unhappy Pedro had been after their parents' death when he thought he was alone with his secret. Her face grew red with shame when she realized how selfishly she and Pedro had helped and supported each other, drawing strength from each other, and how they had left Pepita to struggle alone.

"If you become one of us, Pedro will be the happiest man on earth," she said. "We will go to stay with Uncle Jaime until Pedro comes back from abroad. He may be gone till the end of the year. Uncle Jaime can tell you all you need to know. But Pepita, I hope you realize that we must never talk about this anymore. No one must know, or we will end up burning at the stake. Do you think you can live like that?"

"Have I not hidden my true feelings all my life?"

"You must go on doing it. You must remain exactly as you were, going to church, and all the rest. Even Teresa must not notice any difference in you."

"It will be so much easier, knowing I am not alone."

# 12.

Never had Isabel known such relief as when they reached Toledo and the security of Uncle Jaime's home safely. She loved her life, with its duplicities and dangers, but she now placed the responsibility for Pepita's well-being gratefully onto her uncle's shoulders. He could instruct her in the faith of the Marranos; he could take her to underground meetings; he could explain to her the whole background of the Benahavels. She intended to leave Pepita at Toledo and to return to Madrid alone.

Contrary to her expectations, Uncle Jaime strictly opposed her wish. He could see no reason why she had to return to Madrid to live there alone.

"Why can't you wait for Pedro's return?"

"I miss Madrid; I miss the Court."

"The Court?"

She missed Rafael. She longed to be reunited with him; she must find a reason convincing enough.

"Uncle Jaime, don't you see I have to know what is going on? There may be new intrigues against the Count-Duke. I should stay in contact with everyone during Pedro's absence."

"What will they think of you? A young woman living alone! In the eyes of the nobles, a stain on the honor of our name can only be washed away with the blood of the offender. You know that! I do not want Pedro to get into a situation where he would have to shed blood to clear our name."

"Uncle Jaime, we are different."

"But we live in their world. No, I cannot let you go."

"Uncle Jaime, just for a week. Let me go to get the things I need. My dresses, my books."

"We can send for them. José Caietano will be returning to Madrid; he can go to talk to Teresa."

"Please, Uncle Jaime."

"Who is it, Isabel?"

"What do you mean?"

"Who is the man you want to see?"

"Carlos de Queras." Now why on earth had she said that? It had slipped out of her quite naturally, and it was completely stupid. She hated Carlos and everyone knew it.

"I seem to remember hearing that you disliked him."

"Precisely, but I must know what he is up to. You see, he told Pepita that he had seen me in Paris. I must talk to him again. He could be dangerous." Her mind worked perfectly well, independently of the truth.

The old man thought for a moment, then his stern glance softened.

"All right, you may go. But I expect you back here as soon as possible. And please be careful."

Ana elected to stay at Toledo. She had taken an immediate liking to Uncle Jaime, and she felt well protected in his house. She offered to become Pepita's personal maid, when Isabel told them that Teresa planned to marry Alfonso. Pasquito also stayed at Toledo. Maria, of course, would accompany Isabel to Madrid.

Before they left, José Caietano had a long conference with Uncle Jaime, but when Isabel tried to wheedle out of him what this was all about, he remained surprisingly tight-lipped.

During their last night of camping outside, before reaching Madrid, José took Isabel aside and told her that he had fallen in love with Ana and wanted to marry her. Strangely, she felt a little stab of jealousy.

"How can you do that? She is already married."

"She can change her name, and no one will be the wiser."

"But José, you do not know her past. You do not know all the things she did."

He looked at her, and his mouth twisted wryly. "I am the one who watched what that witch did to the girls who lived with her, remember? I also know about the priest-devil. Ana told me everything."

"And you still want to marry her, have children with her?"

"She has had a horrible life. Not everyone has your courage, nor your opportunities for courage. I love her and I want to marry her."

"They why do you ask me, or is that not what you are doing?"

"Yes, that is what I am doing. I know my father is going to talk this over with you."

"With me. Why would he do that?"

"My father thinks highly of you. He would respect your opinion."

"Just because I read Galileo? I think you overestimate my importance."

"No, Doña Isabel, you underestimate yourself. You are quite an intimidating person, you know."

"Not so long ago you thought differently of me."

"But I have gotten to know you better. Your delicate exterior is deceiving. Underneath you are so stubborn, I do not think a man lives who could dominate you."

He lives, she thought. He lives but he doesn't want to dominate me. Oh Rafael, where are you? I am so tired of being strong and stubborn.

"Why can't you just live with her," she said. "Why must you marry her?"

"Isabel! For whom do you take me? Don Juan Tenorio? I love her. I want to marry her."

"Do not get angry. It is your affair. I hope you realize that you will have to leave Madrid and your family, if you marry her. Unless you want her to be a stranger in your family, never knowing whom she married."

"She knows. I told her."

"José!" All blood drained from her face, and her heart stood still. "How could you! I have scolded Manuela, I have scolded Diego, but I thought surely you would be smarter. You Caietanos talk too much! It is going to be your downfall yet. Wait until your father hears that. I hope he is going to flog you. How could you trust her like that? She is practically a stranger to you. And an Old Christian."

"No. You see, she trusted me first. She comes from a family of sanbenito wearers."

"I thought Maria said she was an orphan from an Old Christian family."

"You would not expect her to advertise that her parents were Marranos, would you?"

Suddenly, Isabel understood why Ana was staying at Toledo.

"You asked Uncle Jaime to turn her into a full-fledged Jewess," she said, and she felt the familiar fear gnawing at her stomach. So many people to share a secret, if anything went wrong . . .

"Yes, and in my own way, I am a proud man. I don't give a

damn what anyone else thinks of her. But my father is old,
and you know how he feels about his own family. I told you
how Manuela is watched and protected. He is willing to make
exceptions, it is true, for instance he admires you, although
you are certainly breaking the code of honor. But all this
counts for naught when his own family is concerned. I have
not a shred of doubt that he would kill any man who dared
molest Manuela, and he would expect virginal purity from a
girl intended to become his daughter-in-law. He is my father,
and I love him and honor him, and I want him to accept my
wife."

"So what do you want me to do?"

"If he should ask you, I want you to tell him that Ana is a
sweet pure New Christian orphan and that she would be an
honorable addition to the Caietano family, to your knowledge."

Isabel had tears in her eyes. She would help Pedro get
Pepita, and she would help José to get Ana, and they would
all form a happy clan of friends, while she would remain the
outsider, the woman without a husband. She could not even
talk about Rafael; she must never even mention his name.

"I hope you will be very happy," she said with a choke in
her voice. "I will do as you say."

"What is it? You aren't crying, are you?"

"It is nothing. I suppose I am scared."

"You must not be." He grinned. "If worse comes to worst,
we can always run to the Serranía and ask for Zamoro."

She dried her tears and smiled.

"I will never forget this voyage, José. Please remain my
friend . . . my brother." She gave him her hand, and he bent
over it.

"Thank you, Doña Isabel, it was a privilege to serve you."


# 13.


There was no news from Pedro.

The Court was spending a few weeks at the Escorial. No
one of importance had stayed at Madrid.

In her room, Isabel found an envelope bearing the royal

seal. She broke it hastily. Two lines on parchment: "I keep
my promises. What about you?" Signed: Yo El Rey. She tore
the paper into small pieces and burned them on a silver tray.

At the apartment she also found a letter. "Where are you,
darling? I have come back from Córdoba. I am worried about
you. Rome is out for now. Our employers have sent me on a
special trip. They want maps of all major Spanish cities. I do
not know how long I will be gone. I think you should
accompany Señora V. to Toledo and wait for me there. Be
good."

Rafael was on a voyage. Major cities: that must mean he
was visiting the seats of the inquisitorial tribunals. He wanted
her with Uncle Jaime. To please him she would go back to
Toledo. To please him, she would do anything.

This letter, too, she tore up. As she did so, she had to make
an effort to keep herself from breaking down with disappointment and exhaustion.

Would this moving about, this uncertainty never end?
Would she never have a place where she belonged?

## ~❦ *1635* ❦~

## 1.

The Valderocas wedding at the beginning of the new year would have been a spectacular event had it been held in Madrid, but Pedro and Pepita chose to marry quietly in Toledo, where two days later José Caietano married Ana, to whom Isabel had given a dowry.

When the newlyweds arrived at the capital, the gossip-mongers were so engrossed in the latest blatant crime of the Royal Favorite that they hardly took notice of anything else.

Carlos de Queras was the first one to tell Isabel all about it. The Count-Duke, it seemed, was entertaining Jews at Court. Not New Christians, but true and recognizable Jews from an Oriental country, some of whom even had the audacity to wear turbans, an unforgivable insult to Spain whose glory had after all been founded on the expulsion of infidels.

In addition, one morning posters had been found all over Madrid, proclaiming "Long Live Mosaic Law—Down with Christian Law."

"It is the most disgraceful, sickening sight my eyes have ever seen," Carlos said. "I swear from now on I will spend all my energies to bring about the downfall of the dictator. I know that your brother is Olivares's protégé, but you have to start putting some distance between yourself and the Olivares couple." He apparently did not know and no one else did either, that Pedro himself had brought the unwelcome guests to the capital.

"Why?" Isabel asked. She conversed with Carlos most politely, upon Pedro's instructions.

"Because I intend, hard as it is for me since I consider it a stupid custom, to woo you according to all the rules of *galantear en palacio*." And with these words, he slipped down on one knee and placed his right hand upon his heart.

"My dearest Doña Isabel, your eyes are purer than emeralds, your hair is spun of gold, your cheeks are prettier than carnations. Do you not know how you have enchanted my heart? Do you not know how cruelly you have trampled upon my sincere feelings of adoration for you? Day and night I meditate upon your charms, thoughts of you rob me of my senses. I forget even the most elementary forms of courtesy. I do not remove my hat for anyone but you, and I will surely die a slow and painful death if you do not relent and concede to do me the great honor of becoming the future Countess de Queras."

Much as she tried, Isabel could not repress a giggle. Carlos, he of the pointed chin, the reptile eyes, the sparse hair and slight body, Carlos trying to become a romantic hero in the tradition of Burgundian Court ceremonial. It was enough to break up anyone's countenance.

"Don Carlos, get up immediately," she said in a low voice, so that none of the servants would hear her ungrateful reception of his ardor. "You look appalling like this, and I have told you what I think of these customs. Have I not once taken your defense when His Majesty teased you into making a fool of yourself? Why do you think I did that?"

"To draw His Majesty's attention upon yourself," Carlos said and sat again on the chair he had abandoned for his kneefall. "But have you gotten very far with him? And what do you promise yourself from becoming his very impermanent mistress? All it can possibly bring you is the honor of giving birth to a bastard and ending up in a convent."

"You ungrateful wretch!" Isabel countered. "I did it out of respect for you, but I see even that small emotion was wasted on you."

"Is that true?" Carlos asked. "Out of respect for me? I did not think you respected anyone."

"Whoever put that notion into your brain? I respect a great number of people."

"Well you hardly respect our Spanish rules and customs. Perhaps all the persons you respect are abroad?"

This was the first time Carlos had mentioned to her face that he knew about her trip with Pedro, and she was eager to find out how much he knew.

"As a matter of fact, I found Parisian customs far more delightful than our own, I admit. How come, if indeed you saw me in Paris, did you not care to make known your presence? If you are as enchanted by me as you pretend to be, why did you not approach me there? I can only conclude that you must have been spying on me, a most distasteful act, for which I shall punish you at the proper opportunity."

"But what were you doing in Paris?" Carlos asked. "I hope Don Pedro is not embroiled in the childish plot to eliminate Richelieu. We know that Olivares entertains this idiotic project, but it will come to naught."

"Saints protect me!" Isabel countered with the proper show of fright. "You cannot be speaking the truth." She longed to get rid of Carlos, but she also dimly sensed that he could be much more dangerous than she had formerly suspected, and she forced herself to sound dignified and Old Christian.

"I realize it is none of my affair," Carlos said, "but I warn you that very soon everything you do will be entirely my affair. Her Majesty is not too happy about your status. You are neither a Lady-in-Waiting, nor the daughter of a courtier. You have no business being at Court, and Her Majesty entirely approves of my intention to marry you."

There were several possible answers to this, but they would all serve only to alienate Carlos, when she needed more than ever to find out what he and his friends planned to do to the Count-Duke.

"Her Majesty," she said with an enigmatic smile, trying to gain time, "Her Majesty you say?"

"What about Her Majesty?"

She had to mystify him, keep him guessing, keep him in suspense. And she also must say something to reduce his cocky self-assurance.

"Oh Don Carlos, one can see that you know very little about feminine guiles. Have you ever considered that even Her Majesty is a woman?"

"I do not know what you are talking about," Carlos said curtly.

"I can see that. Especially since you seem ignorant of my true mission to Paris. Can it be that you are really so uninformed? I thought Her Majesty was putting her full trust in you."

"What are you trying to say?"

"That although you want to marry me, you hide your true activities from me and I, of course, hide mine. You know that I am not the woman ever to surrender her independence to a husband. Life is too exciting to be spent on a velvet cushion under a canopy. The best thing would be for you to go on with your intrigues, and I will go on with mine. I shall give you just one more hint: my affairs and my brother's affairs are not always compatible."

Carlos glanced swiftly about the room. Pedro and Pepita had left him alone with Isabel on purpose. Pedro had received a word from the Count-Duke that Isabel's friendship with Carlos was to be furthered. Maria, however, hovered nearby on a floor cushion. She would never get used to sitting on chairs. Isabel noticed his glance.

"Maria, leave us alone." Maria left. There were still two footmen standing immobile on each side of the door leading from the sitting room to the entrance hall. Servants were generally considered part of a house's furnishings, and their masters usually spoke in their presence as if they did not have ears. Now Isabel motioned for them to leave. They closed the door. She was alone with Carlos.

"The Count-Duke has few friends left, and one of these days even His Majesty is going to realize that," Carlos now said. "Very soon the true Grandees will take over, and I shall be one of them. I knew from the first time I met you that you are an exceptional woman, Doña Isabel, and I want you to be my wife. I have told you before that you will be free to continue your studies and—who knows—if our plans agree perhaps even what you call your intrigues. It is a marriage of convenience, not a love match, but we will both profit by it. You have had time enough to think it over."

"You know my answer, Don Carlos. I stand to gain nothing from this match. I can have all you offer me without becoming your wife."

"Nobody else is willing to offer you a Grandeeship, you must admit," Carlos said, never tiring in his efforts to persuade her. "Well then, if you will not relent when I treat you as an intelligent human being, I shall have to resort to the procedure we both detest, and let me warn you, in this test of nerves, I shall prove stronger than you. You will become my wife, whether you want it or not."

He left her with a bow of great flourish, and she remained perplexed as to what he intended to do.

# 2.

Finally, finally Rafael returned to Madrid. She rushed to the apartment as soon as she received a note from Francisco Molina telling her he was waiting for her. He was busier than ever, and they could meet less often, but they did meet, whenever it was possible for him.

"It is beyond me how you can slip away so easily," he said to her when she came. "Don't they suspect anything?"

It was hard to find a logical explanation. Rafael still assumed that Pedro and Isabel were of impeccable Old Christian stock, and he could not know that they and Pepita were all bound by a trust born of their basic difference from their countrymen. He did not know that she worked with Pedro on a special project of subversion and that she was therefore free to come and go when and where she pleased.

She could tell Rafael only certain selections from her life, for instance, she had to omit the trip to the Netherlands. He thought she had stayed at a convent while he was in Italy. The effort to remember her lies was a strain on her love for him. She wanted so much to trust him and confide everything, but how could she, when he spoke of his hopes that Olivares would disregard the stipulation that Inquisitors had to be forty years of age and agree to Sotomayor's proposal to make him an Inquisitor as soon as he reached thirty, which would be in another year.

There was one aspect of her life she could talk about, and that was her trip to find Pepita. She told him about Sor Angela and the priest of Jaén, and she was indignant and self-righteous about it. How could such things go on right under the nose of the all-powerful Inquisition, she asked him scornfully.

"That witch," he answered, "is a mentally deranged person, and I agree that something ought to be done about her. I will see whether she can be placed in a hospital, perhaps a few good blood-lettings will help. The priest I am afraid we cannot touch. Unless there are two witnesses, respectable witnesses testifying against him, the Inquisition will not even consider an inquiry into the affair. Can you procure such witnesses?"

"No, of course not," she said, "unless I testified myself. Everything else I know is hearsay, although I believe every word I heard."

"There you are!" Rafael said. "And you went to see him in search of a Moor. So where does that place you? Besides, why are you so shocked about the priest? Are you not a concubine of a priest yourself?"

"How can you be so callous? I love you. There is all the difference in the world."

"And I love you. But if I had not been so lucky to find you, God knows what I would do to get a woman to sleep with me. A priest can be as sensually aroused as our monarch. Priests are men, not freaks. I deplore the tactics of that particular Don Juan of Jaén, but how can I condemn him for desiring you, when I have tried a million times to forget you and have not succeeded?"

Instantly she grew alarmed. "What is that? Why would you try to forget me? You must not. I cannot live without you. Oh Rafael, don't you know how much I love you? Promise you will never stop seeing me."

"On the contrary, I promise you that I will stop seeing you the minute you get married to Carlos de Queras, and never forget it."

Her panicky expression brightened. "Thank God that will never happen."

"I am afraid it will, my dear, and much sooner than you think."

"Why?"

"Because he wants you, isn't that obvious? You met him the first time three years ago, when you met me. You must admit that he has been singularly persistent in his pursuit of you."

"So has the King," Isabel replied, "and I have not given in to him either."

"Perhaps that too will come one day."

"I really don't know why you tease me like this."

"I am only trying to point out the inevitable. I adore you, as much as any man can adore a woman. You give me the greatest happiness and making love to you is such a benediction that I can understand the Illuminists. It is a state of special grace. Yet, I would be a liar if I said that my highest goal on earth was to make love to you, or even to have children with you. I believe I was put into this world for a special purpose and I have chosen, I think, the best possible way to achieve this goal."

"I think we have talked about this before," Isabel muttered, "and it doesn't lead anywhere. I will not marry, and that is that." In her mind she added: and even if I did I would still find a way to make you want me, and I would still sleep with you!

They were lying under three woolen blankets. It was a cold day in March, and the apartment could not be heated. They had made love twice already and each time, as usual, Isabel spilled herself before Rafael drew out of her to lose his seed on her belly instead of inside her. Even during his most arduous lovemaking, when Isabel was sure he would forget himself, he remained master over his body and never weakened in this one form of self-discipline. He had explained to her why this was necessary, but she often wondered why he was so afraid of getting her with child. If he really loved her so much, he should want to have a child by her. Other priests had bastards by their concubines. She finally concluded that the true reason was fear. He was afraid he would be so attached to her if she bore him a child that he would be too tempted to leave the order and marry her.

"I don't see why you would refuse to make love to me I were married," she said. "Wouldn't it mean that you could then give yourself completely? You would not have to be afraid of getting me pregnant if I had a husband."

"You belonged to me first, and I would never share you with anyone," he answered.

"Oh, you are so Spanish!" she said in exasperation.

"Well what else could I be? What a strange remark. Do you know any foreigners intimately? Are they different? And if so, in what way?"

"Confound your devilish objectivity! I am taunting you! I am challenging you! I want you to belong to me more than you do. I want to be like fire in your veins. I want you to think of me when you kneel down on your cold monastery floor to mumble your prayers. I want you to think of my body when you celebrate mass. I want you to imagine your hands on my thighs when you carry wax candles in some stupid procession. I want you to dream of my Reina when you go to bed at night and when you wake up in the morning. I want you to compose a love letter in your mind when you are asked to address a missive to His Holiness. I want you to be utterly intoxicated with me as I am with you."

He laughed silently. "Here we go again, our little scene of blasphemy. But sweetness, I am intoxicated. I do think of you, more than I want to. I count the beads on my rosary and it is like counting your kisses. There are just two ideas in me, but one is more important than the other. One is my love for you. . . ."

"That is the less important one," Isabel said.

"Yes, my dearest, and then there is my desire for power, as you know."

"But that power, what for?"

He did not answer.

"I believe you when you say you want to be Inquisitor General of Spain," she said. "Next to the King, the man holding that position wields the ultimate power. But you never told me why you want this."

"It is something I cannot talk about," he said. "And even if I could, you would not understand me." He looked into her eyes and his burned fiercely and fanatically. "This goal of mine is holy to me. Holy, holy, holy."

They remained close to each other, without talking. Isabel reflected that her only weapon was her sexuality. She must never quarrel with him, she must never never appear to become a burden, she must give him nothing but delight and ecstasy; it was her only hope to keep him. She wondered what she could do for him. Since their one excursion into Sodom, he had never asked for any special caresses. Now, as she let her mind wander over events of the past, she remembered her evening at Juliana's, and suddenly the murals were brought back before her inner eye. One scene she remembered above all others: the shepherdess about to touch the priapic erection with her lips. Slowly, she let her fingers wander over his body, and her own lust swelled immediately when she thought of what she would do for him.

He had been satisfied enough, but with her tongue she coaxed desire back into his loins until he was hard enough for her to slide astride him and move rhythmically and determinedly until he moaned, "Please come, my love, please come," but she smiled maliciously at his closed eyes and did not stop until he tried to push her off. Then she pulled away rapidly and, bending down over him, she took the tip of his penis in her mouth until his quivering and trembling stopped. She swallowed the strange bitter taste in her mouth and thought lucidly and coldly that if she could get him accustomed to trusting her to do this, she could one day conveniently forget to pull away, and then . . .

"Who taught you this?" he asked, after lying for a long time with his eyes closed.

He is suspicious like a jealous husband, she thought. "No one," she said. "I wanted to taste you. Is that bad?"

"Bad? My dearest beloved, it is paradise." He reached out to pull her in his arms and covered her face with kisses.

Again she tried to achieve at least a semblance of permanence in their relationship.

"Can I remain your mistress even if you do become Inquisitor?" she asked. The more she repeated the despicable title in her mind, the more it sounded just like any other profession. "Or would you have to leave Madrid?"

"I hope that a tribunal will be instituted in Madrid," he said. "There are plans for this. Until then, I might try to get to Toledo, but, of course, I might be sent to Valladolid, or to Seville, or anywhere, for that matter, even overseas perhaps. I have to take what I can get."

My God, she thought, dear God, if you exist, why did you let me fall in love with this man? Why me? Why him?

"It is late," he said. "We must leave."

They dressed.

"By the way," he asked, "do you still see the Caietanos?"

"From time to time. Manuela is my friend. Why?"

"I do not like you to associate with New Christians."

"Do not worry about me."

"But I do! I do!" he said. "Nothing must happen to you, ever!"

No, she thought, because it might upset your precious career. But she was determined not to quarrel with him. She would go on loving him, if it caused her death.

# 3.

All through the spring and summer Madrid was the playground for spectacular festivities. The Buen Retiro had finally been completed, and its theater lagoon served as the stage for one of Calderon's most imaginative plays, called "Love—the Greatest Enchanter," which was performed on gondolas and at least so enchanted the King that he granted its author the coveted Order of Santiago.

A note of sadness amidst the joy was the passing away of Lope de Vega, Spain's most popular poet, but Philip had already decided that Calderon was a worthy replacement and also awarded him the position of official Court dramatist.

Calderon, in turn, wrote the thought-provoking "Surgeon of His Honor," depicting the tragic fate of an innocent wife whose husband murders her—with the approval of his king as well as of the spectators—for an entirely imagined affront to his honor.

Other frequent amusements that year, including elaborate hunting parties, often led to the woods of the Pardo in the north of Madrid where the Cardinal Infante Ferdinand owned a small palace. Since Olivares had finally relented and permitted that young would-be warrior to exchange clerical garb for a general's uniform, Ferdinand had left for Flanders, and Philip had taken over the Pardo palace and enlarged it to lodge the throngs of hunting companions who shared his outdoor pleasures. As these woods abounded in brambles, or *zarzas*, the place became popularly known as La Zarzuela. Subsequently, when Philip brought companies of actors there to amuse his guests, the musical comedies they performed were also called *zarzuelas*. Calderon, a hunter as well as a poetic jack-of-all-trades, was careful not to be upstaged by another playwright, and upon a wink from his monarch, went to work to compose a series of delightful *zarzuelas*.

For a stranger arriving at Madrid, it would have been difficult to conceive that Spain was a country at war with several nations, and moreover a country virtually starving to death. Yet, even while enormous sums were wasted on fireworks, theater machinery, clothes, horses, gilt carriages, artwork, and church pageantry, the peasants and simple folk were restless.

The Catalans especially had become more and more disenchanted with their monarch who seemed to trample on their century-old citizens' rights, and they steadfastly refused to contribute to the costly upkeep of fortresses along the French border. They even refused to participate in the defense of the Spanish homeland when French troops attacked. This behavior enraged the Count-Duke, because he had as usual grandiose plans to make Castile once again the head of the world. All he needed was forty thousand troops.

He never quite grasped that troops on paper were not troops of flesh and blood. So he gave orders that forty thousand troops must be raised, if not from Catalonia then from elsewhere. Castile, however, was as drained of manpower as of other resources. Hopton, still English Ambassador at Madrid, reported home that he found the few horses available so weak that most of them would never be able to go to the rendezvous. He also remarked that the infantry were unwilling to serve and were carried like galley slaves. The Spanish, he said, are far so short in number of the soldiers they need that they have only one out of three.

Olivares prepared one master plan after another to finish the wars quickly, because he knew that Spain's only salvation lay in a rapid end to her participation in international hostilities. But whether he employed *blandura* or *rigor,* the results were always the same: Catalonia, the only rich part of the country, was not willing to provide more than a few hundred amnestied criminals for service in the royal armies.

Even if the dreadful shadow of the fast-approaching monster called defeat could be seen rising on the horizon, Olivares knew that in addition to his serious task, he was also responsible for the happiness of his monarch, and that he must give his utmost attention to royal entertainment.

Where did the millions of ducats needed for elaborate feasts come from? A large part out of the coffers of desperate New Christians desiring to remain in the good graces of the King. The numbers of *conversos* burned at the stake had gone down considerably since Olivares's tacit agreement with Sotomayor, but the Count-Duke's spy in the Inquisition was forever ready with tips as to who needed to be alerted in time and could pay for the warning with a goodly sum of ducats.

In the meantime, some of the Oriental Jews were still

residing at Madrid, no one knew where, and Olivares continued to receive them and carry on the King's business with
them—at least that was the explanation he gave, high-
handedly, to the members of the Suprema who questioned
the necessity of keeping descendants of Judas Iscariot at the
Most Catholic Court of the World.

"The Count-Duke is trying to sell Christ anew," Olivares's
detractors were muttering, "by order of the little devil in his
walking stick." That indeed was the latest crazy notion of the
superstitious populace. Olivares had a demon, a little devil,
residing in his walking stick. According to some, he was
under the spell of this demon and had to carry out his orders.
According to others, on the contrary, the demon was the
Count-Duke's slave and granted his every wish, guaranteeing
his power over the King and over Spain, in exchange for
Olivares's soul.

# 4.

The perennial Corpus Christi play by Calderon, this year
entitled "The Theater of The World," was being staged on
the great palace square in front of the south façade of the
Alcázar. This façade was of white stone and richly embellished with pilasters, casements, and mouldings of white
marble. The many gilded balconies were transformed by
tapestries and canopies into theater boxes for the royal
household.

Prior to the spectacle, the King, the Count-Duke, and all
the Grandees were riding on horseback in a slow ceremonious
procession around the great place, and, as usual, they were
followed by the dignitaries of the Church.

Isabel sat with Pedro and Pepita in the part of the grandstand reserved for *letrados* and watched the procession.
When she saw the King she smiled, because he had talked to
her during a private soirée held the previous night, and taken
away her fears that he would send for her.

"You know, of course," he had said, "that a royal summons is equivalent to an order. If I sent for you, you would
have to come. But this has become a matter of pride with me:

I want you to come willingly. I am tired of command performances, of services rendered to the Crown. Also, it would hardly please me to see you in a convent. But one day, I shall have you, and you will be mine, and gladly." His words had evoked the familiar response in her body, for despite his ugly face, she found him full of masculine allure, and she could not help smiling flirtatiously whenever their eyes met.

She knew she would see Rafael in the procession, and she looked out for him, but great was her surprise, nay her shock, when she perceived Carlos on horseback.

Carlos had indeed made true his threat and had started his official courtship. The first utterly impossible part of it had been midnight serenades under her window. Next he paid her outrageous compliments in front of courtiers and nobles. Then he got himself further into debt by sending her expensive gifts which she kept returning only to find them again brought back to her, an exchange which lasted until Pedro finally accepted the presents in her name. Rare books from Italy, golden cages with colorful birds, rich brocade dress lengths, crystal containers with foreign cosmetics, these were but a few of the gifts, and Pedro had thanked Carlos by offering him an unlimited low-interest loan. Much to her annoyance, Pedro had begun to look upon Carlos as a possible future brother-in-law.

After the play, she went with Pedro, Pepita, the Velázquez couple, and Don Francisco de Quevedo to the "Emperor's Garden," a terrace so called for its collection of marble statues of the Roman Emperors from Caesar to Domitian. Quevedo, who had been named royal secretary three years ago when Isabel had first met him at the Olivares' reception, was making no secret today of his growing distaste for the Royal Favorite.

"Our politics stink," he said. "Our dissipation is sinful. Ceremonious behavior and inbred laziness are the marks of our ruling class, while our people are starving in the streets. Our chief statesman is an inept bungler. The man covers up his mistakes by catering to His Majesty's every whim. The devil himself would rule better than he does. It is time someone opened the King's eyes."

"Careful now," Velázquez said. "You are too harsh again. Be sure you are not the one to do the eye-opening."

"And why not?" Quevedo countered. "No one else around here dares anything. Cowards all of them. You, of course, do not know how the simple people feel. You have lived in his company for so long, you have succumbed completely to the Count-Duke's false charm."

"Don Francisco, please, keep your tongue harnessed," Velázquez said.

"Well you know my motto," Quevedo said. *"Muchos dicen mal de mi, y yo digo mal de muchos.* But he is one man I would enjoy dragging in the dirt. Oh, he is as clever as the devil's tax collector. For a while, he even had me fooled. I was wary from the first, when he screamed, 'All is mine!' after hearing of the good Philip's demise. I mistrusted him, and I was right. And he was afraid of me. I was banned from Court on his order. But then he changed his mind. He called me back, and he talked to me so reasonably, so earnestly concerned about waste—oh how he would economize, how he would reform the country, how he would wield us into one strong, proud, healthy nation. I listened to him, and I was won over, like most of us were. But look at him now; what a costly mistake he has become. The money he presses out of the people, the taxes he imposes, it is a wonder he lets us breathe. But I'm sure he will think of that yet."

"Of what?" Velázquez asked with the slightly bored smile of someone who had heard the same rousing speech too often.

"Of taxing us for the air we breathe and for the tears we cry. Or at least for the salt content in our tears."

"Well, I am not a politician," Velázquez remarked. "I can only say that I try to be honest and friendly with everyone. His Excellency has shown me nothing but friendship and kindness."

"Yes, indeed," Quevedo snickered, "and our new financial wizard Valderocas will surely agree with you, won't you, Don Pedro?"

Pedro answered quietly: "It is hard for a man who has few helpers to carry out his plans. You yourself, Don Francisco, told us how His Excellency's ideas sounded seducing to your ears. Perhaps he has had no help with them. Perhaps, if we all tried harder . . ."

"Listen to him," Quevedo interrupted. "The fine Christian idealist. I thought your brand had died out with Don Quixote."

"You are among friends," Velázquez reminded him again. "I beseech you, Don Francisco, do not commit any folly. The King listens to no one but Olivares."

"He listens to you," Quevedo countered. "What if you painted some misery for a change? You are out of touch with life. Go back to Seville. Go back to the old street corners. Hear what the people grumble."

"If His Majesty listens to me, it is because I am his friend. That friendship is valuable to me."

"Why? Do you think some of his divinity will rub off on you?"

"Don Francisco, watch your tongue. I simply believe that every man needs a friend, especially a man as lonely and as guileless as our monarch."

"Then tell him what is wrong, if you want to be a true friend."

"I also happen to be a true friend of the Count-Duke, and I shall not seed any discord between my two best friends."

"I could have spared myself the words. I knew it would be hopeless," Quevedo said, turning to a newcomer to their group. He was the Duke of Medina-Celi whose family had been for many generations Grandees of Spain and who shared the general distaste of his class for the upstart Olivares. When at Madrid, Quevedo often stayed at Medina-Celi's house. Now he made the introductions, and the Duke took a careful look at Isabel.

"You are the young heiress Count de Queras is courting, I believe?"

She could still blush, and now she did so most becomingly.

"By my troth, I must be losing my perspicacity after all," Quevedo said. "Here I am standing next to the lady who is the talk of the town, the toast of Madrid I should say, the pink carnation of Rioja's latest poem, and I do not even realize it. So you are *the* Doña Isabel."

"I swear I do not know what you mean, Don Francisco," Isabel said quickly. "But since you so kindly give me the opportunity to talk, I do want to tell you how much I have admired your books."

"Which books?"

"All of them," she said enthusiastically. "And during a recent pilgrimage, when I crossed the countryside, I have found many of the things you describe to be true."

Quevedo stared at her through his thick spectacles and seemed to weigh the value of her words, but Velázquez was faster to point out their implication. "There you are, hombre," he said. "An unexpected advocate for you opinions, and one, may I add, in whom our gracious monarch is not uninterested."

She felt a stab of apprehension. Was he going to tell about the meeting of hers with Philip at his studio? That would be absurd. Did he know anything else? Had Philip talked to him perhaps?

"You are flattering me," she said.

"Not at all. His Majesty would like me to paint your portrait."

Quevedo and Medina-Celi exchanged knowing glances, but Pedro was there, Pedro her brother, the champion of her honor, and when he spoke up, his voice was cold and measured.

"I would like to have a portrait of my sister painted. I was afraid you might refuse my wish, Don Diego, knowing how busy you are, so I mentioned it to His Majesty, who, with his usual kindness, must have prevailed upon you to fulfill my wish."

"I beg your pardon. It was not my intention to cast any shadow of a doubt upon your honor, Don Pedro," Velázquez said smoothly.

"Honor, honor!" Quevedo muttered. "Would you not think Calderon had sufficiently saturated us with those delicate honor orgies of his?"

"I daresay you should paint her portrait," the Duke of Medina-Celi now said. "It seems incredible that the reputedly best-educated woman of Spain can at the same time be the most beautiful one. Don Pedro, rest assured, there is not a nobleman in Spain who would not risk his life to defend your honor."

"Thank you, Your Lordships, I am satisfied," Pedro said, but Isabel doubted the truth of that statement.

They were joined by Carlos de Queras and the Count of Villaquemada, and their talk turned again to politics. Villaquemada said he was just returning from a voyage through Andalusia and Portugal and that he had met with the Marquis de Ayamonte, the Duke of Medina Sidonia, and the Duke of Braganza who was married to a daughter of Medina Sidonia.

"And so, what is the feeling in the air?" Medina-Celi inquired.

"Much unrest and speculation," Villaquemada said.

"Then we are farther along than I thought," Quevedo remarked. "Perhaps if all the old Grandees approached His Majesty . . ."

Velázquez bowed with a sweeping flourish of his plumed hat; their *tertulia* had become too anti-Olivares for his taste. He and Juana left in search of a more congenial group.

"Don't you think that all this is largely a question of economics?" Pedro asked. "We need to stimulate industry and commerce; we stagnate. We should pull ourselves out of this morass of ancient glory and start to work."

If all the devils of Quevedo's "Visions" had appeared right before their eyes, it would not have caused half the consternation provoked by Pedro's innocent remark.

"Work?" Medina-Celi said with raised eyebrows.

"Industry?" Villaquemada asked, as perplexed as if he had never heard the word.

"Commerce," Carlos finally said. "Yes, of course. You must forgive my dear friend Pedro's strange ideas. He is a banker, a merchant. Fine Old Christian family, of course. The Valderocases ought to have been ennobled a long time ago."

"Oh," Medina-Celi said with a face as if he had been handed a worm.

"Of course, he does not care to be ennobled at this particular time," Carlos added quickly, obviously striving to make his future brother-in-law presentable to his own class of friends. "You understand."

"Oh, oh, of course," Medina-Celi now said. Isabel was reminded of Lope de Vega's popular verses:

> *Do you know, oh Fabio, what I mean?*
> *Of course, of course, I understand.*
> *No you lie! For I myself*
> *Who said it, cannot understand it.*

"Personal wealth is what distinguishes a nobleman from a *pícaro*," Quevedo said, knowing his fame to allow him such statements. "Both abhor honest work; one can afford it, the other cannot. Don Pedro Valderocas needs no further title. He is a *letrado*, that is sufficient."

"Alcalá or Salamanca?" Medina-Celi asked, naming the two most famous universities.

"Casa de Contratación," Pedro replied, and Carlos de Queras looked definitely crushed. Pedro's honesty was devastating. He continued, however, to hang on gingerly to one end of Isabel's lace scarf, and when they were joined by Their Majesties, he resolutely kept his hat on.

# 5.

As Isabel had guessed, Pedro was still furious when they got home.

"Either you marry that insufferable fool and stay at Court, or you retire from Madrid. This was too much! Do you realize that I might get killed over a ridiculous thing like that? If we want to beat them at their games, we must not break their rules; that will disqualify us."

"Those delicate honor orgies," Isabel mimicked Quevedo. "I like that man."

"I wish you would like someone who wants to marry you. You do not have to take Queras; there must be many others."

"Yes, fops," she said. "At least Carlos has a certain dignity, although he is trying his best to lose it. But I vow and swear I will not marry him, nor anyone else."

"Then go to live with Uncle Jaime! You become a nuisance here!"

"Pedro!"

"You know he does not mean it," Pepita said softly. "But please, Isabel, why could you not marry someone like Diego Caietano? At least he is good-looking, and he is one of us, and he used to be in love with you."

Isabel shot her an oblique look.

"He is too soft," she said. "If he were a little more like his brother José or like Duarte Perez."

"You are strangely attracted to men you cannot have," Pedro said.

"I think the only man who ever really impressed her was that monk," Pepita said. "You know, Rafael Cortes. I saw him in the procession today."

"Rafael Cortes," Pedro said. "Look at me, Isabel!"

She did, but her face turned white.

"Rafael Cortes," Pedro repeated. "All my life it seems I have contrived for him not to meet Isabel. All the years we were friends I never brought him home, or if I did I made sure he did not meet her. Then Olivares had to send him to Father.

But it is insane! It is insane. You had no time to fall in love with him. And anyway, he is a fanatic. You saw him today, so did I. A black friar, hanging around the old Inquisitor like a dog around his master. God, Isabel, I will buy you any husband you desire. Even him, if I could. He need not be noble, he need not be rich, he need not even be a *letrado*, just make up your mind."

"There is one thing I do not understand," Pepita said. "Why did you make so sure he would not meet her?"

"Because he has always been a fanatic, and at the same time the biggest wencher I knew. I was afraid that if he met Isabel, one day I would have to kill him."

"Would you?" Isabel asked softly. "Would you kill a friend?"

"No, I suppose not. That is why I did not want to have to defend your honor. I hate to kill."

"Have you ever killed anyone?" Pepita asked.

"Certainly. Pirates. Oh, I am a good swordsman, but I hate it. That is why I must stop Isabel's independence. She must marry. Then her husband can worry about her honor."

His determination scared Isabel. By law she had to obey her brother until she acquired a husband.

"Please Pedro, I will behave myself. I will stay home. Please do not force me to marry anyone."

Impulsively, Pepita flung her arms around Isabel.

"Leave her alone, Pedro. It is perfectly honorable for her to live with us. She will simply have to stop riding about town. . . ."

After that, Isabel was more careful when she slipped away to meet Rafael, but meet him she did.

# 6.

The war with France caused many complications for maritime commerce, and Pedro was acting once more as agent for Olivares when he took with him to Seville the royal instructions that the Casa de Contratación was from now on expected to provide the warships urgently needed to defend the Biscay coastline. The necessary vessels were to be withdrawn from their usual duty of protecting the merchant galleons bound for the Indies. In order to protect themselves, merchantmen were urged to sail in a single convoy.

Pedro expected an obstinate—and to his mind justified—refusal on the part of the Casa to accede to so uneconomic a measure, but Olivares said he trusted Pedro's diplomatic talents, especially when dealing with the members of his alma mater, and he insisted that Pedro personally present the plans to the directors of the great maritime clearinghouse.

Since all Spaniards loved long drawn-out discussions, Pedro expected to be gone for two or three months. He made both his wife and his sister promise that they would attend absolutely no festivities during his absence and would not show themselves in public except on holidays on the balconies of Valderocas House. He would have preferred to leave them at Toledo, but Pepita was with child and could not undergo the rigor of travel.

More than his wife, Pedro was concerned about leaving Isabel without his constant supervision. But this time, she could promise him sincerely that she would not leave the house in his absence and would not get into any trouble. Madrid was well-nigh void of dangers or temptations. The royal family preferred the cool stony vastness of the Escorial at the foot of the Sierra de Guadarrama to their uncomfortable Alcázar, and most of the nobles had also fled from the heat of the capital to their various country estates. Carlos de Queras had been summoned home by his father, who apparently had heard of Carlos's extravagances in the matter of his courtship. Rafael Cortes left town to accompany His Eminence Fray Antonio de Sotomayor to a cool mountain retreat. So there was indeed nothing for Isabel to do but behave herself impeccably. This she did, and the only excursions she undertook now and then were to visit Señor Caietano's bookshop. Here, toward the end of September, she heard for the first time about Diego Ximenes.

Diego Ximenes, it seemed, was an incredibly active Marrano who had decided that it was time the Madrid Marrano community organized itself more explicitly. Toward this goal, he had offered his house—or rather its ample cellar—as a meeting place for regular prayer services.

Señor Caietano told Isabel that he and his whole family—save Diego who was with Pedro at Seville—planned to attend Yom Kippur services there. He offered to come and fetch Isabel and Pepita, so they could all ride together to Señor

Ximenes's house under some pretext. Lope Silva, the Portuguese merchant, would also be there. His wife had died a year ago, and he was now courting Manuela. There would be a few other completely trustworthy friends.

Isabel thanked him and said she would talk it over with her sister-in-law. She and Pepita discussed the matter without coming to any solution. Pepita wanted to go badly, for sharing his religion was what had finally made her Pedro's wife, and she wanted to become as good a helpmate as Catalina had been to Fernando Valderocas. On the other hand, she did not know whether Pedro would approve of it, for there was, of course, always the danger of discovery. That was what worried Isabel most. She had never forgotten the seven condemned Judaizers at the great *auto de fé*. Cold logic told her that attending even a simple prayer meeting would doubtless earn them a death sentence if they were caught. However, someone had to make a beginning. It was time to test the situation. Jews had finally been received by the King and given letters of invitation to take back to their communities. The winds of change were blowing strongly. If Sotomayor, as rumors had it, was Olivares's man, perhaps inquisitorial vigilance had slackened. They finally thought that if Señor Caietano was going and taking his whole family with him, it must be safe enough. So they agreed to attend at least one service, on the eve of the Day of Atonement.

But on that day, still called day of purity by those Marranos who had forgotten its true meaning, Pepita awoke from her siesta so nauseated that she could barely lift her head from the pillow. She insisted that Isabel go anyway; Isabel, however, refused to leave her bedside, and when José and Ana came to fetch her, she told them she dare not leave Pepita alone. If she felt better, she would join them later. She knew very well the location of Señor Ximenes's house.

Toward nine, with the approach of night, when a fresh breeze came down from the mountains, Pepita felt better, and Isabel was torn between her desire to join the group of Judaizers and her natural impulse to give in to the gnawing fear in her stomach. Yet, when she pondered that these people were probably the core of the resistance group and that it was her only chance to see them face to face, her spirit of adventure took over. Unable to resist the challenge, she called Maria and asked for a simple dark street dress and a heavy black lace mantilla. She was going to a secret assignation with a man of great nobility. Let Maria spread the word

to the other servants. By now they were all so used to her
extravagances, they would take this at face value.

Once in the street, she walked rapidly and determinedly
through the crowds of idlers, pretending to be unaware of the
many shameless propositions she received from hot-blooded
loiterers who could not afford the prices of regular establish-
ments such as Juliana's. Twice she had to flatten herself
against the wall of a house to get past a knife battle of two
cut-throats defending some outrageous affront to their honor,
and once someone tried to pull her veil off, but she gave him a
sharp tongue lashing, calling him a "flap-eared, beetle-
headed whoreson" to the delight of a more gallant gang of
mad-cap knaves.

She had almost reached the house of Señor Ximenes,
congratulating herself upon her courage, when it occurred to
her that if she were really clever, she would not throw herself
head over heels into this dangerous situation. Something
inside her told her that, on the contrary, it would be most
prudent to inspect what could be a trap before she walked
into it. So she slowed down and came to lean against a corner
house from where she could observe the Ximenes residence.

The street was well lighted with various types of torchlights, for this was the hour when Madrileños loved to sit in
front of their houses to chat. What if some of the innocently
occupied neighbors were spies? Isabel asked herself. She
decided to walk up and down the street several times to see
whether she could notice anything unusual and also whether
she could detect any guards put out by the Ximenes household. She assumed that natural precaution would impose the
use of guards. To be less conspicuous herself, she rearranged
her veil in a coquettish way, leaving one eye free in the
fashion of professional girls of light virtue. Swaying her hips
provocatively, she walked down the street past Diego Ximenes's house. Nothing happened, except that two pustule-faced
youngsters asked for her price. She did not bother to answer.
There was no one sitting or standing outside the Ximenes
house, a very bad sign, she felt, since the house was thus
singled out as being different.

At the corner of the street she stopped and turned to walk
along the walls of the houses on the opposite side. Nothing
unusual here, just a few well-worn compliments such as,
"Your eyes are brighter than the stars," and a hissed, "This is
my hunting ground," from a similarly dressed young woman.
This other girl was obviously trying to get the attention of two

men sitting on the front steps of a house obliquely across from the Ximenes residence. Isabel also walked, meticulously hip-swaying past these two men, but they did not even follow her with their eyes. She made sure of that by turning back as soon as she was past them. Could they be so engrossed in their conversation? She tried the experiment again, this time almost touching their faces with a flourish of her perfumed handkerchief. No reaction at all.

All right then. These men in all probability did not belong in this street. Why then were they here? To observe the Ximenes house? Were they suspecting neighbors, perhaps, or Familiars of the Inquisition? Or were they guards put out by Ximenes? She walked a little further down the street to reflect upon the problem. Finally, she ruled out the possibility that they were guards. They were too far from the house to be of any real help if something happened. When she had reasoned to this point she found herself all at once faced with a terrible test of courage. Should she go in and warn her friends? Or should she disappear from the scene as quickly as possible? Suppose she went in, a woman, interrupting the holiest of holy services, to seed panic, and then suppose that she was wrong, would they forgive her? What would Pedro do in her place? José Caietano? Duarte Perez?

No! That was the wrong way to reason. She was alone and she must rely on no one's judgment but her own. The basic problem was clear enough: she must protect the precious name of Valderocas or all of Pedro's efforts would have been for naught. Yes! But of course. She must leave immediately; she must at all costs avoid being caught here. Pedro would be wroth to know she had even come.

But there was something else. Something more important perhaps than the name of Valderocas, something having to do with loving your fellowmen, with what Duarte Perez would call basic human decency. How would she ever be able to face herself if her friends got caught, and she could have warned them?

She would try just one more time to test those two men. She would walk slowly by the house of Ximenes, stopping for a minute right in front of it, and she would observe the two men.

She approached the house from the side where she could best see the two. Then she stopped and pretended to look at the door. One of the men got up and started to walk over. With trembling fingers she re-adjusted her veil.

"Looking for someone?" the man asked.

She must not be scared. She must sound natural, like a saucy tart, like a born chatterbox, like a professional harlot.

"That depends," she said, giving herself a thick Andalusian accent. "Would you think this was a good place to look for someone?"

"You are not from here?" he asked.

"Don't you like a new face in your street now and then? How about introducing me to your friend? I'm pretty good at trios. We might have some fun."

She expected him to grin at least, but he pointed with a movement of his head toward the Ximenes house.

"Do you know who lives here?"

"No. Who?"

"I don't know. I just thought you were looking for someone."

He apparently was not a resourceful wit, but she beamed at him nevertheless.

"How clever of you," she said, batting her eyelashes. "I just knew I'd meet somebody like you in the capital. How about taking me to a little *tasca*, eh, just for a few *tapas* and some fun."

By now a shade of regret was creeping into his voice. "Sorry my beauty, tonight I'm on duty."

"Oh, and you are a poet, too. How witty, how very charmingly you said that. Well, I must be on my way now, since you are unavailable, I better start looking elsewhere."

He gave a stupid self-satisfied chortle and tried to pinch her behind as she turned away, but she had too many petticoats under her skirt to feel more than a little tuck.

She was about to leave the street, when a gasp of horror arose around her and she suddenly found herself confronted by the armed guards of the Inquisition. And now, for the first time in her life, she witnessed the power of this institution in all its well-planned terror. The street was quickly barricaded at both ends by mounted guardsmen, while an orderly line of armed Familiars descended into the Ximenes house, after demanding that the door be opened in the name of the Holy Office. She stood petrified with the rest of the people, watching how all the secret worshippers were led away, one by one, each between two armed men.

There were many whom she did not know, but there were also many whom she loved dearly: Old Señor Caietano with his bushy white mane walked less erect than usual, his hands were bound behind his back. Manuela was pushed rudely and spat in her tormentor's face, for which she received such a blow that she fell and had to be helped up. Ana walked proudly upright, but tears were streaming down her face; José's bound hands were balled into fists; old birdlike Angelita Caietano, the bookseller's wife from Córdoba, mumbled continuously; Antonio Caietano, his wife Serena, and Juanito the youngest of the Caietano sons showed no emotion at all; Lope Silva's head hung down.

At first the crowd in the street had been quiet, gripped by the eerie spectacle, but all of a sudden, as if they remembered that they had better make a convincing show of their own staunch Catholicism, they started to insult the prisoners.

"Jew pigs, Christ killers, well poisoners, carriers of black death, scum of humanity!"

No one was allowed to leave the street without stating who they were, so Isabel had to turn back to her erstwhile gallant.

"A fine street you live in," she said in her broadest, most contemptuously slurred Andalusian. "With Jews for neighbors. By God's wounds I swear I have never found myself so near bad company. And now my whole evening's earning will be gone. If I hadn't stopped to talk to you I could already be sitting in a fine *tasca*. To repair the damage, how about taking me to one now?"

To her surprise, he did have some authority. He took her to a guard who apparently recognized him and dismounted to salute.

"Eh, Llorente, let the little whore go. I vouch for her."

"Bueno, Capitán."

She thanked both of them with a little curtsy and a blown kiss and walked away, humming and swaying her hips. But as soon as she had put two blocks between herself and them, she started to run and run and she never stopped running until she reached Valderocas House.

# 7.

She was completely out of breath and it took her some time to be able to talk coherently. Pepita guessed immediately that something must have gone terribly wrong and shooed the servants out of the room.

"Now," she whispered, "try to compose yourself and tell me what's wrong."

"The Inquisition got all of them," Isabel whispered back. "Everyone. We are lost. Lost! You understand?"

"It is not possible! What happened?"

Isabel told her hurriedly. When Pepita grasped the situation, she became unusually quiet, staring at Isabel while her mind worked.

"The Caietanos will not talk," she said finally.

"Not the old man, no! Nor José. They would rather let themselves be torn to pieces. But what about Ana? She will not stand the idea of torture; she will talk. And Manuela! Proud enough to spit in their face. She will talk just for the satisfaction of telling the whole world that she is a Jewess. No, it will be a matter of days, and they will come for us."

Pepita turned white and quietly fainted in Isabel's arms. Dragging her to the bed, Isabel called out for Teresa and Maria.

Then, while the women revived Pepita, Isabel's mind began to race. Pedro was presumably still at Seville, too far to be reached. Uncle Jaime was in mortal danger himself if Ana talked. Rafael was practically at the head of the enemy forces, and even if he were not, even if she could trust him, he would not be able to do much. He had warned her repeatedly not to get involved with the Caietanos. In this situation he could do nothing, except possibly help her to flee, and that she could do by herself. Should she ride with Pepita on horseback to Seville to board whatever Valderocas ship was available and sail for Amsterdam? No, Pepita would miscarry for sure. And what good was it to save just Pepita, Pedro, and herself? No, she must first save her friends. Save them, before they could talk and implicate the Valderocases.

She realized that she could not have warned them in time, and she was tremendously relieved that she had stayed outside in the street. For if she had been captured with them, it would have been the end.

But now, to whom could she turn? Who was likely to help a bunch of ill-starred Marranos?

Then it came to her in a flash. Why of course, the Count-Duke. The man who had invited Jews to Madrid. Who had promised them a synagogue. The only man strong enough to challenge the Inquisition.

It took an hour to get dressed for Court, to paint her face, to arrange her hair, but in the end she sat impeccably attired in the Valderocas town coach and asked to be driven to the Alcázar. At the main gate, under the arch, the coach was stopped by the royal halberdiers, and she had to descend and was then handed on from usher to usher until she reached the antechamber of the Count-Duke's office on the second floor.

She could hardly believe her good luck when she was told that he was still working, and she bore the curious glances of the pages and footmen with equanimity. It did not matter what anyone thought of her, if she could only talk to him. She waited by a window and looked down into the *Patio de las Covachuelas* where shopkeepers were only now closing their booths, bookstalls, and jewelry displays for the night. During the day, there was a constant stream of visitors passing to and from the offices and audience chambers of the boards for Castile, Aragon, Italy, Portugal, and Flanders, which were located around the patio on the ground floor, but at this late hour no one was working save the tireless Count-Duke. When she heard a door and hurried footsteps behind her, she thought her time had come, but it was a courier, arriving in great haste, who was immediately admitted to Olivares's office. A few seconds later, she heard a savage roar.

"The devil take the Catalans! The devil take the constitutions! I will crush Barcelona to the ground! When I say Catalonia becomes the parade-ground of Spain, I mean exactly that! I'm sick of their excuses! And I'm sick of hearing the Grandees sympathize with Catalan policy. I rule this country! And may the devil shit on their prerogatives!"

There was a pause during which someone must have tried to calm the minister, for now his voice rang out louder than before:

"Whoreson! Traitor! How dare you answer me like that? Idiots you are! Bungling idiots. Is that why I made Cardona viceroy for Catalonia? In his place I'd have an army standing in rank and file by now. By God, I swear I will get His Majesty himself to move into that confounded province and at the head of all our troops. The Catalans are enemies of God, King, and Fatherland, and if they persist in their obstinacy, they shall pay for it!"

Another courier arrived and was also shown into the Count-Duke's office to be received by a shower of different abuses:

"How dare you pester me with this pettiness at an hour like that. Tell the stupid woman I will have no more to do with her. My God, that happened years ago. Enough I say!" A bell rang and two footmen precipitated themselves into the office to drag away the second distraught courier who did not seem to grasp what was happening to him.

Shortly thereafter, the door opened and Olivares stepped into the well-lighted antechamber, followed by the Protonotario for Aragon and another worried little man who was apparently the unfortunate victim of the minister's rage. Since all three looked as if they were about to leave, Isabel boldly stepped in their way and curtsied. Yet, inside herself she trembled with fear. When Olivares rudely inquired, "What do you want?" she found that she had momentarily lost her voice. "Whatever it is, it will have to wait. Come back tomorrow."

"Your Excellency, it cannot wait," she managed to say.

"What an uncivil presumption!" He beckoned to a footman. "Show her out."

"But Your Excellency, it is I, Isabel Valderocas."

"And who do you think you are? The patron saint of Madrid?"

He stormed out of the chamber, calling down curses and insults upon each and every member of the State Council for Aragon.

This was the Olivares she had never seen, the one people gossiped about, the one Quevedo despised, the man of senseless rages and gross injustice.

She hung her head and felt the first tears of discouragement blur her vision, when she was touched on the shoulder by the Count-Duke's favorite valet, Simón Rodriguez. She knew him to be a man of no mean importance who could make or break appointments with the chief minister and was widely courted by favor-seekers. He smiled at her and gave her a brief word of encouragement: "Try to forgive him. He has had a very bad day."

She nodded blindly.

"He sometimes arrives as early as seven in the morning," Simón Rodriguez added. "At that hour you could be the first petitioner and perhaps see him before he leaves to wake His Majesty."

"Thank you," she said so softly he could barely hear her. Then, remembering that Simón Rodriguez's good will could be worth more than a royal decree, she dropped a formal curtsy to Olivares's chief lackey.

That night she did not sleep but argued with Pepita about the possible consequences of the Caietanos' arrest. They did not know how grave the accusation would be. Neither of them had ever been in Diego Ximenes's house; they did not know whether the cellar had contained any symbols of Judaism for the prayer service, or whether the men and women had only stood there surrounded by empty walls. Had they taken any precautions to make this appear like a party or other innocent festive gathering? And how much were they incriminating themselves?

Pepita said leaving Madrid would only draw attention upon them; they would have to stay and pretend nothing was amiss. But Isabel knew that even if the prisoners did not talk, sooner or later all of Caietano's regular customers would be questioned. Toward morning, before the throngs of servants arrived, she asked Alfonso to drive her back to the Alcázar. She told him she had received news from Pedro which she simply must communicate to His Excellency.

There was a new shift of ushers, and the great palace lay completely silent and deserted. Not a soul in the patio or on the great staircase. The page who took her to the audience chamber was young and gave her a look of puzzled curiosity.

Simón Rodriguez was already with Olivares, but when he saw her arrive, he gave her a little wink and beckoned her to come through the open door into the office. He left, closing the door behind him, so that she found herself alone with the dictator.

Olivares had been sitting at his desk, but now he rose and came toward her with an expression of frank surprise.

"Not you again?" he said, but his voice was calm and beautifully modulated, and through it lightly flew the soft

Andalusian accent she loved to hear. She sank into a deep curtsy.

"Your Excellency, please forgive me for my boldness." He interrupted her and drew her up.

"Doña Isabel, if I remember correctly, it is up to me to beg your forgiveness. I am touched that you are back so soon after the rude reception I gave you last night."

She looked into his dark sad eyes and saw a new puffiness around them and lines forming on his well-shaped forehead. He is getting old, she thought.

"I understand, Your Excellency. You work much too hard, and you do not have enough helpers."

He nodded absentmindedly and walked to a window inviting her by a gesture to follow him. Looking down over the western ramparts, they saw the popular park, "Jardin del Moro," stretching to the banks of the Manzanares.

"Spain is asleep," he said. "The beautiful country of Spain is asleep. I alone am awake, all the time, planning, watching, hoping to wake up our people. But they do not want to wake up. They dream of good old times, of Emperor Charles, and King Philip the Second, of the epoch when Spain knew nothing but victories. They don't want to hear about economy, canalizing rivers, new industries, cultivating the soil. They want to go on dreaming of martial glory, of conquests . . . We aren't strong enough for that, but they don't want to hear it. They dream that a universal monarchy under Habsburg kings is near at hand. They looked up to me to give them back their unquestionable supremacy. I am leading a nation of dreamers." His shoulders sagged and he shook his head. "My dear Doña Isabel," he said and took both her hands in his, "I cannot tell you how good it feels to see you come back to me this morning. I surely thought I had alienated you forever."

"Please do not mention it anymore, Excellency."

"All right," he said softly. "Now what can I do for you? Is His Majesty giving you trouble?"

"Oh no, I would not disturb Your Excellency for something like that! It's . . ." She looked around to see whether there were any servants standing nearby, but he guessed her thoughts and assured her that it was too early for spying ears. "You can speak freely."

"A group of friends of ours were arrested last night," she said in a low voice, "by the Holy Office."

He was visibly taken aback.

"How do you know?"

"I was there."

The seriousness of her words did not fail to reflect in his features. He knitted his brows and his dark eyes bored into her.

"What were you doing?"

Any lie, she feared, might eventually be discovered and used against her. If she expected Olivares to help her, she must trust him enough to tell him the truth and nothing but the truth, though perhaps not the whole truth.

"I was supposed to meet them at the house of a certain Diego Ximenes, whom I do not know personally. As I was approaching his house, the guards of the Holy Office arrived, and I just stood there and saw them being taken away."

"Did anybody recognize you?"

"No, I was veiled."

"Who are your friends?"

"Señor Caietano and his family."

"Not the bookseller?"

"Yes, him."

He let out a low whistle.

"Do you know him?" she asked.

"He works for one of my agents. This is serious. Very serious. Have you told anyone about it?"

"My sister-in-law."

"Is she a gossip?"

"No."

"No one else knows?"

"I don't think so. I suppose they have confiscated the bookshop by now, and the news will spread like wildfire."

He looked at her in a speculative way. "So you want me to get you and Pedro and your sister-in-law safely out of Spain, because you think your friends may incriminate you?"

Her heart sank. Dear God, please let me persuade him. Dear God, please, he must save them.

"Your Excellency, I cannot let my friends perish. I thought, I thought, you could, possibly, intervene. . . ." Her voice trailed off. She was asking him to do the unthinkable, to take accused Judaizers out of the dungeon and send them to freedom. He had done it before, notably in the case of Duarte Perez, for a considerable monetary gain to the Crown. Would he do it again?

He remained silent and observed her, as if trying to make up his mind about her.

"Doña Isabel, there are a few things I would like to know about you before I give you an answer. Will you be honest with me?"

"Why, of course I will!"

"I have heard rumors that you accompanied Don Pedro abroad last year. Why did you do that?"

"I was curious. I wanted to see whether I would like to live outside Spain."

"Why?"

"Because I had heard women have more freedom elsewhere."

His mouth creased in a fatherly smile.

"And what did you find?"

"That I want to live in Spain."

"You want to remain in Madrid."

"Yes, Your Excellency."

"Are you prepared to join a convent?"

"If that would save my friends, yes."

"But you would not like it?"

"No, Excellency."

"Give me the names of your friends."

She gave him all the names, starting with Señor Caietano, his wife, his sons Antonio, José, and Juanito, Ana and Serena, Manuela and her fiancé Lope Silva. At the last name he looked up from the paper onto which he was writing the names.

"Lope Silva. He is the spokesman of the Portuguese Marranos, is he not?"

"I would not know, Excellency."

"What about Diego Caietano?"

She was surprised that he noticed Diego's name was missing on the list, but then she had always heard that his memory was phenomenal.

"He is with Pedro at Seville."

"That complicates matters even further. It is a nasty business, coming at a bad time. Why do these Jews have to be so impatient?"

He did not expect an answer, but Isabel spoke up anyway. "Perhaps they, too, are dreamers, like the rest of us Spaniards. Perhaps they, too, dream of ancient glory."

His thoughts were already somewhere else.

"I have many enemies, and the ranks of my friends are dwindling. I need people like your brother, like the Caietanos. I also need more agents, more people I can trust."

What was he talking about?

"I will try to get your friends out, but they must leave the country immediately. I will notify Pedro to wait for them at Seville."

She was so relieved, she had to hold herself by leaning on his desk.

"Oh, Your Excellency, I do not know how to thank you."

"I do," he said. "You must become one of my agents. You must also help make the name Valderocas less vulnerable. Your association with the Caietanos must be completely forgotten; your life must be irreproachable."

"How can I do that?"

"By marrying into an old noble family."

She stared at him, utterly bewildered. He got up from his desk, slowly took her in his arms, and held her close as if to shield her against the world.

"My dear child, I want you to marry Carlos de Queras." Her body stiffened in revolt, but he did not release her. The top of her head reached to the level of his mouth, and he spoke softly, brushing her hair with his lips.

"Just pretend for a minute that you are my beloved daughter and listen to my reasons. Carlos's family is one of the oldest in Spain. After the reconquest of Granada, the Queras's were given vast stretches of land in the eastern part of Andalusia, and Carlos is the only heir. They are not rich in money, for they have contributed heavily to the Crown before the ascension of our present monarch. But they are rich in land and in prestige. Carlos, I know, is on excellent terms with the Duke of Medina Sidonia and the Marquis of Ayamonte—two individuals who heartily desire to see me fall flat on my face. I even suspect, but I have no proof, that he has on occasion acted as a go-between for the Duke of Braganza of Portugal and the French Cardinal Richelieu. Carlos, in short, is an enemy of mine and getting more so every day. But he is immensely shrewd, never underestimate him, and stands in the favor of the Queen. I would love to ban him from Court, but far from Madrid, he may do greater harm than right under my eyes. I know you detest him. You have made your position quite clear to all of Madrid. However, I now beseech you to reconsider it. You would greatly oblige me."

He released her but continued to hold her hands.

And so the mosaic of her life was smashed. Her beautiful well-organized, exciting life was broken to pieces which could never again be fitted together. Ashen-faced she looked up at the man whom she had so often admired.

"I have long thought that you must be in love with someone else," he said. "I am sure of it now. Who is he?"

"No one knows him," she said, "and he cannot marry me. So his name is of no importance."

"Then I advise you to forget him. I know this sounds harsh; I was young once and in love, but what cannot be helped cannot be helped. We must concentrate on the work at hand. I want you to go home now and stay there. Do not leave the house and receive no guests except Carlos if he should call. Be nicer with him than usual. We do not want him to give up his courtship. Then, as soon as Pedro returns home and tells you that your friends are safely en route to Amsterdam, you will accept Carlos's proposal. After that, the Countess, my wife, will see to it that you are given a position in Her Majesty's entourage. Thus, you will have ample opportunity to come to Court and pass on your reports to me. Do we understand each other?"

"I think so, Your Excellency."

"Good." He went to his desk and rang his silver bell. Simón Rodriguez came back.

"Send for Fray Rafael Cortes, secretary to his Eminence the Inquisitor General. It is a matter of utmost importance."

Hearing his name hit her like a bolt of lightning. She had not known that he was back in Madrid. Olivares's mind was already working on the next stage of his scheme; he walked her to the door absentmindedly. Then, as she curtsied goodbye, his eyes focused again on her face, and he gave a sigh.

"To think that Carlos will never know what a brilliant wife he is getting."

She did not hear his remark. The mere name of Rafael had erased all other problems from her mind. Forget him, Olivares had said, forget him? Never, never would she forget him. Even if she did finally marry Carlos, she would find ways and means to make love to Rafael.

# 8.

After Isabel left him, Olivares went to the private chamber of the King to draw the curtains with his own hands and then inform Philip of the newest world events and Court gossip, before the other gentlemen of the King's chamber got a chance to wish Philip good morning.

Philip usually faced the daylight sullenly, unless he could look forward to a pleasant interruption from the boredom of being His Majesty, but today was another day of trouble to judge by his chief minister's grave expression.

"All right, let's have the devil's breakfast," he said to Olivares after ungraciously tending him the royal hand to kiss.

"The breakfast could be called cooked in heaven," Olivares answered shrewdly. "I even feel tempted to congratulate Your Majesty, if that meant not inviting bad luck."

"How's that?"

"There is a considerable amount of revenue from confiscations about to flow into the coffers of His Eminence. I think some people are up to their old tricks of trapping New Christians. I have heard from a reliable source that a well-to-do merchant, as well as a bookseller and his family, were lured into a frame-up and are now being held for interrogation. They have connections among other wealthy Marranos. If these men are convicted, it will spread a panic."

"Find a remedy," Philip said. "You shouldn't bother me with these details."

"All I need is your signature, Sire. Then I could induce His Eminence to release these persons. You know that they would be more than glad to leave a token of appreciation to the crown. That means . . ."

". . . that we can have a gala at the Buen Retiro," the King interrupted as his face brightened. "In honor of," he thought for a moment. "It doesn't matter in whose honor, I'll find something. Great idea, Count, go ahead. But be diplomatic about it will you. Quevedo has been grumbling too much lately. Any gossip?"

"A great courtship is rumored to end successfully."

"Whose?"

"Carlos de Queras's."

Philip's lower lip hung open for an instant, then a lewd smile started to creep over his face.

"Would I like to place a pair of horns on him."

"If you wait till it is announced, you may find the placing easier."

"She dislikes him that much?"

"She loathes him."

"Then why does she accept?"

"His father is a Grandee. It would give her a better standing at Court. I think she has finally realized that."

"If I asked my wife to take her as Lady-in-Waiting, I could see her every day. Count, that is what I call an angel's breakfast."

Olivares saw with satisfaction that Philip's thoughts would be happily occupied with the stalking of a prey he had long coveted. Moreover, as usual when contemplating a new cardinal sin, His Majesty would avoid talking too much to Sotomayor for fear of hearing another sermon on the evil temptations of the flesh. That gave Olivares the chance to influence Sotomayor without running the danger of Sotomayor's consulting with Philip.

As for the girl, the prospect of becoming Carlos's wife was so grisly that an affair with her monarch might prove a welcome divertissement.

# 9.

Olivares was back at his desk in time to receive the secretary of His Eminence. He handed him the list of names and demanded to be given all available information on the prisoners.

Rafael's eyes skimmed over the list without hesitation. His face showed not the slightest emotion.

"I will try to have the information for you as soon as possible."

Olivares did not take his eyes off Rafael's calm features; he recalled his own involuntary reaction when he had received the bad news, and he never ceased to marvel at the self-discipline and cool efficiency of his former secretary. Even now he could not completely suppress his own apprehension.

"Do you expect His Eminence to balk at my request?" he asked.

Rafael looked up quickly and their eyes met.

"But, of course," Rafael said evenly. "And who is the true master of Spain?"

At that the Count-Duke's sunken lips curled upward causing a barely perceptible movement in his beard.

"Why did you not inform me of this?" Olivares inquired and pointed to the list.

"It must have happened recently. I did not know about it."

"You are not afraid of me," Olivares said in a detached way, as if he merely stated an established fact. "Doesn't it bother you to serve two masters?"

"I serve no masters," Rafael said. "I serve a cause."

"My cause!"

This time it was Rafael who allowed himself the relief of a smile.

"Let us say that our views on certain affairs coincide."

Again their eyes met, but much as Olivares stared at him from under knitted black brows, the Dominican friar did not avert his gaze. Now Olivares got up from his chair to walk around the desk and offer Rafael his hand.

"You are still my friend, though?"

Quickly Rafael grasped the hand and bent over it to bring it to his lips.

"I will always be your friend, Don Gaspar."

Here is one of the few men, Olivares thought, who dared call him by his first name, while at the same time kissing his hand in a gesture uncalled for by etiquette but full of tenderness and completely surprising in a man known for his aloofness and self-control.

"I want you to make clear to His Eminence that I intend to have these people released and shipped out of the country. I suppose this will harm your standing with him and might reduce some of your usefulness in this position."

"If I could give you ten years of my life right now as a present, I would do so," Rafael said.

The Count-Duke knew what he meant.

"His Eminence has been pressing me for the establishment

of an inquisitorial tribunal at Madrid. Perhaps we could find an interim solution. Have an extra inquisitor added to the staff at Toledo to help with the affairs of Madrid," Olivares talked pensively, as if he were alone. "Some wording might be found to give that person slightly less than full rank, thereby circumventing the age requirement. . . . Anyway, it is time for me to exert some of my power in that direction. Sotomayor alone is not enough, we need Inquisitors with progressive ideas. Fray Rafael, I count on you."

Rafael bowed formally before leaving the Count-Duke's office. If he continued on his narrow path, avoiding pitfalls and ravines, it would eventually lead him to his goal: he would become Inquisitor General of Spain. By then Olivares would be old and Rafael Cortes would be the most powerful man in the land. It was a goal worth working for and waiting for; it was a goal justifying any lie, dissimulation, or sacrifice along the way.

# 10.

The procession slowly wound up the large marble staircase to the office of the Royal Favorite. The ushers, young and old, stared with curiosity at the odd spectacle. Preceded by incense-waving monks, the old Inquisitor General himself, Fray Antonio de Sotomayor, personal confessor to His Majesty Philip the Great, walked up in measured steps, carrying an elaborately carved and painted wooden crucifix. Behind him walked his personal secretary, Fray Rafael Cortes, carrying a black box painted with little flames and no doubt containing materials pertaining to the worst of heresies. Both men were flanked and followed by Dominican friars chanting mournful melodies.

The procession continued through the antechambers and petitioners crossed themselves on its passage. Then the carved doors swung open, and doormen briefly bent their knees and made the sign of the cross.

Olivares stood behind his desk and clenched his teeth. Sotomayor knew him to be a religious man, with a good portion of fear of the unknown, and he was now playing on this fear, an audacity Olivares was not inclined to forgive.

As in any great man, two souls were wrestling in the body of the Royal Favorite: the first one was the inborn superstitious soul who demanded occasional excesses of religious fervor. When it took the upper hand, Olivares would lie down in a coffin which he kept in a corner of his bedroom and would ask his personal confessor to absolve him and have candles lit and have priests chant over him, a procedure that inevitably calmed his frayed nerves by reminding him of his own mortality and the eternal peace that would come with death. The other soul was an intrepid heroic one which knew that goodness and righteousness required a steady vigilance and an occasional exertion of brute power for their ultimate triumph.

Sotomayor placed the crucifix on Olivares's desk and motioned Rafael to hand him the box. He opened it and took from it several rolls of parchment. He then placed these papers at the feet of his crucified Savior and turned to the Count-Duke.

"I place in your hand the lives of heinous criminals, of men who have flogged the image of God, men descended from God's own murderers, men whose ancestors screamed: May His blood come over us and over our children; men who would not hesitate—nay who would enjoy—to kill Christ anew; infamous Judaizers whose souls might yet be saved if they were but kept in the care of the Holy Office."

"Thank you, Father. I trust this is all the information you have on these people," Olivares said lightly, while facing the Inquisitor and his attendants with all the haughty indifference he held in store for the few occasions when he had to restrain himself from abusing the perpetrators of an unwelcome attack on his projects. "You may leave," he said to the friars. "I would like to have a word with His Eminence."

The men looked at Sotomayor, but he, with a wave of his hand, permitted them to stay.

"As you wish," Olivares said and took up the parchments to glance through them. "Have any of them been tortured yet?"

"Do you take the Holy Office for an assembly of monsters?" Sotomayor countered. "They are being detained and are more comfortable at this moment than they could be in a public jail. They are being given time to think about their sins."

"They are people who have served our monarch long and

well," Olivares said, "and His Majesty is keenly interested in their welfare."

"They are heretics who will contaminate the very air His Majesty breathes," Sotomayor said.

"They shall not contaminate it for very long," Olivares replied. "I shall personally see to it that they are exiled from Spain. His Majesty himself has signed a letter of safe-conduct for them. I expect you to release them into my custody before you undertake to transfer them to the dungeons of Toledo."

"If the Crown derives any money from this, it will be a deal worthy of Judas Iscariot," Sotomayor intoned. Olivares wished he were alone with the old man, so he could tell him to stop his foolish imitation of Torquemada, but in front of the monks, he had to keep his temper.

"There is no money involved," he said. "Such an insinuation is an insult to His Most Catholic Majesty. We are merely correcting an error. These people have been mistakenly arrested. We know they were lured into a trap, and His Majesty is concerned that there should be strict justice for all his subjects."

"What about the others who were discovered at the same time?"

"Deal with them according to your mercy," Olivares said curtly.

Then, without further ado, he walked to the nearest monk bearing a burning wax candle, and, imperturbably, he placed the first parchment into the flame. When the paper started to singe and curl, he walked over to the fireplace with it, holding it in front of him like a torch, and then, one by one, he burned all of the incriminating documents. Because of Sotomayor's insistence on keeping the Dominican friars with him, the deed would soon be told in all the drawing rooms of Madrid.

"May Our Savior relieve your conscience," Sotomayor said. "We will leave Him with you." And he started to lead the procession away from the minister's office, leaving the crucifix on the desk.

On their way through the *Patio de las covachuelas,* where all the merchants and their customers made room for them, Sotomayor turned to Rafael. "My son, do you wish to supervise the transfer of the prisoners to His Excellency?"

"Father, I wish you could spare me this task. It grieves me that I cannot save their souls."

"I am glad you side with me," Sotomayor said. "Some of

the brothers have warned me that you seem to harbor liberal ideas. I see they are wrong."

"I am dedicated to the Holy Office," Rafael said, "and I am committed to high ideals. I believe that the wicked must be punished so that the righteous may triumph."

"I will designate another brother for the ungrateful task," Sotomayor said. "As for you, I will recommend your name to the Suprema, as a brother qualified to become Inquisitor. I am old and the Lord may soon call me. It would please me to have helped you along on the arduous path that is ours."

Rafael lowered his head as an outward sign of humble gratitude. "Thank you, Father."

# 11.

The news of the popular bookseller's disappearance was received by many Madrileños with apprehension. But soon a rumor spread that the Caietanos had not been arrested at all but had fled before the Inquisition could touch them. Then, a few weeks later, that rumor too was updated, for Diego Caietano came back to Madrid and reopened not only the bookshop, but also a stall in the *Patio de las Covachuelas* and acquired the right to import books for the royal library. It was all very confusing, but since more important events took place every day, the whole Caietano affair soon receded into the background. The new talk of the town centered around a more substantial event: the impending marriage of Doña Isabel Valderocas Sanchez, heiress to tremendous wealth, and Don Carlos de Queras, scion of one of the noblest families of Spain.

To her friends and acquaintances at Court, Isabel gave no explanation of her sudden turnabout. After Pedro had come home from Seville and told her of their friends' safe departure, Pepita was eager to inform him how Isabel had bravely saved the situation, and for a few days Isabel had hoped that Pedro would offer to get her released from her promise to the Count-Duke. Her hopes were in vain. Pedro, on the contrary, approved of the project, and she realized, once again, that she was completely alone and could never rely on anyone but herself.

Finally, the day came when she had to tell Rafael.

They were lying on their bed in the small apartment, under a pile of blankets, caressing and kissing each other softly. She spoke timidly, dreading each word, yet no longer able to keep the truth to herself.

"Rafael, I have always accepted you unconditionally. I have not asked questions. I have loved you without really knowing you, because I cannot help loving you." She had turned to him and was tracing patterns in the curly black hair on his chest, but she avoided looking into his eyes.

"When are you getting married?" he asked brusquely, and she was startled by the hoarseness in his voice.

"How do you know I am getting married?" she murmured.

"All Madrid knows."

"How? It hasn't even been announced. I can still change my mind."

"No, you cannot. I don't blame you. I knew the pressure would become overwhelming. I told you so from the very beginning."

"Well, we also knew that we could never marry each other since you persist in wanting to live your own life. So, why can't I live my life and still meet you here? I promise you I will find a way to come to you, as often as you want me. Carlos is getting enough money from this arrangement; he really does not care about me, only about my money. I will be able to do what I want."

"You have not answered me. When?"

"It will be announced tomorrow."

"That is when the marriage contract will be signed?"

She nodded.

"Then this means good-bye? Oh Isabel!" He suddenly buried his face between her breasts and she felt him swallow hard, twice in a row. Her arms went around him, and she hugged him fiercely.

"No, I will come here again. Perhaps not tomorrow, but the day after. The wedding will take place a month from now, around the first of the year, and even then I will come."

He did not listen to her. He covered her face with kisses, then her throat, her breasts; his hands went all over her in a sudden hunger and she thought quickly, happily, that he loved her and wanted her as much as she loved him, and when he entered her again she felt surge within her the violent hope that he would for once forget himself and perhaps get her with child. After that she was beyond the stage of thinking. Too many delicious sensations churned higher and higher until she spilled over. At the same time, there was a marvelous feeling of contentment and then a slow and peaceful return to calm. It was then that she realized that Rafael was still inside her, that he had finally given himself to her. They had come together, and she at last possessed him the way he had always possessed her.

After a long time of silent closeness, he left her and got up. She observed him through half-closed lids. He washed himself carefully, slipped into his fine white silk shirt, his tight breeches, and she thought she would let him talk first, let him propose a plan of action, let him decide how they would flee together. She would not suggest anything; she would not even offer financial help. She would do nothing ever to hurt his feelings. When he was all dressed, he combed his fine short black beard, his curly hair. If El Greco had known him, he would never have painted anyone else, Isabel thought with pride. He turned around and smiled at her.

"Good-bye, my love. Try to be happy."

Instantly, she sat up, fear showing in her eyes.

"Where are you going? When do I see you again?"

"Never, if I can help it. I will ask to be sent away from Madrid. You knew it would happen one day."

"What do you mean? I don't understand you. Aren't you going to take me with you? Aren't we going together? Not after this! You can't leave me now. You can't, you can't . . ." Her voice died away. He came back to the bed and took both her hands in his.

"I can and I must." He pulled her up quickly and bent over to kiss her mouth a last time. Then he released her suddenly, pushing her back down on the bed, and a second later he was gone. The door slammed shut and she could hear him running downstairs, his shoes beating a fast rhythm on the wooden stairs. She jumped out of bed and ran to the window to catch a last glimpse of him, but he was already turning around the corner and she clenched her left hand into a fist and bit her knuckles to stifle the scream she felt surging up in her throat.

He was gone, and she knew with absolute certainty that he would not come back. Twice before she had thought she had lost him, the first time when he had left Seville abruptly, and the second when he went to Italy. But both times hope and determination had overcome her fear. This time it was different. She was so stunned by his deliberate departure, so mortified in her deepest feelings, that she could neither sob nor cry. On the contrary, the wave streaming through her body was made of a sensation closer to hatred than to despair, a hatred born of the ominous feeling that she had only gotten what she deserved. Pedro had warned her over and over again. He knew that Rafael was a fanatic, and she should have listened to him and believed him. Now it was too late. Too late. Too late. . . . For a time, while she dressed, her mind kept repeating those words until their meaning became lost. Then suddenly she stopped herself. "Too late for what?" she asked aloud, accusingly, "Too late for what?"

She stared at the empty walls of the bedroom and she thought she would perhaps never again set foot in this place, although she would keep it forever. She had spent too many happy moments here to ever give it up.

They had never really decorated the apartment, because they always thought they might one day have to leave it hurriedly. The bedroom contained nothing but the bed and a washstand, the living room a table, two chairs, and a wallshelf filled with maps and a few books on geography. The only personal touch, the only valuable, was a small but heavy sculpture of a nude couple, perhaps Adam and Eve, standing casually together, the woman glancing at a fruit in her right hand, the man placing his arm around the woman's shoulder as if to protect her. Both figures were well proportioned, and the details, faces and hands, exquisitely well worked. Rafael had brought the piece from Rome, and it was the only present he had ever given to Isabel. The sculpture was made of bronze, less than a foot high, and stood in the center of the shelf. Isabel was ready to leave when her eyes fell on it. Impulsively, she reached out for it and was surprised by its weight. She wrapped it in a map, making a parcel.

"A wedding gift for Doña Isabel Valderocas Sanchez," she said sarcastically, "from the future Inquisitor General of Spain."

She locked the door carefully, thinking, as she did so, that she must similarly lock the door to her heart. She would try to bury her feelings, she would try to think only cold and logical thoughts, and she would concentrate upon her new task: espionage for the Count-Duke. Olivares had kept his part of the deal. He had arranged for her friends to reach safety, now she must keep her part.

If Rafael had ambition and pride, so would she have ambition and pride. Rafael, always Rafael! Would his face be forever imprinted upon every facet of her mind?

When she reached Valderocas House and the privacy of her own room, she unwrapped the sculpture and placed it on the ebony chest containing her jewelry, not far from the framed Tiziano sketch of the hand with the rabbit.

# 12.

The Count of Villaquemada was amusing himself in the enclosed courtyard of his rural estate in the north of Madrid. After whipping a fourteen-year-old servant girl for scorching one of his favorite lace collars while ironing it, he now watched contentedly as two of his half-savage field hands were wrestling for the honor of being the first one to ravish the beaten girl. The men had taken their shirts off, and despite the cool December weather, sweat was streaking their unwashed bodies. Half a dozen dogs jumped and barked around the pair, taking as much joy in the spectacle as their master. The girl lay whimpering in a corner. No one else assisted the match. All the other servants knew better than to get in the way of their master's wrath.

Suddenly, a voice spoke up behind the Count.

"I am surprised you still have servants around this place. How can they stand you?"

Villaquemada gave a start as if bitten by a viper, but when he perceived the identity of the intruder, his frown resolved into a smile.

"I certainly think *you* should enjoy this wrestling match," he said, "although of course the brutes are too heavy for your taste."

"What's the matter with the girl?"

"She's the prize over which these two pigs are fighting. Not very funny, eh? What I'd really like to do is mate a girl with one of my hounds. I've been thinking of buying a bawd and paying her for it, although that wouldn't be as much fun as fighting the female's repulsion. I always enjoy a good rape, but some of these country wenches are too filthy for myself.

However, I wouldn't mind guiding a dog's prick. Vicarious rape, eh?"

Carlos didn't answer.

"Well, I see I'm boring you. What brings you here?"

"A matter that can hardly be discussed in this situation," Carlos de Queras replied with cold dignity.

"Up on your high horse again? All right." Villaquemada clapped his hands, and the two men stopped their fight and stared at him with idiotic grins.

"You can both have her and share her," the Count decided, and they let out a wild shout and carried the struggling girl to the servant quarters.

"So, what's new at Court?" Villaquemada asked when he led his guest into an entrance hall furnished with Old Castilian oak pieces and wall hangings depicting martial scenes taken from the victorious past of the conquering family of Villaquemada. From a fireplace, flickering lights danced over the tapestry, making the hall seem alive with galloping knights and fleeing Moors.

"We signed the marriage contract last week," Carlos said.

"Well, congratulations. But I cannot believe it. After three years!"

"It's true."

"How did you manage to succeed? What follies have you committed?"

"Honestly, I don't know myself. I haven't even talked to her alone. Her brother informed me that he accepted my proposal, after that our lawyers worked out the contract. I saw her for exactly five minutes while she signed it, and she has not received me since under the pretext of being indisposed."

"How considerate of her. So you won't even be troubled with a nagging wife. I have a feeling she'll keep much to herself. That's a better deal than I got."

"I haven't much time for pleasantries," Carlos said. "I have money now, and I want to pay you back the monstrous amounts I owe you."

"Yes, I did furnish you with a good many pleasures," Villaquemada said, "and expensive ones at that. There was this young bullfighter, too bad he had to kill himself. . . ."

"A bull killed him!"

"Let's not quarrel over interpretations. Then there was Villanueva's young cousin, and the valet of the Duke of

Medina-Celi, and two pageboys of Her Majesty. You kept them lavishly, didn't you? You spoiled them with expensive presents. It'll take some time to add it all up. Your tastes have cost me larger sums than my own pleasures."

Carlos's mouth twitched in disgust.

"I know what you think," Villaquemada continued. "You think you are more refined than I, because you happen to like innocent young men in whose seduction you take an aesthetic as well as a sexual satisfaction. You think I am crude, because my normal hot-blooded tastes are painful to your delicate senses."

Villaquemada had teased Carlos in the past, now to his astonishment, he discovered that Carlos was no longer in a mood to endure his railleries.

"Enough of this, Enrique. I have other things on my mind. You have just come back from Catalonia. How are things going there?"

Villaquemada assumed a serious tone.

"It couldn't be better, for us, that is. I expect the worst of rebellions to break out in the next few years. I wager the life of my mother that Catalonia will break away from Spain. Any idiot can see it coming."

"So will Portugal," Carlos said. "I am sure of it. Therefore, I see no reason for Andalusia not to declare her independence, eventually. After all, it was an independent kingdom long ago. What the Moors could do, an honest Old Christian could do, too."

"Do what?"

"Declare himself King of Granada, for instance."

"Carlos, you are insane! Your new wealth is turning your head."

"Not at all. This is why I waited patiently to get my hands on this wealth. I have planned it for years. Medina Sidonia, who owns most of western Andalusia, is very much toying with the idea of breaking away from Spain. Now you tell me who is the biggest landowner in eastern Andalusia?"

"Why, your family, of course."

"So if the people of Granada should be inclined to revolt against the central government of Spain, don't you think a Queras should be their leader?"

Enrique shook his head.

"Carlos, I vow and swear I underestimated you," he said with awe in his voice.

"I don't mind that," Carlos answered serenely. "What I want to know is whether I can count on you."

"In what way?"

"I must become the sole owner of all the Valderocas holdings. There is still an uncle at Toledo, and there is Pedro, and his wife, who, by the way, expects an heir."

"But of course," Villaquemada said with a grin as he discovered familiar ground. "Accidents happen; women die in childbirth; assassins are for hire. It takes time, of course, but after a few years, I don't see why your wife should not also conveniently pass away, thus leaving the whole Valderocas estate to you. Then nothing would stand in the way of your contracting a new marriage with a lady of royal blood. The making of a king demands a judicious sense of timing and a superb skill with poison. Even the old Romans knew that."

"I am glad you understand me," Carlos said. "Then I can count on you?"

"Can't you always?"

Carlos nodded. He would use Villaquemada to do his dirty work for him, and he would promise to pay whatever price he asked. Later, if the price were too high, he would have to think of eliminating Villaquemada. Carlos I, King of Granada. That end justified any means.

"There is one warning I must give you," Enrique de Villaquemada crassly interrupted Carlos's self-admiration. "You must lead an exemplary married life. There must be no rumors. Your wife must not be involved in any scandals. I realize that you cannot shut her up, the way I do mine, but you must keep tight reins on her."

"I do not think that will be a problem. She is very much the intellectual type," Carlos said, "not a flighty female. No, I have other plans. If she is at all ambitious, I might hint at my objective. The Duke of Braganza, for example, is not half as ambitious as his wife, you know, Medina Sidonia's daughter. She is the driving force in Portugal. I think she wants to be Queen. Well, we will see. At any rate, I expect to have you often as our guest."

"That should be a real pleasure," Villaquemada said. "By the way, does your betrothed still keep her pet Moor?"

"I think so."

"Then, why don't you suggest she give him to you as a wedding gift?"

Carlos smiled sourly. When Enrique invited him over to

the servants' quarters to watch how the field hands were getting along with the girl, he looked nauseated and begged to be excused.

On his way back to Madrid, Carlos reflected that in all truth he would have preferred to keep Villaquemada ignorant of his plans, had it not been for the fact that Enrique was a Familiar of the Inquisition and therefore immune from prosecution and practically free to commit any crime he pleased.

# 13.

The wedding ceremony was performed in the royal chapel. Their Majesties attended, and the Count-Duke and Countess of Olivares, the Count and Countess of Monterrey, the Duke of Medina de las Torres, the Duke of Medina-Celi, Don Luis de Haro, the Count of Villaquemada, the Court painter Velázquez, the Court poet Calderon de la Barca, the self-styled Court critic Francisco de Quevedo, as well as a host of other nobles and letrados taken almost equally from the pro-Olivares and anti-Olivares camps. Noted absentees were the bride's uncle, Don Jaime Valderocas Dominguez from Toledo and the groom's father, Count de Queras from Granada. Both had given old age and ill health as an excuse.

Isabel wore thick make-up and a brocade wedding gown encrusted with pearls and precious stones. Her farthingale was six feet wide, and her finery weighed over twenty pounds. She looked tired and somehow defeated when she walked down the aisle, and all who witnessed the event needed no guesswork to realize that this was a match of convenience. There was not a man in the crowd who did not think that if he walked in Carlos's place, the bride would look happier.

In spite of the cold January weather, a large crowd had assembled in the Patio de las Covachuelas, and when the couple stepped outside, Isabel was momentarily blinded by the bright sun, and she blinked her eyes at the sea of faces belonging to the common folk who had come to watch. Looking neither left nor right, she glided slowly over the cobblestones, holding herself erect, her elbows close to her sides, as prescribed by etiquette, with her hands resting lightly and elegantly on the huge heavy skirt. It was important that her feet should not be seen when she climbed into the coach, and that maneuver, too, she managed gracefully. She wore black slippers without heels made from the finest glove leather; they were pretty and comfortable, but they must not be seen.

Only after the carriage door with the wide Venetian glass window was closed and Carlos sat across from her, did she allow herself a glance over the gaping crowd. There, near the coach, she recognized the bewildered face of a young man, staring at her with dark, yearning eyes: Diego Caietano, her old friend whom she had purposely avoided, on the Count-Duke's orders.

Then the coach started to move. They left the Alcázar through the main gate and rolled slowly across the palace square toward the Calle Mayor; from there they went to the elegant town palace of the Counts de Queras, where Isabel's servants had already arrived a week earlier and had begun to prepare their lady's quarters.

For Isabel, the first moments in the closed coach were the most difficult, for now the inevitability of her imprisonment became a crushing reality. In the beginning of her betrothal, when her flux was a few days late, she had wildly hoped to be carrying Rafael's child, and she had consented to talk to Carlos and had even tried to flirt with him, reasoning that if she wanted him to accept a bastard as his own child, she would have to get him to make love to her quickly. Carlos, however, had responded with his usual haughtiness, and again she had been perplexed as to why he wanted to marry at all. When her period came, her need to please Carlos had vanished. Now she was ready to shrink back should he make the least attempt to touch her. She could feel his arrogant glance on her face and body, and she had never hated him more than at this moment when she had legally become his property.

"Look at me," Carlos said harshly. She lifted her head slowly to meet his cold glance. "I have given orders to leave us undisturbed for the next few days. As you must know by now, I detest pomp and ceremony, and even more than that, I detest the crude curiosity and practical jokes usually showered upon newlyweds. At the end of the week, there will be a reception in honor of your being named Lady-in-Waiting to

Her Majesty. After that, I hope to be able to avoid Court functions."

"Does not my new position require my frequent presence at the Alcázar?" Isabel asked quietly.

"It is largely an honorary title. I presume Her Majesty is thanking me for past services," Carlos replied.

For the first time since her separation from Rafael, she felt an emotion resembling amusement. She knew that the Countess Olivares had obtained this honor for her, and she smiled inwardly when Carlos went on to explain that the old black dragon was losing some of her influence.

"Soon you will be Countess de Queras, and, by God, our family is as old as hers."

"I am sorry that your father was too ill to come. I would have liked to meet him," Isabel said in an attempt to establish friendly relations with the man destined by fate to rule her life.

"You are better off without meeting him," Carlos said. "I do not think he will forgive me for marrying below my class."

"He might disinherit you," Isabel remarked maliciously.

"He'd rather try to kill you first," Carlos answered.

"Well, I certainly didn't force you to marry me," she snapped.

He squinted until his eyes became two small slits, and the corners of his small mouth twisted off in different directions.

"I told you, I always get what I want," he said. "From the first time I saw you, I knew that I wanted to marry you, and you must admit that I have been persistent."

"I never knew why, but perchance I shall find out."

"Why? Because you had all the prerequisites a woman needs to be successful. Wealth, beauty, intelligence. All but one, you were not noble. Now that you are, what remains to be seen is whether you have ambitions."

"In what way?"

"Are you willing to help your husband achieve a position of power?"

"I thought you detested the Court and politics."

"The Court, yes, in so far as it is run by the Olivares couple—politics, if you will remember your first reception in the capital, has always been a favorite pastime of mine."

As she watched him, a plan started to unfold in Isabel's mind and, almost unconsciously, she slipped into her new role.

"Now that you are my husband," she mumbled, looking demurely into her lap, "I would like to confide something very private to you." She glanced up quickly and saw him look at her in an uncomfortable way, as if he expected the revelation of some physical shortcoming. So she went on, bending forward and lightly laying her hand on his, in an intimate gesture which seemed to further confound him. "Frankly, I have been tired of the Olivares couple for a long time, but since my brother is the Count-Duke's protégé, I never dared admit it to anyone. Of course, I do not expect this to make any difference in our relationship, but I thought you should know. I will try to be a good wife to you, even though I do not particularly like you."

Carlos took a deep breath.

"Well," he said, "well." Then a smile spread over his narrow face, making his chin look more pointed than ever. "Did I not always tell you we would get along famously?"

Her mind pictured two snakes, coiled and ready to strike at each other, but then the carriage stopped. A footman opened the door and unfolded the stairs. Carlos stepped down quickly and held up his hand to help her down, while two other footmen unfurled a small carpet with the shield of arms of the Queras family in front of the folding stairs, so that Isabel could descend without showing her feet.

This was the first time Isabel had come to the palace whose mistress she was to become, and her first impression was that of a huge entrance hall with beautiful plants and priceless wall hangings. There were throngs of servants bowing to her, and a few women curtsied. The women were all from her own staff. An impressive marble staircase was lined on both sides by pages in velvet liveries.

"Your summer apartments are on the second floor of the west wing, your winter apartments are two stories higher, so unfortunately you have quite a climb ahead of you," Carlos informed her. "You will have the apartments of the past Countesses de Queras, and I trust you will find them comfortably furnished and large enough for all of your women. The layout of both apartments is the same. If you wish to redecorate them, you may do so."

They walked upstairs and passed the third floor.

"Whose apartments are here?" Isabel asked.

"Guest rooms and servants' quarters."

"Are there many sleep-in servants?"

"About forty."

She could not quite suppress a gasp. Most of the men appeared to be very young. Was Carlos running a school for pageboys?

"My apartments are in the east wing of the second and fourth floors respectively, right across the hall from yours. I should appreciate if you and your women kept out of them completely."

Her rooms were separated from the rest of the house by a special heavily carved entrance door. Carlos led her into an elegant sitting room from which other doors led to the bedroom, the music room, and her servants' quarters.

Carlos must have given strict instructions to her women, for all of them had followed the couple upstairs and now disappeared through one of the doors. Upon a sign from Carlos, two pages closed the entrance door from the outside, and Isabel found herself alone with her husband in the sitting room.

"My men have also been ordered to keep out of here," Carlos told her. "You will be in charge of your own quarters, and you may keep as many women as you wish to lodge here. There will be no female servants constantly coming and going, you may keep whom you wish and dismiss whom you wish. Your meals will be brought up here by the kitchen hands, except for the evening meal at eleven o'clock which we shall take in the main dining room on the first floor. In the morning, you may visit the library on the first floor. There is also a small chapel on the first floor, but I think it might be more convenient if you designed one of your rooms for that purpose, and we will have it furnished accordingly. You may choose your own confessor who will visit you whenever you desire. This will eliminate the need for you to drive to church. I realize that we must make some concessions to custom, and I will ride with you along the promenade of the Prado once a month."

"You mean I am a prisoner here?" Isabel inquired without hiding her mounting incredulity. "You propose to regulate every moment of my life? This is preposterous."

"I see you are not used to the way of life of quality," Carlos said. "You will have to learn."

"Udsdaggers, Carlos!"

"And please leave His Majesty's swearwords out of our conversation."

"Just a while ago you said you wanted a helpmate—a wife

who will help you achieve a position of power. Were those not your very words?"

"We may have different ideas on how you can help me. Your main task is to make a good impression upon our dinner guests, who I assure you will be the most distinguished noblemen of Spain. I also count on your intellectual brilliance to attract and entertain a genius like Quevedo. So you will have no grounds to complain that I shut you off from stimulating human company. You have to realize that you can no longer consider yourself the *enfant terrible* of Madrid. I am sure you have noticed that your cousin leads a very retired life since she married your brother."

"Yes, but . . ." Isabel stopped short. She was going to say "but she loves him," hardly a remark a proper young wife should address to her husband shortly after the wedding.

"But what?"

"But she does not wish to go out," she finished her sentence lamely.

"Neither should you. You will, of course, have to serve Her Majesty whenever she summons you, but, as I said, that should not be too often."

Isabel hoped it could be as often as once a day. She would never be a willing partner to the absurd game Carlos proposed.

"Tonight we will dine alone," Carlos said. "Until then, you may inspect your apartments and make yourself comfortable. Should anything be amiss, let me know tonight." He bowed formally over her hand and walked toward the door which seemed to open by itself, proof enough that the two young doormen outside had been eavesdropping.

"My God," Isabel said aloud when the door closed behind him, "My God!"

At these words Maria burst into the room and behind her, tumbling in, came the rest of Isabel's personal servants: her wardrobe keeper, her seamstress, her hairdresser and make-up woman, her cook, two chambermaids, and two cleaning women. Maria, since accompanying Isabel on her trip to Granada, had become more and more of a confidante and less of a maid.

Instead of coming forward in an orderly way, to curtsy and present her with their best wishes for coming happiness, the young women squabbled wildly, and each demanded to be the first one to tell her grievances.

"Señora, I wish to leave."

"Me too."

"Señora, I want to go back to Valderocas House."

"Señora, I quit."

"My husband was not allowed to see me."

"My boyfriend was beaten and thrown out."

"Señora, I cannot stand it."

"I was only waiting for you to come."

"They have kept us like prisoners."

Isabel covered her ears with her hands. *"Chito!"* quiet! she snapped, *"Chito! Chito!"* But there was no quiet. Each woman went on to present her case with many woeful interjections, protesting her mistreatment and calling upon God, the Holy Virgin, and all the Saints, to protect her from any further dealings with the inhabitants of the Queras town palace.

"Maria!"

"Yes, Doña Isabel?"

"What happened? Quiet, you others!"

The women, one after another, fell into silence, as Maria told how they had been shut and locked into these apartments since their arrival at the palace. They had been furnished with equipment to clean the place and with food; and, regular as clockwork three times a day, an old man had come to collect the used chamberpots and bring in clean ones. The women had screamed and knocked at the door, but the majordomo had threatened to kill each one of them if they did not shut up and go about their work. They had finally decided to do the best they could: all of Isabel's dresses and lingerie and personal effects were clean and in good repair, her *estrado* with its wall mirrors and velvet floor cushions and ebony jewelry chest was the most beautiful any countess could wish for, and there was not a speck of dust anywhere. Even her bronze statue of Adam and Eve and the Tiziano drawing of the hand with the rabbit had been placed where they belonged among the valuables on the ebony chest. They felt they had done their duty and wished to be released immediately. Five of them were married and anxious to get home to their husbands, two had *novios* and feared to lose them if they remained cooped up in a house full of male servants, and the cook felt that her presence was in any event completely superfluous, since she was not even allowed near the kitchen.

"What happened to my men?" Isabel demanded with a tremor of horror running through her low voice.

"They were sent back upon our arrival here. Don Pedro

was informed that there were more than enough menservants in the house."

"Insane," Isabel whispered, "absolutely insane!"

"That is what we think," Maria said.

Isabel sank down on a low, satin-covered daybed.

"Summon the majordomo," she said to Maria.

"The door is locked," Maria answered.

"How do you know?"

"It always is."

"Not when I am here!" Isabel screamed angrily.

Maria smiled and motioned a chambermaid to the door. It was locked.

"And where is the bell?"

"There is no bell."

"That is not possible." Isabel looked up into the faces of the serving women who watched her with a kind of grim curiosity. Most of them had been hired since the Valderocases's arrival at Madrid, some fairly recently; none were the kind of faithful servants who grew up with the families of their masters. None had any special reason to be fond of Isabel, except that she had treated them kindly and paid them good wages. Ungrateful wretches, Isabel thought, but she did not say it. One did not insult servants unless one felt invulnerable, a feeling Isabel had not enjoyed since her father's death.

"You may all go back to Valderocas House," she now said quietly. "I will ask my husband to hire new servants for me."

"Your husband!" one of the married cleaning women snarled insolently. "Why don't you also ask him to hire you a lover?"

The others grinned, but Maria swung around and slapped the woman's face. "Shut up, old whore!"

The woman quickly grabbed Maria's hair and pulled it so that the girl let out a scream. Immediately, the others started taking sides, and the next instant they were all fighting like cats and dogs.

At that precise moment the door opened, and Carlos appeared.

"Madame, what a perfectly revolting spectacle. I did not know you shared Her Majesty's taste for female wrestling matches." It was a well-known fact that at the theater Queen Isabelle loved to sit behind the louvered shutters of the royal box and amuse herself during intermission by asking her servants to provoke quarrels among the common women.

Isabel had a sharp reply on her tongue but repressed it, because her immediate concern was to placate the madman she had married.

The women stopped their vicious fighting, obviously intimidated by Carlos's presence.

Isabel rose, as gracefully as she could in her heavy clothes, and with sliding steps glided over to her husband's side.

"I would appreciate if you dismissed all of them, all except my personal maid Maria."

"As you wish, Madame. Are you sure though that you can get along with only one maid? I do not think that is quite in keeping with etiquette."

"Neither is locking the doors of women's quarters. It has gone out of fashion since the last Moorish king left Granada," Isabel remarked.

"Were the doors locked? Now that is strange," Carlos said.

"Indeed it is."

"Well, from the behavior of your women, I trust you can see why it was necessary during the past week. My well-behaved personnel would have been spoiled by your rotten creatures."

"You may go," Isabel said to the women.

"What about our wages?" one of them inquired.

Isabel looked at Carlos.

"If I pay you," he said, "I will consider myself your employer. In that case I shall send the whole lot of you to my friend the Count of Villaquemada. He needs more servants."

The women cleared out in a trice. Villaquemada's reputation was bad enough to make any female servant run. They hurried down the stairs helter-skelter; one more eager than the next to reach the freedom of the streets.

"I must say I am shocked at your cruelty," Isabel remarked when Carlos, Maria, and she remained alone.

"You are not defending those good-for-nothings, I hope."

"I have a terrible headache," Isabel said. "I would like to rest for a while. Maria, go prepare my bed."

Maria left, and Isabel turned to Carlos, "You need not lock the door," she said. "It is degrading. I will not leave the house without your permission, and I will not intrude upon your apartments. I should like to reserve the right to enter the library whenever I wish, and I should like to choose a new staff of servants. I hear that my cook was not allowed in the kitchen; it is all right with me. I shall not trouble myself with any household problems."

Carlos looked at her in a speculative way. "Good," he said. "You may come to the library any time. As for the servants, I would prefer you to employ dwarfs. They are more expensive but worth it."

"As you wish."

"But since you will have no cleaning women, I would still prefer you came to the library regularly from eleven to one, accompanied by Maria. During that time, my men could clean your apartments."

A staccato rhythm hammered in Isabel's temples; she readily agreed to anything Carlos proposed. She wondered whether she was going mad, or whether he was really insane to bother her with such details when all she wanted was to be rid of her twenty pounds of finery and climb into her bed. But perhaps this was what Carlos waited for, that they go to bed to consummate the marriage. Perhaps he could not enjoy his rights unless he first reduced her to utter misery. Perhaps he expected her to put up a big resistance. Oh, but she was too exhausted to care. Besides, it had to happen sooner or later, so why prolong the agony?

"Would you like to help me get undressed?" she asked him. "It is a lot of work, and I have only Maria to help me."

"I am afraid that is your problem," Carlos answered stiffly. "I hardly think I would make a good chambermaid. I shall expect to see you for dinner at eleven."

He left again, and Isabel walked sideways through the door which led to her bedroom. Then she sank onto a large beautifully carved and painted four-poster and called for Maria. The girl came immediately.

"Am I waking or dreaming?" Isabel asked her.

"Oh, Doña Isabel, you are awake, unfortunately," Maria said, "but you are living in a nightmare."

"Just get me out of these garments."

It took a long time, but finally she lay on the bed in nothing but her fine lace shirt.

"Do you suppose he will come in, all of a sudden?" Maria asked in a whisper.

"I don't think so."

"You know what I think. I think he is a sinner against nature," Maria whispered again.

Isabel motioned her to sit on the bed.

"Why do you think so?"

"This house," Maria whispered. "Something is wrong.

He's either a sorcerer or a sodomist. Why does he employ only men? Why did he lock us up in here?"

Isabel would have dismissed these ideas, had she not remembered Maria's youthful experience with the witch of Jaén. Now she shuddered with a chill of fear. She would give a fortune to have someone like José Caietano at her side. How easy it had been to brave the unknown in the company of that strong and shrewd young man. How easy also to promise the Count-Duke to become his agent. Even her secret Jewishness had never held the dread she now felt. There had always been men in her life, men she could rely on. And she had not realized it. She had thought herself very brave and superior, and now she was trapped worse than when she had been caught by Juliana.

Juliana! Isabel closed her eyes, and she saw herself again in the small room above the patio of the whorehouse. She saw again the tall blond man with the face mask come into the courtyard. She saw him take off his mask. . . . Why, of course, Philip. She could always complain to Philip. As long as he desired her—and she knew well that he still did—she had a trump card up her sleeve. And Philip was highly accessible, too, because after all, she would be summoned to the Court in a matter of days. She was Lady-in-Waiting to Her Majesty. She took a deep breath and slowly the beating in her temples receded.

"He is a dangerous man, your husband," Maria continued, "and you may be worse off with him than Ana ever was with her stinking old miser of Alcalde." She remained silent for a moment. "You should never have married him." She pronounced her final conclusion as if she were reading a death sentence.

"You do not have to stay with me. You can go back to Valderocas House."

Maria bent down and kissed Isabel on both cheeks. "I would rather die than leave you. We'll be in this together. But do we really need dwarfs? Just to look at them gives me the vapors."

All of a sudden, a terrible suspicion hit Isabel. She sat up brusquely.

"Where is Pasquito? I had sent him here with the menservants. He was supposed to come right back and tell me what the house was like. Then I forgot all about it. Have you seen him here? Or heard of him?"

Maria shook her head. "He arrived with us," she said, "but we were shown up here and stayed here until you and His Lordship arrived this morning."

"Was he among the other men? Did you see him downstairs today?"

"No."

"My God, I hope nothing happened to him."

"Could be they raped him," Maria said matter-of-factly, and again Isabel was reminded that rape had been a common occurrence in Maria's troubled past.

"Why don't we simply both go back to Valderocas House," Maria proposed. "When Don Pedro hears how you are being treated, he'll raise the devil."

"How am I being treated?"

"Well . . ." Maria stared at her mistress and slowly she began to grasp that Isabel had no reason at all to complain. Her own women had made a scandal upon her arrival and had run away. Her husband expected her to keep to her quarters, a most reasonable request any Spanish husband could, in fact, should make. Moreover, her husband had invited her to eat dinner with him, showing him to be of the most liberal intentions. She had been furnished with a large and comfortable winter apartment and had been promised that she could redecorate it, as well as her summer apartment, to her own taste. What could she really complain about?

"He locks you in," Maria said.

"I doubt that."

Isabel got up from her bed and walked barefoot through the sitting room to the entrance door. She pushed the door handle down, lightly, and opened the door an inch just to assure herself that it was unlocked. Immediately, she heard someone come to attention outside, and she closed the door.

"You are being guarded," Maria whispered. "There!"

Isabel shrugged. "A servant on call. A thoughtful gesture and nothing to complain about. Carlos may yet serve me disaster for dinner, but so far, I'm afraid, he has shown himself no more than slightly eccentric."

"If he refuses to sleep with you, you can have the marriage annulled," Maria said, happy to have found such a fine solution.

"Have you lost your mind? I hope he never touches me!"

"But you invited him to undress you," Maria said reproachfully.

"I thought he was shy, and I made an effort to act like a

good wife. But I begin to think you are right; he doesn't like women."

"That's a crime!" Maria said. "You could denounce him to the Inquisition."

"Did you denounce the priest of Jaén?" Isabel countered, and Maria fell silent. They looked at each other, and despite her nervousness, Isabel yawned. She had carried over twenty extra pounds for most of the day, and she was tired.

"Don't you want to see the rest of the apartment? It's beautiful," Maria said, but Isabel closed her eyes. "I wish I could sleep," she mumbled. Maria tiptoed out of the room.

She slept soundly and awoke several hours later, not only refreshed, but also in possession of some of her usual energy and optimism. Despite all the dangers inherent in the life of a crypto-Jewess, she had always held onto her secret conviction that nothing really bad could happen to a Valderocas. When a family owned six galleons, three sugar plantations, two silver mines, not to count silk factories and olive groves, its members simply expected to buy themselves out of any undesirable situation. So it would indeed be easy enough to buy an annulment, but what purpose would that serve? It would make her the object of so much vicious gossip that she would be forced to leave the country or retire to a convent. It would upset Pedro's plans and position by damaging the respectability of the Valderocas name. And worse, she would have broken a solemn promise made to the man on whom they were all counting, the Count-Duke of Olivares. No, it was absolutely necessary that she make the most of this wretched situation by gaining Carlos's trust.

The apartment, as Maria had said, was beautiful. She saw no need to change anything. Her bedroom walls were covered with pale pink silk to match the sheets and canopy of the carved bed. The bed was painted white and gold. Her bedroom also held a large *estrado* with magnificent thick carpets, velvet and silk cushions, Chinese chests holding jewelry and cosmetics, and her precious ebony chest with Rafael's statue. The sitting room was divided into two separate portions, one with modern French chairs, an exquisitely carved cupboard and wall hangings depicting scenes from a ballroom; the other part, the old-fashioned *estrado*, again had many many pillows covered with brocade and damask; it was obviously the place to entertain visiting ladies. The music room contained a harp, an assortment of flutes, two guitars, and a violin. The harp was hidden under an embroidered fitted cover; the other instruments lay in a rosewood cabinet with stained glass doors. The previous countesses Queras must have been music lovers. Adjoining her bedroom was a dressing room. Then there was a narrow hallway leading to three rooms for servants. But nowhere could Isabel detect a bathroom or any container vaguely resembling a bathtub. Apparently, people of quality did not get dirty.

"What do you think, Maria, how many women will we need?"

"If you want the truth, Doña Isabel, I'd rather do everything alone. I cannot stand dwarfs. Except, I hate to sleep alone. It always scares me."

"You can sleep in my room."

"What if His Lordship objects?"

"May it spite His Lordship."

Her first evening meal with Carlos was completely uneventful. He came to call for her at a quarter to eleven to guide her to the formal dining room where they each sat at one end of the table, to be served by a dozen waiters. The men all stared at Isabel with such piercing insistence that she found herself unable to enjoy any of the twelve-course dinner. Carlos was silent, and Isabel racked her mind for some harmless invitation to talk. Finally, she asked him whether it had always been a custom in the Queras family for the wives to eat with their husbands. He looked up at her, startled as if he had forgotten her presence, then he smiled.

"No, it is a custom I intend to introduce. I think it was time we did away with some of the old Moorish manners."

"I am relieved to find you less conservative than I feared."

"And what, Madame, is that supposed to mean?"

She found his way of calling her Madame disconcerting, but she decided she would not object to it.

"Well, if you do not insist too much upon convention, I thought I might get along with only my personal maid, unless you expect me to entertain, in which case I would need additional help."

"Do I infer that you are opposed to hiring dwarfs?"

"No, but you see I have always been able to get along without ostentation."

To judge by his sour expression, her barb had landed in the center of his sensibilities.

"What about your other needs? You had sent us a whole crew of servants."

"If you permit me to send my personal laundry once a week to Valderocas House and to use my cousin's seamstress, I think I could get along with just Maria."

She could see that he was bewildered, and she wondered which of his two desires would triumph, the one for the least amount of female intrusion into his male household, or the wish to act correctly in the eyes of the world. Almost predictably the former won, proving that Carlos had not much respect for the ways of the other noble houses of Spain, although he meant to keep up the necessary pretenses.

"What excuse could you possibly have for that?" he asked, his hopeful tone giving away the turn his inner struggle was taking.

"They know my tastes, and it would save me the trouble of training new personnel. Pepita knows I detest all that."

"Will that necessitate visits from you over there?"

"Well, I expect to visit Pepita about twice a week anyway. It would be most rude not to do so."

Carlos's fingers nervously hammered on the table. He did not answer, and they finished their meal in silence.

Afterwards, he asked her to come to the library, a not too large room with shelves on all four walls from floor to ceiling. He closed the door, drew a curtain, and then closed another, inner door. Isabel gathered that this time he intended to speak to her alone, whereas so far all his remarks had been made more for the consumption of his servants. He pointed to an armchair, and she sat down. Walking up and down, and rhythmically tapping the handle of a sharp paper knife onto the palm of his left hand, he spoke in an abrupt manner.

"I suppose this is the time we have to come to an understanding. You always asked me why I needed a wife, and perhaps you were right. In a way, I may not need a wife. I should have entered an order. However, I have obligations, being the only surviving heir of the Queras family. It is expected of me to marry. I now have fulfilled part of the family obligation and hope to live without harassment for the next few years. Now, to your question why specifically I chose you. You must understand that my alliance with the heiress of our only Old Christian banking family has important implications. Through you I have access to tremendous wealth, and through my family, I have the right to aspire to the highest offices of the kingdom, and perhaps more. We are neither

Trastámaras nor Habsburgs; still, the blood of other ancient royal houses of Spain flows in my veins, and my descendants might yet rule again one day."

"I believe you," Isabel said. It was probably true, and at any rate, she did not care.

"What position would you like to occupy?" she asked him, because it was the obvious question to ask. What she really wanted to know was what had happened to Pasquito, but somehow she did not dare bring that up. She would find out sooner or later. In the meantime, it was essential to gain Carlos's full trust, for after all, she had married him in order to spy on him.

"First and foremost we must rid ourselves of Olivares," Carlos said. "There can be no position for us as long as he is in power."

"It is in my interest to see you rise to power," Isabel said. "And Carlos, you, too, must realize that I married you for more than your title. I gambled on you, because your insistence persuaded me that you had the potential and the willpower necessary for success, and I think that in spite of everything, His Majesty does not really dislike you."

Carlos stopped his nervous wanderings.

"Madame, if you are not too tired, I would like to tell you a few things about the people who I hope will become our allies."

"Nothing would fascinate me more," Isabel said truthfully.

He looked at her for a long time, and when she looked into his almost lashless eyes, she resolutely pushed away her feelings of distaste and held his glance until he turned around to pull another chair nearer to hers.

"Well, then, listen," he said.

And so she spent her wedding night listening to the sinuous intrigues and audacious conspiracies spun here, there, and everywhere—notably in Catalonia, Portugal, and Andalusia —by a handful of Grandees of Spain.

# 14.

It took Isabel a whole month before she found her first opportunity to speak to Olivares alone.

As Carlos had predicted, she spent all of her time in her apartments, except for the programmed visit to the library every morning, when her rooms were being cleaned, and a few short visits to Pepita in the company of her husband. Even if she had wanted to, she would not have found anyone to whom she could complain that she had made a horrendous mistake, that her life was at its bleakest. The heaviest burden of all was her separation from Rafael. The more she tried to eliminate him from her memory, the more her whole being cried out for him. For over three years she had been his mistress. Now, every day the certainty that she would never see him again made her more irritable.

The door to her cage finally opened with the long-awaited summons to call upon Her Majesty. Isabel drove to the Alcázar in a flurry of excitement. The Countess of Olivares greeted her in the antechamber of the Queen and took her aside to tell her that after the theatrical she must inconspicuously slip over to the Velázquez home where the Count-Duke would meet her, hopefully without attracting attention.

During the play, she found herself unable to concentrate. She felt the Queen's questioning glance on her face, and she knew that Isabelle de Bourbon must wonder how well she got along with Carlos. During intermission, Her Majesty spoke to her.

"I hope your husband will not be too inconvenienced if I expect you from now on to assume some of your duties at the palace. I shall see you every Tuesday and Thursday at eleven o'clock."

"Thank you, Your Majesty, I shall endeavor to serve you well."

Refreshments were brought, almond water and sweet meats, and Her Majesty proposed a few changes in the play, for this was only a dress rehearsal.

"Who wrote it?" Isabel asked of a courtesan sitting at her side.

"Hush, His Majesty did," the young lady whispered back.

"Then why isn't he here?"

"Her Majesty plans this as a surprise for him."

"Oh!"

After this bit of information, Isabel paid more attention to the play and found it witty and graceful.

Olivares waited for her in the Velázquez drawing room. Juana Pacheco was spending the day in the country with her children, and somehow the Count-Duke had contrived for them to be left alone. He took her to the studio. As usual, there were many royal portraits standing about on easels, the most remarkable being a completely finished equestrian portrait of Philip and—vying for admiration with it—a sequel showing the Count-Duke in the pose of a victorious general on horseback. But the most delightful canvas by far was a portrait of Prince Balthasar Carlos in hunting costume with two dogs.

The Royal Favorite laid a heavy hand on Isabel's shoulder.

"Is it very hard on you?"

"Your Excellency . . ." Isabel started but did not know what to say. What could she really complain about? That she had lost her lover and that her Moorish slave had apparently run away?

"I am your friend," he said.

All of a sudden there was a lump in her throat.

"I do need a friend."

"Does he treat you all right?"

"He pays no attention to me whatsoever. You could say that he keeps me a prisoner."

"So I gathered. That is why I asked my wife to get you over here twice a week."

"Thank you so much."

"Anything to report?"

"We've had the Duke of Medina-Celi for dinner and Don Francisco Quevedo who swears he will open His Majesty's eyes as to the miseries of the country."

"Who else?"

"Carlos is in contact with the Marquis of Ayamonte and the Duke of Medina Sidonia. We have also received a Señor Pinto Ribeiro from Portugal. He is some sort of agent to the Duke of Braganza."

"And what do they all plan?"

"First, to oust you by all means."

Olivares threw his head back and laughed. "That should prove very difficult."

"They also say that your power over His Majesty is unnatural and that your habit of receiving and keeping Jews at Court proves that you have heretical tendencies."

This time Olivares did not laugh.

"I shall see to it that the Inquisition finds quite a different scandal to uncover," he growled. "Quite different. But keep your ears open. And thank you for your hint. I will have to find out more about this Pinto. Leave now, and I will follow in a little while."

He touched her cheek briefly and smiled at her. She dropped him a curtsy and left.

Moving swiftly along the dark and drafty hallways that were the scourge of the royal Alcázar, she had almost reached the great staircase when a man stepped out of a side door and pulled her into a dark chamber she did not know existed. Before she could even think of pushing him away, she felt his mouth on hers, his thick tongue pushing her lips apart, and his muscular body pressing against hers. His mouth tasted sweet and fresh. He must have prepared himself for this encounter and without thinking any further, she found herself melting into his embrace. Her arms went around him, and she kissed him back with a moan of pleasure in her throat.

"I want you," he whispered hoarsely. "I have waited long enough, I want you now." His tongue went to her ears and penetrated first one and then the other, sending shivers of anticipation through her body.

"You want me," he said. "Say that you want me."

"Yes," she whispered. "Yes I want you. Oh, Felipe, I want you."

He continued to kiss her, his body pressing more urgently against hers, then abruptly he let her go and pulled her through another door and another dark hallway into a small bedroom. He locked the door, all the time holding onto her with one hand, as if he was afraid she might escape him again.

"I could have sent for you," he said, "but I wanted to catch you myself. If my memory serves me right, you have promised me a lot over the years, but you have given me nothing." His breathing was fast and irregular, and he pulled her in his arms again and kissed her as she had never been kissed before. Desire danced through her blood like sparkling wine. She had a brief vision of Rafael, but Rafael seemed to have nothing to do with this. He was the now unreachable ideal of her heart. Philip, however, was here and real and mad with passion. She sank down on the bed with him. He could not wait to get her undressed. He simply pushed up her skirts and before she knew what was really happening, she felt his strong member moving deep inside her body, and again she moaned with pleasure. He made love to her in such a way that all his desire seemed to pour into her, and she responded wildly. Even after she spent herself, he continued his almost savage thrusting awakening deep within her a new passion that demanded still greater satisfaction. Twice more he made her come before joining with her in a last bout of sheer ecstasy.

They were lying on the bed, her head resting on his arm, and his fingers traced over her face and her lips.

"I am not always so brutal," he said. "Remember that night at Juliana's? I was prepared to be gentle with you then and not to hurt you. I wanted to be your first lover. Udsdaggers, I cannot stand the idea that you belong to that mealymouthed Queras. But gentleness and patience did not seem to work with you. And I had to have you."

"Why?"

"I have thought of nothing else since I saw you walk by me in your wedding gown. I could have screamed that you must be mine, that no one had the right to take you away from me. I wanted you from the time I first saw you at a reception years ago."

"And now that you have had me?" Isabel asked softly.

"Now, I want you more than before. It enrages me to think that every night you share Carlos's bed. I wanted to make sure you knew that there is no better lover than I. And now I have spoiled it all by my rashness."

"Oh no, you haven't," she said. "I have never been loved like that." It was true. Until now she had been the mistress of only one man whom she worshiped with every fiber of her body, and she had actually thought it impossible to ever belong to another man. Yet, there was in her relation with the King an entirely different element. There was no love here, only pure sexual allure, but there could be no doubt that Philip was the more experienced lover, the man who lived for his sensual pleasures, whereas Rafael, even in his most tender moments, was always partially preoccupied with his ideas.

"At least there will be no problem now if I get you with child," Philip whispered in her ear.

"What if Her Majesty finds out?" Isabel asked.

"Worse. What if your husband finds out?" Philip countered.

Isabel smiled, and with her slender fingers twirled his moustache. Seen from very near, he did not look ugly. His eyes were as clear as hers, and his skin was white and free of blemishes.

"You will soon tire of me," she said. "Until then, we must be careful."

"I will never tire of you," he protested. "Come let me look at you."

He undressed her with agile hands and when finally the last lace shirt was undone, he pulled her again into his arms and his hands traveled over her body. He kissed her small erect pink nipples, his hand moved her thighs, and soon she was again united with him in a violent embrace.

"How did you know I was coming along this way?" she asked, after his appetite was appeased, and they huddled together under the silken sheets.

"I knew you were coming today to the rehearsal. I know every step you took since then."

"But the rehearsal is supposed to be a surprise for you. And how could you know I would go to visit Doña Juana?"

"I know everything I want to know," he said, "except one thing. Will you come back if I send for you?"

A voice inside Isabel said no, never, I belong to Rafael, but she suppressed that voice ruthlessly and nodded assent. Her body was starved for love; she was bored and unhappy. Anyway, one could not refuse the King.

# 15.

Yet, when she was on her way home, the first scruples started to creep into her mind. She had sinned. She had given herself to a man she did not love. She was a slut, no better than the whores she had seen in Juliana's patio.

But whose fault was it? If she came right down to it, it was Rafael's fault. His refusal to see her after her marriage. She did not even know his whereabouts. She could not even tell him that Carlos never touched her. He could have gone on being her only lover. But no, he had to be proud and exclusive.

Carlos. What if Carlos found out? What was the matter with that man? Was he impotent? Was he a sodomist as Maria thought? Did he trust her, as it certainly seemed when he let her listen in on all his schemes with his Grandee friends, or did he have some plan to exploit her?

She sat thus thinking in her town coach, the one used by previous Countesses de Queras, when the coach suddenly stopped, and she saw her footmen wrestling with a bunch of beggars. She opened the door to look out.

"What is the matter?"

Before the chief groom could close the door again, someone threw a piece of paper onto her lap. A whip cracked, and a familiar voice cried out. Then the coach started to roll on. She unfolded the note:

"Dear Doña Isabel: If you ever need help, real help, contact Pasquito El Moro at the Bodegon de San Gil. I know that you are a prisoner in your house and bear you no grudge. Your husband is a liar and a murderer and upon a word from you, I shall be obliged to dispatch him straight to the devil's own stewpot."

She recognized the handwriting, of course. Everything that boy knew she had taught him herself. Pasquito, her little brother, her little slave. Pasquito, a member of the *germanía?* What had Carlos done to him?

Her own scruples and ill feelings were forgotten. As soon as she would get home, she would confront Carlos in righteous anger and demand an explanation as to what had happened to Pasquito. Or perhaps it would be better if she talked to the boy first. Yes. She would not return home until she had found out the truth. She rapped at the window and the coach stopped.

"Take me to Valderocas House," she ordered.

Pedro was not home, and Isabel hesitated when she saw Pepita. There had always been a sort of friction between Pasquito and Pepita, and she did not know how much, if anything, she could tell her sister-in-law about her suspicions. Pepita was visibly pregnant now; her baby was due in another two months. Nevertheless, she rose from her floor cushion and came forward to kiss Isabel.

"What is wrong?"

"Wrong? Nothing. I am just paying you a visit."

"Come, Isabel, I thought there were to be no more secrets between us."

Isabel, too, was tired of secrets.

"Do you know where Pasquito is?"

"No, why?"

Wordlessly Isabel handed her the note.

"Bodegon de San Gil," Pepita said softly, "that horrible place."

"What do you know about it?"

"I was there for the first couple of days when I ran away. It is an old inn where *pícaros* meet."

"All right. I will have to go there."

"Oh, but you cannot. If anyone found out! It is impossible."

"I must talk to the boy. I must know what he means. If you do not want to come, I will have to borrow some of your clothes and a pillow."

For a moment Pepita looked perplexed, then she understood. For a pregnant woman, it was perfectly safe to go anywhere she pleased. She could even ask to see the King, and he would have to come out on his balcony and show himself, for an unwritten law said that expecting mothers were never to be refused anything they desired. Pepita had never felt any strange cravings, to be Pedro's wife was the epitome of her desires, but Isabel was right. If she wanted to go to the Bodegon de San Gil, there was no better way to do it than in the company of a pregnant woman, or in the disguise of one.

"I will come with you," Pepita said. "Why don't you call the coach while I get ready."

Isabel dismissed her own driver and footmen, telling them that she would come home later in the day with the Valderocas coach.

The main room of the inn smelled of rancid olive oil, onions, garlic, and unwashed bodies. The windows were few and dirty to the point of uselessness, and the sole source of light consisted of a couple of oil lamps on two tables where a dozen slovenly unkempt youths rolled dice and played cards. In a corner, a blind man was mumbling to himself. A formidable fat maidservant with coarse black hair on her upper lip asked them what they wanted.

"I want to talk to Pasquito El Moro," Pepita announced brashly.

Some boys looked up and snickered.

"He is not here," the woman said.

"He better be here real fast," Pepita said, "or he'll smoke for it."

"Oh, did that little rascal get you in trouble?" A big man with a face hideously patched up from too many knife wounds rose from the table where he had been teaching dice tricks to the youngsters.

"Yes, and unless he gets me out of it, my baby will be born cross-eyed," Pepita said. "And I'll call down on Pasquito all the curses of Sodom and Gomorrha."

"Jesus protect me," the big man muttered. "We'll get him for you."

"Better hurry," Pepita said and flicked him a small silver coin.

In spite of the dark, the man caught it expertly.

"What was that all about?" Isabel whispered when a few of the youngsters had left to look for Pasquito.

"Just to show them we know our way around," Pepita whispered back. "Among *pícaros*, talk like *pícaros*, I learned that from Zamoro."

"But what about the cross-eyed baby?"

"You have to mystify them," Pepita explained. "Show them you are not afraid, and they will think they have reason to be afraid of you. Come, let us sit at a table."

They sat down, and Pepita snapped her fingers. "Eh *Gorda*, I'm thirsty. What have you got?"

"Wine," the fat woman answered.

"Water is what I want," Pepita said, "nice cool, fresh water."

"We're out of it."

"Then get some."

Obediently, the fat one walked to the door, but at that moment Pasquito came in, followed by a gang of juvenile *pícaros*.

"Where's that pinch-prick says I got her pregnant?" he shouted angrily, and, "Yeah, where is she now?" the others behind him echoed in chorus.

"Pasquito!" Pepita shouted in angry indignation.

"Doña Pepita!" Pasquito exclaimed, "and Doña Isabel."

"Come with us, Pasquito," Isabel said quietly.

"You are taking him nowhere!" the big man interrupted

harshly. "He's got a job to do. A job that brings twenty ducats. He stays right here."

Pasquito turned around to face the man. "I think you better let Farino do that one. I have a hunch I'll be after bigger game."

"How much bigger?"

"Five times at least," Pasquito said.

"Ten times, if he does it right," Isabel said, trying to make her voice sound as brash as Pepita's.

"Go then," the man said and they left.

They drove back to Valderocas House in silence, for Isabel had smothered her first impulse to interrogate Pasquito on the spot, and Pepita guessed intuitively that he did not want to talk in front of her. Isabel took him to her room.

"What happened?" she asked him when they were finally alone.

"Why did you marry that monster?" Pasquito asked.

Isabel was taken aback, by his hard masculine voice, as well as by the impudence of his question. Nevertheless, she answered softly.

"I had to. You must understand Pasquito, there are things one cannot choose. He was picked for me by the Queen. As you know, I fought it as long as I could."

"One of these days I am going to kill him," Pasquito said slowly, "unless you tell me that you love him."

"Pasquito, you are out of your mind! You must not say such things. What has he done to you?"

"He has humiliated me and misused me, and he has asked his friends to humiliate me and misuse me," Pasquito said with trembling nostrils, "and he has driven other young men to kill themselves from shame. But I will not kill myself. I will kill him instead. I will kill him as one kills a vicious dog; he is evil."

"Pasquito, my little brother, do not do such a foolish thing, I am sorry he mistreated you, but I don't think he is evil. It is like a sickness. There are other men like him."

"No," Pasquito said, "no, Doña Isabel. There are other men who seduce boys, but they do it kindly. He is twisted and ugly inside and out, and he wants to make twisted and ugly everything that he touches. He and his friend Villaquemada."

"Why didn't you come back to Valderocas House?"

"Without you, there was nothing here for me."

Pasquito had grown up to be slightly taller than Isabel. A svelte body, curly black hair, dark skin, expressive eyes, and even teeth made him a most handsome lad by any standards of beauty.

"Leave the country," Isabel proposed. "I will give you all the money you want. You could go to North Africa, if you like, or to the New World."

"No. I have found some of my people," Pasquito said.

"Moors, you mean? Heretics?"

"Yes."

"Pasquito, you should not even be telling me this. And you should not call yourself El Moro. You cannot go around telling people you are an Arab. It is madness. You will be caught by the Inquisition."

"I do not go around telling people. El Moro is just a nickname they gave me. Besides, I know I can trust you."

"Even though I am married to a monster?"

"Are you really married to him? Or are you just living in his house?" he asked quickly. She was surprised by the maturity of his question.

"I just live in his house," she said.

"I like to be independent," Pasquito said. "It was rough at first, but now I've made friends, and I'm going to stay with them."

"To live as a criminal?"

"I am not such a criminal as your husband, Doña Isabel. He is worse than you can possibly imagine, worse than even his friend Villaquemada. At the Bodegon de San Gil, we know everything that is going on in Madrid, all the so-called crimes of passion and vengeance. And what we don't know, Juliana knows."

"Who is Juliana?" Isabel asked and looked straight into his eyes. To her joy he blushed. He was trying hard to lose the remainder of his innocence, but he could still blush.

"I don't think Don Carlos will ever harm me," she said. "He is highly eccentric, but that is all."

"His friend Villaquemada has paid for several murders recently committed in the city," Pasquito informed her, "and birds of a feather flock together."

"Let us talk about you," Isabel suggested. "How does this criminal brotherhood work? Do you have to turn over the money you make, or the loot, or whatever, to a leader?"

"Yes."

"And he pays you?"

"Yes, according to the quality of our accomplishments."

"Good God, you were made for a better life, Pasquito."

"I am not a slave anymore. I am free! The *germanía* protects me."

She took off a pearl necklace she was wearing that day and handed it to him. "Here, this is worth far more than two hundred ducats, and you can tell them it is not stolen, so they can sell it for an honest price. If I need help, I will come to you, but only if you promise that you will also come to me if you need help."

"I will, Doña Isabel, I promise." He bowed to her, a little awkwardly, and then, impulsively, he kissed her hand. There was a wistful smile on her lips as she watched him leave.

# 16.

Pedro came home while she was still telling Pepita a few truths about her life with Carlos. Both Pepita and Pedro insisted that she could not go back to him. She should stay at Valderocas House, and Pedro would challenge Carlos to a duel.

"Flimflam. Don't be so dramatic. Of course, I will go back. Olivares needs me there. And at least Carlos will never touch me."

"You mean he hasn't," Pedro began haltingly.

"Of course, he hasn't. He married me for our money, and he wants to be King of Andalusia. He is completely crazy but harmless as far as I am concerned. I saw Olivares today, and I will go on reporting to him."

She wondered for an instant whether she should mention her new relationship with the King, but then she decided that it was a very personal matter, and she omitted it from her story about gossip at the palace.

"Olivares is finally convinced he can do away with the Holy Office altogether," Pedro said. "That is a goal worth all our trouble. Imagine religious liberty in Spain. Freedom to worship, does that not mean freedom of speech?"

"Well, that plan of his is being talked about," Isabel told him. "Carlos's friends intend to inform the Papal Nuncio of his schemes. If he isn't careful, he is going to be in trouble with Rome."

"Did you tell him?"

"No, I wanted to ask your advice first. We don't want to discourage him."

"I'll see that he hears of this."

"Oh Pedro, I get so disheartened sometimes. Here it has been almost four years since we came to Madrid with basketfuls of hopes, and so far none of them has materialized."

"How can you say that? Before I went to Oran and to Salonica, not one Jew was permitted in the entire kingdom. Now we are receiving them at Court, and the Count-Duke talks of giving them a synagogue and a Jewish quarter. What do you expect? A revocation of the expulsion order overnight?"

"No, but look whom we have lost. Our best friends had to leave, and I was almost caught with them. We still cannot say what we think; we cannot even admit to being Marranos, and the more I listen to Carlos and his group, the more I think that they are stronger than the Count-Duke, because there are many of them and only one of him. They are like the waves that hollow out the rocks from underneath. I am afraid for him. I want him to succeed, but no one helps him."

"You help him. I do. And so do a few others."

"Who are they?"

"I don't know."

"Then how do you know they exist?"

"I take his word."

Pepita listened to them. She was well informed now, and she approved of their work, but she never gave any advice unless it concerned the family welfare. She strove hard to become as calm and serene as Catalina had been.

"I do not see how you two can sit here and discuss the Count-Duke's mysterious friends, when you know that something else is so much more important," she now interjected.

"What is that, dear?" Pedro asked.

"Why, Isabel's safety, of course. Imagine what will happen to her if Carlos finds out what she has been up to. Spying on him! He is liable to kill her. You know he would be in his right. He can do to her . . . why . . . just about anything. It is insane for her to go back."

"I will go with her and talk to Carlos," Pedro said.

"I assure you I can shift for myself," Isabel demurred, but Pedro insisted that he personally wished to visit her apartments.

The Queras doorman looked somewhat surprised to see Isabel arrive with her brother, but since it was not his place to make any remarks, he signaled to a few pages to accompany them upstairs. The pages opened the entrance door for them.

Maria was in a state of utmost anxiety.

"Thank God, you are home," the girl exclaimed.

"What happened?" Isabel asked.

"Downstairs. In the apartments below ours. The most terrifying screams, and laughter, and strange noises—like whips. It scared me nearly to death."

Pedro looked at Isabel. She shrugged.

"Where are your other servants?" Pedro inquired.

"Oh, I forgot to tell you. I only have Maria."

There was exasperation in his voice. "By God, Isabel, I have a feeling you have forgotten to tell me a lot of things. What happened to all the women who came here with you?"

"They did not like to be confined to my quarters."

"So he does keep you all imprisoned here!" He walked up and down, frowning, chewing his upper lip and balling his fists. "That whoreson, I swear I will . . ."

"You will what?" Carlos's voice came to them with a cold nasal twang. Both Isabel and Pedro turned to see him stand in the doorway, just as if he had listened outside, which was not possible because the door had been closed.

"I swear I will avenge our honor!" Pedro said. "My sister is used to more than one servant, and she is used to complete liberty of movement, and so are her servants."

"I do not care what she is used to. She is my wife now, and if she complains, it is my honor that must be avenged, not yours. Get out of my house."

"Yes, I will, and I will take Isabel with me."

"Pedro, what are you talking about? Carlos, stop it! I have not complained about a thing. I would not dream of leaving my husband."

Both men looked at her, and she returned their stares proudly. Pictures of men swirled through her mind: Rafael, Philip, Duarte Perez, Diego Caietano, his brother José, the Jews of Amsterdam, Calderon, Quevedo, Velázquez, Rembrandt, her own father, but above all, Olivares. Olivares, the only possible savior of the Marranos, the man who must be helped beyond personal sacrifice. She had no illusions as to Olivares's true motives: he was not interested in Jews or Marranos. He was interested in getting Spain's economy back in shape. But if the end result was liberty, what did it matter? Carlos was the Count-Duke's enemy. She had to stay with him and watch him. In a men's world, this was her only chance to play a decisive role.

Pedro's hand had instinctively reached for his sword during his exchange with Carlos. Now he dropped it, and he also dropped his eyes. If Isabel took her husband's side, a quick retreat was the best policy.

"Good-bye, Isabel," he said and kissed her hand. Then he bowed to Carlos, "Your servant, Don Carlos." He left abruptly. Isabel knew she had hurt his feelings. Damn men, she thought, why are they so stupid?

"Now, Madame, would you kindly tell me, what was this all about?"

"I do not really know, Carlos," Isabel said, forcing herself to sound bored. "It seems that there are rumors in town that you have mistreated one of my former slaves, Pasquito. I did not know until today. I thought he had just run away with the others."

"What kind of rumors?"

"I don't know. That you flogged him perhaps. I had gone to see my sister-in-law, because she has found this marvelous new dressmaker, and then Pedro insisted he had to drive me home and inspect my apartments. He was shocked to find no more servants than Maria, and knowing the reputation of our friend Don Enrique"—she stressed the word "our"—"he must have imagined you habitually mistreat the servants and perhaps even your wife."

"You had never told him that you have only Maria?"

"Of course not! I have not told them anything about the way we live. My place is with you."

Carlos had listened attentively but apparently was satisfied with her explanation. His limited experience with women was a trump card Isabel held smilingly in her hand.

He pulled some clay pellets from his pocket and started to chew them, a gesture Isabel found revolting and effeminate, for the masticating of clay was mostly a female vice.

"I have thought it over," he said. "You may hire as many servants, male or female, as you desire to employ. I find you to be a discreet and irreproachable spouse, and I must admit you are fulfilling all my expectations. Now tell me a bit about your day at Court." He sat down primly in one of the armchairs. Then, realizing that Isabel was still standing, he got up again and gallantly led her to the chair, taking another one for himself.

"Thank you, Carlos. Well, to begin at the beginning, I assisted at a new play His Majesty had written. It was a rehearsal, and Her Majesty directed the players." She went on to tell him the details of the plot and concluded, "It was quite witty and charming, but of course, a Quevedo he is not."

"If only he could put his mind to matters of government. Did you see the Count-Duke?"

This was a tricky question. Naturally, Carlos kept spies at the Alcázar, as any other Grandee or would-be-Grandee, and it would never do to get caught in a lie.

"Yes, I did, very briefly. I was on my way to visit Doña Juana de Velázquez, and it turned out that the Count-Duke had gone to visit Don Diego at the same time. So we met one another, but since neither of the Velázquez's were at their apartments, all we exchanged was a greeting."

"Nothing more?"

"You know him! I do not know what he hates more, chitchat or women. I found him to be looking tired and shaky. Confidentially, Carlos, I don't think he is going to last too long. I don't even think you and our friends have to try so hard to oust him. It would be much better to let him fall by himself. The King may not take too kindly to anyone who directly upsets his regime. You should, of course, encourage His Majesty to govern when Olivares goes, or perhaps you should even try to become a Royal Favorite yourself, but do not be the one who pushed the Count-Duke. Don't get too involved. Just be there at the right moment."

"You are a shewd woman, Madame. You have a mind I much admire."

"Thank you."

"I have some interesting news myself," Carlos continued. "Things in Catalonia go from bad to worse. Olivares has been trying for years to get the Catalans to speak Castilian. Now it seems the priests refuse to preach their sermons in any language but Catalan. And God knows what they are telling their fellow Catalans."

"Well, but how can we achieve the unity of Spain, if we persist in speaking different languages? Castilian is the language of the empire," Isabel repeated one of the Count-Duke's much-quoted sayings.

"Who needs an Empire? I think we would do much better as a federation of different states. Portugal, Aragon, Catalonia, Andalusia, and, of course, Castile. But why should Castile dominate the others?"

"You really think it will come then, the dissolution of the nation? When we have tried so hard, since the Catholic Kings, to achieve unity of state and of religion? If we have different states, might we not also get different religions?"

"Oh no!" Carlos exclaimed indignantly. "Religion has nothing to do with it. Do not suppose I am advocating any *blandura* for heretics. No, we simply would have a separate Inquisition for each state, just as now we have a separate Inquisition for Portugal. Do you realize that Andalusia is the richest province of Spain? To rule over Andalusia, even over the former Moorish kingdom of Granada, is better than to rule over any other land."

"That is what you want," Isabel said. "You are serious, aren't you?"

"Are you going to help me?"

"Of course, I am your wife, am I not?"

"You . . ."

Before he could finish his sentence, a courier rushed in with a rolled-up parchment in his hands.

Carlos took it and unrolled it slowly. Isabel watched his face, and she thought he looked like a prisoner who had been given his freedom. Turning to the usher who had admitted the courier, he said, "See that the man gets well fed, well treated, and well rewarded."

When the two had left, he turned again to Isabel, rose from his seat, extended his hand to her ceremoniously, and helped her up.

"Yes, you are my wife," he said, stressing each word, "and that makes you Countess de Queras and wife of a Grandee of Spain. My father is dead."

"Oh, Carlos, I am sorry," she said impulsively.

"Well, I am not. And if you had known him, you would not be sorry either."

"You will want to go to Court today?" she asked, for Carlos would not officially be Grandee as long as the King had not granted him permission—in front of the other Grandees—to cover his head in the royal presence.

"First, we want to be sure he knows," Carlos said.

"His Majesty's play will be presented next Tuesday following a midnight supper. I did not know whether you wanted to attend, knowing how you detest such functions, but . . ."

"But thank you, Count and Countess de Queras will attend with pleasure," Carlos finished with a smug and superior smile. "By then he will know. I will make sure of that."

# 17.

Carlos's elevation to the ranks of the Grandees was a very simple matter. After the play, the Count-Duke gave a reception in his apartments, and throughout the evening, Carlos walked around with a gorgeously plumed hat in his left hand, almost despairing because the King seemed to avoid him, but finally, just as he was preparing to leave, His Majesty spoke the magical words, "Don Carlos, cover yourself."

Carlos sank onto one knee, and as he rose again, he put on his hat with great flourish. Isabel curtsied very low as etiquette demanded, in gratitude for the great honor bestowed upon her husband, and Philip gallantly helped her up.

"Countess, it is a pleasure to see you."

She dropped her eyes demurely, and no one guessed that she had lain in the King's bed for an hour earlier that day, when she had been summoned to the palace by a royal page.

On the way home, Carlos spoke at length about his plans for the future, and Isabel took mental notes for her next report to Olivares.

A week later, Philip fell in love with a young actress, and Isabel's role as royal mistress was, at least temporarily, finished. Her peace of mind, in that respect, was restored with the arrival of her monthly flux.

Once again her life seemed to settle into a pattern, but this time a dull and dreary one. There were no social events during Lent, and the only times she left Queras House were to hear the first and second Edict of Faith and the Anathema. But by now she had gotten so used to the yearly threats of eternal hellfire that she hardly listened anymore. She continued to report to the Count-Duke all the moves prepared by Carlos and his dinner guests, but even that began to bore her.

When she complained about that to Pepita, her sister-in-law shook her head.

"Isabel," Pepita said, "I am afraid you are not happy unless you can court some deathly danger. Is it not enough that our life is constantly threatened? And yours in particular?"

"Flimflam."

# 18.

Everywhere in Spain, Passion Week was the time of interminable processions, but none were as flamboyant in their interpretation of suffering as the Good Friday procession of Madrid. To do public penitence was an art taught by masters, just like dancing or fencing. There were rules to be observed, and an adroit disciplinarian could capture a lady's heart by lashing his skin so that the blood splattered all about him without falling on his long pleated gown.

Early on Good Friday morning, Isabel had a surprise visit by her husband. She was still in bed, half-awake, half-adream, thinking about Rafael and herself, reviewing in her mind all the perfect moments of her past love, when Maria came in to tell her that Carlos wished to talk to her.

"Tell him to come in."

"Here?"

"Well, he *is* my husband. It won't harm him to see me in my nightgown."

But Carlos refused, and she had to dress before meeting him in the sitting room.

"Madame, I expect you to be ready in one hour at the latest."

"What for?"

"To sit on the balcony."

"You mean I have to watch the procession?"

"Naturally. I did not think I would have to remind you of your duties. Just be sure you wear the new brocade gown, the one with the rubies, and have all your women sit behind you." She had hired a half-dozen new servants after Carlos promised that the women could go and come as they pleased.

"Where will you be?" she asked him, almost expecting to hear him say he would be part of the processions.

"I have an appointment. I will tell you about it later. But I want you to watch both the morning and the afternoon processions. That is an order."

The insufferable fool! How long would she have to live with him? How long? Good God, for the rest of her life! How could she have accepted that arrangement? Why did she have to suffer for the freedom of her friends? Why not simply run away and join them?

The streets were lined with gaping crowds, and all the balconies were graced with ladies in their best finery, while dark sounds of drums and high sounds of clarions filled the air with lamenting rhythms. Hundreds of disciplinarians filed by, barefoot with long gowns of fine cloth, on their heads conical mitres from which loose pieces of cloth fell to their shoulders, so that their faces were hidden except for two holes for the eyes. On their backs and shoulders three big holes were cut into the fabric, so that their skin showed. Each man had an abundance of ribbons tied to his sleeves and most of them also had a ribbon tied to their whip. To be admired, a penitent must discipline himself by a quick flick of his wrist. The blows must fall in a measured cadence, and the blood must spurt out but never soil his clothes. It was fashionable to give oneself expert cuts and lashes on one's shoulders and to go hence before one's mistress's window and patiently whip oneself, hoping that the adored lady watched through the lattice of her chamber if she were not out on the balcony. Many disciplinarians whipped themselves furiously whenever they saw a pretty lass pass by in the street, as if to splash her with their blood, and the girl was supposed to acknowledge this homage and thank them with a smile or a nod.

Isabel was familiar with the sight of these gentlemen disciplinarians, and she did not mind watching them; what she dreaded was the passing of the true penitents, those who repented their real or imagined sins to the point of taking the advice of their confessors who enjoined them to undergo such severe martyrdom that they often did not live out the year. The true penitents could easily be recognized, for they were naked from the shoulders to the waist, their faces also being hidden by a hood, and their arms and body were swaddled tightly with thin strips of fabric so that their flesh turned black and blue. These victims of their own ignorance carried from

three to seven swords which seemed to stick in their backs
and arms and hurt them terribly whenever they fell, a
frequent occurrence, since they were unable to see the road.
They usually cut their feet on the street litter and stumbled
over stones, and they left traces of blood where they passed.
Others carried crosses so heavy that they could only advance
slowly and had to be helped by servants who accompanied
them. The servants' faces were also covered, lest they and
therefore their masters be recognized, for these repentant
sinners were of the highest quality and never ordinary folk.

After watching hour after hour of this grievous spectacle,
with only one interruption for a fast-like midday meal and a
short siesta, Isabel was most irritable when Carlos joined her
in the late afternoon.

"There ought to be a law against this nonsense," she said
moodily. "Our religious fanaticism is disgraceful."

"You are perfectly right, Madame. I just heard the Papal
Nuncio pronounce himself very strongly against these prac-
tices. But I don't think anybody is going to listen to Cardinal
Monti."

"Of course not. As long as there are husbands who force
their wives to see this butchery, common sense remains
buried."

"You don't even ask me where I heard the Nuncio," Carlos
chided, unruffled by her barb. Her fits of bad humor never
touched him in the least.

"It would not surprise me if he was a new friend of yours."

"How perceptive of you. I hope he is going to be. I am
coming from his house now. I met someone else there, whom
I think you know."

"Oh?"

"Yes, the new Inquisitor in charge of Madrid affairs."

"Who is that?" she asked idly, thinking he might be one of
the guests they had entertained for dinner.

"A certain Fray Rafael Cortes."

Instantly, the blood drained from her face, and there was a
gnawing feeling of imminent doom in the pit of her stomach.

He mistook her silence for lack of memory.

"Don't you recall? The man who had come from Madrid to
your father's reception. The night I met you. Well, I suppose
you haven't seen him since. He is a Dominican, and now he
has become an Inquisitor. A thoroughly insufferable fellow."

"Why?" Isabel managed to ask, although she felt perfectly
numb.

"I didn't like the way he looked at me."

So Rafael had advanced a giant step toward his goal, while she perished in the morass of daily dreariness. What was he doing to forget her? Immersing himself in his work? Burning heretics? Sneaking out at night in secular clothes to visit such places as La Casa de Celestina? No, not that. He never paid for a wench. He had said so himself. How could he live without her? Or had she become a burden, had he been glad to find the pretext of her marriage to get rid of her? If only she could be sure of the truth, life would be easier to bear. She thought of contacting him somehow. After all, an Inquisitor was someone no Countess need be ashamed to receive. Invite him. But no, that was pointless; he would not come. He would send an excuse. If only she could let him know somehow that she did not really belong to Carlos.

# 19.

Shortly after Easter, Pepita gave birth to a son. He was named Fernando and baptized at a splendid ceremony during which Isabel held him, since she was to be his godmother. This time Uncle Jaime had come from Toledo and with him the Raíz family and other friends, for the sole purpose of holding a secret prayer meeting at night in the cellar of Valderocas House. They would pass a sponge over little Fernando's forehead and they would give him his Hebrew name. They would recite a few short blessings, just as they had done the night Isabel had first met her fellow Marranos of Toledo. She could not assist for lack of a good excuse, but that night, lying alone in her bed, she earnestly prayed to the God of her fathers, begging Him, pleading with Him, to speedily bring about the time when they would have to hide no longer.

But when Carlos informed her, two weeks later, that he had to leave on an extended trip to Andalusia, she could think of nothing else but how she would use his absence to contact Rafael. The idea of greater freedom for herself brought a smile to her lips.

"You will receive no one in my absence," Carlos said, "and I expect you to lead the same retired life as when I am here."

"I will go nowhere but to Valderocas House and to the

Palace should I be summoned by Her Majesty," Isabel promised.

Pepita welcomed the opportunity to see Isabel more often, because Pedro was once more being sent abroad by the Count-Duke. The two women were sitting on Pepita's *estrado*, Isabel rocking baby Fernando in her lap, Pepita embroidering a tiny shirt for him, when the door opened and Alfonso came in.

The mere sight of Alfonso, a manservant in Pepita's bedroom, spelled trouble.

Moreover, he closed the door after him.

"Alfonso, what is it?" Pepita asked, looking alarmed.

"Fray Gabriel Ortiz and Fray Jesus Dominguin of the Holy Office wish to speak to Her Ladyship, Countess de Queras," Alfonso announced stiffly.

Isabel stopped rocking Fernando and over his fuzzy head stared at Alfonso. Her heart stood still. This could be the end! Someone had betrayed them!

"The Holy Office?" she whispered. "Are you sure?"

"Yes, Doña Isabel, very sure."

Pepita took the baby and held him tightly.

"Just now, when Pedro is abroad. I hope it is nothing serious."

"The Inquisition is always serious," Isabel hissed, thinking that perhaps Pedro was not abroad, that perhaps they had caught him and now came for her. She turned to Alfonso, "I will come immediately. Do not let them come into the house."

The guards greeted her with utmost civility and informed her that she was invited to appear as a witness at a special hearing.

"Can I not go home first? My servants will worry about my absence."

She was assured there was no need for that. She would not be detained. She remembered that this was the way the Inquisition acted, never giving victims the time to inform anyone or to call for help.

The guards handed her into a simple oilcloth-covered coach and sat across from her, watching her politely. She was deeply worried. Who had talked? What did they know? Would Olivares be informed, and would he help her? Had Pedro been arrested or Uncle Jaime? What was going on? She remembered how the Caietanos had been handcuffed and mistreated, and she wondered whether titled people were arrested with more respect. At any rate, she walked between the two friars into the building housing the Madrid offices of the Inquisition, just like any other prisoner.

When she was finally ushered into the audience chamber, it appeared that she was, indeed, only a witness and had a right to be treated with all the politeness due to a person of quality.

It was a large room with a high ceiling and stark white walls, contrasting with the dark wood of the doors and window frames. One end of the room consisted of a raised platform, and on it, behind a long table, there sat six Dominican friars. In the center of the otherwise empty hall stood an armchair for the witness. Behind the friars a life-size crucifix hung on the wall. There were doors on each side of the cross.

She curtsied to the monks and sat down, feeling small and insignificant. The two friars who had brought her remained standing behind her chair. All six sitting at the table wore the white gown and black cloak of the Dominican order, but the three on her right were young and eager-looking, while the three on her left had gray hair and wrinkled skin. None of them even glanced at her. They seemed busy taking and comparing notes. The center chair between the two groups was empty. Suddenly, there was a shuffling of chairs. They all rose to their feet, and one of Isabel's guards asked her to rise. The door on the right side of the crucifix opened, and the Friar Inquisitor arrived, walked to his chair, and Isabel found herself staring unbelievably into Rafael's eyes. For the first time in her life, she was utterly unable to hold herself erect, and with a little moan, she slumped into the chair.

His voice came to her, as through a fog.

"Countess, are you feeling all right?"

"Yes." She could not bring herself to call him Your Illustrious Lordship, a title given dignitaries of the rank of bishop. "Quite well, thank you."

"Then we shall proceed with the hearing. Fray Gabriel, your turn."

The young friar at the far right started to take down her name, age, and address. Then the next friar informed her that whatever she said would be kept entirely confidential and that she was to conceal nothing. The third one made her swear on the Holy Bible that she would reveal to the Holy Tribunal all she knew regarding the matters which would be under discussion and that she would not tell anyone about her interrogation, under pain of excommunication and of eternal hellfire. Therewith the role of the three younger men seemed to be ended, and the older monks began the interrogation proper. But the first question, "Countess, are you happy with your husband?" startled her so visibly that the Inquisitor, Rafael, who up until now had just watched her, lifted his right hand to interrupt.

"Countess, I would like to deviate from our normal procedure to give you a brief idea of why you were convoked here today. It has come to our attention that there exists in Madrid a group of a most heinous nature, namely a group of sodomists and similarly perverted creatures. Your husband is one of the persons who was denounced to us, but, as you surely know, the Holy Office is the most just tribunal existing on this earth, and we never proceed hastily. We realize that as a Grandee of Spain, your husband has many enemies who would take great pleasure in his arrest, and we want to avoid any rash and scandalous act. We are therefore conducting a confidential investigation, and your cooperation will be most valuable."

Good God, Rafael investigating Carlos. Rafael probing into her conjugal affairs. Rafael discovering the truth. Rafael discovering the truth! The undreamed of opportunity! The unique occasion to rid herself of Carlos. One word from her, one word of the truth, and Carlos was finished. Who had denounced him? Pasquito perhaps? Other young *pícaros?* What did it matter? She could finish him off, easily, painlessly. He would be picked up at Granada or at Seville, and she would never have to face him again. He would rot in some dungeon forever. The implications were staggering.

She stared into Rafael's eyes, but suddenly she was frightened. He had always been able to read her mind. He must know what she was thinking now. It must be obvious to him. If he gave her but one small sign of encouragement, she would go ahead. She stared at him, for what seemed an eternity, but his glance remained cool and a little bit sad. He did not love her anymore. For if he did, he could surely have found a way of letting her know about this, they could have planned it together. Instead, the whole responsibility lay on her own shoulders. Once again she must make a decision. Oh, she was so tired of making all the decisions; she wished she could find a man with whom she could make decisions.

The old friar at Rafael's right now repeated his question: "Are you happy with your husband?"

"Happy? Your Lordship, who is ever happy? I am an average wife, no happier, or unhappier than others, I suppose."

"You think that you have a normal marriage?"

"I think so."

"You consider your husband a good husband?"

"He gives me no reason to complain." Would Rafael understand this? Would he understand that, since she loathed Carlos, his abstention from husbandly duties was a great joy to her?

"Have you observed in your husband or in his friends any abnormal behavior?"

"No."

"He keeps only menservants, does he not?"

"We also have womenservants, Your Lordship."

The questions became annoying. She hated to submit to their probings. If they asked any intimate details in front of Rafael, she would turn about and take Carlos's side.

The whole procedure was revolting. Once she realized that her fears had been unfounded, that this had nothing to do with her family or her work for Olivares, she was appalled by their audacity. The nerve to interrogate a wife about her husband. The cynical callousness of it all. And this was what Rafael preferred to living with her? This was what he preferred to an honorable life abroad?

Did he really expect her to denounce her husband? He looked tired. Overworked. No. She must not think that way. She must not let her love for him gain the upper hand. The more she looked at him, the more she knew that she loved him and would never stop loving him. She was angry with him, furious even, but she loved him. She loved every wrinkle on his forehead—God, he was getting wrinkles! And on his temples she could detect some gray hair. . . .

"Do you spend much time with your husband?"

The old men had prepared all their questions. Did they interrogate all the wives of suspected sodomists in this manner?

"We have many discussions."

"What about?"

"The Court, politics."

"Do you share the same bed?"

She looked at Rafael, and she felt her face getting hot. If

only he would give her a sign, an imperceptible nod or a *no* formed with silent lips. But nothing. Then she remembered that two guards were standing behind her. He could not signal to her even if he wanted to. Should she tell the truth? She recalled how concerned he had been when Pepita had run away. How he had deplored that her mother had talked too much. He had said how he wished people would not give away their secrets.

But if Pasquito was right, Carlos deserved to be arrested. She must think of that, too. She must not forget that Carlos, indeed, was a criminal. However, what could she say without dragging Pasquito into this affair? The Inquisition must never touch that boy, lest they find out that he was a secret believer in Mohammed.

On the other hand, what had Carlos actually done to her? Nothing that warranted his rotting in a dungeon. No. She could not do it. She could not send a human being to torture, even if she hated him and despised him.

The interrogators regarded her silence as embarrassment. The oldest one spoke to her, softly, fatherly. "My dear Countess, please speak to us as freely as to your own confessor."

The one who had asked the question repeated it now, "Do you share the same bed?"

The crucial question. The one she wanted to etch into Rafael's mind. The long-awaited opportunity to let him know that her body did not belong to Carlos. She could not let it slip through her fingers. She looked at their faces, into their eyes. There was no morbid curiosity here, just professional concern. They did not know about herself and their new Inquisitor: they did not know that her personal integrity was at stake; they purely asked one of the routine questions prepared for wives of alleged homosexuals. At last, she looked into Rafael's eyes and then she answered while holding his glance, "Yes, we do." She almost whispered her monstrous lie, and the old interrogator was perhaps hard of hearing for he admonished her to speak louder.

"Yes," she said in a firm hard voice, "we do share the same bed. Your Lordship, I do not know why you think that my husband might be involved with the group you are investigating, but I can assure you that he is a wonderful husband, and it grieves me to imagine that he could have enemies who go around spreading lies about him. I swear on the Holy Cross and by all saints and by Our Lord's wounds that I have no complaint against him."

All of a sudden there came a spark of life into Rafael's somber eyes. She half-expected him to break into his usual silent laughter, and with relief she realized that she had done the right thing, the one thing he had hoped she would do. She had once made fun of people who swore elaborate oaths, and he had said he would know not to believe her if she ever used one. He remembered now, and he did not believe one word of what she had said.

"Thank you, Countess," he said, before the interrogator could launch into the next question. "I think we have heard all the testimony we need to have. We would like to advise you not to disturb the Count's peace of mind. The less said, the better it is. We thank you for your kind cooperation." He rose and left the room. The guards told her that she, too, could leave, and they accompanied her back to the coach and took her back to Valderocas House.

She had time to think of an explanation to give Pepita. She told her it was a completely harmless case of mistaken identity. The Inquisition was interested in a person whom they believed to be in her service. It was nothing at all, not worth mentioning.

Pepita let out a sigh of relief. "That's wonderful," she said. "It proves they are not as infallible as all that."

Her unexpected encounter with Rafael had shaken her so much that instead of driving back to Queras House, Isabel left through the back door and took a hackney to the promenade of the Prado.

While riding up and down the famous *paseo*, she tried to organize her thoughts. Foremost in her mind was an overwhelming sadness, a dull pain, the perception of the uselessness of her life. Nothing was left of the intricate mosaic, nothing but a pile of shattered tiles. Hope, love, trust, exuberance, adventure—all these had intermingled before her marriage—making her life exciting, even happy. Now they were gone forever. She might as well not exist. Would anyone miss her if she disappeared? Really miss her? Pedro was happy with Pepita. He did not need her anymore for moral support, and Rafael had his career. And did Olivares really need her services, or was it all merely a political game?

Rafael, oh Rafael! A sentence came back to her, a few words from the past. "Watch out, Don Rafael, for I am not done with you." Had she said those words? Had she ever been so determined? Then why had she given him up without a struggle? Why had she bowed to his order not to see him anymore? If she could tempt him in the past, why had she ceased to tempt him? He had once said that if her life were in danger, she would be more important to him than his work. Well, today she had been convoked by the Inquisition. Might that not bring her life in danger, eventually? Should she not contact him to find out what this was truly about?

I will see him, she said to herself, I will see him. *I will see him*. The words were magic, filling her with energy. She believed them, she repeated them, and the more she repeated them, the more they became a simple truth. She would see him again, and he would love her again.

She told the driver to take her immediately to the Alcázar. There she descended in front of the main gate and walked past the royal halberdiers into the *Patio de las Covachuelas*. At the stall of the public scribe, she had to stand in line. She had never realized that so many illiterates came here to have their letters written. The scribe, an old man, first told a heart-rending story about the miseries of his life to every prospective customer. That way he could ask for a higher price and not be refused. He gave Isabel a lewd smile of anticipation, obviously expecting a love letter.

"Please take your best parchment," she said, "and write: Francisco Molina is expected at nine o'clock at the second bookstall of the *Patio de las Covachuelas*."

"Not so fast, my Lady. First tell me to whom this letter is addressed."

"It is not a letter. It is a reminder. A message I was asked to give to someone. Just write it down as I said."

He was about to open his mouth to start a discussion when she placed a gold coin in front of him. He took it and with great embellishing strokes wrote exactly what she had said.

"Now roll it up and seal it three times."

She found another hackney and drove back to the building where the Inquisitorial Tribunal met. There she asked the driver whether he would consider the equivalent of his monthly intake a good price for a little errand.

"What is it?" the man asked suspiciously.

"I want you to deliver a message to his Illustrious Lordship the Inquisitor, Fray Rafael Cortes. I must be sure that it gets into his hands. I want you to go in and find out if the tribunal is still in session. If it is, we will wait until the friars come out. If it is not, I want you to find out where the Inquisitor is and give him the message. Now I want you to understand that it is just as important for me to know that you could not find him or could not give it to him. Therefore, I shall pay you just as well if you come out without having delivered the note. You understand? Either way, it is the same to me."

"Yes, my Lady."

He took the parchment, looked at it carefully from all sides, and then looked at the building. She could guess his thoughts.

"It is not a denunciation," she said. "It has nothing to do with the matters of the Holy Office. It is a personal note from a friend who had to leave Madrid. That is why I want to get it into the hands of the Inquisitor himself. You need not be afraid. It does not require an answer."

"What if someone else takes it from me?"

"If they insist, you let them have it and tell me about it. You will still be paid."

"And if I am asked who sends me, what do I say?"

"Just tell them the Duchess de Miraflores." She smiled, not at him but at an inner vision of José Caietano's laughing face. The driver smiled back at her and bowed. She watched him disappear behind the gray stone portal.

He was gone for about half an hour, and she started to worry. But, when he came back, she could see right away that his hands were empty.

"I gave it to him," he informed her.

"What did he look like?"

He was surprised. "You do not know him?" Then suddenly he turned pale. "Jesus protect me, perhaps that wasn't him. He looked young. Not at all what I thought an Inquisitor would look like. Tall, black hair, a black beard. ¡Válgame Dios! What if it wasn't him?"

She shrugged, "Oh well, if it was not he, we cannot help it, can we? We did our best. Here is your money."

In accordance with Pedro's instructions, Isabel never went anywhere without a good supply of ducats, so she would be able to bribe herself out of any dangerous situation. Now she handed him a small leather bag, and when he opened it, his eyes bulged.

"My Lady, Manolo will always be at your service. You can find me every morning at ten at the Puerta del Sol."

"Thank you Manolo. I will remember it. Now please drive me to Calle Santiago."

She told Pepita that she was going to a secret assignation, and she wore her old hooded cloak and veil when she walked back to the Alcázar. She had made up her mind that she would wait for him every day at nine o'clock, for as long as Carlos was out of town. If he had gotten the note, he would come, if not today then tomorrow or the day thereafter.

In addition to a reliable and expensive new clock, Valderocas House had many hourglasses, and so she knew that it was not quite nine when she entered the patio. All the stalls were open. Jewelry glittered in the torchlights; the pastry cooks were praising their wares; young budding painters exhibited their latest efforts; only the bookstalls were quiet. Isabel walked around the patio, nervous and apprehensive: Dear God, please let him come. Dear God, I cannot stand this waiting anymore. Dear God, I simply must speak to him, if only for a few minutes. Please dear God.

When he finally came, she did not recognize him right away, because he wore secular clothes and a full vizard, but as soon as he approached her, she recognized his step, and she hastened to lift her veil.

"I must talk to you. It is important," she whispered.

"Please hurry. I don't have much time." The same husky voice, giving his answer as normally as if they had never been separated.

"Where can we go?" she asked.

"Let us take a hackney."

He walked quickly taking long steps, and she had trouble keeping up with him. He handed her into a coach for hire and asked the driver to take them toward the Buen Retiro.

"Why did you call me?" he whispered when they were sitting side by side.

"Because I am afraid. Could you not avoid interrogating me? What is going to happen to Carlos?"

"Nothing, I hope. I had to call on you. There is a big scandal about to break, and Carlos is deeply enmeshed in it. I hope that your testimony will save him."

"Why do you care to save him?" she asked, her voice low but contemptuous.

"For the same reason you do. He talks a lot to you, and you talk a lot to Olivares. You are too valuable."

More than a dozen times Rafael had surprised her by his

perspicacity, but never as much as this time. She caught her breath and gripped his hands.

"Rafael, I do not understand."

"I don't quite understand it myself, Isabel. I don't know why or how you got into this, and I don't know what exactly you are doing, but I got a hint from the Count-Duke to keep you and Carlos out of this matter, to hush it up, you understand, and I am trying my best."

"Why didn't you contact me beforehand?"

"I had considered it, but I thought it was safer this way. I counted on your natural indignation and possibly your hatred for me."

"Hatred? Rafael, you know I could not hate you if you killed me. I cannot stop thinking about you. I will never stop loving you, I can't."

"Even when you are with Philip?"

"Who told you that? The Count-Duke?"

"It does not matter. It is true, isn't it?"

"Not anymore. It happened, yes. But that is your fault."

"If it helps you to think that way. I could not know that Carlos was a sodomist."

"Carlos has never touched me and never will."

"And Philip?"

"Oh Rafael. Only a few times. I now wish it hadn't happened."

"Don't worry about it. I understand. He is a good lover they say. And, of course, he is the King."

"Rafael, Rafael, you are torturing me."

She leaned against him, letting her head rest on his chest, and finally he took her in his arms and started to kiss her face, gently at first, then hungrily searching for her mouth, and as their tongues met, the long waiting was over. She clung to him, trying to melt into his body, and then she had to bury her face against the side of his neck, and she was shaken by sobs of relief and joy.

"My dearest beloved, my wonderful girl, what shall I do with you?" he whispered in her ear.

"Keep me near you. Let me be with you again. I have missed you so. Oh Rafael, don't you know how much I've missed you?"

He hugged her tightly for a brief moment.

"I have to go back now. We still have work to do. I only took a break. I said I had been summoned to the Alcázar.

You must not send me any more notes like this. It could have fallen into the wrong hands. You are not careful enough."

"When will I see you again?"

"Darling, you only make it harder for yourself. You know I can never belong to you. Now it is more difficult than ever."

"Do you like your work? Snooping into other people's lives?"

"You do not understand what I am doing. I want to combat a great evil, and I am doing the best I can."

She remembered that he did not like to be questioned, and she quickly repressed the one she had in her mind. A theological discussion would do nothing but widen the gulf between them.

"If I invited you to Queras House, would you come? Could you become a friend of the family? Carlos might not object."

He shook his head. "Carlos and his friends have a terrible reputation. I could not even entertain such a thought."

"Then tell me when I can see you. Please Rafael, I have to see you again. If you refuse, I will leave Spain. I swear I will run away and never come back. I cannot stand this life."

"No! You must not do that. You must continue to work for the Count-Duke. It is important. Already there are too few Old Christians helping him."

There it was again. The eternal barrier between them. Churning up within her she felt the wild impulse of shouting "But I am a Jewess!" How could she love someone she would never be able to trust?

"Why are you on such intimate terms with the Count-Duke?" she asked.

"Here we go again. You are as nosy as ever. You cannot have forgotten that I used to work for him. That I always had much admiration for him."

He stuck his head through the glassless window and shouted to the driver to take them back to the Alcázar.

The coach turned, and for a brief moment, a shaft of moonlight fell on Rafael's face, and when she saw his determined features and somber eyes, a shiver of premonition ran up Isabel's spine. A wild, an absolutely mad notion formed in the back of her mind, a notion too exotic to be true, and yet too enticing to be discarded.

"Rafael," she said slowly in a low, almost eery voice, "Rafael, I think I finally know what you are up to."

"I should hope not," he said lightly.

"Oh, but I do. Wait, there was this book on your shelf, and you knew the Caietanos, and you worked for Olivares, and then you became Secretary to his Eminence, and now you . . ."

"Stop!" he interrupted her by clapping his palm over her mouth, much as Pedro used to do. "Do not play that game. It is dangerous. Do not talk. How often must I tell you that? Keep your thoughts to yourself. I never question what you do, so do not speculate about me."

"You questioned plenty today," she reminded him.

"I only listened."

"Yes, someone else did the asking for you."

"You were tempted to give away Carlos, weren't you?"

"Of course I was."

"Isabel, if something similar ever happens when I am not with you, if you are ever interrogated by the Holy Office, about anything or anyone, do not tell them a thing. Never, never talk. Try to remain silent. Tell them you do not know."

"Rafael, whose side are you on?" It was a stupid question, she thought. He would not like it.

"Yours. Always."

Never had she so strongly wished to tell him the truth. To tell him who she was, to test his trust. If it did not involve other lives, she knew she would do it. But she did not have the right to betray other human beings. She did not have the right to tell him, even though she now strongly suspected that he really was on their side.

"Rafael, I cannot stand this life anymore! If you refuse to meet me, I will run away. Count-Duke or not, I do not care to sacrifice my life for Spain."

He touched her hand with his lips, and she shivered from wanting him so much. Then at last he gave in.

"All right. Find a place where we can meet."

"I still have the apartment."

"You do? Why?"

"I couldn't give it up. Before I was married, I paid the rent for a whole year. I have never gone there though. I could not bear it."

"I still have the key," he said, "But I have not gone there either. I once passed by in the street, and the memories were painful."

They kissed the rest of the way, until the coach pulled up in front of the royal palace. Then he spoke quickly.

"I may not be able to see you more often than once or twice a month. I do not have much freedom anymore. I am constantly surrounded."

"Oh, Rafael, you sacrifice yourself. Is it really worth your life?"

"It is, to me."

"Your ultimate goal means that much?"

"Yes."

"Nothing will ever be more important to you?"

"Your life is."

"But not my happiness."

"No."

"What good is my life if I am unhappy?"

"Your happiness lies in your own hands."

"Then even if it is once a month, please try to meet me. There is no other happiness for me but to be with you."

"All right sweetness. I will try to get away. I will let you know when." He kissed her once more hungrily, then jumped out of the carriage before she could say another word.

# 1637

## 1.

Carnival at Madrid! Masquerades and torchlight parades. Riotous carousing and drunken sordid street orgies. Courtly merrymaking and wanton revels. Here elegant mirth, there contumelious ditties. Brutal games and savage practical jokes.

Every year it was the same, only more of it. Life itself had become a perpetual carnival, and the most extraordinary feats were not exciting enough to titillate the jaded senses of the populace. Not enough were age-old jokes such as tying strings across streets to make passengers fall and then to empty contents of chamber pots and ashtrays over them, not enough to release maimed dogs and cats into dense crowds, nor to stuff hot wax into horses' and mules' ears—new brutalities had to be invented every year. One of the favorite attractions was the rooster game. A fowl was buried in the ground so that only the neck and head were free, and the game consisted of gouging the rooster's eyes in the most rapid and skillful manner, or cutting off its head while galloping by at full speed. This was the poor man's bullfight, and the winner called himself king of the roosters.

Isabel had been brought up to abhor the carnival season and to avoid setting foot into the street during the days preceding Ash Wednesday. She had assumed that all people of quality felt likewise, and so it greatly surprised her when

Carlos came to discuss with her the plans for the coming festivities. He brought with him various invitations from Court, and she learned that in accordance with Their Majesties' wishes, the Carnival of 1637 would be a carnival to end all carnivals and would be crowned by the most magnificent festivities ever planned by men. The outrageous sum of three hundred thousand ducats had been allocated by the royal treasury to cover the expenses, and every person of quality was expected to outdo the others in elaborate costumes and masks. The jollities would last for more than a week and start with an extravagant feast on Sunday the fifteenth of February.

"Good God, why all this ostentation? I thought we did not have enough money to pay our troops in Catalonia. Now there is your opportunity to form an opposition and protest," Isabel said to Carlos.

"On the contrary, I could not be more pleased to see the master of the little devil in the walking stick ruin himself. Let Castile bleed to death, as long as Andalusia stays strong. I'll tell you what this is all about. The Princess Carignnano is visiting Madrid, and it is our monarch's fondest wish to honor and impress her."

Isabel lowered her lashes and fought with herself. Should she admit her ignorance? Carlos, as often when dealing with extemporaneous matters, was astute enough to guess her reason for hesitating.

"She is a sister of the Count of Soissons. The Count is a French nobleman who would be completely unimportant, if it were not for the fact that he is in arms against Richelieu. And you know our Favorite's motto: any enemy of Richelieu's is a friend of mine. I agree with you that the whole undertaking is an exercise in futility, but as I often say, the greater Olivares's follies, the harder his inevitable downfall."

"So if I understand correctly, the whole event has no other purpose than to show Richelieu that we still have plenty of money to punish France?"

Carlos gave her the speculative look she so hated, "Madame, it is a pity you are not a man."

She smiled, thinking if only he knew how much she was a woman, and she wondered at the same time whether the festivities would give her an opportunity to spend a few hours with Rafael. Since she had found him again, they had been able to meet from time to time, and thanks to their continued illicit affair, she had found life more bearable.

The homosexual scandal had exploded and rocked the Court to such an extent that the shock waves reached London and Paris in the form of outrageous rumors filling diplomatic pouches, but finally only minor noblemen and a few pages had been openly punished, and Carlos had never known how close he had come to being publicly shamed.

"Since I am one of the true Grandees living in Madrid," he said, "I will unfortunately not be able to avoid appearing with His Majesty in the horseback parade. There will be a sort of masquerade tourney in front of the Buen Retiro, on scaffolds two stories high—it frightens me just to think of it—and, in addition, we will be surrounded by so many torchlights that the Roman saturnalia were bleak by comparison. Velázquez and Olivares have given their full attention to every minute detail, and the spectacle will be unsurpassed."

"It seems to me the main thing for you to do is to secure a reliable horse," Isabel said. "It would not do at all for you to be thrown at a critical moment."

Carlos gave her a pleased glance.

"Villaquemada has a good mare for me, a splendid-looking dapple gray, tame as a mule. He has been riding her through fireworks. I think she will not disappoint me."

"Don Carlos, do I really have to come? Could I not stay at home? Everyone will be masked. I don't see what difference it makes."

"All the difference in the world. I count on you to take my place that day among our friends. Villaquemada will not be in the parade, and I expect you to stay at his side. The general disguise will help some of the Count-Duke's enemies to slip into town. You absolutely must report to me everything that is said and planned in my absence."

"Do you not trust Don Enrique?"

"I do not trust anyone."

"Neither do I," Isabel said.

"That is what makes us alike."

Carlos left the house on Sunday afternoon to assemble with the other nobles chosen to participate in the masked tourney, while Isabel, fully dressed, hooded, and masked, waited for the arrival of Enrique de Villaquemada. The notorious Count had not changed since she had first met him at the opening of the Buen Retiro. His sallow face had grown a bit fatter, but his stiletto beard was as black as ever, and his hair as bushy. He had chosen an animal mask for his face, a bull with

viciously pointed horns, and when he held it up, she compli-
mented him.

"An excellent woodcarver made this for me," he said.
"You'll see more masks like this next Sunday at the *mojiganga*
of the Protonotario of Aragon. It'll be the fun of the
century."

"Why? What makes a *mojiganga* different from other
masquerades?"

"The refinement of the disguises. Villanueva told me all
about it, and I expect this week to become the most memorable of my life."

"Again why?"

He bent toward her and blinked rakishly.

"Can't you guess, fair lass? Carlos must have told you that I
am going to be your escort for the duration of the festivities,
and believe me, I am going to show you a carnival the like
you've never seen. You know that everything is permitted
these days; all carnal sins will be forgotten and forgiven, and
with you in my arms, I intend to commit enough sins to last
me till next carnival."

"*¡Válgame Dios!* What if Carlos heard you?" Isabel drew
back in mock fright.

He laughed while handing her into the gilded town coach of
the Villaquemadas. She decided to act as naturally and
pleasantly as possible under the circumstances, because she
was well aware that she was riding in the company of the most
brutal nobleman of Madrid, and only her hope of extracting
from him some information valuable to Olivares had kept her
from feigning an attack of migraine or acute melancholia—
the latest fashions in sickness.

As soon as the coach started rolling, he placed his hand on
her thigh. "Your dear husband wants me to believe that you
are entirely impervious to male charms, but, of course, you
and I know better, don't we?"

"I don't know what you mean," she said, trying to push his
hand away, but he caught hers and brought it to his lips.

"You know what I mean," he said, and a hot flash of fear
tore through her body. Did he know about Rafael?

"We all have spies at the palace, but mine are a lot better
informed than your husband's. Thus, I know that you have
not been able to resist Philip's courtship, and I also know
that—for the moment at least—you have fallen from royal
favor. So you should be happy about my proposition. My

dear," he bent to whisper into her ear. "I intend to shove my good hot prick into you, and I guarantee that you'll enjoy it."

Isabel stiffened, "Get away from me. I shall tell this to Carlos."

"You would not dare, and he wouldn't believe you. Besides, he would have you killed if he finds out about Philip. He can't make love to a woman and you know it, but he is insanely jealous, and he would personally avenge his honor upon a word from me."

"You are a vile coarse creature," she hissed. "I hate you, and if you dare touch me, I shall have you killed, for I am richer than you are, and I can buy the whole *germanía*, if I so please."

"*¡Y olé!* I like a high-spirited mare. I think I shall take you straight to my country estate and mount you there and to hell with the carnival."

She felt a strong impulse to open the door and jump out of the coach, but a mere look at the street made her shudder. From all sides there came screams and raucous laughter. *Pícaros* shouted obscene ditties, masked men were catching masked women and all but raping them in the open; courtiers on horseback were provoking the simple folk; whips cracked; stones, garbage, foul eggs, ashes, and pieces of coal formed a deathly blizzard; bags of powder exploded under the hoofs of mules and horses. Reason was dead. Unlimited passion had raised its ugly scepter.

"It's a pity I can't give in to my lust and ravish you on the spot," Villaquemada continued, "but I promised your husband that you would watch his equestrian feats, and so I'm afraid we will have to proceed to the Buen Retiro. That, however, doesn't mean you can't entertain me until we get there."

With these words he grabbed both her hands and held them in the iron grip of his left. At the same time he pulled off her mask with his right hand and held her neck so that she was unable to move, while his face came nearer and nearer and finally his mouth pressed on hers and his tongue pushed beyond her teeth. It was then that she bit him with all her strength, and he pulled away with an outcry of pain.

"Bitch! I'll get you for that. I vow and swear that I will have you, come what may."

She shrugged and put her mask back in place.

The square in front of the Buen Retiro was already packed

with spectators, but they had reserved seats at one of the windows, and Isabel was firmly guided by the Count who held onto her elbow so tightly that she could not have broken away without a struggle.

"I am not going to let you out of my sight," Villaquemada whispered in her ear when they took their seats at the window. "You are a most precious charge. Have you ever thought that if anything happened to Don Pedro Valderocas, you would be the richest woman of Spain?"

"I don't know what you mean. Why would anything happen to my brother?"

"Because he is too closely connected with the Count-Duke. You should tell him to take heed."

She did not answer, but somehow, immediately, Pasquito's remarks jumped to her mind. Villaquemada had extensive contacts in the underworld; could there be any intentions of harming Pedro? Had he heard of such a plan? Was he trying to warn her? Or was it something he merely invented in order to make her more susceptible to his crude advances? To show her that he was her friend?

For the moment, she did not have to pay any more attention to her escort, however, for two triumphal chariots representing war and peace entered the plaza, each drawn by twenty-four oxen and surrounded by a hundred masked horsemen—one group was led by the King and the other by the Count-Duke. A well-choreographed play of charges and counter-charges began, a fantastic, colorful spectacle illuminated by thousands and thousands of huge yellow wax candles. The chariots had been built according to the instructions of Cosme Loti and were now drawn together to serve as a stage for a play by Calderon.

The outdoor events were followed by a ball in the halls of the Retiro Palace. Isabel knew that somewhere in the crowd must be Pedro and Pepita, for they, too, had received invitations to the ball, but the confusion was so great that she was not able to find them. Moreover, Enrique de Villaquemada never left her side and took a wicked pleasure in whispering more and more shameless propositions as soon as they were alone for a minute.

Philip and Olivares spent the whole night entertaining their guest of honor, the Princess Carignano, and for the first time Isabel found herself clearly on the side of the disfavored. She longed to join the circle around Their Majesties, to exchange at least a quick glance with the Count-Duke, to intercept an encouraging smile from the Countess, but she knew that it would spoil all her efforts to gain the confidence of their enemies, and so she had to stay close to Villaquemada. They were waiting for Carlos when Don Francisco de Quevedo joined them to comment in his usual biting way upon the follies of the carnival season.

"Look at the fools! This has become the true face of Spain. Masquerades, mummeries, foolishness!"

"But Don Francisco," Villaquemada said, "this is the carnival season."

"We are so steeped in depravity, carnival has become our normal way of life. What a disgusting waste." He pointed to Olivares, "Look at him smiling broadly, the black devil, presiding over this dissipation. This is the antechamber of hell. For every wax candle burning here, a child starves to death, for every face mask, a peasant has to leave his home, for every bullfight, a battle is lost."

"There have been several attempts on his life," Villaquemada said, "but none have succeeded. It is because of his knowledge of the black arts. He knows how to conjure up the dark powers that protect him."

"If you feel that strongly about him, Don Francisco," Isabel said, "why don't you simply talk to him? If you have good suggestions, perhaps he might listen to you, especially if you tried to serve him."

"The naïveté of an innocent soul!" Quevedo laughed drily. "My dear Doña Isabel, charming hostess of many dinners I enjoyed, do you think that man is still normal? Capable of listening to anyone but his own inflated ego? Why doesn't your brother talk to him? I cannot imagine a Valderocas approving of so much waste. Wasn't Don Pedro supposed to be his financial advisor? Is this what he advises?"

At this point Carlos finally arrived. He appeared breathless and had taken off his mask.

"Isabel, come quickly. Pedro's coach was attacked on his way here."

"Carlos! What happened? Is he hurt?"

"I don't know. I suggest we leave at once for Valderocas House. Don Francisco, Enrique, please excuse us."

They were virtually pushing their way through the dense crowds, and it took them some time to get to their coach.

"What happened exactly?" Isabel kept asking. "How did you find out? Who told you?" But Carlos only pushed on and pulled her behind him. He handed her into the coach.

"Hurry," he told the driver. "Run over the people if you must, but for God's sake hurry!"

He took the seat across from her, he never sat close to her if he could avoid it.

"Alfonso, your brother's man came to inform the Count-Duke, who, in turn, told me. It seems that two masked men jumped into Pedro's coach and that there was a fight. Pedro was hurt, but we don't know how badly. His men, of course, tried to defend him, but the would-be assassins got away."

"Why do you think someone would want to kill Pedro?" Isabel asked.

"I don't know. Some personal vengeance perhaps. A point of honor. Someone jealous of his wealth. There could be a number of reasons."

She wanted to tell him what Villaquemada had said, that Pedro was too closely associated with the Count-Duke, but her inbred hesitation of talking too much made her decide to remain silent. It was too unlikely a coincidence that such an attempt on Pedro's life should have been made right after Enrique's warnings. He must have known something. And if he knew, Carlos must have known. Then why hadn't Carlos warned her? To keep her from worrying perhaps? If it was a political move, who could gain by it?

As soon as she saw Pepita's calm and determined face, Isabel knew that Pedro was not hurt too badly. She had been afraid of finding her sister-in-law in hysterics; instead Pepita appeared as collected as if they were paying her a normal social visit. She led them to the bedroom, where they found Pedro propped up against several pillows.

"Pedro, darling, what happened?" Isabel ran toward him and bent over him to kiss him.

"I wish I knew. Someone obviously hired two cutthroats to do away with me. I have yet to figure out why."

"But are you hurt?"

"Oh, just a scratch. I have a tough skin, a fast fist, and fortunately an agile wife who picked up a few good tricks from a gypsy she knew. Between the two of us, we succeeded in scaring off those wretches."

Pedro looked at his wife, and they exchanged a glance so full of love and trust and mutual admiration that Isabel felt like a stranger.

"Do you think it might have to do with your work for the Count-Duke?" Carlos asked.

"Perhaps. But whoever it was, he better not try again.

From now on I am going to be protected, and the next one who tries is going to get caught and be made to talk. Then we shall see who pays for my demise and why."

"This is the carnival season. It may have been a mistake or perhaps just a practical joke, for after all, you weren't really hurt," Carlos said.

"Those men meant business," Pedro said. "But you shouldn't worry about it. Thank you for coming so quickly."

"I will call on you tomorrow morning early, while the streets are empty," Isabel said. "Now you had better rest."

"I am glad to see it is less serious than I feared," Carlos said, "I was worried."

## 2.

Isabel went to see Pedro early the next morning, as she had promised, and since Pepita was busy with little Fernando, she had an opportunity to talk to him alone.

"Villaquemada knew something," she said right away. "He practically warned me yesterday that something might happen to you. He made it sound like a political thing."

"That proves everything I have figured out," Pedro said. "Listen carefully. This was not the first time someone tried to kill me. I haven't told Pepita, because she would worry herself sick. But we must find out who it is. It cannot concern our special work, because if anyone knew about that, they could denounce me to the Inquisition and that would finish us. No, it must be something personal. I have been thinking and thinking, and the only person who would greatly benefit by my death would be you. You would inherit all of the Valderocas wealth if anything happened to Pepita and me. And if you get it all, that means Carlos gets it. So, Isabel, I think your husband is trying to have me murdered. I don't have a shred of proof, though. What do we do?"

"Leave Spain!"

"Are you mad? I am expecting a delegation of our brethren from Oran. I must see this through."

"Tell Olivares."

"He's already beset with troubles. Besides, what could he do? Carlos is a Grandee."

"I could denounce Carlos to the Inquisition as a sodomist."

"You know we cannot risk getting involved with the Holy Office. What if they probed into our lives?"

"Well, Pedro, we cannot let them kill you!"

"Or you! Because you must realize that you are going to be the next victim. First me, then Uncle Jaime and Pepita, and my baby son, and finally you. Thus, Carlos will inherit everything to the last *maravedí*."

Little by little, the monstrosity of what they were thinking filled Isabel's mind with horror. Her eyes opened wide, and she stared at Pedro, and she knew she was frightened as she had never been frightened before. Until now, all her fears had been general fears based on dangers inherent in her everyday life: the danger of being tried for heresy, the danger of being discovered with Rafael, the danger of becoming pregnant by Philip, the danger of having Carlos discover her duplicity. All these dangers might possibly cause her death. But never, never had there been the thought that someone might deliberately plan to murder her family and herself.

"What do you want me to do?" she finally asked in a whisper.

"You must get in touch with Pasquito and tell him to warn us if he can find out anything."

"Yes. But, why don't you do that?"

"Because I am going to leave Madrid. I will bring Pepita and baby Fernando to Uncle Jaime, and I will stay with them at Toledo until it is time for me to pick up our brethren from Oran. You are safe, as long as nothing happens to me. But if I should die, I want you to take Pepita and leave for Amsterdam immediately. In the meantime, if you could find anything to compromise Carlos politically, tell Olivares. And now try to compose yourself and look normal."

Pedro still wore his neatly trimmed beard, but there were wrinkles around his downward-slanted eyes, and some gray hair had crept into his chestnut locks. As she looked at him, he crinkled his nose at her, and in spite of her fears, he brought a smile to her face.

# 3.

For the *mojiganga* at the Country Estate of Geronimo de Villanueva, Marquis of Villalba and Protonotario of Aragon, Carlos bought Isabel an expensive ivory mask with a head-gear of silver bells, a rarity that had once belonged to an East Indian temple dancer. It hid her head and all her hair so completely that she was well protected from recognition.

This *mojiganga* was indeed a masquerade to outmask all others. There were masks and costumes representing just about every animal known to man; there were ancient pagan gods and goddesses; there were persons of literature and fable; and there were even parodies of famous contemporaries.

But there was only one chiming East Indian temple dancer, and Philip, with his eye for rarities, had hardly spied her, when he gallantly offered her his arm to lead her to the dance floor.

"If you are who I think you are—and I would know your charming figure anywhere—I have a mind to make your husband's horns grow a little bigger," he murmured to her.

Now that she had found Rafael again, even though she saw him so seldom, she was determined not to give in to Philip's desire. He, however, pressed on, "I will ask the Protonotario to lead you to a place where I shall meet you, for I am again in love with you. You will come, won't you?"

She nodded assent without speaking, but when he accompanied her back to Carlos at the end of the dance, she excused herself, telling her husband that the Queen had asked for her. Then she rushed on through the crowd until she saw the Countess of Olivares, who wore her usual black dress and a simple black face mask. She curtsied and then spoke in a low urgent voice.

"Your Grace, I do not know whether you recognize me, but I am in trouble. His Majesty just gave me an assignation, and I am afraid my husband will kill me if he learns of it. I must get out of this mask before the Protonotario finds me. Please, what shall I do?"

"Doña Isabel, I have a good mind to give His Majesty a lesson. Listen . . ." the older woman pulled the young one aside and whispered a few words. A short while later, both ladies accompanied Her Majesty to an upstairs room where refreshments had been laid out for the Queen and her entourage.

After many years as chief Lady-in-Waiting, Inés de Zúñiga was an expert on court procedure. She knew that if the Queen could be brought to admire Isabel's mask, Isabel would have to offer it to her instantly as a gift. All that was necessary then was to persuade the Queen to wear the ivory mask and the silver headdress. She had imparted her plan to Isabel and between the two of them, they found it easy enough to convince Isabelle de Bourbon that she should try the exotic adornment.

"Imagine the fun of walking out there incognito," the Countess suggested.

"I shall do it," said the Queen.

They also exchanged their starched lace collars, and then both countesses watched their Queen walk down the marble staircase right into the arms of their host, the Protonotario of Aragon.

Isabel could not help a feeling of apprehension.

"Perhaps I should leave now?" she asked of Doña Inés.

"At least you should not be recognized anymore. Let me ask one of my women for her mask and cloak." They went back to the refreshment room, and the Countess helped Isabel adjust a plain brown silk mask and slip into a hooded cloak.

"I am sorry to hear that your brother had an unfortunate accident," Doña Inés said. "I want you to know that the Count and I value Don Pedro as a good friend. I was happy to discover tonight that you have courage and high moral standards. It is something not often found at this Court."

Isabel was glad that the mask hid her face, for she could feel herself blushing from the unearned compliment.

Carlos and Enrique were still standing where she had left them, staring at a door through which presumably the Queen had followed the Protonotario. Isabel passed behind them but they remained unaware of her. Too many people were swirling about. Who would pay attention to one of the Countess Olivares' attendants?

"You shouldn't have warned her," Carlos was saying. "It wasn't necessary."

"Right now you should be worried that she'll give you a royal heir," Enrique snickered, "for look who is leaving in the same direction."

"If she lays with the King right here, I swear I will kill her."

"The brother first."

"I wonder what incompetent idiots you hired."

"I am sorry. I hope tonight will be more successful."

Isabel's heart stood still. Whatever could that mean? Pedro was not here. What did they plan for tonight? How could she warn Pedro? Villaquemada was bending and whispering into Carlos's ear. She dared not approach them. Already if they turned around, she was lost. She retreated hastily back to the refreshment room. There she shed the brown mask and cloak and took up the gold-embroidered mask left by the Queen.

This time she walked straight toward her husband and made him a deep reverence. Both he and Enrique bowed to her and she forced herself to laugh out loud.

"I am glad you are not angry with me for having lost my beautiful mask."

"Isabel! You! What happened?"

"The Queen admired it so much, I was forced to give it to her, and she decided to wear it."

"Oh, oh . . . the Queen," Carlos said.

"You sound relieved," Isabel chided.

"Where were you all this time?" Villaquemada asked.

"Upstairs with the Ladies-in-Waiting."

"Did you see the black dragon?"

"Yes, briefly, why?"

"I wondered whether they had left. I cannot see the Count-Duke anywhere."

"I didn't know you to be such an admirer of the Count-Duke," Isabel said.

"Perhaps tonight I am," Villaquemada said with a short ugly laughter, and Isabel noticed that Carlos gave him an angry look.

Tonight, she thought, and with a sudden flash of intuition she knew what was planned. They hadn't meant Pedro at all. Tonight they would try to kill the Count-Duke! There it was again, that uncanny feeling of impending horror. Was that how a fortune-teller felt who knew a tragic event was about to happen? Or was it just her own feverish imagination, the lack of sleep during this past week, the lack of food, the constant fear, the nightmares of murder? She looked around the vast hall, desperately seeking an excuse to slip away, but all the costumes were incredibly elaborate and meant to completely disguise the wearers; she could not even pretend to recognize anyone. Doña Inés had been easy to spot, because she had never worn any color but black since the death of her daughter.

"What did I tell you?" Villaquemada now said to her, blinking with one eye. "Did you ever see such ingenuity? Calderon's plays aren't as well staged as this festivity."

"But where is Calderon? And Quevedo? And Velázquez? Let us guess who is who," Isabel suggested. However, the effort of appearing natural became too much, and she felt faint and dizzy and had to lean against Carlos.

"Madame, what is the matter?"

"I feel dizzy. Please accompany me upstairs."

He led her stiffly upstairs and to the *estrado* in the room reserved for Her Majesty's entourage. She sank down on a floor cushion and leaned back against the wall. Yet, the minute he left, she revived miraculously.

"Go fetch the Countess," she ordered a woman servant, "but do not be conspicuous about it. I have a message for her from Her Majesty."

It took a few minutes, and Doña Inés came.

"Doña Isabel, what now?"

Isabel rose swiftly.

"Your Grace," she drew Doña Inés most unceremoniously toward her and talked into her ear, "I must see His Excellency at once. It is very important. But he must not be seen coming in here."

"Why don't you tell me?"

Indeed why not? The two women looked at each other, and somehow Isabel understood that whatever Olivares did, his wife knew. Whatever he hoped to accomplish, his wife prayed for him to succeed. Whatever became of him, his wife would always remain at his side, loyal, loving, the crutch on which he could lean.

Isabel admired Olivares, she was fond of him, but this woman, his old homely wife loved him deeply. She loved him, as Isabel loved Rafael.

"Your Grace," Isabel said, "I may sound terribly foolish to you, and you may think I have taken leave of my senses because of what happened to my brother the other day, but I assure you I am completely aware of what I am saying, although I can furnish no proof for the veracity of my suspicions."

"Doña Isabel, my husband trusts you, I know. What is it?"

"I have a feeling, Doña Inés, I have a terrible feeling that someone is trying to assassinate His Excellency."

The Countess smiled. "My dear child, that is nothing new. We live with threats all the time. You have heard someone menacing him? Do not pay any attention to it. It happens every day."

"Doña Inés, I beseech you, do not ride home in your usual coach tonight. Please, send the coach alone and ride home with Their Majesties or with someone else."

"I will ride in my own coach or with Her Majesty, I always do. My husband will ride in his special coach where he can work."

"Yes, that is it. Don't let him ride in it tonight. Please Doña Inés?"

"But why? What did you hear?"

Isabel only stared at her.

"All right, child. Come with me." The Countess led her through a side door into another room, and then into another and still into another. "Wait here, I shall try to find my husband."

Isabel waited and worried, hoping that Carlos would not come to look for her, and above all that he had not noticed that she had spoken to the Countess.

Finally, after what seemed an eternity, the Count-Duke himself came in. He walked less jauntily than usual, perhaps his elaborate costume was heavy. He did not wear a mask.

Isabel curtsied to him, but he drew her up. "My wife tells me you are terribly worried. What is it?"

"Your Excellency, I think my husband and the Count of Villaquemada have hired assassins to kill you tonight. I know they tried to kill my brother. I have no proof, but I overheard some remarks, and I am sick with fear. Please Your Excellency, you may laugh about me tomorrow, but please, do not ride back to the Alcázar in your regular coach tonight."

Olivares looked at her sadly. "The bastard," he said, "after you saved him from public shame. The whoreson."

"Please, Your Excellency?"

"All right." He took both her hands in his and then pulled her near him and kissed her on the forehead. "Be careful yourself." He pointed to another door. "You can go down that way." She curtsied again and turned to go, when he caught her hand. "By the way, I hear it is a mean trick you played on His Majesty just now. Let's hope he takes it kindly." He grinned, and she left with a lighter heart.

The door led to the servants' stairs and at the bottom she found herself in a narrow hallway. As she walked toward the direction from where the most noise came, she passed a door behind which she could hear muffled sounds of laughter. There was a dark smooth voice and then a cascade of silvery giggles: Felipe de Habsburg and Isabelle de Bourbon did seem to enjoy each other's company.

Before entering the ballroom, Isabel slipped her mask back in place. It took some time to locate Carlos and Enrique, but finally she found them in a political conversation with Quevedo and the Duke of Medina-Celi.

"I keep telling him, it is not necessary to risk his neck," Medina-Celi was saying, "but he won't listen. Don Francisco, if you go on ranting like that, you'll end up minus your head."

"Two more days of this madness, and then it will be Ash Wednesday, and I'll mark my forehead and repent," Quevedo answered. "Too bad the real sinners never repent."

They went on talking, and after a while they were joined by two dwarfs, small creatures with big heads and sad eyes. One of them was Quevedo's pet dwarf, the other El Primo, so called because his ancestors were of noble background. El Primo was the favorite of the King and a good friend of Velázquez. Isabel was amazed to hear both of them discuss matters of state with great wisdom and insight.

The sound of clarions and an announcement by the King's heralds interrupted their talk. The *mojiganga* of the Protonotario of Aragon had found such favor in His Majesty's eyes, said the herald, that His Majesty had decided the whole affair would be repeated the coming Tuesday at the Alcázar.

"That will cost another two hundred thousand ducats," Quevedo grumbled, "bringing the whole expense to half a million. Half a million ducats for a masquerade! Oh God, when will you send us a responsible ruler?"

It was almost dawn when the feast ended, and a long line of coaches rolled back toward Madrid. Isabel could hardly keep her eyes open, and in the end, the even rattling of the carriage made her doze off. She sat up brusquely when some shots tore through the night.

"What's that?"

The coach stopped as all the other carriages came to a halt. Footmen and pages were sent running, and soon everyone was informed that assassins had shot several times through the Count-Duke's coach.

Was he hurt?

No, the coach had been empty.

# 4.

"It seems as if I am forever saying good-bye to you," Isabel complained as she lay in Rafael's arms. "Why, why, did I have to fall in love with you?"

He hugged her and kissed her eyes.

"Darling, don't make it so hard for yourself. We two have had so much more love and happiness than most other Spaniards. Look, you are the wife of a Grandee of Spain, and a woman of significance at Court; how many are there like you? I am about to become a full-fledged Inquisitor, at Toledo yet, the most important tribunal of Spain. And here we are lying together in the same bed. You are simply asking for the impossible."

"I am not. I am simply asking to be the wife of the man I love, to bear his children, to keep his home, and to share his bed every night. Millions of women enjoy this much. Why can't you be like other men?"

"For the same reason that you are not like other women."

They had been through the same argument before; like their love, it had been continuing for over five years. She thought she knew everything there was to know about him: above all his ambition, his boundless ambition, but there always remained a small mystery, the mystery she dared not think about. The incongruities she had observed over the years, the inconsistencies of some of his actions. Perhaps this was only her own conscience bothering her, the knowledge that she was keeping from him the very essence of her being, that he would never know her, because he would never know that she was a heretic. He, on the other hand, must think that he knew everything about her, especially since he had found out that she was spying for the Count-Duke.

She had never been able to figure out why Olivares would have told him so much, unless, of course, the Count-Duke

had no other way to save Carlos from being publicly exposed
as a sodomist. That proved that her work was important to
Olivares, far more important than she herself had thought.

Gaspar de Guzmán and his wife Inés de Zúñiga were the
only persons to know that Isabel had once saved the Count-
Duke's life, and this was certainly of enormous credit to her.
In addition, she had gained the special favor of the Queen,
because thanks to Isabel's mask, Her Majesty had spent a
most pleasurable tête-à-tête with her own husband. And the
King, far from being angry with Isabel, had sent her another
Tiziano drawing, with a note asking her to remain his friend.

Yes, Rafael was right, she had become a personage to be
reckoned with at Court. And no one knew that underneath it
all, she was really Sarita Benahavel, a Jewess from Seville.

But Rafael, her lover, her formidable, awe-inspiring,
fiercely ambitious lover, Rafael was being sent to Toledo as
Inquisitor of the Holy Office. Only a few steps remained, and
he would become the most powerful man in Spain. Fray
Antonio de Sotomayor was eighty-two years old; he could not
last forever, and then, with the grace of Olivares, Fray Rafael
Cortes might be suggested to take his place. Who was Isabel
Valderocas to stop him? What could she offer him in exchange for the tremendous power within his grasp? She would
have to give him up.

"Do you know that Carlos is after our wealth?" she asked
him, propping herself on one elbow and anxiously scanning
his face. "Do you know that he is trying to have Pedro
murdered, and then probably me, so he can inherit our
wealth?"

"I thought that was his plan all along," Rafael said.

"Rafael! So you would let me be killed and just stand by
and watch?"

"No. We have informers among all classes of the population, even among the lowest of ne'er-do-wells. I've kept an
eye on Carlos. He won't do a thing to you as long as Pedro is
alive."

"But couldn't he kill Pedro any day?"

"He'd have to hire someone. It would have to be above
suspicion. At any rate, your former slave Pasquito is also
watching out for your interests. I do not think you need to be
too worried."

"Pasquito! What do you know about him?"

"He brought us some of the charges against Carlos at the
time of the sodomy trials."

"Yes, I thought so. He hates him."

They looked at each other, and for a brief moment, Isabel thought that his eyes asked her for the final test of trust and perhaps her eyes asked him for the same, but generations of Benahavels called out to her to beware, and she averted her glance.

"Pasquito El Moro," Rafael said softly.

"That is just a name he gives himself to brag," Isabel said defensively.

"Of course, dear. Do not torment yourself so much."

"Nothing really torments me, except the fact that I lose you again. Rafael, what will my life be like without you? One day, I swear, I will leave Spain."

"To go where?"

"To Amsterdam!" She said it quickly and naturally, and only when she saw his pensive eyes on her did she realize what she had done. She had given herself away, just as a criminal gave himself away eventually if he was interrogated for too long. Amsterdam was heretic ground. To want to go to Amsterdam could mean only one thing. And Rafael of all men must know exactly what it meant.

He did not say anything. He stood up from the bed and started to dress himself.

"Where are you going? Rafael. Say something. You scare me."

He finished dressing. Then, when he was ready to leave, he sat down on the edge of the bed and took her in his arms.

"Isabel, I love you more than you will ever know. I love you so much I would give my life for you. It is precisely because I love you, that I have to do the work I am doing. I try to make Spain a better place to live in."

"Oh Rafael! When will I see you again?"

"When you come to Toledo. Can't you visit your Uncle Jaime once in a while? Pepita is living with him now; you could visit her."

"Do you want me to come to Toledo?"

"I know by now that I will never cease wanting you."

"I will try to talk Carlos into letting me go."

He kissed her again and left. It was always the same. It was always he who left first, striding away purposefully.

## 1.

There had not been a great *auto de fé* since the one at Madrid in the summer of 1632, and therefore many important persons of Castile were assembled at Toledo on this thirteenth of January 1638 to witness the public Act of Faith to take place in the former capital of Spain. It would be the first *auto de fé* organized by the new Inquisitor of Toledo, Fray Rafael Cortes, and it was to be celebrated in the Church of San Pedro Mártir. Twenty-two persons, mostly Judaizers, would appear to be sentenced in public.

Among the noble spectators were the Grandee of Spain, Count Carlos de Queras and his wife Isabel Valderocas Sanchez. They shared a pew with the Countess's uncle, Don Jaime Valderocas Dominguez, her brother Don Pedro Valderocas Sanchez, who had recently returned from an overseas voyage, his wife Doña Pepita, and the family of one Pablo Raíz, a distant relative of the Countess.

It had taken Isabel some effort to talk Carlos into undertaking this voyage, but she had been determined to make it. It was her first opportunity to come to Toledo since Rafael's departure. During the remainder of the previous year, Carlos had been rigorously opposed to her traveling alone, and she had actually welcomed the *auto de fé* as a good opportunity to force her husband to take the trip to Toledo.

"What kind of Old Christian are you, anyway," she had asked him. "It would be most insulting to my uncle if you did not accept his hospitality." Since the elderly Jaime was still a partner in the vast holdings of the family, Carlos had judged it useful to give in to his wife's demands.

So they had traveled the muddy road to Toledo in rainy winter weather. Carlos had caught a cold and was consequently in a ghastly humor, but Isabel could hardly control her elation at the prospect of seeing Rafael again.

Pedro could not understand her eagerness to attend another *auto*. Before they left for church, he talked to her alone.

"Good God, Isabel, how can you come expressly from Madrid to witness such a horror."

"I have my reasons."

"We are lucky there will not be anyone 'relaxed in person.'"

"How do you know?"

"I know all about this *auto*. We succeeded in buying off quite a number of Judaizers. The only ones who will be actually sentenced to lose wealth—and that is more than three hundred thousand ducats—are Juan Nuñez Saravia and his brother, but even they will not have to wear sanbenitos in public. Of course, we will all donate money to help them back on their feet."

"Pedro, that is wonderful. Do you realize what that means? You have made more progress than we hoped for. Judaizers, and they won't be burned! Why it is unheard of!"

"I wish I could be as optimistic as you are. But this time I hesitate to take any credit for what happened. We offered the money to Olivares, and he took it, but that in itself is strange. The Crown, or the Count-Duke for that matter, has never before consented to intervene in an *auto de fé*. They have helped our friends the Caietanos and other groups, yes, but that was always in the early stages of the process. I do not know how these men were saved—at the last minute, so to speak, from being burned alive. It is a miracle."

"Well, I prefer to think our work has finally paid off," Isabel maintained stubbornly.

Neither of them alluded to the fact that the Inquisitor in this case was a man they both knew.

But later in the day, when they sat silently in their pew and watched the solemn proceedings and listened to the oaths, they exchanged a brief glance when Rafael Cortes mounted the pulpit and began his great sermon against the evils threatening mankind in the guise of harmless eccentricities.

He thundered against superstitions and blasphemies, reciting the well-known lists of religious crimes that formed the backbone of most Edict of Faith and Anathema sermons, and he reaffirmed that all the heinous sinners before him had earned no less than eternal hellfire for their contumacious devilish behavior. He ranted on like that until Isabel was brought to the verge of disowning him in her heart, and Pedro's face had turned into a mask of contempt. Then, after exhausting his audience, he suddenly changed his tone of voice, as he started preaching about love and forgiveness. It seemed to Isabel that he had found her face in the multitude and that he was talking to her alone, when he said that the Holy Office, instead of saving the poor sinners' souls by releasing them from their criminal bodies, had decided this time to give the penitents a chance to redeem themselves by leading a good and exemplary life from now on.

In the end, it turned out that the practitioners of various modes of black magic, as well as a couple of sodomists, got sentences no worse than those of the Judaizers, an unprecedented occurrence.

"Most unsatisfying *auto* I have ever attended," Carlos muttered, when they returned to Uncle Jaime's house. "Not even a chance to see a Jew burn. Why did we come here? To hear a sermon about forgiveness? Ha! I told you I couldn't stand that man when I met him at Cardinal Monti's. Good Lord, if that's our new breed of Inquisitors, I swear it is the last *auto* I will ever attend." He was seized by a coughing spell, and Isabel insisted that he go to bed as soon as the room was prepared for him.

"I'm afraid Carlos is coming down with a bad ague," she told everyone and no one in particular. "It might be better if he slept alone until he is feeling better."

"That is no problem," Pepita said. "Pedro can share Uncle Jaime's room, and you can sleep with me. Thus, Carlos will have the guest room to himself."

Carlos only sneezed and coughed and was beyond putting up any resistance when they bedded him. Pepita motioned for Isabel to follow her into the kitchen.

"We must put something potent into this herb infusion," she whispered. "We have an underground meeting tonight, and if you want to come, we have to be sure Carlos does not wake up."

"Of course, I want to come. What do you have in mind?"

"Uncle Jaime keeps a foreign powder he sometimes uses in his hot chocolate at night, because he has a hard time falling asleep. If it is all right with you, we could physic Carlos's drink."

"Do be sure to use enough of it."

Isabel took the hot herb infusion to him on a tray and watched him drink it with wifely concern. It was the first time that she saw her husband in bed, and she was happy she did not have to share it with him. He continued to sneeze and cough and complain, but finally the potion did its work, and he fell asleep.

It had been years since Isabel had last attended a Marrano service, and she felt out of place in the underground meeting hall. But when plump and motherly Juana Sanchez de Raíz kissed her on both cheeks and gaunt Pablo Raíz shook her hand and the others smiled at her, a sensation of peace and well-being came over her. She was once again among her own people. This was where she belonged, among the secret Jews of Spain, among people like the Raízes, and the Caietanos, and the Perezes, and the cousins of the Portuguese who had figured in this afternoon's *auto de fé*. Here she belonged. Or perhaps at Amsterdam where she could openly worship the God of her fathers, but never, never among the Court society of His Most Catholic Majesty. And yet, her own people would not want her, would cast her out, if they knew that she was the mistress of the man they most hated: the new Inquisitor of Toledo.

They had no prayer books as they did in Amsterdam, where Menasseh ben Israel had printed a Hebrew-Spanish version for the ignorant newcomers from Spain. Here they had to rely on their memories.

The service was brief. The purpose of the meeting was not to worship but to talk. They wanted to assess the new inquisitor. Would there be a new rigorous policy of spying and persecution, or could they all rest easy for a while?

"Rest easy?" Pedro said: "Don't you see, he has been here only a few months, and already we've got an *auto*. That man, I know him personally, is the most ambitious, the most power-hungry man I have ever met. He will stop at nothing to get ahead, and if he did not burn anyone today, it may well be because the Count-Duke gave a warning to Sotomayor, and Sotomayor, in turn, warned Cortes. It is Sotomayor who is the moderate. You remember, perhaps, that the great *auto* of

Madrid took place before Sotomayor became Inquisitor
General. We must all work for the Count-Duke, as I have
done. It is our only hope. And let me tell you right now,
never, never try to bribe Fray Rafael Cortes. He does not
want money. He wants power."

Isabel said nothing. At Court she would have spoken up, at
Court she had a right to her opinion, at Court she could and
had talked back to people like Calderon de la Barca and
Francisco Quevedo. Here, in a meeting hall two stories under
her uncle's house, she kept her silence. Even though she had
never and would never betray them, she felt like a traitor.
And as Pedro spoke, her feeling of oneness with them was
gone. Again she was alone. She did not belong anywhere. She
fitted into no mold.

The musty air became oppressive. She wished their meeting were over and done with; why did they want to expose
themselves to the danger of discovery on a night when the
town was full of strangers and full of monks? She grew
impatient with their slow way of speech, their long argu-
ments, and she finally whispered to Pedro that she wanted to
leave. She said she feared Carlos might wake up and call for
her.

Back in the patio, she breathed deeply to fill her lungs with
fresh air. The January night was crisp, but not biting, and she
lingered in the empty courtyard. All of Jaime's servants were
Marranos, like their master, and they participated in the
meeting. Only the doorman had been left as a guard. When
Isabel asked him in a low voice whether everything was all
right, he told her he was not sure.

"What do you mean, not sure?"

"There is someone standing outside in the street, watching
our house."

"How do you know?"

Her question was understandable, for the wooden portal
leading to the street was closed and bolted. The doorman
beckoned her to follow him halfway up the stairs. There was a
small window, more a hole in the thick stone wall, through
which one could look down into the street without being seen.
In a niche in the wall opposite their house was a statue of
Mary, Mother of God; at its feet burned oil lamps and wax
candles, giving a faint glimmer of light in all directions. It was
in this dim light that Isabel could make out the figure of a
man, a tall man in riding breeches and a short cloak and a
hunting cap. She had seen him too often in this disguise to

have the least doubt: she was looking down on Fray Rafael Cortes, the new Inquisitor of Toledo.

To spite the Holy Ghost! she thought. He must be mad to come here. Whom was he waiting for?

To the guard she said, "It looks like he is waiting for someone. I wonder who he is. From where could I see the whole street?"

"Don Jaime's bedroom window goes out that way."

"Good. I will try to watch the man from there, while you go downstairs and tell Don Jaime about this." She could think of no better excuse to get rid of the doorman, and she hoped her plan would succeed. He nodded and left. She dashed upstairs and into her uncle's bedroom. She opened the window and leaned out as far as the iron grille permitted. Then she softly called his name.

"Francisco Molina!"

With a few steps he was under her window.

"I must see you," he said.

"You are out of your mind to come here! The doorman saw you. You must hurry away quickly."

"I must see you."

"Tomorrow then. But where?"

"Come to confession at the cathedral. At nine in the morning, after the second mass."

"I will be there. Leave now. Quickly!"

He blew her a kiss. The fool, what if anyone saw him? Her heart cried out as she saw him hurry up the street and around the corner of the Tránsito.

She closed her eyes for a minute. Dear God, help me to compose myself. Dear God, I do not know whether You exist, it is so hard to believe in You, but please, if You do exist, please help me now. I am trying to be good. I really am. I am trying to be helpful. I am trying to think that You sent me to this earth for a reason, and that You have a purpose to all You do. Please dear God, if only I knew Your purpose, I could try to serve You. But it is so hard. And I love him so much.

Jaime Valderocas came into the bedroom.

"What is it, Isabel?"

"I don't know, Uncle. There was a man watching the house. Or so it seemed. But then he turned to that statue of Mary and made a sign of the cross, and then he left. So maybe it was nothing after all. What do you think?"

Jaime looked out the window.

"*¡Válgame Dios!* I don't know. He left, just like that? Perhaps a spy. Perhaps just a lost soul praying to Mary."

"Don't you think it is dangerous to have a meeting tonight? Uncle Jaime, are you careful enough?"

"You are right. I will tell everyone to leave. But you must understand that they needed reassurance. After what happened today."

"Let us hope that was the last *auto de fé* at Toledo."

"I wish it were the last one in Spain."

"We are working for this goal, Uncle Jaime. By the way, tomorrow morning I am going to visit the cathedral and a few other churches."

"Why?"

"Well, Carlos is sick. And I think as the Countess de Queras, I should be seen in church. Don't you agree? There are other noble folk in town. I think I am expected to go to a morning mass. I think I had better."

"Do whatever you think you must. You have done very well, so far."

# 2.

It was shortly before nine when Isabel approached the imposing cathedral of Toledo. She entered through a gate leading to the cloisters and from there passed into the vast dome itself. The mass was just over. She dipped her fingers in holy water and crossed herself, she curtsied to the main altar, and she looked around for the confessionals. She walked all around the side altars, hesitating now and then, feeling awkward and ill at ease. It was too early for the Toledans; there were few people in the tremendous gothic basilica. She could not go on turning around and around, she would make herself conspicuous. Finally, she knelt in a pew in front of the main altar.

Putting her forehead upon her folded hands she prayed:

"Dear God, Adonai, God of Abraham, God of Isaac, and God of Jacob, dear God of my ancestors, we believe You to be everywhere, so You must be here too, although this is the abode of the one they call Your son. Please dear God, I am so confused, I do not know what to believe, and I wish You would help me. I do not know what is right. Is it right for me to love the man I love? I love him so much, dear God, how can that be wrong? But I love Pedro too, and Uncle Jaime, and I know our work is right. And I love Pasquito, and why should it be wrong for him to believe in Mohammed? And I love the Count-Duke, and I wish he would succeed in repealing the expulsion order. For can we not all live together in peace? Are we not all Your children? Is it not more important for us to do right by our fellowmen, than to despise them because they think differently about You? Can I not love and respect my fellowmen, whether they be Catholics or Protestants, or Moslems, or Marranos, or Jews? Please, dear God, I wish You would tell me what to do, as You told the prophets. . . ."

Here she felt a hand touching her shoulder, and looking up she saw Rafael in the simple habit of a Dominican friar.

"Come along," he said softly.

She followed him to a confessional.

As soon as they had taken their respective places, it was Rafael who confessed. He finally confessed that he could not live without her, that he needed her.

"Isabel, I must see you alone. Tell me where to meet you, and I will be there. You must help me, dearest, I cannot stand it anymore. You must help me, I need you. I need you."

She could hear from his voice that he was desperate. He truly needed her. But why? Why all of a sudden did he have to meet her? And why here, at Toledo, where he wielded the power of life or death over all of her friends and relatives?

"Why can you not come to Madrid?" she asked him. "How can I meet you here without being watched? What is it, tell me."

"I love you. I want to hold you once more. Just once."

"You know Toledo better than I do," she said. "Where can we meet?"

"I don't know. I cannot even get a room at an inn. It is such a small town, my face is known. Besides we would not find a room if we tried. Everything is taken because of the *auto*."

His hands reached up to the carved wooden grille separating them, and Isabel reached up until their fingertips met.

"Please, Isabel, think of something."

A small current seemed to leap from his fingertips to hers. She could almost feel his desperate need for love and support.

"Come during the siesta," she whispered. "Everyone will be sleeping then, and I will let you in."

"But your house is full of guests."

"Never mind."

"But where do we go from there?"

"Let that be my worry."

She fretted the rest of the morning, hovering now over Carlos, now over Uncle Jaime, helping to prepare dinner so that they could eat on time, telling everyone they should get a good rest after the excitement of the previous day. By three o'clock they were finally all in their rooms. Pepita had fallen asleep, when little Fernando started to cry. Instantly she was wide awake and found Isabel dressed and ready to go out.

She picked up her son first, then asked, "Where are you going?"

Isabel put a finger to her lips.

"What are you up to now?" Pepita whispered.

"Hush! Remember the many times I have been up to something? You know how complicated my life has become, so do not ask any questions. Just see to it that no one notices my absence."

Pepita put the baby down on her own bed and rushed up to Isabel, flinging both arms around her.

"Be careful that no one sees you. I will swear you are asleep in my room."

Isabel kissed her and left.

Again the patio was empty. She opened the door to the basement, before pulling the bolt from the main entrance gate. It was only a few yards from one door to the other, and it took no more than three seconds for Rafael and her to disappear in the dark of Don Jaime's wine cellar. Isabel had prepared an oil lamp, and now she guided Rafael quickly along the racks with jugs and wine skins to the great vat, and through it into the first subterranean hallway. He followed her silently.

They came to a crossroads where a straight air shaft brought in some daylight.

"This is as far as I dare go," Isabel whispered. She shook with fear. She had taken him into the ancient underground of Toledo. She was betraying the secret of the Marranos.

He took the oil lamp from her and placed it on the ground. Then his arms went around her, and for a long time neither of them spoke, while their tongues met, and their bodies strained toward each other in the same untameable desire they had never been able to conquer.

"I must have you now, here, or I will lose my mind," Rafael said in her ear. "Come, my beloved."

They made love, and it was more passionate and complete than it had ever been.

Afterward, she waited for him to speak, to admit now that they were meant for each other, that nothing could ever keep them apart. She was ready with a dozen practical plans of how to get out of Spain, but he buried his face on her breasts and sobbed.

"If only I could talk to you," he said, "if only I could talk to someone. . . . It is hell, Isabel, it is hell this life. But I have to go through with it." He stood up.

"But why? Why?"

"Because it is a necessary step toward my goal."

"Your goal. Your goal! You never think of anything else except when we make love. Can't you see that we cannot live without each other? Why don't you give in and admit that you are human? You can burn me for the blasphemy, but I tell you, you have a rotten life, and it is immoral work that you do. Sending people to their deaths!"

"I have not sent anyone to death," he said quietly. "I thought you understood that."

He buttoned his breeches and smoothed his coat.

When he helped her up, she looked at the damp muddy walls around her, the dim oil lamp, and a wave of desperation and shame engulfed her. Was this her life? Was this the happiest moment of her life? To meet the Inquisitor of Toledo in a dirty underground hole?

Yes, she wanted him. Yes, she thought of him day and night. Yes, she dreamed of him when she lay in her bed. Yes, yes, she worshiped him beyond rationality. Yes, she would die for him. . . . But where did it lead? To a quick embrace whenever he had a chance? No! No! She could not go on like this. Suddenly, she felt old. Old and beyond passion. Too old to continue such a reckless way of life.

"Rafael, I have known you for almost six years now. And we have loved each other for all that time. That is why I ask you now, for the last time, to make a choice. We can go abroad; we can go to Jamaica, or to Brazil, or to France, or to the Netherlands, or even to Turkey, where no one could reach us. We can go to any place on earth, and we can build a new life together. Abandon your ambition. Forget the Church and your goal. You say yourself that you cannot bear it. You say yourself that it is hell. Well, my life is hell, too. I live with a husband who surely intends to kill me one day, and my standing at Court depends upon the quality of my espionage for the Count-Duke. I have had enough, Rafael, and so have you. We must escape. We are not capable of living without one another. So why can we not go?"

He had taken her hands; he had listened quietly. Now he encircled her waist with his arms and held her tenderly.

"You are a splendid woman, Isabel, and I do love you, and I do understand you, and I agree with you. But you see, if I left Spain, I would be nothing. I would no longer be the man you love. I have dedicated my whole life to one goal, and if I give it up, I will not be myself anymore."

"And your goal has not changed?"

"It never will."

She detested saying it, but she had to hear him confirm it once more.

"You still want to become Inquisitor General of Spain?"

"Yes."

You are mad, she thought, Don Rafael Cortes, you are truly mad. But she did not say it, she did not let out the scream that welled up in her throat; she wanted to summon enough strength to match his own. She disengaged herself from his hold, and when she thought she could be sure of her voice, she spoke.

"I will guide you upstairs. I trust you will forget that you have ever set foot in this underground passage. If someone meets us on our way out, my uncle, or the doorman, or a servant, I will say that you were a messenger from the Count-Duke. You must disappear as quickly as possible."

"When will I see you again?"

"Never." Her voice almost broke, but she forced herself to repeat the painful word: "Never! I will not come back to Toledo for as long as I know you are here."

When he did not answer, she turned around, picked up the oil lamp and led the way upstairs.

He slipped away from the house as easily as he had come, and she went back up to Pepita's room to change her clothes. Pepita immediately recognized what had caused the soiled condition of her dress.

"So that is what it was," she said, sounding relieved. "You took a peek at the treasure chamber. And I was afraid you had gone to meet a spy of the Count-Duke's."

"I wanted to be sure I still knew my way around," Isabel said, but she felt too weak and unhappy to talk and went to bed, saying she feared she had caught her husband's illness.

# 3.

Upon her return to Madrid, Isabel threw herself into a whirl of social events. The best excuse she could find for escaping the gloominess of her husband's palace was the reinstatement of the nunnery of San Plácido. The house where the nuns went into residence on Calle de Madera adjoined the town house of Geronimo de Villanueva, the Protonotario of Aragon, with whom Enrique de Villaquemada had struck up a friendship of sorts. So while Carlos and Enrique were visiting the Protonotario, trying to wheedle out of him the latest gossip about the Count-Duke—and Villanueva feeding them the wrong information, since he was loyal to Olivares—Isabel sat in the drawing room of the young nuns and sipped refreshments with the other ladies of Madrid's society. Following her visits there, she often drove to the Alcázar to chat with the Queen, because Isabelle de Bourbon wanted to hear a detailed description of how the nuns were acting, what they talked about, and whether they seemed normal or likely to become demonically possessed again.

"Frankly, to me they seem like charming well-bred young ladies, Your Majesty, and we must not forget that these nuns are not the same ones who were dispersed ten years ago."

"What about the Abbess?"

"I would think her to be of the highest moral character. She is motherly with her young charges, yet she inspires respect. She looks intelligent."

The Queen made a moue. She liked tales of secret debaucheries as long as they did not involve her own husband, and she hated Villanueva almost as much as she hated Olivares. She had not forgotten the unsavory role he had played in the scandal that had led to the original dispersion of the nuns, and somehow she gave the impression that she would welcome a similar story.

"Well," she said, "I am sure Villanueva has a good reason for having the nunnery reinstated, in a house that belongs to him. I only hope I find out what it is." She shrugged and took up a sheaf of papers from her harpsichord. "In the meantime," she said, "we haven't had a private theatrical in a long time. Just the other day, Calderon let me have copies of a delightful play of his. It is about a man who murders his wife because he thinks she has given herself to the King. But she was actually innocent, just as in the play about the surgeon and his honor. There is that wonderful scene when she slowly bleeds to death. It is very romantic. In the end, the man is forgiven and marries someone else. I would like to direct the play myself, and His Majesty could play the King." Here she interrupted herself to giggle, "And you, Doña Isabel, could play the lady who is slain in passion. What do you think? Shall we read through it? I will read the part of the King, until His Majesty has time to join us." She handed Isabel a copy. Isabel stretched out her hand to receive it, when suddenly the room began to spin around her, and she heard several cries of "What is it?" before fainting away.

The smelling salts of the Countess of Monterrey brought her back to her senses and, with the facility of lying she had acquired when she first came to Madrid, she told them that she had fainted once before, because she was suffering from the greensickness.

She was not sure whether the ladies believed her, but Her Majesty called for a sedan chair, and she was carried to her coach. She found the street odors more repulsive than usual, but with a supreme effort, she made it safely to her own apartment before starting to vomit. Then she retched and retched until she was completely exhausted and fell on her bed.

At first she thought that Carlos had tried to poison her, because she had never in her life felt so nauseated. But thinking back, she remembered how often she had been tired since coming back from Toledo, and she remembered certain violent headaches. When she started to count, she realized the true reason for her sickness. After her departure from Toledo she had banned all thoughts concerning Rafael from her mind so deliberately that she had almost succeeded in eliminating their ecstatic moment from her memory. Now it came back to her with the force of a lightning bolt, and she knew without doubt that she was with child.

Her first concern was to reassure her maids who cluttered helplessly about her that her vomiting was a consequence of the atrocious sweetmeats she had been served at the palace.

But what next? Calderon's play was no mere playwright's exaggeration. Wronged husbands were slaying their wives every day. Society approved of these crimes, encouraged them, glorified them, and if Villaquemada's assessment of Carlos was correct, he would kill her without mercy. How long would she be able to hide her condition? Not at all, if she continued vomiting like this. She must leave as soon as possible. She would go to Seville, back to her old home. Pasquito's parents would take care of her, and from there she would board a ship for Amsterdam. It was the only sensible thing to do.

She knew she would not be able to hide her condition from Maria, and there was no reason to do so. On the contrary, the girl would be of great help in preparing for their flight. She therefore lost no time in telling her that she was pregnant by an old friend whom she had met again at Toledo, and she asked Maria to tell Carlos that she was too sick to come down to dinner.

"Oh no, Doña Isabel, you must behave as if nothing is amiss. Especially today, when the Count of Villaquemada will come for dinner." Maria was more afraid of the notorious knave than of Carlos. "You must find an excuse to undertake a trip to Toledo as soon as possible, and your husband will be less likely to refuse when there is company."

"Yes, I suppose you are right. In the meantime, I want you to plan what we need to take along." She sat up in her bed but was forced to lie down again. "Maria, I don't even know how I can go downstairs without fainting again."

"You need some salt," Maria said. "That is what the girls in Jaén used to do when they got pregnant. Chew salted meat. I will get some for you and some smelling salts, too. Perhaps you could tell them that you ate too many clay pellets."

"No, Carlos knows I abhor eating clay. He would never believe that."

Maria left and came back with dried pieces of salted beef, and she instructed Isabel to chew them slowly and to avoid rapid movements. She also told her to keep a perfumed handkerchief between her breasts and to carry a little flask of smelling salts in her pocket.

"And remember, if your husband finds out about this, you'll be dead," Maria whispered. "That should scare you enough to keep you from fainting."

Isabel gave her a tired look and shrugged. She had lived for too long now with the knowledge that Carlos might want to murder her. She had lived for too long with the knowledge that the Holy Office might want to burn her. She had lived for too long without any semblance of security that one more danger no longer made much of a difference. She would outlive them all, she thought dully, and she would go to Amsterdam and see Duarte Perez again, and José Caietano, and perhaps she would even meet Uriel Acosta, that mysterious outcast from Christianity and Judaism. She felt like an outcast herself, perhaps she would be happier living among outcasts.

Punctually at eleven o'clock she entered the formal dining room where she was met by her husband, Enrique de Villaquemada, and a young woman called Esperanza whom Enrique presented as a cousin of his.

"Your Grace, I am happy to see you are feeling better, after your misfortune in Her Majesty's drawing room," Villaquemada drawled with exaggerated concern.

Isabel's eyebrows shot up. "I was terribly tired," she said, "but I have rested and feel fine."

"On the contrary, you look pale," Carlos said. "And it was rather embarrassing for me to be told by others that you have the greensickness."

"Well, I have not had much fresh air recently," Isabel countered. "I suppose a little trip to the country would do me good."

"I would be delighted to receive you on my estate," Enrique offered immediately. "Esperanza is living there with me now, and we would certainly do our best to entertain you, would we not, Esperanza?"

Esperanza smiled, and Isabel thought there was a vulgar look about her. Her clothes were fashionable, she wore the wide blonde wig now coming *en vogue,* and her face was painted correctly. There was nothing obviously wrong with her. It was that somehow she reminded Isabel of the creatures she had seen at Juliana's. A lack of quality.

"Thank you so much. I think I would prefer to go south. We are in the middle of March, and it is spring in Andalusia. I would like to go there."

"Right now, you are not going anywhere," Carlos said, and Isabel shut her lips tightly to keep from letting a scornful reply escape.

During the dinner, she ate little and said less. Villaquemada explained that his cousin would like to enter the nunnery of San Plácido.

"But why San Plácido?" Isabel asked, not quite able to picture the vigorous flashy Esperanza among the dainty nuns of Villanueva's convent.

"It is an ingenious plan," Carlos said, "and you are going to play a part in it. That is why you cannot possibly leave Madrid at this time."

After dinner, they went to the library, where Carlos again closed the outer door, the curtain, and the inner door, as he had done on their wedding night.

"Now," he said, turning around, "Enrique has found a fool-proof plan to rid us of our hated dictator and his abject creature the Protonotario of Aragon with one stroke. You tell the ladies, Enrique."

"First," Villaquemada said, "I want to recapitulate a few facts our ladies may not know. Ten years ago, we had several black magic and sorcery scandals involving the Protonotario. Olivares, at that time, used all his influence to keep Villanueva from being persecuted by the Inquisition. A short while later, and not everyone knows this, Olivares himself was taken in by a common criminal, one Gerónimo de Liébana. That man had been condemned to the galleys when he managed to convince the Count-Duke that he was a first-rate sorcerer and had buried on the beach of Málaga a small box containing magic objects that would give another nobleman, the Marquis de Valenzuela, demonical powers over the Count-Duke. The stupidity of that story cries to high heaven, but Olivares fell right into the trap. He is so superstitious, that man, so easily duped, he even convinced the King that they should send a committee to the beach of Málaga to dig up that nonexistent box! You can well imagine that the Inquisition did not wait long to put its nose into the affair, and Liébana was condemned as a sorcerer to four hundred lashes and a prison term for life. For all we know, he still rots in the dungeon of Córdoba. That was the second time Olivares came into conflict with the Holy Office. In addition, we all know that he has interfered in that Caietano affair, and I have the feeling that the recent fiasco at Toledo, where not a single Jew was burned, is also of his doing. In short, all we need is another well-documented scandal involving sorcery or sacrilege, and Olivares will be finished."

"And where do I come in?" Isabel asked, apprehension showing in her voice.

"Oh, do not worry, Doña Isabel," Villaquemada said with a lewd grin. "Nothing will happen to your precious person. All you will have to do is spread gossip. But that comes last. No, the idea is to get the nuns of San Plácido sufficiently possessed to lure the Count-Duke into believing that if he and his wife have intercourse at the convent, the Countess will conceive and present him with an heir."

Despite her predicament, despite her fears, despite her revulsion of remaining in the same room with them, Isabel could not help a short explosive laugh.

"That is the most preposterous thing I have ever heard! Why, the Count-Duke is in his fifties, and Doña Inés cannot be much younger. They would laugh hysterically at such a proposition."

Carlos nodded, "I think she is right, Enrique."

"Ha! But they do not have to do it. It will be enough if one of the nuns spreads that rumor. Can you imagine how it will fly all over the country? The Count-Duke mounting his wife surrounded by black candles and chanting nuns! It will be the story of the century."

Catching the smirk on Esperanza's face, Isabel understood their plot.

"And I suppose you will be the nun peddling the saucy details," she said to the girl. She was sure now, that far from being Villaquemada's cousin, she was a wench he had picked up somewhere and was grooming and paying for the job.

"I prefer your other plan," Carlos said, "the one involving Villanueva and the King."

"That one is more difficult though. First of all, the young nun Villanueva mentioned must really be as beautiful as he says. Second, she must be made willing to listen to Philip's advances, provided we can get Philip interested in her in the first place. Then, of course, if Villanueva helps Philip seduce a nun within the confines of the convent, it would work for our purpose only if the Holy Office can be convinced that the King was acting under the demonical influence of Olivares and Villanueva. It is a risky business, because it involves His Majesty, but at any rate, it would make a splendid rumor, just like the Olivares holy coitus."

They tossed the two ideas back and forth, adding so many promiscuous details that Isabel thought it would be grotesque if anyone would ever seriously believe such a rumor. She would not even take the trouble of warning the Olivares couple about it. Still, she wondered why they trusted her so much. Either they took her to be a fool, or they were sure they could silence her if they ever caught her betraying their plans.

At the end of the evening, after hours of discussion, they made her sign a statement saying that she testified to the high moral standards of Esperanza Flores Fuente, cousin of the Count of Villaquemada.

## 4.

Every passing day brought greater fear. She complained about the climate, but Carlos remained adamant, and she thought she would finally have to flee without taking anything along, because she would have no reason to prepare her bags and baskets.

It was a month after the revelation of Villaquemada's plans that Pedro came to visit her. He had to spend a few days at Madrid to confer with the Count-Duke, and he brought her the latest news concerning the efforts of his Marrano group. "We are still pressing for permission to build a synagogue at Madrid," he whispered into her ear. "If we can only get that much granted, the rest will come easily."

Her mind was elsewhere.

"How are things at Toledo?" she asked in a normal tone, indicating she meant everyday life and not their secret work.

"Fine, just fine. Pepita is with child. I hope it is a girl this time."

To his surprise, she burst into tears and threw herself into his arms.

"Pedro, Pedro . . ."

"Isabel, my God, what is it?"

"I am with child myself. . . ."

He held her at arm's length, staring into her face, unbelieving, disgusted. "Carlos?" he asked.

"Of course not."

"Who then?"

"A man I love."

As soon as she had said that, a sigh of relief went through his body, and he pulled her back into his arms.

"Darling, why didn't you let us know? We'll have to get you out of here quickly. I will take you with me to Toledo."

"You don't mind?" she sobbed. "You are not going to abandon me?"

"Of course not. You know I am your best friend. Do you want to keep the child? If not, I am sure we can arrange for you to lose it."

"I want to keep it."

"Is it the King's?"

She only shook her head.

"Well," he said, "what do you want to do?"

"I want to go abroad. Let me go to Amsterdam."

"All right. I will leave for Toledo at the end of the week. Can you be ready by then?"

"Yes. Any time."

"Friday then. At siesta time. Around three in the afternoon."

After that, she felt much better, almost cheerful. What until now had been a burden, a dread, suddenly became the blessing it was meant to be. She would have a child. She would have Rafael's child. She carried part of him deep within her, a part no one could ever take away. Even if she had lost him forever, she would finally have a human being to love, a human being who would love her without qualification.

# 5.

Friday she dismissed all her maids, except Maria, giving them the whole day off, because she wanted a few hours to rest and pack a few essentials for the trip before Pedro came to pick her up. Carlos had left the house early, leaving a message that he would not be back until dinner time, that meant eleven at night. He, too, had given leave to most of his servants.

At two o'clock she was ready and dressed and she told

Maria to wait for Pedro at the street corner and to tell him not even to come into the house. She gave Maria the one bag she had packed. Thus, she would be able to leave with empty hands, as if she were going out for a visit. She knew that the doorman reported every one of her moves to Carlos.

Her impending departure made her so happy that she was humming to herself while going for a last time through all her rooms. Everything looked the same as usual, none of the servants had realized that she was going to leave. As she glanced over her bedroom *estrado,* her semiprecious stones carelessly arranged in crystal bowls, her perfume flasks, her jewelry boxes, her fans and Chinese vases, she reflected how easily she could leave all this. It meant nothing to her.

Then her eyes fell upon the statue Rafael had given her. Slowly she ascended the one step onto the *estrado* and bent to pick up the bronze sculpture of the man and the woman. She held it against her chest and stopped her humming, for she realized that this was the one object she did not want to live without. She would have to wrap it up, make a parcel to take with her. She turned around. . . .

. . . Then she saw him! He stood in the doorway and drew his sword. She wanted to scream, but she could not. It seemed to her that her blood had stopped flowing, that her heart had stopped beating. Every hair on her body was raised in horror. . . . Carlos de Queras had come to kill her.

They stood still, both of them, not moving a muscle, just staring at each other. There was murderous hatred in his eyes, the righteous hatred of a Spaniard whose wife had been unfaithful. Whatever else he might have planned with Villa-quemada, this was his own doing. He had finally come to kill her.

But perhaps, perhaps she could still placate him. She opened her mouth, her tongue was dry, her throat would not obey, she did not know how to speak.

He stood perfectly still, the sword in his hand.

Finally, she found a semblance of voice, "Carlos, what are you doing?"

"What I should have done when I first heard that you lay with the King."

So that was it. He had learned about Philip. Probably from Villaquemada. That was much better than the truth. She must not show her fear. She must drag this on. She must make him talk, until someone came. Until Pedro came.

"How do you know it is true?" she asked.

"I do not wish to discuss that. If it had been anyone but Philip, the man would be dead by now. Since I cannot kill the King, I have to kill you. Only your blood can wash my honor. You know that as well as I do."

"But who says anything happened?"

"Your pregnancy does. I will be damned if I bring up a royal bastard."

He took a step nearer, the unsheathed sword in his right hand.

"But Carlos, how else are you going to have an heir? Why, I think you should thank me."

"That you made me the laughingstock of Madrid?"

"No! But that I saved your life when the Inquisition was investigating you. You didn't know that, did you? You don't know that you would have figured in the private *auto* with the other sodomists if it had not been for my testimony!"

He laughed sarcastically. "What a vivid imagination, Madame! It was my friend Enrique who saved me, thanks to his influence. You know that he is a Familiar of the Inquisition."

"And how do you know I am with child? Is that also Villaquemada who told you?"

"No, for that you have yourself to thank. You told your brother. Do you not know that anything spoken in your sitting room can be heard in the hall outside? It was planned that way."

He took another step nearer, and she clutched the statue in her trembling hands. She was still on the *estrado,* a step higher than he, but she was cornered. She would never be able to get past him and to the door.

"You will not get away with this," she said. "You can kill me now, but Pedro will come any minute, and he will avenge me."

"Pedro is dead," he said. "He was killed by assassins two days ago."

She looked at him but did not see him. He repeated his words, "Pedro is dead."

"No!" She gave a sudden blood-curdling scream. A scream so high, so piercing, so unnatural, that for an instant Carlos was taken off guard. At the same time, she lunged forward, and without knowing how, she lifted her hands with the bronze statue and smashed it down on Carlos's skull.

He fell immediately and without a sound. She stared at

him, her hands hanging loosely at her sides, her mouth slightly open, her mind beyond comprehension. A puddle of blood formed under his head, and he did not move.

Mechanically, she walked past him, but when she reached the door, she was confronted by three young men, and the mere prospect of having her way barred again was too much. She fainted, falling against the nearest one.

When she opened her eyes she was lying on the floor; their faces were huge and distorted. Then she heard a familiar voice.

"Doña Isabel, it's me, Pasquito."

Pasquito?

Yes, it was he. Pasquito El Moro, almost unrecognizable because of a thin black beard covering most of his face. It took Isabel a few moments to realize where she was, and what had happened.

"What are you doing here?" she asked. She stretched out her hand, and he helped her to her feet.

"I am sorry we came late. Only today Don Pedro told me about you."

"Pedro? Pedro? He is alive?"

"He was alive when we left him. Not very much alive, but alive."

"Where is he?"

"A woman called Juliana is taking care of him."

"Juliana? Not the one of Casa Celestina?"

"The same. She has patched up many of us in her time."

"But why? I don't understand. If he is hurt, why isn't he at the hospital? The best doctors should take care of him. Why is he not at Valderocas House?"

Pasquito shook his head. "Look, there is no time now for explanations. We must get out of here. You come with me, and my friends will take care of him." With a movement of his head he pointed to Carlos who still lay exactly as he had fallen, his sword by his side.

"Be sure to clean up the blood," he told them.

"But how will they get him out of here?"

"Don't worry, they are experts."

The staircase was empty, not surprisingly at this time of day. But where was the doorman?

"The doorman? He was one of Villaquemada's henchmen. I have taken pleasure in dispatching him to the devil," Pasquito said.

Maria was waiting for them in a hackney. Pasquito and his friends had met her at the street corner and told her to call a coach for hire.

The hackney took them to a narrow alley on the outskirts of town and stopped before a one-story house. Pasquito asked the driver to wait outside with Maria.

They entered a dark hallway smelling of urine and spoiled food. Isabel, however, was still in such a state of shock that her senses remained immune. Pasquito knocked at a door and a husky alto voice answered, "Come in."

The room was as dark as the hallway, for there was but one dirt-encrusted window, but finally Isabel could distinguish a bed, a table, two chairs, and a washstand of sorts. A man was lying on the bed, and a woman held his hand.

"How is he?" Pasquito asked.

"Better, I think."

Isabel came nearer and stared at the woman. By God, it was her! The fox-faced Juliana. She would never forget that face for as long as she lived. But Juliana had seen too many girls to remember one face seen briefly many years ago. She gave no sign of recognizing Isabel.

Then Isabel bent over the man. Pedro! She softly kissed his forehead. He stirred.

"Pasquito, now tell me what this is all about."

"Well, about three days ago, Villaquemada paid a huge sum to a villain called El Cuchillo, with a promise of more if he promptly removed Pedro Valderocas from this earth. When I heard of this, I went to warn Pedro, and I told him that he was as good as dead unless he disappeared quickly. He said he could not go; he had to take his chances. So all I could do was offer my services to El Cuchillo, saying I had a personal account to settle with Valderocas. They know, of course, that I used to be your slave, so I seemed a natural choice for the part. My plan was to stab El Cuchillo in such a way that it would appear that Pedro had done it. Unfortunately, I was not experienced enough for one like him, because although I stabbed him first, he managed to get his knife well into Pedro. My two friends, the ones you have seen, finished off El Cuchillo, and we dragged Pedro in here."

"But why not home? Why not to a doctor?"

"It would have meant the police on our backs and given Villaquemada or Queras a chance to finish him off. Besides, Juliana knows more about knife wounds than any doctor in Madrid."

"But this El Cuchillo, didn't he have friends? Won't this slaughter go on?"

"Him, friends?" Juliana laughed. "He was the most brutal baggage alive. He terrorized all of us."

"And Pedro? Will he be all right?"

"We hope so," Pasquito said. "I had intended to come and tell you that the rumor of Pedro's death was not true, but I didn't know how to go about it. We wanted to be sure first that Villaquemada thought he had succeeded. There seemed to be no hurry. I did not think that you were in any immediate danger. Then this morning, when Pedro woke up for the first time, he told me that he was supposed to fetch you on Friday afternoon, and that he thought it was a matter of life or death. Well, it's Friday today. That started me running. But I see, you can take care of yourself. I am proud of you."

What could she say to a seventeen-year-old member of the criminal brotherhood who expressed his pride in a good kill?

"Thank you, Pasquito."

From the bed came a barely audible moan. Instantly, Isabel leaned over Pedro.

"Darling, I am here. You will be all right. Pedro . . ."

"Isabel? Is that you?"

"Yes. Oh darling. You must have a doctor."

He shook his head, almost imperceptibly, "Don't tell Pepita."

Isabel turned to Juliana. "His wife. She is expecting a baby. He doesn't want her to worry. But she must have heard the rumors."

"Where is she?"

"At Toledo."

"Mmm. I doubt the rumor travels that fast. Seems to me if he could get rid of that enemy of his, Villaquemada, he could be brought back to his house and taken care of there."

"I don't think Villaquemada will be any more trouble," Isabel said. "I think his real enemy was one Carlos de Queras."

"The sodomist?" Juliana said. "It's time somebody disposed of him."

Isabel and Pasquito looked at each other.

"I think that has been done," Pasquito said.

"¡Y olé!" Juliana said. "Well, if you two are staying here now, I'll be leaving. I can come tomorrow and change the bandage. Unless you want to do it yourself. I've been neglecting my business these past two days."

"Don't worry, I think you'll be paid handsomely," Pasquito assured her.

She left without any greeting.

"Does she know who we are?" Isabel whispered.

"She knows who Pedro is. She knew him, anyway. She knows most of the men of Madrid. But she doesn't know who you are. She thinks you are his paramour."

"It will take some time for Pedro to recover. In the meanwhile, Pepita will worry herself sick. We must get word to her."

"You are right. We will do something. But you must stay here and watch Pedro. If he suffers too much, give him a spoonful of that liquid on the table, a drop at a time so he won't choke. I will go out and bring Maria back to Valderocas House. She can wait for you there. Then I'll go and take care of Villaquemada. It will make an interesting double murder story, and we will have rid Madrid of three of her most undesirable characters."

"Three?"

"Well, El Cuchillo, Queras, and Villaquemada."

"Do you kill easily?"

"Only when it's necessary."

She looked at him. Her eyes were now used to the dim light, and she opened her arms to him, "Pasquito."

He walked into her arms like a brother, and they hugged each other.

"I did not want this life for you, Pasquito. I will go to Amsterdam. Come with me."

"Isabel," he said softly, "my big sister. I can't go. Neither can you."

She gripped his shoulders, "Why can't I go?"

"Because you have to stay in Madrid. At your palace. You are Countess de Queras, your brother could never explain your disappearance. Widow of a Grandee of Spain. The only place you can possibly go to is a convent."

"Oh, but I cannot."

"And why not?"

She might as well tell him. All Madrid would find out sooner or later.

"Because I am with child."

"Doña Isabel!" She could hear a whole gamut of repugnance in his voice, and she was quick to dispel any misconceptions.

"That is why he wanted to kill me. Because I had been unfaithful."

Pasquito swallowed. He felt as protective toward her as Pedro did. He was a Spanish male defending the honor of the family, and to him Isabel was his family.

"And the father of your child?"

"Oh, Pasquito, he is a man I love and he loves me, but he cannot marry me."

"Well then, why would you want to leave? Your child will be a Grandee of Spain. And with Villaquemada dead, you won't have a thing to worry about."

"And why can't you leave?"

"Because I belong here. I am a Spaniard. My ancestors have been Spaniards for eight hundred years." He had not forgotten his history lessons.

"May God be with you, Pasquito."

He kissed her hand and left.

She sat down on the bed and softly stroked Pedro's burning forehead.

# 6.

When the bodies of Villaquemada and Queras were found, the wheels of the rumor mills turned frantically. It seemed that the two had visited la Casa de Celestina, where they had picked a fight, a few days earlier, with a notorious *germanía* chief, named El Cuchillo. They had killed El Cuchillo by stabbing him in the back, and, of course, they had not been able to escape the vengeance of the underground leader's gang.

Similar crimes were committed every week, and the only unusual fact in this one was the high rank of the persons involved. But even persons of high rank were not safe, for there had also been an attempt on Don Pedro Valderocas's life. For a couple of days, rumor had it that Don Pedro was dead. But that, fortunately, turned out to be untrue. It would have been too terrible for the poor Countess de Queras to lose a husband and a brother at the same time. Already she was said to be beside herself with grief.

It was a disgrace. One could not venture into the streets anymore without a bodyguard. Something ought to be done. What good was the old law decreeing that the skin of *pícaros* had to be branded according to the gravity of their crime, what good the law that said in case of relapse branded *pícaros* were to be sent to the galleys? You had to catch a man first before you could punish him, and if one was to rely on current accounts, a third of the Spanish population were vagrants, in other words, *pícaros*.

Several outraged ladies set out to demand that houses such as the Casa de Celestina should be closed forever by royal decree, but to their distress, they found no advocates for their ideas among the lords who had direct access to His Majesty.

After a few weeks, the furor settled, and the gossip mongers turned their attention to other matters. For instance, to the new events at San Plácido, where the newly instated nuns were reportedly engaging in vicarious fertility rites. . . .

Carlos's earthly remains were brought to Granada to be buried in the vault of the Counts de Queras. Isabel said she could not bear to return to Queras House and wished to donate the palace to the religious order of the Barefoot Carmelites. Since a widow in Spain had only three choices: to remarry, to live her life in complete isolation, or enter a convent, the grateful Order of the Carmelites immediately offered her the position of Abbess of the new nunnery. Isabel declined, however, saying she wished to retire to a dark chamber in her brother's residence.

The dark chamber was no caprice or invention on her part. It was custom for a widow to spend her first year of mourning in a room hung with black, preferably where not a glimmer of daylight could seep in. She must sit there, cross-legged on a little quilt, and bewail the death of her departed husband. After a year, she could exchange the black drapes and wall hangings for gray ones, but she, herself, would have to wear black forever, unless she remarried. Isabel could hardly believe her eyes, when Maria and Teresa came with her new garments. A gown and petticoat of black serge and to wear over them a kind of black linen surplice which reached lower than her knees and had long straight sleeves that hung over her hands. A piece of black muslin was supposed to lie over her head, covering her face and neck completely. In addition, when going out—a thing to be avoided if at all possible—she was supposed to wear a hat with a very large brim.

She took one look at the clothes, touched the rough

material, and with a sweep of her arm sent the whole assortment flying to the floor.

"I will never wear that."

"But Doña Isabel, what will your friends say?" Teresa objected softly. Teresa had been with the Valderocas family for so long now that she had assumed the role of arbiter of manners.

"I don't care what they think." Isabel looked at them defiantly. Then she suddenly remembered that she was to them that marvelous human being who could not be contradicted. Almost as holy as the expectant Virgin.

"You cannot have forgotten that I am carrying the future Count de Queras," she said smugly. "If I wear nothing but black and see nothing but black, I will give birth to a melancholic baby. And if I sit in a chamber without daylight, my baby might be born blind. It is out of the question. I must have my old room back, and I must have comfortable clothes. I owe it to the illustrious family of Queras!" None of whom, thank God, remained alive.

"*¡Oh Madre mia!*" Teresa crossed herself, and Maria followed her example.

Since Maria had not seen Carlos at all on the fateful Friday, she believed the general rumor about his death, and so did the other servants.

Pasquito had entreated Isabel not to tell the truth to anyone, not even to her brother and Pepita. The best would be to make believe that Pasquito had arrived in time to fetch her at Queras House and that she had not seen Carlos, either. This fit in with her inbred sense of caution and with all she had ever been taught by Pedro as well as by Rafael. Do not talk! Moreover, Pasquito assured her that it would considerably advance his own standing in the criminal brotherhood if he could claim to have killed both Queras and Villaquemada.

Her refusal to set foot again into Queras House was taken as a natural reaction to the shock of losing her husband, and after it became known that she was with child, she could almost call her life peaceful again. Pedro's wounds healed well, and Pepita moved back to Madrid, accompanied by little Fernando, who had just turned two. The young sisters-in-law found a topic of particular common interest: lying-in practices and child-rearing.

A very few times Pepita tried to bring their talk around to the friends Isabel must have made at Court, but Isabel guessed the reason for these hints, and she smiled and said she would never reveal the true identity of her baby's father. She still wanted to leave for Amsterdam, but her husband's death prevented these plans. If she had left during his lifetime, Pedro could have explained that Carlos had mistreated her, but now she had no such excuse. On one point Isabel did have to give in; child or no child, she was required to wear black. But, at least she had her gowns made of fine silk and lace, and in the end the color was becoming to her fair complexion and red-golden hair.

She received many kind notes: from the Queen, from Inés de Zúñiga, from the Countess of Monterrey, from the Velázquez couple, and even from Quevedo and Calderon, but she never heard from Rafael. Yet, he must know about it! He must know it changed everything. He must also have heard that she was with child, and he certainly must realize that it could only be his child she was carrying. But never a word from him.

Finally, in desperation, she brought up the subject herself one day, while sitting on Pepita's *estrado* and playing with little Fernando.

"What do you hear from Toledo? Are things better under the new Inquisitor?"

Pepita looked up in surprise.

"Rafael Cortes, you mean?"

"Who else?"

"Don't you know he was sent to Italy?"

"How could I?"

"It's true you haven't been very active. But I thought you knew. The other inquisitors of Toledo were not too happy with him, and especially the Archbishop thought he was too lenient. Shortly after the *auto,* he was sent to the Holy See as a special envoy for the Dominican Order. Some say it is a punishment, others say that it is a promotion and that Sotomayor wants to get him into the good graces of the Holy Father, for future advancement."

"How do you know all that?"

"At the last underground meeting, we talked about nothing else."

She had to say something quickly to show it really did not mean much to her.

"Oh! I'm afraid I haven't kept up with the news. What else is there? Have you heard from the Caietanos?"

"Diego has slipped in and out of the country. He says they

are doing very well at Amsterdam." Pepita continued to chat about their other friends at Toledo, but Isabel hardly listened.

So he was gone again. To Rome. To further his ambition. No doubt the Pope would choose his name when it came up among the three possible choices the King could submit to Rome for the position of Inquisitor General of Spain. If not after Sotomayor's death, then later. Rafael was still young, he had time, he would succeed. No, his departure for Rome was no punishment. It was a step forward.

But at least that explained his silence. He was not in Spain. He did not know. And even if by chance he learned from the Spanish Ambassador in Rome that Carlos had died, he would be glad for her, but it would not change anything. He would not know that she carried his child.

They stayed at Madrid through the summer. This year their advanced pregnancies prevented them from participating in any secret services for the High Holy Days.

In September, Pepita gave birth to a girl, who was named Catalina. In the middle of October, Isabel was delivered of a healthy boy. For her the choice of names was much more complicated, since the child was from the day of his birth Count de Queras and Grandee of Spain. The name Carlos was inevitable. The Count-Duke offered to hold the child at the christening ceremony, a kindness calling for the name of Gaspar. A Grandee being officially the cousin of the King, the name Felipe also had to be considered. Finally, Pedro and Pepita expected her to give the child the first name of his real father, whom no one knew, so Isabel was compelled to think of a few first names. She thought of Duarte and of José, but then, the obvious choice occurred to her in a flash. Wasn't the boy Francisco Molina's son?

So the little bastard boy became Carlos Felipe Gaspar Francisco de Queras y Valderocas, owner of vast lands in Andalusia and Grandee of Spain.

But when they came home from the baptism, Isabel herself washed her son's forehead and mumbled, "Adonai, God and God of our Fathers, God of Abraham, God of Isaac, and God of Jacob, please accept this boy as one of your children, and bless him and keep him, and know him by the name of Rafael."

Pedro had asked her which Hebrew name she would prefer and had suggested all those previously used by the Benahavels, but she maintained stubbornly that Rafael, being the name of an archangel, was as good a Hebrew name as any, and she would accept no other.

"But it is such a common Christian name in Spain," Pedro objected. This was so true that Isabel's past infatuation with Rafael Cortes did not seem to enter his mind.

"So much the better. Especially since I intend to call him by that name."

"You'll call him Rafael?" Pedro asked. "How will you explain this to his teachers and to everyone else? I don't like it."

"Pedro Valderocas Sanchez! I will tell you something. I am going to leave this country before my son is old enough to have teachers. I am not going to stay in Spain forever. It is a terrible country."

"But still it is our country."

"It is a country that would not want us if the truth about us were known. And anyway, I would rather be the mother of an honest bastard than of a false Grandee."

"Sarita Benahavel," Pedro said softly, "I still need you in Spain. Your task is not finished. You are a Countess and the mother of a Grandee. After your year of mourning, you will be received at Court again. You are too valuable to our efforts. You must remain in Spain."

"I will stay until Rafaelito is old enough to travel."

So little Rafael became Rafaelito, and finally Elito for short. Elito. The Hebrew word for God and the Spanish diminutive. A most fitting name for a child she worshiped from the day he was born.

Even though Isabel could not go out, her life was far from dull. She was again helping Pedro with the administration of their vast business interests which recently included hidden investments in the Dutch West India Company, a precaution she believed was important. Also, Pedro kept her informed of all political events. She was often amazed how clearly Carlos de Queras had foreseen what would happen. He had often predicted the final doom of the Olivares regime, and as the political news grew worse with every passing month, Isabel felt growing within her the certainty that all their plans would end badly. But whenever she warned Pedro of her fears, he told her it was only the fact that she had a child now and that the responsibility for another human being made her timid.

"I feel like Cassandra," she told him. "I know the disaster

will come, but I don't know how to stop it. And you won't believe me."

"I think Quevedo has been your dinner guest too often," Pedro said. "He talks just like you."

"Yes, he knows that Spain is doomed," Isabel said. "It is too late for reforms."

"It is never too late to work for liberty," Pedro said.

# 1.

For over twenty years war had been raging in large parts of Europe, with Spanish armies involved from Milan to Flanders. In the beginning, Spanish troops had been victorious, especially under the military leadership of Ambrosio Spínola. His successor, the Cardinal Infante Ferdinand, though every bit as ambitious and courageous as Spínola, had neither his genius nor his luck, and victories became sparse.

Theoretically, the Spanish people knew that they were at war with the French and the Dutch, but in practical terms, this knowledge changed their way of life very little. Sometimes one side won a battle, and sometimes the other. If Spain won there was a noisy expensive victory celebration at Madrid, and if Spain lost, nothing was said about it.

In October 1637, for instance, the Dutch had recaptured Breda. No one had made any mention of the fact, although some eight years previously, when Spínola had first conquered Breda, the Spanish had taken this to be the most decisive battle of the war and had celebrated it as if it had the importance of Lepanto. Velázquez had painted his most famous canvas, the Surrender of Breda, transforming the event into an eternal victory for Spain. Now Breda was lost again and remained lost. The year 1638 had also been unfavorable for Spain, except one small victory over the French at Fuenterrabía, which had sent Madrid into a mad victory dizziness and resulted in the Count-Duke's being covered with royal compliments.

But the beginning of 1639 dispelled any further notions of Spanish military supremacy: the road from Milan to Flanders was taken by enemy troops, thus cutting off the Spanish armies in the Netherlands from any kind of reinforcements, unless they could be brought in via the English Channel which was heavily patrolled by the Dutch.

The Count-Duke needed no Cassandra to remind him daily that Spanish foreign policy was courting disaster, but he still remained ignorant of the dangers besetting Spain from within, the brewing discontent of Catalonia, Portugal, and even Andalusia. When Isabel had reported to him the vague plans of rebellion concocted by Carlos and his friends at her dinner table, he had laughed them off as wishful fantasies. Now, he felt, the time had come to show all of Spain that he could impose his will wherever and whenever he needed to do so. He called the Protonotario of Aragon to discuss the affairs of the principality of Catalonia, that eternal thorn in the Count-Duke's political flesh.

"There is no more money in Castile," Olivares said. "Our only hope lies now with the Catalans."

"I doubt the Catalans will donate more money or troops," Villanueva said, "and not unreasonably so. They feel that their constitutions have continuously been violated by Madrid. Why should they come to your aid?"

"Because Catalonia is a rich province, abundant in men and supplies and the most unburdened of all our kingdoms. In addition, Catalonia has a coastline. That means galleys can be brought into Barcelona with troops from Naples and Sicily. We have to open a front in Catalonia, because once the Catalans are attacked by the French, they will turn out gallantly to resist. It is simply necessary that Catalonia should find herself directly involved with the common welfare of the monarchy! Then they will finally be forced to accept my plans for the union of arms. It is our only way to win the war."

"And how do you know Richelieu will attack in Catalonia?" the Protonotario wanted to know.

"Because my agents tell me that the principality is seething with discontent."

The next few months proved that the Count-Duke's political instincts were sound insofar as they concerned his arch-

enemy the French Cardinal Richelieu. But his fond hopes
regarding the reaction of the Catalans were unceremoniously
crushed. Although the new Spanish Viceroy in Catalonia,
Don Dalman de Queralt, Count of Santa Coloma, received
detailed instructions to have six thousand Catalans ready to
defend the border, he was not able to raise the troops, and
when the French onslaught came, the castle of Salces surren-
dered.

Salces had been the centerpiece of the glorious table of
Catalan fortifications, a strongly built fortress which should
have withstood enemy attack had it been properly manned.
Its defeat was the first lethal break in the career of the
Count-Duke. It meant that war had been finally brought into
the Spanish motherland.

## 2.

The military defeat in Catalonia encouraged all conspirators
against the rule of Olivares. Don Francisco Quevedo decided
to make good his threat to open the eyes of the King. In sharp
brilliant verses he exposed all of the Count-Duke's mistakes,
the despair of the educated men who dared not intervene, the
misery of the common masses, the hopelessness of the whole
situation.

Quevedo had strong political theories, but he knew that
Olivares would never permit another man to gain the trust of
the King. He would never share the power he had held alone
for almost twenty years. Quevedo even feared he would not
gain admittance to the King long enough to expound his
ideas. So he bribed a royal lackey to slip his explosive poem
under Philip's napkin at the royal dinner table.

He had been warned often enough by Velázquez and by his
friend the Duke of Medina-Celi not to risk his neck. But just
as Isabel and Pedro wanted to help the Marranos to obtain
religious liberty, Quevedo wanted to help the oppressed
masses to obtain freedom from exploitation.

He had not counted on the extreme loyalty of his King.
Philip had made up his mind, once and for all, that Olivares
was his true friend, and he did not permit any attack on his
Favorite. No one's dupe, Philip recognized immediately that

this poem was not the opinion of one harmless fool. Silence
on his part would only encourage the conspiracy, and permis-
siveness would lead to rebellion. He showed the poem to
Olivares.

"The nerve to spoil my dinner, Count. Who do you think
can have that nerve?"

Two lines immediately jumped at the Count-Duke:

> Ya el pueblo doliente llega a recelar.
> No le echen gabela sobre el respirar.

In dull despair the people were ready to expect to be
taxed for the very air they breathed. Only one man could
have written that, and that same man was the only one in
Spain brilliant enough to become a danger to Olivares. The
Count-Duke looked at his King, and he saw that Philip
was merely waiting to hear the confirmation of his own
suspicion.

"Who else but Quevedo?" Olivares said. "He has been
conspiring for years with the Grandees who have left the
Court. His ideas are contrary to the interests of the Habsburg
monarchy. He is undermining the very ground under Your
Majesty's throne."

"And how do you expect to deal with him, Count?"

Truly, Olivares would have liked to have his head cut off.
But that would have been too extreme; it would only lead
to more trouble. To have him exiled, on the other hand,
would be playing into Quevedo's hands. He could then easily go to France and cause harm by offering his services to
Richelieu.

"I would suggest to have him arrested, his writings confiscated, and have him imprisoned in a monastery." There, that
sounded firm but mild. A sort of house arrest. . . .

Philip looked at Olivares. The arrest would have to be
ordered by the King. Quevedo was quality. Philip could easily
guess what kind of arrest Olivares had in mind. The minister's
vengeance would be terrible. The poet would land in a dark
unwholesome dungeon.

On the other hand, it served him right. He should have put
his brilliant mind to serve the Crown and the Crown's chief
minister, especially at a time when war had come to the
threshold of the country. Anyway, the man had hardly ever
had a good word about Philip's rule.

"I will sign the order for his arrest. After that, I do not wish to be troubled any further about this matter. May it serve as an example to others."

Quevedo was arrested in the dark of night at the house of his friend, the Duke of Medina-Celi, and brought to an underground prison cell in the Monastery of Saint Marc, just outside the city walls of León.

Thus, for the moment at least, the voice of rebellion was silenced.

# 3.

There was much talk about the arrest, and everywhere people took sides. Valderocas House was no exception. Isabel said she thought the Count-Duke had gone too far, and it would in the end turn against him. Pedro, on the contrary, welcomed it as a proof that the Count-Duke's power had not diminished. "Any enemy of Olivares is an enemy of mine," he maintained. "We must help the Count-Duke, now more than ever."

But when he came back from a soirée at the English Embassy, he shook his head in utter bewilderment.

"I don't know what to think anymore. We are on the verge of losing the war and with it a good portion of our prestige. We have such tremendous problems that it staggers the imagination: and what is Madrid talking about? The latest amorous crime of Philip the Lover."

"What is that?" Pepita asked.

"He has fallen in love with one of the nuns at San Plácido," Pedro said. "According to the rumors, he has asked Villanueva and the Count-Duke for help in seducing the lovely virgin. It seems furthermore that Villanueva agreed to have a hole made in the wall leading from his own cellar to the one of the convent next door, and that Philip and Olivares, led by Villanueva, entered the convent through that hole and proceeded to a room where the seduction was to take place. There they found a young nun laid out on a bier, as if she were dead, a crucifix in her folded hands, and tapers burning at the head and the foot of the bier. Philip is said to have fled in terror, followed by the Count-Duke and Villanueva."

Isabel had listened with much interest. The story sounded familiar to her.

"And do you think anyone would believe that?" she asked.

"The English Ambassador did," Pedro said.

"And why not?" Pepita fell in. "If they believe that Olivares made love to his wife in front of those nuns, they are sure to believe this one."

"It is bad," Pedro said.

"Flimflam," said Isabel. "Those lies were invented originally by Villaquemada to get the Count-Duke in trouble with the Inquisition. He and Carlos planned it all with a cousin of Enrique. She actually joined the nunnery. She was to start the rumors. Not even the Inquisition will take that seriously."

"On the contrary," Pedro said. "It may well go down in history as the pure truth about the morals of our time."

"Poor historians," Pepita giggled.

"Poor Spain," Isabel said.

# 1.

The beginning of the new year was a little more promising for the Spanish Viceroy in Catalonia, the Count of Santa Coloma, had finally thought of a clever device to get his Catalan countrymen interested in the fighting. He simply promised preferential treatment in appointment to city offices to all those who would go to relieve Salces, the French occupied fortress. One might have thought all Catalan men had bureaucratic ink in their veins, because enough of them went to fight for Salces that on the sixth of January the fortress was taken back from the French. In addition, new troops arrived from Italy and were billeted in Catalonia, although over the severest protests of the Catalans. For Madrid the victory at Salces was reason enough to forget the war and think of more pleasurable pursuits.

Isabel, after having spent a year and a half in virtual seclusion, was called back to attend to some of her functions as Lady-in-Waiting. Her first assignment was to accompany Her Majesty to a rehearsal of a new Calderon play at the theater of the Buen Retiro. Calderon himself was there to direct the players and to see that Cosme Loti's sensational sceneries did not overpower the message of his play. As soon as the Queen arrived, the actors became agitated, each one trying to upstage the others, because all of them knew that Her Majesty liked nothing as much as seeing a play, or an actor, defeated by catcalls. Calderon himself had begun to resent her frequent presence at rehearsals. In his opinion, the failure of some of his plays could clearly be attributed to the Bourbon Queen's bad mood of the moment. This was her only power. She could make or break a play, and she enjoyed it.

She knew the actors had their minds more on her than on their lines, as she sat lazily smiling and peeling an orange, then tossing the peels onto the stage. One of her peels hit a young actress, said to be the latest conquest of Philip, and the saucy wench, instead of going on with her lines, picked up the peel and with a flick of her wrist threw it smack into the face of the dignified poet laureate of the Spanish Court, Pedro Calderon de la Barca.

This was too much for even the most self-possessed poet, and Calderon was quick to grab her and place a resounding slap on her cheek. Her Majesty was delighted. This much surpassed a fight provoked among the common spectators. She leaned forward excitedly.

The actress, however, screeched, and since she had been liberal with her favors and was very pretty, she had half a dozen actors at her side abusing Calderon and starting to pull the sets apart. This, in turn, angered Cosme Loti, who now threatened to have all of them whipped right in front of Her Majesty. Just as Isabelle de Bourbon turned back to her women to mention that this spectacle promised to be a lot more entertaining than the whole boring lot of Calderon's morality plays, the comedy turned into tragedy.

One of the male actors pulled a knife and charged angrily into the huddle. There was a scream, a gasp, and slowly all of them drew apart to form a circle around the fallen victim.

Calderon had been badly stabbed and was about to bleed as nobly and quietly to death as a character out of one of his own plays. There had often been serious differences of opinion during rehearsals, and more than a few others had ended in duels. So if Calderon died of his wound, it would certainly be said that he had died in defense of a noble idea of his, because the truth would have been too degrading.

But it did not come to that. A court physician was called, arrived in time and, like Pedro Valderocas, Calderon recovered from the knifing.

It all made another good story to tell at a reception, and

life could have continued pleasantly, had it not been for
a fatal misjudgment on the part of the Count-Duke in the
only cause that seemed to occupy his mind: the Catalan
cause.

# 2.

Indeed, a new plan had sprung up in the overworked mind of
the chief minister, a plan to end all his troubles with
Catalonia, and he announced it proudly to the Viceroy:

, "Really," he said, "the Catalans ought to see more of the
world than Catalonia."

A simple statement, an ironic statement, but a statement
destined to cause a revolution, lose a principality, and topple
a government. Since the Count-Duke always tried to back his
words with actions, this was what he had planned: six
thousand Catalan men were to be sent for service in Italy.
After all, he reasoned, Italian troops had come to the aid of
Catalonia, so an exchange would finally integrate the Catalans into the rest of the vast Spanish Empire. His friends
warned him that this would be the final injury to Catalan
pride, but, as usual, he did not heed their warnings.

What Carlos de Queras had predicted as far back as 1632
finally occurred. The Catalans revolted. They threw all
Spaniards out of their country and eventually became so
drunk with their own power that they murdered Don Dalman
de Queralt, Count of Santa Coloma, the gentle Viceroy who
had tried in vain to plead their cause with Olivares.

The report of his death reached Madrid with all the ghastly
details intact. It had been on a hot day during the harvest
festival, and the Count had been warned that the revolution
was out of control. He had tried to flee, but he had fallen to
the ground on the last stretch of beach between him and a
rowboat that was to bring him to a royal galley. There the
pursuing revolutionaries found him and stabbed him to
death.

The stabbing killed not only Santa Coloma but all of the
Count-Duke's hopes regarding Catalonia. The rich province
was lost to Spain. The Catalans would declare for the King of
France.

# 3.

The event was discussed in all the homes of Madrid, but in none with more anxiety than in Valderocas House.

Diego Caietano, who still now and then acted as Pedro's agent, had come back from a trip to Portugal, and the news he brought with him was alarming in view of the apparently successful revolt of the Catalans.

There were still a great number of Marranos living in Portugal, more than in Spain. Over the years, they had managed to buy certain privileges from Philip and Olivares. Several of their deals had been negotiated by Pedro Valderocas and Lope Silva, the Portuguese merchant who had been caught with the Caietanos.

During the years since Portugal first became integrated into Spain, Portuguese wealth had declined considerably. This could be intelligently attributed to the fact that Spanish monarchs were consistently more interested in Castile, the place of their abode, than in the outlying provinces. Also, instead of spending Portuguese money in Portugal, it had been spent mainly on wars fought on foreign soil. As a result, the Portuguese were increasingly unhappy with their lot and eyed the Catalans with admiration.

This would have been of no concern to the Marranos had the priests and discontented nobles not found the easy excuse that the reason for all their troubles was the continued existence of Jews in their midst. These Marranos were not even called New Christians—no matter that they went to church and considered themselves Catholics—the descendants of Jews were Jews, and the Jews were accused of undermining Portuguese virtue and heroic spirit.

Portugal was officially governed by a relative of King Philip, Margaret of Savoy, Duchess of Mantua. But the true head of the Portuguese noblemen was the Duke of Braganza, direct descendant of the last independent King of Portugal and therefore, in many eyes, the legitimate heir to the throne. The Duke loved music and arts, and sometimes hunting; he had no inclination to wield a sceptre. Not so his wife. Doña

Luisa de Guzmán, daughter of the Duke of Medina Sidonia and cousin to the Count-Duke of Olivares, was made of far stronger material. She not only had the will, but also the intellectual capacity to plan the recapture of the Portuguese throne for her husband.

All these facts were known to Pedro and Isabel, but they still could not understand why Diego Caietano insisted that he had uncovered a special plot.

"Have you ever heard of one João Pinto Ribeiro?" Diego asked them in a voice intimating the man must be an advocate of the devil.

"Not I," Pedro said.

But Isabel nodded.

"Pinto Ribeiro. Why, yes, he once came to dinner at Queras House. He is a professor of some kind, and perhaps also an agent of the Duke of Braganza. Wait, now I remember, he was involved in some plot planned by Carlos and Villaquemada, and I believe the Marquis of Ayamonte and also the Duke of Medina Sidonia. I reported it to the Count-Duke at the time."

"So you know him," Diego said. "He is a professor of civil law at Coimbra. Convinced that the Duke of Braganza is the rightful heir to the throne, he will do everything in his power to see Braganza crowned King of Portugal. He plans a revolt, and if we do not warn Olivares immediately, he will succeed. And if he does, it will spell the end of normal life for our Portuguese brethren. He will want recognition from the Pope, and to obtain it, he will cancel every civil right ever bought by the New Christians. We must not forget that the King and Olivares always talk of privileges they granted. What privileges? To be allowed to live in peace? For any other human being that is a right, not a privilege. We must act. We must prevent Braganza from taking over Portugal."

"I believe that Portugal is ripe for a revolution," Isabel said. Much as she had detested Carlos, she had to admit that his political instincts had been sound. Even his dream of becoming King of Granada did not look too eccentric in view of recent events. "But my impression of this Pinto is that he has prepared his plan for many years, and that he has enough support, or in plain language, enough spies in Madrid to let him know immediately who informs against him. There is not a room at the Alcázar that does not have ears. In addition, it

is impossible to get through to Olivares. He is too upset over
the Santa Coloma assassination. And actually what proof do
we have? What new steps has Pinto undertaken? When I gave
his name to Olivares a few years ago, he said that he would
watch him. We must have something more concrete than
rumors."

"I have that, too," Diego said. "Pinto is in the process of
organizing a great hunting party at Vila Vicosa. A harmless-
looking project, eh? Everyone knows how the Duke likes to
hunt. Well, wait until you see the guest list. Every discontented Portuguese noble is on it. If that list does not convince
the Count-Duke that something is amiss, he has no political
instincts left."

"I have tried to see him, but he has not received me,"
Pedro said.

"If he does not receive you, I do not even have a shred of a
chance," Diego said.

Both men looked at Isabel. She was a Lady-in-Waiting. She
had access to the Queen. She was also the mother of a
Grandee of Spain and could even request an audience with
Philip. Via Philip, perhaps she could get to Olivares. It had
gotten to the point where it was easier to speak to His
Majesty than to the minister.

Isabel thought. No one but the Countess Olivares and the
Count-Duke knew that thanks to her Olivares's coach had
been empty on the night of the *mojiganga*. She had possibly
saved the Count-Duke's life, but she had never mentioned
this to anyone, not even to Pedro. Would that be of help
now? Would Olivares remember?

"Give me the list. I will try to warn him."

Diego looked uneasy. "I don't know. If you are caught with
that list . . ."

"Flimflam. Do you think I am going to walk around waving
it on top of a halberd?"

The Alcázar was darker and drearier than ever. Even the
folk in the patio seemed to droop under the weight of the
disastrous news. Wherever a few acquaintances gathered, one
heard undertones of shame and dread. Words like Catalonia,
Barcelona, stabbings, revolt. Was the end of Spain's grandeur
near at hand?

Isabel had to wait for a long time in the antechamber of the
Countess Olivares's drawing room. She, too, was unsure of

herself. How would she be received? Would they give credence to her report? Would she be able to persuade Inés de Zúñiga that her husband had to act quickly if he wanted to save part of the Kingdom and perhaps his own head?

While she waited, she argued again with herself whether it was not finally time to leave and move to Amsterdam. The only reason why she had not given in to her wish to leave was her ever present hope that Rafael would return from Italy and that he would finally see Elito. The child was almost two years old and had his father's dark curly hair and black eyes. She had often thought she should write to Rafael, but she did not know where he was. Even if she could find out his address at Rome, what would she tell him? Francisco Molina has a son? That was the only message she could think of. What if he did not receive it? What if he received it but gave no answer? How would she know the difference? Sometimes she was so discouraged she sobbed for hours into her pillow at night.

Her thoughts turned to another reason why she could not leave Spain: Pedro's work. Pedro was convinced that he was chosen to help his brethren come back to Spain and build a synagogue at Madrid. All events to the contrary only reinforced his opinion that the time of fulfillment was drawing near. The Count-Duke had promised him that by 1642 all difficulties would be cleared away and that he would send him to Oran with firm commitments from the Crown to permit Jews from North Africa to reside at the capital. Now after Diego's revelations, Isábel was afraid. What if Olivares died before that date? What if someone killed him in retribution for what had happened in Catalonia?

She was startled out of her thoughts by a small creature with an enormous head that wobbled with every step of his spindly legs.

"Her Ladyship will receive you," Doña Inés's pet dwarf announced in a high squeaky voice.

Isabel followed him into the drawing room. As usual, the Countess wore black, and her face was thickly painted. Like a mask hiding her true feelings, Isabel thought. Then she curtsied.

"Doña Isabel? What brings you here?"

"My brother has received a portfolio of valuable paintings from Italy, and we would be very honored if His Excellency and Your Grace could spare a few moments to look at them."

Donã Inés's eyebrows shot up questioningly, and Isabel

could feel the curious glances of all her women and dwarfs who busied themselves about the room.

"I thank you for your kind invitation, Doña Isabel, but I hardly think this is the right time for it. There are pressing matters of state, as you may realize. . . ."

Isabel leaned forward.

"There is one painting, in particular, Your Grace. It represents a masquerade scene, a *mojiganga* of sorts, and it is exquisite, delicately drawn, and an eerie atmosphere of danger seems to hang over the scene. We think His Excellency would get great satisfaction from viewing it."

The Countess's expression did not change; she was known to keep perfect control over her emotions, but from a quick widening of her eyes, Isabel could see that she had understood.

She rose. "It is out of the question that my husband leave his office these days, but perhaps we can arrange for you to show him the painting. I will see what I can do." She walked with Isabel to the door, and Isabel let three words escape between her teeth: "It is urgent."

The Countess smiled her masklike smile, "Yes, I know."

They stayed home for the remainder of that day and night, thinking that any time a messenger might come to summon Pedro to Olivares's office. They talked, all four of them, Pepita, Pedro, Diego, and Isabel, until the early hours of dawn. Finally, the doorman announced that a masked stranger wished to speak to Don Pedro.

"I will receive him in the library."

The stranger, a big hulk of a man in a full-length cloak and a full vizard, was led into the library where Pedro met him. Only when he was assured that all doors were locked and that no one could hear them, did he take off his mask.

"Your Excellency," Pedro bowed to him, astonished that the minister ventured alone into the streets.

Olivares threw off his heavy cape and let himself slump into an easy chair. He had aged considerably. His once smooth forehead was deeply lined, his lips were so sunken they could barely be seen; he rested his elbow on the arm of the chair and his head in his hand.

"What now?" he said,

"Diego Caietano is back from Portugal. The Duke of Braganza wants to become King."

"That is no news. That is a slight nuisance. Anyway, he is married to a cousin of mine. The Guzmáns have always been loyal to Spain."

"I am afraid, Your Excellency, that this time hunger for power surpasses loyalty."

Olivares growled. "Do you think the daughter of Medina Sidonia would betray Spain?"

Even her father would, Pedro was tempted to say, but instead he explained, "Your Excellency, all I know is the planning of an intrigue on the largest scale, organized by one Pinto Ribeiro. Diego can tell you the details."

"He is here?"

"Yes, and eager to serve you."

"Let me hear him."

Pedro went to fetch Diego, and together they convinced Olivares that only immediate action could save a desperate situation.

"But what can I do? I cannot send troops into Portugal."

"No, but you could send troops from Portugal to Catalonia," Diego suggested boldly.

"And thus deprive the Duke of military support from his countrymen. Not bad, young man, not bad. But that, I shall keep as a last resort. First, I shall offer the Duke the government of Milan. That is an office usually held by a Royal Prince. He cannot possibly refuse."

The offer was made, but to the general consternation at Madrid, the Duke of Braganza replied most politely that he was too ignorant of Italian politics to accept that high honor, and that he much preferred to stay in his own country.

So there remained for Olivares only the proposition Diego had suggested in the first place. Olivares ordered the Duke and all his men to serve the King against the rebellious Catalans. And to report at once to Madrid. By then it was almost the end of the year.

Madrid was making ready for the winter festivities. In Spain big trouble had a way of announcing itself by small signs. One morning there were no fish on the market. No fish? Well, the fish from Lisbon had not arrived yet. Why not? Who knows!

A few days later, everyone knew. Upon a pistol shot fired by Pinto, the Palace of the Duchess of Mantua had been taken by surprise, the Duchess herself had been escorted to the Spanish border, her most loyal servants had been killed, the fortresses had been delivered to the conspirators, and the

Duke of Braganza had been crowned as John IV, King of Portugal. The Portuguese Cortes was summoned, and every step was taken to assure the world that the Duke was the legal heir to the throne and its rightful occupant.

When the full truth became known, there were grave faces all over Madrid. As usual, the idlers on the Calle Mayor knew everything before the King learned of it. But contrary to usual, no one wanted to be the one to inform His Majesty.

That afternoon a bullfight was held at the Plaza Mayor, but the only person to watch the arena was the King. Everyone else was watching the Count-Duke's somber face. After the fight, back at the Alcázar, Philip sat down to play cards. Finally, the Count-Duke had decided upon his approach. He spoke gaily into the hushed silence.

"I bring great news for Your Majesty."

"What is it?" Philip asked, not even looking up from his cards.

"In one moment, Sire, you have won a great dukedom and vast wealth."

"How is that, Count?" Philip looked up this time, not sure yet what to expect.

"Sire, the Duke of Braganza has gone mad and has proclaimed himself King of Portugal. It will be necessary for you to confiscate all of his possessions."

Pedro was in the room with other courtiers, and he admired Olivares's pluck, thinking that if Philip had the same courage, he should jump up, throw down his cards, and shout: By God, Count, you are right. Off to Portugal!

Philip, however, did nothing of the sort. His face grew cold, and he turned back to his cards.

"Find a remedy," was all he answered.

Olivares left brusquely. On the way out, his glance crossed Pedro's eyes. Seeing the desperation in the Count-Duke's face, Pedro was gripped by anguish. If his plans were to succeed, if his life's work was not to have been in vain, he had to catch the minister now, before he fell again into one of his great depressions. He excused himself from the other courtiers and quickly followed the Favorite.

Despite the chilly fog that had settled over the town, he convinced Olivares to go for a ride in the Count-Duke's office on wheels.

"We must plan a counterrevolution at once," Pedro suggested briskly.

"We need money for that."

"I will raise what is needed. There is one part of the Portuguese population already firmly on our side."

"How is that?"

"The Jews have all to lose and nothing to gain from the new government. The new King will revoke all the concessions made to the New Christians, because he will want to be recognized by the Holy Father."

Olivares nodded. "Yes, that stands to reason."

"Therefore, if we can win over the Grand Inquisitor of Portugal to our way of thinking and induce him to promise the New Christians a cessation of persecution, Your Excellency, you will guarantee much wealth and good will on your side. We must not lose any time." Pedro spoke enthusiastically. He had the weird feeling of holding Olivares in his hand, just as Olivares always held Philip. Diego had told him that the New Christians of Portugal felt the Grand Inquisitor feared he might be replaced if Braganza became King. Therefore, he might be influenced to side with Olivares.

The Count-Duke looked at Pedro. Then he bent forward over the narrow table that separated them and whispered:

"Don Pedro, look into my eyes."

They stared at each other again, as they had done many years ago when they had first met.

"Tell me honestly," Olivares said, "I want to know why you remain with me, when everyone else conspires against me. What do you want from me?"

"The salvation of Spain."

"That is empty flattery."

"It is the truth."

"A truth that requires a miracle."

Pedro took a deep breath. The goal of his life must be reached. He must try for it now. He leaned forward:

"It requires the complete abolition of the Inquisition," he said in a quiet, determined, almost hypnotic voice.

The Count-Duke's gaze did not waver. They still stared at each other in the flickering shine of the oil lamps. The coach continued to move; the earth did not open up to swallow the man who had just proposed the most heretical idea ever submitted to the Royal Favorite.

Olivares, too, breathed deeply and heavily. "So I am not the only one to entertain that thought," he said. "You know, I think I will actually put the question to the Royal Council."

Pedro thought he had not heard correctly. Should it be so easy? A vote in the Royal Council? How many counselors must be bribed? How much would it cost? No matter. No price was too high.

But Olivares's next words made his heart stand still.

"Don Pedro Valderocas Sanchez," the Count-Duke said, emphasizing the maternal surname, "I have a suspicion that you are a Jew."

Pedro did not reply. His tongue found no words. But Olivares did not seem to expect an answer; he continued quietly, "But you have served me well, and I will continue to consider you a fine Old Christian. Yes, your advice is good. I will prepare letters for Dom Sebastião de Tello, the Grand Inquisitor of Portugal, and for other ecclesiastics whom I know to be on our side. This is what must be done: We will have a general uprising for which you will put up all the money. We will capture the Duke of Braganza. And we will thus save Portugal for Spain without spilling the blood of even one Castilian soldier. This victory should give me all the power I need to push for reforms. And one of them will be a severe curtailment of the Inquisition. Do you want to go to Portugal to see that my plans are carried out?"

"I would prefer to entrust that task to Diego Caietano. He knows every person worth knowing in Portugal."

"As you wish. Don Pedro, as soon as this matter is cleared up, I swear to you I shall give orders for the building of a synagogue at Madrid. You will get what you really want: religious liberty for Spain."

Olivares's hand lay on the table between them; now Pedro reached for it and touched it respectfully with his lips.

"Don Gaspar, you are a great man."

## 1.

"Isabel, come at once! Diego is back from Portugal!"

Pedro brought a fresh gust of spring air with him when he entered the nursery. The children jumped up to greet him. His son Fernando was five years old, a little man, dressed in breeches and a soft velvet jacket. He did not belong in the nursery anymore, but he liked to sneak in there when his aunt Isabel was playing with the babies, Catalina and Elito, because she spun marvelous tales for him; tales of heroes and princes who all bowed to the rider of the magic horse, the horse that could only be captured by a boy who learned his lessons as well as Fernando.

Isabel could see from Pedro's grave expression that something had gone wrong, and she called out to Maria to stay with the babies while she followed him to the library.

Diego was covered with a crust of dust and sweat. His story was one of utter defeat.

He had had no trouble entering Portugal, and he had contacted all the right persons. He delivered Olivares's letter to the Grand Inquisitor, won over a host of disappointed nobles, and succeeded in organizing a plot that he thought could not fail.

Just when everything seemed well in hand, disaster had struck. A key conspirator was betrayed, caught, and tortured. He revealed all the names. On the day of the planned uprising, all the noble conspirators were arrested and publicly executed. Diego had already been on his way back to Madrid when he heard about it and had been riding like the devil ever since. There was a price on his head in Portugal, but as far as he knew, Pedro Valderocas was safe. No one was aware of his role behind the scene.

Thus, the Duke of Braganza remained King of Portugal. Spain was shrinking, and so was Valderocas wealth, since a good part of it had gone to pay for the abortive revolution.

## 2.

True to Carlos's earlier predictions, the Duke of Medina Sidonia now tried to carve an independent Kingdom out of Andalusia. Pedro heard of these plans through one of his own agents in Seville and reported the plot to Olivares who, most unceremoniously, gave Medina Sidonia the choice of house arrest at the Royal Alcázar or of losing his head. He chose the former.

Next, the Marquis of Ayamonte attempted to set up an independent Republic of Andalusia with the help of the French. By now, however, Olivares's show of clemency had ended. The Marquis was simply arrested and executed. The loss of both Catalonia and Portugal caused Olivares to rethink his policies. With Spain's military strength depleted, her economy at the nadir, her Court frivolous, what he needed was not more of the same, but a fresh approach, a total overhaul of Spanish attitudes and expectations. Perhaps Pedro Valderocas was right. The Financial Advisor kept insisting that new wealth must be brought in, that rich expatriots must be lured back, that by abolishing the Inquisition and recovering some of the spoils in her coffers, the Count-Duke would gain the means to revive the economy.

Toward the end of 1641, Pedro Valderocas was sent to North Africa to deliver invitations and letters of safe-conduct signed by the King addressed to leaders of Jewish communities. Olivares prepared himself to make his final bid for reversing the fate of Spain.

# 1.

Don Gaspar de Guzmán had no more time to lose. After pleading privately with the now eighty-seven-year-old Inquisitor General to support his opinion that the Inquisition had done its work and was no longer needed, and after asking Philip's permission to address the Royal Council on this subject, he carefully prepared a passionate speech on the political and economic advantages of religious liberty without ever once using the word liberty. Thanks to his oratorical gifts, he was able to convince a majority of Council members that the Inquisition was indeed an institution that had outlived its usefulness.

The news of the Count-Duke's speech had hardly reached the ears of the Madrileños, when Cardinal Monti, the Papal Nuncio, asked to be heard in public audience by His Majesty, King Philip IV. It seemed as if all of Madrid was informed of the impending match of strength, because on the day of the audience, the chamber was overflowing with spectators and among them many estranged Grandees and other enemies of Olivares. Indeed, there was only a small group of friends standing with Pedro Valderocas near the Favorite, to the left of the throne.

Isabel, Countess de Queras, came in the train of the Queen, with the other Ladies-in-Waiting, and they stood on the right side, behind the chair of Her Majesty.

Formerly, Isabelle de Bourbon had not shown herself at such functions, but in recent times she had taken an inordinate interest in politics, and her love for Spain and for her husband had grown in proportion to her hatred for Olivares.

When Philip arrived, every man bent his knee and every woman sank to the ground, but their excited whispers did not stop. It was not until the Cardinal stepped forward that an oppressive silence settled over the chamber. The grim Italian approached the throne slowly with measured steps. He did not bow to His Majesty but stood erect and boldly stared at Philip.

"For hundreds of years Spain has been a model unto the nations, a bastion protecting our Holy Faith from overt and hidden enemies, a staunch defender of Catholicism. Now Spain is losing her power and her glory. . . ." The Cardinal stopped and let his words sink into the assembled courtiers. "And many Spaniards may wonder why. Why are things going badly for Spain? Why does God Almighty permit this great nation to suffer defeat? Why? I can tell you why. Because the bright shield of faith is being tarnished. There is a powerful man at work in Spain, a man who tramples on the rights of the Church. He tries to tear down the mighty building of the Holy Office of the Inquisition. He sows weeds into the fields of the Lord, he is evil and wily. But lo, the wicked shall be destroyed, and the harvest of the Lord must be cleaned of tares, and the purity of the faith must be assured. The perverter of the faith must be dismissed, he must no longer be permitted to serve the Crown. . . ."

The Cardinal would have continued in this manner, had Philip not summoned his courage and put an end to the speech by asking abruptly:

"What exactly do you request?"

"That Don Gaspar de Guzmán be dismissed from Court," the Cardinal answered without hesitation.

A gasp went through the crowd, but the King lifted his hand, and they were silent.

"Anything else?" Philip inquired, without moving a muscle of his impassive face.

"That the power of the Holy Office not be diminished but on the contrary strengthened to insure the absolute purity of the Holy Faith in Spain."

"Thank you for your advice. We shall think about it."

This was one of the most difficult moments of Olivares's career. The eyes of Madrid were upon him, the eyes of his enemies who had no fonder wish than to see him completely defeated and finally without the loving protection of his monarch. He was a man of violent emotions and the effort to hold back his fury hammered on his brains and blurred his vision. But he stood proudly erect, even though everything went dark around him. He forced himself to appear as hard as a block of marble.

The Queen smiled openly at the Cardinal. She had expected a lot from this public audience, but she, as well as the other spectators, were sorely disappointed. Philip treated the matter as lightly as if the Cardinal had asked for a minor favor, and he gave no one a hint of his true thoughts.

Later that day, when he was alone, Philip called Olivares to his bedroom. They had not talked together for a long time, Philip having more and more often turned to his wife for counsel and companionship, as if he had suddenly discovered what a charming, intelligent person he had married. Now he lay on his bed, his hands under his head, and he looked at Olivares in a speculative way.

"Count, once again they ask for your head."

"Sire, are you going to give it to them?"

They had had this exchange before, many times indeed, and Philip's reply had always been the same, a friendly glance telling Olivares that he was and would forever be Philip's best friend. But this time Philip remained pensive.

"I cannot support your views regarding the Inquisition," he said. "I am convinced that the time has not yet come to stop the activities of the Holy Office."

"If I were not directly involved, Sire, I would venture the opinion that Cardinal Monti's request was an unheard of challenge, and that Your Majesty should respond in kind."

"Yes, but the mere fact that the Papal Nuncio dared accuse you in public shows the tremendous strength of his support among the Princes of the Church and the Grandees. No, this is not the time for a duel with the Holy See. We will have to placate them."

Olivares was long used to turning to another direction when he found the road barred on one side.

"We could give the impression of strengthening the Holy Office by naming an additional member to the Supreme Council of the Inquisition," he proposed.

"Do you have someone in mind?"

"A young Inquisitor from Toledo who has just returned from Rome. He is in the good graces of the Holy Father and extremely devoted to Your Majesty. He would doubtless serve us well."

"What family?"

"He has no family. He was orphaned when young and has dedicated his life to the Dominican Order."

"No family, no trouble. But a Dominican? Would he not turn against you?"

"He has been secretary to the Inquisitor General," Olivares said, omitting to mention that the man had previously been his own secretary. "He is intelligent and discreet."

"All right, we will submit his name. Who is he?"

"Fray Rafael Cortes."

"Never heard of him. Go ahead."

"I am sure you will not regret your decision, Sire."

"I hope not. Lately all the news is saddening. My kingdom is shrinking. I wonder how much of it I will be able to leave to my son. I am getting tired, Count, I wish I could rest, but I know I must do my duty. And my duty right now is to reconquer the territories I have lost. God punishes the nation for my sins. I must show myself worthy in order to halt the disastrous course of events. I have decided to go to Catalonia, at the head of all my troops. Then, when I come back after reconquering the rebellious province, I shall be stronger than ever. You stay here and govern, while I go to win the battle."

Up until now, Olivares had found it fairly easy to combat the naïveté of his monarch, but since Philip's self-esteem had been bolstered by the Queen, the Count-Duke was not able to dissuade Philip from this childish project. He spent an hour talking earnestly to the King, but he could not convince him that his presence would hinder military operations more than further them. The King, Olivares knew, would have to be protected and entertained, and valuable troops would have to be used for ceremonial duties and theatrical maneuvers.

His efforts were for naught. Philip thought that only he could lead Spanish soldiers to victory.

So Olivares found himself between two traps. If he stayed at Madrid, he could continue to govern and see that the Queen started no mischief. On the other hand, Philip would be alone and another Grandee would take that opportunity to usurp the position of Favorite. Moreover, if anything happened to Philip, Olivares would be accused of having sent the King to his death. So there was really no choice but to accompany him.

In April, after the end of the spring rains, the King, the

Count-Duke, and a host of knights and nobles left Madrid at the head of a small army, heading in the general direction of Catalonia. They had not gotten far from Madrid, when they had to stop and camp, because the King felt the urgent need to talk to his wife, who rode out to meet him. Shortly thereafter, another stop was necessary, because the King missed his daily sports and insisted on playing tennis.

To informed Madrileños, it looked as if this was going to be a long campaign.

## 2.

Fray Rafael Cortes was named member of the Supreme Council of the Inquisition shortly before His Majesty's departure for Catalonia.

When Isabel heard the news, her first impulse was to send him a letter of congratulations. But, as she started to write, she remembered their last meeting, how she had walked out of his life. All of a sudden she was afraid. Having a son had changed her feelings. Keeping Elito safe was more important than personal happiness. She tore up the letter. If he inquired about her, he would learn that she had had a child and would be the one to approach her. She went to the apartment a few times. She had faithfully kept up paying the rent for it. Now she took the statue back and placed it in the center of the table so his eye would fall on it should he by some chance come back.

In the middle of May, word came from Toledo that Uncle Jaime was feeling weak, and Pedro and Pepita decided to go there immediately. Isabel proposed to stay in Madrid with the three children, Fernando, who had just turned six, and Catalina and Elito who were both three. Leaving the children with Isabel in Madrid made it possible for Pedro and Pepita to ride on horseback instead of taking the coach and to reach Toledo within a few hours.

After their departure, Isabel took the children for a ride along the promenade of the Prado. On her way there she saw Pasquito in the street and stopped to talk to him. He told her that he had acquired quite a following among the members of the *germanía*. He still lived at the Bodegon de San Gil. She pressed her lips together in disapproval.

In the park she met Juana de Velázquez who told her that the Queen was visiting soldiers' barracks and giving patriotic speeches. She met a few other acquaintances, and all talked about the war with Catalonia and the vague hope that things might change for the better since the King had apparently taken over.

Cardinal Monti's request for Olivares's dismissal had been mostly forgotten, and no one was much interested in the Inquisition or the men behind it. Was it a good sign? No one of any importance had been arrested for some time. No *auto de fé* was expected in the near future. As for the new member on the Suprema, no one seemed to know much about him. Rafael Cortes meant nothing to anyone.

Throughout that day, Isabel was nervous and apprehensive. She did not know why. She told herself that she was worried about Uncle Jaime, but in her innermost being, she knew this to be untrue. She loved Uncle Jaime, but she was not at all worried about him. Pepita would take excellent care of him; there was no reason to fret.

She helped Maria put the children to bed and then went to the library to look through a stack of books Diego Caietano had given her before leaving for Amsterdam. It was about ten o'clock when Alfonso came to tell her that a messenger had arrived from Toledo with urgent news.

Uncle Jaime is dead! she thought, and a sudden sadness gripped her heart.

"Show him in."

She did not know the man. He was young and pale, covered with sweat, and completely out of breath.

"Countess de Queras?" he asked, casting furtive glances around him.

"Yes, what is it?"

"I must speak to you alone."

Alfonso was still holding the door open. Upon a sign from Isabel, he left and closed the door.

"Now?"

"Countess, Don Pedro has been arrested, and his wife, and Pablo Raíz and his family, and at least ten other families of Toledo," the man spoke rapidly in a low voice. "You must leave at once."

"My God! When did this happen?"

"This afternoon, during siesta time. Don Pedro had just arrived. We had an underground meeting, and the Inquisition arrested everyone."

"And Don Jaime?"

"They took him too."

"I thought he was sick."

"Not that I know of."

She stared at him in horror. Jaime not sick. That could only mean Pedro and Pepita had walked into a trap. Someone had known ahead of time about the meeting, had known they would attend if they could be brought to Toledo. . . .

"Who are you?"

"Bernardo Raíz Sanchez, a nephew of Pablo. I was one of the guards we had set out. They did not come my way, but when I realized what was happening, I got away through the lower part of the galleries to the river. Once outside I stole a horse and came here as fast as I could."

"How did you know about me?"

"There was no one else to warn. They were all at the meeting. Señora de Valderocas gave instructions before the meeting to all the guards that you must be told immediately if anything went wrong. The guards are always told before the meetings what to do."

As Isabel listened to him, a feeling of complete detachment overcame her. It seemed to her that she had no limbs, no body, no emotion. She was like a third person watching this incredible scene.

This was what she had feared most, ever since she had found out they were Marranos. The Inquisition had finally caught up with the Benahavels. How often had she thought about this moment? How often had she harbored the gnawing knowledge of doom in her stomach? Now it had happened. And there was nothing she could do. Nothing?

"You must flee, Countess, at once." The young man stared anxiously into her white face.

The children! She must save the children, or they would be taken away and given to families far from Madrid to be brought up by strangers, never to see their parents again. The boy was right. They must leave at once. If this had been planned, the guards would come for her tonight. They would come in the middle of night to attract the least attention.

Yes, she must leave at once. But to where? Why, to the apartment! The instant she thought of it, she knew exactly what she must do.

The time had finally come to trust Rafael or to perish.

"Bernardo. I have a place we can go to. An apartment no one knows. We will go there right now with my woman Maria and the children."

"Stay in Madrid? Impossible! We must leave for Seville."

"No! We would be caught right away. Besides, how could we do anything from Seville? We must get them out."

He looked at her as if she had lost her mind.

"Get them out? That is impossible. They are in the dungeon."

"Well, do you think I am going to leave them there? Don't say another word. I know what to do."

It was as if the mere thought of Rafael had given her strength. She rushed to the door and opened it:

"Alfonso! Maria! Teresa!"

"Señora, Doña Isabel?"

"I have just been informed that Doña Pepita has had a bad accident and that I have to leave right away with the children. An overland coach is waiting for me not far out; they are changing the horses. Alfonso, there is no time to get our coach ready, please call a hackney; that will save time. Maria and Teresa, get the children dressed and get a basket ready with a change of clothes and another one with food. Just for the children. But hurry. Maria will come with me. The others stay here. We have no more room."

She gave her orders rapidly and firmly, then she rushed to her room and stuffed whatever jewelry and gold she could find into a soft leather bag.

She had not told Alfonso exactly where the overland coach was waiting for her, but to the hackney driver she gave the distinct order, "Calle de Toledo," and so for all to see and hear, they rattled off in the right direction. Half-way down the road, at the Plazuela de la Cevada, she told the driver to stop and let them off. She paid him and they started to walk. Maria carried Elito, Bernardo carried Catalina, Isabel took the two baskets and to little Fernando she explained that they would visit some friends. It was a good ten-minute walk to the apartment, but finally they were all inside and Isabel bolted the door. From years of experience she knew that none of the neighbors cared in the least about anyone else, and she let out a sigh of relief.

"Maria, think of Jaén, and do not ask any questions," Isabel said. "You and Bernardo stay here with the children, while I go out to get help. Put all three into the big bed, and

Maria sing them to sleep. Bolt the door and let no one come in. Pretend you are a young couple with three children who just moved in. I will be back as soon as I can. If not, Bernardo must take over as head of this family and do whatever he thinks is best."

She left hurriedly. At the street corner, she found another carriage for hire and took it to the Bodegon de San Gil. The place was a hundred times more odious at night than during the day. She asked for Pasquito El Moro, and was told that he wasn't there but would be back in a few hours. At the Puerta del Sol, her next stop, she asked for Manolo the hackney driver, only to find that he had moved away. In the *Patio de las Covachuelas* the guard in front of the chamber where the Suprema met, told her that he had no idea how she could contact an Inquisitor during dinner time. He could be at any of a dozen official dinners. Finally, she went to the building where she had once been interrogated and said that she had an urgent message from a dying man for Fray Rafael Cortes.

"You mean his Illustrious Lordship the Inquisitor?"

"Yes, your Lordship," she made herself sound shy and ignorant, like a maid sent on an errand.

"I think he is at Toledo," the guard said. "Come back in a week."

"Thank you, my Lord,"

She ran along the streets as fast as she could. Her only hope had vanished. Rafael was at Toledo. That meant Rafael knew. He had perhaps even ordered the arrests. No, not that! If he knew he would try to help. She must get back to the apartment. But what then? God, my God, you have forsaken us!

We will have to leave, she thought. But not through Seville! They would have set a trap for them at Seville. They would know that she would try to reach one of the Valderocas ships. No, she must go to Catalonia. To Barcelona. That was French now. And from there through France to the Netherlands. To Amsterdam. To join the Caietanos and Duarte Perez. To find safety at last.

Her throat was dry, she could not swallow, her hands were covered with cold sweat, and her heart beat unbelievably loud and fast. Yet, it no longer occurred to her to look for a hackney. She just ran on and on until she reached the corner of her street. There she slowed down, her inbred caution taking over once more. The street, at twelve midnight, looked busy and normal in the flicker of the torchlights. It was the middle of May, and friends gathered outside after dinner to stand around and chat.

When she entered the house and groped her way up the dark staircase, a man was waiting for her on the landing. She gasped when he stepped suddenly into her way. He caught her and put his hand over her mouth.

"Isabel, quiet, it is I."

"Rafael! Oh, Rafael!"

"I suppose you know what happened," he said softly in her ear, "or you wouldn't be here."

His calm voice soothed her frayed nerves. He was with her, he had come to save her, nothing bad could happen to her now. Without wanting to, she broke into tears of exhaustion.

"There now, Isabel, calm down. I have come as fast as I could. I went to Valderocas House first, where they told me you had left with the children for Toledo because Pepita had had an accident. I was almost ready to turn back, when it occurred to me that you might have come here. But your man had me fooled. Only the fact that he stubbornly refused to open the door made me wonder. So I pretended to leave, but sneaked back up. And then I heard a child's voice calling for Aunt Isabel."

"Oh, Rafael . . ."

"What now?" he asked. "Can we talk in front of them?"

"We will have to," she said. "It is safer here than anywhere else."

She knocked at the door.

"Who is it?"

"It's Isabel. Open quickly."

Bernardo pushed back the bolt and opened the door.

"A fellow was here," he began, but stopped when he saw Rafael come in behind Isabel.

"Yes, he is a friend of mine. But you did well not to open the door."

Then she remembered that Bernardo was from Toledo, and she feared for a moment that he might recognize Rafael. He had been too young, however, to recall the *auto de fé* of Toledo, and he gave no sign of ever having seen Rafael before. Moreover, Rafael wore his hunting costume.

"Are the children asleep?" Isabel asked.

"Almost, Señora, Maria is still with them."

"I would like you to stay in the other room and wait for my

decision. I think my friend can help us. He is Señor Francisco Molina, and he has a great many important friends all over Spain." She turned to Rafael, "Francisco, this young man is Bernardo Raíz, he came to warn us and save us."

Rafael bowed slightly. "For warning my friends, I thank you with all my heart. To save them we still have a lot of work before us."

"Yes, Señor." Bernardo walked softly into the adjoining bedroom and closed the door.

"Who is he?" Rafael asked when they were alone.

"A young man who stood guard while your murderers invaded the underground."

"Isabel, Isabel." He pulled her in his arms, "When will you ever trust me?"

She went limp in his arms. She was so tired, so very tired of fighting the world. She wanted to lay down the burden. And now she was finally free to do it, there was no one else to protect. They had all been caught.

"I am a Jewess, Rafael," she said. "I am a Jewess and you are a Dominican Inquisitor. How can there be trust between us?"

He gripped her shoulders and held her so he could look into her eyes. Then he pulled her back closely against him.

"Isabel, my Isabel. My beloved, how well you held up under so much pressure." He kissed her forehead. "I was called to Toledo a week ago," he continued. "I was told that a great victory for the Inquisition was being prepared, and that I should be there. Well, I had business with Cardinal Monti, and I could not get there until this afternoon. If I had known what it was, I could have prevented it. When I arrived, I learned that Pedro and all your family had been incarcerated. I had the choice of trying to get them out immediately or of coming first to warn you. I felt it was most urgent to get you out of Madrid first."

"But Rafael, I don't understand," Isabel said.

"Isabel! I am on your side! How often did I tell you that?"

"But what do you mean?"

"I am working for the Count-Duke, just like Pedro and you. I was working for him long before you. I once saved his life many years ago, and that is how I became his secretary."

She stared at him, her mouth open, and a shiver ran through her body, and again every hair rose up on her skin. She said slowly and almost inaudibly, "You are the man. The man we wanted to know. The Count-Duke's spy in the Holy Office. The leader of the Marranos."

He smiled wistfully and shook his head. "Yes and no. Yes, I am the Count-Duke's spy, and I am the man the Marranos wanted to know, but I am not a Marrano myself, and I did not know you were one. You have been hiding your true beliefs well. The Inquisition is still in the dark about you. If you had not told me now that you are a Jewess, I would not have known."

"Not known?" she stopped and just looked at him.

"I knew you were working for Olivares, and I knew Pedro was, but I thought it was for political reasons, for patriotic reasons. I knew the Caietanos well; old Caietano worked for me directly, without ever knowing who I was. I went to see him under the pretext of buying books. I knew, of course, that they were Jews, but he never guessed that I was the man he wanted so much to meet. I was also aware that Pedro contacted the Jews abroad and brought them to Madrid, but since Olivares is a true Old Christian concerned about Spain's future, I assumed Pedro was too. Although his hostility toward me when I joined the Dominicans should have been a warning. But by then I knew you, and I so much wanted to believe that you were absolutely safe, I convinced myself that you were Old Christians. I even dug into the past of the Valderocases, but it looked as pure as paradise."

"That is a long story," Isabel said. "Our true name is not Valderocas. We are Jews, Rafael, and since our faith is passed on through the maternal line, your son, too, is a Jew and will be brought up as one."

She had never seen him so shocked, so pushed off balance. Abruptly, he gripped her arm.

"What did you say?"

"That we have a son, whose Christian name is Carlos Felipe Gaspar Francisco de Queras y Valderocas, but whose true name is Rafael Cortes Benahavel."

"Isabel! When? How could you be silent? How could you hide this from me? How could you?" He had raised his voice, and was almost shouting at her. She took a step away from him.

"I thought you did not want to know," she said. "I was afraid of telling you, and then you were gone."

"You could have sent me a letter. You could have let me know."

"What for? It would have made life harder for you."

"Oh Isabel!" He covered his eyes with his hand for a moment, and his shoulders sagged, then he straightened up.

"Where is he?" he asked, and she pointed to the bedroom door.

"In there with the others."

"How old is he? What does he look like?"

"He is three and a half. He looks like you."

She expected him to rush to the door, but instead he turned away from her and walked to the window. He leaned his head against the wooden shutters and stared into the street. For a few minutes neither of them spoke. Isabel went to sit on one of the two chairs in the room.

"I don't know what to say," Rafael began slowly. "For while you know much about me, you do not know all. As I said, I am not a Marrano, I am not a secret Jew, and I don't think there were any Jews among my ancestors. I am an orphan. My real parents died when I was very young. But Church registers show them and their ancestors to have been Old Christians. I was brought up by a very sweet and simple couple, the man was a shoemaker and the woman a cook for hire. They were also good Catholics as far as I can judge. They died before I met you. Your brother and I became friends when we were children, playing ball in the streets. Later, when he went to the Casa de Contratácion, he asked your father to pay for my studies. One day we went for a journey on a galley, and for the first time in my life I saw what it meant to be a galley slave. I saw how they lived like animals, worse than animals, and I asked what they had done. I was told that they were heretics and that they had been condemned by the Inquisition. It was the turning point of my life. It opened my eyes. And from then on I went to Church and I listened and I learned, and the more I listened and learned, the more I became convinced that the so-called Holy Office was the most evil institution on earth. I thought that it had nothing to do with the faith nor with the Catholic Church as such. It was like an evil disease contaminating innocent Christians. And I wondered how I could combat it. This occupied my thoughts, until one day, during a history lesson, we came upon the story of the Trojan horse. That night, not able to sleep, I conceived the idea that has been guiding my life. I was determined to fight the Inquisition from within. More than that, I was determined to rise as high as possible in the hierarchy of the Dominican Order, to have a say in the affairs of the Holy Office. And as I rose to power, the Supreme Office did not seem out of reach.

"When you asked me the first time what I wanted from life, and you yourself had discovered that I wanted power, I realized that what I really wanted was to be Inquisitor General of Spain. I did not tell you then, I told you much later. To become a man almost equal to the Pope, a man able to influence the King. At the *auto de fé* of Madrid, when I saw the Inquisitor General elevated high above His Majesty, I knew that he was a man all-powerful. So now I am a member of the Suprema, and it does not seem impossible that after Sotomayor's death I will inherit his office. Then I can be the one to say to Philip: 'I agree with the Count-Duke. There is no more work for the Holy Office in Spain. It can cease to function.' "

He turned around and walked over to her, pulling her up to stand in front of him.

"Do you know what that means? It means that we would have liberty in Spain. Not only for Jews and descendants of Jews, but for Moors as well, and for Protestants and even atheists. Because I think that may be what I am. I do not believe that there is a God."

"Do you mind if your son is a Jew?" she asked.

He kissed her forehead. "No, I don't mind. I just would not want him to be a fanatic."

"But you are a fanatic," she said.

"Yes. It is very hard. And I may yet be broken."

"No, you won't," she said, strength returning to her voice. "You will reach your goal and no one will break you."

A sigh of relief went through his body.

"Oh Isabel, you understand. Finally, you understand."

"Yes, I understand. And if we were living in a country as free as the one you want to fashion, we would have understood each other a long time ago. Because we could have trusted one another. But in Spain, you cannot trust anyone."

"I had asked you to trust me," he said.

"Yes, but too many lives were depending on me. What if you had turned out to be as trustworthy as the Old Christian lover of la Susana? And you never trusted me enough to be more explicit about your plans. While I trusted you enough to take you into the underground galleries of Toledo."

"I knew those galleries before you took me there."

"You did?"

"Don't forget, I am the Count-Duke's spy."

At his words she put her arms around his neck and they were drawn to each other as they had always been.

Rafael was the first to pull away.

"I want to see my son," he said, "and then we must work out a plan to get Pedro and Pepita out of prison and all of you on your way to Amsterdam."

"Come," she said, and they walked into the bedroom.

Isabel held an oil lamp near Elito's face and Rafael stood for a long time staring at his sleeping son. Then he bent down to kiss his forehead. Elito did not stir. They returned to the sitting room.

"Is it possible to have them released officially?" Isabel asked. "A few years ago Olivares could get the Caietanos out."

"How did you know that?"

"I asked him to do it. That is why I married Carlos. I had pledged myself to do this in order to spy upon Carlos and his group of conspirators, provided the Count-Duke would save my friends."

"So you were the one who told him about the Caietanos? And I thought he had another spy in the Inquisition. But how did you know about it right away?"

"Because I barely escaped being caught with them."

"Isabel! I never knew how deeply involved you were."

"Do you know that I went to Amsterdam once?"

"I guessed that."

"But then you also know how often I lied to you!"

"I realized that you were cautious as I had taught you to be. But I really did believe that the Valderocases were Old Christians."

"Tell me who betrayed us?"

He sat down at the table but did not answer right away. Isabel could tell by his expression that he knew the answer.

"Well, who was it?"

"I wish I could spare you this, but I think that from now on we must be completely honest with one another."

"Yes."

"Diego Caietano was caught as he tried to cross into France. He gave the Inquisitors all the names."

"I don't believe it! Not Diego!"

"He was tortured, Isabel. He went through the whole gamut of tortures. Few human beings can withstand that."

"You could not stop them?"

"I was not there! I read the transcripts of his confession. I read them only this afternoon when I asked why they had arrested your brother and the others. Your name was not on the list, but I knew they would get it from one of the others. It was imperative to warn you right away. So I told the Inquisitor in charge, who is a Fray Gabriel Moreno, that I had to confer in this matter with the Inquisitor General, and I left immediately."

"You must ask Sotomayor to free the prisoners."

"I cannot do that. The old man trusts me completely."

"What if you went to contact the Count-Duke?"

"It would take several days to locate him. What excuse could I give for my absence? You see, the problem is not only how to get them out of the dungeon; I can do that easily by myself. I can walk in there and upon my word they will be released. But I will do this only as a last resort, because . . ."

"Because it would be the end of your career," Isabel finished for him. "You would never become Inquisitor General after that."

"That is the crux of the problem."

"Then you must not do it. We must find another way."

"Yes, but suppose we do, there remains the question of your escape."

"We must get to Seville. There is always a galleon waiting for us."

"But Isabel, dearest, do you not realize that whatever Valderocas ship comes into Seville will be confiscated? That your houses do not belong to you anymore, nor your galleons, nor your plantations, nor your silver mines, nor any of your possessions? What you do not have here, now, with you, you do not have anymore. Unless you have transferred some of your property to the Netherlands or to other countries hostile to Spain. And even to get to that, you must first get safely out of Spain."

This was an idea completely alien to Isabel. She had never considered what life would be like if she were divested of her wealth, of her ability to buy herself out of any disagreeable situation, and of the solid effect the name Valderocas provoked in well-informed circles. Was it all gone at once, the Old Christian magic, the mansions, the vessels, the olive groves, the silver mines, the tremendous assets she had taken for granted? Was she a poor hunted criminal who must run for her life?

"The safest way would be for you to take Maria and Bernardo and the children and travel by coach through

France. You can travel under an assumed name, and I will give you recommendations and letters of safe-conduct. Once I know you are safely out of Spain, I will take care of Pedro and Pepita."

"But what about the others? The Raízes, Uncle Jaime, and all my friends in Toledo?"

"Darling, even I cannot get all of them free. If I had known all along that you were Marranos, I would have watched out for you, but I really had no idea you were in such danger. I thought you might be potential Judaizers—aren't we all?—but I swear I believed your *limpieza* documents. This is my only hope on which to base an official release of Pedro and Pepita. That they were unblemished Old Christians and were lured into a trap. Uncle Jaime was caught in the middle of a Hebrew ceremony. No one could save him."

"I have another plan," she said. "I will ride to Catalonia. I will wear a royal livery and pretend to be a courier. I will talk to His Majesty, and I will obtain the release of everyone and the reinstatement of Pedro as owner of the Valderocas properties."

Rafael shook his head.

"Even if you got through to the King, why do you think he would help you? Because you have been his mistress? He does not care about past amours, and you know it. He wouldn't meddle with the affairs of the Holy Office even if it filled his treasury."

"He has done it in the past."

"Only upon the advice of Olivares."

"Then I will see Olivares."

"He is in enough trouble as it is."

"What do you mean?"

"That the Suprema intends to reexamine all of the old charges brought against him, plus a few recent ones: the affair of San Plácido, the fact that he took money from the Portuguese merchants, the fact that he freed the Caietanos, the fact that he sent letters to the Primate of Portugal asking him to promise new liberties to the New Christians, the fact that he has received Oriental Jews at Court. . . . The list goes on endlessly. I am positive that he would intervene to save Pedro, but I am also convinced that if he does that, it would mean the end for him. Since his speech at the Royal Council, where he asked outright for a curtailment of the Inquisition and for a Jewish quarter and synagogue at Madrid, he has drawn upon him the wrath of the Suprema. And he is well aware of all this, because I told him so myself. He must be careful not to stumble. If he falls, so does Sotomayor, and so do my plans. He must remain chief minister, or all our efforts will have been in vain."

Her thoughts took another direction.

"Why are you so sure that the Inquisition of Seville would already have confiscated our galleons? Does it not take time for instructions to get down there? If I left right away for Seville, perhaps I could still get away with at least one vessel and instead of sailing for Amsterdam, I could sail to the New World, and sell our properties there, and save some of our holdings. Pedro will never forgive me if I give up everything without even attempting to retain some of our property."

Again Rafael shook his head.

"This was a well-premeditated coup. Your brother and his wife were lured to Toledo under the pretext that your uncle was ill, because someone had infiltrated the Marrano group of Toledo and organized it so that there would be a meeting and that they would attend. I would have learned of all this in time, if I had not stayed here to placate the Papal Nuncio. But Olivares has asked me to woo Cardinal Monti. Well, we don't have time to go into all this now, but rest assured that couriers have been sent to Seville and that as of now, the name Valderocas will become anathema in that city."

"Everything is lost then?" she asked, but she still could not grasp the full implications of her question.

"Yes, everything except our lives."

"And you would endanger yourself to save us?"

"You know that."

She walked to the window and stared into the night. The torchlights had been extinguished, the street was quiet and dark, Madrid was finally going to bed. She thought and thought. Rafael said nothing. Slowly, she came to accept the idea of her helplessness. Officially, the name Valderocas did not count anymore. Officially, she could do nothing. But that did not mean that she had lost her powers of reasoning. She must find a way. Others had escaped from dungeons. Rafael said he could walk in and get them out. Suppose he did that. What exactly would happen? If they all left together, nothing. He could flee with them, and they would get away. But he did not want that. He wanted to stay to become Inquisitor General and help Olivares rid Spain of her greatest scourge.

So the problem narrowed down to this: Rafael must get the prisoners out, but no one must know that it was he. That meant whoever recognized him must be eliminated. So . . . A shiver ran up her spine, as it did each time she had an outrageous premonition.

"Rafael. I have an idea. It is crazy and it is dangerous, but I think it will work."

"Tell me."

"If you were to go and request the release of the prisoners yourself, how exactly would you go about it? Would it be sufficient if you spoke to the chief guard, or whoever is in charge of the dungeon, and would he give the order to bring the prisoners up?"

"No, it would not be that easy. I think I would have to go personally down through the various corridors to the cell where they are kept, and I would have to designate the persons I wanted to convoke to my office. This is what I would pretend, that I wanted to have them transferred to Madrid. And I would have to have the written permission to do this from the Inquisitor General."

"Could you forge that?"

"I would have to."

"Are there many guards whom you would have to face personally?"

"Not if I went in the middle of night."

"Would it be normal for you to be accompanied by a number of friars?"

"Not only normal but indispensable. There would have to be two friars to guard each prisoner. But why do you ask?"

"Because I think we can carry it off. I will go with you. I will be one of the friars, and Bernardo could come. And Pasquito could bring his gang. Why, we should have enough friars to kill all the guards in Toledo. You get us in, and we get you out. And no one will know how this jailbreak was accomplished."

"Kill the guards! Isabel, you don't realize what you are saying. You have never killed a man!"

She faced him directly, and her face became hard and contemptuous at the memory of Carlos.

"Yes, I have. I killed Carlos de Queras."

His eyes widened. "I suppose it was necessary," he said.

"Yes, it was self-defense. But I will kill again, before I let my family burn at the stake."

"Not even a *germanía* member will dare break into the dungeon of Toledo. You will not find anyone that courageous."

"Maybe not that courageous but that greedy."

"How will you pay them? You cannot promise a fortune and then not deliver. They would turn against you. You have nothing left."

She thought of a chamber in the underground hallways of Toledo.

"I have plenty left. Gold coins and jewels. Enough to pay a gang of cutthroats and to bribe guards and to get us all to Amsterdam. We have a hidden treasure in Toledo. Just get us into the jail, and everything else will be easy."

Rafael shook his head.

"I have never known another woman like you. You are as ruthless as I am. And you, too, like to live in a whirl of danger."

"We work for the same goal. Only ruthless people succeed."

She expected him to put up a strong resistance, to oppose her going, but instead he took her hands and looked at her for a long time. She thought she could detect a sadness in his eyes.

"How old are you?" he asked finally.

"I just turned thirty."

"So you were not quite twenty when I first met you. We have known each other for ten years. It is incredible."

"What is?"

"All the things we could have done together and did not. Sometimes I wonder. I never did that when I was younger. I was always sure of myself. Only now, I begin to doubt. Will I succeed?"

"Of course, you will."

"I could marry you and go away with you. I love you that much."

They stood still. His words hung between them, finely spun, like a fragile future almost within their reach, yet easily destroyed by a wrong word. Years ago, months ago, Isabel would have pressed her advantage; now she barely dared to breathe. Rafael never spoke in vain, he never uttered a sentence he would not stand by. What would he say next? Would he take back these precious words?

"I love you, Isabel. You are the most wonderful soulmate,

friend, and lover a man could ever wish for. I dearly want to
think that one day you will be my wife."

"It is still possible," she said in a barely audible voice.

"I know. It may even become necessary that I leave
Spain—depending on who recognizes me."

She did not know what to answer. Now that Rafael had
seen his son, he was no longer invulnerable. He had become a
human, a mortal, a man who could be caught, and hurt, and
perhaps killed.

She lifted herself on her toes, her arms went around his
neck and they hugged tightly.

"I love you, Rafael. I love you, and I trust you completely.
I also trust that you will do what is right."

It had taken them ten years to reach this moment, when
they loved and trusted each other. The feeling filled Isabel's
heart with hope. Almost nothing was impossible now. They
would free Pedro and Pepita and all the others, they would
flee together, they would sail to Amsterdam, and from there
to new worlds.

She took a deep breath, and as air rushed into her lungs,
courage seemed to rush into her mind. Resolutely, she
directed her thoughts to the practical matter of summoning
helpers for their venture.

"Let us go to the Bodegon de San Gil. Among Pasquito's
friends, there must be well over a dozen men who have a
grievance against the Holy Office."

# 3.

Following the Queras-Villaquemada murders, Pasquito had
made a name for himself in the underworld of Madrid. When
they explained their plan to him, he promised to bring not
only the men, but even men made to measure.

"What do you mean by that?" Isabel asked.

"That we should have a double for Señor Molina. It is a
trick we use quite often to gain entrance into palaces. One of
us poses as a well-known nobleman, the others are his
attendants. I don't think this has ever been used for a
jailbreak, but so much the better."

"But that was the idea all along," Rafael said. "I will

pretend to be the Inquisitor Fray Rafael Cortes whom I physically resemble enough, and I will get you in."

"Yes, of course, I understand that. However, since you say you cannot flee with us, there will be someone around to testify against you later, unless we kill everyone we come in contact with, and that would leave a goodly number of corpses lying around. In my opinion, it would be better to bind and gag the guards, for them to trade clothes with some prisoners, and take them with us. Then you can return to Madrid immediately, while we dump the guards at a convenient spot, and one of us—your double, Señor Molina—pulls off his false beard and thus dramatically proves to the guards that they have been duped."

"A very ingenious plan," Rafael said.

They were sitting, the three of them, in a bedroom of the inn, Rafael and Pasquito on the edge of the bed, Isabel right next to them on a worm-eaten chair. Isabel had presented Rafael as Francisco Molina, an old friend of Pedro's and a Familiar of the Inquisition, yet a man willing to risk his life to get Pedro out.

"But what about you and your gang? The guards could well testify against you," Isabel said.

Pasquito laughed. "The cutthroats I have in mind for this venture all have good reason to disappear from Madrid for a while. We will all sail with you. No, the only problem is . . ." He stopped and looked sharply at Rafael, then he lowered his voice. "Look, you have come here because Doña Isabel knows she can trust me. And if you have come here with her, it is because you also trust me. You know me, even though I've grown a beard, and I would know you anywhere. This thing about calling yourself Francisco Molina will work well with my men, because they have never seen you before, nor have they ever seen the Inquisitor Fray Rafael Cortes. But I know you are Rafael Cortes. Don't forget I've seen you at Seville when I was just a child, and I've seen you again when I brought you the charges against Queras. Since you didn't do anything to him, I had to kill him myself. What we plan now is so dangerous that we three must trust each other. I have thought for a long time that Doña Isabel was what you would call a heretic. I know I am. And your presence here proves that you are one of us. So the problem, the real problem is not to get Pedro out, but to protect you."

Rafael had listened quietly. His face betrayed no more emotion than when the Count-Duke had handed him the list

of the arrested Caietanos. But Isabel looked at him anxiously.
Would he trust Pasquito? He smiled and laid his hand on the
young man's shoulder.

"Pasquito El Moro," he said. "Would you like to become a
Dominican friar? I could use a man like you."

Isabel took a deep breath. "Rafael knows that I killed
Carlos. I told him," she said. Pasquito acknowledged her
words with a nod.

"Don Rafael, I would very much like to work for you," he
said, "but more than that, I want to see Doña Isabel and her
son safely to Amsterdam."

"He is my son, too," Rafael said.

"Oh, my God," said Pasquito.

Isabel's spirits soared. She was no longer alone, she had
finally found two human beings she could trust completely.

"Let us plan this jailbreak," she said. "Pasquito is right.
Francisco Molina—let's please use that name—is the most
vulnerable person. Yet, he is the only one who can get our
friends released."

"Don't worry about me, I can look after myself," Rafael
said. "To me the greatest problem is still how to get you out of
Spain, assuming we are able to escape from Toledo. Pasquito,
are your men good horsemen?"

"No, I bet they've eaten more horses than they've sat on."

"That means slow travel with wagons and mules. In that
case, you will all have to wear the white gowns and black
cloaks of the Dominicans, and pose as a group of traveling
friars. But which way?"

"To Seville of course," Pasquito said.

"The Valderocas vessels will have been confiscated,"
Rafael said.

"Seville harbor is always full of ships. Don Pedro is the best
sailor in Spain. My men are the best thieves of Spain. Once in
Seville, we'll have no trouble at all."

"Pasquito can get two good wagons and two dozen mules
from our own stables," Isabel said. "Since neither Pedro nor I
am at Madrid, the theft will not be reported."

"That leaves the robes, and perhaps a banner with the
emblem of the Holy Office," Pasquito said.

"I'll provide those," Rafael said.

They went on to discuss every detail of their project: the
amount of food and water needed, the exact time of their
meeting on the road to Toledo, the instructions to be given to

the men on how to comport themselves if they should meet other groups of traveling monks, and the amount of payment to be promised to the men.

"I don't have current money," Isabel said. "It will have to be old gold coins and jewels."

"With the latest devaluation, they will prefer that anyway," Pasquito said.

Rafael accompanied Isabel back to the apartment where Bernardo and Maria were still waiting with the children.

"I am still not too happy about this plan of going to Seville," Rafael said. "We will see what Pedro thinks of it. In any event, I would like to stay with you until you actually leave the soil of Spain."

He was still cautious. Not yet committed to leave with her.

"But how would you explain your absence?"

"I'll think of something."

"Where are you going now?"

"I will bring you back, then go on to my monastery. It is almost morning. You will leave with the others as soon as Pasquito calls for you. I will catch up with you later in the day, after I've arranged for myself to leave on some official mission."

Back at the apartment, he took her in his arms. "Isabel, when you get out of the country, start calling yourself Señora de Cortes. It is a very common name, but the only one I can offer you. I think you agree that a Catholic wedding ceremony means nothing to us. There must be other persons in Spain by the name of Rafael Cortes, so no one will find it strange that your husband bears the same name as the Inquisitor. I will think of you as my wife, and I will be happy to know you are safe."

Tears welled into her eyes. "And if anything goes wrong, you will come with us or join us later? Promise me?"

"Yes, I promise."

# 4.

"Fray Rafael, back from Toledo, so soon?"

Cardinal Monti rose from his seat behind a beautifully carved wooden desk and offered his hand to Rafael, who took it and respectfully kissed the cardinal's ring.

"Your Eminence, I thought you might be interested in the news I bring from Toledo, so I rushed here as fast as I could."

"Good news or bad news?"

"Good news I think. Don Pedro Valderocas has been arrested and all his family with him. They have been discovered to be Judaizers."

The cardinal smiled.

"I did not think you would consider that good news. Are you not the right hand of Fray Antonio de Sotomayor? Your Inquisitor General has yielded to the Count-Duke's demands before. I seem to recall that you, yourself, were present when the Count-Duke burned inquisitorial files and released a group of Judaizers. I have observed you closely, Fray Rafael, especially since the Holy Father has told me of the good impression you made upon him during your stay at Rome. But I daresay I do not know where to place you. You were named to the Suprema with the approval of Olivares, and prior to that, you had been called away from Toledo because of your alleged liberal ideas. Now you tell me the Valderocas arrest—which so obviously goes against the Count-Duke—is good news. Where do you stand?"

"Your Eminence, I must confess that I have sinned. I have overruled my Christian conscience in order to advance myself. In the past, it is true, I have tried to please the Count-Duke and His Eminence the Inquisitor General. But this time, I cannot do it. I know that as soon as the Count-Duke learns of the Valderocas arrest, he will try to have the prisoners released in order to get his hands on their tremendous wealth which would come at an opportune moment for him, because he could use it for the campaign against Catalonia. I will be tempted to accede to his wishes and work for the release of the prisoners, because, Your

Eminence, I am a Spaniard, and I hope that Spain will win the war. But by doing so, I would sin again, and these sins weigh heavily on my conscience. By right, the Valderocas wealth belongs to the Holy Office, and we could use it well for the purification of the faith. I must place my faith before my country, and therefore, Your Eminence, I beeseech you to help me."

"What do you ask?"

"I want to leave Madrid and be unavailable for some time. I did not stay at Toledo, because the prisoners are safely in the dungeon, and my presence there could not serve any purpose except the one that the Count-Duke could reach me there if he wanted to. I also want to atone for past sins. I know that the Valderocases have considerable holdings in Andalusia. They own land, storehouses, and vessels. I would like to see to it personally that all these properties are confiscated and that not one single item escapes our notice."

"What would Sotomayor think of that?"

"He would approve."

"Unless the Count-Duke told him otherwise. As for myself, I must stay out of Spanish squabbles. I am the representative of the Holy See. I can only speak openly as I did at the audience when I asked for Olivares's dismissal. I cannot carry on intrigues."

Intrigues were Cardinal Monti's favorite pastime, but Rafael bowed his head humbly.

"I propose to make a round of the main inquisitorial tribunals. It will get me away from Madrid, and by the time I return, the case will have progressed too far to be stopped. At least I hope so."

"Pedro Valderocas was one of the last crutches on which the Count-Duke could lean," Cardinal Monti said. "If you were named Inquisitor for this case, would you see to it that Pedro Valderocas was relaxed in person?"

"I would."

"Then why do you not defy them openly?"

"Your Eminence, I am young. The Inquisitor General is a very old man. I have to respect his age, if nothing else."

The Cardinal thought it over. He himself had nothing to lose. If Fray Rafael Cortes wanted to detach himself at the last minute from the case of the doomed Royal Favorite, it only showed his astuteness. The man was young and ambitious. He could be used later, perhaps even as a witness against the Count-Duke.

"I think the Inquisitor General has not yet been informed of the Valderocas arrest," Cardinal Monti said, confirming Rafael's suspicion that the whole affair had been plotted by Olivares's enemies in the Inquisition, "so there is no reason why he should object to your plans of visiting the other tribunals. If I were you, I would leave before the news gets to him."

"Thank you for your advice, Your Eminence."

Rafael bent again to kiss the ring, and the Cardinal blessed him with the sign of the cross.

# 5.

They entered Toledo around three in the morning when most people had finally gone to bed. To a cortege of Dominican friars, the gate to the city was opened immediately. The Familiar in charge of inspecting incoming and outgoing travelers was duly informed that the friars would leave immediately after picking up a few prisoners. This was nothing unusual; the Holy Office preferred the darkness of night to cover its operations. Pasquito had been taught by Rafael how to act as official spokesman of the group, so that Rafael would not have to identify himself until it became indispensable.

One wagon had been left outside at a safe distance from the city. In it Maria, Bernardo, and the three children were waiting, guarded by two of Pasquito's men. Rafael's horse had also been left with them.

Into the city went Rafael, Pasquito, Isabel, and six other men. Their wagon and mules had to wait at the city gate, since the streets of Toledo were too narrow for large vehicles.

They carried torchlights, but their faces were hidden in the shadow of their cowls, and they advanced silently to the massive stone building which housed the inquisitorial prison. Rafael knocked three times on the portal and seemingly from out of nowhere a voice called:

"Who is there?"

"His Illustrious Lordship, Fray Rafael Cortes, Inquisitor of Madrid and Toledo," Pasquito answered emphatically.

A friar opened the door and led them into the patio where

they were welcomed by the chief jailer who still rubbed the sleep from his eyes.

When told of their request to transfer 'the Valderocas prisoners to Madrid, the man hesitated. He had to consult with the Inquisitor in charge of the case. Since he had recognized Rafael, this regulation seemed to bother him.

"I am sorry, Father," he said to Rafael, "but you know the rules."

"Of course, my son, I would be the last one to ignore them. But Fray Gabriel Moreno has already been notified of our arrival and will be here in a short while. Since we do not want to rob him of too much sleep, I suggest you bring the prisoners up to the patio, and we will leave as soon as you have his approval."

"But I do not have enough guards."

"I brought enough friars with me."

The jailer, a simple monk, was occupying a place too low in the hierarchy of the Dominicans to contradict a member of the Supreme Council of the Inquisition. He instructed the brother doorman to watch for the arrival of Fray Gabriel Moreno. Then he led Rafael and his friars to a staircase descending into the lower parts of the prison. There were cells on both sides of the hallway; some had doors, some just iron grilles. Each contained a slop-pail and a heap of straw. The air was too foul to breathe. In one of the open cells a woman was wailing: "Oh Lord, oh Lord have mercy. I did it, whatever they say, I did it, just get me out of here, dear Lord, just help me."

"Who is that?" Rafael asked.

"A crazy witch," the jailer answered.

Isabel shuddered. She followed Rafael closely. Her hair was hidden under a short dark wig, and she had pulled the black hood far down over her face. Left and right, moaning like helpless wounded animals, there lay the victims of recent tortures. Would she find Pedro like this? Uncle Jaime? Pepita? Behind her someone was grinding his teeth. Pasquito must feel the same horror. How could they free but a few persons, when so many were suffering? Would it be possible to open the other cells? Did one master key unlock all of them? Or did each one require a different key?

Finally, they reached the end of the corridor, and the jailer unlocked a door. The cell was larger and more comfortable than the others. Even here, a man like Pedro Valderocas obtained preferential treatment.

A candle was burning on the table. Pedro sat on the bed, staring in front of him.

"On your feet, *perro hereje*," the jailer growled.

Pedro stood up, shakily.

Rafael turned to two of Pasquito's men.

"Bind him."

At the sound of his voice, Pedro gave a start, and when he recognized his former friend, his face became a mask of hatred.

"Despicable whoreson!"

"And gag him too," Rafael said. When it was done he turned to the jailer. "Where are the others?"

"The women are upstairs. Except for the crazy witch, she is too noisy."

"Who is guarding them?"

"No one. They are all locked up, and there is never any trouble at night."

"Good! Who else is guarding the men?"

"With your permission, Father, at this hour of night, only the brother doorman and myself are awake. At dawn we get more help."

"So much the better! Pasquito, plan number two."

Plan number one had called for extreme caution. Plan number two meant all caution overboard, full speed ahead. Before the jailer knew what happened, he was gagged, and he felt the point of a dagger in his back. "Open all the doors, you fool," Pasquito grumbled. "And if you fumble, it will be the last time."

With trembling fingers the jailer tried to fit the key into the next door lock, but he was too upset to succeed. Pasquito opened the door. The groaning man on a pile of straw was Uncle Jaime. He was too weak to stand up and two men had to carry him. The next cell contained Pablo Raíz and three of his friends.

"We won't have time to open all the doors," Pasquito said. "Let's just ask who can walk and free those who will be able to flee. And for God's sake, someone untie Don Pedro and take the gag off."

Isabel approached her brother. "Pedro," she whispered, "Rafael is on our side. He is one of us. He always has been. But no one must recognize him."

Pedro's gag was taken off. However, he was too dazed to answer.

Still being pushed at dagger point, the jailer led them

upstairs to the women's section. Pepita and Señora Raíz were the only prisoners of note. Of all the prisoners in the jail, only about twenty were able to walk. Once they were all assembled in the patio, Rafael called the brother doorman, who was also gagged and shown a dagger. He then very obligingly unlocked the portal for them.

Don Jaime's confiscated house was locked. The keys were at the office of Fray Gabriel Moreno, the Inquisitor in charge. All the windows had iron grilles. Yet enter it they must. The majority of the escapees had to flee via the tunnels to the river, and Isabel needed to get to the treasure.

"What the devil are we waiting for?" one of Pasquito's men asked.

"We must get into this house."

"Why didn't you say so? I was convicted for picking locks at the royal Alcázar." The man walked up to the door, pulled up his white robe, and extracted a couple of tools from his trouser pocket. Seconds later the lock sprang open.

They filed silently into the patio.

"We don't have much time left," Pasquito said. "With the coming of dawn, guards will be sent in every direction. We cannot stay as one group. We will be caught right away. Yet, since we must leave the city the way we came, we will take with us the three Valderocases and our two prisoners. All others must flee by themselves and fend for themselves. Who can lead them out of the city?"

"I can," several voices spoke up.

There came a rasping sound from the ground where the men had laid Uncle Jaime on a mat.

"Take Pablo and Juana Raíz with you," Uncle Jaime said, almost inaudibly, "I am dying, you can leave me here."

Isabel went to kneel at his side. "Flimflam, Uncle Jaime, you must not talk like that. You have still many years ahead of you. Till a hundred and twenty," she said in accordance with Jewish tradition. But when she held her torchlight next to his face, she saw that he was suffering.

"Remember the treasure," he said. "Use it wisely. They have broken my back. I cannot sit or stand. Leave me here."

Isabel got up and motioned for Rafael to follow her.

Pablo Raíz led the group of prisoners who were fleeing by themselves into the underground until they came to the general meeting place from where they would find their own way to the river. Then he returned to the patio.

In the meantime Isabel took Rafael to the treasure chamber. She came prepared with a soft leather pouch which they now filled with old gold coins and precious jewels. Rafael looked at everything but said nothing.

On the way back through the narrow tunnels, Isabel held on tightly to his hand. If only he would stay with them. He must want to see them safely out of Spain. Then, at the last minute . . . cross the border with them or board a ship. So often in the past she had willed him into her life, she could not bear to lose him now, when they finally knew all about each other.

Perhaps he guessed her thoughts, for suddenly he gave her hand a rapid squeeze. She vaguely remembered that he had done this before, many years ago.

"Rafael, I am afraid. Come with us. Leave Spain. If anyone finds out that you had anything to do with this, they will burn you alive. My beloved, your son will need you. Come with us."

He did not answer. Her heart swelled with hope. She must give him time to become accustomed to the thought, time to wrestle with his fanatical desire to become the savior of Spain by abolishing the Inquisition, time to come to an understanding that he, too, was mortal.

He was right not to answer her. This was not the moment to linger and talk; they had to move out of the city fast, before the day broke.

When they returned to the patio, Uncle Jaime had died. Rafael went to join Pedro and Pepita at his side and spoke to them in low and urgent tones.

Pasquito whispered to Isabel that he felt the two guards, even though bound and gagged, were a danger to their enterprise.

"For one thing they know Rafael well enough not to be fooled by any double. For another, if they get away from us, we will all be done for. And what if they attract attention and are recognized when we leave the city? It is folly to risk everyone's life. Isabel, my men and I want to kill them. We'll do it quietly and quickly. It is much safer."

"What about their bodies?" she asked, also in a whisper.

"In the cellar, behind the vat."

She glanced around quickly. No one was watching. She nodded. "And take their robes," she said. "We can use them later for Pablo and Juana Raíz."

They left Toledo the way they had come. Pedro, Pablo, Juana, and Pepita were walking each between two false friars,

and Rafael was carrying Uncle Jaime's body. They would
bury him once they had put a safe distance between themselves and Toledo.

Outside the city gate, they all climbed back into the wagon,
except for Pedro and Rafael, who led the way, riding on
mules and conferring rapidly in low voices. Half an hour later
they found Bernardo, Maria, and the children exactly where
they had left them.

By now Pedro had recovered from his ordeal and resumed
his leadership role. He assembled the group around him and
explained crisply why he could not take them to Seville where
everyone wanted to go.

"If we go to Seville, we will be caught. There is not the
least doubt in my mind. Seville is where everyone would
expect us to go, and this is precisely why we must not go
there. It is far, we would be losing a precious amount of time
trying to cross the rivers, there may be guards at the bridges,
and we will have to use the regular passes across the Sierra
Morena. As soon as our jailbreak becomes known, there will
be traps set out for us all along the way. If we turn west
toward Portugal, we run even greater risks. We may be taken
for Spanish spies. The border guards along the Pyrenees will
also have been alerted by the time we get there. The safest
route for us and the most unexpected, I would think, would
be to travel east, cross the Tajo at Aranjuez and keep on a
straight course to Valencia. It is unlikely that anyone at
Valencia has heard of our arrest, and even if they have, I
know the harbor well, I have friends there, and I know we can
get a galley to Italy. What do you say? Are you with me?"

"I'll sail with you, wherever you go!" Pasquito exclaimed.

"If El Moro goes, so do we," shouted Pasquito's gang.

While Pedro was laying out his plans, Rafael had taken
Isabel away from the crowd.

"I have been able to talk to Pedro at last," he said, "and we
understand each other completely. I have also told him that I
love you and would dearly love to marry you. He understands
and knows everything."

"Even about Elito?"

"Yes."

"Oh, Rafael! Then you are finally one of us. You will go
with us to Amsterdam."

For an answer, he pulled her into his arms and held her,
while speaking softly and soothingly.

"Isabel, my beloved. I cannot come with you. I must go

back to Madrid now, immediately, and pretend that I have not left the city, so that I will not be connected with this jailbreak."

"But then, how will you join us? How will you find us?"

"I won't. I will stay in Spain and pursue my quest."

A flash of pain streaked through every fiber of her body. She freed herself from his embrace.

This was the end then. The end of her hope for a normal life, the end of a secret well from which she had drawn power and strength. A few more minutes of being close to the man she had loved for ten years—ever since she first had laid eyes on him—and then she would never see him again. Never! For he would perish in Spain. She was certain of it now. He was too vulnerable. His goal was too ambitious, too impossible to reach.

He took her hands in his and continued to talk to her in his most gentle voice.

"You must understand, my beloved, that if I abandoned my goal, I would not be myself anymore. This idea, this great desire to do what I have to do, it has been with me so long that I cannot give it up without tearing my very soul out of my body. There would be nothing left of me but an empty shell. Many can live without a sense of mission, but some are chosen. Olivares is chosen. You yourself are chosen—you cannot deny how important you have been to Olivares and to so many Marranos. Pedro is chosen—he would not leave now, if he had not been caught—and I am chosen. I have told you that I have a good chance of becoming Inquisitor General when Sotomayor dies, and then confessor to the King. Pedro agrees with me. We have dedicated our lives to abolish a great evil. If I succeed . . ." he stopped, as if searching for the right words.

"You will be remembered in history as a hero," Isabel finished his sentence in a toneless voice.

"A hero? Perhaps. I had not thought of that. I can only think of thousands of galley slaves wasting away, and people rotting in dungeons, and others being burned alive. I must stop it, Isabel. Men called the monster into being, men can stop it. I want to be one of them. For only then will I have lived."

She heard his words, but while her mind agreed with him, her heart could not. She had shared Pedro's strong drive to bring religious liberty back to Spain, but she could not share Rafael's mission. She had helped Pedro. She had done her duty as a sister and as a descendant of a long line of Benahavels and she would continue to do so. But now she felt frail and small and fearful. They had often said goodbye, but never so finally. It was worse than if he were dying. As a dead lover he could live in her memory. To know that he was alive, far away from her, forever in danger, never to be reached, never to be touched again—that was breaking her heart.

"Rafael," she said in a low, low voice, "we may never see each other again."

"I know, my love."

He took her back in his arms, and when he kissed her, her face was suddenly wet with his tears. His voice was choking.

"I love you, Isabel. Knowing that you are safe will give me strength. I will think of you every night before I go to sleep. I will remember everything we have done. I will imagine Elito growing up, safely, taught by you, to become a strong and happy young man. I will try to make Spain a better place to which he can come back one day, if he wants to. I love you."

She knew then, that whether he succeeded or failed, she had lost him forever. If he succeeded, he would have to remain a Dominican priest for the rest of his life. If he failed, he would die.

"I love you, Rafael."

They kissed again, deeply, for nothing more needed to be said. Then he mounted his horse and sped away. She watched him until he disappeared into the dawn.

# 6.

Amsterdam had not changed much during the past ten years, except that its burghers had become still more affluent. Both the Sephardic and Ashkenazic communities had prospered along with their Prostestant neighbors.

Menasseh ben Israel had reached a pinnacle of glory during the state visit of Queen Henriette Marie of England, since Her Majesty had expressed the wish to attend services at the Amsterdam synagogue in order to hear one of Menasseh's famous orations. She had been accompanied by the Stadthol-der of the United Provinces, Fredrick Henry, Prince of Orange, and Menasseh's speech had been printed and dedicated to the Queen and the Stadtholder. The memorable event had taken place on Thursday, May 16, 1642, on the same day that Pedro Valderocas and his family had been arrested at Toledo.

"Just imagine," Isabel said, when the Rabbi showed her a copy of the program, "the sister of Queen Isabelle de Bourbon, visiting a synagogue to hear a sermon at the same time that we had to flee from Spain."

"Forget Spain," Duarte Perez said. "You must think of the future. Now that Pedro has time to look after his investments in the Dutch West India Company, you should think of joining us in the New World."

"Why should she do that?" Pedro asked. "We are Jews, Duarte, and Jews are not welcome at New Amsterdam. I don't understand how you can leave Beatriz there; she must feel so lonely."

"I don't consider myself a Jew," Duarte said, glancing askance at Menasseh. "Not since that terrible day when the narrow-minded rabbis and elders of Amsterdam forced Uriel Acosta to lie down on the threshold of the synagogue so that the members of the congregation could walk over his body. It was the most degrading act I have ever witnessed—despicable and humiliating."

"So you prefer to live as a false Christian, as an eternal Marrano," Menasseh said.

"I would rather be a Marrano in the New World than a Jew among the bigots of Amsterdam," Duarte replied.

Menasseh sighed. "It was not all that easy. Uriel could have recanted."

"He did that once."

"Why then did he repeat his heresies?"

"To say there is no life after death is not contrary to old Jewish doctrine," Duarte pointed out.

"But it directly attacks the basic belief of Christianity."

"So?"

"So we live in a Christian world. Why should we offend those who welcomed us in their midst?"

"Uriel Acosta might have become the greatest Jewish philosopher. Are you going to suffocate every great spirit among us?"

Isabel had listened to their discussion. "Why don't you invite him to the New World?" she now asked of Duarte.

He looked at her in surprise.

"But Uriel Acosta is dead."

"Dead? What happened to him?"

"He shot himself."

"Oh no! When?"

"Three years ago, after he was excommunicated in the most shameful manner."

They were sitting in the drawing room of Menasseh's house on Breestraat. Pedro, Pepita, and Isabel had renewed their friendship with the Spanish-Portuguese community of Amsterdam and found themselves welcome and respected.

After their successful flight to Valencia where they had bought a galley from a fellow trader and old friend of Fernando Valderocas with the rest of Uncle Jaime's gold ducats, Pedro had taken them to Genoa, from where they had planned to travel by land. However, in the harbor of Genoa, they had come upon a royal Spanish galleon, and both Pedro and Isabel had decided that their past services to the Spanish Crown entitled them to a private act of piracy. The underpaid royal sailors were only too glad to serve Pedro Valderocas, and they had boldly sailed back along the coasts of Spain, through the straits of Gibralter and along the coasts of Portugal and France to Amsterdam. There Duarte Perez had offered them his house as a permanent residence, because he had taken his wife Beatriz and their two children, Pedro and Hannah, to New Amsterdam where they lived quietly and, as he said, happily. He had come back only to dispose of any property he still held in the Netherlands.

"But how do you live over there?" Pedro asked, "as Christians?"

Yes, Duarte admitted, they went to Church on Sundays, now and then, not to attract attention, but they did not feel that they were committing any sin. They did not want to be Jews, and they did not particularly want to be Christians. They wanted to live in peace and friendship with their fellowmen.

"We practice a personal religion of common sense and mutual understanding," Duarte said to Pedro. "And if that is heresy, then we are heretics and will always be heretics."

"You are Marranos, and you will always be Marranos," Pedro said.

"If to be an individual with a personal belief is to be a Marrano, then yes, we are Marranos and will remain Marranos. But in New Amsterdam we are considered Christian. I am a highly respected burgher and member of the Dutch West India Company."

"Don't listen to him," Menasseh said to Pedro. "He has a heart of gold but an addled brain. Pedro, you have done well to return to the religion of your fathers. Now you can live a comfortable life among your own people."

A comfortable life among his own people. What a soothing sentence, what a calming thought. Give up the constant fight, leave behind him the troubles of Spain, be a Jew among Jews; it was a proposition Pedro felt he would not be able to resist. What would happen to the Jews from Oran, when they finally arrived at Madrid? Rafael Cortes would have to look after them; there was nothing Pedro could do anymore. He could not even travel through the world inviting people to come back to Spain. How could he invite anyone to a country where he, himself, could not go for fear of being burned alive?

No, his efforts on behalf of Spain were buried. From now on, he would settle down to the life of a prosperous burgher and family man.

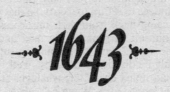

# 1.

Several months after their arrival in Amsterdam, Menasseh ben Israel came to call on them one evening with a new refugee from Madrid. When he introduced the stranger, Isabel could hardly suppress a gasp, because she knew him well, as did all the Ladies-in-Waiting. He was Vicente de Rocamora, a Dominican friar reputed for his education and piety. He had been a fashionable confessor in Court circles and finally received the honor of serving in this capacity to the young Infanta Maria, daughter of King Philip IV.

"Fray Vicente," she said, extending her hand to greet him, "how did you get here?"

"My name is Isaac," he replied, "and I asked Rabbi ben Israel to put me in contact with you as soon as possible. I bring news from Madrid."

He was immediately surrounded by Pedro, Pepita, Isabel, Duarte, Menasseh, and a few other friends who happened to be gathered at the Valderocas residence.

"I think by now you must have heard that Olivares has been banished from Court," he began his tale, but was immediately interrupted by a horrified "No!" from his audience.

"Yes, during his absence from Madrid, the Queen succeeded in amassing a strong opposition. It is said that she even persuaded the King's former wet-nurse, whom he loved like a mother, to intervene and to implore him on her knees to remove Olivares from Madrid. Be this gossip or truth, it is certain that the Queen herself spared no effort to win the admiration of the troops stationed at Madrid, by appearing before them with the Infante Balthasar Carlos to beseech them to save the country for her son. She also encouraged estranged Grandees to return to Court, so that when the King and Olivares came back from their unsuccessful campaign, Philip found himself surrounded by men and women who assured him he would have their undying support, loyalty, and help, if only he dismissed Olivares. Well, you know that Philip never had much character; whatever strength he had came from the Count-Duke. When he realized how weak and old his Favorite had grown, he decided to let him have the long rest the Count-Duke had often sought and requested. We must assume that he told him gently to retire to his country seat at Loeches, because he gave him ample time to put his papers in order—some say to burn all the incriminating ones—and he even went to the Escorial for several days to spare himself the sight of his Favorite's departure. But when he came back to Madrid and found that Olivares had still not left, he must have given him more explicit orders. By then, of course, word that the Count-Duke was falling from grace had spread through all Madrid, and jeering crowds appeared every day in front of the Alcázar to insult the Count-Duke and promise him the worst if he should fall into their hands."

"How did he escape them?" Pedro asked.

"By a ruse. He ostensibly ordered his overland coach and mule train for a certain hour in the evening, and while the crowds waited for his appearance, he left through a back door and hurried away from Madrid in a small unmarked coach, protected by the dark of night."

"When was that?"

"On January twenty-third."

Isabel closed her eyes. While the others asked question after question, she could think of only one thing: If Olivares was defeated, all their plans had failed. What would happen now to Rafael Cortes?

Pedro's thoughts apparently traveled a similar path. He raised his voice above the others, "What about the Inquisitor General?"

"I suppose he will be replaced very soon," the former Court confessor answered. "The Queen and the Grandees alone could never have persuaded Philip to let go of his old friend and mentor; there was a mounting pressure from the Church to punish the Count-Duke. He had come too often in conflict with the Inquisition. Sotomayor will be replaced by a strict anti-Olivares man. This is one of the reasons why I left now rather than later. I have been a Marrano for many years, and I had great hopes that the situation would improve. After your arrest, Don Pedro, I realized that you had been one of our group. I have another sad event to report. Young Diego Caietano was burned alive at a private *auto de fé*. I think his family lives at Amsterdam. I would appreciate it if any of you could help me console them. I dread my duty of having to bring them such terrible news."

Even though Diego had betrayed her family, Isabel felt a stab of pain in her chest. In a flash she remembered his round and happy face when he had confessed that he loved her. Now he had died a martyr's death.

"I will come with you," she said. "They are my best friends."

"Where do they live?"

"Not far from here, on Breestraat. It is only a coincidence that none of them are here tonight."

There was a pause in the conversation, and finally Isabel asked the only question that mattered to her.

"Do you think that Fray Rafael Cortes has a chance of being nominated for the position of Inquisitor General?"

Rocamora looked at her with a frown of surprise.

"Rafael Cortes? Fray Rafael tried to switch camps at the last minute. He came to talk to me one day. Very distressed. If only I had known that he was on our side, I would have been able to counsel him. If only we had all been able to trust one another, we might have succeeded. He told me he was thinking of supporting the Papal Nuncio, Cardinal Monti, against the Count-Duke. How could I guess that it was a ruse? I only realized that after he was arrested."

"Arrested! Rafael?" With effort she kept her voice steady.

"Yes, and I could have warned him. I could have told him that Monti is shrewd. Rafael needed help, but I think he always acted alone."

"I don't understand," Pedro said. "How could he detach himself from the Count-Duke and Sotomayor? It was against all our interests."

"No, it was a very clever ruse. I think he did it to keep Olivares completely informed of all the moves prepared against him by the Inquisition. I don't know what happened;

frankly, I dared not inquire into it, but I suspect that Cardinal Monti, or someone else, finally realized that Rafael Cortes was the spy in their midst. He was arrested and is being held in the prison of Valladolid."

Pedro glanced at Isabel. She sat quite still. All the blood seemed to have drained from her face. He knew she wanted to hear all that Rocamora could tell them.

"Why in Valladolid?" he asked.

"Because that is where they are holding another very distinguished prisoner, a man called Don Lope de Vera y Alarcon. Don Lope is only twenty-three, of unblemished Old Christian ancestry, and a distinguished theologian. His constant reading of the Old Testament in Hebrew caused him to have doubts regarding the truth of Christian doctrine. Most members of the Inquisition have been following his case with the greatest concern. He defended himself brilliantly in the beginning—he has been imprisoned since 1639—but two years ago he circumsized himself with a bone he had kept for this purpose from his food. Now he calls himself Judah the Believer and maintains that he is a Jew."

"And all these years he was not tortured?" Menasseh interjected.

"Not that I know of. On the contrary, in a case like that, the Inquisitors are extremely eager to convince the prisoner of the error of his ways by reasoning with him. Torture would only turn him into a stubborn martyr."

"But for four years?"

"Oh yes. Our foremost theologians are constantly being sent to Valladolid to argue with him. I suppose for that reason it was decided to incarcerate Rafael Cortes in the same prison. The Inquisitors and theologians can work on him at the same time. These are special cases."

"Then you do not assume Rafael will be tortured or relaxed in the near future?" Pedro asked, while still keeping an eye on Isabel.

"Definitely not. The case will probably drag on for years. Since he was a member of the Suprema, it will have to go to Rome. I expect his case will become as famous as the trial of Archbishop Carranza."

Their talk drifted on to other topics, and after a while, Isabel rose quietly and went upstairs to her room.

Since her separation from Rafael, she had lived in a world of her own where nothing could hurt her very much. She had lost her spontaneity, her quick tongue, her adventurous spirit. Both joy and fear had given away to a sense of composure and equanimity, as if all her real feelings were suspended. She loved Elito, but he was a healthy and happy boy who required no special mothering, and he caused her neither worry nor grief. She was friendly with everyone, but she no longer held learned discussions with rabbis and writers, nor did she take any interest in Pedro's new investments or in his business with the Dutch West India Company. She lived the quiet life of a wealthy young widow.

The sudden news of Rafael's imprisonment plunged like a double-edged knife into her heart, tearing open old wounds, calling forth her former strengths, reaffirming her will to live, reawakening her indomitable desire to forge her own destiny.

Rafael had lost his quest! And so, they had all lost. Even Olivares. But Rafael alone would also lose his life. And all of this, because too many Spaniards had not been able to trust one another. So many secret Marranos, so many valiant fighters—and yet each of them fighting alone. Without mutual support, without a well-organized effort, they had been doomed to failure.

The knife turned in her heart. Anger welled up, pent-up anger that swept away the walls she had built, and her real feelings came rushing back so fast that she was caught by a dizzy spell and had to lie down.

"Rocamora is right," she said to Pedro, when he and Pepita came to look in on her after their guests had left. "We might have succeeded if only we had been able to trust one another."

"Isabel, don't make it harder for yourself by dwelling on it. We have done our best. We are here now. We will help those who come here, and we will build a new life for all of us."

She closed her eyes. All of us, she thought, except Rafael, and the fierce storm inside her began to rage again. Pedro fell silent. He and Pepita exchanged a helpless glance. What could they say that would not sound foolish?

Isabel's mind was in turmoil. Never in her life had she been able to accept defeat. Passivity was foreign to her nature. Obstacles were to be overcome, problems to be solved, events to be bent and shaped to her will. She had not given up when Pepita had disappeared, nor when the Caietanos had been arrested, nor when Pedro and all their Toledo family and friends had been thrown into a dungeon. She had tried to wrest Rafael loose from his cause, but for a while it had seemed that the cause might win. Now the cause had lost.

Now Rafael himself would want to escape. He had even promised her that he would try to join them if anything went wrong. How could she not rush to his help?

She opened her eyes and looked at her brother.

"I must go back to Spain. I must try to free him."

Pedro shook his head, and his eyes filled with tears.

"Isabel, my brave sister, it is not possible."

"Oh yes, it must be! I know that he will try to escape. If he succeeds, I will hear about it; it will be the talk of Madrid. If he is still in jail by the time I get there, I will go to Valladolid and use all my wits to get him out. If he is transferred to Rome, I will go to Rome. I will not rest until he is free or one of us perishes. Pedro, what I did for you, I must do for him."

One look at her determined face told Pedro and Pepita that she would not listen to reasoning. By pointing out that she had saved them, she had effectively stalemated their opposition.

"I have helped our cause, your cause, Rafael's cause, Olivares's cause, I have done the best I could, always. Now, this is my cause: I will go to free my child's father, or die in the attempt."

"But, before, you had others," Pepita whispered. "Now you are alone with no one to help you."

"You are helping. You will bring up Elito. You and Pedro. I know you will not let him forget me, and you will tell him that his father was a great man."

"Pepita is right," Pedro said. "You cannot attempt it alone. This is madness. You are pronouncing your own death sentence."

"Pasquito will come with me. He would risk his life for me. We both ride well. We will take the shortest route through France. Once in Spain, we will find others. Imagine Rocamora a Marrano! The Infanta's own confessor. There are still Marranos in Spain. And there are still enough desperate men such as those who fled with us. Pasquito will find them."

Pepita broke into tears. "Oh Isabel, don't go, we love you, stay here where you belong. Remember what a dungeon is like. What if you get caught?"

"No, my dearest Pepita, I am going. For if I stay, I will die of heartbreak."

Their argument continued for another two weeks, the time it took Isabel and Pasquito to make their preparations and to wait for the weather to clear. In the end, Isabel won, as she knew she would.

# 2.

It was a beautiful morning in April. The meadows were green and covered with flowers. After a fortnight of stormy weather, the sky had cleared. Amsterdam's gabled roofs glistened in the sun, a breeze ran through the forest of masts in the harbor and through the wide wings of the windmills.

Two young men on horseback galloped away from the city across the fertile land, unaware of the lovely countryside, as if nothing mattered but speed. Only after they had lost the city from sight did they stop for a moment to confer about the direction to take. They wore similar hunting clothes and seemed to be of equal status, but otherwise they did not resemble each other in the least.

"If only we could go on like this until we reach Madrid," said the one who was slim and delicate with short reddish hair and big gray eyes. "Let's keep on a straight southwestern course."

"Yes, but we must slow down, Doña Isabel, or we'll tire the horses," said the swarthy, masculine one.

"Pasquito! I am José Molina, younger brother of Francisco Molina, a mapmaker searching his fortune."

"I know. I won't forget. Be of good cheer, José Molina, we will succeed."

"We must and we will."

They exchanged a warm glance of friendship and settled down to an easy canter.

# 1656

## 1.

Elito Cortes Benahavel stood at the crowded rail of the ship, his mind teeming with thoughts. He was a dark, serious young man of seventeen—too young his aunt Pepita had said to travel so far from home. But his uncle Pedro had supported his decision, pointing out that master traders and navigators had to learn early to sail the oceans. What better way to introduce Elito to the workings of the great Dutch West India Company than to let him sail with Duarte Perez, an old family friend, to New Amsterdam to settle a company dispute with Peter Stuyvesant, governor of the Dutch colony.

Two years earlier the first Jews had landed in New Amsterdam. The governor had wanted them to leave, but the Company insisted that they must stay. And now an order was on its way directing Stuyvesant to permit Jews to own land and to establish a quarter in New Amsterdam. Elito's heart swelled with pride that he was one of the bearers of this important news. He thought that his parents would have approved of his decision to become one of the first Jews to own property in North America.

So many times he had heard the tale of his parents' tragic fate, so many times he had talked with his beloved uncle and aunt about their love and courage and determination, that it seemed to him he knew them well and even shared the sense of mission which had made them a legend. He could no longer remember when his uncle Pedro had first told him, but their story was known to every Jew who lived in or visited Amsterdam.

She had almost succeeded—this tempestuous woman he had known as his mother for such a short time. Together with her trusted friend Pasquito, she had ridden all the way to Valladolid. By a ruse that only a woman of her ingenuity and intelligence could maneuver, she had stolen into the prison and set his father free.

But the joy of their reunion was shortlived. Rafael's escape did not go unnoticed for long. During a brief rest on the outskirts of the city they were overwhelmed by mounted guards and brought back to the prison. Once Isabel's identity was established, the trail had been swift and the sentence terrible.

And so it was that his mother, the Jewess who was known as Isabel Valderocas, and his father, an Old Christian and an Inquisitor of Spain, were publicly denounced and died at the stake.

Pasquito, the intrepid Moor who had barely escaped with his own life, came back to tell the story. Hidden in the crowd that villified them on their way to the *quemadero,* he saw them mount their separate pyres which had been built side by side, and proudly turn their heads to look at each other. Their eyes seemed to lock in a bond of love that would carry them beyond the smoke and flames to a death that finally united them.

All of Spain was publicly scandalized, but beneath the surface, in hushed and secret conversation, a story of true martyrdom slowly emerged. Neither had sought it, but both had dedicated their lives in their own ways to the betterment of their countrymen. Isabel Valderocas and Rafael Cortes. By now it was clear that they would be remembered more for their audacious deeds than for their private sins. Isabel and Rafael. Already their names evoked two spirits of great passion and great purpose.

Elito took from his pocket the worn and faded parchment letter his mother had written before she set out on the fateful journey.

"My beloved son, I write this letter knowing that I may never again see your beautiful face that has so often reminded me of your father. You will only read this letter in the event that I do not return. I hope that when you are older you will be able to understand and forgive me for leaving you. Above all, my Elito, and no matter what else you may hear, I want you to know what a great and brave man your father was. For ten years I loved him with all my heart and soul without even understanding the mission of his life. I could not help loving him, even when I thought his personal ambition was selfish. In truth, he was the noblest of men, seeking justice and freedom for all those who were, unlike himself, not born of Christian blood and therefore treated cruelly.

"To fully appreciate his courage you should know that he risked his own life to save all of us: Uncle Pedro, Aunt Pepita, your cousins, you and me. I am going now to try to save him.

"I have asked that you be reared a Jew in the tradition of the generations of Benahavels before us, but I hope that you will never forget that your father was a Christian. May you strive, as he did, for the tolerance of all faiths. I hope that you will be courageous in your beliefs, but treat with justice and compassion even those who do not share them. To be able to love and trust other human beings is more valuable than all worldly possessions. May God bless you and keep you."

Elito carefully folded the letter and returned it to his pocket. In the distance he could see land and his heart beat faster with excitement. He looked around him at other eager faces. He was not the only Jew among the Dutch merchants on this voyage. There were about a dozen others going to join the few Jewish families who had fled to New Amsterdam two years earlier from Brazil where the Inquisition still ruled in full force. Here, in the new land, they would live in peace.

Courage, trust, love, justice, compassion. Elito promised himself to make these values his own for as long as he lived. Then, as the land drew nearer, his thoughts could no longer dwell on the past. For here, finally, was his own future, a great adventure about to begin.

# *Epilogue*

The following news bulletin was published on the seventeenth of December 1968 by the *Washington Post* and other major newspapers around the world:

### Spain Formally Removes 476-Year-Old Ban on Jews
(Reuters)

MADRID, Dec. 16—Spain today formally lifted its expulsion order against the Jews—made 476 years ago and long ago abolished in practice—to mark the opening of the first synagogue built in Madrid.

A Ministry of Justice decree read at the synagogue inauguration officially recognized the Jewish community and "acknowledged the abolition" of the 1492 decree.

Madrid did not possess a synagogue before the expulsion of the Jews in 1492. The city became the capital of Spain 69 years later.

Queen Isabella, known as "The Catholic Queen," expelled Spain's flourishing Jewish community as a measure aimed at creating political and religious unity, but Jews started to drift back to Spain late in the 19th century. Today the number is about 8500, according to Madrid's first rabbi since the 15th century, Benito Garzon.

Jews have been shown tolerance under the government of Gen. Francisco Franco and their position was strengthened by new religious liberty laws, approved last year, which allow Protestants, Jews, and other non-Catholics to hold and advertise public services and obtain official recognition for their communities.

From the beginning of civilization down to our own time, men and women of good will have tried to free the world of superstition, narrow-mindedness, bigotry, persecution, and hatred. Few ever lived to see their efforts bear fruit, because human understanding ripens too slowly. But that does not mean their work was in vain.

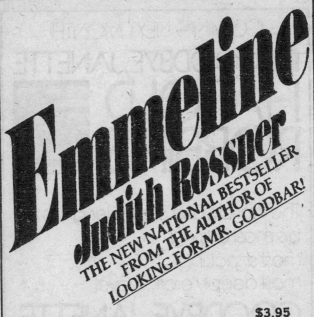